OXFORD WORLD'S CLASSICS

STORIES AND POEMS

RUDYARD KIPLING was born in Bombay (now Mumbai) in 1865. He was brought to England at the age of 5 with his younger sister Alice, and left for a miserable six years with a foster family, followed by a happier period at school in Devon, where his precocious literary gifts flourished. In 1882 he returned to India as a journalist on the *Civil and Military Gazette* in Lahore (now in Pakistan) and from 1887 on the Allahabad *Pioneer*. He became a Freemason in 1886. His poems and stories of Anglo-Indian life, first published in India and then, from 1890, in England, made him famous. He left India in 1889 (never to return) and travelled in the Far East and America. In January 1892 he married Caroline Balestier, the sister of a close friend, Wolcott Balestier, who had died suddenly a few weeks earlier. The Kiplings settled in Brattleboro, Vermont, where their first two children, Josephine and Elsie, were born. After a bitter quarrel with Carrie's brother Beatty, the Kiplings left America in 1896 and returned to England, eventually settling at 'Bateman's', near Burwash in Sussex, in 1902. Their son John was born in 1897. Kipling's last visit to America, in the winter of 1899, was marked by the death from pneumonia of Josephine, the 'Best Beloved' of the *Just So Stories*; he himself nearly died from the same illness. Kipling's popularity reached its peak from 1899 (with the phenomenal success of 'The Absent-Minded Beggar', the verses he wrote to raise money for soldiers' families in the Boer War) to the award of the Nobel Prize in 1907 (the first to a British writer). His work continued to sell but he became an embattled partisan of Imperialism and Unionism, though he was never an unthinking or uncritical apologist. His son John died in the Great War at the battle of Loos in 1915. Kipling's last years, though still productive, were shadowed by grief, by illness, and by his prophetic fear of another war with Germany, for which he thought Britain ill-prepared. He died in 1936 and was buried in Westminster Abbey.

DANIEL KARLIN is Winterstoke Professor of English at the University of Bristol and has previously taught at University College London, Boston University, and the University of Sheffield. His publications include *The Figure of the Singer* (2013), editions of Robert Browning, and editions of Rider Haggard's *She* and Edward FitzGerald's *Rubáiyát of Omar Khayyám* for Oxford World's Classics.

OXFORD WORLD'S CLASSICS

For over 100 years Oxford World's Classics have brought readers closer to the world's great literature. Now with over 700 titles—from the 4,000-year-old myths of Mesopotamia to the twentieth century's greatest novels—the series makes available lesser-known as well as celebrated writing.

The pocket-sized hardbacks of the early years contained introductions by Virginia Woolf, T. S. Eliot, Graham Greene, and other literary figures which enriched the experience of reading. Today the series is recognized for its fine scholarship and reliability in texts that span world literature, drama and poetry, religion, philosophy, and politics. Each edition includes perceptive commentary and essential background information to meet the changing needs of readers.

OXFORD WORLD'S CLASSICS

RUDYARD KIPLING

Stories and Poems

Edited with an Introduction and Notes by
DANIEL KARLIN

UNIVERSITY PRESS

OXFORD
UNIVERSITY PRESS

Great Clarendon Street, Oxford OX2 6DP
United Kingdom

Oxford University Press is a department of the University of Oxford. It furthers the University's objective of excellence in research, scholarship, and education by publishing worldwide. Oxford is a registered trade mark of Oxford University Press in the UK and in certain other countries.

First published 1999
First published, with revisions, as an Oxford World's Classics paperback 2015
Impression: 5

Published in the United States of America by Oxford University Press
198 Madison Avenue, New York, NY 10016, United States of America

British Library Cataloguing in Publication Data
Data available

Library of Congress Control Number: 2015931302

ISBN 978–0–19–872343–1

Printed in Great Britain by
Clays Ltd, St Ives plc

PREFACE

All anthologists cower at the thought of their omissions and hard choices, but the selector of Kipling fears hate-mail. A complete and magnificent volume could be compiled from what I have left out—certainly as far as the stories are concerned. I hasten to say that I do not claim to present the best of Kipling, but only some of the best, and that my choices have been circumscribed by principles which may explain, if not excuse, a number of missing items.

To begin with, this is a selection of short stories and poems, not of other kinds of writing. Kipling's novels, travel-writing, journalism, political speeches, autobiographical writings, and correspondence are not represented. *Kim* is too good to be done justice by extracts, and neither *The Light that Failed* nor *The Naulahka* are good enough to justify them. Kipling's non-fiction deserves an anthology of its own; combining it with the fiction would mean that neither could be properly sampled. (It has been hard enough to combine fiction and poetry, for that matter.) The *Kim* of such a non-fiction anthology would be *Something of Myself*, Kipling's posthumously published memoir and one of his greatest works, in places limpid and rancid in others, haunted always by the lost paradise of which I say something in my introduction.

Within the category of fiction, I have tried to include something from each of Kipling's published volumes (of his uncollected work only 'Proofs of Holy Writ' really pressed for a place, and comes high on the list of my own regrets). Again there are some exceptions. *Under the Deodars* (1888) and *Actions and Reactions* (1909) have no representatives (I gesture sorrowfully at 'At the Pit's Mouth', 'A Deal in Cotton', and 'The House Surgeon' . . .). I came to the view that the stories in *The Jungle Book* (1894) and *The Second Jungle Book* (1895), and the stories of *Stalky & Co.* (1899), *Puck of Pook's Hill* (1906), and *Rewards and Fairies* (1910), were too dependent on each other for individual tales to be taken out of the frame.[1] The test-case was a *Stalky* story which I originally intended to include, called 'The Moral

[1] I take *Stalky & Co.* to include the other stories which Kipling published in subsequent collections, and which were subsequently brought together in a volume called *The Complete Stalky & Co.* (1929, and excellently edited by Isabel Quigly in Oxford World's Classics).

Reformers': I realized that in order to understand this extraordinary tale you need to be familiar not only with the events of the tale which immediately precedes it, but with what the boys would call 'the whole biznai' of the school, their lives, characters, and backgrounds as the whole collection displays them. The same is true of the linked, interwoven tales of English history in *Puck of Pook's Hill* and *Rewards and Fairies*. In a sense I have treated these collections as though they were novels, feeling that individual editions of them would serve the reader far better than extracts.

What remains constitutes a wide enough arena for debate. I can say that the only even-handedness I enjoined on myself was chronological: I did not set out to 'cover' different genres, themes, or styles, but to choose the works that would, in my view, give the greatest pleasure.

In one sense this was an easier task with the stories than the verse. This is because some of Kipling's most famous and memorable phrases come from poems which are not (again in my view) his best. With some doubts I have included 'The Betrothed', 'Recessional', and 'The White Man's Burden', but left out 'The Ballad of East and West' and 'The Winners' ('Down to Gehenna or up to the Throne | He travels the fastest who travels alone'); and I have doubts about my doubts. A poem like 'The Absent-Minded Beggar', by which Kipling raised £250,000 for relief of soldiers' families in the Boer War, poses a real difficulty by being so important in the popular culture of its time and so mediocre as verse. I confess it was a relief to omit 'Ulster' on the same consideration.

I have acknowledged, in my notes, the help of the *Readers' Guide to Rudyard Kipling's Works*, and the bibliography will direct readers to many other useful biographical, critical, and contextual studies. Among them will be found a book called *The Art of Rudyard Kipling* by J. M. S. Tompkins. It was first published in 1959 (when my father was reading the *Just So Stories* to me) and remains the finest general critical book on Kipling, acute and illuminating at every point it touches. Joyce Tompkins, whom I never had the pleasure of knowing, died in 1986. I commend her work to readers of this volume, and I dedicate my share in it to her memory.

CONTENTS

VERSE

INTRODUCTION

Kipling's Brilliant Career

Kipling began as a sensation, almost a scandal; he rose like a rocket, and was expected to fall like a stick; he baffled prediction, and is still up there. But his trajectory has been uneven. He is no longer the fashion, as he was for a few brief years in the 1890s, when he was decorated with an epigram by Oscar Wilde and elicited a typically nuanced compliment from Henry James.[1] Nor does he command the devotion of the general, middle-class reading public, as he did for the first thirty years of the century. The economic and cultural interests of this class have shifted, if indeed it can be said to be composed of the same kinds of people. The authenticity and immediacy of *Kim* are as remote as those of *The Pilgrim's Progress*. On the other hand, the decline of Kipling's critical reputation has been reversed in recent years; his admirers may cling to the superstition that a drowned man brought back to life won't sink again.

We can plot the swings in Kipling's fortune against the graph of history, though there is a problem with plotting his literary achievement and significance on the same graph. I suggest later on in this introduction that we ought not to reckon Kipling's value (indeed that of any artist) by tallying his ideas, opinions, and attitudes against our own. Nevertheless few writers have been so engaged, so identified with the public life of their time, or have been so insistently praised and blamed as a spokesman and prophet. It was a position of Kipling's own making, too, as much as that of his critics. It may be true that, like Uncle Toby's elaborate entrenchments and fortifications in *Tristram Shandy*, Kipling's embattled participation in public affairs masks or displaces a different preoccupation, but it is also true that the

[1] Wilde: 'As one turns over the pages of his *Plain Tales from the Hills*, one feels as if one were seated under a palm tree reading life by superb flashes of vulgarity' ('The True Function and Value of Criticism', *Nineteenth Century* (Sept. 1891), repr. in *Intentions*, 1892). James: 'Kipling strikes me personally as the most complete man of genius (as distinct from "fine intelligence,") that I have ever known' (*Correspondence of William James*, ed. I. K. Krupsjelis and E. M. Berkley, vol. ii (Charlottesville: University Press of Virginia, 1993), 200). If Kipling knew of Wilde's remark it does not seem to have inspired him with lifelong gratitude: he refers in *Something of Myself* to the 'suburban Toilet-Club school favoured by the late Mr. Oscar Wilde'. For James, on the other hand, see p. xx below.

entrenchments and fortifications took on a life of their own and constituted an end in themselves.

The public world in which Kipling's career took shape, from the 1870s to the 1930s, saw the climax of British imperial power and the beginning of its decline, passing through the ordeal of the Great War. Queen Victoria was declared Empress of India in 1877; Kipling lived to record, in *Something of Myself*, his contempt for the 'great and epoch-making India Bill' of 1935, which gave self-government to the Indian provinces and seemed to most Conservatives to open the door to independence. He also lived long enough after the Great War, which claimed the life of his only son, to recognize the threat of Nazism and to warn, as he thought unavailingly, of the need to rearm. This political context is also, of course, a social and cultural one. No literary career which lasts, as Kipling's did, for half a century, can escape bearing witness to social history: patterns of change and continuity are vividly realized in, for example, his portrayal of a restless class-consciousness in the aftermath of the Boer War ('Chant-Pagan', p. 480). R. L. Green pays personal tribute to Kipling's evocation of rural Sussex, a culture to which Kipling came as an outsider in 1902, and he reminds us that there is plenty of similar testimony to the accuracy of outline and detail in the Indian stories.[2]

Kipling himself would probably enjoy being thought of as a political and social chronicler, if only because, like Pau Amma in 'The Crab that Played with the Sea' (*Just So Stories*, 1902), such an image would give him the hard shell he needed to 'play his play'. His sense of writing as work, producing social value for material reward, though perfectly sincere, also helped him to baffle and deflect any attempt to pluck out the heart of his mystery. It ought not to seem strange that a great artist should love his art, but Kipling's love was fiercely self-protecting, so much so that at times it resembles its opposite. His hatred of 'artiness' has sometimes led to the absurd charge of philistinism, but a philistine hates art as much as artiness because he cannot tell the difference. Kipling's hatred of artiness is that of a jealous lover of art; he cannot bear that his god should be mocked by the worship of idols.

It seems at first as though this love of art has a genetic or hereditary source. Kipling's family had artistic leanings and connections: his

[2] 'The Countryman' in John Gross (ed.), *Rudyard Kipling and His World* (1972), 120–5.

father was a talented draughtsman, designer, teacher, and curator, one of his mother's sisters married the President of the Royal Academy and another the painter Edward Burne-Jones, at whose house Kipling gained enchanting childhood glimpses of Victorian celebrities such as William Morris and Robert Browning. But he did not come to art through these double doors; he came in at the tradesman's entrance. Like many Anglo-Indian children,[3] he was sent home for his education, but not to a grand public school followed by Oxford or Cambridge. His parents could not afford it, and Kipling's cleverness had not revealed itself in any scholarly form. The school he attended, the United Services College at Westward Ho! in Devon, was a businesslike establishment whose main objective was to get the boys through the Army entrance examination, though its headmaster, Cormell Price, had been a friend of William Morris and Edward Burne-Jones at Oxford in the 1850s and was by no means an unsympathetic figure. Kipling, whose short-sightedness precluded him from a military career, stood out in the school as a brilliant, obstreperous asset and nuisance, but for all his creative ferment (skits and sketches, parodies and pastiches for the school mag.), no one envisaged him making a living from such materials. Kipling himself did not envisage it. He did not, like Robert Browning, declare himself a poet and oblige his family to accept (and fund) his vocation. When his schooling came to an end he returned to India to work as a journalist on the *Civil and Military Gazette*, the house journal of the Anglo-Indian community of Lahore.[4]

Kipling's apprenticeship as a journalist left lasting marks on his development as an artist (he strongly anticipates Hemingway in this respect as in many others). It gave focus and direction to his restless, inquisitive nature (the nature he celebrates in Rikki-tikki-tavi, who like all mongooses is 'eaten up from nose to tail with curiosity', and in the ''Satiable Curtiosity' of the Elephant's Child). Journalism was his profession, his craft, the only work of which he had inside knowledge to compare with that of the soldier, the engineer, the doctor, or the

[3] The term 'Anglo-Indian', here and elsewhere in this volume, denotes British people born or settled in India, not people of mixed race. For details of Kipling's birthplace and family background, see the Chronology, p. xxix. For his experiences on being brought to England as a small child, and their effect on him, see below, p. xxi.

[4] Lahore is now in Pakistan; 'India' in this volume denotes British India. British rule extended directly and indirectly over most of the subcontinent. See Appendix A, p. 525.

businessman.[5] Admittedly the journalist was not a man of action, but he was something more than a bystander: he was a witness and recording angel. It came naturally to Kipling to publish his verses in newspapers and to find friends, as he did throughout his life, amongst journalists, editors, and proprietors; he retained to the end the journalist's cynicism about the motives of those in power, adding to it a thoroughly modern cynicism about the power of the press itself.[6]

The profession of journalism also endowed Kipling with what today's recruitment consultants like to call 'transferable skills'. It trained him in faculties of observation, concentration, and economy of means which served him well at the outset of his literary career.[7] Perhaps even more important, it gave him a definite, if limited, audience for his work. Kipling did not begin by having to impress the whole world, but only a portion of it, and one which he knew intimately. When he left India in March 1889, Kipling abandoned the Anglo-Indian public (the public which had given *Departmental Ditties* its local, word-of-mouth fame), but he carried with him the confidence and determination of a successful professional career.

Journalism had another and complex effect on Kipling's art. He had private and peculiar reasons for a hunger which is also, for journalists, a professional hunger: the desire to be in the know, to gain access to an inner circle, to belong to a privileged group. Journalists often experience a conflict between the duty, or pleasure, of keeping things to themselves (their 'sources') and the pleasure, or duty, of broadcasting what they know (their 'stories'). Kipling's art shows how closely the passions of secrecy and revelation are entwined. He loved to be in the know, and he loved to tell what he knew: many of his stories are 'inside stories', stories of what 'really happened', as opposed to what a deluded or indifferent public believes. Yet the storyteller who brings us such news has also broken out of the circle which he took such

[5] See, in this selection, 'The Man Who Would Be King' (p. 57), in which Kipling draws on his experience both as sub-editor of the *Gazette* and as roving correspondent of its larger sister-paper, the Allahabad *Pioneer*, and 'The Village that Voted the Earth was Flat' (p. 293), in which Kipling lovingly and fearfully documents a press campaign from the first planted story to the point at which the world's merciless attention is focused on the puny victims. Among his poems on the subject, 'The Files' (p. 484) is outstanding: by turns acute, ironic, and melancholy, and written from within.

[6] See for example the comments on the behaviour of the reporters on a juicy murder case in 'Fairy-Kist' (p. 410).

[7] For the famous 'turn-overs' in the *Civil & Military Gazette*, the original format of many of the stories in *Plain Tales from the Hills*, see *Kipling's India*, ed. Pinney, pp. 10–11.

pains to penetrate. Kipling's engagement with Freemasonry has a similar doubleness about it. He became a Mason shortly after his return to India; Freemasonry offered the delights and rituals of belonging and fellowship, and did so promiscuously, as Kipling emphasizes in chapter 3 of *Something of Myself*: 'Here I met Muslims, Hindus, Sikhs, members of the Araya and Brahmo Samaj, and a Jew tyler, who was priest and butcher to his little community in the city. So yet another world opened to me which I needed'.[8] But Kipling in turn opens this world to us: there are Masonic plots and conspiracies in his work, not in the vulgar but the elevated dimension, the dimension of artistic design and emotional conviction which is at the heart of what a writer 'means'.

The focus of Kipling's passion for inside knowledge—at any rate in his fiction—is not on the rulers of the earth but on the doers and makers. 'The Bridge-Builders' (in the significantly titled collection *The Day's Work*, 1898) juxtaposes two worlds, that of the engineer Findlayson and that of the pantheon of the Indian gods, but the other pantheon—the imperial government—appears only in refracted glimpses of its corruption and do-nothingism. There are a few tales about the corridors of power, but they are mostly early and burlesque, or tilted towards odd points of view.[9] Kings and rulers are relegated to a vague distance, or if they do appear it is in conversation with the subalterns or craftsmen in whom Kipling was really interested. The best story he ever wrote in which royalty features is 'In the Presence' (*A Diversity of Creatures*, 1917), where the king is an honoured corpse. As his career advanced and his reputation grew he became the friend of great men and a partisan for their causes, but they never people his fiction. He hero-worshipped Cecil Rhodes, for example, and paid tribute to him in numerous public ways (including the inscription on the Rhodes Memorial in Cape Town), but it would never have occurred to him to make Rhodes the subject of a story.

Kipling's engagement with social and political questions, especially those of the British Empire, accordingly looks very different in his public speeches, articles, and correspondence than it does in his

[8] The little Jewish community of Lahore is commemorated in the brief and bleak tale 'Jews in Shushan' (*Life's Handicap*, 1891). The 'tyler' is the doorkeeper of a Masonic Lodge.

[9] In *Plain Tales from the Hills* the Viceroy of India appears in a farce of mistaken identity ('A Germ-Destroyer') and the ruling Council is influenced in passing important legislation by the 'inside knowledge' of native opinion supplied by a child ('Tod's Amendment').

fiction. He detested the Liberal politicians who came to power in the aftermath of the Boer War and whom he attacked with bigoted virulence for their supposed betrayal of England's mission and the selling of her national soul; such polemic finds its way into his 'occasional' verse, especially in reference to Irish nationalism (a persistent theme from 'Cleared' in 1890 to 'Ulster' in 1912), but in his fiction it is present, if at all, in indirect and ambivalent forms.

It is true that Kipling's contemporaries were reluctant to make this distinction. He came to be identified as a writer with the political tendencies he espoused, or was thought to espouse; nor was this identification affected in people's minds by his refusal of public office or honours (he would not stand for Parliament and even declined the award of the Order of Merit from King George V, who had become a personal friend; the only honours he accepted were the Nobel Prize, and honorary degrees from universities). The perception was that Kipling's immersion in reactionary prophecy and apologetics involved the whole of his writing. This perception constitutes a prejudice, hard to overcome because Kipling kept the means of overcoming it to himself. There is, in other words, an 'inside story' to Kipling himself, without which the case for his art cannot be convincingly made.

Kipling's Secret

Lovers and admirers of Kipling may well feel exasperation at having to make the case at all. Kipling is one of the three best short story writers in English, along with Henry James and Hemingway, his contemporaries in a golden age of the genre. Admittedly he could not write 'real' novels or plays (though *Kim* is a true romance) but he is a very fine poet; not many writers have such a second string to their bow. His travel writing (especially in the early years) and some of his journalism are also of high quality. Among his many achievements is one book for children—the *Just So Stories*—which for sheer intensity of imagination, vivid realization, comic ingenuity, intuitive understanding and uncondescending delight in the child's point of view, has never been, and never will be surpassed. Altogether he is one of a handful of writers in English without a knowledge of whose work a person's literary education is defective. Great writers are like great cities: they may be dirty, noisy, and crowded with people you don't like and wouldn't be happy to live with, but you can't claim to know the country without at least paying them a visit.

And Kipling is worth more than a visit. Take, as just one example, his descriptive power, the faculty which took his first readers by surprise and storm. His touch is uncanny: he can evoke a taste, a smell, a look, a human expression with immediate and infallible conviction, so that reading him is often a series of delighted assentings. Nor is this descriptive art an art of surfaces. In 'The Wrong Thing' (*Rewards and Fairies*, 1910), Hal, the Tudor craftsman, criticizes a fresco by his rival Benedetto by saying 'it goes no deeper than the plaster'; technical skill by itself produces pictures 'which all men praised and none looked at twice'. But we do look twice at Kipling's pictures, because he looked twice at what he painted. He strives for the effect he describes in 'The Courting of Dinah Shadd' (*Life's Handicap*, 1891) of 'the wonderful Indian stars, which are not all pricked in our one plane, but, preserving an orderly perspective, draw the eye through the velvet darkness of the void up to the barred doors of heaven itself' (the void is part of it, and the barring of heaven, too; for as Kipling said of Kim, 'his limitations were as curious and sudden as his expansions'). Where description merges into symbol, Kipling's reach is bold, he is not afraid of grandeur, but he never gesticulates: he is like Daniel Dravot, in 'The Man who would be King', singing and whistling among the mountains in defiance of the 'tremenjus avalanches'.[10] Like the machines he admired, his prose is both powerful and finely calibrated. As with his descriptive faculty, so with his narrative skill, his range of mood and tone, and, above all, his supreme playful verbal intelligence.

And yet—and yet. Lovers and admirers of Kipling usually end up having to apologize for him—for those of his opinions which were either deplorable to begin with, or have become so with changes in fashion. What is powerful and convincing in Kipling's art is so mixed with what is repellent and sometimes mad in his outlook (like his theory that the suffragette movement was Nature's way of ridding the country of its surplus women by 'getting 'em to slay themselves')[11] that it is hard to make the case for him as an artist without engaging in a defence of his politics.

The defence, these days, usually takes one of two forms. First, Kipling's enemies are accused of reductive and simplistic readings of his work, and the argument is made that his views on, say, Empire are much more subtle and complex than they are made out to be. This is

[10] See p. 71 in this edition.

[11] See headnote to 'The Female of the Species', p. 681.

undoubtedly true, but it only gets you so far: 'Recessional' (p. 478) may well be a solemn warning against the dangers of imperial arrogance, but after all it is an imperialist's warning; if you believe that all magic is evil, then a white witch isn't much better than the traditional kind with broomstick and cauldron. A variant of the first defence is the argument that some of Kipling's most offensive sayings have simply been misunderstood. 'Recessional', again, has the notorious line about 'lesser breeds without the Law'. George Orwell claimed this line was 'always good for a snigger in pansy-left circles' (there's nothing like fighting fire with fire) because it conjured up an image of a white man beating a native, whereas what Kipling actually meant by 'lesser breeds' was the Germans.[12] So that's all right! It should be pointed out that the date of the poem, 1897, gives Kipling less reason than the date of Orwell's essay, 1942.

In any case, the truth that Kipling has been misunderstood or misrepresented is only a partial truth: on some questions his opinions and attitudes never altered and are never other than dishonouring to him. To take an example which matters just because it is so local and casual: in one of his last stories, 'A Naval Mutiny' (*Limits and Renewals*, 1932), which is set in Bermuda, it is said of a retired bo'sun who has set up home close to the naval dockyard: ''No more keepin' Daddy away from there than land-crabs off a dead nigger.' This image is Kipling's in all but name; there is no suggestion that the author distances himself in any way from the character who utters it. (And 'A Naval Mutiny' is a good story, too, a farcical yarn twisted with threads of old men's memories.)

The second defence is one of mitigation by appeal to biographical or historical context: if you understand the particular circumstances in which Kipling was living and working, you will see what is disagreeable about him 'in context' or 'in proportion'. His anti-Semitism, for example, is nothing special, a common-or-garden weed of the time; moreover (here the second defence rejoins the first) a character like Kadmiel in 'The Treasure and the Law' (*Puck of Pook's Hill*, 1906) troubles the surface of our judgement and suggests that Kipling as an artist is comfortingly complex and ambivalent about his prejudices. In the same way, the character of Hurree Chunder Mookerjee in *Kim* is offered as a ransom for the portrayal of his near-namesake Harendra Mukerji in 'The Ballad of Boh Da Thone' (*Barrack-Room Ballads*,

[12] 'Rudyard Kipling', *Horizon* (Feb. 1942), in *Collected Essays, Journalism and Letters*, ii. 215–16.

1892) and a dozen other caricatures of the Bengali 'babu'. It sometimes seems as if Kipling is to take the credit for the prejudices he did see through—the scorn of the respectable classes for the social dregs who made up the 'Tommies' of the British Army, for example—while being excused for those he embraced, on the grounds that he was possessed by the *Zeitgeist*.

Of course Kipling *is* a more complex figure than his enemies allow, and there *is* a historical dimension to his thought and writing which he deserves to have taken into account as much as any other writer. Yet none of this would make much difference if there were not a larger and more comprehensive reason for reading him. The truth is that Kipling is indefensible on any other ground than the pleasure he offers his readers, and there he is impregnable. It is no good wishing we lived in a world where great artists were lovable human beings with opinions which coincided in all respects with our own (at whatever period we happen to encounter them). The Gods of the Copybook Headings limp up to explain it once more: artists who please in this way don't last; they are fellow-travellers, and lay down their burden when we ourselves cease. On the other hand, as Kipling knew well, artists who don't please don't last either. He does, and he has.

The problem we have with Kipling is partly of his own making. In his delightful skit about literary rivalry, 'In the Neolithic Age' (p. 451), the lesson hammered home is that '*There are nine and sixty ways of constructing tribal lays* | *And-every-single-one-of-them-is-right*'. Yet this easygoing principle depends on an unspoken agreement about what constitutes a 'tribal lay' and gives it value. The 'ways' of writing are not the same as its purposes, and Kipling eventually found himself engaging, with a will, in literary warfare for political or ideological ends. Letters written during the period between the Boer War and the First World War, in particular, often imply that his vocation was the inculcating of home-truths in palatable form, the smuggling of messages disguised as entertainment. As a consequence he was prepared, in certain moods, to accept exactly the kind of hostile criticism to which we object on his behalf. As he wrote to a friend in 1909 about an unfavourable review of *Actions and Reactions*: 'The review wasn't exactly laudatory but I can perfectly see what the man meant and felt. A lot of my stuff to be any good at all in certain quarters must offend and arride in others. And there is no "belt" in this war [i.e. no rule about hitting below the belt]. We got to the stage of poisoning the wells long ago' (*Letters*, iii. 395). We are very far here from the aesthetic principle that all 'tribal lays' are of equal validity, and from the rollicking depiction of disputes within a single literary tribe.

And yet—and yet. In a letter written three days before this dispatch from the ideological front, Kipling wrote to thank the American critic Henry Seidel Canby for sending him his book *The Short Story in English*. After complimenting Canby in familiar style for recognizing 'that loose-lipped old frump Aphra Behn as a workman in her particular—or unparticular style',[13] Kipling goes on:

> In spite of all you say about Henry James you don't seem to me to admit what I believe to be the case—that he is head and shoulders the biggest of them all and will in the end be found to be perhaps the most enduring influence. It's very amusing to see men who, so to say, blaspheme his manner unconsciously saturated with his technical methods. I should have liked a long chapter on him. (*Letters*, iii. 394)

It was James who eight years earlier, in raptures over *Kim*, had advised Kipling to 'chuck public affairs, which are an ignoble scene'[14]—to no avail. Yet the influence of which Kipling speaks in this letter is everywhere in his own work, especially, as might be expected, in post-war fiction such as 'Dayspring Mishandled' (p. 391), but also in 'My Sunday at Home' (p. 209), in 'They' (p. 256), and in 'Mrs Bathurst' (p. 276). Not that Kipling needed the lesson of the Master to learn the love of literary language and the craft of style. But his obsession with craftsmanship, though it has some affinity with the aestheticism of the 1880s and 1890s, springs from a fundamentally different and personal source. It is Kipling's secret—the figure in his carpet, to quote James again. It is the confiding (and withholding, for something is always kept back) of this secret which, in the work of every great writer, fascinates readers, arouses their desire, and enriches their own imaginative life. The curious thing is that the process is renewable—in the case of writers as good as Kipling, endlessly so. His best stories, from *Plain Tales from the Hills* to *Limits and Renewals*, are as fresh, as astonishing, as moving, as funny, as darkling at the twentieth reading as at the first. What is his secret? What, then, does he know?

[13] It is rare to find references to Behn by an Edwardian writer outside the academy. Kipling added: 'I've often thought that she in *Oroonookoo* [*sic*] and Defoe in many tales drew from the same inkpot if with different pens.'

[14] *Letters*, ed. L. Edel, vol. iv (1984), 212.

The Outsider

What Kipling knows, first of all, is that he does not belong. His stories and poems are filled with images of belonging: family, school, village, church, club, regiment, class, caste, tribe, nation; wolf-pack, beehive, seal-herd; horses in a pasture, locomotives in a shed; even a steamship offers its boilerplates and rivets the chance to participate in a collective identity.[15] Solidarity with one's kind is the most precious gift in Kipling's world: he founded a fictional Masonic Lodge, 'Faith and Works 5837', to offer the characters in his stories about the Great War and its aftermath the comfort he knew they deserved.[16] But Kipling's emblem is the Cat that Walked by Himself, who is both inside and outside the warm cave and the ordered lives of beasts and men.

The roots of this knowledge lie where we might expect, in the first place of belonging, the family. Kipling was born in Bombay, the elder of two children; his sister Alice ('Trix') was two years younger than him. His father, John Lockwood Kipling, had come out to India with his wife Alice, in order to take up a post as principal of a Bombay art school. He eventually became curator of the Lahore Museum, an occupation at which he excelled and for which he would still be remembered even without the loving tribute to the 'Treasure-house' and its guardian in the opening chapter of *Kim*. The Kiplings were ordinary, middle-class Anglo-Indians, not settlers: most English people who came to India to work, whether in business or the civil administration, did so with the intention of returning home, either after their tour of duty or, if they were there for the longer term, on retirement, as Kipling's parents were to do. Like other Anglo-Indians (all those who could afford it), they sent their children home to be educated, and this is what happened to Rudyard and his sister. Readers will find the details in the headnote to 'Baa Baa, Black Sheep' (p. 559), but briefly what happened was that the children were taken to England and left in lodgings at Southsea, to be looked after by the owners of the house as paying guests. Rudyard was 5 and a half, Trix not quite 3. For the next five years, the only contact Kipling had with his parents was by letter. He was subjected to physical and emotional humiliation, some of which was to do with the monstrous pettiness of

15 'The Ship that Found Herself' (*The Day's Work*, 1898), not in this edition.

16 The Lodge first appears in 'In the Interests of the Brethren' and three other stories in *Debits and Credits* (1926): 'The Janeites', 'A Madonna of the Trenches', and 'A Friend of the Family'. Members of the Lodge appear also in 'Fairy-Kist' and 'The Tender Achilles' (*Limits and Renewals*, 1932; 'Fairy-Kist' is included in this edition, p. 409).

domestic Calvinism, but above all he felt himself cut off, separated, estranged—a feeling which was confirmed (and allegorized) by the delayed discovery of his extreme short-sightedness. Something broke in him which was never made whole. All his life he was drawn to stories of benign surrogacy and adoption, in which the cast-out were fostered and cherished as he had not been. *The Jungle Books* are founded on this pattern: Mowgli, lost (or abandoned) by his parents is rescued by Mother Wolf and Father Wolf; Rikki-tikki-tavi is adopted by a human family after a flood washes him out of his mother's burrow; Little Toomai is taken to witness the elephants' dance; Purun Bhagat becomes the presiding deity of a Himalayan village. Stories of white men who are loved and worshipped by native tribes belong to this pattern, whatever other white man's burden they bear; so do the Masonic stories I have mentioned, in which the waifs and strays of the War are cared for, often by men who have lost their own children. As for *Kim*, the orphan hero is spoiled for choice, and can take his pick of the Lama, the 'Sahiba', the Regiment, and the Secret Service as a substitute family. Yet in all these stories there are figures, or traces, of isolation, of exclusion, of the self-contained or the unassimilable. For Kipling knew, also, that solidarity was an illusion, sometimes a treacherous one, that he at least was alone and shiftless, like Mowgli, cast out by wolf-pack and village alike. In one of the most poignant passages of *Something of Myself*, Kipling describes the brief respite from the 'House of Desolation' at Southsea given by holidays at The Grange, his beloved Aunt Georgy's house in London:[17]

> At first I must have been escorted there, but later I went alone, and arriving at the house would reach up to the open-work iron bell-pull on the wonderful gate that let me in to all felicity. When I had a house of my own, and The Grange was emptied of meaning, I begged for and was given that bell-pull for my entrance, in the hope that other children might also feel happy when they rang it.

There would be an incalculable difference to that second sentence if it simply read: 'When I had a house of my own, I begged for and was given . . .' In the modulation from 'felicity' to 'hope', the intervening note of pain, *and the Grange was emptied of meaning*, is gratuitous, chilling, and apt (for a grange should be stored, should be filled with good things); readers of Kipling will recognize as characteristic both the stroke of knowledge and the refusal to flinch.

[17] Aunt Georgy was his mother's sister, married to the painter Edward Burne-Jones.

Surrogacy fails in the end, and the original bond cannot be renewed. The last lines of 'Baa, Baa, Black Sheep' (p. 113) declare this principle, by which Kipling's art would always abide. The child cannot belong again to his mother *as if she had never gone*. After the Fall, *all the Love in the world will not take away that knowledge*. These are the 'limits' which, as the title of Kipling's final book suggests, attend the most longed-for 'renewals'.

Not belonging is a curse, but also a privilege. Kim's bazaar nickname is 'Little Friend of all the World'; Mowgli is 'of one blood' with all the peoples of the Jungle; Kotick, the White Seal, leads his people to salvation; Strickland, the police officer whose mastery of disguise is also an attribute of Sherlock Holmes, goes 'deeper than the skin' among the natives of India;[18] the narrator in 'My Sunday at Home' (p. 209) revels in his apartness from the two cultures which he sees enmeshed in each other's coils beneath him; the cat knows both the warm cave and the wild wet woods; the speaker of 'Chant-Pagan' (p. 480) is self-emancipated from the social niceties and nastiness of 'awful old England'. The privilege of not belonging is that you notice things: as Kipling says in *Something of Myself*, his time in the 'House of Desolation' at Southsea was a '[not] unsuitable preparation for my future, in that it demanded constant wariness, the habit of observation, and attendance on moods and tempers'. Accordingly Kipling's stories are full of self-contained people, especially men and children, who watch and listen and hold their tongues; effusiveness is for him the sin against the Holy Ghost. Often the narrator himself is such a tacit figure, a scene-setter and enabler rather than a participant (examples in this edition include 'With the Main Guard', 'Mrs Bathurst', and 'The Bull that Thought'), but even when he does take part in the action he may give himself the least conspicuous role, as he does in 'The Village that Voted the Earth was Flat' (p. 293). An outsider is often best placed to 'realize' (be conscious of, and bring to consciousness) the fellowship from which he is excluded.

Not belonging is a privilege, but also a curse. It leads ultimately to scepticism about identity itself. Kipling's stories are filled with divided or multiple selves, and with doubts about the validity of the 'self'. 'The Jungle is shut to me and the village gates are shut to me,' Mowgli

[18] 'Miss Youghal's Sais', *Plain Tales from the Hills* (1888); Strickland also appears in 'The Bronckhorst Divorce Case' and (a cameo role) in 'To Be Filed for Reference' in the same collection; later in 'The Mark of the Beast' and 'The Return of Imray' (*Life's Handicap*, 1891), *Kim* (1901, ch. 12) and 'A Deal in Cotton' (*Actions and Reactions*, 1909).

sings. 'As Mang [the bat] flies between the beasts and birds so fly I between the village and the Jungle. . . . These two things fight together in me as the snakes fight in the spring.' Georgy, the 'Brushwood Boy' (*The Day's Work*, 1898) leads a life divided between the exemplary performance of his duty, and a dream-world in which his identity undergoes fantastic transformations and is supernaturally linked to the dream-life of the woman he will eventually marry. (He is an especially significant figure in this context because he so truly belongs to his class and profession, he is so wholly integrated into the collective life of school and army; the self is not cut off or cast out, but implodes.) In another story from this collection, 'The Bridge-Builders' (p. 163), the engineer Findlayson is precipitated by a flood (both literal and symbolic) into another dimension of identity and existence, in which he witnesses a conclave of the Indian gods. In the midst of his shape-changes, his delighted adoption of one disguise after another, Kim is arrested by fits of self-unseeing: 'Who is Kim—Kim—Kim?' St Paul, in 'The Manner of Men' (*Limits and Renewals*, 1932) is disparaged by one of the characters for having 'the woman's trick of taking the tone and colour of whoever he talked to'.[19] He does this, as he tells us himself in the poem which follows the story, to draw people to Christ: he has been 'made all things to all men', crossing the boundaries of race and nationality, speaking in every language, so that he can enter the identities of others and bend them to his purpose:

Since I was overcome
By that great Light and Word,
I have forgot or forgone
The self men call their own
(Being made all things to all men)
So that I might save some
At such small price, to the Lord,
As being all things to all men.

The title of the poem is 'At His Execution'. On the point of death, Paul prays for release from his shifting, groundless identity:

I was made all things to all men,
But now my course is done—
And now is my reward—
Ah, Christ, when I stand at Thy Throne

[19] The events of the story are based on Acts 27 and 28: 1–11, the account of the shipwreck of the vessel in which Paul was being transported as a prisoner to Rome. The story is told by the captain and second-in-command of the vessel.

With those I have drawn to the Lord,
Restore me my self again!

Only after death can such a restoration be imagined. If, as M. Voiron says in 'The Bull that Thought', 'Life is sweet to us all; to the artist who lives many lives in one, sweetest' (p. 379), it is equally true that 'many lives in one' may make life itself unbearable.

The Blissful Seat

England was not, and never became, Kipling's native land. In chapter 3 of *Something of Myself*, he describes his 'joyous homecoming' to India—more particularly to Lahore and his family, his 'people':

> I found myself at Bombay where I was born, moving among sights and smells that made me deliver in the vernacular sentences whose meaning I knew not. Other Indian-born boys have told me how the same thing happened to them.
>
> There were yet three or four days' rail to Lahore, where my people lived. After these, my English years fell away, nor ever, I think, came back in full strength.

Although mysteriously potent, the imprint of India is no more permanent than that of England. Already, in the sentence which speaks of the English years falling away, their return is envisaged. What India does is to limit their capacity to come back 'in full strength'. Kipling would not be absorbed by England; on the contrary, he would cultivate, deliberately, the attitude of a stranger and pilgrim. In 'The Prophet and the Country' (*Debits and Credits*, 1926) the narrator meets an American nomad, exiled from his native land; but he himself is comically estranged, as the opening of the story makes clear:

> North of London stretches a country called 'The Midlands,' filled with brick cities, all absolutely alike, but populated by natives who, through heredity, have learned not only to distinguish between them but even between the different houses; so that at meals and at evening multitudes return, without confusion or scandal, each to the proper place.

By the time he wrote this Kipling had elected Sussex as his home, though when he first settled there he wrote that it was 'the most marvellous of all foreign countries that I have ever been in' (*Letters*, iii. 113).[20] His evocations of Sussex life have the eagerness, the loving

[20] The remark is often taken to apply to England as a whole, but the context makes it clear that 'England' is a synecdoche for Sussex, and indeed for a particular part of it.

accuracy of a naturalized, not a native son. Moreover they are profoundly literary. The main use of the motor car, he claimed, was 'the discovery of England', and in a letter to the journalist Filson Young he described 'a day in the car in an English county' as

a day in some fairy museum where all the exhibits are alive and real and yet none the less delightfully mixed up with books. For instance, in six hours, I can go from the land of the *Ingoldsby Legends* by way of the Norman Conquest and the Barons' War into Richard Jefferies' country, and so through the Regency, one of Arthur Young's less known tours, and *Celia's Arbour*, into Gilbert White's territory.[21]

This sense of life being 'delightfully mixed up with books' is a constant preoccupation in Kipling's work. His stories are alive with storytelling, with characters who frame and interpret their experiences through their reading. Books, sometimes real and sometimes imagined (like 'M. de C.'s' pamphlet in 'The Bonds of Discipline', p. 234) form the starting point of many stories and poems and sometimes their subject-matter (in one of his last stories, 'Proofs of Holy Writ', Shakespeare and Ben Jonson discuss the translation of a passage from the Bible intended for the Authorized Version; 'The Coiner', p. 503 is about the genesis of *The Tempest*).[22] His characters often describe each other in terms of characters from stories they know: the boys in *Stalky & Co.* do this obsessively, drawing on the Latin classics and the works of Bret Harte with impartial glee.

The bookishness of Kipling's work has a 'period' feel to it—he was, to use the old-fashioned term, a 'man of letters', writing in the last phase of a homogeneous literary culture; and it has a contemporary feel, confirming, to use the new-fangled term, the 'intertextuality' of all writing; but it is also, I would suggest, peculiar to him, and marks his work in a completely personal sense. It gives us a key to the problem of origins, of belonging, and of identity which shapes his art.

The key opens a door in time from Kipling's late fiction to the source of his imaginative life. 'Fairy-Kist', published in 1927 and

The poem 'Sussex' (*The Five Nations*, 1903) attempts an impossible synthesis between the *choice* to live in one place rather than another and the *fate* which makes you a native of one place and no other, whether you like it or not.

[21] For a longer extract from this letter, see headnote to 'They' (pp. 606–7).

[22] 'Proofs of Holy Writ' was not published separately in Kipling's lifetime and first appeared in the Sussex Edition. As you might expect, the stories in *Puck of Pook's Hill* (1906) and *Rewards and Fairies* (1910) are especially literary, indeed Shakespearian—the whole idea for them came from the Kipling children getting up a performance of *A Midsummer Night's Dream* in the garden at Bateman's.

included in Kipling's last collection, *Limits and Renewals*, depends for its plot and interpretation on a story by the Victorian children's author Juliana Horatia Ewing.[23] This story, called *Mary's Meadow*, itself tells us about life shaped by literature, for the children in the story make up a game with characters from an old herbal. Mrs Ewing is not the only author whose work enters into the design of 'Fairy-Kist'—she is strangely opposed, in the interpretative scheme of the tale, to Sir Arthur Conan Doyle and the figure of Sherlock Holmes—but she is more important than Conan Doyle because of the genre in which she wrote and because she is one of the morning stars of Kipling's creativity.

In the opening chapter of *Something of Myself* Kipling describes reading as his 'salvation' in the House of Desolation at Southsea, the 'means to everything that would make me happy'. He goes on:

> As soon as my pleasure in this was known, deprivation from reading was added to my punishments. I then read by stealth and the more earnestly.
>
> There were not many books in that house, but Father and Mother as soon as they heard I could read sent me priceless volumes. One I have still, a bound copy of *Aunt Judy's Magazine* of the early 'seventies, in which appeared Mrs. Ewing's *Six to Sixteen*. I owe more in circuitous ways to that tale than I can tell. I knew it, as I know it still, almost by heart. Here was a history of real people and real things.

The truthfulness of this (truth to the psychology of childhood, to the *priceless* intensity of early reading, to the bond between pleasure and transgression) seems indisputable and of central significance. We take our divinities where we find them. The subject of Mrs Ewing's book is an Anglo-Indian tale about two sisters sent to be educated in England; its title covers the years of Kipling's life between his abandonment in England and his return to India. She, then, is Kipling's true foster-mother, and literature his only home. The implications of this are spelled out in another passage from the same chapter:

> When my Father sent me a *Robinson Crusoe* with steel engravings I set up in business alone as a trader with savages (the wreck parts of the tale never much interested me), in a mildewy basement room where I stood my solitary confinements. My apparatus was a coconut shell strung on a red cord, a tin trunk, and a piece of packing-case which kept off any other world. Thus fenced about, everything inside the fence was quite real, but mixed with the smell of damp cupboards. If the bit of board fell, I had to begin the magic all

[23] For details see the headnote, pp. 643–4.

over again. I have learned since from children who play much alone that this rule of 'beginning again in a pretend game' is not uncommon. The magic, you see, lies in the ring or fence that you take refuge in.

This is where Kipling belongs: his family, his race, his people. His tribe is the tribe of writers, who 'set up in business alone', who 'trade with savages' (that's you and me, incidentally); in his basement he joins an underground nation of 'children who play much alone'.[24] No wonder Kipling's writing pullulates, from his schooldays forward, with imitations, pastiches, parodies, literary burglaries and crimes of passion; no wonder he was untroubled by plagiarism, whether his own or others', since literary theft is all in the family; on the other hand he foamed with rage at the illegitimate piracy of unscrupulous publishers (*outsiders*, *intruders*). No bond in life could ever be as authentic as that which, dimensionless and fictive, bound him to the other members of his craft.

Of course literature is not a proper place, not a real community; but then, nor is any other. At least the writer knows, in advance of his people, what David knew: 'we are strangers before thee, and sojourners, as were all our fathers: our days on the earth are as a shadow, and there is none abiding' (1 Chronicles 29: 15). The passion with which Kipling creates and recreates the paradise of belonging is the passion of exile. In *Paradise Lost*, Milton writes that the Fall

> Brought death into the world, and all our woe,
> With loss of Eden, till one greater Man
> Restore us, and regain the blissful seat.

But that lies in the future. Kipling found his 'blissful seat' in hell, in the mildewy basement of the House of Desolation—a refuge which never ceased to depend, fortunately for us, on his 'beginning again in a pretend game'.

[24] 'The Story of Muhammad Din' (p. 20) is (in one of its aspects) a fable on this subject.

CHRONOLOGY OF KIPLING'S LIFE AND WORK

(Kipling is referred to as RK, his father as JLK. Alice is always Kipling's mother; his sister Alice is referred to by her nickname Trix. Entries for each year after 1886 start with the major publication(s) of that year).

1865 30 December. Born in Bombay. Named Joseph Rudyard, after his Kipling grandfather and Lake Rudyard, near Burslem, in Staffordshire, where his parents met in 1863. Baptized in Bombay Cathedral.

RK's father, John Lockwood Kipling, born 1837, the son of a Methodist minister; attended art school in Stoke and worked for a firm of architectural sculptors in London. In 1864 he took up a post at the School of Art in Bombay; shortly before leaving he married Alice Macdonald, also born 1837, the daughter of a famous Wesleyan preacher, George Browne Macdonald. Alice's four sisters all played an important part in RK's early life, esp. Georgiana (Aunt Georgy), who had married the painter Edward Burne-Jones in 1860.

1868 February. The Kiplings travel to England for the birth (11 June) of their second child, Alice (Trixie or Trix); return to India in November.

1870 April. John, the Kipling's third child, dies shortly after birth.

1871 15 April. The Kiplings sail to England, with the intention of leaving their children there (for health reasons and to have them educated at home, a common practice among English families in India).

3 October. RK and Trix are placed as paying boarders with a family in Southsea (for details see headnote to 'Baa Baa, Black Sheep', p. 559). In the years which follow RK suffers, by his own account, physical and emotional abuse. His eyesight deteriorates but his short-sightedness is not diagnosed until 1877.

1872 RK attends Hope House day-school in Southsea. At this period he has not yet learned to read or write; he will not learn until 1874.

1873 December. RK pays the first of four Christmas visits to the Burne-Jones's house, The Grange, in North End Road, Fulham, a haven from his Southsea misery.

1875 JLK appointed Principal of the New Mayo School of Art in Lahore, and Curator of the Museum.

1877 January. Aunt Georgie, alarmed by evidence of RK's short-sightedness, writes to Alice urging her to return to England.

March. Alice arrives and takes RK and Trix away from Southsea. The children spend the summer holidays at Goldings Hill, a farm near Loughton, Essex. Trix, however, returns to Southsea where she remains until 1880.

1878 January. RK starts at United Services College at Westward Ho!, Devon; the headmaster, Cormell Price, was a friend of RK's parents. RK meets George Beresford (M'Turk in *Stalky & Co.*) and later Lionel Charles Dunsterville (Stalky); he himself is nicknamed 'Gigger' from his spectacles or 'gig-lamps'.

Summer. JLK takes RK to Paris where he is organizing the Indian section of the Arts and Manufactures display at the International Exposition. RK dates his lifelong love of France from this trip.

1879 Begins writing poems (only a few of which find their way into his own collected edition).

June. First known story, 'My First Adventure', published under the pen-name 'Nickson' in *The Scribbler*, a family magazine compiled by RK with the Burne-Jones and Morris children.

1880 RK goes to Southsea to take Trix away; meets Florence Garrard (Flo), two years older than him, with whom he falls in love.

1881 Edits United Services College Chronicle, producing seven issues June 1881–July 1882. A further fourteen issues contain contributions by him.

December. *Schoolboy Lyrics* printed by RK's parents unbeknownst to him. Twenty-two of the twenty-three poems later collected in *Early Verse* (vol. xvii of Outward Bound edition, 1897).

1882 Easter. Meets Stephen Wheeler, editor of the *Civil and Military Gazette* in Lahore (*CMG*), who is in England on leave, and at JLK's request agrees to consider RK for a job.

July. Leaves United Services College. Spends his last summer holiday partly at Rottingdean with the Burne-Joneses. Before leaving for India (20 September), RK proposes to Flo Garrard and believes they have an 'understanding' amounting to an engagement.

November. Begins work at the *CMG* as sub-editor on monthly salary of 100 rupees (approx £6 13*s* 4*d*.). The paper is owned by local lawyers and businessmen including Sir George Allen, owner of the national daily, the Allahabad *Pioneer*.

8 November. RK's sonnet 'Two Lives' published in *The World*, his first commercial publication (one guinea).

During this period RK writes a group of poems which he calls 'Sundry Phansies' and dedicates to Flo Garrard. Eight are reprinted in subsequent collections.

1883 Summer. First visit to Simla, the hill-station where the government of India takes up residence in the hot weather.

Late July. Alice Kipling travels to England.

1884 January. Alice returns with Trix. The family are together in a permanent location for the first time since childhood.

July. Flo Garrard writes to end their relationship, which she does not consider to have amounted to an engagement.

November. RK and Trix print *'Echoes' by Two Writers*, a series of verse skits and parodies.

1885 March. Travels to Rawalpindi and the North-West Frontier to cover the Viceroy's reception for Abdur Rahman, Amir of Afghanistan. This is RK's only visit to the frontier. He ventures across the border at Jumrood and is fired on by a tribesman hiding among the rocks in the Pass.

Summer. Assigned to Simla to cover the social season. Meets Mrs Burton (possibly a model for Mrs Hauksbee). The Viceroy, Lord Dufferin, is a friend of the Kipling family.

Autumn. Works on 'Mother Maturin', his novel of Indian life, which he will never finish but some of whose material he will use in other stories and in *Kim*.

December. Publication of *Quartette*, the Christmas annual of the *CMG*, written by the four members of the Kipling family; RK's contributions include 'The Strange Ride of Morrowbie Jukes' and 'The Phantom 'Rickshaw'.

1886 Publications: *Departmental Ditties*. The volume, printed on the *CMG* press, is made up to look like an official envelope tied with red tape. The first edition sells out quickly and a second with additional poems is published by a Calcutta firm, Thacker, Spink & Co.; the volume makes Kipling's local name.

5 April. Admitted as Freemason to the Lodge Hope and Perseverance, no. 782, EC, at Lahore, eight months short of minimum age of 21. A month later passes to second degree.

Autumn. His friend Sir Ian Hamilton sends the manuscript of 'The Mark of the Beast' to England where it is rejected by Andrew Lang and William Sharp.

October. Lang reviews *Departmental Ditties* in *Longman's Magazine*, the first English review of RK's work.

6 December. Raised to Master Mason, Sublime Degree, at Lahore; is Acting Secretary of the Lodge and becomes Secretary in January 1887.

1887 Stephen Wheeler retires as editor of *CMG*; replaced by E. Kay Robinson, who unlike Wheeler encourages RK to write stories as well as articles and remodels the paper with new type and layout. RK undertakes series of 'turn-overs' (pieces of both fiction and non-fiction, beginning on page 1 and continuing on the next page) in which many of the stories of *Plain Tales from the Hills* make their first appearance.

7 November. Resigns as Secretary of Lodge and asks for a Clearance Certificate to join Lodge Independence with Philanthropy in Allahabad, where he is to edit *The Week's News*, the magazine supplement of the *Pioneer*.

Writes series of articles about a trip to the native states of Rajputana (modern Rajasthan), published in the *Pioneer* Dec. 1887–Feb. 1888 and collected in *Letters of Marque*.

1888 Publications: *Plain Tales from the Hills*; *Soldiers Three*, *The Story of the Gadsbys*, *In Black and White*, *Under the Deodars*, *The Phantom 'Rickshaw*, and *Wee Willie Winkie* published by A. H. Wheeler and Co. in their 'Indian Railway Library' series.

Trix becomes engaged to John Fleming, an officer seconded from the Queen's Own Borderers to the Survey department. After a break the engagement is renewed and the couple marry in 1889.

1889 A combination of personal and professional reasons persuades RK to leave India. He funds his trip in part by selling the copyrights of his published volumes.

Leaves by ship (3 March) from Calcutta; visits Rangoon, Singapore, Hong Kong, and Canton, where he joins a steamer to Japan, arriving 15 April. Leaves Japan (11 May) for San Francisco, arriving 28 May. Visits Portland, Tacoma, Yellowstone Park; travels via Salt Lake City, Omaha, and Chicago to Pennsylvania, where he stays with Professor Aleck Hill and his wife Edmonia (close friends met in India). Visits Washington, Philadelphia, Boston, and other places in New England. In Elmira (New York) meets Mark Twain.

Briefly engaged to Caroline Taylor, younger sister of Mrs Hill; the engagement is broken off on religious grounds.

25 September. Leaves for England.

5 October. Arrives Liverpool; travels on to London where he finds rooms at 19 Villiers Street, off the Strand.

Andrew Lang introduces RK at the Savile Club. Begins publishing verse in *Macmillan's Magazine* whose editor used to work for the *Pioneer*; another Indian contact, Stephen Wheeler, introduces RK to the editor of the *St James's Gazette*. Lang advises the publishing firm of Sampson Low, for whom he is a reader, to take over the Indian Railway Library volumes.

1890 Publications: first English editions of *Plain Tales from the Hills* and the Indian Railway Library volumes.

Mrs K. W. Clifford, a successful minor novelist, introduces RK to Macmillan, who will eventually become his main English publishers; Walter Besant introduces him to the firm of literary agents A. P. Watt and Son.

22 February. First of the poems which later make up *Barrack-Room Ballads* published in *Scots Observer*, whose editor, W. E. Henley, has become a friend of RK. Other poems appear in American newspapers.

Spring. Forms close friendship with Wolcott Balestier, an American literary agent working in London, from a wealthy and well-connected New England family. Wolcott's brother, Beatty, has the reputation of a ne'er-do-well; he has two sisters, Caroline (Carrie) and Josephine.

May. Visits Flo Garrard at her studio in Paris which she shares with a friend, Mabel Price.

Kipling's father and mother arrive from India on leave (to late summer 1891).

June. Wolcott's mother, his brother Beatty, and his sisters arrive in London; RK does not yet meet them. Beatty returns to America in July.

July. Agrees to collaborate with Wolcott on a novel, an adventure story of which Wolcott will write the chapters set in America and Kipling the ones set in India. This will become *The Naulahka* (see below). Meets Wolcott's sister Josephine.

August. Completes a draft of *The Light that Failed*. The stress of overwork aggravated by fictionalizing of his relationship with Flo Garrard in the novel brings him close to breakdown.

October. RK suffers from influenza and depression; is advised to travel and goes to Naples and Sorrento, where he stays with former Viceroy Lord Dufferin, now Italian Ambassador.

25 October. Proposed for membership of the Savile (elected 30 January 1891). The proposal is supported by, among others, Walter Besant, Edmund Gosse, Rider Haggard, Thomas Hardy, W. E. Henley, Henry James, and George Saintsbury.

Winter. Meets Caroline (Carrie) Balestier, Wolcott's sister; she is three years older than he, mannish, and disliked by RK's family.

Corresponds with Robert Louis Stevenson, who writes from Samoa praising *Soldiers Three*.

1891 Publications: *The Light that Failed*. The novel first appeared in *Lippincott's Magazine*, and the magazine text was separately issued; this version was in twelve chapters and had a happy ending. Later in the year the first English trade edition appeared with fifteen chapters and the unhappy ending which had been RK's original version (see preface) and which is retained in subsequent editions. Both versions had been prepared for copyright purposes by the end of 1890. It has been suggested that Carrie Balestier was responsible for persuading RK to publish the version with the happy ending. Also: *The City of Dreadful Night and Other Places*; *Life's Handicap*—a number of the stories in this volume were also published in America by RK's authority under the title *Mine Own People*, with an introduction by Henry James.

RK suppresses publication in India and England of two collections of stories, articles, and travel sketches, *The Smith Administration* and *Letters of Marque*, later included in *From Sea to Sea* (1899).

Publication of *Beast and Man in India* by JLK to which RK contributes poems and verse chapter headings; the book is also an important source for the *Jungle Books*.

May–June. Brief trip to United States to visit Harry Macdonald, RK's eldest uncle. Harry dies while RK is at sea and RK is indignant at being met by reporters at the dock.

July. Leaves his rooms in Villiers Street.

August. Travels to South Africa, and then on to New Zealand, arriving at Wellington on 18 October.

6 November. Leaves New Zealand for Australia; arrives Sydney, and a week later travels by ship to Melbourne and Adelaide. From Adelaide the ship continues to Colombo, Ceylon, arriving early December. From Colombo RK travels to Tuticorin at the southern tip of India, and then across the country by train to Lahore, arriving a few days before Christmas. There he learns of the death from typhoid of Wolcott Balestier. Immediately leaves Lahore for Bombay, and from there (27 December) travels to England.

1892 Publications: *The Naulahka*, the adventure story on which he had collaborated with Wolcott; the misspelling is probably Wolcott's, perhaps preserved by RK out of affection. *Barrack-Room Ballads and Other Verses* : some of the material had been published in America in 1890 (see above); the American edition of the 1892 volume was called *Ballads and Barrack-Room Ballads*.

10 January. Arrives at Victoria Station and is met by Mrs Balestier, Carrie, and Josephine.

18 January. Marries Carrie at All Souls' Church, Langham Place.

2 February. The Kiplings sail from Liverpool to New York. From there they travel to the Balestier family home in Brattleboro, Vermont.

20 February. RK travels to New York, Chicago, and as far west as the Rocky Mountains to write travel sketches for the *CMG* and other papers.

March. Buys land in Brattleboro for house, to be called 'Naulakha' (the name means 'nine lakhs of rupees', a 'lakh' being 100,000).

4 April. The Kiplings travel to Japan, arriving Yokohama 20 April.

9 June. RK's bank fails and he looses nearly £2,000; the Kiplings are forced to cut their trip short and return to the United States.

Summer. The Kiplings live in Bliss Cottage while Naulakha is being built.

29 December. Birth of Josephine Kipling.

1893 Publications: *Many Inventions*.

Summer. The Kiplings move into Naulakha.

November. Kipling's father retires from his post at the Lahore art school and museum.

1894 Publications: *The Jungle Book*.

March. RK visits Bermuda.

April–August. The Kiplings visit England, where RK's parents are living at Tisbury, Wiltshire.

July. Buys back British copyright of Indian Railway Library volumes.

1895 Publications: *The Second Jungle Book*.

January. Meets Theodore Roosevelt in Washington, where Carrie is recovering from severe burns in a domestic accident.

July–August. The Kiplings travel to England for their summer holiday.

Winter. The American publishing firm Scribner's offers to issue RK's complete works. Their agent in the negotiations, Frank N. Doubleday, later sets up his own firm and takes over the publishing of RK's work in America.

1896 Publications: *The Seven Seas*.

The Kiplings quarrel with Beatty over his superintending of the building work at Naulakha, his alleged misappropriation of funds, and his drinking. In March Beatty petitions for bankruptcy, blaming his sister for his plight. On 6 May RK and Beatty are involved in a brawl in which Beatty threatens RK with personal violence; RK presses a charge of assault and Beatty is arrested on 9 May. The hearing on 12 May is swamped by reporters and sightseers, and RK is deeply hurt by the publicity, much of it hostile and finger-pointing; local opinion is also against him. Beatty is ordered to give bail to keep the peace and to appear again in court in September, but RK will by this time have left America.

2 February. Birth of Elsie Kipling.

March. RK travels with his friend Dr Conland to Gloucester, Massachusetts, and to Boston harbour to gather material for deep-sea fishing scenes in *Captains Courageous*.

29 August. The Kiplings leave the United States, arriving Southampton on 9 September.

Autumn. The Kiplings rent Rock House, in Maidencombe, near Torquay, in Devon but spend a miserable winter there and abandon it in the spring.

1897 Publications: *Captains Courageous.*

2 April. RK elected to the *Athenaeum* (at 32 the youngest member).

11 May. The Kiplings leave Rock House and move to London, where they stay at a hotel in Kensington.

Summer. The Kiplings stay at North End House, Rottingdean (see above). RK forms close friendship with his cousin Stanley Baldwin, though he will later become a violent political opponent.

17 July. Publication of 'Recessional' in *The Times.*

17 August. Birth of John Kipling.

25 September. The Kiplings move to a rented house in Rottingdean, The Elms.

A. P. Watt, RK's agent, buys back the copyright of *Departmental Ditties.*

1898 Publications: *An Almanac of Twelve Sports* (verses written for William Nicholson's calendar prints); *A Fleet in Being: Notes of Two Trips with the Channel Squadron*; *The Day's Work.*

January–April. The Kiplings visit South Africa, travelling via Madeira, and staying at a boarding-house in Cape Town. RK's friends include the High Commissioner, Sir Alfred Milner, and Cecil Rhodes, both of whom he had met before in London. In March Kipling visits Rhodesia and returns to Cape Town via Johannesburg.

December. Trix suffers breakdown and spends next three years in nursing homes.

1899 Publications: *Stalky & Co.*; *From Sea to Sea*, containing material previously suppressed by Kipling in 1891.

20 January. The Kiplings sail for New York, where Carrie wants to see her mother and RK to settle publishing arrangements. Both RK and his daughter Josephine fall seriously ill; RK recovers from his lung-complaint, but Josephine dies (6 March). RK is advised to rest for six months and not to spend winters in England.

June. Return to England. Andrew Carnegie offers the Kiplings the use of a small house in the Highlands during the summer.

October. Beginning of the Boer War. Publication of 'The Absent-Minded Beggar' (31 October) which, set to music by Sir Arthur Sullivan, enjoys enormous popular success, and raises £250,000 for soldiers' families.

RK's passion for motoring sparked by visit of Lord Rothermere in 'one of those motor-car things'. He hires his first car and driver.

December. Refuses offer of knighthood (KCB) from Lord Salisbury's government.

1900 20 January. The Kiplings leave England for South Africa, arriving Cape Town 5 February. RK visits military hospitals and meets Lord Roberts before Roberts leaves to take up command of British forces. Cecil Rhodes plans to build a house on his 'Groote Schuur' estate in Cape Town for use by writers and artists; he offers the first tenure to the Kiplings.

March. RK contributes to *The Friend*, a newspaper publication for the British forces occupying Bloemfontein (some of his contributions will be published the following year in fellow-journalist Julian Ralph's volume *War's Brighter Side*). Witnesses an engagement at Karee Siding, his only first-hand experience of combat.

April. The Kiplings return to England. During the summer RK organizes a volunteer rifle company at Rottingdean. He also acquires his first motor-car, a steam-driven 'Locomobile'. (In subsequent years he will own a succession of Lanchesters and Rolls-Royces.)

December. The Kiplings travel to South Africa, arriving on Christmas Day. They take up residence at 'The Woolsack', the cottage near 'Groote Schuur' which Rhodes has built. For the next few years (to 1908) they will spend their winters in South Africa. As well as Rhodes himself RK meets Jameson and Baden-Powell.

1901 Publications: *Kim*.

1902 Publications: *Just So Stories*.

1 June. Boer War ends.

10 June. The Kiplings buy 'Bateman's' at Burwash in Sussex; they move in on 2 September. The pattern of their life for the next five years alternates between Sussex and South Africa; in subsequent years they travel extensively and RK discovers new activities and interests (especially skiing and motoring) but Bateman's remains their permanent home, gradually extended by the purchase of surrounding land to a small estate; RK's interest in the rural community embraces both its working life (agriculture and crafts) and the history which is inscribed in its landscape and buildings, and which will provide him with material for much of his pre-war poetry and fiction.

1903 Publications: *The Five Nations*.

November. Again refuses offer of knighthood (KCMG), from Arthur Balfour's government.

1904 Publications: *Traffics and Discoveries*.

RK refuses the first of several requests to stand for Parliament (he is offered a safe Conservative seat in Edinburgh).

First series of 'The Muse among the Motors' (literary pastiches and parodies) appears in the *Daily Mail*; not published in volume form until 1919.

1906 Publications: *Puck of Pook's Hill.*

1907 June. Accepts honorary degrees from Durham and Oxford.

September. Visits Canada and accepts honorary degree from McGill University in Montreal.

December. Awarded Nobel Prize for Literature, the first award to an English writer; travels to Sweden to accept the prize; the occasion is overshadowed by the death of the King of Sweden.

1908 Publications: *Letters to the Family: Notes on a Recent Trip to Canada.*

1909 Publications: *Actions and Reactions*; *Abaft the Funnel* (a 'spoiler' for an unauthorized American edition of early stories and journalism; the title had originally been used for a series of stories in the *CMG*).

Supports the recently founded Boy Scout movement and writes a 'Patrol Song' for Baden-Powell; visits one of the early Scout camps in the New Forest and will appear at Scout rallies in the future.

1910 Publications: *Rewards and Fairies.*

November. Death of RK's mother.

1911 Publications: *A History of England* (with C. R. L. Fletcher).

January. Death of RK's father.

RK and Carrie visit Ireland; the 'dirt and slop and general shiftlessness of Dublin' confirms RK in his support for Ulster and opposition to Home Rule. Up to the beginning of the War he will engage in violent polemic against the Liberal government on behalf of the extreme 'Ulster Covenant'.

John Kipling, whose eyesight will not permit him to follow a career in the Navy, starts at Wellington College with a view to entering the Army.

1913 Visits Egypt.

John Kipling leaves Wellington and attends a 'crammer' at Bournemouth.

1914 4 August. Beginning of First World War. Following Kitchener's appeal for volunteers, John Kipling (a week before his seventeenth birthday) offers himself for a commission but is rejected and proposes to enlist as a private; at RK's request, however, Lord Roberts nominates John to his own regiment, the Irish Guards, and John reports for duty at Warley Barracks on 14 September. Kipling is active in recruitment and appeals for funds.

1915 Publications: *The Fringes of the Fleet.*

12 August. RK travels to France to report on the war; he meets Clemenceau and visits the front.

15 August. John Kipling's battalion leaves for France.

2 October. John Kipling is reported missing at the Battle of Loos (27 September). Carrie persists in hoping he may have been taken prisoner but RK knows better. John's body is not found in his parents' lifetime (his grave was only recently identified).

At the request of the Admiralty, RK reports on activity of the Navy in home waters in a series of articles.

At about this period RK begins to suffer from the abdominal pain, eventually (but too late for effective treatment) diagnosed as duodenal ulcers; the last twenty years of his life are spent in continual bouts of illness.

1916 Publications: *Sea Warfare*, including *The Fringes of the Fleet* and other pieces about the Navy.

1917 Publications: *A Diversity of Creatures.*

May. Refuses offer, conveyed by Stanley Baldwin, of 'pretty much any honour he will accept' from Bonar Law's government; later in the same year engages in protracted correspondence to ensure his name is not put forward for the Companion of Honour.

Becomes a member of the Imperial (later Commonwealth) War Graves Commission, for which he works tirelessly, devising many of the memorial inscriptions including the one set up in every war cemetery, 'Their name liveth for evermore'.

Becomes one of the trustees of the Rhodes Scholarships at Oxford (in July 1925 he will resign over the appointment of a Liberal, Philip Kerr, as Secretary).

1919 Publications: *The Years Between.*

Death of Mrs Balestier, Carrie's mother. Her estate has been considerably diminished by gifts to the incorrigible Beatty.

1920 Publications: *Letters of Travel*, containing three series of letters: 'From Tideway to Tideway', referring to RK's travels in the Orient in 1892; 'Letters to the Family' (referring to Canada; see above, 1908); and 'Egypt of the Magicians', referring to his 1914 trip. In later collected editions a fourth series, 'Brazilian Sketches', was added.

February. RK revisits Southsea with Carrie; his painful memories are undiminished.

Autumn. The Kiplings tour the battlefields over which the Irish Guards had fought, including the site of their son's death.

1921 November. Visits France and accepts honorary degrees from Paris and Strasbourg.

December. Refuses the offer from King George V of the Order of Merit, and is annoyed when news of his refusal is leaked by the Palace.

1922 May. Accompanies the King on pilgrimage to the war graves in France, and ghost-writes the King's speech.

1923 Publications: *Land and Sea Tales for Scouts and Guides*; *The Irish Guards in the Great War*.

October. Elected Rector of St Andrews University.

1924 May. Elsie Kipling announces her engagement to Captain George Bambridge, like her brother an officer in the Irish Guards. The marriage takes place in October. RK, though stoical, is desolate at departure of his last child.

1926 Publications: *Debits and Credits*.

1927 Foundation of the Kipling Society.

1928 January. Acts as one of the pallbearers at Thomas Hardy's funeral at Westminster Abbey.

1930 Publications: *Thy Servant a Dog*.

1932 Publications: *Limits and Renewals*.

Writes 'Proofs of Holy Writ', his last story (collected in Sussex Edition). Begins to write *Something of Myself*, part of a deliberate process of gathering and reflecting on his life's work.

Christmas. King George V makes the first royal broadcast to the Commonwealth; his speech is written by RK.

1933 Publications: *Souvenirs of France*.

1936 13 January. RK taken to hospital with haemorrhage from ulcers.

18 January. RK dies shortly after midnight. His ashes buried (23 January) in Westminster Abbey.

NOTE ON THE TEXT

The text of the stories, including the verse which in some cases accompanies them, is that of *Works* ('Uniform Edition', 1899–1938). The text of the poems is that of the 'Definitive Edition' (1940). Obvious misprints have been silently corrected and a small amount of house-styling has been imposed (e.g. the standard use of single inverted commas); otherwise the text is unchanged. These editions have been chosen because they combine good, though not absolute, authority with the widest dissemination.

Almost all of Kipling's work exists in multiple states: manuscripts and typescripts, magazine versions of the stories, revisions for collected editions, variations in title and wording between Indian, English, and American printings, etc. In many cases the textual history has significance (and certainly interest) but in a selection such as the present, covering the whole of Kipling's career, it would simply not have been practical to attempt to incorporate it in a critical apparatus.

The degree sign (°) indicates a note at the end of the book.

From PLAIN TALES FROM THE HILLS (1888)

Lispeth

Look, you have cast out Love! What Gods are these
You bid me please?
The Three in One, the One in Three? Not so!
To my own gods I go.
It may be they shall give me greater ease
Than your cold Christ and tangled Trinities.

The Convert

She was the daughter of Sonoo, a Hill-man of the Himalayas, and Jadéh his wife. One year their maize failed, and two bears spent the night in their only opium poppy-field just above the Sutlej Valley on the Kotgarh side;° so, next season, they turned Christian, and brought their baby to the Mission to be baptized. The Kotgarh Chaplain christened her Elizabeth, and 'Lispeth' is the Hill or *pahari*° pronunciation.

Later, cholera came into the Kotgarh Valley and carried off Sonoo and Jadéh, and Lispeth became half servant, half companion, to the wife of the then Chaplain of Kotgarh. This was after the reign of the Moravian missionaries° in that place, but before Kotgarh had quite forgotten her title of 'Mistress of the Northern Hills'.

Whether Christianity improved Lispeth, or whether the gods of her own people would have done as much for her under any circumstances, I do not know; but she grew very lovely. When a Hill-girl grows lovely, she is worth travelling fifty miles over bad ground to look upon. Lispeth had a Greek face—one of those faces people paint so often, and see so seldom. She was of a pale, ivory colour, and, for her race, extremely tall. Also, she possessed eyes that were wonderful; and, had she not been dressed in the abominable print-cloths affected by Missions, you would, meeting her on the hillside unexpectedly, have thought her the original Diana of the Romans° going out to slay.

Lispeth took to Christianity readily, and did not abandon it when she reached womanhood, as do some Hill-girls. Her own people hated her because she had, they said, become a white woman and washed herself daily; and the Chaplain's wife did not know what to do with her. One cannot ask a stately goddess, five feet ten in her shoes, to clean plates and dishes. She played with the Chaplain's children and took classes in the Sunday School, and read all the books in the house, and grew more and more beautiful, like the Princesses in fairy tales. The Chaplain's wife said that the girl ought to take service in Simla° as a nurse or something 'genteel'. But Lispeth did not want to take service. She was very happy where she was.

When travellers—there were not many in those years—came in to Kotgarh, Lispeth used to lock herself into her own room for fear they might take her away to Simla, or out into the unknown world.

One day, a few months after she was seventeen years old, Lispeth went out for a walk. She did not walk in the manner of English ladies—a mile and half out, with a carriage-ride back again. She covered between twenty and thirty miles in her little constitutionals, all about and about, between Kotgarh and Narkunda.° This time she came back at full dusk, stepping down the break-neck descent into Kotgarh with something heavy in her arms. The Chaplain's wife was dozing in the drawing-room when Lispeth came in breathing heavily and very exhausted with her burden. Lispeth put it down on the sofa, and said simply, 'This is my husband. I found him on the Bagi° Road. He has hurt himself. We will nurse him, and when he is well your husband shall marry him to me.'

This was the first mention Lispeth had ever made of her matrimonial views, and the Chaplain's wife shrieked with horror. However, the man on the sofa needed attention first. He was a young Englishman, and his head had been cut to the bone by something jagged. Lispeth said she had found him down the hillside, and had brought him in. He was breathing queerly and was unconscious.

He was put to bed and tended by the Chaplain who knew something of medicine; and Lispeth waited outside the door in case she could be useful. She explained to the Chaplain that this was the man she meant to marry; and the Chaplain and his wife lectured her severely on the impropriety of her conduct. Lispeth listened quietly, and repeated her first proposition. It takes a great deal of Christianity to wipe out uncivilised Eastern instincts, such as falling in love at first sight. Lispeth, having found the man she worshipped, did not see why she should keep silent as to her choice. She had no intention of being sent away, either. She was going to nurse that Englishman until he was well enough to marry her. This was her programme.

After a fortnight of slight fever and inflammation, the Englishman recovered coherence and thanked the Chaplain and his wife, and Lispeth—especially Lispeth—for their kindness. He was a traveller in the East, he said—they never talked about 'globe-trotters' in those days, when the P. & O. fleet° was young and small—and had come from Dehra Dun° to hunt for plants and butterflies among the Simla hills. No one at Simla, therefore, knew anything about him. He fancied that he must have fallen over the cliff while reaching out for a fern on a rotten tree-trunk, and that his coolies must have stolen his baggage and fled. He thought he would go back to Simla when he was a little stronger. He desired no more mountaineering.

He made small haste to go away, and recovered his strength slowly. Lispeth objected to being advised either by the Chaplain or his wife; therefore the latter spoke to the Englishman, and told him how matters stood in Lispeth's heart. He laughed a good deal, and said it was very pretty and romantic, but, as he was engaged to a girl at Home, he fancied that nothing would happen. Certainly he would behave with discretion. He did that. Still he found it very pleasant to talk to Lispeth, and walk with Lispeth, and say nice things to her, and call her pet names while he was getting strong enough to go away. It meant nothing at all to him, and everything in the world to Lispeth. She was very happy while the fortnight lasted, because she had found a man to love.

Being a savage by birth, she took no trouble to hide her feelings, and the Englishman was amused. When he went away, Lispeth walked with him up the Hill as far as Narkunda, very troubled and very miserable. The Chaplain's wife, being a good Christian and disliking anything in the shape of fuss or scandal—Lispeth was beyond her management entirely—had told the Englishman to tell Lispeth that he was coming back to marry her. 'She is but a child, you know, and, I fear, at heart a heathen,' said the Chaplain's wife. So all the twelve miles up the Hill the Englishman, with his arm round Lispeth's waist, was assuring the girl that he would come back and marry her; and Lispeth made him promise over and over again. She wept on the Narkunda Ridge till he had passed out of sight along the Muttiani path.°

Then she dried her tears and went in to Kotgarh again, and said to the Chaplain's wife, 'He will come back and marry me. He has gone to his own people to tell them so.' And the Chaplain's wife soothed Lispeth and said, 'He will come back.' At the end of two months Lispeth grew impatient, and was told that the Englishman had gone over the seas to England. She knew where England was, because she had read little geography primers; but, of course, she had no conception of the nature of the sea, being a Hill-girl. There was an old puzzle-map of the World in the house. Lispeth had played with it when she was a child. She unearthed it again, and put it together of evenings, and cried to herself, and tried to imagine where her Englishman was. As she had no ideas of distance or steamboats her notions were somewhat wild. It would not have made the least difference had she been perfectly correct; for the Englishman had no intention of coming back to marry a Hill-girl. He forgot all about her by the time he was butterfly-hunting in Assam. He wrote a book on the East afterwards. Lispeth's name did not appear there.

At the end of three months Lispeth made daily pilgrimage to Narkunda to see if her Englishman was coming along the road. It gave her comfort, and the Chaplain's wife finding her happier thought that she was getting over her 'barbarous and most indelicate folly.' A little later the walks ceased to help Lispeth, and her temper grew very bad. The Chaplain's wife thought this a profitable time to let her know the real state of affairs—that the Englishman had only promised his love to keep her quiet—that he had never meant anything, and that it was wrong and improper of Lispeth to think of marriage with an Englishman, who was of a superior clay, besides being promised in marriage to a girl of his own people. Lispeth said that all this was clearly impossible because he had said he loved her, and the Chaplain's wife had, with her own lips, asserted that the Englishman was coming back.

'How can what he and you said be untrue?' asked Lispeth.

'We said it as an excuse to keep you quiet, child,' said the Chaplain's wife.

'Then you have lied to me,' said Lispeth, 'you and he?'

The Chaplain's wife bowed her head, and said nothing. Lispeth was silent too for a little time; then she went out down the valley, and returned in the dress of a Hill-girl—infamously dirty, but without the nose-stud and ear-rings. She had her hair braided into the long pigtail, helped out with black thread, that Hill-women wear.

'I am going back to my own people,' said she. 'You have killed Lispeth. There is only left old Jadéh's daughter—the daughter of a *pahari* and the servant of *Tarka Devi*.° You are all liars, you English.'

By the time that the Chaplain's wife had recovered from the shock of the announcement that Lispeth had 'verted to her mother's gods the girl had gone; and she never came back.

She took to her own unclean people savagely, as if to make up the arrears of the life she had stepped out of; and, in a little time, she married a woodcutter who beat her after the manner of *paharis*, and her beauty faded soon.

'There is no law whereby you can account for the vagaries of the heathen,' said the Chaplain's wife, 'and I believe that Lispeth was always at heart an infidel.' Seeing she had been taken into the Church of England at the mature age of five weeks, this statement does not do credit to the Chaplain's wife.

Lispeth was a very old woman when she died. She had always a perfect command of English, and when she was sufficiently drunk could sometimes be induced to tell the story of her first love-affair.

It was hard then to realise that the bleared, wrinkled creature, exactly like a wisp of charred rag, could ever have been 'Lispeth of the Kotgarh Mission'.

Three and—an Extra

When halter and heel-ropes are slipped, do not give chase with sticks but with *gram*.°

Punjabi Proverb

After marriage arrives a reaction, sometimes a big, sometimes a little one; but it comes sooner or later, and must be tided over by both parties if they desire the rest of their lives to go with the current.

In the case of the Cusack-Bremmils this reaction did not set in till the third year after the wedding. Bremmil was hard to hold at the best of times; but he was a beautiful husband until the baby died and Mrs Bremmil wore black, and grew thin, and mourned as though the bottom of the Universe had fallen out. Perhaps Bremmil ought to have comforted her. He tried to do so, but the more he comforted the more Mrs Bremmil grieved, and, consequently, the more uncomfortable grew Bremmil. The fact was that they both needed a tonic. And they got it. Mrs Bremmil can afford to laugh now, but it was no laughing matter to her at the time.

Mrs Hauksbee appeared on the horizon; and where she existed was fair chance of trouble. At Simla her by-name was the 'Stormy Petrel'. She had won that title five times to my own certain knowledge. She was a little, brown, thin, almost skinny, woman, with big, rolling, violet-blue eyes, and the sweetest manners in the world. You had only to mention her name at afternoon teas for every woman in the room to rise up and call her not blessed.° She was clever, witty, brilliant, and sparkling beyond most of her kind; but possessed of many devils of malice and mischievousness. She could be nice, though, even to her own sex. But that is another story.°

Bremmil went off at score after the baby's death and the general discomfort that followed, and Mrs Hauksbee annexed him. She took no pleasure in hiding her captives. She annexed him publicly, and saw that the public saw it. He rode with her, and walked with her, and talked with her, and picnicked with her, and tiffined at Peliti's° with her, till people put up their eyebrows and said, 'Shocking!' Mrs Bremmil stayed at home, turning over the dead baby's frocks and crying into the empty cradle. She did not care to do anything else. But some eight dear, affectionate lady-friends explained the situation at length to her in case she should miss the cream of it. Mrs Bremmil listened quietly, and thanked them for their good offices. She was not as clever as Mrs Hauksbee, but she was no fool. She kept her own counsel, and did not speak to Bremmil of what she had heard. This is worth remembering. Speaking to or crying over a husband never did any good yet.

When Bremmil was at home, which was not often, he was more affectionate than usual; and that showed his hand. The affection was forced, partly to soothe his own conscience and partly to soothe Mrs Bremmil. It failed in both regards.

Then 'the A.-D.-C. in Waiting° was commanded by Their Excellencies, Lord and Lady Lytton, to invite Mr and Mrs Cusack-Bremmil to Peterhoff on July 26 at 9-30 P.M.'—'Dancing' in the bottom-left-hand corner.

'I can't go,' said Mrs Bremmil, 'it is too soon after poor little Florrie . . . but it need not stop you, Tom.'

She meant what she said then, and Bremmil said that he would go just to put in an appearance. Here he spoke the thing which was not; and Mrs Bremmil knew it. She guessed—a woman's guess is much more accurate than a man's certainty—that he had meant to go from the first, and with Mrs Hauksbee. She sat down to think, and the outcome of her thoughts was that the memory of a dead child was worth considerably less than the affections of a living husband. She made her plan and staked her all upon it. In that hour she discovered that she knew Tom Bremmil thoroughly, and this knowledge she acted on.

'Tom,' said she, 'I shall be dining out at the Longmores' on the evening of the 26th. You'd better dine at the Club.'°

This saved Bremmil from making an excuse to get away and dine with Mrs Hauskbee, so he was grateful, and felt small and mean at the same time—which was wholesome. Bremmil left the house at five for a ride. About half-past five in the evening a large leather-covered basket came in from Phelps's° for Mrs Bremmil. She was a woman who knew how to dress; and she had not spent a week on designing that dress and having it gored, and hemmed, and herring-boned, and tucked and rucked (or whatever the terms are), for nothing. It was a gorgeous dress—slight mourning.° I can't describe it, but it was what *The Queen* calls 'a creation'—a thing that hit you straight between the eyes and made you gasp. She had not much heart for what she was going to do; but as she glanced at the long mirror she had the satisfaction of knowing that she had never looked so well in her life. She was a large blonde and, when she chose, carried herself superbly.

After the dinner at the Longmores' she went on to the dance—a little late—and encountered Bremmil with Mrs Hauksbee on his arm. That made her flush, and as the men crowded round her for dances she looked magnificent. She filled up all her dances except three, and those she left blank. Mrs Hauksbee caught her eye once; and she knew it was war—real war—between them. She started handicapped in the struggle, for she had ordered Bremmil about just the least little bit in the world too much, and he was beginning to resent it. Moreover, he had never seen his wife look so lovely. He stared at her from doorways, and glared at her from passages as she went about with her partners; and the more he stared, the more taken was he. He could scarcely believe that this was the woman with the red eyes and the black stuff gown who used to weep over the eggs at breakfast.

Mrs Hauksbee did her best to hold him in play, but, after two dances, he crossed over to his wife and asked for a dance.

'I'm afraid you've come too late, *Mister* Bremmil,' she said, with her eyes twinkling.

Then he begged her to give him a dance, and, as a great favour, she allowed him the fifth waltz. Luckily Five stood vacant on his programme. They danced it together, and there was a little flutter round the room. Bremmil had a sort of a notion that his wife could dance, but he never knew she danced so divinely. At the end of that waltz he asked for another—as a favour, not as a right; and Mrs Bremmil said, 'Show me your programme, dear!' He showed it as a naughty little schoolboy hands up contraband sweets to a master. There was a fair sprinkling of 'H' on it, besides 'H' at supper. Mrs Bremmil said nothing, but she smiled contemptuously, ran her pencil through Seven and Nine—two 'H's'—and returned the card with her own name written above—a pet name that only she and her husband used. Then she shook her finger at him, and said laughing, 'Oh, you silly, *silly* boy!'

Mrs Hauksbee heard that, and—she owned as much—felt she had the worst of it. Bremmil accepted Seven and Nine gratefully. They danced Seven, and sat out Nine in one of the little tents. What Bremmil said and what Mrs Bremmil did is no concern of any one.

When the band struck up 'The Roast Beef of Old England,'° the two went out into the verandah, and Bremmil began looking for his wife's dandy (this was before 'rickshaw° days) while she went into the cloak-room. Mrs Hauksbee came up and said, 'You take me in to supper, I think, Mr Bremmil?' Bremmil turned red and looked foolish. 'Ah—h'm! I'm going home with my wife, Mrs Hauksbee. I think there has been a little mistake.' Being a man, he spoke as though Mrs Hauksbee were entirely responsible.

Mrs Bremmil came out of the cloak-room in a swan's-down cloak with a white 'cloud'° round her head. She looked radiant; and she had a right to.

The couple went off into the darkness together, Bremmil riding very close to the dandy.

Then said Mrs Hauksbee to me—she looked a trifle faded and jaded in the lamplight—'Take my word for it, the silliest woman can manage a clever man; but it needs a very clever woman to manage a fool.'

Then we went in to supper.

In the House of Suddhoo

A stone's throw out on either hand
From that well-ordered road we tread,
And all the world is wild and strange:
Churel and ghoul and *Djinn* and sprite°
Shall bear us company to-night,
For we have reached the Oldest Land
Wherein the Powers of Darkness range.

From the Dusk to the Dawn

The house of Suddhoo, near the Taksali Gate,° is two-storied, with four carved windows of old brown wood, and a flat roof. You may recognise it by five red hand-prints arranged like the Five of Diamonds on the whitewash between the upper windows. Bhagwan Dass the grocer and a man who says he gets his living by seal-cutting° live in the lower story with a troop of wives, servants, friends, and retainers. The two upper rooms used to be occupied by Janoo and Azizun, and a little black-and-tan terrier that was stolen from an Englishman's house and given to Janoo by a soldier. To-day, only Janoo lives in the upper rooms. Suddhoo sleeps on the roof generally, except when he sleeps in the street. He used to go to Peshawar° in the cold weather to visit his son who sells curiosities near the Edwardes' Gate,° and then he slept under a real mud roof. Suddhoo is a great friend of mine, because his cousin had a son who secured, thanks to my recommendation, the post of head-messenger to a big firm in the Station.° Suddhoo says that God will make me a Lieutenant-Governor one of these days. I daresay his prophecy will come true. He is very, very old, with white hair and no teeth worth showing, and he has outlived his wits—outlived nearly everything except his fondness for his son at Peshawar. Janoo and Azizun are Kashmiris, Ladies of the City, and theirs was an ancient and more or less honourable profession; but Azizun has since married a medical student from the North-West and has settled down to a more respectable life somewhere near Bareilly.° Bhagwan Dass is an extortionate° and an adulterator.° He is very rich. The man who is supposed to get his living by seal-cutting pretends to be very poor. This lets you know as much as is necessary of the four principal tenants in the house of Suddhoo. Then there is Me of course; but I am only the chorus that comes in at the end to explain things. So I do not count.

Suddhoo was not clever. The man who pretended to cut seals was the cleverest of them all—Bhagwan Dass only knew how to lie—except Janoo. She was also beautiful, but that was her own affair.

Suddhoo's son at Peshawar was attacked by pleurisy, and old Suddhoo was troubled. The seal-cutter man heard of Suddhoo's anxiety and made capital out of it. He was abreast of the times. He got a friend in Peshawar to telegraph daily accounts of the son's health. And here the story begins.

Suddhoo's cousin's son told me, one evening, that Suddhoo wanted to see me; that he was too old and feeble to come personally, and that I should be conferring an everlasting honour on the House of Suddhoo if I went to him. I went; but I think, seeing how well off Suddhoo was then, that he might have sent something better than an *ekka*, which jolted fearfully, to haul out a future Lieutenant-Governor to the City on a muggy April evening. The *ekka* did not run quickly. It was full dark when we pulled up opposite the door of Ranjit Singh's Tomb° near the main gate of the Fort. Here was Suddhoo, and he said that by reason of my condescension, it was absolutely certain that I should become a Lieutenant-Governor while my hair was yet black. Then we talked about the weather and the state of my health, and the wheat crops, for fifteen minutes, in the Huzuri Bagh,° under the stars.

Suddhoo came to the point at last. He said that Janoo had told him that there was an order of the *Sirkar*° against magic, because it was feared that magic might one day kill the Empress of India.° I didn't know anything about the state of the law; but I fancied that something interesting was going to happen. I said that so far from magic being discouraged by the Government it was highly commended. The greatest officials of the State practised it themselves. (If the Financial Statement° isn't magic, I don't know what is.) Then, to encourage him further, I said that, if there was any *jadoo*° afoot, I had not the least objection to giving it my countenance and sanction, and to seeing that it was clean *jadoo*—white magic, as distinguished from the unclean *jadoo* which kills folk. It took a long time before Suddhoo admitted that this was just what he had asked me to come for. Then he told me, in jerks and quavers, that the man who said he cut seals was a sorcerer of the cleanest kind; that every day he gave Suddhoo news of the sick son in Peshawar more quickly than the lightning could fly, and that this news was always corroborated by the letters. Further, that he had told Suddhoo how a great danger was threatening his son, which could be removed by clean *jadoo*; and, of course, heavy payment. I began to see exactly how the land lay, and told Suddhoo that I also understood a little *jadoo* in the Western line, and would go to his house to see that everything was done decently and in order. We set off together; and on the way Suddhoo told me that he had paid the seal-cutter between one hundred and two hundred rupees° already; and the *jadoo* of that night would cost two hundred more. Which was cheap, he said, considering the greatness of his son's danger; but I do not think he meant it.

The lights were all cloaked in the front of the house when we arrived. I could hear awful noises from behind the seal-cutter's shop-front, as if some one were groaning his soul out. Suddhoo shook all over, and while we groped our way upstairs told me that the *jadoo* had begun. Janoo and Azizun met us at the stair-head, and told us that the *jadoo*-work was coming off in their rooms, because there was more space there. Janoo is a lady of a free-thinking turn of mind. She whispered that the *jadoo* was an invention to get money out of Suddhoo, and that the seal-cutter would go to a hot place when he died. Suddhoo was nearly crying with fear and old age. He kept walking up and down the room in the half-light, repeating his son's name over and over again, and asking Azizun if the seal-cutter ought not to make a reduction in the case of his own landlord. Janoo pulled me over to the shadow in the recess of the carved bow-windows. The boards were up, and the rooms were only lit by one tiny oil-lamp. There was no chance of my being seen if I stayed still.

Presently, the groans below ceased, and we heard steps on the staircase. That was the seal-cutter. He stopped outside the door as the terrier barked and Azizun fumbled at the chain, and he told Suddhoo to blow out the lamp. This left the place in jet darkness, except for the red glow from the two *huqas*° that belonged to Janoo and Azizun. The seal-cutter came in, and I heard Suddhoo throw himself down on the floor and groan. Azizun caught her breath, and Janoo backed on to one of the beds with a shudder. There was a clink of something metallic, and then shot up a pale blue-green flame near the ground. The light was just enough to show Azizun, pressed against one corner of the room with the terrier between her knees; Janoo, with her hands clasped, leaning forward as she sat on the bed; Suddhoo, face down, quivering, and the seal-cutter.

I hope I may never see another man like that seal-cutter. He was stripped to the waist, with a wreath of white jasmine as thick as my wrist round his forehead, a salmon coloured loin-cloth round his middle, and a steel bangle on each ankle. This was not awe-inspiring. It was the face of the man that turned me cold. It was blue-gray in the first place. In the second, the eyes were rolled back till you could only see the whites of them; and, in the third, the face was the face of a demon—a ghoul—anything you please except of the sleek, oily old ruffian who sat in the daytime over his turning-lathe downstairs. He was lying on his stomach with his arms turned and crossed behind him, as if he had been thrown down pinioned. His head and neck were the only parts of him off the floor. They were nearly at right angles to the body, like the head of a cobra at spring. It was ghastly. In the centre of the room, on the bare earth floor, stood a big, deep, brass basin, with a pale blue-green light floating in the centre like a night-light. Round that basin the man on the floor wriggled himself three times. How he did it I do not know. I could see the muscles ripple along the spine and fall smooth again; but I could not see any other motion. The head seemed the only thing alive about him, except that slow curl and uncurl of the labouring back-muscles. Janoo from the bed was breathing seventy to the minute; Azizun held her hands before her eyes; and old Suddhoo, fingering at the dirt that had got into his white beard, was crying to himself. The horror of it was that the creeping, crawly thing made no sound—only crawled! And, remember, this lasted for ten minutes, while the terrier whined, and Azizun shuddered, and Janoo gasped, and Suddhoo cried.

I felt the hair lift at the back of my head, and my heart thump like a thermantidote paddle.° Luckily, the seal-cutter betrayed himself by his most impressive trick and made me calm again. After he had finished that unspeakable triple crawl, he stretched his head away from the floor as high as he could, and sent out a jet of fire from his nostrils. Now I knew how fire-spouting is done—I can do it myself—so I felt at ease. The business was a fraud. If he had only kept to that crawl without trying to raise the effect, goodness knows what I might not have thought. Both the girls shrieked at the jet of fire and the head dropped, chin-down on the floor, with a thud; the whole body lying then like a corpse with its arms trussed. There was a pause of five full minutes after this, and the blue-green flame died down. Janoo stooped to settle one of her anklets, while Azizun turned her face to the wall and took the terrier in her arms. Suddhoo put out an arm mechanically to Janoo's *huqa*, and she slid it across the floor with her foot. Directly above the body and on the wall were a couple of flaming portraits, in stamped-paper frames, of the Queen and the Prince of Wales. They looked down on the performance, and to my thinking, seemed to heighten the grotesqueness of it all.

Just when the silence was getting unendurable, the body turned over and rolled away from the basin to the side of the room, where it lay stomach-up. There was a faint 'plop' from the basin—exactly like the noise a fish makes when it takes a fly—and the green light in the centre revived.

I looked at the basin, and saw, bobbing in the water, the dried, shrivelled, black head of a native baby—open eyes, open mouth, and shaved scalp. It was worse, being so very sudden, than the crawling exhibition. We had no time to say anything before it began to speak.

Read Poe's account of the voice that came from the mesmerised dying man,° and you will realise less than one-half of the horror of that head's voice.

There was an interval of a second or two between each word, and a sort of 'ring, ring, ring,' in the note of the voice, like the timbre of a bell. It pealed slowly, as if talking to itself, for several minutes before I got rid of my cold sweat. Then the blessed solution struck me. I looked at the body lying near the doorway, and saw, just where the hollow of the throat joins on the shoulders, a muscle that had nothing to do with any man's regular breathing twitching away steadily. The whole thing was a careful reproduction of the Egyptian teraphin° that one reads about sometimes; and the voice was as clever and as appalling a piece of ventriloquism as one could wish to hear. All this time the head was 'lip-lip-lapping' against the side of the basin, and speaking. It told Suddhoo, on his face again whining, of his son's illness and of the state of the illness up to the evening of that very night. I always shall respect the seal-cutter for keeping so faithfully to the time of the Peshawar telegrams. It went on to say that skilled doctors were night and day watching over the man's life; and that he would eventually recover if the fee to the potent sorcerer, whose servant was the head in the basin, were doubled.

Here the mistake from the artistic point of view came in. To ask for twice your stipulated fee in a voice that Lazarus might have used when he rose from the dead, is absurd. Janoo, who is really a woman of masculine intellect, saw this as quickly as I did. I heard her say, '*Asli nahin! Fareib!*'° scornfully under her breath; and just as she said so the light in the basin died out, the head stopped talking, and we heard the room door creak on its hinges. Then Janoo struck a match, lit the lamp, and we saw that head, basin, and seal-cutter were gone. Suddhoo was wringing his hands, and explaining to anyone who cared to listen, that, if his chances of eternal salvation depended on it, he could not raise another two hundred rupees. Azizun was nearly in hysterics in the corner; while Janoo sat down composedly on one of the beds to discuss the probabilities of the whole thing being a *bunao*, or 'make-up.'

I explained as much as I knew of the seal-cutter's way of *jadoo*; but her argument was much more simple—'The magic that is always demanding gifts is no true magic,' said she. 'My mother told me that the only potent love-spells are those which are told you for love. This seal-cutter man is a liar and a devil. I dare not tell, do anything, or get anything done, because I am in debt to Bhagwan Dass the *bunnia*° for two gold rings and a heavy anklet. I must get my food from his shop. The seal-cutter is the friend of Bhagwan Dass, and he would poison my food. A fool's *jadoo* has been going on for ten days, and has cost Suddhoo many rupees each night. The seal-cutter used black hens and lemons and *mantras*° before. He never showed us anything like this till to-night. Azizun is a fool, and will be a *purdahnashin*° soon. Suddhoo has lost his strength and his wits. See now! I had hoped to get from Suddhoo many rupees while he lived, and many more after his death; and behold, he is spending everything on that offspring of a devil and a she-ass, the seal-cutter!'

Here I said, 'But what induced Suddhoo to drag me into the business? Of course I can speak to the seal-cutter, and he shall refund. The whole thing is child's talk—shame—and senseless.'

'Suddhoo *is* an old child,' said Janoo. 'He has lived on the roofs these seventy years and is as senseless as a milch-goat. He brought you here to assure himself that he was not breaking any law of the *Sirkar*, whose salt he ate many years ago. He worships the dust off the feet of the seal-cutter, and that cow-devourer° has forbidden him to go and see his son. What does Suddhoo know of your laws or the lightning-post?° I have to watch his money going day by day to that lying beast below.'

Janoo stamped her foot on the floor and nearly cried with vexation; while Suddhoo was whimpering under a blanket in the corner, and Azizun was trying to guide the pipe-stem to his foolish old mouth.

Now, the case stands thus. Unthinkingly, I have laid myself open to the charge of aiding and abetting the seal-cutter in obtaining money under false pretences, which is forbidden by Section 420 of the Indian Penal Code. I am helpless in the matter for these reasons. I cannot inform the Police. What witnesses would support my statements? Janoo refuses flatly, and Azizun is a veiled woman somewhere near Bareilly—lost in this big India of ours. I dare not again take the law into my own hands, and speak to the seal-cutter; for certain am I that, not only would Suddhoo disbelieve me, but this step would end in the poisoning of Janoo, who is bound hand and foot by her debt to the *bunnia*. Suddhoo is an old dotard; and whenever we meet mumbles my idiotic joke that the *Sirkar* rather patronises the Black Art than otherwise. His son is well now; but Suddhoo is completely under the influence of the seal-cutter, by whose advice he regulates the affairs of his life. Janoo watches daily the money that she hoped to wheedle out of Suddhoo taken by the seal-cutter, and becomes daily more furious and sullen.

She will never tell, because she dare not; but, unless something happens to prevent her, I am afraid that the seal-cutter will die of cholera—the white arsenic kind—about the middle of May. And thus I shall be privy to a murder in the House of Suddhoo.

Beyond the Pale

> Love heeds not caste nor sleep a broken bed. I went in search of love and lost myself.
>
> *Hindu Proverb*

A man should, whatever happens, keep to his own caste, race, and breed. Let the White go to the White and the Black to the Black. Then, whatever trouble falls is in the ordinary course of things—neither sudden, alien, nor unexpected.

This is the story of a man who wilfully stepped beyond the safe limits of decent everyday society, and paid for it heavily.

He knew too much in the first instance; and he saw too much in the second. He took too deep an interest in native life; but he will never do so again.

Deep away in the heart of the City, behind Jitha Megji's *bustee*,° lies Amir Nath's Gully,° which ends in a dead-wall pierced by one grated window. At the head of the Gully is a big cowbyre, and the walls on either side of the Gully are without windows. Neither Suchet Singh nor Gaur Chand approve of their women-folk looking into the world. If Durga Charan had been of their opinion he would have been a happier man to-day, and little Bisesa would have been able to knead her own bread. Her room looked out through the grated window into the narrow dark Gully where the sun never came and where the buffaloes wallowed in the blue slime. She was a widow, about fifteen years old, and she prayed the Gods, day and night, to send her a lover; for she did not approve of living alone.

One day, the man—Trejago his name was—came into Amir Nath's Gully on an aimless wandering; and, after he had passed the buffaloes, stumbled over a big heap of cattle-food.

Then he saw that the Gully ended in a trap, and heard a little laugh from behind the grated window. It was a pretty little laugh, and Trejago, knowing that, for all practical purposes, the old *Arabian Nights* are good guides, went forward to the window, and whispered that verse of 'The Love Song of Har Dyal'° which begins:—

> Can a man stand upright in the face of the naked Sun; or a Lover in the Presence of his Beloved?
>
> If my feet fail me, O Heart of my Heart, am I to blame, being blinded by the glimpse of your beauty?

There came the faint *tchink* of a woman's bracelets from behind the grating, and a little voice went on with the song at the fifth verse:—

> Alas! alas! Can the Moon tell the Lotus of her love when the Gate of Heaven is shut and the clouds gather for the rains?
>
> They have taken my Beloved, and driven her with the pack-horses to the North.
>
> There are iron chains on the feet that were set on my heart.
>
> Call to the bowmen to make ready—

The voice stopped suddenly, and Trejago walked out of Amir Nath's Gully, wondering who in the world could have capped 'The Love Song of Har Dyal' so neatly.

Next morning, as he was driving to office, an old woman threw a packet into his dogcart. In the packet was the half of a broken glass-bangle, one flower of the blood-red *dhak*,° a pinch of *bhusa* or cattle-food, and eleven cardamoms. That packet was a letter—not a clumsy compromising letter, but an innocent unintelligible lover's epistle.

Trejago knew far too much about these things, as I have said. No Englishman should be able to translate object-letters. But Trejago spread all the trifles on the lid of his office-box and began to puzzle them out.

A broken glass-bangle stands for a Hindu widow all India over; because, when her husband dies, a woman's bracelets are broken on her wrists. Trejago saw the meaning of the little bit of the glass. The flower of the *dhak* means diversely 'desire', 'come,' 'write,' or 'danger,' according to the other things with it. One cardamom means 'jealousy'; but when any article is duplicated in an object-letter, it loses its symbolic meaning and stands merely for one of a number indicating time, or, if incense, curds, or saffron be sent also, place. The message ran then—'A widow—*dhak* flower and *bhusa*,—at eleven o'clock.' The pinch of *bhusa* enlightened Trejago. He saw—this kind of letter leaves much to instinctive knowledge—that the *bhusa* referred to the big heap of cattle-food over which he had fallen in Amir Nath's Gully, and that the message must come from the person behind the grating; she being a widow. So the message ran then—'A widow, in the Gully in which is the heap of *bhusa*, desires you to come at eleven o'clock.'

Trejago threw all the rubbish into the fireplace and laughed. He knew that men in the East do not make love under windows at eleven in the forenoon, nor do women fix appointments a week in advance. So he went, that very night at eleven, into Amir Nath's Gully, clad in a *boorka*,° which cloaks a man as well as a woman. Directly the gongs of the City made the hour, the little voice behind the grating took up 'The Love Song of Har Dyal' at the verse where the Pathan girl calls upon Har Dyal to return. The song is really pretty in the Vernacular.° In English you miss the wail of it. It runs something like this—

Alone upon the housetops, to the North
  I turn and watch the lightning in the sky,—
The glamour of thy footsteps in the North.
  Come back to me, Beloved, or I die!

Below my feet the still bazar is laid—
  Far, far, below the weary camels lie,—
The camels and the captives of thy raid.
  Come back to me, Beloved, or I die!

My father's wife is old and harsh with years,
  And drudge of all my father's house am I.—
My bread is sorrow and my drink is tears.
  Come back to me, Beloved, or I die!

As the song stopped, Trejago stepped up under the grating and whispered—'I am here.'

Bisesa was good to look upon.

That night was the beginning of many strange things, and of a double life so wild that Trejago to-day sometimes wonders if it were not all a dream. Bisesa, or her old handmaiden who had thrown the object-letter, had detached the heavy grating from the brick-work of the wall; so that the window slid inside, leaving only a square of raw masonry into which an active man might climb.

In the day-time, Trejago drove through his routine of office-work, or put on his calling-clothes and called on the ladies of the Station, wondering how long they would know him° if they knew of poor little Bisesa. At night, when all the City was still, came the walk under the evil-smelling *boorka*, the patrol through Jitha Megji's *bustee*, the quick turn into Amir Nath's Gully between the sleeping cattle and the dead walls, and then, last of all, Bisesa, and the deep, even breathing of the old woman who slept outside the door of the bare little room that Durga Charan allotted to his sister's daughter. Who or what Durga Charan was, Trejago never inquired; and why in the world he was not discovered and knifed never occurred to him till his madness was over, and Bisesa. . . . But this comes later.

Bisesa was an endless delight to Trejago. She was as ignorant as a bird; and her distorted versions of the rumours from the outside world, that had reached her in her room, amused Trejago almost as much as her lisping attempts to pronounce his name—'Christopher.' The first syllable was always more than she could manage, and she made funny little gestures with her roseleaf hands, as one throwing the name away, and then, kneeling before Trejago, asked him, exactly as an Englishwoman would do, if he were sure he loved her. Trejago swore that he loved her more than any one else in the world. Which was true.

After a month of this folly, the exigencies of his other life compelled Trejago to be especially attentive to a lady of his acquaintance. You may take it for a fact that anything of this kind is not only noticed and discussed by a man's own race, but by some hundred and fifty natives as well. Trejago had to walk with this lady and talk to her at the Band-stand, and once or twice to drive with her; never for an instant dreaming that this would affect his dearer, out-of-the-way life. But the news flew, in the usual mysterious fashion, from mouth to mouth, till Bisesa's duenna heard of it and told Bisesa. The child was so troubled that she did the household work evilly, and was beaten by Durga Charan's wife in consequence.

A week later Bisesa taxed Trejago with the flirtation. She understood no gradations and spoke openly. Trejago laughed, and Bisesa stamped her little feet—little feet, light as marigold flowers, that could lie in the palm of a man's one hand.

Much that is written about Oriental passion and impulsiveness is exaggerated and compiled at second-hand, but a little of it is true; and when an Englishman finds that little, it is quite as startling as any passion in his own proper life. Bisesa raged and stormed, and finally threatened to kill herself if Trejago did not at once drop the alien

Memsahib who had come between them. Trejago tried to explain, and to show her that she did not understand these things from a Western standpoint. Bisesa drew herself up, and said simply—

'I do not. I know only this—it is not good that I should have made you dearer than my own heart to me, *Sahib*. You are an Englishman. I am only a black girl'—she was fairer than bar-gold in the Mint,—'and the widow of a black man.'

Then she sobbed and said—'But on my soul and my Mother's soul, I love you. There shall no harm come to you, whatever happens to me.'

Trejago argued with the child, and tried to soothe her, but she seemed quite unreasonably disturbed. Nothing would satisfy her save that all relations between them should end. He was to go away at once. And he went. As he dropped out of the window she kissed his forehead twice, and he walked home wondering.

A week, and then three weeks, passed without a sign from Bisesa. Trejago, thinking that the rupture had lasted quite long enough, went down to Amir Nath's Gully for the fifth time in the three weeks, hoping that his rap at the sill of the shifting grating would be answered. He was not disappointed.

There was a young moon, and one stream of light fell down into Amir Nath's Gully, and struck the grating which was drawn away as he knocked. From the black dark Bisesa held out her arms into the moonlight. Both hands had been cut off at the wrists, and the stumps were nearly healed.

Then, as Bisesa bowed her head between her arms and sobbed, some one in the room grunted like a wild beast, and something sharp—knife, sword, or spear,—thrust at Trejago in his *boorka*. The stroke missed his body, but cut into one of the muscles of the groin, and he limped slightly from the wound for the rest of his days.

The grating went into its place. There was no sign whatever from inside the house,—nothing but the moonlight strip on the high wall, and the blackness of Amir Nath's Gully behind.

The next thing Trejago remembers, after raging and shouting like a madman between those pitiless walls, is that he found himself near the river as the dawn was breaking, threw away his *boorka* and went home bareheaded.

What was the tragedy—whether Bisesa had, in a fit of causeless despair, told everything, or the intrigue had been discovered and she tortured to tell; whether Durga Charan knew his name and what became of Bisesa—Trejago does not know to this day. Something horrible had happened, and the thought of what it must have been comes upon Trejago in the night now and again, and keeps him company till the morning. One special feature of the case is that he does not know where lies the front of Durga Charan's house. It may open on to a courtyard common to two or more houses, or it may lie behind any one of the gates of Jitha Megji's *bustee*. Trejago cannot tell. He cannot get Bisesa—poor little Bisesa—back again. He has lost her in the City where each man's house is as guarded and as unknowable as the grave; and the grating that opens into Amir Nath's Gully has been walled up.

But Trejago pays his calls regularly, and is reckoned a very decent sort of man.

There is nothing peculiar about him, except a slight stiffness, caused by a riding-strain, in the right leg.

The Story of Muhammad Din

Who is the happy man? He that sees in his own house at home,
little children crowned with dust, leaping and falling and crying.

Munichandra, translated by Professor Peterson°

The polo-ball was an old one, scarred, chipped, and dinted. It stood on the mantelpiece among the pipe-stems which Imam Din, *khitmatgar*, was cleaning for me.

'Does the Heaven-born want this ball?' said Imam Din deferentially.

The Heaven-born set no particular store by it; but of what use was a polo-ball to a *khitmatgar*?°

'By Your Honour's favour, I have a little son. He has seen this ball, and desires it to play with. I do not want it for myself.'

No one would for an instant accuse portly old Imam Din of wanting to play with polo-balls. He carried out the battered thing into the verandah; and there followed a hurricane of joyful squeaks, a patter of small feet, and the *thud-thud-thud* of the ball rolling along the ground. Evidently the little son had been waiting outside the door to secure his treasure. But how had he managed to see that polo-ball?

Next day, coming back from office half an hour earlier than usual, I was aware of a small figure in the dining-room—a tiny, plump figure in a ridiculously inadequate shirt which came, perhaps, half-way down the tubby stomach. It wandered round the room, thumb in mouth, crooning to itself as it took stock of the pictures. Undoubtedly this was the 'little son'.

He had no business in my room, of course; but was so deeply absorbed in his discoveries that he never noticed me in the doorway. I stepped into the room and startled him nearly into a fit. He sat down on the ground with a gasp. His eyes opened and his mouth followed suit. I knew what was coming, and fled, followed by a long, dry howl which reached the servants' quarters far more quickly than any command of mine had ever done. In ten seconds Imam Din was in the dining-room. Then despairing sobs arose, and I returned to find Imam Din admonishing the small sinner who was using most of his shirt as a handkerchief.

'This boy,' said Imam Din judicially, 'is a *budmash*—a big *budmash*.° He will, without doubt, go to the *jail-khana*° for his behaviour.' Renewed yells from the penitent, and an elaborate apology to myself from Imam Din.

'Tell the baby,' said I, 'that the *Sahib* is not angry, and take him away.' Imam Din conveyed my forgiveness to the offender, who had now gathered all his shirt round his neck, stringwise, and the yell subsided into a sob. The two set off for the door. 'His name,' said Imam Din, as though the name were part of the crime, 'is Muhammad Din, and he is a *budmash*.' Freed from present danger, Muhammad Din turned round in his father's arms, and said gravely, 'It is true that my name is Muhammad Din, *Tahib*, but I am not a *budmash*. I am a *man*!'

From that day dated my acquaintance with Muhammad Din. Never again did he come into my dining-room, but on the neutral ground of the garden we greeted each other with much state, though our conversation was confined to '*Talaam, Tahib*' from his side, and '*Salaam, Muhammad Din*' from mine. Daily on my return from office, the little white shirt and the fat little body used to rise from the shade of the creeper-covered trellis where they had been hid; and daily I checked my horse here, that my salutation might not be slurred over or given unseemly.

Muhammad Din never had any companions. He used to trot about the compound, in and out of the castor-oil bushes, on mysterious errands of his own. One day I stumbled upon some of his handiwork far down the grounds. He had half buried the polo-ball in dust, and struck six shrivelled old marigold flowers in a circle round it. Outside that circle again was a rude square, traced out in bits of red brick alternating with fragments of broken china; the whole bounded by a little bank of dust. The water-man from the well-curb° put in a plea for the small architect, saying that it was only the play of a baby and did not much disfigure my garden.

Heaven knows that I had no intention of touching the child's work then or later; but, that evening, a stroll through the garden brought me unawares full on it; so that I trampled, before I knew, marigold-heads, dust-bank, and fragments of broken soap-dish into confusion past all hope of mending. Next morning, I came upon Muhammad Din crying softly to himself over the ruin I had wrought. Some one had cruelly told him that the *Sahib* was very angry with him for spoiling the garden, and had scattered his rubbish, using bad language the while. Muhammad Din laboured for an hour at effacing every trace of the dust-bank and pottery fragments, and it was with a tearful and apologetic face that he said, '*Talaam Tahib*,' when I came home from office. A hasty inquiry resulted in Imam Din informing Muhammad Din that, by my singular favour, he was permitted to disport himself as he pleased. Whereat the child took heart and fell to tracing the ground-plan of an edifice which was to eclipse the marigold-polo-ball creation.

For some months the chubby little eccentricity revolved in his humble orbit among the castor-oil bushes and in the dust; always fashioning magnificent palaces from stale flowers thrown away by the bearer, smooth water-worn pebbles, bits of broken glass, and feathers pulled, I fancy, from my fowls, always alone, and always crooning to himself.

A gaily-spotted sea-shell was dropped one day close to the last of his little buildings; and I looked that Muhammad Din should build something more than ordinarily splendid on the strength of it. Nor was I disappointed. He meditated for the better part of an hour, and his crooning rose to a jubilant song. Then he began tracing in the dust. It would certainly be a wondrous palace, this one, for it was two yards long and a yard broad in ground-plan. But the palace was never completed.

Next day there was no Muhammad Din at the head of the carriage-drive, and no '*Talaam Tahib*' to welcome my return. I had grown accustomed to the greeting, and its omission troubled me. Next day Imam Din told me that the child was suffering slightly from fever and needed quinine. He got the medicine, and an English Doctor.

'They have no stamina, these brats,' said the Doctor, as he left Imam Din's quarters.

A week later, though I would have given much to have avoided it, I met on the road to the Mussulman burying-ground Imam Din, accompanied by one other friend, carrying in his arms, wrapped in a white cloth, all that was left of little Muhammad Din.

From SOLDIERS THREE (1888)

With the Main Guard

Der jungere Uhlanen°
Sit round mit open mouth
While Breitmann tell dem stories
Of fightin' in the South;°
Und gif dem moral lessons,
How before der battle pops,
Take a little prayer to Himmel°
Und a goot long drink of Schnapps.

Hans Breitmann's Ballads

'Mary, Mother av Mercy, fwhat the divil possist us to take an' kape this melancolious counthry? Answer me that, Sorr.'

It was Mulvaney who was speaking. The time was one o'clock of a stifling June night, and the place was the main gate of Fort Amara,° most desolate and least desirable of all fortresses in India. What I was doing there at that hour is a question which only concerns M'Grath the Sergeant of the Guard, and the men on the gate.

'Slape,' said Mulvaney, 'is a shuparfluous necessity. This gyard'll shtay lively till relieved.' He himself was stripped to the waist; Learoyd on the next bed-stead was dripping from the skinful of water which Ortheris, clad only in white trousers, had just sluiced over his shoulders; and a fourth private was muttering uneasily as he dozed open-mouthed in the glare of the great guard-lantern. The heat under the bricked archway was terrifying.

'The worrst night that iver I remimber. Eyah! Is all Hell loose this tide?' said Mulvaney. A puff of burning wind lashed through the wicket-gate like a wave of the sea, and Ortheris swore.

'Are ye more heasy, Jock?' he said to Learoyd. 'Put yer 'ead between your legs. It'll go orf in a minute.'

'Ah don't care. Ah would not care, but ma heart is plaayin' tivvy-tivvy° on ma ribs. Let me die! Oh, leave me die!' groaned the huge Yorkshireman, who was feeling the heat acutely, being of fleshly build.

The sleeper under the lantern roused for a moment and raised himself on his elbow.—'Die and be damned then!' he said. '*I'm* damned and I can't die!'

'Who's that?' I whispered, for the voice was new to me.

'Gentleman born,'° said Mulvaney; 'Corp'ril wan year, Sargint nex'. Red-hot on his C'mission, but dhrinks like a fish. He'll be gone before the cowld weather's here. So!'

He slipped his boot, and with the naked toe just touched the trigger of his Martini.° Ortheris misunderstood the movement, and the next instant the Irishman's rifle was dashed aside, while Ortheris stood before him, his eyes blazing with reproof.

'You!' said Ortheris. 'My Gawd, *you*! If it was you, wot would *we* do?'

'Kape quiet, little man,' said Mulvaney, putting him aside, but very gently; ''tis not me, nor will ut be me whoile Dinah Shadd's here.° I was but showin' something.'

Learoyd, bowed on his bedstead, groaned, and the gentleman-ranker sighed in his sleep. Ortheris took Mulvaney's tendered pouch, and we three smoked gravely for a space while the dust-devils danced on the glacis and scoured the red-hot plain.

'Pop?' said Ortheris, wiping his forehead.

'Don't tantalise wid talkin' av dhrink, or I'll shtuff you into your own breech-block an'—fire you off!' grunted Mulvaney.

Ortheris chuckled, and from a niche in the verandah produced six bottles of gingerade.

'Where did ye get ut, ye Machiavel?'° said Mulvaney. ''Tis no bazar pop.'

''Ow do *Hi* know wot the Orf'cers drink?' answered Ortheris. 'Arst the mess-man.'

'Ye'll have a Disthrict Coort-Martial settin' on ye yet, me son,' said Mulvaney, 'but'—he opened a bottle—'I will not report ye this time. Fwhat's in the mess-kid° is mint° for the belly, as they say, 'specially whin that mate° is dhrink. Here's luck! A bloody war or a—°no, we've got the sickly season. War, thin!'—he waved the innocent 'pop' to the four quarters of Heaven. 'Bloody war! North, East, South, an' West! Jock, ye quakin' hayrick, come an' dhrink.'

But Learoyd, half mad with the fear of death presaged in the swelling veins of his neck, was begging his Maker to strike him dead, and fighting for more air between his prayers. A second time Ortheris drenched the quivering body with water, and the giant revived.

'An' Ah divn't see thot a mon is i' fettle for gooin' on to live; an' Ah divn't see thot there is owt for t' livin' for. Hear now, lads! Ah'm tired—tired. There's nobbut watter i' ma bones. Let me die!'

The hollow of the arch gave back Learoyd's broken whisper in a bass boom. Mulvaney looked at me hopelessly, but I remembered how the madness of despair had once fallen upon Ortheris, that weary, weary afternoon on the banks of the Khemi River, and how it had been exorcised by the skilful magician Mulvaney.°

'Talk, Terence!' I said, 'or we shall have Learoyd slinging loose, and he'll be worse than Ortheris was. Talk! He'll answer to your voice.'

Almost before Ortheris had deftly thrown all the rifles of the guard on Mulvaney's bedstead, the Irishman's voice was uplifted as that of one in the middle of a story, and, turning to me, he said—

'In barricks or out of it, as *you* say, Sorr, an Oirish rig'mint is the divil an' more. 'Tis only fit for a young man wid eddicated fisteses. Oh the crame av disruption is an Oirish rig'mint, an' rippin', tearin', ragin' scattherers in the field av war! My first rig'mint was Oirish—Faynians° an' rebils to the heart av their marrow was they, an' *so* they fought for the Widdy° betther than most, bein' contrairy—Oirish. They was the Black Tyrone. You've heard av thim, Sorr?'

Heard of them! I knew the Black Tyrone for the choicest collection of unmitigated blackguards, dog-stealers, robbers of hen-roosts, assaulters of innocent citizens, and recklessly daring heroes in the Army List. Half Europe and half Asia has had cause to know the Black Tyrone—good luck be with their tattered Colours as Glory has ever been!

'They *was* hot pickils an' ginger! I cut a man's head tu deep wid my belt° in the days av my youth, an', afther some circumstances which I will oblitherate, I came to the Ould Rig'mint,° bearin' the character av a man wid hands an' feet. But, as I was goin' to tell you, I fell acrost the Black Tyrone agin wan day whin we wanted thim powerful bad. Orth'ris, me son, fwhat was the name av that place where they sint wan comp'ny av us an' wan av the Tyrone roun' a hill an' down again, all for to tache the Paythans something they'd niver learned before? Afther Ghuzni° 'twas.'

'Don't know what the bloomin' Paythans called it. We called it Silver's Theayter.° You know that, sure!'

'Silver's Theatre—so 'twas. A gut° betune two hills, as black as a bucket, an' as thin as a girl's waist. There was over-many Paythans for our convaynience in the gut, an' begad they called thimselves a Reserve—bein' impident by natur! Our Scotchies an' lashins av

Gurkys° was poundin' into some Paythan rig'ments, I think 'twas. Scotchies an' Gurkys are twins bekaze they're so onlike, an' they get dhrunk together whin God plazes. As I was sayin', they sint wan comp'ny av the Ould an' wan av the Tyrone to double up the hill an' clane out the Paythan Reserve. Orf'cers was scarce in thim days, fwhat wid dysintry an' not takin' care av thimselves, an' we was sint out wid only wan orf'cer for the comp'ny; but he was a Man that had his feet beneath him an' all his teeth in their sockuts.'

'Who was he?' I asked.

'Captain O'Neil—Old Crook—Cruikna-bulleen°—him that I tould ye that tale av whin he was in Burma.[1] Hah! He was a Man. The Tyrone tuk a little orf'cer bhoy, but divil a bit was he in command, as I'll dimonstrate presintly. We an' they came over the brow av the hill, wan on each side av the gut, an' there was that ondacint Reserve waitin' down below like rats in a pit.°

'"Howld on, men," sez Crook, who tuk a mother's care av us always. "Rowl some rocks on thim by way av visitin'-kyards." We hadn't rowled more than twinty bowlders, an' the Paythans was beginnin' to swear tremenjus, whin the little orf'cer bhoy av the Tyrone shqueaks out acrost the valley:—"Fwhat the divil an' all are you doin', shpoilin' the fun for my men? Do ye not see they'll stand?"

'"Faith, that's a rare pluckt wan!"° sez Crook. "Niver mind the rocks, men. Come along down an' take tay wid thim!"

'"There's damned little sugar in ut!" sez my rear-rank man; but Crook heard.

'"Have ye not all got spoons?" he sez, laughin', an' down we wint as fast as we cud. Learoyd bein' sick at the Base, he, av coorse, was not there.'

'Thot's a lie!' said Learoyd, dragging his bedstead nearer. 'Ah gotten *thot* theer, an' you knaw it, Mulvaney.' He threw up his arms, and from the right arm-pit ran, diagonally through the fell of his chest, a thin white line terminating near the fourth left rib.

'My mind's goin',' said Mulvaney, the unabashed. 'Ye were there. Fwhat was I thinkin' of? 'Twas another man, av coorse. Well, you'll remimber thin, Jock, how we an' the Tyrone met wid a bang at the bottom an' got jammed past all movin' among the Paythans?'

[1] Now first of the foemen of Boh Da Thone
Was Captain O'Neil of the Black Tyrone.
The Ballad of Boh Da Thone

'Ow! It *was* a tight 'ole. I was squeezed till I thought I'd bloomin' well bust,' said Ortheris, rubbing his stomach meditatively.

''Twas no place for a little man, but *wan* little man'—Mulvaney put his hand on Ortheris's shoulder—'saved the life av me. There we shtuck, for divil a bit did the Paythans flinch, an' divil a bit dare we; our business bein' to clear 'em out. An' the most exthryordinar' thing av all was that we an' they just rushed into each other's arrums, an' there was no firing for a long time. Nothin' but knife an' bay'nit when we cud get our hands free: an' that was not often. We was breast-on to thim, an' the Tyrone was yelpin' behind av us in a way I didn't see the lean av at first. But I knew later, an' so did the Paythans.

'"Knee to knee!" sings out Crook, wid a laugh whin the rush av our comin' into the gut shtopped, an' he was huggin' a hairy great Paythan, neither bein' able to do anything to the other, tho' both was wishful.

'"Breast to breast!" he sez, as the Tyrone was pushin' us forward closer an' closer.

'"An' hand over back!"° sez a Sargint that was behin'. I saw a sword lick out past Crook's ear, an' the Paythan was tuk in the apple av his throat like a pig at Dromeen Fair.°

'"Thank ye, Brother Inner Guard,"° sez Crook, cool as a cucumber widout salt. "I wanted that room." An' he wint forward by the thickness av a man's body, havin' turned the Paythan undher him. The man bit the heel off Crook's boot in his death-bite.

'"Push, men!" sez Crook. "Push, ye paper-backed beggars!" he sez. "Am I to pull ye through?" So we pushed an' we kicked, an' we swung, an' we swore, an' the grass bein' slippery, our heels wouldn't bite, an' God help the front-rank man that wint down that day!'

''Ave you ever bin in the Pit hentrance o' the Vic.° on a thick night?' interrupted Ortheris. 'It was worse nor that, for they was goin' one way, an' we wouldn't 'ave it. Leastaways, I 'adn't much to say.'

'Faith, me son, ye said ut, thin. I kep' the little man betune my knees as long as I cud, but he was pokin' roun' wid his bay'nit, blindin' an' stiffin'° feroshus. The devil of a man is Orth'ris in a ruction—aren't ye?' said Mulvaney.

'Don't make game!' said the Cockney. 'I knowed I wasn't no good then, but I guv 'em compot° from the lef' flank when we opened out. No!' he said, bringing down his hand with a thump on the bedstead, 'a bay'nit ain't no good to a little man—might as well 'ave a bloomin' fishin'-rod! I 'ate a clawin', maulin' mess, but gimme a breech that's wore out a bit an' hamminition one year in store, to let the powder kiss the bullet,° an' put me somewheres where I ain't trod on by 'ulkin swine like you, an' s'elp me Gawd, I could bowl you over five times outer seven at height 'undred. Would yer try, you lumberin' Hirishman?'

'No, ye wasp. I've seen ye do ut. I say there's nothin' better than the bay'nit, wid a long reach, a double twist av ye can, an' a slow recover.'

'Dom the bay'nit,' said Learoyd, who had been listening intently. 'Look a-here!' He picked up a rifle an inch below the foresight with an underhanded action, and used it exactly as a man would use a dagger.

'Sitha,' said he softly, 'thot's better than owt, for a mon can bash t' faace wi' thot, an', if he divn't, he can breeak t' forearm o' t' gaard. 'Tis not i' t' books, though. Gie me t' butt.'

'Each does ut his own way, like makin' love,' said Mulvaney quietly; 'the butt or the bay'nit or the bullet accordin' to the natur' av the man. Well, as I was sayin', we shtuck there breathin' in each other's faces an' swearin' powerful; Orth'ris cursin' the mother that bore him bekaze he was not three inches taller.

'Prisintly he sez:—"Duck, ye lump, an' I can get at a man over your shouldher!"

'"You'll blow me head off," I sez, throwin' my arm clear; "go through under my arm-pit, ye blood-thirsty little scutt,"° sez I, "but don't shtick me or I'll wring your ears round."

'Fwhat was ut ye gave the Paythan man forninst me, him that cut at me whin I cudn't move hand or foot? Hot or cowld was ut?'

'Cold,' said Ortheris, 'up an' under the rib-jint. 'E come down flat. Best for you 'e did.'

'Thrue, my son! This jam thing that I'm talkin' about lasted for five minutes good, an' thin we got our arms clear an' wint in. I misremimber exactly fwhat I did, but I didn't want Dinah to be a widdy at the depot. Thin, after some promishkuous hackin' we shtuck again, an' the Tyrone behin' was callin' us dogs an' cowards an' all manner av names; we barrin' their way.

'"Fwhat ails the Tyrone?" thinks I; "they've the makin's av a most convanient fight here."

'A man behind me sez beseechful an' in a whisper:—"Let me get at thim! For the love av Mary give me room beside ye, ye tall man!"

'"An' who are you that's so anxious to be kilt?" sez I, widout turnin' my head, for the long knives was dancin' in front like the sun on Donegal Bay whin ut's rough.

'"We've seen our dead,"° he sez, squeezin' into me; "our dead that was men two days gone! An' me that was his cousin by blood could not bring Tim Coulan off! Let me get on," he sez, "let me get to thim or I'll run ye through the back!"

'"My troth," thinks I, "if the Tyrone have seen their dead, God help the Paythans this day!" An' thin I knew why the Oirish was ragin' behind us as they was.

'I gave room to the man, an' he ran forward wid the Haymakers' Lift° on his bay'nit an' swung a Paythan clear off his feet by the belly-band av the brute, an' the iron bruk at the lockin'-ring.

'"Tim Coulan 'll slape easy to-night," sez he wid a grin; an' the next minut his head was in two halves and he wint down grinnin' by sections.

'The Tyrone was pushin' an' pushin' in, an' our men was swearin' at thim, an' Crook was workin' away in front av us all, his sword-arm swingin' like a pump-handle an' his revolver spittin' like a cat. But the strange thing av ut was the quiet that lay upon. 'Twas like a fight in a drame—except for thim that was dead.

'Whin I gave room to the Oirishman I was expinded an' forlorn in my inside. 'Tis a way I have, savin' your presince, Sorr, in action. "Let me out, bhoys," sez I, backin' in among thim. "I'm goin' to be onwell!" Faith they gave me room at the wurrd, though they would not ha' given room for all Hell wid the chill off. When I got clear, I was, savin' your presince, Sorr, outragis sick bekaze I had dhrunk heavy that day.

'Well an' far out av harm was a Sargint av the Tyrone sittin' on the little orf'cer bhoy who had stopped Crook from rowlin' the rocks. Oh, he was a beautiful bhoy, an' the long black curses was sliding out av his innocint mouth like mornin'-jew from a rose!

'"Fwhat have you got there?" sez I to the Sargint.

'"Wan av Her Majesty's bantams wid his spurs up," sez he. "He's goin' to Coort-Martial me."

'"Let me go!" sez the little orf'cer bhoy. "Let me go and command my men!" manin' thereby the Black Tyrone which was beyond any command—ay, even av they had made the Divil a Field-Orf'cer.

'"His father howlds my mother's cow-feed° in Clonmel," sez the man that was sittin' on him. "Will I go back to *his* mother an' tell her that I've let him throw himself away? Lie still, ye little pinch of dynamite, an' Coort-Martial me aftherwards."

'"Good," sez I; "'tis the likes av him makes the likes av the Commander-in-Chief, but we must presarve thim. Fwhat d'you want to do, Sorr?" sez I, very politeful.

' "Kill the beggars—kill the beggars!" he shqueaks, his big blue eyes brimmin' wid tears.

' "An' how'll ye do that?" sez I. "You've shquibbed off your revolver like a child wid a cracker; you can make no play wid that fine large sword av yours; an' your hand's shakin' like an asp on a leaf.° Lie still and grow," sez I.

' "Get back to your comp'ny," sez he; "you're insolint!"

' "All in good time," sez I, "but I'll have a dhrink first."

'Just thin Crook comes up, blue an' white all over where he wasn't red.

' "Wather!" sez he; "I'm dead wid drouth! Oh, but it's a gran' day!"

'He dhrank half a skinful, and the rest he tilts into his chest, an' it fair hissed on the hairy hide av him. He sees the little orf'cer bhoy undher the Sargint.

' "Fwhat's yonder?" sez he.

' "Mutiny, Sorr," sez the Sargint, an' the orf'cer bhoy begins pleadin' pitiful to Crook to be let go; but divil a bit wud Crook budge.

' "Kape him there," he sez, "'tis no child's work this day. By the same token," sez he, "I'll confishcate that iligant nickel-plated scent-sprinkler av yours, for my own has been vomitin' dishgraceful!"

'The fork av his hand was black wid the back-spit av the machine. So he tuk the orf'cer bhoy's revolver. Ye may look, Sorr, but, by my faith, *there's a dale more done in the field than iver gets into Field Ordhers!*

' "Come on, Mulvaney," sez Crook; "is this a Coort-Martial?" The two av us wint back together into the mess an' the Paythans were still standin' up. They was not *too* impart'nint though, for the Tyrone was callin' wan to another to remimber Tim Coulan.

'Crook stopped outside av the strife an' looked anxious, his eyes rowlin' roun'.

' "Fwhat is ut, Sorr?" sez I; "can I get ye anything?"

' "Where's a bugler?" sez he.

'I wint into the crowd—our men was dhrawin' breath behin' the Tyrone who was fightin' like sowls in tormint—an' prisintly I came acrost little Frehan, our bugler bhoy, pokin' roun' among the best wid a rifle an' bay'nit.

' "Is amusin' yoursilf fwhat you're paid for, ye limb?" sez I, catchin' him by the scruff. "Come out av that an' attind to your duty," I sez; but the bhoy was not pleased.

' "I've got wan," sez he, grinnin', "big as you, Mulvaney, an' fair half as ugly. Let me go get another."

'I was dishpleased at the personability av that remark, so I tucks him under my arm an' carries him to Crook who was watchin' how the fight wint. Crook cuffs him till the bhoy cries, an' thin sez nothin' for a whoile.

'The Paythans began to flicker onaisy, an' our men roared. "Opin ordher! Double!" sez Crook. "Blow, child, blow for the honour av the British Arrmy!"

'That bhoy blew like a typhoon, an' the Tyrone an' we opined out as the Paythans broke an' I saw that fwhat had gone before wud be kissin' an' huggin' to fwhat was to come. We'd dhruv thim into a broad part av the gut whin they gave, an' thin we opined out an' fair danced down the valley, dhrivin' thim before us. Oh, 'twas lovely, an' stiddy, too! There was the Sargints on the flanks av what was left av us, kapin' touch, an' the fire was runnin' from flank to flank, an' the Paythans was dhroppin'. We opined out wid the widenin' av the valley, an' whin the valley narrowed we closed again like the shticks on a lady's fan, an' at the far ind av the gut where they thried to stand, we fair blew them off their feet, for we had expinded very little ammunition by reason av the knife work.'

'Hi used thirty rounds goin' down that valley,' said Ortheris, 'an' it was gentleman's work. Might 'a' done it in a white 'andkerchief an' pink silk stockin's, that part. Hi was on in that piece.'

'You could ha' heard the Tyrone yellin' a mile away,' said Mulvaney, 'an' 'twas all their Sargints cud do to get thim off. They was mad—mad—mad! Crook sits down in the quiet that fell whin we had gone down the valley, an' covers his face wid his hands. Prisintly we all came back again accordin' to our natures and disposishins, for they, mark you, show through the hide av a man in that hour.

'"Bhoys! bhoys!" sez Crook to himself. "I misdoubt we could ha' engaged at long range an' saved betther men than me." He looked at our dead an' said no more.

'"Captain dear," sez a man av the Tyrone, comin' up wid his mouth bigger than iver his mother kissed ut, spittin' blood like a whale; "Captain dear," sez he, "if wan or two in the shtalls have been discommoded, the gallery have enjoyed the performinces av a Roshus."°

'Thin I knew that man for the Dublin dock-rat he was—wan av the bhoys that made the lessee av Silver's Theatre gray before his time wid tearin' out the bowils av the benches an' t'rowin' thim into the pit. So I passed the wurrud that I knew when I was in the Tyrone an' we lay in Dublin. "I don't know who 'twas," I whispers, "an' I don't care, but anyways I'll knock the face av you, Tim Kelly."

'"Eyah!" sez the man, "was you there too? We'll call ut Silver's Theatre." Half the Tyrone, knowin' the ould place, tuk ut up: so we called ut Silver's Theatre.

'The little orf'cer bhoy av the Tyrone was thremblin' an' cryin'. He had no heart for the Coort-Martials that he talked so big upon. "Ye'll do well later," sez Crook, very quiet, "for not bein' allowed to kill yourself for amusemint."

'"I'm a dishgraced man!" sez the little orf'cer bhoy.

'"Put me undher arrest, Sorr, if you will, but, by my sowl, I'd do ut again sooner than face your mother wid you dead," sez the Sargint that had sat on his head, standin' to attention an' salutin'. But the young wan only cried as tho' his little heart was breakin'.

'Thin another man av the Tyrone came up, wid the fog av fightin' on him.'

'The what, Mulvaney?'

'Fog av fightin'. You know, Sorr, that, like makin' love, ut takes each man diff'rint. Now I can't help bein' powerful sick whin I'm in action. Orth'ris here, niver stops swearin' from ind to ind, an' the only time that Learoyd opins his mouth to sing is whin he is messin' wid other people's heads; for he's a dhirty fighter is Jock. Recruities sometime cry, an' sometime they don't know fwhat they do, an' sometime they are all for cuttin' throats an' such-like dirtiness; but some men get heavy-dead-dhrunk on the fightin'. This man was. He was staggerin', an' his eyes were half shut, an' we cud hear him dhraw breath twinty yards away. He sees the little orf'cer bhoy, an' comes up, talkin' thick an' drowsy to himsilf. "Blood the young whelp!" he sez; "blood the young whelp"; an' wid that he threw up his arms, shpun roun', an' dropped at our feet, dead as a Paythan, an' there was niver sign or scratch on him. They said 'twas his heart was rotten, but oh, 'twas a quare thing to see!

'Thin we wint to bury our dead, for we wud not lave thim to the Paythans, an' in movin' among the haythen we nearly lost that little orf'cer bhoy. He was for givin' wan divil wather and layin' him aisy against a rock. "Be careful, Sorr," sez I; "a wounded Paythan's worse than a live wan." My troth, before the words was out of my mouth, the man on the ground fires at the orf'cer bhoy lanin' over him, an' I saw the helmit fly. I dropped the butt on the face av the man an' tuk his pistol. The little orf'cer bhoy turned very white, for the hair av half his head was singed away.

'"I tould you so, Sorr!" sez I; an', afther that, whin he wanted to help a Paythan I stud wid the muzzle contagious to the ear. They dare not do anythin' but curse. The Tyrone was growlin' like dogs over a bone that has been taken away too soon, for they had seen their dead an' they wanted to kill ivry sowl on the ground. Crook tould thim that he'd blow the hide off any man that misconducted himself; but, seeing that ut was the first time the Tyrone had iver seen their dead, I do not wondher they were on the sharp.° 'Tis a shameful sight! Whin I first saw ut I wud niver ha' given quarter to any man north of the Khaibar —no, nor woman either, for the women used to come out afther dhark°—Auggrh!

'Well, evenshually we buried our dead an' tuk away our wounded, an' come over the brow av the hills to see the Scotchies an' the Gurkys taking tay with the Paythans in bucketsfuls. We were a gang av dissolute ruffians, for the blood had caked the dust, an' the sweat had cut the cake, an' our bay'nits was hangin' like butchers' steels betune ur legs, an' most av us were marked one way or another.

'A Staff Orf'cer man, clean as a new rifle, rides up an' sez: "What damned scarecrows are you?"

'"A comp'ny av Her Majesty's Black Tyrone an' wan av the Ould Rig'mint," sez Crook very quiet, givin' our visitors the flure as 'twas.

'"Oh!" sez the Staff Orf'cer; "did you dislodge that Reserve?"

'"No!" sez Crook, an' the Tyrone laughed.

'"Thin fwhat the divil have ye done?"

'"Disthroyed ut," sez Crook, an' he took us on, but not before Toomey that was in the Tyrone sez aloud, his voice somewhere in his stummick: "Fwhat in the name av misfortune does this parrit widout a tail mane by shtoppin' the road av his betthers?"

'The Staff Orf'cer wint blue, an' Toomey makes him pink by changin' to the voice av a minowderin'° woman an' sayin': "Come an' kiss me, Major dear, for me husband's at the wars an' I'm all alone at the Depot."

'The Staff Orf'cer wint away, an' I cud see Crook's shoulthers shakin'.

'His Corp'ril checks Toomey. "Lave me alone," sez Toomey, widout a wink. "I was his bâtman° before he was married an' he knows fwhat I mane, av you don't. There's nothin' like livin' in the hoight av society." D'you remimber that, Orth'ris!'

'Hi do. Toomey, 'e died in 'orspital, next week it was, 'cause I bought 'arf his kit; an' I remember after that—'

'GUARRD, TURN OUT!'

The Relief had come; it was four o'clock. 'I'll catch a kyart° for you, Sorr,' said Mulvaney, diving hastily into his accoutrements. 'Come up to the top av the Fort an' we'll pershue our invistigations into M'Grath's shtable.' The relieved guard strolled round the main bastion on its way to the swimming-bath, and Learoyd grew almost talkative. Ortheris looked into the Fort ditch and across the plain. 'Ho! it's weary waitin' for Ma-ary!"° he hummed; 'but I'd like to kill some more bloomin' Paythans before my time's up. War! Bloody war! North, East, South, and West.'

'Amen,' said Learoyd slowly.

'Fwhat's here?' said Mulvaney, checking at a blur of white by the foot of the old sentry-box. He stooped and touched it. 'It's Norah—Norah M'Taggart! Why, Nonie darlin', fwhat are ye doin' out av your mother's bed at this time?'

The two-year-old child of Sergeant M'Taggart must have wandered for a breath of cool air to the very verge of the parapet of the Fort ditch. Her tiny night-shift was gathered into a wisp round her neck and she moaned in her sleep. 'See there!' said Mulvaney; 'poor lamb! Look at the heat-rash on the innocint skin av her. 'Tis hard—crool hard even for us. Fwhat must it be for these? Wake up, Nonie, your mother will be woild about you. Begad, the child might ha' fallen into the ditch!'

He picked her up in the growing light, and set her on his shoulder, and her fair curls touched the grizzled stubble of his temples. Ortheris and Learoyd followed snapping their fingers, while Norah smiled at them a sleepy smile. Then carolled Mulvaney, clear as a lark, dancing the baby on his arm—

'If any young man should marry you,°
  Say nothin' about the joke;
That iver ye slep' in a sinthry-box,
  Wrapped up in a soldier's cloak.'

'Though, on my sowl, Nonie,' he said gravely, 'there was not much cloak about you. Niver mind, you won't dhress like this ten years to come. Kiss your friends an' run along to your mother.'

Nonie, set down close to the Married Quarters, nodded with the quiet obedience of the soldier's child, but, ere she pattered off over the flagged path, held up her lips to be kissed by the Three Musketeers. Ortheris wiped his mouth with the back of his hand and swore sentimentally; Learoyd turned pink; and the two walked away together. The Yorkshireman lifted up his voice and gave in thunder the chorus of *The Sentry-Box*, while Ortheris piped at his side.

''Bin to a bloomin' sing-song, you two?' said the Artilleryman, who was taking his cartridge down to the Morning Gun.° 'You're over merry for these dashed days.'

> 'I bid ye take care o' the brat, said he,
> For it comes of a noble race,'

Learoyd bellowed. The voices died out in the swimming-bath.

'Oh, Terence!' I said, dropping into Mulvaney's speech, when we were alone, 'it's you that have the Tongue!'

He looked at me wearily;° his eyes were sunk in his head, and his face was drawn and white. 'Eyah!' said he; 'I've blandandhered° thim through the night somehow, but can thim that helps others help thimselves? Answer me that, Sorr!'

And over the bastions of Fort Amara broke the pitiless day.°

From IN BLACK AND WHITE (1888)

On the City Wall

Then she let them down by a cord through the window; for her house was upon the town-wall, and she dwelt upon the wall.

Joshua ii. 15

Lalun is a member of the most ancient profession in the world. Lilith was her very-great-grand-mamma, and that was before the days of Eve,° as every one knows. In the West, people say rude things about Lalun's profession, and write lectures about it, and distribute the lectures to young persons in order that Morality may be preserved. In the East, where the profession is hereditary, descending from mother to daughter, nobody writes lectures or takes any notice; and that is a distinct proof of the inability of the East to manage its own affairs.

Lalun's real husband, for even ladies of Lalun's profession in the East must have husbands, was a big jujube-tree. Her Mamma, who had married a fig-tree, spent ten thousand rupees on Lalun's wedding, which was blessed by forty-seven clergymen of Mamma's Church, and distributed five thousand rupees in charity to the poor. And that was the custom of the land. The advantages of having a jujube-tree for a husband are obvious. You cannot hurt his feelings, and he looks imposing.

Lalun's husband stood on the plain outside the City walls, and Lalun's house was upon the east wall facing the river.° If you fell from the broad window-seat you dropped thirty feet sheer into the City Ditch. But if you stayed where you should and looked forth, you saw all the cattle of the City being driven down to water, the students of the Government College playing cricket, the high grass and trees that fringed the river-bank, the great sand-bars that ribbed the river, the red tombs of dead Emperors° beyond the river, and very far away through the blue heat-haze a glint of the snows of the Himalayas.

Wali Dad used to lie in the window-seat for hours at a time watching this view. He was a young Muhammadan who was suffering acutely from education of the English variety and knew it. His father had sent him to a Mission-school to get wisdom, and Wali Dad had absorbed more than ever his father or the Missionaries intended he should. When his father died, Wali Dad was independent and spent two years experimenting with the creeds of the Earth and reading books that are of no use to anybody.

After he had made an unsuccessful attempt to enter the Roman Catholic Church and the Presbyterian fold at the same time (the Missionaries found him out and called him names, but they did not understand his trouble), he discovered Lalun on the City wall and became the most constant of her few admirers. He possessed a head that English artists at home would rave over and paint amid impossible surroundings—a face that female novelists would use with delight through nine hundred pages. In reality he was only a clean-bred young Muhammadan, with pencilled eyebrows, small-cut nostrils, little feet and hands, and a very tired look in his eyes. By virtue of his twenty-two years he had grown a neat black beard which he stroked with pride and kept delicately scented. His life seemed to be divided between borrowing books from me and making love to° Lalun in the window-seat. He composed songs about her, and some of the songs are sung to this day in the City from the Street of the Mutton-Butchers to the Copper-Smiths' ward.°

One song, the prettiest of all, says that the beauty of Lalun was so great that it troubled the hearts of the British Government and caused them to lose their peace of mind. That is the way the song is sung in the streets; but, if you examine it carefully and know the key to the explanation, you will find that there are three puns in it—on 'beauty,' 'heart,' and 'peace of mind,'—so that it runs: 'By the subtlety of Lalun the administration of the Government was troubled and it lost such and such a man.' When Wali Dad sings that song his eyes glow like hot coals, and Lalun leans back among the cushions and throws bunches of jasmine-buds at Wali Dad.

But first it is necessary to explain something about the Supreme Government which is above all and below all and behind all. Gentlemen come from England, spend a few weeks in India, walk round this great Sphinx of the Plains, and write books upon its ways and its works, denouncing or praising it as their own ignorance prompts. Consequently all the world knows how the Supreme Government conducts itself. But no one, not even the Supreme Government, knows everything about the administration of the Empire. Year by year England sends out fresh drafts for the first fighting-line, which is officially called the Indian Civil Service. These die, or kill themselves by overwork, or are worried to death, or broken in health and hope in order that the land may be protected from death and sickness, famine and war, and may eventually become capable of standing alone. It will never stand alone, but the idea is a pretty one, and men are willing to die for it, and yearly the work of pushing and coaxing and scolding and petting the country into good living goes forward. If an advance be made all credit is given to the native, while the Englishmen stand back and wipe their foreheads. If a failure occurs the Englishmen step forward and take the blame. Overmuch tenderness of this kind has bred a strong belief among many natives that the native is capable of administering the country, and many devout Englishmen believe this also, because the theory is stated in beautiful English with all the latest political colour.

There be other men who, though uneducated, see visions and dream dreams,° and they, too, hope to administer the country in their own way—that is to say, with a garnish of Red Sauce.° Such men must exist among two hundred million people, and, if they are not attended to, may cause trouble and even break the great idol called *Pax Britannic*,° which, as the newspapers say, lives between Peshawar and Cape Comorin.° Were the Day of Doom to dawn to-morrow, you would find the Supreme Government 'taking measures to allay popular excitement,' and putting guards upon the graveyards that the Dead might troop forth orderly. The youngest Civilian° would arrest Gabriel on his own responsibility if the Archangel could not produce a Deputy Commissioner's permission to 'make music or other noises' as the license says.

Whence it is easy to see that mere men of the flesh who would create a tumult must fare badly at the hands of the Supreme Government. And they do. There is no outward sign of excitement; there is no confusion; there is no knowledge. When due and sufficient reasons have been given, weighed and approved, the machinery moves forward, and the dreamer of dreams and the seer of visions is gone from his friends and following. He enjoys the hospitality of Government; there is no restriction upon his movements within certain limits; but he must not confer any more with his brother dreamers. Once in every six months the Supreme Government assures itself that he is well and takes formal acknowledgement of his existence. No one protests against his detention, because the few people who know about it are in deadly fear of seeming to know him; and never a single newspaper 'takes up his case' or organises demonstrations on his behalf, because the newspapers of India have got behind° that lying proverb which says the Pen is mightier than the Sword, and can walk delicately.

So now you know as much as you ought about Wali Dad, the educational mixture, and the Supreme Government.

Lalun has not yet been described. She would need, so Wali Dad says, a thousand pens of gold and ink scented with musk. She has been variously compared to the Moon, the Dil Sagar Lake,° a spotted quail, a gazelle, the Sun on the Desert of Kutch,° the Dawn, the Stars, and the young bamboo. These comparisons imply that she is beautiful exceedingly according to the native standards, which are practically the same as those of the West. Her eyes are black and her hair is black, and her eyebrows are black as leeches; her mouth is tiny and says witty things; her hands are tiny and have saved much money; her feet are tiny and have trodden on the naked hearts of many men. But, as Wali Dad sings: 'Lalun *is* Lalun, and when you have said that, you have only come to the Beginnings of Knowledge.'

The little house on the City wall was just big enough to hold Lalun, and her maid, and a pussy-cat with a silver collar. A big pink and blue cut-glass chandelier hung from the ceiling of the reception room. A petty Nawab° had given Lalun the horror, and she kept it for politeness' sake. The floor of the room was of polished chunam,° white as curds. A latticed window of carved wood was set in one wall; there was a profusion of squabby pluffy cushions and fat carpets everywhere, and Lalun's silver *huqa*,° studded with turquoises, had a special little carpet all to its shining self. Wali Dad was nearly as permanent a fixture as the chandelier. As I have said, he lay in the window-seat and meditated on Life and Death and Lalun—specially Lalun. The feet of the young men of the City tended to her doorways and then—retired, for Lalun was a particular maiden, slow of speech, reserved of mind, and not in the least inclined to orgies which were nearly certain to end in strife. 'If I am of no value, I am unworthy of this honour,' said Lalun. 'If I am of value, they are unworthy of Me.' And that was a crooked sentence.

In the long hot nights of latter April and May all the City seemed to assemble in Lalun's little white room to smoke and to talk. Shiahs° of the grimmest and most uncompromising persuasion; Sufis° who had lost all belief in the Prophet and retained but little in God; wandering Hindu priests passing southward on their way to the Central India fairs and other affairs; Pundits° in black gowns, with spectacles on their noses and undigested wisdom in their insides; bearded headmen of the wards; Sikhs with all the details of the latest ecclesiastical scandal in the Golden Temple;° red-eyed priests from beyond the Border,° looking like trapped wolves and talking like ravens; M.A.'s of the University, very superior and very voluble—all these people and more also you might find in the white room. Wali Dad lay in the window-seat and listened to the talk.

'It is Lalun's *salon*,' said Wali Dad to me, 'and it is electic°—is not that the word? Outside of a Freemasons' Lodge I have never seen such gatherings. *There* I dined once with a Jew°—a Yahoudi!' He spat into the City Ditch with apologies for allowing national feelings to overcome him. 'Though I have lost every belief in the world,' said he, 'and try to be proud of my losing, I cannot help hating a Jew. Lalun admits no Jews here.'

'But what in the world do all these men do?' I asked.

'The curse of our country,' said Wali Dad. 'They talk. It is like the Athenians°—always hearing and telling some new thing. Ask the Pearl and she will show you how much she knows of the news of the City and the Province. Lalun knows everything.'

'Lalun,' I said at random—she was talking to a gentleman of the Kurd persuasion who had come in from God-knows-where—'when does the 175th Regiment go to Agra?'

'It does not go at all,' said Lalun, without turning her head. 'They have ordered the 118th to go in its stead. That Regiment goes to Lucknow in three months, unless they give a fresh order.'

'That is so,' said Wali Dad, without a shade of doubt. 'Can you, with your telegrams and your newspapers, do better? Always hearing and telling some new thing,' he went on. 'My friend, has your God ever smitten a European nation for gossiping in the bazars? India has gossiped for centuries—always standing in the bazars until the soldiers go by. Therefore—you are here to-day instead of starving in your own country, and I am not a Muhammadan—I am a Product—a Demnition Product.° That also I owe to you and yours: that I cannot make an end to my sentence without quoting from your authors.' He pulled at the *huqa* and mourned, half feelingly, half in earnest, for the shattered hopes of his youth. Wali Dad was always mourning over something or other—the country of which he despaired, or the creed in which he had lost faith, or the life of the English which he could by no means understand.

Lalun never mourned. She played little songs on the *sitar*, and to hear her sing, '*O Peacock, cry again*,'° was always a fresh pleasure. She knew all the songs that have ever been sung, from the war-songs of the South, that make the old men angry with the young men and the young men angry with the State, to the love-songs of the North, where the swords whinny-whicker like angry kites in the pauses between the kisses, and the Passes fill with armed men, and the Lover is torn from his Beloved and cries, *Ai! Ai! Ai!* evermore. She knew how to make up tobacco for the *huqa* so that it smelt like the Gates of Paradise and wafted you gently through them. She could embroider strange things in gold and silver, and dance softly with the moonlight when it came in at the window. Also she knew the hearts of men, and the heart of the City, and whose wives were faithful and whose untrue, and more of the secrets of the Government Offices than are good to be set down in this place. Nasiban, her maid, said that her jewelry was worth ten thousand pounds, and that, some night, a thief would enter and murder her for its possession; but Lalun said that all the City would tear that thief limb from limb, and that he, whoever he was, knew it.

So she took her *sitar* and sat in the window-seat, and sang a song of old days° that had been sung by a girl of her profession in an armed camp on the eve of a great battle—the day before the Fords of the Jumna° ran red and Sivaji° fled fifty miles to Delhi with a Toorkh stallion at his horse's tail° and another Lalun on his saddle-bow. It was what men call a Mahratta *laonee*, and it said:—

Their warrior forces Chimnajee
 Before the Peishwa led,
The Children of the Sun and Fire
 Behind him turned and fled.

And the chorus said:—

With them there fought who rides so free
 With sword and turban red,
The warrior-youth who earns his fee
 At peril of his head.

'At peril of his head,' said Wali Dad in English to me. 'Thanks to your Government, all our heads are protected, and with the educational facilities at my command'—his eyes twinkled wickedly—'I might be a distinguished member of the local administration. Perhaps, in time, I might even be a member of a Legislative Council.'

'Don't speak English,' said Lalun, bending over her *sitar* afresh. The chorus went out from the City wall to the blackened wall of Fort Amara which dominates the City. No man knows the precise extent of Fort Amara.° Three kings built it hundreds of years ago, and they say that there are miles of underground rooms beneath its walls. It is peopled with many ghosts, a detachment of Garrison Artillery, and a

Company of Infantry. In its prime it held ten thousand men and filled its ditches with corpses.

'At peril of his head,' sang Lalun again and again.

A head moved on one of the Ramparts—the gray head of an old man—and a voice, rough as shark-skin on a sword-hilt, sent back the last line of the chorus and broke into a song that I could not understand, though Lalun and Wali Dad listened intently.

'What is it?' I asked. 'Who is it?'

'A consistent man,' said Wali Dad. 'He fought you in '46, when he was a warrior-youth; refought you in '57, and he tried to fight you in '71,° but you had learned the trick of blowing men from guns° too well. Now he is old; but he would still fight if he could.'

'Is he a Wahabi,° then? Why should he answer to a Mahratta *laonee* if he be Wahabi—or Sikh?' said I.

'I do not know,' said Wali Dad. 'He has lost, perhaps, his religion. Perhaps he wishes to be a King. Perhaps he is a King. I do not know his name.'

'That is a lie, Wali Dad. If you know his career you must know his name.'

'That is quite true. I belong to a nation of liars. I would rather not tell you his name. Think for yourself.'

Lalun finished her song, pointed to the Fort, and said simply: 'Khem Singh.'

'Hm,' said Wali Dad. 'If the Pearl chooses to tell you the Pearl is a fool.'

I translated to Lalun, who laughed. 'I choose to tell what I choose to tell. They kept Khem Singh in Burma,'° said she. 'They kept him there for many years until his mind was changed in him. So great was the kindness of the Government. Finding this, they sent him back to his own country that he might look upon it before he died. He is an old man, but when he looks upon this his country his memory will come. Moreover, there be many who remember him.'

'He is an Interesting Survival,' said Wali Dad, pulling at the *huqa*. 'He returns to a country now full of educational and political reform, but, as the Pearl says, there are many who remember him. He was once a great man. There will never be any more great men in India. They will all, when they are boys, go whoring after strange gods,° and they will become citizens—"fellow-citizens"—"illustrious fellow-citizens". What is it that the native papers call them?'

Wali Dad seemed to be in a very bad temper. Lalun looked out of the window and smiled into the dust-haze. I went away thinking about

Khem Singh who had once made history with a thousand followers, and would have been a princeling but for the power of the Supreme Government aforesaid.

The Senior Captain commanding Fort Amara was away on leave, but the Subaltern, his Deputy, had drifted down to the Club, where I found him and inquired of him whether it was really true that a political prisoner had been added to the attractions of the Fort. The Subaltern explained at great length, for this was the first time that he had held Command of the Fort, and his glory lay heavy upon him.

'Yes,' said he, 'a man was sent in to me about a week ago from down the line—a thorough gentleman, whoever he is. Of course I did all I could for him. He had his two servants and some silver cooking-pots, and he looked for all the world like a native officer. I called him Subadar Sahib;° just as well to be on the safe side, y'know. "Look here, Subadar Sahib," I said, "you're handed over to my authority, and I'm supposed to guard you. Now I don't want to make your life hard, but you must make things easy for me. All the Fort is at your disposal, from the flagstaff to the dry ditch, and I shall be happy to entertain you in any way I can, but you mustn't take advantage of it. Give me your word that you won't try to escape, Subadar Sahib, and I'll give you my word that you shall have no heavy guard put over you." I thought the best way of getting at him was by going at him straight, y'know; and it was, by Jove! The old man gave me his word, and moved about the Fort as contented as a sick crow. He's a rummy chap—always asking to be told where he is and what the buildings about him are. I had to sign a slip of blue paper when he turned up, acknowledging receipt of his body and all that, and I'm responsible, y'know, that he doesn't get away. Queer thing, though, looking after a Johnnie old enough to be your grandfather, isn't it? Come to the Fort one of these days and see him?'

For reasons which will appear, I never went to the Fort while Khem Singh was then within its walls. I knew him only as a gray head seen from Lalun's window—a gray head and a harsh voice. But natives told me that, day by day, as he looked upon the fair lands round Amara, his memory came back to him and, with it, the old hatred against the Government that had been nearly effaced in far-off Burma. So he raged up and down the West face of the Fort from morning till noon and from evening till the night, devising vain things° in his heart, and croaking war-songs when Lalun sang on the City wall. As he grew more acquainted with the Subaltern he unburdened his old heart of some of the passions that had withered it. 'Sahib,' he used to say, tapping his stick against the parapet, 'when I was a young man I was one of twenty thousand horsemen who came out of the City and rode round the plain here. Sahib, I was the leader of a hundred, then of a thousand, then of five thousand, and now!'—he pointed to his two servants. 'But from the beginning to to-day I would cut the throats of all the Sahibs in the land if I could. Hold me fast, Sahib, lest I get away and return to those who would follow me. I forgot them when I was in Burma, but now that I am in my own country again, I remember everything.'

'Do you remember that you have given me your Honour not to make your tendance a hard matter?' said the Subaltern.

'Yes, to you, only to you, Salhib,' said Khem Singh. 'To you because you are of a pleasant countenance.° If my turn comes again, Sahib, I will not hang you nor cut your throat.'

'Thank you,' said the Subaltern gravely, as he looked along the line of guns that could pound the City to powder in half an hour. 'Let us go into our own qurters, Khem Singh. Come and talk with me after dinner.'

Khem Sigh would sit on his own cushion at the Subaltern's feet, drinking heavy, scented anise-seed brandy in great gulps, and telling strange stories of Fort Amara, which had been a palace in the old days, of Begums and Ranees tortured to death°—ay, in the very vaulted chamber that now served as a Mess-room; would tell stories of Sobraon° that made the Subaltern's cheeks flush and tingle with pride of race, and of the Kuka rising° from which so much was expected and the fore-knowledge of which was shared by a hundred thousand souls. But he never told tales of '57 because, as he said, he was the Subaltern's guest, and '57 is a year that no man, Black or White, cares to speak of. Once only, when the anise-seed brandy had slightly affected his head, he said: 'Sahib, speaking now of a matter which lay between Sobraon and the affair of the Kukas, it was ever a wonder to us that you stayed your hand at all, and that, having stayed it, you did not make the land one prison. Now I hear from without that you do great honour to all men of our country and by your own hands are destroying the Terror of your Name which is your strong rock and defence. This is a foolish thing. Will oil and water mix? Now in '57—'

'I was not born then, Subadar Sahib,' said the Subaltern, and Khem Singh reeled to his quarters.

The Subaltern would tell me of these conversations at the Club, and my desire to see Khem Singh increased. But Wali Dad, sitting in the window-seat of the house on the City wall, said that it would be a cruel thing to do, and Lalun pretended that I preferred the society of a grizzled old Sikh to hers.

'Here is tobacco, here is talk, here are many friends and all the news of the City, and, above all, here is myself. I will tell you stories and sing you songs, and Wali Dad will talk his English nonsense in your ears. Is that worse than watching the caged animal yonder? Go to-morrow then, if you must, but to-day such and such an one will be here, and he will speak of wonderful things.'

It happened that To-morrow never came, and the warm heat of the latter Rains gave place to the chill of early October almost before I was aware of the flight of the year. The Captain commanding the Fort returned from leave and took over charge of Khem Singh according to the laws of seniority. The Captain was not a nice man. He called all natives 'niggers,' which, besides being extreme bad form, shows gross ignorance.

'What's the use of telling off two Tommies to watch that old nigger?' said he.

'I fancy it soothes his vanity,' said the Subaltern. 'The men are ordered to keep well out of his way, but he takes them as a tribute to his importance, poor old wretch.'

'I won't have Line men taken off regular guards in this way. Put on a couple of Native Infantry.'

'Sikhs?' said the Subaltern, lifting his eyebrows.

'Sikhs, Pathans, Dogras°—they're all alike, these black vermin,' and the Captain talked to Khem Singh in a manner which hurt that old gentleman's feelings. Fifteen years before, when he had been caught for the second time, every one looked upon him as a sort of tiger. He liked being regarded in this light. But he forgot that the world goes forward in fifteen years, and many Subalterns are promoted to Captaincies.

'The Captain-pig is in charge of the Fort?' said Khem Singh to his native guard every morning. And the native guard said: 'Yes, Subadar Sahib,' in deference to his age and his air of distinction; but they did not know who he was.

In those days the gathering in Lalun's little white room was always large and talked more than before.

'The Greeks,' said Wali Dad who had been borrowing my books, 'the inhabitants of the city of Athens, where they were always hearing and telling some new thing, rigorously secluded their women—who were fools. Hence the glorious institution of the heterodox women°—is it not?—who were amusing and *not* fools. All the Greek philosophers delighted in their company. Tell me, my friend, how it goes now in Greece and the other places upon the Continent of Europe. Are your women-folk also fools?'

'Wali Dad,' I said, 'you never speak to us about your women-folk and we never speak about ours to you. That is the bar between us.'

'Yes,' said Wali Dad, 'it is curious to think that our common meeting-place should be here, in the house of a common—how do you call *her*?' He pointed with the pipe-mouth to Lalun.

'Lalun is nothing but Lalun,' I said, and that was perfectly true. 'But if you took your place in the world, Wali Dad, and gave up dreaming dreams—'

'I might wear an English coat and trouser. I might be a leading Muhammadan pleader. I might be received even at the Commissioner's tennis-parties where the English stand on one side and the natives on the other, in order to promote social intercourse throughout the Empire. Heart's Heart,' said he to Lalun quickly, 'the Sahib says that I ought to quit you.'

'The Sahib is always talking stupid talk,' returned Lalun with a laugh. 'In this house I am a Queen and thou art a King. The Sahib'—she put her arms above her head and thought for a moment—'the Sahib shall be our Vizier—thine and mine, Wali Dad—because he has said that thou shouldst leave me.'

Wali Dad laughed immoderately, and I laughed too. 'Be it so,' said he. 'My friend, are you willing to take this lucrative Government appointment? Lalun, what shall his pay be?'

But Lalun began to sing, and for the rest of the time there was no hope of getting a sensible answer from her or Wali Dad. When the one stopped, the other began to quote Persian poetry with a triple pun in every other line. Some of it was not strictly proper, but it was all very funny, and it only came to an end when a fat person in black, with gold *pince-nez*, sent up his name to Lalun, and Wali Dad dragged me into the twinkling night to walk in a big rose-garden and talk heresies about Religion and Governments and a man's career in life.

The Mohurrum, the great mourning-festival of the Muhammadans, was close at hand, and the things that Wali Dad said about religious fanaticism would have secured his expulsion from the loosest-thinking Muslim sect. There were the rose-bushes round us, the stars above us, and from every quarter of the City came the boom of the big Mohurrum drums. You must know that the City is divided in fairly equal proportions between the Hindus and the Musalmans, and where both creeds belong to the fighting races, a big religious festival gives ample chance for trouble. When they can—that is to say, when the authorities are weak enough to allow it—the Hindus do their best to arrange some minor feast-day of their own in time to clash with the period of general mourning for the martyrs Hasan and Hussain, the heroes of the Mohurrum. Gilt and painted paper presentations of their tombs are borne with shouting and wailing, music, torches, and yells, through the principal thoroughfares of the City; which fakements° are called *tazias*. Their passage is rigorously laid down beforehand by the Police, and detachments of Police accompany each *tazia* lest the Hindus should throw bricks at it and the peace of the Queen and the heads of Her loyal subjects should thereby be broken. Mohurrum time in a 'fighting' town means anxiety to all the officials, because, if a riot breaks out, the officials and not the rioters are held responsible. The former must foresee everything, and while not making their precautions ridiculously elaborate, must see that they are at least adequate.

'Listen to the drums!' said Wali Dad. 'That is the heart of the people—empty and making much noise. How, think you, will the Mohurrum go this year? *I* think that there will be trouble.'

He turned down a side-street and left me alone with the stars and a sleepy Police patrol. Then I went to bed and dreamed that Wali Dad had sacked the City and I was made Vizier, with Lalun's silver *huqa* for mark of office.

All day the Mohurrum drums beat in the City, and all day deputations of tearful Hindu gentlemen besieged the Deputy Commissioner with assurances that they would be murdered ere next dawning by the Muhammadans. 'Which,' said the Deputy Commissioner, in confidence to the Head of Police, 'is a pretty fair indication that the Hindus are going to make 'emselves unpleasant. I think we can arrange a little surprise for them. I have given the heads of both Creeds fair warning. If they choose to disregard it, so much the worse for them.'

There was a large gathering in Lalun's house that night, but of men that I had never seen before, if I except the fat gentleman in black with the gold *pince-nez*. Wali Dad lay in the window-seat, more bitterly scornful of his Faith and its manifestations than I had ever known him. Lalun's maid was very busy cutting up and mixing tobacco for the guests. We could hear the thunder of the drums as the processions accompanying each *tazia* marched to the central gathering-place in the plain outside the City, preparatory to their triumphant re-entry and circuit within the walls. All the streets seemed ablaze with torches, and only Fort Amara was black and silent.

When the noise of the drums ceased, no one in the white room spoke for a time. 'The first *tazia* has moved off,' said Wali Dad, looking to the plain.

'That is very early,' said the man with the *pince-nez*. 'It is only half-past eight.' The company rose and departed.

'Some of them were men from Ladakh,' said Lalun, when the last had gone. 'They brought me brick-tea such as the Russians sell,° and a tea-urn from Peshawur. Show me, now, how the English *Memsahibs* make tea.'

The brick-tea° was abominable. When it was finished Wali Dad suggested going into the streets. 'I am nearly sure that there will be trouble to-night,' he said. 'All the City thinks so, and *Vox Populi* is *Vox Die*, as the Babus say.° Now I tell you that at the corner of the Padshahi Gate° you will find my horse all this night if you want to go about and to see things. It is a most disgraceful exhibition. Where is the pleasure of saying "*Ya Hasan, Ya Hussain*" twenty thousand times in a night?'

All the processions—there were two-and-twenty of them—were now well within the City walls. The drums were beating afresh, the crowd were howling '*Ya Hasan! Ya Hussain!*' and beating their breasts, the brass bands were playing their loudest, and at every corner where space allowed, Muhammadan preachers were telling the lamentable story of the death of the Martyrs. It was impossible to move except with the crowd, for the streets were not more than twenty feet wide. In the Hindu quarters the shutters of all the shops were up and cross-barred. As the first *tazia*, a gorgeous erection ten feet high, was borne aloft on the shoulders of a score of stout men into the semi-darkness of the Gully of the Horsemen, a brickbat crashed through its talc° and tinsel sides.

'Into thy hands, O Lord!'° murmured Wali Dad profanely, as a yell went up from behind, and a native officer of Police jammed his horse through the crowd. Another brickbat followed, and the *tazia* staggered and swayed where it had stopped.

'Go on! In the name of the *Sirkar*,° go forward!' shouted the Policeman; but there was an ugly cracking and splintering of shutters, and the crowd halted, with oaths and growlings, before the house whence the brickbat had been thrown.

Then, without any warning, broke the storm—not only in the Gully of the Horsemen, but in half-a-dozen other places. The *tazias* rocked like ships at sea, the long pole-torches dipped and rose round them while the men shouted: 'The Hindus are dishonouring the *tazias!* Strike! strike! Into their temples for the Faith!' The six or eight Policemen with each *tazia* drew their batons, and struck as long as they could in the hope of forcing the mob forward, but they were overpowered, and as contingents of Hindus poured into the streets, the fight became general. Half a mile away where the *tazias* were yet untouched the drums and the shrieks of '*Ya Hasan! Ya Hussain!*' continued, but not for long. The priests at the corners of the streets knocked the legs from the bedsteads that supported their pulpits and smote for the Faith, while stones fell from the silent houses upon friend and foe, and the packed streets bellowed: '*Din! Din! Din!*' A *tazia* caught fire, and was dropped for a flaming barrier between Hindu and Musalman at the corner of the Gully. Then the crowd surged forward, and Wali Dad drew me close to the stone pillar of a well.

'It was intended from the beginning!' he shouted in my ear, with more heat than blank unbelief should be guilty of. 'The bricks were carried up to the houses beforehand. These swine of Hindus! We shall be gutting kine in their temples to-night!'°

Tazia after *tazia*, some burning, others torn to pieces, hurried past us and the mob with them, howling, shrieking, and striking at the house doors in their flight. At last we saw the reason of the rush. Hugonin, the Assistant District Superintendent of Police, a boy of twenty, had got together thirty constables and was forcing the crowd through the streets. His old gray Police-horse showed no sign of uneasiness as it was spurred breast-on into the crowd, and the long dog-whip with which he had armed himself was never still.

'They know we haven't enough Police to hold 'em,' he cried as he passed me, mopping a cut on his face. 'They *know* we haven't! Aren't any of the men from the Club coming down to help? Get on, you sons of burnt fathers!'° The dog-whip cracked across the writhing backs, and the constables smote afresh with baton and gun-butt. With these passed the lights and the shouting, and Wali Dad began to swear under his breath. From Fort Amara shot up a single rocket; then two side by side. It was the signal for troops.

Petitt, the Deputy Commissioner, covered with dust and sweat, but calm and gently smiling, cantered up the clean-swept street in rear of the main body of the rioters. 'No one killed yet,' he shouted. 'I'll keep 'em on the run till dawn! Don't let 'em halt, Hugonin! Trot 'em about till the troops come.'

The science of the defence lay solely in keeping the mob on the move. If they had breathing-space they would halt and fire a house, and then the work of restoring order would be more difficult, to say the least of it. Flames have the same effect on a crowd as blood has on a wild beast.

Word had reached the Club° and men in evening-dress were beginning to show themselves and lend a hand in heading off and breaking up the shouting masses with stirrup-leathers, whips, or chance-found staves. They were not very often attacked, for the rioters had sense enough to know that the death of a European would not mean one hanging but many, and possibly the appearance of the thrice-dreaded Artillery. The clamour in the City redoubled. The Hindus had descended into the streets in real earnest and ere long the mob returned. It was a strange sight. There were no *tazias*—only their riven platforms—and there were no Police. Here and there a City dignitary, Hindu or Muhammadan, was vainly imploring his co-religionists to keep quiet and behave themselves—advice for which his white beard was pulled. Then a native officer of Police, unhorsed but still using his spurs with effect, would be borne along, warning all the crowd of the danger of insulting the Government. Everywhere men struck aimlessly with sticks, grasping each other by the throat, howling and foaming with rage, or beat with their bare hands on the doors of the houses.

'It is a lucky thing that they are fighting with natural weapons,' I said to Wali Dad, 'else we should have half the City killed.'

I turned as I spoke and looked at his face. His nostrils were distended, his eyes were fixed, and he was smiting himself softly on the breast. The crowd poured by with renewed riot—a gang of Musalmans hard pressed by some hundred Hindu fanatics. Wali Dad left my side with an oath, and shouting: '*Ya Hasan! Ya Hussain!*' plunged into the thick of the fight where I lost sight of him.

I fled by a side alley to the Padshahi Gate where I found Wali Dad's horse, and thence rode to the Fort. Once outside the City wall, the tumult sank to a dull roar, very impressive under the stars and reflecting great credit on the fifty thousand angry able-bodied men who were making it. The troops who, at the Deputy Commissioner's instance, had been ordered to rendezvous quietly near the Fort, showed no signs of being impressed. Two companies of Native Infantry, a squadron of Native Cavalry, and a company of British Infantry were kicking their heels in the shadow of the East face, waiting for orders to march in. I am sorry to say that they were all pleased, unholily pleased, at the chance of what they called 'a little fun.' The senior officers, to be sure, grumbled at having been kept out of bed, and the English troops pretended to be sulky, but there was joy in the hearts of all the subalterns, and whispers ran up and down the line: 'No ball-cartridge—what a beastly shame!' 'D'you think the beggars will really stand up to us?' ''Hope I shall meet my money-lender there. I owe him more than I can afford.' 'Oh, they won't let us even unsheathe swords.' 'Hurrah! Up goes the fourth rocket. Fall in, there!'

The Garrison Artillery, who to the last cherished a wild hope that they might be allowed to bombard the City at a hundred yards' range, lined the parapet above the East gateway and cheered themselves hoarse as the British Infantry doubled along the road to the Main Gate of the City.° The Cavalry cantered on to the Padshahi Gate, and the Native Infantry marched slowly to the Gate of the Butchers.° The surprise was intended to be of a distinctly unpleasant nature, and to come on top of the defeat of the Police, who had been just able to keep the Muhammadans from firing the houses of a few leading Hindus. The bulk of the riot lay in the north and north-west wards. The east and south-east were by this time dark and silent, and I rode hastily to Lalun's house for I wished to tell her to send some one in search of Wali Dad. The house was unlighted, but the door was open, and I climbed upstairs in the darkness. One small lamp in the white room showed Lalun and her maid leaning half out of the window, breathing heavily and evidently pulling at something that refused to come.

'Thou art late—very late,' gasped Lalun without turning her head. 'Help us now, O Fool, if thou hast not spent thy strength howling among the *tazias*. Pull! Nasiban and I can do no more! O Sahib, is it you? The Hindus have been hunting an old Muhammadan round the Ditch with clubs. If they find him again they will kill him. Help us to pull him up.'

I put my hands to the long red silk waist-cloth that was hanging out of the window, and we three pulled and pulled with all the strength at our command. There was something very heavy at the end, and it swore in an unknown tongue as it kicked against the City wall.

'Pull, oh, pull!' said Lalun at the last. A pair of brown hands grasped the window-sill and a venerable Muhammadan tumbled upon the floor, very much out of breath. His jaws were tied up, his turban had fallen over one eye, and he was dusty and angry.

Lalun hid her face in her hands for an instant and said something about Wali Dad that I could not catch.

Then, to my extreme gratification, she threw her arms round my neck and murmured pretty things. I was in no haste to stop her; and

Nasiban, being a handmaiden of tact, turned to the big jewel-chest that stands in the corner of the white room and rummaged among the contents. The Muhammadan sat on the floor and glared.

'One service more, Sahib, since thou hast come so opportunely,' said Lalun. 'Wilt thou'—it is very nice to be thou-ed° by Lalun—'take this old man across the City—the troops are everywhere, and they might hurt him for he is old—to the Kumharsen Gate?° There I think he may find a carriage to take him to his house. He is a friend of mine, and thou art—more than a friend—therefore I ask this.'

Nasiban bent over the old man, tucked something into his belt, and I raised him up, and led him into the streets. In crossing from the east to the west of the City there was no chance of avoiding the troops and the crowd. Long before I reached the Gully of the Horsemen I heard the shouts of the British Infantry crying cheerily: 'Hutt,° ye beggars! Hutt, ye devils! Get along! Go forward, there!' Then followed the ringing of rifle-butts and shrieks of pain. The troops were banging the bare toes of the mob with their gun-butts—for not a bayonet had been fixed. My companion mumbled and jabbered as we walked on until we were carried back by the crowd and had to force our way to the troops. I caught him by the wrist and felt a bangle there—the iron bangle of the Sikhs°—but I had no suspicions, for Lalun had only ten minutes before put her arms round me. Thrice we were carried back by the crowd, and when we made our way past the British Infantry it was to meet the Sikh Cavalry driving another mob before them with the butts of their lances.

'What are these dogs?' said the old man.

'Sikhs of the Cavalry, Father,' I said, and we edged our way up the line of horses two abreast and found the Deputy Commissioner, his helmet smashed on his head, surrounded by a knot of men who had come down from the Club as amateur constables and had helped the Police mightily.

'We'll keep 'em on the run till dawn,' said Petitt. 'Who's your villainous friend?'

I had only time to say: 'The Protection of the *Sirkar!*' when a fresh crowd flying before the Native Infantry carried us a hundred yards nearer to the Kumharsen Gate, and Petitt was swept away like a shadow.

'I do not know—I cannot see—this is all new to me!' moaned my companion. 'How many troops are there in the City?'

'Perhaps five hundred,' I said.

'A lakh of men° beaten by five hundred—and Sikhs among them!

Surely, surely, I am old man, but—the Kumharsen Gate is new. Who pulled down the stone lions? Where is the conduit? Sahib, I am a very old man, and, alas, I—I cannot stand.' He dropped in the shadow of the Kumharsen Gate where there was no disturbance. A fat gentleman wearing gold *pince-nez* came out of the darkness.

'You are most kind to bring my old friend,' he said suavely. 'He is a landholder of Akala.° He should not be in a big City when there is religious excitement. But I have a carriage here. You are quite truly kind. Will you help me to put him into the carriage? It is very late.'

We bundled the old man into a hired victoria that stood close to the gate, and I turned back to the house on the City wall. The troops were driving the people to and fro, while the Police shouted, 'To your houses! Get to your houses!' and the dog-whip of the Assistant District Superintendent cracked remorselessly. Terror-stricken *bunnias*° clung to the stirrups of the cavalry, crying that their houses had been robbed (which was a lie), and the burly Sikh horsemen patted them on the shoulder and bade them return to those houses lest a worse thing should happen.° Parties of five or six British soldiers, joining arms, swept down the side-gullies, their rifles on their backs, stamping, with shouting and song, upon the toes of Hindu and Musalman. Never was religious enthusiasm more systematically squashed; and never were poor breakers of the peace more utterly weary and footsore. They were routed out of holes and corners, from behind well-pillars and byres, and bidden to go to their houses. If they had no houses to go to, so much the worse for their toes.

On returning to Lalun's door I stumbled over a man at the threshold. He was sobbing hysterically and his arms flapped like the wings of a goose. It was Wali Dad, Agnostic and Unbeliever, shoeless, turbanless, and frothing at the mouth, the flesh on his chest bruised and bleeding from the vehemence with which he had smitten himself. A broken torch-handle lay by his side, and his quivering lips murmured, '*Ya Hasan! Ya Hussain!*' as I stooped over him. I pushed him a few steps up the staircase, threw a pebble at Lalun's City window and hurried home.

Most of the streets were very still, and the cold wind that comes before the dawn whistled down them. In the centre of the Square of the Mosque° a man was bending over a corpse. The skull had been smashed in by gun-butt or bamboo-stave.

'It is expedient that one man should die for the people,'° said Petitt grimly, raising the shapeless head. 'These brutes were beginning to show their teeth too much.'

And from afar we could hear the soldiers singing 'Two Lovely Black Eyes,'° as they drove the remnant of the rioters within doors.

Of course you can guess what happened? I was not so clever. When the news went abroad that Khem Singh had escaped from the Fort, I did not, since I was then living this story, not writing it, connect myself, or Lalun, or the fat gentleman of the gold *pince-nez*, with his disappearance. Nor did it strike me that Wali Dad was the man who should have convoyed him across the City, or that Lalun's arms round my neck were put there to hide the money that Nasiban gave to Khem Singh, and that Lalun had used me and my white face as even a better safeguard than Wali Dad who proved himself so untrustworthy. All that I knew at the time was that, when Fort Amara was taken up with the riots, Khem Singh profited by the confusion to get away, and that his two Sikh guards also escaped.

But later on I received full enlightenment; and so did Khem Singh. He fled to those who knew him in the old days, but many of them were dead and more were changed, and all knew something of the Wrath of the Government. He went to the young men, but the glamour of his name had passed away, and they were entering native regiments or Government offices, and Khem Singh could give them neither pension, decorations, nor influence—nothing but a glorious death with their back to the mouth of a gun. He wrote letters and made promises, and the letters fell into bad hands, and a wholly insignificant subordinate officer of Police tracked them down and gained promotion thereby. Moreover, Khem Singh was old, and aniseseed brandy was scarce, and he had left his silver cooking-pots in Fort Amara with his nice warm bedding, and the gentleman with the gold *pince-nez* was told by Those who had employed him° that Khem Singh as a popular leader was not worth the money paid.

'Great is the mercy of these fools of English!' said Khem Singh when the situation was put before him. 'I will go back to Fort Amara of my own free will and gain honour. Give me good clothes to return in.'

So, at his own time, Khem Singh knocked at the wicket-gate of the Fort and walked to the Captain and the Subaltern, who were nearly gray-headed on account of correspondence that daily arrived from Simla marked 'Private.'

'I have come back, Captain Sahib,' said Khem Sigh. 'Put no more guards over me. It is no good out yonder.'

A week later I saw him for the first time to my knowledge, and he made as though there were an understanding between us.

'It was well done, Sahib,' said he, 'and greatly I admired your astuteness in thus boldly facing the troops when I, whom they would have doubtless torn to pieces, was with you. Now there is a man in Fort Ooltagarh° whom a bold man could with ease help to escape. This is the position of the Fort as I draw it on the sand—'

But I was thinking how I had become Lalun's Vizier after all.

From THE PHANTOM RICKSHAW (1888)

The Man who would be King

Brother to a Prince and fellow to a beggar if he be found worthy.

The Law, as quoted, lays down a fair conduct of life, and one not easy to follow. I have been fellow to a beggar again and again under circumstances which prevented either of us finding out whether the other was worthy. I have still to be brother to a Prince, though I once came near to kinship with what might have been a veritable King, and was promised the reversion of a Kingdom—army, law-courts, revenue, and policy all complete. But, to-day, I greatly fear that my King is dead, and if I want a crown I must go hunt it for myself.

The beginning of everything was in a railway train upon the road to Mhow from Ajmir. There had been a Deficit in the Budget,° which necessitated travelling, not Second-class, which is only half as dear as First-class, but by Intermediate, which is very awful indeed. There are no cushions in the Intermediate class, and the population are either Intermediate, which is Eurasian, or native, which for a long night journey is nasty, or Loafer, which is amusing though intoxicated. Intermediates do not buy from refreshment-rooms. They carry their food in bundles and pots, and buy sweets from the native sweetmeat-sellers, and drink the road-side water. That is why in the hot weather Intermediates are taken out of the carriages dead, and in all weathers are most properly looked down upon.

My particular Intermediate happened to be empty till I reached Nasirabad, when a big black-browed gentleman in shirt-sleeves entered, and, following the custom of Intermediates, passed the time of day. He was a wanderer and a vagabond like myself, but with an educated taste for whisky. He told tales of things he had seen and done, of out-of-the-way corners of the Empire into which he had penetrated, and of adventures in which he risked his life for a few days' food.

'If India was filled with men like you and me,° not knowing more than the crows° where they'd get their next day's rations, it isn't seventy millions of revenue° the land would be paying—it's seven hundred millions,' said he; and as I looked at his mouth and chin I was disposed to agree with him.

We talked politics—the politics of Loaferdom, that sees things from the underside where the lath and plaster is not smoothed off—and we talked postal arrangements because my friend wanted to send a telegram back from the next station to Ajmir, the turning-off place from the Bombay to the Mhow line as you travel westward. My friend had no money beyond eight annas, which he wanted for dinner, and I had no money at all, owing to the hitch in the Budget before mentioned. Further, I was going into a wilderness where, though I should resume touch with the Treasury, there were no telegraph offices. I was, therefore, unable to help him in any way.

'We might threaten a Station-master, and make him send a wire on tick,' said my friend, 'but that'd mean inquiries for you and for me, and *I*'ve got my hands full these days. Did you say you are travelling back along this line within any days?'

'Within ten,' I said.

'Can't you make it eight?' said he. 'Mine is rather urgent business.'

'I can send your telegram within ten days if that will serve you,' I said.

'I couldn't trust the wire to fetch him now I think of it. It's this way. He leaves Delhi on the 23rd for Bombay. That means he'll be running through Ajmir about the night of the 23rd.'

'But I'm going into the Indian Desert,' I explained.

'Well *and* good,' said he. 'You'll be changing at Marwar Junction to get into Jodhpore territory—you must do that—and he'll be coming through Marwar Junction in the early morning of the 24th by the Bombay Mail. Can you be at Marwar Junction on that time? 'Twon't be inconveniencing you because I know that there's precious few pickings to be got out of these Central India States—even though you pretend to be correspondent of the *Backwoodsman*."°

'Have you ever tried that trick?' I asked.

'Again and again, but the Residents° find you out, and then you get escorted to the Border before you've time to get your knife into them. But about my friend here. I *must* give him a word o' mouth to tell him what's come to me or else he won't know where to go. I would take it more than kind of you if you was to come out of Central India in time to catch him at Marwar Junction, and say to him: "He has gone South for the week." He'll know what that means. He's a big man with a red beard, and a great swell he is. You'll find him sleeping like a gentleman with all his luggage round him in a Second-class compartment. But don't you be afraid. Slip down the window, and say: "He has gone South for the week," and he'll tumble. It's only cutting your time of stay in those parts by two days. I ask you as a stranger—going to the West,' he said with emphasis.

'Where have *you* come from?' said I.

'From the East,' said he, 'and I am hoping that you will give him the message on the Square—for the sake of my Mother° as well as your own.'

Englishmen are not usually softened by appeals to the memory of their mothers, but for certain reasons, which will be fully apparent, I saw fit to agree.

'It's more than a little matter,' said he, 'and that's why I asked you to do it—and now I know that I can depend on you doing it. A Second-class carriage at Marwar Junction, and a red-haired man asleep in it. You'll be sure to remember. I get out at the next station, and I must hold on there till he comes or sends me what I want.'

'I'll give the message if I catch him,' I said, 'and for the sake of your Mother as well as mine I'll give you a word of advice. Don't try to run the Central India States just now as the correspondent of the *Backwoodsman*. There's a real one knocking about here, and it might lead to trouble.'

'Thank you,' said he simply, 'and when will the swine be gone? I can't starve because he's ruining my work. I wanted to get hold of the Degumber Rajah down here about his father's widow, and give him a jump.'

'What did he do to his father's widow, then?'

'Filled her up with red pepper and slippered her to death as she hung from a beam. I found that out myself, and I'm the only man that would dare going into the State to get hush-money for it. They'll try to poison me, same as they did in Chortumna° when I went on the loot there. But you'll give the man at Marwar Junction my message?'

He got out at a little roadside station, and I reflected. I had heard, more than once, of men personating corrrespondents of newspapers and bleeding small Native States with threats of exposure, but I had never met any of the caste before. They led a hard life, and generally die with great suddenness. The Native States have a wholesome horror of English newspapers which may throw light on their peculiar methods of government, and do their best to choke correspondents with champagne, or drive them out of their mind with four-in-hand barouches.° They do not understand that nobody cares a straw for the internal administration of Native States so long as oppression and crime are kept within decent limits, and the ruler is not drugged, drunk, or diseased from one end of the year to the other. They are the dark places of the earth, full of unimaginable cruelty, touching the Railway and the Telegraph on one side, and, on the other, the days of Harun-al-Raschid.° When I left the train I did business with divers Kings, and in eight days passed through many changes of life. Sometimes I wore dress-clothes and consorted with Princes and Politicals,° drinking from crystal and eating from silver. Sometimes I lay out upon the ground and devoured what I could get, from a plate made of leaves,° and drank the running water, and slept under the same rug as my servant. It was all in the day's work.

Then I headed for the Great Indian Desert upon the proper date, as I had promised, and the night Mail set me down at Marwar Junction, where a funny, little, happy-go-lucky, native-managed railway runs to Jodhpore. The Bombay Mail from Delhi makes a short halt at Marwar. She arrived as I got in, and I had just time to hurry to her platform and go down the carriages. There was only one Second-class on the train. I slipped the window and looked down upon a flaming red beard, half covered by a railway rug. That was my man, fast asleep, and I dug him gently in the ribs. He woke with a grunt, and I saw his face in the light of the lamps. It was a great and shining face.

'Tickets again?' said he.

'No,' said I. 'I am to tell you that he is gone South for the week. He has gone South for the week!'

The train had begun to move out. The red man rubbed his eyes. 'He has gone South for the week,' he repeated. 'Now that's just like his impidence. Did he say that I was to give you anything? 'Cause I won't.'

'He didn't,' I said, and dropped away, and watched the red lights die out in the dark. It was horribly cold because the wind was blowing off the sands. I climbed into my own train—not an Intermediate Carriage this time—and went to sleep.

If the man with the beard had given me a rupee I should have kept it as a memento of a rather curious affair. But the consciousness of having done my duty was my only reward.

Later on I reflected that two gentlemen like my friends could not do any good if they forgathered and personated correspondents of newspapers, and might, if they black-mailed one of the little rat-trap states of Central India or Southern Rajputana, get themselves into serious difficulties. I therefore took some trouble to describe them as accurately as I could remember to people who would be interested in deporting them; and succeeded, so I was later informed, in having them headed back from the Degumber borders.

Then I became respectable, and returned to an Office where there were no Kings and no incidents outside the daily manufacture of a newspaper. A newspaper office seems to attract every conceivable sort of person, to the prejudice of discipline. Zenana-mission° ladies arrive, and beg that the Editor will instantly abandon all his duties to describe a Christian prize-giving in a back-slum of a perfectly inaccessible village; Colonels who have been overpassed for command sit down and sketch the outline of a series of ten, twelve, or twenty-four leading articles on Seniority *versus* Selection; Missionaries wish to know why they have not been permitted to escape from their regular vehicles of abuse and swear at a brother-missionary under special patronage of the editorial We; stranded theatrical companies troop up to explain that they cannot pay for their advertisements, but on their return from New Zealand or Tahiti will do so with interest; inventors of patent punkah-pulling machines, carriage couplings, and unbreakable swords and axle-trees, call with specifications in their pockets and hours at their disposal; tea-companies enter and elaborate their prospectuses with the office pens; secretaries of ball-committees clamour to have the glories of their last dance more fully described; strange ladies rustle in and say, 'I want a hundred lady's cards printed *at once*, please,' which is manifestly part of an Editor's duty; and every dissolute ruffian that ever tramped the Grand Trunk Road° makes it his business to ask for employment as a proof-reader. And, all the time, the telephone-bell is ringing madly, and Kings are being killed on the Continent, and Empires are saying, 'You're another,' and Mister Gladstone is calling down brimstone upon the British Dominions,° and the little black copy-boys are whining, '*kaa-pi chay-ha-yeh*' (copy wanted) like tired bees, and most of the paper is as blank as Modred's shield.°

But that is the amusing part of the year. There are six other months when none ever comes to call, and the thermometer walks inch by inch up to the top of the glass, and the office is darkened to just above reading-light, and the press-machines are red-hot of touch, and nobody writes anything but accounts of amusements in the Hill-stations or obituary notices. Then the telephone becomes a tinkling terror, because it tells you of the sudden deaths of men and women that you knew intimately, and the prickly-heat covers you with a garment, and you sit down and write: 'A slight increase of sickness is reported from the Khuda Janta Khan District.° The outbreak is purely sporadic in its nature, and, thanks to the energetic efforts of the District authorities, is now almost at an end. It is, however, with deep regret we record the death, etc.'

Then the sickness really breaks out, and the less recording and reporting the better for the peace of the subscribers. But the Empires and the Kings continue to divert themselves as selfishly as before, and the Foreman thinks that a daily paper really ought to come out once in twenty-four hours, and all the people at the Hill-stations in the middle of their amusements say: 'Good gracious! Why can't the paper be sparkling? I'm sure there's plenty going on up here.'

That is the dark half of the moon, and, as the advertisements say, 'must be experienced to be appreciated.'

It was in that season, and a remarkably evil season, that the paper began running the last issue of the week on Saturday night, which is to say Sunday morning, after the custom of a London paper. This was a great convenience, for immediately after the paper was put to bed, the dawn would lower the thermometer from 96° to almost 84° for half an hour, and in that chill—you have no idea how cold is 84° on the grass until you begin to pray for it—a very tired man could get off to sleep ere the heat roused him.

One Saturday night it was my pleasant duty to put the paper to bed alone. A King or courtier or a courtesan or a Community was going to die or get a new Constitution, or do something that was important on the other side of the world,° and the paper was to be held open till the latest possible minute in order to catch the telegram.

It was a pitchy black night, as stifling as a June night can be, and the *loo*, the red-hot wind from the westward, was booming among the tinder-dry trees and pretending that the rain was on its heels. Now and again a spot of almost boiling water would fall on the dust with the flop of a frog, but all our weary world knew that was only pretence. It was a shade cooler in the press-room than the office, so I sat there, while the type ticked and clicked, and the night-jars hooted at the windows, and the all but naked compositors wiped the sweat from their foreheads, and called for water. The thing that was keeping us back, whatever it was, would not come off, though the *loo* dropped and the last type was set, and the whole round earth stood still in the choking heat, with its finger on its lip, to wait the event. I drowsed, and wondered whether the telegraph was a blessing, and whether this dying man, or struggling people, might be aware of the inconvenience the delay was causing. There was no special reason beyond the heat and worry to make tension, but, as the clock-hands crept up to three o'clock, and the machines spun their fly-wheels two or three times to see that all was in order before I said the word that would set them off, I could have shrieked aloud.

Then the roar and rattle of the wheels shivered the quiet into little bits. I rose to go away, but two men in white clothes stood in front of me. The first one said: 'It's him!' The second said: 'So it is!' And they both laughed almost as loudly as the machinery roared, and mopped their foreheads. 'We seed there was a light burning across the road, and we were sleeping in that ditch there for coolness, and I said to my friend here, The office is open. Let's come along and speak to him as turned us back from the Degumber State,' said the smaller of the two. He was the man I had met in the Mhow train, and his fellow was the red-bearded man of Marwar Junction. There was no mistaking the eyebrows of the one or the beard of the other.

I was not pleased, because I wished to go to sleep, not to squabble with loafers. 'What do you want?' I asked.

'Half an hour's talk with you, cool and comfortable, in the office,' said the red-bearded man. 'We'd *like* some drink—the Contrack doesn't begin yet, Peachey, so you needn't look—but what we really want is advice. We don't want money. We ask you as a favour, because we found out you did us a bad turn about Degumber State.'

I led from the press-room to the stifling office with the maps on the walls, and the red-haired man rubbed his hands. 'That's something like,' said he. 'This was the proper shop to come to. Now, Sir, let me introduce to you Brother Peachey Carnehan, that's him, and Brother Daniel° Dravot, that is *me*, and the less said about our professions the better, for we have been most things in our time. Soldier, sailor, compositor, photographer, proof-reader, street-preacher, and correspondents of the *Backwoodsman* when we thought the paper wanted one. Carnehan is sober, and so am I. Look at us first, and see that's sure. It will save you cutting into my talk. We'll take one of your cigars apiece, and you shall see us light up.'

I watched the test. The men were absolutely sober, so I gave them each a tepid whisky and soda.

'Well *and* good,' said Carnehan of the eyebrows, wiping the froth from his moustache. 'Let me talk now, Dan. We have been all over India, mostly on foot. We have been boiler-fitters, engine-drivers, petty contractors, and all that, and we have decided that India isn't big enough for such as us.'

They certainly were too big for the office. Dravot's beard seemed to fill half the room and Carnehan's shoulders the other half, as they sat on the big table. Carnehan continued: 'The country isn't half worked out because they that governs it won't let you touch it. They spend all their blessed time in governing it, and you can't lift a spade, nor chip a rock, nor look for oil, nor anything like that, without all the Government saying, "Leave it alone, and let us govern." Therefore, such *as* it is, we will let it alone, and go away to some other place where a man isn't crowded and can come to his own. We are not little men, and there is nothing that we are afraid of except Drink, and we have signed a Contrack on that. *Therefore* we are going away to be Kings.'

'Kings in our own right,' muttered Dravot.

'Yes, of course,' I said. 'You've been tramping in the sun, and it's a very warm night, and hadn't you better sleep over the notion? Come to-morrow.'

'Neither drunk or sunstruck,' said Dravot. 'We have slept over the notion half a year, and require to see Books and Atlases, and we have decided that there is only one place now in the world that two strong men can Sar-a-*whack*.° They call it Kafiristan. By my reckoning it's the top right-hand corner of Afghanistan, not more than three hundred miles from Peshawar.° They have two-and-thirty heathen idols there, and we'll be the thirty-third and fourth. It's a mountainous country, and the women of those parts are very beautiful.'

'But that is provided against in the Contrack,' said Carnehan. 'Neither Woman nor Liqu-or, Daniel.'

'And that's all we know, except that no one has gone there, and they fight, and in any place where they fight a man who knows how to drill men can always be a King. We shall go to those parts and say to any King we find—"D'you want to vanquish your foes?" and we will show him how to drill men; for that we know better than anything else. Then we will subvert that King and seize his Throne and establish a Dy-nasty.'

'You'll be cut to pieces before you're fifty miles across the Border,' I said. 'You have to travel through Afghanistan to get to that country. It's one mass of mountains and peaks and glaciers, and no Englishman has been through it. The people are utter brutes, and even if you reached them you couldn't do anything.'

'That's more like,' said Carnehan. 'If you could think us a little more mad we would be more pleased. We have come to you to know about this country, to read a book about it, and to be shown maps. We want you to tell us that we are fools and to show us your books.' He turned to the bookcases.

'Are you at all in earnest?' I said.

'A little,' said Dravot sweetly. 'As big a map as you have got, even if it's all blank where Kafiristan is, and any books you've got. We can read, though we aren't very educated.'

I uncased the big thirty-two-miles-to-the-inch map of India,° and two smaller Frontier maps, hauled down volume INF–KAN of the *Encyclopædia Britannica*,° and the men consulted them.

'See here!' said Dravot, his thumb on the map. 'Up to Jagdallak, Peachey and me know the road. We was there with Roberts' Army.° We'll have to turn off to the right at Jagdallak through Laghmann territory. Then we get among the hills—fourteen thousand feet—fifteen thousand—it will be cold work there, but it don't look very far on the map.'

I handed him Wood on the *Sources of the Oxus*.° Carnehan was deep in the *Encyclopædia*.

'They're a mixed lot,' said Dravot reflectively; 'and it won't help us to know the names of their tribes. The more tribes the more they'll fight, and the better for us. From Jagdallak to Ashang. H'mm!'

'But all the information about the country is as sketchy and inaccurate as can be,' I protested. 'No one knows anything about it really. Here's the file of the *United Services' Institute*.° Read what Bellew° says.'

'Blow Bellew!' said Carnehan. 'Dan, they're a stinkin' lot of heathens, but this book here says they think they're related to us English.'

I smoked while the men pored over Raverty,° Wood, the maps, and the *Encyclopædia*.

'There is no use your waiting,' said Dravot politely. 'It's about four o'clock now. We'll go before six o'clock if you want to sleep, and we won't steal any of the papers. Don't you sit up. We're two harmless lunatics, and if you come to-morrow evening down to the Serai° we'll say good-bye to you.'

'You *are* two fools,' I answered. 'You'll be turned back at the Frontier or cut up the minute you set foot in Afghanistan. Do you want any money or a recommendation down-country? I can help you to the chance of work next week.'

'Next week we shall be hard at work ourselves, thank you,' said

Dravot. 'It isn't so easy being a King as it looks. When we've got our Kingdom in going order we'll let you know, and you can come up and help us to govern it.'

'Would two lunatics make a contrack like that?' said Carnehan, with subdued pride, showing me a greasy half-sheet of notepaper on which was written the following. I copied it, then and there, as a curiosity—

This Contract between me and you persuing witnesseth in the name of God—Amen and so forth.

(*One*) *That me and you will settle this matter together;* i.e. *to be Kings of Kafiristan.*

(*Two*) *That you and me will not, while this matter is being settled, look at any Liquor, nor any Woman black, white, or brown, so as to get mixed up with one or the other harmful.*

(*Three*) *That we conduct ourselves with Dignity and Discretion, and if one of us gets into trouble the other will stay by him.*

Signed by you and me this day.
Peachey Taliaferro Carnehan.
Daniel Dravot.
Both Gentlemen at Large.

'There was no need for the last article,' said Carnehan, blushing modestly; 'but it looks regular. Now you know the sort of men that loafers are—we *are* loafers, Dan, until we get out of India—and *do* you think that we would sign a Contrack like that unless we was in earnest? We have kept away from the two things that make life worth having.'

'You won't enjoy your lives much longer if you are going to try this idiotic adventure. Don't set the office on fire,' I said, 'and go away before nine o'clock.'

I left them still poring over the maps and making notes on the back of the 'Contrack'. 'Be sure to come down to the Serai to-morrow,' were their parting words.

The Kumharsen Serai is the great four-square sink of humanity where the strings of camels and horses from the North load and unload. All the nationalities of Central Asia may be found there, and most of the folk of India proper. Balkh and Bokhara there meet Bengal and Bombay, and try to draw eye-teeth.° You can buy ponies, turquoises, Persian pussy-cats, saddle-bags, fat-tailed sheep and musk in the Kumharsen Serai, and get many strange things for nothing. In the afternoon I went down to see whether my friends intended to keep their word or were lying there drunk.

A priest attired in fragments of ribbons and rags stalked up to me, gravely twisting a child's paper whirligig. Behind him was his servant bending under the load of a crate of mud toys. The two were loading up two camels, and the inhabitants of the Serai watched them with shrieks of laughter.

'The priest is mad,' said a horse-dealer to me. 'He is going up to Kabul to sell toys to the Amir. He will either be raised to honour or have his head cut off. He came in here this morning and has been behaving madly ever since.'

'The witless are under the protection of God,' stammered a flat-cheeked Usbeg in broken Hindi. 'They foretell future events.'

'Would they could have foretold that my caravan would have been cut up by the Shinwaris° almost within shadow of the Pass!'° grunted the Eusufzai agent of a Rajputana trading-house° whose goods had been diverted into the hands of other robbers just across the Border, and whose misfortunes were the laughing-stock of the bazar. 'Ohé, priest, whence come you and whither do you go?'

'From Roum° have I come,' shouted the priest, waving his whirligig; 'from Roum, blown by the breath of a hundred devils across the sea! O thieves, robbers, liars, the blessing of Pir Khan° on pigs, dogs, and perjurers! Who will take the Protected of God to the North to sell charms that are never still to the Amir? The camels shall not gall, the sons shall not fall sick, and the wives shall remain faithful while they are away, of the men who give me place in their caravan. Who will assist me to slipper the King of the Roos° with a golden slipper with a silver heel? The protection of Pir Khan be upon his labours!' He spread out the skirts of his gaberdine and pirouetted between the lines of tethered horses.

'There starts a caravan from Peshawar to Kabul in twenty days, *Huzrut*,'° said the Eusufzai trader. 'My camels go therewith. Do thou also go and bring us good luck.'

'I will go even now!' shouted the priest. 'I will depart upon my winged camels, and be at Peshawar in a day! Ho! Hazar Mir Khan,' he yelled to his servant, 'drive out the camels, but let me first mount my own.'

He leaped on the back of his beast as it knelt, and, turning round to me, cried: 'Come thou also, Sahib, a little along the road, and I will sell thee a charm—an amulet that shall make thee King of Kafiristan.'

Then the light broke upon me, and I followed the two camels out of the Serai till we reached open road and the priest halted.

'What d'you think o' that?' said he in English. 'Carnehan can't talk their patter, so I've made him my servant. He makes a handsome servant. 'Tisn't for nothing that I've been knocking about the country for fourteen years. Didn't I do that talk neat? We'll hitch on to a caravan at Peshawar till we get to Jagdallak, and then we'll see if we can get donkeys for our camels, and strike into Kafiristan. Whirligigs for the Amir, O Lor! Put your hand under the camel-bags and tell me what you feel.'

I felt the butt of a Martini,° and another and another.

'Twenty of 'em,' said Dravot placidly. 'Twenty of 'em and ammunition to correspond, under the whirligigs and the mud dolls.'

'Heaven help you if you are caught with those things!' I said. 'A Martini is worth her weight in silver among the Pathans.'

'Fifteen hundred rupees of capital—every rupee we could beg, borrow, or steal—are invested on these two camels,' said Dravot. 'We won't get caught. We're going through the Khaiber with a regular caravan. Who'd touch a poor mad priest?'

'Have you got everything you want?' I asked, overcome with astonishment.

'Not yet, but we shall soon. Give us a memento of your kindness, *Brother*. You did me a service, yesterday, and that time in Marwar. Half my Kingdom shall you have,° as the saying is.' I slipped a small charm compass° from my watch-chain and handed it up to the priest.

'Good-bye,' said Dravot, giving me hand cautiously. 'It's the last time we'll shake hands with an Englishman these many days. Shake hands with him, Carnehan,' he cried, as the second camel passed me.

Carnehan leaned down and shook hands. Then the camels passed away along the dusty road and I was left alone to wonder. My eye could detect no failure in the disguises. The scene in the Serai proved that they were complete to the native mind. There was just the chance, therefore, that Carnehan and Dravot would be able to wander through Afghanistan without detection. But, beyond, they would find death—certain and awful death.

Ten days later a native correspondent giving me the news of the day from Peshawar, wound up his letter with: 'There has been much laughter here on account of a certain mad priest who is going in his estimation to sell petty gauds and insigificant trinkets which he ascribes as great charms to H. H. the Amir of Bokhara. He passed through Peshawar and associated himself to the Second Summer caravan that goes to Kabul. The merchants are pleased because through superstition they imagine that such mad fellows bring good fortune.'

The two, then, were beyond the Border. I would have prayed for them, but, that night, a real King died in Europe,° and demanded an obituary notice.

The wheel of the world swings through the same phases again and again. Summer passed and winter thereafter, and came and passed again. The daily paper continued and I with it, and upon the third summer there fell a hot night, a night-issue, and a strained waiting for something to be telegraphed from the other side of the world, exactly as had happened before. A few great men had died in the past two years, the machines worked with more clatter, and some of the trees in the office garden were a few feet taller. But that was all the difference.

I passed over to the press-room, and went through just such a scene as I have already described. The nervous tension was stronger than it had been two years before, and I felt the heat more acutely. At three o'clock I cried, 'Print off,' and turned to go, when there crept to my chair what was left of a man. He was bent into a circle, his head was sunk between his shoulders, and he moved his feet one over the other like a bear. I could hardly see whether he walked or crawled—this rag-wrapped, whining cripple who addressed me by name, crying that he was come back. 'Can you give me a drink?' he whimpered. 'For the Lord's sake give me a drink!'

I went back to the office, the man following with groans of pain, and I turned up the lamp.

'Don't you know me?' he gasped, dropping into a chair, and he turned his drawn face, surmounted by a shock of gray hair, to the light.

I looked at him intently. Once before had I seen eyebrows that met over the nose in an inch-broad black band, but for the life of me I could not tell where.

'I don't know you,' I said, handing him the whisky. 'What can I do for you?'

He took a gulp of the spirit raw, and shivered in spite of the suffocating heat.

'I've come back,' he repeated; 'and I was the King of Kafiristan—me and Dravot—crowned Kings we was! In this office we settled it—you setting there and giving us the books. I am Peachey—Peachey Taliaferro Carnehan, and you've been setting here ever since—O Lord!'

I was more than a little astonished, and expressed my feelings accordingly.

'It's true,' said Carnehan, with a dry cackle, nursing his feet, which were wrapped in rags. 'True as gospel. Kings we were, with crowns upon our heads—me and Dravot—poor Dan—oh, poor, poor Dan, that would never take advice, not though I begged of him!'

'Take the whisky,' I said, 'and take your own time. Tell me all you can recollect of everything from beginning to end. You got across the Border on your camels, Dravot dressed as a mad priest and you his servant. Do you remember that?'

'I ain't mad—yet, but I shall be that way soon. Of course I remember. Keep looking at me, or maybe my words will go all to pieces. Keep looking at me in my eyes and don't say anything.'

I leaned forward and looked into his face as steadily as I could. He dropped one hand upon the table and I grasped it by the wrist. It was twisted like a bird's claw, and upon the back was a ragged red diamond-shaped scar.

'No, don't look there. Look at *me*,' said Carnehan. 'That comes afterwards, but for the Lord's sake don't distrack me. We left with that caravan, me and Dravot playing all sorts of antics to amuse the people we were with. Dravot used to make us laugh in the evenings when all the people was cooking their dinners—cooking their dinners, and . . . what did they do then? They lit little fires with sparks that went into Dravot's beard, and we all laughed—fit to die. Little red fires they was, going into Dravot's big red beard—so funny.' His eyes left mine and he smiled foolishly.

'You went as far as Jagdallak with that caravan,' I said at a venture, 'after you had lit those fires. To Jagdallak, where you turned off to try to get into Kafiristan.'

'No, we didn't neither. What are you talking about? We turned off before Jagdallak, because we heard the roads were good. But they wasn't good enough for our two camels—mine and Dravot's. When we left the caravan, Dravot took off all his clothes and mine too, and said we would be heathen, because the Kafirs didn't allow Mohammedans to talk to them. So we dressed betwixt and between, and such a sight as Daniel Dravot I never saw yet nor expect to see again. He burned half his beard, and slung a sheep-skin over his shoulder, and shaved his head into patterns. He shaved mine, too, and made me wear outrageous things to look like a heathen. That was in a most mountaineous country, and our camels couldn't go along any more because of the mountains. They were tall and black, and coming home I saw them fight like wild goats—there are lots of goats in Kafiristan.

And these mountains, they never keep still, no more than the goats. Always fighting they are, and don't let you sleep at night.'

'Take some more whisky,' I said very slowly. 'What did you and Daniel Dravot do when the camels could go no further because of the rough roads that led into Kafiristan?'

'What did which do? There was a party called Peachey Taliaferro Carnehan that was with Dravot. Shall I tell you about him? He died out there in the cold. Slap from the bridge fell old Peachey,° turning and twisting in the air like a penny whirligig that you can sell to the Amir.—No; they was two for three-ha'pence, those whirligigs, or I am much mistaken and woful sore. . . . And then these camels were no use, and Peachey said to Dravot—"For the Lord's sake let's get out of this before our heads are chopped off," and with that they killed the camels all among the mountains, not having anything in particular to eat, but first they took off the boxes with the guns and the ammunition, till two men came along driving four mules. Dravot up and dances in front of them, singing,—"Sell me four mules." Says the first man—"If you are rich enough to buy, you are rich enough to rob;" but before ever he could put his hand to his knife, Dravot breaks his neck over his knee, and the other party runs away. So Carnehan loaded the mules with the rifles that was taken off the camels, and together we starts forward into those bitter cold mountaineous parts, and never a road broader than the back of your hand.'

He paused for a moment, while I asked him if he could remember the nature of the country through which he had journeyed.

'I am telling you as straight as I can, but my head isn't as good as it might be. They drove nails through it to make me hear better how Dravot died. The country was mountaineous and the mules were most contrary, and the inhabitants was dispersed and solitary. They went up and up, and down and down, and that other party, Carnehan, was imploring of Dravot not to sing and whistle so loud, for fear of bringing down the tremenjus avalanches. But Dravot says that if a King couldn't sing it wasn't worth being King, and whacked the mules over the rump, and never took no heed for ten cold days. We came to a big level valley all among the mountains, and the mules were near dead, so we killed them, not having anything in special for them or us to eat. We sat upon the boxes, and played odd and even° with the cartridges that was jolted out.

'Then ten men with bows and arrows ran down that valley, chasing twenty men with bows and arrows, and the row was tremenjus. They was fair men°—fairer than you or me—with yellow hair and remarkable well built. Says Dravot, unpacking the guns—"This is the beginning of the business. We'll fight for the ten men," and with that he fires two rifles at the twenty men, and drops one of them at two hundred yards from the rock where he was sitting. The other men began to run, but Carnehan and Dravot sits on the boxes picking them off at all ranges, up and down the valley. Then we goes up to the ten men that had run across the snow too, and they fires a footy° little arrow at us. Dravot he shoots above their heads and they all falls down flat. Then he walks over them and kicks them, and then he lifts them up and shakes hands all round to make them friendly like. He calls them and gives them the boxes to carry, and waves his hand for all the world as though he was King already. They takes the boxes and him across the valley and up the hill into a pine wood on the top, where there was half-a-dozen big stone idols. Dravot he goes to the biggest—a fellow they call Imbra—and lays a rifle and a cartridge at his feet, rubbing his nose respectful with his own nose, patting him on the head, and saluting in front of it. He turns round to the men and nods his head, and says—"That's all right. I'm in the know, too, and all these old jim-jams° are my friends." Then he opens his mouth and points down it, and when the first man brings him food, he says—"No"; and when the second man brings him food he says—"No"; but when one of the old priests and the boss of the village brings him food, he says—"Yes," very haughty, and eats it slow. That was how we came to our first village, without any trouble, just as though we had tumbled from the skies. But we tumbled from one of those damned rope-bridges, you see, and—you couldn't expect a man to laugh much after that?'

'Take some more whisky and go on,' I said. 'That was the first village you came into. How did you get to be King?'

'I wasn't King,' said Carnehan. 'Dravot he was the King, and a handsome man he looked with the gold crown on his head and all. Him and the other party stayed in that village, and every morning Dravot sat by the side of old Imbra, and the people came and worshipped. That was Dravot's order. Then a lot of men came into the valley, and Carnehan and Dravot picks them off with the rifles before they knew where they was, and runs down into the valley and up again the other side and finds another village, same as the first one, and the people all falls down flat on their faces, and Dravot says—"Now what is the trouble between you two villages?" and the people points to a woman, as fair as you or me, that was carried off,° and Dravot takes her back to the first village and counts up the dead—eight there was. For each dead man Dravot pours a little milk on the ground and waves his arms like a whirligig, and "That's all right," says he. Then he and Carnehan takes the big boss of each village by the arm and walks them down into the valley, and shows them how to scratch a line with a spear right down the valley, and gives each a sod of turf from both sides of the line. Then all the people comes down and shouts like the devil and all, and Dravot says—"Go and dig the land, and be fruitful and multiply,"° which they did, though they didn't understand. Then we asks the names of things in their lingo—bread and water and fire and idols and such, and Dravot leads the priest of each village up to the idol, and says he must sit there and judge the people, and if anything goes wrong he is to be shot.

'Next week they was all turning up the land in the valley as quiet as bees and much prettier, and the priests heard all the complaints and told Dravot in dumb show what it was about. "That's just the beginning," says Dravot. "They think we're Gods." He and Carnehan picks out twenty good men and shows them how to click off a rifle, and form fours, and advance in line, and they was very pleased to do so, and clever to see the hang of it. Then he takes out his pipe and his baccy-pouch and leaves one at one village, and one at the other, and off we two goes to see what was to be done in the next valley. That was all rock, and there was a little village there, and Carnehan says—"Send 'em to the old valley to plant," and takes 'em there, and gives 'em some land that wasn't took before. They were a poor lot, and we blooded 'em with a kid before letting 'em into the new Kingdom. That was to impress the people, and then they settled down quiet, and Carnehan went back to Dravot who had got into another valley, all snow and ice and most mountaineous. There was no people there and the Army got afraid, so Dravot shoots one of them, and goes on till he finds some people in a village, and the Army explains that unless the people wants to be killed they had better not shoot their little matchlocks; for they had matchlocks. We makes friends with the priest, and I stays there alone with two of the Army, teaching the men how to drill, and a thundering big Chief comes across the snow with kettle-drums and horns twanging, because he heard there was a new God kicking about. Carnehan sights for the brown° of the men half a mile across the snow and wings one of them. Then he sends a message to the Chief that, unless he wished to be killed, he must come and shake hands with me and leave his arms behind. The Chief comes along first, and Carnehan shakes hands with him and whirls his arms about, same as Dravot used, and very much surprised that Chief was, and strokes my eyebrows. Then Carnehan goes alone to the Chief, and asks him in dumb show if he had an enemy he hated. "I have," says the Chief. So Carnehan weeds out the pick of his men, and sets the two of the Army to show them drill, and at the end of two weeks the men can manœuvre about as well as Volunteers.° So he marches with the Chief to a great big plain on the top of a mountain, and the Chief's men rushes into a village and takes it; we three Martinis firing into the brown of the enemy. So we took that village too, and I gives the Chief a rag from my coat and says, "Occupy till I come"; which was scriptural.° By way of a reminder, when me and the Army was eighteen hundred yards away, I drops a bullet near him standing on the snow, and all the people falls flat on their faces. Then I sends a letter to Dravot wherever he be by land or by sea.'

At the risk of throwing the creature out of train I interrupted—'How could you write a letter up yonder?'

'The letter?—Oh!—The letter! Keep looking at me between the eyes, please. It was a string-talk letter, that we'd learned the way of it from a blind beggar in the Punjab.'

I remember that there had once come to the office a blind man with a knotted twig and a piece of string which he wound round the twig according to some cipher of his own. He could, after the lapse of days or hours, repeat the sentence which he had reeled up. He had reduced the alphabet to eleven primitive sounds, and tried to teach me his method, but I could not understand.

'I sent that letter to Dravot,' said Carnehan; 'and told him to come back because this Kingdom was growing too big for me to handle, and then I struck for the first valley, to see how the priests were working. They called the village we took along with the Chief, Bashkai, and the first village we took, Er-Heb. The priests at Er-Heb° was doing all right, but they had a lot of pending cases about land to show me, and some men from another village had been firing arrows at night. I went out and looked for that village, and fired four rounds at it from a thousand yards. That used all the cartridges I cared to spend, and I waited for Dravot, who had been away two or three months, and I kept my people quiet.

'One morning I heard the devil's own noise of drums and horns, and Dan Dravot marches down the hill with his Army and a tail of hundreds of men, and, which was the most amazing, a great gold crown on his head. "My Gord, Carnehan," says Daniel, "this is a tremenjus business, and we've got the whole country as far as it's worth having. I am the son of Alexander by Queen Semiramis,° and you're my younger brother and a God too! It's the biggest thing we've ever seen. I've been marching and fighting for six weeks with the Army, and every footy little village for fifty miles has come in rejoiceful; and more than that, I've got the key of the whole show, as you'll see, and I've got a crown for you! I told 'em to make two of 'em at a place called Shu, where the gold lies in the rock like suet in mutton. Gold I've seen, and turquoise I've kicked out of the cliffs, and there's garnets in the sands of the river, and here's a chunk of amber that a man brought me. Call up all the priests and, here, take your crown."

'One of the men opens a black hair bag, and I slips the crown on. It was too small and too heavy, but I wore it for the glory. Hammered gold it was—five pound weight, like a hoop of a barrel.

'"Peachey," says Dravot, "we don't want to fight no more. The Craft's the trick,° so help me!" and he brings forward that same Chief that I left at Bashkai—Billy Fish we called him afterwards, because he was so like Billy Fish that drove the big tank-engine at Mach on the Bolan° in the old days. "Shake hands with him," says Dravot, and I shook hands and nearly dropped, for Billy Fish gave me the Grip. I said nothing, but tried him with the Fellow Craft Grip. He answers all right, and I tried the Master's Grip,° but that was a slip. "A Fellow Craft he is!" I says to Dan. "Does he know the word?"—"He does," says Dan, "and all the priests know. It's a miracle! The Chiefs and the priests can work a Fellow Craft Lodge° in a way that's very like ours, and they've cut the marks on the rocks, but they don't know the Third Degree, and they've come to find out. It's Gord's Truth. I've known these long years that the Afghans knew up to the Fellow Craft Degree, but this is a miracle. A God and a Grand-Master of the Craft am I, and a Lodge in the Third Degree I will open, and we'll raise the head priests and the Chiefs of the villages."

'"It's against all the law," I says, "holding a Lodge without warrant from any one; and you know we never held office in any Lodge."

'"It's a master-stroke o' policy," says Dravot. "It means running the country as easy as a four-wheeled bogie° on a down grade. We can't stop to inquire now, or they'll turn against us. I've forty Chiefs at my heel, and passed and raised° according to their merit they shall be. Billet these men on the villages, and see that we run up a Lodge of some kind. The temple of Imbra will do for the Lodge-room. The women must make aprons° as you show them. I'll hold a levee of Chiefs to-night and Lodge to-morrow."

'I was fair run off my legs, but I wasn't such a fool as not to see what a pull this Craft business gave us. I showed the priests' families how to make aprons of the degrees, but for Dravot's apron the blue border and marks was made of turquoise lumps on white hide, not cloth. We took a great square stone in the temple for the Master's chair, and little stones for the officers' chairs, and painted the black pavement with white squares, and did what we could to make things regular.

'At the levee which was held that night on the hillside with big bonfires, Dravot gives out that him and me were Gods and sons of Alexander, and Past Grand-Masters° in the Craft, and was come to make Kafiristan a country where every man should eat in peace and drink in quiet, and specially obey us. Then the Chiefs come round to shake hands, and they were so hairy and white and fair it was just shaking hands with old friends. We gave them names according as they was like men we had known in India—Billy Fish, Holly Dilworth, Pikky Kergan, that was Bazar-master° when I was at Mhow, and so on, and so on.

'*The* most amazing miracles was at Lodge next night. One of the old priests was watching us continuous, and I felt uneasy, for I knew we'd have to fudge the Ritual, and I didn't know what the men knew. The old priest was a stranger come in from beyond the village of Bashkai. The minute Dravot puts on the Master's apron that the girls had made for him, the priest fetches a whoop and a howl, and tries to overturn the stone that Dravot was sitting on. "It's all up now," I says. "That comes of meddling with the Craft without warrant!" Dravot never winked an eye, not when ten priests took and tilted over the Grand-Master's chair—which was to say the stone of Imbra. The priests begins rubbing the bottom end of it to clear away the black dirt, and presently he shows all the other priests the Master's Mark, same as was on Dravot's apron, cut into the stone. Not even the priests of the temple of Imbra knew it was there. The old chap falls flat on his face at Dravot's feet and kisses 'em. "Luck again," says Dravot, across the Lodge to me; "they say it's the missing Mark that no one could understand the why of. We're more than safe now." Then he bangs the butt of his gun for a gavel and says: "By virtue of the authority vested in me by my own right hand and the help of Peachey, I declare myself Grand-Master of all Freemasonry in Kafiristan in this the Mother Lodge o' the country,° and King of Kafiristan equally with Peachey!" At that he puts on his crown and I puts on mine—I was doing Senior Warden°—and we opens the Lodge in most ample form.° It was a amazing miracle! The priests moved in Lodge through the first two degrees almost without telling, as if the memory was coming back to them. After that, Peachey and Dravot raised such as was worthy°—high priests and Chiefs of far-off villages. Billy Fish was the first, and I can tell you we scared the soul out of him. It was not in any way according to Ritual, but it served our turn. We didn't raise more than ten of the biggest men, because we didn't want to make the Degree common. And they was clamouring to be raised.

'"In another six months," says Dravot, "we'll hold another Communication,° and see how you are working." Then he asks them about their villages, and learns that they was fighting one against the other, and were sick and tired of it. And when they wasn't doing that they was fighting with the Mohammedans. "You can fight those when they come into our country," says Dravot. "Tell off every tenth man of your tribes for a Frontier guard, and send two hundred at a time to this valley to be drilled. Nobody is going to be shot or speared any more so long as he does well, and I know that you won't cheat me, because you're white people—sons of Alexander—and not like common, black Mohammedans. You are *my* people, and by God," says he, running off into English at the end—"I'll make a damned fine Nation of you, or I'll die in the making!"

'I can't tell all we did for the next six months, because Dravot did a lot I couldn't see the hang of, and he learned their lingo in a way I never could. My work was to help the people plough, and now and again go out with some of the Army and see what the other villages were doing, and make 'em throw rope-bridges across the ravines which cut up the country horrid. Dravot was very kind to me, but when he walked up and down in the pine wood pulling that bloody red beard of his with both fists I knew he was thinking plans I could not advise about, and I just waited for orders.

'But Dravot never showed me disrespect before the people. They were afraid of me and the Army, but they loved Dan. He was the best of friends with the priests and the Chiefs; but any one could come across the hills with a complaint, and Dravot would hear him out fair, and call four priests together and say what was to be done. He used to call in Billy Fish from Bashkai, and Pikky Kergan from Shu, and an old Chief we called Kafuzelum°—it was like enough to his real name—and hold councils with 'em when there was any fighting to be done in small villages. That was his Council of War, and the four priests of Bashkai, Shu, Khawak, and Madora was his Privy Council. Between the lot of 'em they sent me, with forty men and twenty rifles and sixty men carrying turquoises, into the Ghorband country° to buy those hand-made Martini rifles, that come out of the Amir's workshops at

Kabul, from one of the Amir's Herati regiments° that would have sold the very teeth out of their mouths for turquoises.

'I stayed in Ghorband a month, and gave the Governor there the pick of my baskets for hush-money, and bribed the Colonel of the regiment some more, and, between the two and the tribes-people, we got more than a hundred hand-made Martinis, a hundred good Kohat Jezails° that'll throw to six hundred yards, and forty man-loads of very bad ammunition for the rifles. I came back with what I had, and distributed 'em among the men that the Chiefs sent in to me to drill. Dravot was too busy to attend to those things, but the old Army that we first made helped me, and we turned out five hundred men that could drill, and two hundred that knew how to hold arms pretty straight. Even those cork-screwed, hand-made guns was a miracle to them. Dravot talked big about powder-shops and factories, walking up and down in the pine wood when the winter was coming on.

'"I won't make a Nation," says he. "I'll make an Empire! These men aren't niggers; they're English! Look at their eyes—look at their mouths. Look at the way they stand up. They sit on chairs in their own houses. They're the Lost Tribes,° or something like it, and they've grown to be English. I'll take a census in the spring if the priests don't get frightened. There must be a fair two million of 'em in these hills. The villages are full o' little children. Two million people—two hundred and fifty thousand fighting men—and all English! They only want the rifles and a little drilling. Two hundred and fifty thousand men, ready to cut in on Russia's right flank when she tries for India! Peachey, man," he says, chewing his beard in great hunks, "we shall be Emperors—Emperors of the Earth! Rajah Brooke° will be a suckling to us. I'll treat with the Viceroy on equal terms. I'll ask him to send me twelve picked English—twelve that I know of—to help us govern a bit. There's Mackray, Sergeant-pensioner at Segowli—many's the good dinner he's given me, and his wife a pair of trousers. There's Donkin, the Warder of Tounghoo Jail;° there's hundreds that I could lay my hand on if I was in India. The Viceroy shall do it for me. I'll send a man through in the spring for those men, and I'll write for a dispensation from the Grand Lodge for what I've done as Grand-Master. That—and all the Sniders° that'll be thrown out when the native troops in India take up the Martini. They'll be worn smooth,° but they'll do for fighting in these hills. Twelve English, a hundred thousand Sniders run through the Amir's country in driblets—I'd be content with twenty thousand in one year—and we'd be an Empire. When everything was shipshape, I'd hand over the crown—this crown I'm wearing now—to Queen Victoria on my knees, and she'd say: 'Rise up, Sir Daniel Dravot.' Oh, it's big! It's big, I tell you! But there's so much to be done in every place—Bashkai, Khawak, Shu, and everywhere else."

'"What is it?" I says. "There are no more men coming in to be drilled this autumn. Look at those fat, black clouds. They're bringing the snow."

'"It isn't that," says Daniel, putting his hand very hard on my shoulder; "and I don't wish to say anything that's against you, for no other living man would have followed me and made me what I am as you have done. You're a first-class Commander-in-Chief, and the people know you; but—it's a big country, and somehow you can't help me, Peachey, in the way I want to be helped."

'"Go to your blasted priests, then!" I said, and I was sorry when I made that remark, but it did hurt me sore to find Daniel talking so superior when I'd drilled all the men, and done all he told me.

'"Don't let's quarrel, Peachey," says Daniel without cursing. "You're a King too, and the half of this Kingdom is yours; but can't you see, Peachey, we want cleverer men than us now—three or four of 'em, that we can scatter about for our Deputies. It's a hugeous great State, and I can't always tell the right thing to do, and I haven't time for all I want to do, and here's the winter coming on and all." He put half his beard into his mouth, all red like the gold of his crown.

'"I'm sorry, Daniel," says I. "I've done all I could. I've drilled the men and shown the people how to stack their oats better; and I've brought in those tinware rifles from Ghorband—but I know what you're driving at. I take it Kings always feel oppressed that way."°

'"There's another thing too," says Dravot, walking up and down. "The winter's coming and these people won't be giving much trouble, and if they do we can't move about. I want a wife."

'"For Gord's sake leave the women alone!" I says. "We've both got all the work we can, though I *am* a fool. Remember the Contrack, and keep clear o' women."

'"The Contrack only lasted till such time as we was Kings; and Kings we have been these months past," says Dravot, weighing his crown in his hand. "You go get a wife too, Peachey—a nice, strappin', plump girl that'll keep you warm in the winter. They're prettier than English girls, and we can take the pick of 'em. Boil 'em once or twice in hot water and they'll come out like chicken and ham."°

'"Don't tempt me!" I says. "I will not have any dealings with a woman not till we are a dam' side more settled than we are now. I've been doing the work o' two men, and you've been doing the work o' three. Let's lie off a bit, and see if we can get some better tobacco from Afghan country and run in some good liquor; but no women."

'"Who's talking o' *women?*" says Dravot. "I said *wife*—a Queen to breed a King's son for the King. A Queen out of the strongest tribe, that'll make them your blood-brothers, and that'll lie by your side and tell you all the people thinks about you and their own affairs. That's what I want."

'"Do you remember that Bengali woman I kept at Mogul Serai° when I was a plate-layer?" says I. "A fat lot o' good she was to me. She taught me the lingo and one or two other things; but what happened? She ran away with the Station-master's servant and half my month's pay. Then she turned up at Dadur Junction° in tow of a half-caste, and had the impidence to say I was her husband—all among the drivers in the running-shed too!"

'"We've done with that," says Dravot; "these women are whiter than you or me, and a Queen I will have for the winter months."

'"For the last time o' asking, Dan, do *not*," I says. "It'll only bring us harm. The Bible says° that Kings ain't to waste their strength on women, 'specially when they've got a new raw Kingdom to work over."

'"For the last time of answering I will," said Dravot, and he went away through the pine-trees looking like a big red devil, the sun being on his crown and beard and all.

'But getting a wife was not as easy as Dan thought. He put it before the Council, and there was no answer till Billy Fish said that he'd better ask the girls. Dravot damned them all round. "What's wrong with me?" he shouts, standing by the idol Imbra. "Am I a dog° or am I not enough of a man for your wenches? Haven't I put the shadow of my hand over this country? Who stopped the last Afghan raid?" It was me really, but Dravot was too angry to remember. "Who bought your guns? Who repaired the bridges? Who's the Grand-Master of the sign cut in the stone?" says he, and he thumped his hand on the block that he used to sit on in Lodge, and at Council, which opened like Lodge always. Billy Fish said nothing and no more did the others. "Keep your hair on, Dan," said I; "and ask the girls. That's how it's done at Home, and these people are quite English."

'"The marriage of the King is a matter of State," says Dan, in a white-hot rage, for he could feel, I hope, that he was going against his better mind. He walked out of the Council-room, and the others sat still, looking at the ground.

'"Billy Fish," says I to the Chief of Bashkai, "what's the difficulty here? A straight answer to a true friend."

'"You know," says Billy Fish. "How should a man tell you who knows everything? How can daughters of men marry Gods or Devils? It's not proper."

'I remembered something like that in the Bible;° but if, after seeing us as long as they had, they still believed we were Gods, it wasn't for me to undeceive them.

'"A God can do anything," says I. "If the King is fond of a girl he'll not let her die."—"She'll have to," said Billy Fish. "There are all sorts of Gods and Devils in these mountains, and now and again a girl marries one of them and isn't seen any more. Besides, you two know the Mark cut in the stone. Only the Gods know that. We thought you were men till you showed the sign of the Master."

'I wished then that we had explained about the loss of the genuine secrets of a Master-Mason at the first go-off; but I said nothing. All that night there was a blowing of horns in a little dark temple half-way down the hill, and I heard a girl crying fit to die. One of the priests told us that she was being prepared to marry the King.

'"I'll have no nonsense of that kind," says Dan. "I don't want to interfere with your customs, but I'll take my own wife."—"The girl's a little bit afraid," says the priest. "She thinks she's going to die, and they are a-heartening of her up down in the temple."

'"Hearten her very tender, then," says Dravot, "or I'll hearten you with the butt of a gun so you'll never want to be heartened again." He licked his lips, did Dan, and stayed up walking about more than half the night, thinking of the wife that he was going to get in the morning. I wasn't any means comfortable, for I knew that dealings with a woman in foreign parts, though you was a crowned King twenty times over, could not but be risky. I got up very early in the morning while Dravot was asleep, and I saw the priests talking together in whispers, and the Chiefs talking together too, and they looked at me out of the corners of their eyes.

'"What is up, Fish?" I say to the Bashkai man, who was wrapped up in his furs and looking splendid to behold.

'"I can't rightly say," says he; "but if you can make the King drop all this nonsense about marriage, you'll be doing him and me and yourself a great service."

'"That I do believe," says I. "But sure, you know, Billy, as well as me, having fought against and for us, that the King and me are nothing more than two of the finest men that God Almighty ever made. Nothing more, I do assure you."

'"That may be," says Billy Fish, "and yet I should be sorry if it was." He sinks his head upon his great fur cloak for a minute and thinks. "King," says he, "be you man or God or Devil, I'll stick by you to-day. I have twenty of my men with me, and they will follow me. We'll go to Bashkai until the storm blows over."

'A little snow had fallen in the night, and everything was white except the greasy fat clouds that blew down and down from the north. Dravot came out with his crown on his head, swinging his arms and stamping his feet, and looking more pleased than Punch.

'"For the last time, drop it, Dan," says I in a whisper, "Billy Fish here says that there will be a row."

'"A row among my people!" says Dravot. "Not much. Peachey, you're a fool not to get a wife too. Where's the girl?" says he with a voice as loud as the braying of a jackass. "Call up all the Chiefs and priests, and let the Emperor see if his wife suits him."

'There was no need to call any one. They were all there leaning on their guns and spears round the clearing in the centre of the pine wood. A lot of priests went down to the little temple to bring up the girl, and the horns blew fit to wake the dead. Billy Fish saunters round and gets as close to Daniel as he could, and behind him stood his twenty men with matchlocks. Not a man of them under six feet. I was next to Dravot, and behind me was twenty men of the regular Army. Up comes the girl, and a strapping wench she was, covered with silver and turquoises, but white as death, and looking back every minute at the priests.

'"She'll do," said Dan, looking her over. "What's to be afraid of, lass? Come and kiss me." He puts his arm round her. She shuts her eyes, gives a bit of a squeak, and down goes her face in the side of Dan's flaming red beard.

'"The slut's bitten me!" says he, clapping his hand to his neck, and, sure enough, his hand was red with blood. Billy Fish and two of his matchlock-men catches hold of Dan by the shoulders and drags him into the Bashkai lot, while the priests howl in their lingo—"Neither God nor Devil but a man!" I was all taken aback, for a priest cut at me in front, and the Army behind began firing into the Bashkai men.

'"God A'mighty!" says Dan. "What is the meaning of this?"

'"Come back! Come away!" says Billy Fish. "Ruin and Mutiny is the matter. We'll break for Bashkai if we can."

'I tried to give some sort of orders to my men—the men o' the regular Army—but it was no use, so I fired into the brown of 'em with an English Martini and drilled three beggars in a line. The valley was full of shouting, howling creatures, and every soul was shrieking, "Not a God nor a Devil but only a man!" The Bashkai troops stuck to Billy Fish all they were worth, but their matchlocks wasn't half as good as the Kabul breech-loaders, and four of them dropped. Dan was bellowing like a bull, for he was very wrathy; and Billy Fish had a hard job to prevent him running out at the crowd.

'"We can't stand," says Billy Fish. "Make a run for it down the valley! The whole place is against us." The matchlock-men ran, and we went down the valley in spite of Dravot. He was swearing horrible and crying out he was a King. The priests rolled great stones on us, and the regular Army fired hard, and there wasn't more than six men, not counting Dan, Billy Fish, and Me, that came down to the bottom of the valley alive.

'Then they stopped firing and the horns in the temple blew again. "Come away—for God's sake come away!" says Billy Fish. "They'll send runners out to all the villages before ever we get to Bashkai. I can protect you there, but I can't do anything now."

'My own notion is that Dan began to go mad in his head from that hour. He stared up and down like a stuck pig. Then he was all for walking back alone and killing the priests with his bare hands; which he could have done. "An Emperor am I," says Daniel, "and next year I shall be a Knight of the Queen."

'"All right, Dan," says I; "but come along now while there's time."

'"It's your fault," says he, "for not looking after your Army better. There was mutiny in the midst, and you didn't know—you damned engine-driving, plate-laying, missionary's-pass-hunting hound!"° He sat upon a rock and called me every foul name he could lay tongue to. I was too heart-sick to care, though it was all his foolishness that brought the smash.

'"I'm sorry, Dan," says I, "but there's no accounting for natives. This business is our Fifty-Seven.° Maybe we'll make something out of it yet, when we've got to Bashkai."

'"Let's get to Bashkai, then," says Dan, "and, by God, when I come back here again I'll sweep the valley so there isn't a bug in a blanket left!"

'We walked all that day, and all that night Dan was stumping up and down on the snow, chewing his beard and muttering to himself.

'"There's no hope o' getting clear," said Billy Fish. "The priests will have sent runners to the villages to say that you are only men.

Why didn't you stick on as Gods till things was more settled? I'm a dead man," says Billy Fish, and he throws himself down on the snow and begins to pray to his Gods.

'Next morning we was in a cruel bad country—all up and down, no level ground at all, and no food either. The six Bashkai men looked at Billy Fish hungry-way as if they wanted to ask something, but they said never a word. At noon we came to the top of a flat mountain all covered with snow, and when we climbed up into it, behold, there was an Army in position waiting in the middle!

'"The runners have been very quick," says Billy Fish, with a little bit of a laugh. "They are waiting for us."

'Three or four men began to fire from the enemy's side, and a chance shot took Daniel in the calf of the leg. That brought him to his senses. He looks across the snow at the Army, and sees the rifles that we had brought into the country.

'"We're done for," says he. "They are Englishmen, these people, —and it's my blasted nonsense that has brought you to this. Get back, Billy Fish, and take your men away; you've done what you could, and now cut for it. Carnehan," says he, "shake hands with me and go along with Billy. Maybe they won't kill you. I'll go and meet 'em alone. It's me that did it. Me, the King!"

'"Go!" says I. "Go to Hell, Dan! I'm with you here. Billy Fish, you clear out, and we two will meet those folk."

'"I'm a Chief," says Billy Fish, quite quiet. "I stay with you. My men can go."

'The Bashkai fellows didn't wait for a second word, but ran off, and Dan and Me and Billy Fish walked across to where the drums were drumming and the horns were horning. It was cold—awful cold. I've got that cold in the back of my head now. There's a lump of it there.'

The punkah-coolies had gone to sleep. Two kerosene lamps were blazing in the office, and the perspiration poured down my face and splashed on the blotter as I leaned forward. Carnehan was shivering, and I feared that his mind might go. I wiped my face, took a fresh grip of the piteously mangled hands, and said: 'What happened after that?'

The momentary shift of my eyes had broken the clear current.

'What was you pleased to say?' whined Carnehan. 'They took them without any sound. Not a little whisper all along the snow, not though the King knocked down the first man that set hand on him—not though old Peachey fired his last cartridge into the brown of 'em. Not a single solitary sound did those swines make. They just closed up tight, and I tell you their furs stunk. There was a man called Billy

Fish, a good friend of us all, and they cut his throat, Sir, then and there, like a pig; and the King kicks up the bloody snow and says: "We've had a dashed fine run for our money. What's coming next?" But Peachey, Peachey Taliaferro, I tell you, Sir, in confidence as betwixt two friends, he lost his head, Sir. No, he didn't neither. The King lost his head, so he did, all along o' one of those cunning rope-bridges. Kindly let me have the paper-cutter, Sir. It tilted this way. They marched him a mile across that snow to a rope-bridge over a ravine with a river at the bottom. You may have seen such. They prodded him behind like an ox. "Damn your eyes!" says the King. "D'you suppose I can't die like a gentleman?" He turns to Peachey—Peachey that was crying like a child. "I've brought you to this, Peachey," says he. "Brought you out of your happy life to be killed in Kafiristan, where you was late Commander-in-Chief of the Emperor's forces. Say you forgive me, Peachey,"—"I do," says Peachey. "Fully and freely do I forgive you, Dan."—"Shake hands, Peachey," says he. "I'm going now." Out he goes, looking neither right nor left, and when he was plumb in the middle of those dizzy dancing ropes—"Cut, you beggars," he shouts; and they cut, and old Dan fell, turning round and round and round, twenty thousand miles, for he took half an hour to fall till he struck the water, and I could see his body caught on a rock with the gold crown close beside.

'But do you know what they did to Peachey between two pine-trees? They crucified him, Sir, as Peachey's hands will show. They used wooden pegs for his hands and his feet; and he didn't die. He hung there and screamed, and they took him down next day, and said it was a miracle that he wasn't dead. They took him down—poor old Peachey that hadn't done them any harm—that hadn't done them any—'

He rocked to and fro and wept bitterly, wiping his eyes with the back of his scarred hands and moaning like a child for some ten minutes.

'They was cruel enough to feed him up in the temple, because they said he was more of a God than old Daniel that was a man. Then they turned him out on the snow, and told him to go home, and Peachey came home in about a year, begging along the roads quite safe; for Daniel Dravot he walked before and said: "Come along, Peachey. It's a big thing we're doing." The mountains they danced at night, and the mountains they tried to fall on Peachey's head, but Dan he held up his hand, and Peachey came along bent double. He never let go of Dan's hand, and he never let go of Dan's head. They gave it to him as a present in the temple, to remind him not to come again, and though the crown was pure gold, and Peachey was starving, never would Peachey sell the same. You knew Dravot, Sir! You knew Right Worshipful Brother° Dravot! Look at him now!'

He fumbled in the mass of rags round his bent waist; brought out a black horsehair bag embroidered with silver thread, and shook therefrom on to my table—the dried, withered head of Daniel Dravot! The morning sun that had long been paling the lamps struck the red beard and blind sunken eyes; struck, too, a heavy circlet of gold studded with raw turquoises, that Carnehan placed tenderly on the battered temples.

'You be'old now,' said Carnehan, 'the Emperor in his 'abit as he lived°—the King of Kafiristan with his crown upon his head. Poor old Daniel that was a monarch once!'

I shuddered, for, in spite of defacements manifold, I recognised the head of the man of Marwar Junction. Carnehan rose to go. I attempted to stop him. He was not fit to walk abroad. 'Let me take away the whisky, and give me a little money,' he gasped. 'I was a King once. I'll go to the Deputy Commissioner and ask to set in the Poorhouse till I get my health. No, thank you, I can't wait till you get a carriage for me. I've urgent private affairs—in the south—at Marwar.'

He shambled out of the office and departed in the direction of the Deputy Commissioner's house. That day at noon I had occasion to go down the blinding hot Mall, and I saw a crooked man crawling along the white dust of the roadside, his hat in his hand, quavering dolorously after the fashion of street-singers at Home. There was not a soul in sight, and he was out of all possible ear-shot of the houses. And he sang through his nose, turning his head from right to left:—

'The Son of Man goes forth to war,°
A golden crown to gain;
His blood-red banner streams afar—
Who follows in his train?'

I waited to hear no more, but put the poor wretch into my carriage and drove him off to the nearest missionary for eventual transfer to the Asylum. He repeated the hymn twice while he was with me whom he did not in the least recognise, and I left him singing it to the missionary.

Two days later I inquired after his welfare of the Superintendent of the Asylum.

'He was admitted suffering from sunstroke. He died early yesterday morning,' said the Superintendent. 'Is it true that he was half an hour bare-headed in the sun at mid-day?'

'Yes,' said I, 'but do you happen to know if he had anything upon him by any chance when he died?'

'Not to my knowledge,' said the Superintendent.

And there the matter rests.

A Skeleton Map of India (Punjab), India Survey, 1886. Bodleian Library, Map Room, D10(312). Reproduced by permission of the Bodleian Library.

74°
76°
78°
80°
82
K S H M I R
KASHMIR
LEH
JHELUM
SIALKOT
CHAMBA
AMRITSAR
LAHORE
KAPURTHALA
LUDHIANA
J A B
PATIALA
UMBALLA
SIRSA
NAINITAL
MEERUT
DELHI
W.
PROVINCES
Sheet I.—India. 1 Inch = 32 Miles.

From WEE WILLIE WINKIE (1888)

Baa Baa, Black Sheep

Baa Baa, Black Sheep,
Have you any wool?
Yes, Sir, yes, Sir, three bags full.
One for the Master, one for the Dame—
None for the Little Boy that cries down the lane.

Nursery Rhyme

The First Bag

When I was in my father's house, I was in a better place.°

They were putting Punch to bed—the *ayah*° and the *hamal*° and Meeta, the big *Surti* boy,° with the red and gold turban. Judy, already tucked inside her mosquito-curtains, was nearly asleep. Punch had been allowed to stay up for dinner. Many privileges had been accorded to Punch within the last ten days, and a greater kindness from the people of his world had encompassed his ways and works, which were mostly obstreperous. He sat on the edge of his bed and swung his bare legs defiantly.

'Punch-*baba* going to bye-lo?' said the *ayah* suggestively.

'No,' said Punch. 'Punch-*baba* wants the story about the Ranee° that was turned into a tiger. Meeta must tell it, and the *hamal* shall hide behind the door and make tiger-noises at the proper time.'

'But Judy-*baba* will wake up,' said the *ayah*.

'Judy-*baba* is waked,' piped a small voice from the mosquito-curtains. 'There was a Ranee that lived at Delhi. Go on, Meeta,' and she fell fast asleep again while Meeta began the story.

Never had Punch secured the telling of that tale with so little opposition. He reflected for a long time. The *hamal* made the tiger-noises in twenty different keys.

' 'Top!' said Punch authoritatively. 'Why doesn't Papa come in and say he is going to give me *put-put*?'°

'Punch-*baba* is going away,' said the *ayah*. 'In another week there will be no Punch-*baba* to pull my hair any more.' She sighed softly, for the boy of the household was very dear to her heart.

'Up the Ghauts in a train?' said Punch, standing on his bed. 'All the way to Nassick° where the Ranee-Tiger lives?'

'Not to Nassick this year, little Sahib,' said Meeta, lifting him on his shoulder. 'Down to the sea where the cocoa-nuts are thrown, and across the sea in a big ship. Will you take Meeta with you to *Belait*?'°

'You shall all come,' said Punch, from the height of Meeta's strong arms. 'Meeta and the *ayah* and the *hamal* and Bhini-in-the-Garden, and the salaam-Captain-Sahib-snake-man.'°

There was no mockery in Meeta's voice when he replied—'Great is the Sahib's favour,' and laid the little man down in the bed, while the *ayah*, sitting in the moonlight at the doorway, lulled him to sleep with an interminable canticle such as they sing in the Roman Catholic Church at Parel.° Punch curled himself into a ball and slept.

Next morning Judy shouted that there was a rat in the nursery, and thus he forgot to tell her the wonderful news. It did not much matter, for Judy was only three and she would not have understood. But Punch was five; and he knew that going to England would be much nicer than a trip to Nassick.

Papa and Mamma sold the brougham and the piano, and stripped the house, and curtailed the allowance of crockery for the daily meals, and took long counsel together over a bundle of letters bearing the Rocklington° postmark.

'The worst of it is that one can't be certain of anything,' said Papa, pulling his moustache. 'The letters in themselves are excellent, and the terms are moderate enough.'

'The worst of it is that the children will grow up away from me,' thought Mamma; but she did not say it aloud.

'We are only one case among hundreds,' said Papa bitterly. 'You shall go Home again in five years, dear.'

'Punch will be ten then—and Judy eight. Oh, how long and long and long the time will be! And we have to leave them among strangers.'

'Punch is a cheery little chap. He's sure to make friends wherever he goes.'

'And who could help loving my Ju?'

They were standing over the cots in the nursery late at night, and I think that Mamma was crying softly. After Papa had gone away, she knelt down by the side of Judy's cot. The *ayah* saw her and put up a prayer that the *memsahib* might never find the love of her children taken away from her and given to a stranger.

Mamma's own prayer was a slightly illogical one. Summarised it ran: 'Let strangers love my children and be as good to them as I should be, but let *me* preserve their love and their confidence for ever and ever. Amen.' Punch scratched himself in his sleep, and Judy moaned a little.

Next day they all went down to the sea, and there was a scene at the Apollo Bunder° when Punch discovered that Meeta could not come too, and Judy learned that the *ayah* must be left behind. But Punch found a thousand fascinating things in the rope, block, and steam-pipe line on the big P. and O. Steamer long before Meeta and the *ayah* had dried their tears.

'Come back, Punch-*baba*,' said the *ayah*.

'Come back,' said Meeta, 'and be a *Burra Sahib*' (a big man).

'Yes,' said Punch, lifted up in his father's arms to wave good-bye. 'Yes, I will come back, and I will be a *Burra Sahib Bahadur!*' (a very big man indeed).

At the end of the first day Punch demanded to be set down in England, which he was certain must be close at hand. Next day there was a merry breeze, and Punch was very sick. 'When I come back to Bombay,' said Punch on his recovery, 'I will come by the road—in a broom-*gharri*.° This is a very naughty ship.'

The Swedish boatswain consoled him, and he modified his opinions as the voyage went on. There was so much to see and to handle and ask questions about that Punch nearly forgot the *ayah* and Meeta and the *hamal*, and with difficulty remembered a few words of the Hindustani once his second-speech.

But Judy was much worse. The day before the steamer reached Southampton, Mamma asked her if she would not like to see the *ayah* again. Judy's blue eyes turned to the stretch of sea that had swallowed all her tiny past, and she said: '*Ayah! What ayah?*'

Mamma cried over her and Punch marvelled. It was then that he heard for the first time Mamma's passionate appeal to him never to let Judy forget Mamma. Seeing that Judy was young, ridiculously young, and that Mamma, every evening for four weeks past, had come into the cabin to sing to her and Punch to sleep with a mysterious rune that he called 'Sonny, my soul,'° Punch could not understand what

Mamma meant. But he strove to do his duty; for, the moment Mamma left the cabin, he said to Judy: 'Ju, you bemember Mamma?'

''Torse I do,' said Judy.

'Then *always* bemember Mamma, 'r else I won't give you the paper ducks that the red-haired Captain Sahib cut out for me.'

So Judy promised always to 'bemember Mamma.'

Many and many a time was Mamma's command laid upon Punch, and Papa would say the same thing with an insistence that awed the child.

'You must make haste and learn to write, Punch,' said Papa, 'and then you'll be able to write letters to us in Bombay.'

'I'll come into your room,' said Punch, and Papa choked.

Papa and Mamma were always choking in those days. If Punch took Judy to task for not 'bemembering', they choked. If Punch sprawled on the sofa in the Southampton lodging-house and sketched his future in purple and gold, they choked; and so they did if Judy put up her mouth for a kiss.

Through many days all four were vagabonds on the face of the earth—Punch with no one to give orders to, Judy too young for anything, and Papa and Mamma grave, distracted, and choking.

'Where,' demanded Punch, wearied of a loathsome contrivance on four wheels with a mound of luggage atop—'*where* is our broom-*gharri?* This thing talks so much that *I* can't talk. Where is our *own* broom-*gharri*? When I was at Bandstand before we comed away, I asked Inverarity Sahib why he was sitting in it, and he said it was his own. And I said, "I will *give* it you"—I like Inverarity Sahib—and I said, "Can you put your legs through the pully-wag loops by the windows?" And Inverarity Sahib said No, and laughed. *I* can put my legs through the pully-wag loops. I can put my legs through *these* pully-wag loops. Look! Oh, Mamma's crying again! I didn't know I wasn't not to do *so*.'

Punch drew his legs out of the loops of the four-wheeler: the door opened and he slid to the earth, in a cascade of parcels, at the door of an austere little villa whose gates bore the legend 'Downe Lodge'. Punch gathered himself together and eyed the house with disfavour. It stood on a sandy road, and a cold wind tickled his knickerbockered legs.

'Let us go away,' said Punch. 'This is not a pretty place.'

But Mamma and Papa and Judy had left the cab, and all the luggage was being taken into the house. At the doorstep stood a woman in black, and she smiled largely, with dry chapped lips. Behind her was a man, big, bony, gray, and lame as to one leg—behind him a boy of twelve, black-haired and oily in appearance. Punch surveyed the trio, and advanced without fear, as he had been accustomed to do in Bombay when callers came and he happened to be playing in the verandah.

'How do you do?' said he. 'I am Punch.' But they were all looking at the luggage—all except the gray man, who shook hands with Punch, and said he was 'a smart little fellow.' There was much running about and banging of boxes, and Punch curled himself up on the sofa in the dining-room and considered things.

'I don't like these people,' said Punch. 'But never mind. We'll go away soon. We have always went away soon from everywhere. I wish we was gone back to Bombay *soon*.'

The wish bore no fruit. For six days Mamma wept at intervals, and showed the woman in black all Punch's clothes—a liberty which Punch resented. 'But p'raps she's a new white *ayah*,' he thought. 'I'm to call her Antirosa, but she doesn't call *me* Sahib. She says just Punch,' he confided to Judy. 'What is Antirosa?'

Judy didn't know. Neither she nor Punch had heard anything of an animal called an aunt. Their world had been Papa and Mamma, who knew everything, permitted everything, and loved everybody—even Punch when he used to go into the garden at Bombay and fill his nails with mould after the weekly nail-cutting, because, as he explained between two strokes of the slipper to his sorely-tried Father, his fingers 'felt so new at the ends.'

In an undefined way Punch judged it advisable to keep both parents between himself and the woman in black and the boy in black hair. He did not approve of them. He liked the gray man, who had expressed a wish to be called 'Uncleharri.' They nodded at each other when they met, and the gray man showed him a little ship with rigging that took up and down.

'She is a model of the *Brisk*—the little *Brisk* that was sore exposed that day at Navarino.'° The gray man hummed the last words and fell into a reverie. 'I'll tell you about Navarino, Punch, when we go for walks together; and you mustn't touch the ship, because she's the *Brisk*.'

Long before that walk, the first of many, was taken, they roused Punch and Judy in the chill dawn of a February morning to say Good-bye; and of all people in the wide earth to Papa and Mamma—both crying this time. Punch was very sleepy and Judy was cross.

'Don't forget us,' pleaded Mamma. 'Oh, my little son, don't forget us, and see that Judy remembers too.'

'I've told Judy to bemember,' said Punch, wriggling, for his father's beard tickled his neck, 'I've told Judy—ten—forty—'leven thousand times. But Ju's so young—quite a baby—isn't she?'

'Yes,' said Papa, 'quite a baby, and you must be good to Judy, and make haste to learn to write and—and—and—'

Punch was back in his bed again. Judy was fast asleep, and there was the rattle of a cab below. Papa and Mamma had gone away. Not to Nassick; that was across the sea. To some place much nearer, of course, and equally of course they would return. They came back after dinner-parties, and Papa had come back after he had been to a place called 'The Snows,'° and Mamma with him, to Punch and Judy at Mrs Inverarity's house in Marine Lines. Assuredly they would come back again. So Punch fell asleep till the true morning, when the black-haired boy met him with the information that Papa and Mamma had gone to Bombay, and that he and Judy were to stay at Downe Lodge 'for ever'. Antirosa, tearfully appealed to for a contradiction, said that Harry had spoken the truth, and that it behoved Punch to fold up his clothes neatly on going to bed. Punch went out and wept bitterly with Judy, into whose fair head he had driven some ideas of the meaning of separation.

When a matured man discovers that he has been deserted by Providence, deprived of his God, and cast without help, comfort, or sympathy, upon a world which is new and strange to him, his despair, which may find expression in evil-living, the writing of his experiences, or the more satisfactory diversion of suicide, is generally supposed to be impressive. A child, under exactly similar circumstances as far as its knowledge goes, cannot very well curse God and die.° It howls till its nose is red, its eye are sore, and its head aches. Punch and Judy, through no fault of their own, had lost all their world. They sat in the hall and cried; the black-haired boy looking on from afar.

The model of the ship availed nothing, though the gray man assured Punch that he might pull the rigging up and down as much as he pleased; and Judy was promised free entry into the kitchen. They wanted Papa and Mamma gone to Bombay beyond the seas, and their grief while it lasted was without remedy.

When the tears ceased the house was very still. Antirosa had decided that it was better to let the children 'have their cry out,' and the boy had gone to school. Punch raised his head from the floor and sniffed mournfully. Judy was nearly asleep. Three short years had not taught her how to bear sorrow with full knowledge. There was a distant, dull boom in the air—a repeated heavy thud. Punch knew that sound in Bombay in the Monsoon. It was the sea—the sea that must be traversed before any one could get to Bombay.

'Quick, Ju!' he cried, 'we're close to the sea. I can hear it! Listen! That's where they've went. P'raps we can catch them if we was in time. They didn't mean to go without us. They've only forgot.'

'Iss,' said Judy. 'They've only forgotted. Less go to the sea.'

The hall-door was open and so was the garden-gate.

'It's very, very big, this place,' he said, looking cautiously down the road, 'and we will get lost; but *I* will find a man and order him to take me back to my house—like I did in Bombay.'

He took Judy by the hand, and the two ran hatless in the direction of the sound of the sea. Downe Villa was almost the last of a range of newly-built houses running out, through a field of brick-mounds, to a heath where gypsies occasionally camped and where the Garrison Artillery of Rocklington practised. There were few people to be seen, and the children might have been taken for those of the soldiery who ranged far. Half an hour the wearied little legs tramped across heath, potato-patch, and sand-dune.

'I'se so tired,' said Judy, 'and Mamma will be angry.'

'Mamma's *never* angry. I suppose she is waiting at the sea now while Papa gets tickets. We'll find them and go along with them. Ju, you mustn't sit down. Only a little more and we'll come to the sea. Ju, if you sit down I'll *thmack* you!' said Punch.

They climbed another dune, and came upon the great gray sea at low tide. Hundreds of crabs were scuttling about the beach, but there was no trace of Papa and Mamma, not even of a ship upon the waters—nothing but sand and mud for miles and miles.

And 'Uncleharri' found them by chance—very muddy and very forlorn—Punch dissolved in tears, but trying to divert Judy with an 'ickle trab,' and Judy wailing to the pitiless horizon for 'Mamma, Mamma!'—and again 'Mamma!'

The Second Bag

> Ah, well-a-day, for we are souls bereaved!
> Of all the creatures under Heaven's wide scope
> We are most hopeless, who had once most hope,
> And most beliefless, who had most believed.
>
> *The City of Dreadful Night*

All this time not a word about Black Sheep. He came later, and Harry the black-haired boy was mainly responsible for his coming.

Judy—who could help loving little Judy?—passed, by special permit, into the kitchen and thence straight to Aunty Rosa's heart. Harry was Aunty Rosa's one child, and Punch was the extra boy about the house. There was no special place for him or his little affairs, and he was forbidden to sprawl on sofas and explain his ideas about the manufacture of this world and his hopes for his future. Sprawling was lazy and wore out sofas, and little boys were not expected to talk. They were talked to, and the talking to was intended for the benefit of their morals. As the unquestioned despot of the house at Bombay, Punch could not quite understand how he came to be of no account in this his new life.

Harry might reach across the table and take what he wanted; Judy might point and get what she wanted. Punch was forbidden to do either. The gray man was his great hope and stand-by for many months after Mamma and Papa left, and he had forgotten to tell Judy to 'bemember Mamma.'

This lapse was excusable, because in the interval he had been introduced by Aunty Rosa to two very impressive things—an abstraction called God, the intimate friend and ally of Aunty Rosa, generally believed to live behind the kitchen-range because it was hot there—and a dirty brown book filled with unintelligible dots and marks. Punch was always anxious to oblige everybody. He therefore welded the story of the Creation on to what he could recollect of his Indian fairy tales, and scandalised Aunty Rosa by repeating the result to Judy. It was a sin, a grievous sin, and Punch was talked to for a quarter of an hour. He could not understand where the iniquity came in, but was careful not to repeat the offence, because Aunty Rosa told him that God had heard every word he had said and was very angry. If this were true why didn't God come and say so, thought Punch, and dismissed the matter from his mind. Afterwards he learned to know the Lord as the only thing in the world more awful than Aunty Rosa

—as a Creature that stood in the background and counted the strokes of the cane.

But the reading was, just then, a much more serious matter than any creed. Aunty Rosa sat him upon a table and told him that A B meant ab.

'Why?' said Punch. 'A is a and B is bee. *Why* does A B mean ab?'

'Because I tell you it does,' said Aunty Rosa, 'and you've got to say it.'

Punch said it accordingly, and for a month, hugely against his will, stumbled through the brown book, not in the least comprehending what it meant. But Uncle Harry, who walked much and generally alone, was wont to come into the nursery and suggest to Aunty Rosa that Punch should walk with him. He seldom spoke, but he showed Punch all Rocklington, from the mud-banks and the sand of the back-bay to the great harbours where ships lay at anchor, and the dockyards where the hammers were never still, and the marine-store shops, and the shiny brass counters in the Offices where Uncle Harry went once every three months with a slip of blue paper and received sovereigns in exchange; for he held a wound-pension.° Punch heard, too, from his lips the story of the battle of Navarino, where the sailors of the Fleet, for three days afterwards, were deafs as posts and could only sign to each other. 'That was because of the noise of the guns,' said Uncle Harry, 'and I have got the wadding of a bullet somewhere inside me now.'

Punch regarded him with curiosity. He had not the least idea what wadding was, and his notion of a bullet was a dockyard cannon-ball bigger than his own head. How could Uncle Harry keep a cannon-ball inside him? He was ashamed to ask, for fear Uncle Harry might be angry.

Punch had never known what anger—real anger—meant until one terrible day when Harry had taken his paint-box to paint a boat with, and Punch had protested. Then Uncle Harry had appeared on the scene and, muttering something about 'strangers' children,'° had with a stick smitten the black haired boy across the shoulders till he wept and yelled, and Aunty Rosa came in and abused Uncle Harry for cruelty to his own flesh and blood, and Punch shuddered to the tips of his shoes. 'It wasn't my fault,' he explained to the boy, but both Harry and Aunty Rosa said that it was, and that Punch had told tales, and for a week there were no more walks with Uncle Harry.

But that week brought a great joy to Punch.

He had repeated till he was thrice weary the statement that 'the Cat lay on the Mat and the Rat came in.'

'Now I can truly read,' said Punch, 'and now I will never read anything in the world.'

He put the brown book in the cupboard where his school-books lived and accidentally tumbled out a venerable volume without covers, labelled *Sharpe's Magazine.*° There was the most portentous picture of a griffin on the first page, with verses below. The griffin carried off one sheep a day from a German village, till a man came with a 'falchion' and split the griffin open. Goodness only knew what a falchion was, but there was the Griffin, and his history was an improvement upon the eternal Cat.

'This,' said Punch, 'means things, and now I will know all about everything in all the world.' He read till the light failed, not understanding a tithe of the meaning, but tantalised by glimpses of new worlds hereafter to be revealed.

'What is a "falchion"? What is a "e-wee lamb"? What is a "base *uss*urper"? What is a "verdant me-ad"?' he demanded with flushed cheeks, at bedtime, of the astonished Aunty Rosa.

'Say your prayers and go to sleep,' she replied, and that was all the help Punch then or afterwards found at her hands in the new and delightful exercise of reading.

'Aunty Rosa only knows about God and things like that,' argued Punch. 'Uncle Harry will tell me.'

The next walk proved that Uncle Harry could not help either; but he allowed Punch to talk, and even sat down on a bench to hear about the Griffin. Other walks brought other stories as Punch ranged farther afield, for the house held large store of old books° that no one ever opened—from *Frank Fairlegh* in serial numbers, and the earlier poems of Tennyson, contributed anonymously° to *Sharpe's Magazine*, to '62 Exhibition Catalogues,° gay with colours and delightfully incomprehensible, and odd leaves of *Gulliver's Travels.*

As soon as Punch could string a few pot-hooks together he wrote to Bombay, demanding by return of post 'all the books in all the world.' Papa could not comply with this modest indent, but sent *Grimm's Fairy Tales*° and a Hans Anderson.° That was enough. If he were only left alone Punch could pass, at any hour he chose, into a land of his own, beyond reach of Aunty Rosa and her God, Harry and his teasements, and Judy's claims to be played with.

'Don't disturve me, I'm reading. Go and play in the kitchen,' grunted Punch. 'Aunty Rosa lets *you* go there.' Judy was cutting her second teeth and was fretful. She appealed to Aunty Rosa, who descended on Punch.

'I was reading,' he explained, 'reading a book I *want* to read.'

'You're only doing that to show off,' said Aunty Rosa. 'But we'll see. Play with Judy now, and don't open a book for a week.'

Judy did not pass a very enjoyable playtime with Punch, who was consumed with indignation. There was a pettiness at the bottom of the prohibition which puzzled him.

'It's what I like to do,' he said, 'and she's found out that and stopped me. Don't cry, Ju—it wasn't your fault—*please* don't cry, or she'll say I made you.'

Ju loyally mopped up her tears, and the two played in their nursery, a room in the basement and half underground, to which they were regularly sent after the mid-day dinner while Aunty Rosa slept. She drank wine—that is to say, something from a bottle in the cellaret—for her stomach's sake, but if she did not fall asleep she would sometimes come into the nursery to see that the children were really playing. Now bricks, wooden hoops, ninepins, and chinaware cannot amuse for ever, especially when all Fairyland is to be won by the mere opening of a book, and, as often as not, Punch would be discovered reading to Judy or telling her interminable tales. That was an offence in the eyes of the law, and Judy would be whisked off by Aunty Rosa, while Punch was left to play alone, 'and be sure that I hear you doing it.'

It was not a cheering employ, for he had to make a playful noise. At last, with infinite craft, he devised an arrangement whereby the table could be supported as to three legs on toy bricks, leaving the fourth clear to bring down on the floor. He could work the table with one hand and hold a book with the other. This he did till an evil day when Aunty Rosa pounced upon him unawares and told him that he was 'acting a lie.'

'If you're old enough to do that,' she said—her temper was always worst after dinner—'you're old enough to be beaten.'

'But—I'm—I'm not an animal!' said Punch aghast. He remembered Uncle Harry and the stick, and turned white. Aunty Rosa had hidden a light cane behind her, and Punch was beaten then and there over the shoulders. It was a revelation to him. The room-door was shut, and he was left to weep himself into repentance and work out his own gospel of life.

Aunty Rosa, he argued, had the power to beat him with many stripes. It was unjust and cruel, and Mamma and Papa would never have allowed it. Unless perhaps, as Aunty Rosa seemed to imply, they had sent secret orders. In which case he was abandoned indeed. It would be discreet in the future to propitiate Aunty Rosa, but, then again, even in matters in which he was innocent, he had been accused of wishing to 'show off.' He had 'shown off' before visitors when he had attacked a strange gentleman—Harry's uncle, not his own—with requests for information about the Griffin and the falchion, and the precise nature of the Tilbury in which Frank Fairlegh rode—all points of paramount interest which he was bursting to understand. Clearly it would not do to pretend to care for Aunty Rosa.

At this point Harry entered and stood afar off, eyeing Punch, a dishevelled heap in the corner of the room, with disgust.

'You're a liar—a young liar,' said Harry, with great unction, 'and you're to have tea down here because you're not fit to speak to us. And you're not to speak to Judy again till Mother gives you leave. You'll corrupt her. You're only fit to associate with the servant. Mother says so.'

Having reduced Punch to a second agony of tears, Harry departed upstairs with the news that Punch was still rebellious.

Uncle Harry sat uneasily in the dining-room. 'Damn it all, Rosa,' said he at last, 'can't you leave the child alone? He's a good enough little chap when I meet him.'

'He puts on his best manners with you, Henry,' said Aunty Rosa, 'but I'm afraid, I'm very much afraid, that he is the Black Sheep of the family.'

Harry heard and stored up the name for future use. Judy cried till she was bidden to stop, her brother not being worth tears; and the evening concluded with the return of Punch to the upper regions and a private sitting at which all the blinding horrors of Hell were revealed to Punch with such store of imagery as Aunty Rosa's narrow mind possessed.

Most grievious of all was Judy's round-eyed reproach, and Punch went to bed in the depths of the Valley of Humiliation.° He shared his room with Harry and knew the torture in store. For an hour and a half he had to answer that young gentleman's questions as to his motives for telling a lie, and a grievous lie, the precise quantity of punishment inflicted by Aunty Rosa, and had also to profess his deep gratitude for such religious instruction as Harry thought fit to impart.

From that day began the downfall of Punch, now Black Sheep.

'Untrustworthy in one thing, untrustworthy in all,' said Aunty

Rosa, and Harry felt that Black Sheep was delivered into his hands. He would wake him up in the night to ask him why he was such a liar.

'I don't know,' Punch would reply.

'Then don't you think you ought to get up and pray to God for a new heart?'

'Y-yess.'

'Get out and pray, then!' And Punch would get out of bed with raging hate in his heart against all the world, seen and unseen. He was always tumbling into trouble. Harry had a knack of cross-examining him as to his day's doings, which seldom failed to lead him, sleepy and savage, into half-a-dozen contradictions—all duly reported to Aunty Rosa next morning.

'But it *wasn't* a lie,' Punch would begin, charging into a laboured explanation that landed him more hopelessly in the mire. 'I said that I didn't say my prayers *twice* over in the day, and *that* was on Tuesday. *Once* I did. I *know* I did, but Harry said I didn't,' and so forth, till the tension brought tears, and he was dismissed from the table in disgrace.

'You usen't to be as bad as this,' said Judy, awe-stricken at the catalogue of Black Sheep's crimes. 'Why are you so bad now?'

'I don't know,' Black Sheep would reply. 'I'm not, if I only wasn't bothered upside down. I knew what I *did*, and I want to say so; but Harry always makes it out different somehow, and Aunty Rosa doesn't believe a word I say. Oh, Ju! don't *you* say I'm bad too.'

'Aunty Rosa says you are,' said Judy. 'She told the Vicar so when he came yesterday.'

'Why does she tell all the people outside the house about me? It isn't fair,' said Black Sheep. 'When I was in Bombay, and was bad—*doing* bad, not made-up bad like this—Mamma told Papa, and Papa told me he knew, and that was all. *Outside* people didn't know too—even Meeta didn't know.'

'I don't remember,' said Judy wistfully. 'I was all little then. Mamma was just as fond of you as she was of me, wasn't she?'

''Course she was. So was Papa. So was everybody.'

'Aunty Rosa likes me more than she does you. She says that you are a Trial and a Black Sheep, and I'm not to speak to you more than I can help.'

'Always? Not outside of the times when you mustn't speak to me at all?'

Judy nodded her head mournfully. Black Sheep turned away in despair, but Judy's arms were round his neck.

'Never mind, Punch,' she whispered. 'I *will* speak to you just the same as ever and ever. You're my own own brother though you are—though Aunty Rosa says you're bad, and Harry says you are a little coward. He says that if I pulled your hair hard, you'd cry.'

'Pull, then,' said Punch.

Judy pulled gingerly.

'Pull harder—as hard as you can! There! I don't mind how much you pull it *now*. If you'll speak to me same as ever I'll let you pull it as much as you like—pull it out if you like. But I know if Harry came and stood by and made you do it I'd cry.'

So the two children sealed the compact with a kiss, and Black Sheep's heart was cheered within him, and by extreme caution and careful avoidance of Harry he acquired virtue, and was allowed to read undisturbed for a week. Uncle Harry took him for walks, and consoled him with rough tenderness, never calling him Black Sheep. 'It's good for you, I suppose, Punch,' he used to say. 'Let us sit down. I'm getting tired.' His steps led him now not to the beach, but to the Cemetery of Rocklington, amid the potato-fields. For hours the gray man would sit on a tombstone, while Black Sheep would read epitaphs, and then with a sigh would stump home again.

'I shall lie there soon,' said he to Black Sheep, one winter evening, when his face showed white as a worn silver coin under the light of the lych-gate. 'You needn't tell Aunty Rosa.'

A month later he turned sharp round, ere half a morning walk was completed, and stumped back to the house. 'Put me to bed, Rosa,' he muttered. 'I've walked my last. The wadding has found me out.'

They put him to bed, and for a fortnight the shadow of his sickness lay upon the house, and Black Sheep went to and fro unobserved. Papa had sent him some new books, and he was told to keep quiet. He retired into his own world, and was perfectly happy. Even at night his felicity was unbroken. He could lie in bed and string himself tales of travel and adventure while Harry was downstairs.

'Uncle Harry's going to die,' said Judy, who now lived almost entirely with Aunty Rosa.

'I'm very sorry,' said Black Sheep soberly. 'He told me that a long time ago.'

Aunty Rosa heard the conversation. 'Will nothing check your wicked tongue?' she said angrily. There were blue circles round her eyes.

Black Sheep retreated to the nursery and read *Cometh up as a*

Flower° with deep and uncomprehending interest. He had been forbidden to open it on account of its 'sinfulness,' but the bonds of the Universe were crumbling, and Aunty Rosa was in great grief.

'I'm glad,' said Black Sheep. 'She's unhappy now. It wasn't a lie, though. *I* knew. He told me not to tell.'

That night Black Sheep woke with a start. Harry was not in the room, and there was a sound of sobbing on the next floor. Then the voice of Uncle Harry, singing the song of the Battle of Navarino,° came through the darkness:—

'Our vanship was the Asia—
The Albion and Genoa!'

'He's getting well,' thought Black Sheep, who knew the song through all its seventeen verses. But the blood froze at his little heart as he thought. The voice leapt an octave and rang shrill as a boatswain's pipe:—

'And next came on the lovely Rose,
The Philomel, her fire-ship, closed,
And the little Brisk was sore exposed
That day at Navarino.'

'That day at Navarino, Uncle Harry!' shouted Black Sheep, half wild with excitement and fear of he knew not what.

A door opened, and Aunty Rosa screamed up the staircase: 'Hush! For God's sake hush, you little devil. Uncle Harry is *dead!*'

The Third Bag

Journeys end in lovers' meeting,
Every wise man's son doth know.°

'I wonder what will happen to me now,' thought Black Sheep, when semi-pagan rites peculiar to the burial of the Dead in middle-class houses had been accomplished, and Aunty Rosa, awful in black crape, had returned to this life. 'I don't think I've done anything bad that she knows of. I suppose I will soon. She will be very cross after Uncle Harry's dying, and Harry will be cross too. I'll keep in the nursery.'

Unfortunately for Punch's plans, it was decided that he should be sent to a day-school which Harry attended. This meant a morning walk with Harry, and perhaps an evening one; but the prospect of freedom in the interval was refreshing. 'Harry'll tell everything I do, but I won't do anything,' said Black Sheep. Fortified with this virtuous resolution, he went to school only to find that Harry's version of his character had preceded him, and that life was a burden in consequence. He took stock of his associates. Some of them were unclean,° some of them talked in dialect, many dropped their h's, and there were two Jews and a negro, or some one quite as dark, in the assembly. 'That's a *hubshi*,'° said Black Sheep to himself. 'Even Meeta used to laugh at a *hubshi*. I don't think this is a proper place.' He was indignant for at least an hour, till he reflected that any expostulation on his part would be by Aunty Rosa construed into 'showing off,' and that Harry would tell the boys.

'How do you like school?' said Aunty Rosa at the end of the day.

'I think it is a very nice place,' said Punch quietly.

'I suppose you warned the boys of Black Sheep's character?' said Aunty Rosa to Harry.

'Oh yes,' said the censor of Black Sheep's morals. 'They know all about him.'

'If I was with my father,' said Black Sheep, stung to the quick, 'I shouldn't *speak* to those boys. He wouldn't let me. They live in shops. I saw them go into shops—where their fathers live and sell things.'

'You're too good for that school, are you?' said Aunty Rosa, with a bitter smile. 'You ought to be grateful, Black Sheep, that those boys speak to you at all. It isn't every school that takes little liars.'

Harry did not fail to make much capital out of Black Sheep's ill-considered remark; with the result that several boys, including the *hubshi*, demonstrated to Black Sheep the eternal equality of the human race by smacking his head, and his consolation from Aunty Rosa was that it 'served him right for being vain.' He learned, however, to keep his opinions to himself, and by propitiating Harry in carrying books and the like to get a little peace. His existence was not too joyful. From nine till twelve he was at school, and from two to four, except on Saturdays. In the evenings he was sent down into the nursery to prepare his lessons for the next day, and every night came the dreaded cross-questionings at Harry's hand. Of Judy he saw but little. She was deeply religious—at six years of age Religion is easy to come by—and sorely divided between her natural love for Black Sheep and her love for Aunty Rosa, who could do no wrong.

The lean woman returned that love with interest, and Judy, when she dared, took advantage of this for the remission of Black Sheep's penalties. Failures in lessons at school were punished at home by a week without reading other than school-books, and Harry brought the news of such a failure with glee. Further, Black Sheep was then bound to repeat his lessons at bedtime to Harry, who generally succeeded in making him break down, and consoled him by gloomiest forebodings for the morrow. Harry was at once spy, practical joker, inquisitor, and Aunty Rosa's deputy executioner. He filled his many posts to admiration. From his actions, now that Uncle Harry was dead, there was no appeal. Black Sheep had not been permitted to keep any self-respect at school: at home he was, of course, utterly discredited, and grateful for any pity that the servant girls—they changed frequently at Downe Lodge because they, too, were liars—might show. 'You're just fit to row in the same boat with Black Sheep,' was a sentiment that each new Jane or Eliza might expect to hear, before a month was over, from Aunty Rosa's lips; and Black Sheep was used to ask new girls whether they had yet been compared to him. Harry was 'Master Harry.' in their mouths; Judy was officially 'Miss Judy'; but Black Sheep was never anything more than Black Sheep *tout court*.

As time went on and the memory of Papa and Mamma became wholly overlaid by the unpleasant task of writing them letters, under Aunty Rosa's eye, each Sunday, Black Sheep forgot what manner of life he had led in the beginning of things. Even Judy's appeal to 'try and remember about Bombay' failed to quicken him.

'I can't remember,' he said. 'I know I used to give orders and Mamma kissed me.'

'Aunty Rosa will kiss you if you are good,' pleaded Judy.

'Ugh! I don't want to be kissed by Aunty Rosa. She'd say I was doing it to get something more to eat.'

The weeks lengthened into months, and the holidays came; but just before the holidays Black Sheep fell into deadly sin.

Among the many boys whom Harry had incited to 'punch Black Sheep's head because he daren't hit back,' was one more aggravating then the rest, who, in an unlucky moment, fell upon Black Sheep when Harry was not near. The blows stung, and Black Sheep struck back at random with all the power at his command. The boy dropped and whimpered. Black Sheep was astounded at his own act, but, feeling the unresisting body under him, shook it with both his hands in blind fury and then began to throttle his enemy; meaning honestly to slay him. There was a scuffle, and Black Sheep was torn off the body by Harry and some colleagues, and cuffed home tingling but exultant. Aunty Rosa was out: pending her arrival, Harry set himself to lecture Black Sheep on the sin of murder—which he described as the offence of Cain.

'Why didn't you fight him fair? What did you hit him when he was down for, you little cur?'

Black Sheep looked up at Harry's throat and then at a knife on the dinner-table.

'I don't understand,' he said wearily. 'You always set him on me and told me I was a coward when I blubbed. Will you leave me alone until Aunty Rosa comes in? She'll beat me if you tell her I ought to be beaten; so it's all right.'

'It's all wrong,' said Harry magisterially. 'You nearly killed him, and I shouldn't wonder if he dies.'

'Will he die?' said Black Sheep.

'I daresay,' said Harry, 'and then you'll be hanged, and go to Hell.'

'All right,' said Black Sheep, picking up the table-knife. 'Then I'll kill *you* now. You say things and do things and—and *I* don't know how things happen, and you never leave me alone—and I don't care *what* happens!'

He ran at the boy with the knife, and Harry fled upstairs to his room, promising Black Sheep the finest thrashing in the world when Aunty Rosa returned. Black Sheep sat at the bottom of the stairs, the table-knife in his hand, and wept for that he had not killed Harry. The servant-girl came up from the kitchen, took the knife away, and consoled him. But Black Sheep was beyond consolation. He would be badly beaten by Aunty Rosa; then there would be another beating at Harry's hands; then Judy would not be allowed to speak to him; then the tale would be told at school, and then—

There was no one to help and no one to care, and the best way out of the business was by death. A knife would hurt, but Aunty Rosa had told him a year ago, that if he sucked paint he would die. He went into the nursery, unearthed the now disused Noah's Ark, and sucked the paint off as many animals as remained. It tasted abominable, but he had licked Noah's Dove clean by the time Aunty Rosa and Judy returned. He went upstairs and greeted them with: 'Please, Aunty Rosa, I believe I've nearly killed a boy at school and I've tried to kill Harry, and when you've done all about God and Hell, will you beat me and get it over?'

The tale of the assault as told by Harry could only be explained on the ground of possession by the Devil. Wherefore Black Sheep was not only most excellently beaten, once by Aunty Rosa and once, when thoroughly cowed down, by Harry, but he was further prayed for at family prayers, together with Jane who had stolen a cold rissole from the pantry, and snuffled audibly as her sin was brought before the

Throne of Grace. Black Sheep was sore and stiff but triumphant. He would die that very night and be rid of them all. No, he would ask for no forgiveness from Harry, and at bed-time would stand no questioning at Harry's hands, even though addressed as 'Young Cain.'

'I've been beaten,' said he, 'and I've done other things. I don't care what I do. If you speak to me to-night, Harry, I'll get out and try to kill you. Now you can kill me if you like.'

Harry took his bed into the spare room, and Black Sheep lay down to die.

It may be that the makers of Noah's Arks know that their animals are likely to find their way into young mouths, and paint them accordingly. Certain it is that the common, weary next morning broke through the windows and found Black Sheep quite well and a good deal ashamed of himself, but richer by the knowledge that he could, in extremity, secure himself against Harry for the future.

When he descended to breakfast on the first day of the holidays, he was greeted with the news that Harry, Aunty Rosa, and Judy were going away to Brighton, while Black Sheep was to stay in the house with the servant. His latest outbreak suited Aunty Rosa's plans admirably. It gave her good excuse for leaving the extra boy behind. Papa in Bombay, who really seemed to know a young sinner's wants to the hour, sent, that week, a package of new books. And with these, and the society of Jane on board-wages, Black Sheep was left alone for a month.

The books lasted for ten days. They were eaten too quickly in long gulps of twelve hours at a time. Then came days of doing absolutely nothing, of dreaming dreams and marching imaginary armies up and downstairs, of counting the number of banisters, and of measuring the length and breadth of every room in handspans—fifty down the side, thirty across, and fifty back again. Jane made many friends, and, after receiving Black Sheep's assurance that he would not tell of her absences, went out daily for long hours. Black Sheep would follow the rays of the sinking sun from the kitchen to the dining-room and thence upward to his own bedroom until all was gray dark, and he ran down to the kitchen fire and read by its light. He was happy in that he was left alone and could read as much as he pleased. But, later, he grew afraid of the shadows of window-curtains and the flapping of doors and the creaking of shutters. He went out into the garden, and the rustling of the laurel-bushes frightened him.

He was glad when they all returned—Aunty Rosa, Harry, and Judy—full of news, and Judy laden with gifts. Who could help loving loyal little Judy? In return for all her merry babblement, Black Sheep confided to her that the distance from the hall-door to the top of the first landing was exactly one hundred and eighty-four handspans. He had found it out himself.

Then the old life recommenced; but with a difference, and a new sin. To his other iniquities Black Sheep had now added a phenomenal clumsiness—was as unfit to trust in action as he was in word. He himself could not account for spilling everything he touched, upsetting glasses as he put his hand out, and bumping his head against doors that were manifestly shut. There was a gray haze upon all his world, and it narrowed month by month, until at last it left Black Sheep almost alone with the flapping curtains that were so like ghosts, and the nameless terrors of broad daylight that were only coats on pegs after all.

Holidays came and holidays went, and Black Sheep was taken to see many people whose faces were all exactly alike; was beaten when occasion demanded, and tortured by Harry on all possible occasions; but defended by Judy through good and evil report, though she hereby drew upon herself the wrath of Aunty Rosa.

The weeks were interminable, and Papa and Mamma were clean forgotten. Harry had left school and was a clerk in a Banking-Office. Freed from his presence, Black Sheep resolved that he should no longer be deprived of his allowance of pleasure-reading. Consequently when he failed at school he reported that all was well, and conceived a large contempt for Aunty Rosa as he saw how easy it was to deceive her. 'She says I'm a little liar when I don't tell lies, and now I do, she doesn't know,' thought Black Sheep. Aunty Rosa had credited him in the past with petty cunning and stratagem that had never entered into his head. By the light of the sordid knowledge that she had revealed to him he paid her back full tale. In a household where the most innocent of his motives, his natural yearning for a little affection, had been interpreted into a desire for more bread and jam, or to ingratiate himself with strangers and so put Harry into the background, his work was easy. Aunty Rosa could penetrate certain kinds of hypocrisy, but not all. He set his child's wits against hers and was no more beaten. It grew monthly more and more of a trouble to read the school-books, and even the pages of the open-print story-books, danced and were dim. So Black Sheep brooded in the shadows that fell about him and cut him off from the world, inventing horrible punishments for 'dear Harry,' or plotting another line of the tangled web of deception that he wrapped round Aunty Rosa.

Then the crash came and the cobwebs were broken. It was impossible to foresee everything. Aunty Rosa made personal inquiries as to Black Sheep's progress and received information that startled her. Step by step, with a delight as keen as when she convicted an underfed housemaid of the theft of cold meats, she followed the trail of Black Sheep's delinquencies. For weeks and weeks, in order to escape banishment from the book-shelves, he had made a fool of Aunty Rosa, of Harry, of God, of all the world! Horrible most horrible, and evidence of an utterly depraved mind.

Black Sheep counted the cost. 'It will only be one big beating and then she'll put a card with "Liar" on my back, same as she did before. Harry will whack me and pray for me, and she will pray for me at prayers and tell me I'm a Child of the Devil and give me hymns to learn. But I've done all my reading and she never knew. She'll say she knew all along. She's an old liar too,' said he.

For three days Black Sheep was shut in his own bedroom—to prepare his heart. 'That means two beatings. One at school and one here. *That* one will hurt most.' And it fell even as he thought. He was thrashed at school before the Jews and the *hubshi* for the heinous crime of carrying home false reports of progress. He was thrashed at home by Aunty Rosa on the same count, and then the placard was produced. Aunty Rosa stitched it between his shoulders and bade him go for a walk with it upon him.

'If you make me do that,' said Black Sheep very quietly, 'I shall burn this house down, and perhaps I'll kill you. I don't know whether I *can* kill you—you're so bony—but I'll try.'

No punishment followed this blasphemy, though Black Sheep held himself ready to work his way to Aunty Rosa's withered throat, and grip there till he was beaten off. Perhaps Aunty Rosa was afraid, for Black Sheep, having reached the Nadir of Sin, bore himself with a new recklessness.

In the midst of all the trouble there came a visitor from over the seas to Down Lodge, who knew Papa and Mamma, and was commissioned to see Punch and Judy. Black Sheep was sent to the drawing-room and charged into a solid tea-table laden with china.

'Gently, gently, little man,' said the visitor, turning Black Sheep's face to the light slowly. 'What's that big bird on the palings?'

'What bird?' asked Black Sheep.

The visitor looked deep down into Black Sheep's eyes for half a minute, and then said, suddenly: 'Good God, the little chap's nearly blind!'

It was a most business-like visitor. He gave orders, on his own responsibility, that Black Sheep was not to go to school or open a book until Mamma came home. 'She'll be here in three weeks, as you know of course,' said he, 'and I'm Inverarity Sahib. I ushered you into this wicked world, young man, and a nice use you seem to have made of your time. You must do nothing whatever. Can you do that?'

'Yes,' said Punch in a dazed way. He had known that Mamma was coming. There was a chance, then, of another beating. Thank Heaven, Papa wasn't coming too. Aunty Rosa had said of late that he ought to be beaten by a man.

For the next three weeks Black Sheep was strictly allowed to do nothing. He spent his time in the old nursery looking at the broken toys, for all of which account must be rendered to Mamma. Aunty Rosa hit him over the hands if even a wooden boat were broken. But that sin was of small importance compared to the other revelations, so darkly hinted at by Aunty Rosa. 'When your Mother comes, and hears what I have to tell her, she may appreciate you properly,' she said grimly, and mounted guard over Judy lest that small maiden should attempt to comfort her brother, to the peril of her soul.

And Mamma came—in a four-wheeler—fluttered with tender excitement. Such a Mamma! She was young, frivolously young, and beautiful, with delicately-flushed cheeks, eyes that shone like stars, and a voice that needed no appeal of outstretched arms to draw little ones to her heart. Judy ran straight to her, but Black Sheep hesitated. Could this wonder be 'showing off'? She would not put out her arms when she knew of his crimes. Meantime was it possible that by fondling she wanted to get anything out of Black Sheep? Only all his love and all his confidence; but that Black Sheep did not know. Aunty Rosa withdrew and left Mamma, kneeling between her children, half laughing, half crying, in the very hall where Punch and Judy had wept five years before.

'Well, chicks, do you remember me?'

'No,' said Judy frankly, 'but I said, "God bless Papa and Mamma" ev'vy night.'

'A little,' said Black Sheep. 'Remember I wrote to you every week, anyhow. That isn't to show off, but 'cause of what comes afterwards.'

'What comes after? What should come after, my darling boy?' And she drew him to her again. He came awkwardly, with many angles. 'Not used to petting,' said the quick Mother-soul. 'The girl is.'

'She's too little to hurt any one,' thought Black Sheep, 'and if I said I'd kill her, she'd be afraid. I wonder what Aunty Rosa will tell.'

There was a constrained late dinner, at the end of which Mamma picked up Judy and put her to bed with endearments manifold. Faithless little Judy had shown her defection from Aunty Rosa already. And that lady resented it bitterly. Black Sheep rose to leave the room.

'Come and say good-night,' said Aunty Rosa, offering a withered cheek.

'Huh!' said Black Sheep. 'I never kiss you, and I'm not going to show off. Tell that woman what I've done, and see what she says.'

Black Sheep climbed into bed feeling that he had lost Heaven after a glimpse through the gates. In half a hour 'that woman' was bending over him. Black Sheep flung up his right arm. It wasn't fair to come and hit him in the dark. Even Aunty Rosa never tried that. But no blow followed.

'Are you showing off? I won't tell you anything more than Aunty Rosa has, and *she* doesn't know everything,' said Black Sheep as clearly as he could for the arms round his neck.

'Oh, my son—my little, little son! It was my fault—*my* fault, darling—and yet how could we help it? Forgive me, Punch.' The voice died out in a broken whisper, and two hot tears fell on Black Sheep's forehead.

'Has she been making you cry too?' he asked. 'You should see Jane cry. But you're nice, and Jane is a Born Liar—Aunty Rosa says so.'

'Hush, Punch, hush! My boy, don't talk like that. Try to love me a little bit—a little bit. You don't know how I want it. Punch-*baba*, come back to me! I am your Mother—your own Mother—and never mind the rest. I know—yes, I know, dear. It doesn't matter now. Punch, won't you care for me a little?'

It is astonishing how much petting a big boy of ten can endure when he is quite sure that there is no one to laugh at him. Black Sheep had never been made much of before, and here was this beautiful woman treating him—Black Sheep, the Child of the Devil and the inheritor of undying flame—as though he were a small God.

'I care for you a great deal, Mother dear,' he whispered at last, 'and I'm glad you've come back; but are you sure Aunty Rosa told you everything?'

'Everything. What *does* it matter? But—' the voice broke with a sob that was also laughter—'Punch, my poor, dear, half-blind darling, don't you think it was a little foolish of you?'

'*No*. It saved a lickin'.'

Mamma shuddered and slipped away in the darkness to write a long letter to Papa. Here is an extract:—

. . . Judy is a dear, plump little prig who adores the woman, and wears with as much gravity as her religious opinions—only eight, Jack!—a venerable horse-hair atrocity which she calls her Bustle! I have just burnt it, and the child is asleep in my bed as I write. She will come to me at once. Punch I cannot quite understand. He is well nourished, but seems to have been worried into a system of small deceptions which the woman magnifies into deadly sins. Don't you recollect our own upbringing, dear, when the Fear of the Lord was so often the beginning of falsehood?° I shall win Punch to me before long. I am taking the children away into the country to get them to know me, and, on the whole, I am content, or shall be when you come home, dear boy, and then, thank God, we shall be all under one roof again at last!

Three months later, Punch, no longer Black Sheep, has discovered that he is the veritable owner of a real, live, lovely Mamma, who is also a sister, comforter, and friend, and that he must protect her till the Father comes home. Deception does not suit the part of a protector, and, when one can do anything without question, where is the use of deception?

'Mother would be awfully cross if you walked through that ditch,' says Judy, continuing a conversation.

'Mother's never angry,' says Punch. 'She'd just say, "You're a little *pagal*;"° and that's not nice, but I'll show.'

Punch walks through the ditch and mires himself to the knees. 'Mother, dear,' he shouts, 'I'm just as dirty as I can pos-*sib*-ly be!'

'Then change your clothes as quickly as you pos-*sib*-ly can!' Mother's clear voice rings out from the house. 'And don't be a little *pagal!*'

'There! 'Told you so,' says Punch. 'It's all different now, and we are just as much Mother's as if she had never gone.'

Not altogether, O Punch, for when young lips have drunk deep of the bitter waters of Hate, Suspicion, and Despair, all the Love in the world will not wholly take away that knowledge; though it may turn darkened eyes for a while to the light, and teach Faith where no Faith was.

From LIFE'S HANDICAP (1891)

On Greenhow Hill

To Love's low voice she lent a careless ear;
Her hand within his rosy fingers lay,
A chilling weight. She would not turn or hear;
But with averted face went on her way.
But when pale Death, all featureless and grim,
Lifted his bony hand, and beckoning
Held out his cypress-wreath, she followed him,
And Love was left forlorn and wondering,
That she who for his bidding would not stay,
At Death's first whisper rose and went away.

Rivals

'*Ohé, Ahmed Din! Shafiz Ullah ahoo!* Bahadur Khan, where are you? Come out of the tents, as I have done, and fight against the English. Don't kill your own kin! Come out to me!'

The deserter from a native corps was crawling round the outskirts of the camp, firing at intervals, and shouting invitations to his old comrades. Misled by the rain and the darkness, he came to the English wing of the camp, and with his yelping and rifle-practice disturbed the men. They had been making roads all day, and were tired.

Ortheris was sleeping at Learoyd's feet. 'Wot's all that?' he said thickly. Learoyd snored, and a Snider° bullet ripped its way through the tent wall. The men swore. 'It's that bloomin' deserter from the Aurangabadis,'° said Ortheris. 'Git up, some one an' tell 'im 'e's come to the wrong shop.'

'Go to sleep, little man,' said Mulvaney, who was steaming nearest the door. 'I can't arise an' expaytiate with him. 'Tis rainin' entrenchin' tools outside.'

' 'Tain't because you bloomin' can't. It's 'cause you bloomin' won't, ye long, limp, lousy, lazy beggar, you. 'Ark to 'im 'owlin'!'

'Wot's the good of argifying? Put a bullet into the swine! 'E's keepin' us awake!' said another voice.

A subaltern shouted angrily, and a dripping sentry whined from the darkness—

‘’Tain’t no good, sir. I can’t see ’im. ’E’s ’idin’ somewhere down ’ill.’

Ortheris tumbled out of his blanket. ‘Shall I try to get ’im, sir?’ said he.

‘No,’ was the answer. ‘Lie down. I won’t have the whole camp shooting all round the clock. Tell him to go and pot his friends.’

Ortheris considered for a moment. Then, putting his head under the tent wall, he called, as a ’bus conductor calls in a block, ‘’Igher up, there! ’Igher up!’

The men laughed, and the laughter was carried down wind to the deserter, who, hearing that he had made a mistake, went off to worry his own regiment half a mile away. He was received with shots; the Aurangabadis were very angry with him for disgracing their colours.

‘An’ that’s all right,’ said Ortheris, withdrawing his head as he heard the hiccough of the Sniders in the distance. ‘S’elp me Gawd, tho’, that man’s not fit to live—messin’ with my beauty-sleep this way.’

‘Go out and shoot him in the morning, then,’ said the subaltern incautiously. ‘Silence in the tents now. Get your rest, men.’

Ortheris lay down with a happy little sigh, and in two minutes there was no sound except the rain on the canvas and the all-embracing and elemental snoring of Learoyd.

The camp lay on a bare ridge of the Himalayas, and for a week had been waiting for a flying column to make connection. The nightly rounds of the deserter and his friends had become a nuisance.

In the morning the men dried themselves in hot sunshine and cleaned their grimy accoutrements. The native regiment was to take its turn of road-making that day while the Old Regiment loafed.

‘I’m goin’ to lay for a shot at that man,’ said Ortheris, when he had finished washing out his rifle. ‘’E comes up the watercourse every evenin’ about five o’clock. If we go and lie out on the north ’ill a bit this afternoon we’ll get ’im.’

‘You’re a bloodthirsty little mosquito,’ said Mulvaney, blowing blue clouds into the air. ‘But I suppose I will have to come wid you. Fwhere’s Jock?’

‘Gone out with the Mixed Pickles, ’cause ’e thinks ’isself a bloomin’ marksman,’ said Ortheris with scorn.

The ‘Mixed Pickles’ were a detachment of picked shots, generally employed in clearing spurs of hills when the enemy were too impertinent. This taught the young officers how to handle men, and did not do the enemy much harm. Mulvaney and Ortheris strolled out of camp, and passed the Aurangabadis going to their road-making.

'You've got to sweat to-day,' said Ortheris genially. 'We're going to get your man. You didn't knock 'im out last night by any chance, any of you?'

'No. The pig went away mocking us. I had one shot at him,' said a private. 'He's my cousin, and *I* ought to have cleared our dishonour. But good luck to you.'

They went cautiously to the north hill, Ortheris leading, because, as he explained, 'this is a long-range show, an' I've got to do it.' His was an almost passionate devotion to his rifle, whom, by barrack-room report, he was supposed to kiss every night before turning in. Charges and scuffles he held in contempt, and, when they were inevitable, slipped between Mulvaney and Learoyd, bidding them to fight for his skin as well as their own. They never failed him. He trotted along, questing like a hound on a broken trail, through the wood of the north hill. At last he was satisfied, and threw himself down on the soft pine-needled slope that commanded a clear view of the watercourse and a brown, bare hillside beyond it. The trees made a scented darkness in which an army corps could have hidden from the sun-glare without.

''Ere's the tail o' the wood,' said Ortheris. ''E's got to come up the watercourse, 'cause it gives 'im cover. We'll lay 'ere. 'Tain't not arf so bloomin' dusty neither.'

He buried his nose in a clump of scentless white violets. No one had come to tell the flowers that the season of their strength was long past, and they had bloomed merrily in the twilight of the pines.

'This is something like,' he said luxuriously. 'Wot a 'evinly clear drop for a bullet acrost. How much d'you make it, Mulvaney?'

'Seven hunder. Maybe a trifle less, bekaze the air's so thin.'

Wop! wop! wop! went a volley of musketry on the rear face of the north hill.

'Curse them Mixed Pickles firin' at nothin'! They'll scare arf the country.'

'Thry a sightin' shot in the middle of the row,' said Mulvaney, the man of many wiles.° 'There's a red rock yonder he'll be sure to pass. Quick!'

Ortheris ran his sight up to six hundred yards and fired. The bullet threw up a feather of dust by a clump of gentians at the base of the rock.

'Good enough!' said Ortheris, snapping the scale down. 'You snick your sights to mine or a little lower. You're always firin' high. But remember, first shot to me. O Lordy! but it's a lovely afternoon.'

The noise of the firing grew louder, and there was a tramping of men in the wood. The two lay very quiet, for they knew that the British soldier is desperately prone to fire at anything that moves or calls. Then Learoyd appeared, his tunic ripped across the breast by a bullet, looking ashamed of himself. He flung down on the pine-needles, breathing in snorts.

'One o' them damned gardeners o' th' Pickles,' said he, fingering the rent. 'Firin' to th' right flank, when he knowed I was there. If I knew who he was I'd 'a' rippen the hide offan him. Look at ma tunic!'

'That's the spishil trustability av a marksman. Train him to hit a fly wid a stiddy rest at seven hunder, an' he'll loose on anythin' he sees or hears up to th' mile. You're well out av that fancy-firin' gang, Jock. Stay here.'

'Bin firin' at the bloomin' wind in the bloomin' treetops,' said Ortheris with a chuckle. 'I'll show you some firin' later on.'

They wallowed in the pine-needles, and the sun warmed them where they lay. The Mixed Pickles ceased firing, and returned to camp, and left the wood to a few scared apes. The watercourse lifted up its voice in the silence, and talked foolishly to the rocks. Now and again the dull thump of a blasting charge three miles away told that the Aurangabadis were in difficulties with their road-making. The men smiled as they listened and lay still, soaking in the warm leisure. Presently Learoyd, between the whiffs of his pipe—

'Seems queer—about 'im yonder—desertin' at all.'

''E'll be a bloomin' side queerer when I've done with 'im,' said Ortheris. They were talking in whispers, for the stillness of the wood and the desire of slaughter lay heavy upon them.

'I make no doubt he had his reasons for desertin'; but, my faith! I make less doubt ivry man has good reason for killin' him,' said Mulvaney.

'Happen there was a lass tewed up wi' it. Men do more than more for th' sake of a lass.'

'They make most av us 'list. They've no manner av right to make us desert.'

'Ah; they make us 'list, or their fathers do,' said Learoyd softly, his helmet over his eyes.

Ortheris's brows contracted savagely. He was watching the valley. 'If it's a girl I'll shoot the beggar twice over, an' second time for bein' a fool. You're blasted sentimental all of a sudden. Thinkin' o' your last near shave?'

'Nay, lad; ah was but thinkin' o' what has happened.'

'An' fwhat has happened, ye lumberin' child av calamity,° that you're lowing like a cow-calf at the back av the pasture, an' suggestin' invidious excuses for the man Stanley's goin' to kill. Ye'll have to wait anther hour yet, little man. Spit it out, Jock, an' bellow melojus to the moon. It takes an earthquake or a bullet graze to fetch aught out av you. Discourse, Don Juan! The a-moors av Lotharius Learoyd! Stanley, kape a rowlin' rig'mental eye on the valley.'

'It's along o' yon hill there,' said Learoyd, watching the bare sub-Himalayan spur that reminded him of his Yorkshire moors. He was speaking more to himself than his fellows. 'Ay,' said he, 'Rumbolds Moor stands up ower Skipton town, an' Greenhow Hill stands up ower Pately Brig.° I reckon you've never heeard tell o' Greenhow Hill, but yon bit o' bare stuff if there was nobbut a white road windin' is like ut; strangely like. Moors an' moors an' moors, wi' never a tree for shelter, an' gray houses wi' flagstone rooves, and pewits cryin', an' a windhover goin' to and fro just like these kites. And cold! A wind that cuts you like a knife. You could tell Greenhow Hill folk by the red-apple colour o' their cheeks an' nose tips, and their blue eyes, driven into pin-points by the wind. Miners mostly, burrowin' for lead i' th' hillsides, followin' the trail of th' ore vein same as a field-rat. It was the roughest minin' I ever seen. Yo'd come on a bit o' creakin' wood windlass like a well-head, an' you was let down i' th' bight of a rope, fendin' yoursen off the side wi' one hand, carryin' a candle stuck in a lump o' clay with t'other, an' clickin'° hold of a rope with t'other hand.'

'An' that's three of them,' said Mulvaney. 'Must be a good climate in those parts.'

Learoyd took no heed.

'An' then yo' came to a level, where you crept on your hands and knees through a mile o' windin' drift, an' you come out into a cave-place as big as Leeds Townhall,° with a engine pumpin' water from workin's 'at went deeper still. It's a queer country, let alone minin', for the hill is full of those natural caves, an' the rivers an' the becks drops into what they call pot-holes, an' come out again miles away.'

'Wot was yo doin' there?' said Ortheris.

'I was a young chap then, an' mostly went wi' 'osses, leadin' coal and lead ore; but at th' time I'm tellin' on I was drivin' the waggon-team i' th' big sumph.° I didn't belong to that country-side by rights.

I went there because of a little difference at home, an' at fust I took up wi' a rough lot. One night we'd been drinkin', an' I must ha' hed more than I could stand, or happen th' ale was none so good. Though i' them days, By for God, I never seed bad ale.' He flung his arms over his head, and gripped a vast handful of white violets. 'Nah,' said he, 'I never seed the ale I could not drink, the bacca I could not smoke, nor the lass I could not kiss. Well, we mun have a race home, the lot on us. I lost all th' others, an' when I was climbin' ower one of them walls built o' loose stones, I comes down into the ditch, stones and all, an' broke my arm. Not as I knawed much about it, for I fell on th' back of my head, an' was knocked stupid like. An' when I come to mysen it were mornin', an' I were lyin' on the settle i' Jesse Roantree's house-place, an' 'Liza Roantree was settin' sewin'. I ached all ovver, and my mouth were like a lime-kiln. She gave me a drink out of a china mug wi' gold letters—"A Present from Leeds"—as I looked at many and many a time at after. "Yo're to lie still while Dr Warbottom comes, because your arm's broken, and father has sent a lad to fetch him. He found yo' when he was goin' to work, an' carried you here on his back," sez she. "Oa!" sez I; an' I shet my eyes, for I felt ashamed o' mysen. "Father's gone to his work these three hours, an' he said he'd tell 'em to get somebody to drive the tram." The clock ticked, an' a bee comed in the house, an' they rung i' my head like mill-wheels. An' she give me another drink an' settled the pillow. "Eh, but yo're young to be getten drunk an' such like, but yo' won't do it again, will yo'?" —"Noa," sez I, "I wouldn't if she'd not but stop they mill-wheels clatterin'."'

'Faith, it's a good thing to be nursed by a woman when you're sick!' said Mulvaney. 'Dir' cheap at the price av twenty broken heads.'

Ortheris turned to frown across the valley. He had not been nursed by many women in his life.

'An' then Dr Warbottom comes ridin' up, an' Jesse Roantree along with 'im. He was a high-larned doctor, but he talked wi' poor folk same as theirsens. "What's ta bin agaate on naa?" he sings out. "Brekkin' tha thick head?" An' he felt me all ovver. "That's none broken. Tha' nobbut knocked a bit sillier than ordinary, an' that's daaft eneaf." An' soa he went on, callin' me all the names he could think on, but settin' my arm, wi' Jesse's help, as careful as could be. "Yo' mun let the big oaf bide here a bit, Jesse," he says, when he hed strapped me up an' given me a dose o' physic; "an' you an' 'Liza will tend him, though he's scarcelins worth the trouble. An' tha'll lose tha work," sez he, "an' tha'll be upon th' Sick Club for a couple o' months an' more. Doesn't tha think tha's a fool?"'

'But whin was a young man, high or low, the other av a fool, I'd like to know?' said Mulvaney. 'Sure, folly's the only safe way to wisdom, for I've thried it.'

'Wisdom!' grinned Ortheris, scanning his comrades with uplifted chin. 'You're bloomin' Solomons, you two, ain't you?'

Learoyd went calmly on, with a steady eye like an ox chewing the cud.

'And that was how I comed to know 'Liza Roantree. There's some tunes as she used to sing—aw, she was always singin'—that fetches Greenhow Hill before my eyes as fair as yon brow across there. And she would learn me to sing bass, an' I was to go to th' chapel wi' 'em, where Jesse and she led the singin', th' old man playin' the fiddle. He was a strange chap, old Jesse, fair mad wi' music, an' he made me promise to learn the big fiddle when my arm was better. It belonged to him, and it stood up in a big case alongside o' th' eight-day clock,° but Willie Satterthwaite, as played it in the chapel, had getten deaf as a door-post, and it vexed Jesse, as he had to rap him ower his head wi' th' fiddle-stick to make him give ower sawin' at th' right time.

'But there was a black drop in it all, an' it was a man in a black coat that brought it. When th' Primitive Methodist° preacher came to Greenhow, he would always stop wi' Jesse Roantree, an' he laid hold of me from th' beginning. It seemed I wor a soul to be saved, and he meaned to do it. At th' same time I jealoused 'at he were keen o' savin' 'Liza Roantree's soul as well, and I could ha' killed him many a time. An' this went on till one day I broke out, an' borrowed th' brass for a drink from 'Liza. After fower days I come back, wi' my tail between my legs, just to see 'Liza again. But Jesse were at home an' th' preacher—th' Reverend Amos Barraclough. 'Liza said naught, but a bit o' red come into her face as were white of a regular thing. Says Jesse, tryin' his best to be civil, "Nay, lad, it's like this. You've getten to choose which way it's goin' to be. I'll ha' nobody across ma doorstep as goes a-drinkin', an' borrows my lass's money to spend i' their drink. Ho'd tha tongue, 'Liza," sez he, when she wanted to put in a word 'at I were welcome to th' brass, and she were none afraid that I wouldn't pay it back. Then the Reverend cuts in, seein' as Jesse were losin' his temper, an' they fair beat me among them. But it were 'Liza, as looked an' said naught, as did more than either o' their tongues, an' soa I concluded to get converted.'

'Fwhat!' shouted Mulvaney. Then, checking himself, he said softly,

'Let be! Let be! Sure the Blessed Virgin is the mother of all religion an' most women; an' there's a dale av piety in a girl if the men would only let ut stay there. I'd ha' been converted myself under the circumstances.'

'Nay, but,' pursued Learoyd with a blush, 'I meaned it.'

Ortheris laughed as loudly as he dared, having regard to his business at the time.

'Ay, Ortheris, you may laugh, but you didn't know yon preacher Barraclough—a little white-faced chap, wi' a voice as 'ud wile a bird off an a bush and a way o' layin' hold of folks as made them think they'd never had a live man for a friend before. You never saw him, an'—an'—you never seed 'Liza Roantree—never seed 'Liza Roantree . . . Happen it was as much 'Liza as th' preacher and her father, but anyways they all meaned it, an' I was fair shamed o' mysen, an' so I become what they called a changed character. And when I think on, it's hard to believe as yon chap going to prayer-meetin's, chapel, and class-meetin's were me. But I never had naught to say for mysen, though there was a deal o' shoutin', and old Sammy Strother, as were almost clemmed° to death and doubled up with the rheumatics, would sing out, "Joyful! Joyful!" and 'at it were better to go up to heaven in a coal-basket than down to hell i' a coach an' six. And he would put his poor old claw on my shoulder, sayin', "Doesn't tha feel it, tha great lump? Doesn't tha feel it?" An' sometimes I thought I did, and then again I thought I didn't, an' how was that?'

'The iverlastin' nature av mankind,' said Mulvaney. 'An' furthermore, I misdoubt you were built for the Primitive Methodians. They're a new corps anyways. I hold by the Ould Church, for she's the mother of them all—ay, an' the father, too. I like her bekaze she's most remarkable regimental in her fittings. I may die in Honolulu, Nova Zambra,° or Cape Cayenne,° but wherever I die, me being' fwhat I am, an' a priest handy, I go under the same orders an' the same words an' the same unction as tho' the Pope himself come down from the roof av St Peter's to see me off. There's neither high nor low, nor broad nor deep, nor betwixt nor between wid her, an' that's that I like. But mark you, she's no manner av Church for a wake man, bekaze she takes the body and the soul av him, onless he has his proper work to do. I remember when my father died that was three months comin' to his grave; begad he'd ha' sold the shebeen° above our heads for ten minutes' quittance of purgathory. An' he did all he could. That's why I say ut takes a strong man to deal with the Ould Church, an' for that reason you'll find so many women go there. An' that sames a conundrum.'

'Wot's the use o' worrittin' 'bout these things?' said Ortheris. 'You're bound to find all out quicker nor you want to, any'ow.' He jerked the cartridge out of the breech-block into the palm of his hand. ''Ere's my chaplain,' he said, and made the venomous black-headed bullet bow like a marionette. ''E's goin' to teach a man all about which is which, an' wot's true, after all, before sundown. But wot 'appened after that, Jock?'

'There was one thing they boggled at, and almost shut th' gate i' my face for, and that were my dog Blast, th' only one saved out o' a litter o' pups as was blowed up when a keg o' minin' powder loosed off in th' store-keeper's hut. They liked his name no better than his business, which were fightin' every dog he comed across; a rare good dog, wi' spots o' black and pink on his face, one ear gone, and lame o' one side wi' being driven in a basket through an iron roof, a matter of half a mile.

'They said I mun give him up 'cause he were worldly and low; and would I let mysen be shut out of heaven for the sake on a dog? "Nay," says I, "if th' door isn't wide enough for th' pair on us, we'll stop outside, for we'll none be parted." And th' preacher spoke up for Blast, as had a likin' for him from th' first—I reckon that was why I come to like th' preacher—and wouldn't hear o' changin' his name to Bless, as some o' them wanted. So th' pair on us became reg'lar chapel-members. But it's hard for a young chap o' my build to cut traces from the world, th' flesh, an' the devil all uv a heap. Yet I stuck to it for a long time, while th' lads as used to stand about th' town-end an' lean ower th' bridge, spittin' into th' beck o' a Sunday, would call after me, "Sitha, Learoyd, when's ta bean to preach, 'cause we're comin' to hear tha."—"Ho'd tha jaw. He hasn't getten th' white choaker° on ta morn," another lad would say, and I had to double my fists hard i' th' bottom of my Sunday coat, and say to mysen, "If 'twere Monday and I warn't a member o' the Primitive Methodists, I'd leather all th' lot of yond'." That was th' hardest of all—to know that I could fight and I mustn't fight.'

Sympathetic grunts from Mulvaney.

'So what wi' singin', practisin', and class-meetin's, and th' big fiddle, as he made me take between my knees, I spent a deal o' time i' Jesse Roantree's house-place. But often as I was there, th' preacher fared° to me to go oftener, and both th' old man an' th' young woman were pleased to have him. He lived i' Pately Brig, as were a goodish step off, but he come. He come all the same. I liked him as well or better as any man I'd ever seen i' one way, and yet I hated him wi' all my heart i' t'other, and we watched each other like cat and mouse, but civil as you please, for I was on my best behaviour, and he was that fair and open that I was bound to be fair with him. Rare good company he was, if I hadn't wanted to wring his cliver little neck half of the time. Often and often when he was goin' from Jesse's I'd set him a bit on the road.'

'See 'im 'ome, you mean?' said Ortheris.

'Ay. It's a way we have i' Yorkshire o' seein' friends off. Yon was a friend as I didn't want to come back, and he didn't want me to come back neither, and so we'd walk together towards Pately, and then he'd set me back again, and there we'd be wal two o'clock i' the mornin' settin' each other to an' fro like a blasted pair o' pendulums twixt hill and valley, long after th' light had gone out i' 'Liza's window, as both on us had been looking at, pretending to watch the moon.'

'Ah!' broke in Mulvaney, 'ye'd no chanst against the maraudin' psalm-singer. They'll take the airs an' the graces instid av the man nine times out av ten, an' they only find the blunder later—the wimmen.'

'That's just where yo're wrong,' said Learoyd, reddening under the freckled tan of his cheeks. 'I was th' first wi' 'Liza, an' yo'd think that were enough. But th' parson were a steady-gaited sort o' chap, and Jesse were strong o' his side, and all th' women i' the congregation dinned it to 'Liza 'at she were fair fond to take up wi' a wastrel ne'er-do-weel like me, as was scarcelins respectable an' a fighting dog at his heels. It was all very well for her to be doing me good and saving my soul, but she must mind as she didn't do herself harm. They talk o' rich folk bein' stuck up an' genteel, but for cast-iron pride o' respectability there's naught like poor chapel folk. It's as cold as th' wind o' Greenhow Hill—ay, and colder, for 'twill never change. And now I come to think on it, one at strangest things I know is 'at they couldn't abide th' thought o' soldiering.° There's a vast o' fightin' i' th' Bible, and there's a deal of Methodists i' th' army; but to hear chapel folk talk yo'd think that soldierin' were next door, an' t'other side, to hangin'. I' their meetin's all their talk is o' fightin'. When Sammy Strother were stuck for summat to say in his prayers, he'd sing out, "Th' sword o' th' Lord and o' Gideon."° They were allus at it about puttin' on th' whole armour o' righteousness,° an' fightin' the good fight o' faith.° And then, atop o' 't all, they held a prayer-meetin' ower a young chap as wanted to 'list, and nearly deafened him, till he picked up his hat and fair ran away. And they'd tell tales in th' Sunday-school o' bad lads as had been thumped and brayed for bird-nesting o' Sundays and playin' truant o' week-days, and how they took to wrestlin', dog-fightin', rabbit-runnin', and drinkin', till at last, as if 'twere a hepitaph on a gravestone, they damned him across th' moors wi', "an' then he went and 'listed for a soldier," an' they'd all fetch a deep breath, and throw up their eyes like a hen drinkin'.'

'Fwhy is ut?' said Mulvaney, bringing down his hand on his thigh with a crack. 'In the name av God, fwhy is ut? I've seen ut, tu. They cheat an' they swindle an' they lie an' they slander, an' fifty things fifty times worse; but the last an' the worst by their reckonin' is to serve the Widdy° honest. It's like the talk av childer—seein' things all round.'

'Plucky lot of fightin' good fights of whatsername they'd do if we didn't see they had a quiet place to fight in. And such fightin' as theirs is! Cats on the tiles. T'other callin' to which to come on. I'd give a month's pay to get some o' them broad-backed beggars in London sweatin' through a day's road-makin' an' a night's rain. They'd carry on a deal afterwards—same as we're supposed to carry on. I've bin turned out of a measly arf-license pub° down Lambeth way, full o' greasy kebmen, 'fore now,' said Ortheris with an oath.

'Maybe you were dhrunk,' said Mulvaney soothingly.

'Worse nor that. The Forders° were drunk. *I* was wearin' the Queen's uniform.'

'I'd no particular thought to be a soldier i' them days,' said Learoyd, still keeping his eye on the bare hill opposite, 'but this sort o' talk put it i' my head. They was so good, th' chapel folk, that they tumbled ower t'other side. But I stuck to it for 'Liza's sake, specially as she was learning me to sing the bass part in a horotorio as Jesse were gettin' up. She sung like a throstle hersen, and we had practisin's night after night for a matter of three months.'

'I know what a horotorio is,' said Ortheris pertly. 'It's a sort of chaplain's sing-song—words all out of the Bible, and hullabaloojah choruses.'°

'Most Greenhow Hill folks played some instrument or t'other, an' they all sung so you might have heard them miles away, and they were so pleased wi' the noise they made they didn't fare to want anybody to listen. The preacher sung high seconds° when he wasn't playin' the flute, an' they set me, as hadn't got far with big fiddle, again Willie Satterthwaite, to jog his elbow when he had to get a' gate playin'. Old Jesse was happy if ever a man was, for he were th' conductor an' th' first fiddle an' th' leadin' singer, beatin' time wi' his fiddle-stick, till at times he'd rap with it on the table, and cry out, "Now, you mun all stop; it's my turn." And he'd face round to his front, fair sweating wi' pride, to sing th' tenor solos. But he were grandest i' th' choruses, waggin' his head, flinging his arms round like a windmill, and singin' hisself black in the face. A rare singer were Jesse.

'Yo' see, I was not o' much account wi' 'em all exceptin' to 'Liza Roantree, and I had a deal o' time settin' quiet at meetings and horotorio practises to hearken their talk, and if it were strange to me at beginnin', it got stranger still at after, when I was shut on it, and could study what it meaned.

'Just after th' horotorios came off, 'Liza, as had allus been weakly like, was took very bad. I walked Dr Warbottom's horse up and down a deal of times while he were inside, where they wouldn't let me go, though I fair ached to see her.

'"She'll be better i' noo, lad—better i' noo," he used to say. "Tha mun ha' patience." Then they said if I was quiet I might go in, and th' Reverend Amos Barraclough used to read to her lyin' propped up among th' pillows. Then she began to mend a bit, and they let me carry her on to th' settle, and when it got warm again she went about same as afore. Th' preacher and me and Blast was a deal together i' them days, and i' one way we was rare good comrades. But I could ha' stretched him time and again with a good will. I mind one day he said he would like to go down into th' bowels o' th' earth, and see how th' Lord had builded th' framework o' th' everlastin' hills.° He were one of them chaps as had a gift o' sayin' things. They rolled off the tip of his clever tongue, same as Mulvaney here, as would ha' made a rare good preacher if he had nobbut given his mind to it. I lent him a suit o' miner's kit as almost buried th' little man, and his white face down i' th' coat-collar and hat-flap looked like the face of a boggart,° and he cowered down i' th' bottom o' the waggon. I was drivin' a tram as led up a bit of an incline up to th' cave where the engine was pumpin', and where th' ore was brought up and put into th' waggons as went down o' themselves, me puttin' th' brake on and th' horses a-trottin' after. Long as it was daylight we were good friends, but when we got fair into th' dark and could nobbut see th' day shinin' at the hole like a lamp at a street-end, I feeled down-right wicked. Ma religion dropped all away from me when I looked back at him as were always comin' between me and 'Liza. The talk was 'at they were to be wed when she got better, an' I couldn't get her to say yes or nay to it. He began to sing a hymn in his thin voice, and I came out wi' a chorus that was all cussin' an' swearin' at my horses, an' I began to know how I hated him. He were such a little chap, too. I could drop him wi' one hand down Garstang's Copper-hole—a place where th' beck slithered ower th' edge on a rock, and fell wi' a bit of a whisper into a pit as no rope i' Greenhow could plump.'

Again Learoyd rooted up the innocent violets. 'Ay, he should see th' bowels o' th' earth an' never naught else. I could take him a mile or two along th' drift, and leave him wi' his candle doused to cry hallelujah, wi' none to hear him and say amen. I was to lead him down th' ladder-way to th' drift where Jesse Roantree was workin', and why shouldn't he slip on th' ladder, wi' my feet on his fingers till they loosed grip, and I put him down wi' my heel? If I went fust down th' ladder I could click hold on him and chuck him over my head, so as he should go squshin' down the shaft, breakin' his bones at ev'ry timberin' as Bill Appleton did when he was fresh,° and hadn't a bone left when he wrought to th' bottom. Niver a blasted leg to walk from Pately. Niver an arm to put round 'Liza Roantree's waist. Niver no more—niver no more.'

The thick lips curled back over the yellow teeth, and that flushed face was not pretty to look upon. Mulvaney nodded sympathy, and Ortheris, moved by his comrade's passion, brought up the rifle to his shoulder, and searched the hillside for his quarry, muttering ribaldry about a sparrow, a spout, and a thunder-storm.° The voice of the watercourse supplied the necessary small talk till Learoyd picked up his story.

'But it's none so easy to kill a man like yon. When I'd given up my horses to th' lad as took my place and I was showin' th' preacher th' workin's, shoutin' into his ear across th' clang o' th' pumpin' engines, I saw he were afraid o' naught; and when the lamplight showed his black eyes, I could feel as he was masterin' me again. I were no better nor Blast chained up short and growlin' i' the depths of him while a strange dog went safe past.

'"Th'art a coward and a fool," I said to mysen; an' I wrestled i' my mind again' him till, when we come to Garstang's Copper-hole, I laid hold o' the preacher and lifted him up over my head and held him into the darkest on it. "Now, lad," I says, "it's to be one or t'other on us—thee or me—for 'Liza Roantree. Why, isn't thee afraid for thysen?" I says, for he were still i' my arms as a sack. "Nay; I'm but afraid for thee, my poor lad, as knows naught," says he. I set him down on th' edge, an' th' beck run stiller, an' there was no more buzzin' in my head like when th' bee come through th' window o' Jesse's house. "What dost tha mean?" says I.

'"I've often thought as thou ought to know," says he, "but 'twas hard to tell thee. 'Liza Roantree's for neither on us, nor for nobody o' this earth.° Dr Warbottom says—and he knows her, and her mother before her—that she is in a decline, and she cannot live six months longer. He's known it for many a day. Steady, John! Steady!" says he. And that weak little man pulled me further back and set me agin' him, and talked it all over quiet and still, me turnin' a bunch o' candles in my hand, and counting them ower and ower again as I listened. A deal on it were th' regular preachin' talk, but there were a vast lot as made me begin to think as he were more of a man than I'd ever given him credit for, till I were cut as deep for him as I were for mysen.

'Six candles we had, and we crawled and climbed all that day while they lasted, and I said to mysen, "'Liza Roantree hasn't six months to live." And when we came into th' daylight again we were like dead men to look at, an' Blast come behind us without so much as waggin' his tail. When I saw 'Liza again she looked at me a minute and says, "Who's telled tha? For I see tha knows." And she tried to smile as she kissed me, and I fair broke down.

'Yo'see, I was a young chap i' them days, and had seen naught o' life, let alone death, as is allus a-waitin'. She telled me as Dr Warbottom said as Greenhow air was too keen, and they were goin' to Bradford, to Jesse's brother David, as worked i' a mill, and I mun hold up like a man and a Christian, and she'd pray for me. Well, and they went away, and the preacher that same back end o' th' year were appointed to another circuit, as they call it, and I were left alone on Greenhow Hill.

'I tried, and I tried hard, to stick to th' chapel, but 'tweren't th' same thing at after. I hadn't 'Liza's voice to follow i' th' singin', nor her eyes a-shinin' acrost their heads. And i' th' class-meetings they said as I mun have some experiences to tell, and I hadn't a word to say for mysen.

'Blast and me moped a good deal, and happen we didn't behave ourselves over well, for they dropped us and wondered however they'd come to take us up. I can't tell how we got through th' time, while i' th' winter I gave up my job and went to Bradford. Old Jesse were at th' door o' th' house, in a long street o' little houses. He'd been sendin' th' children 'way as were clatterin' their clogs in th' causeway, for she were asleep.

'"Is it thee?" he says; "but you're not to see her. I'll none have her wakened for a nowt like thee. She's goin' fast, and she mun go in peace. Thou'lt never be good for naught i' th' world, and as long as thou lives thou'll never play the big fiddle. Get away, lad, get away!" So he shut the door softly i' my face.

'Nobody never made Jesse my master, but it seemed to me he was about right, and I went away into the town and knocked up against a recruiting sergeant. The old tales o' th' chapel folk came buzzin' into my head. I was to get away, and this were th' regular road for the likes o' me. I 'listed there and then, took th' Widow's shillin',° and had a bunch o' ribbons pinned i' my hat.

'But next day I found my way to David Roantree's door, and Jesse came to open it. Says he, "Thou's come back again wi' th' devil's colours flyin'—thy true colours, as I always telled thee."

'But I begged and prayed of him to let me see her nobbut to say good-bye, till a woman calls down th' stair-way, "She says John Learoyd's to come up." Th' old man shifts aside in a flash, and lays his hand on my arm, quite gentle like. "But thou'lt be quiet, John," says he, "for she's rare and weak. Thou was allus a good lad."

'Her eyes were all alive wi' light, and her hair was thick on the pillow round her, but her cheeks were thin—thin to frighten a man that's strong. "Nay, father, yo mayn't say th' devil's colours. Them ribbons is pretty." An' she held out her hands for th' hat, an' she put all straight as a woman will wi' ribbons. "Nay, but what they're pretty," she says. "Eh, but I'd ha' liked to see thee i' thy red coat, John, for thou was allus my own lad—my very own lad, and none else."

'She lifted up her arms, and they come round my neck i' a gentle grip, and they slacked away, and she seemed fainting. "Now yo' mun get away, lad," says Jesse, and I picked up my hat and I came downstairs.

'Th' recruiting sergeant were waitin' for me at th' corner public-house. "Yo've seen your sweetheart?" says he. "Yes, I've seen her," says I. "Well, we'll have a quart now, and you'll do your best to forget her," says he, bein' one o' them smart, bustlin' chaps. "Ay, sergeant," says I. "Forget her." And I've been forgettin' her ever since.'

He threw away the wilted clump of white violets as he spoke. Ortheris suddenly rose to his knees, his rifle at his shoulder, and peered across the valley in the clear afternoon light. His chin cuddled the stock, and there was a twitching of the muscles of the right cheek as he sighted; Private Stanley Ortheris was engaged on his business. A speck of white crawled up the watercourse.

'See that beggar? . . . Got 'im.'

Seven hundred yards away, and a full two hundred down the hillside, the deserter of the Aurangabadis pitched forward, rolled down a red rock, and lay very still, with his face in a clump of blue gentians, while a big raven flapped out of the pine wood to make investigation.

'That's a clean shot, little man,' said Mulvaney.

Learoyd thoughtfully watched the smoke clear away. 'Happen there was a lass tewed up wi' him, too,' said he.

Ortheris did not reply. He was staring across the valley, with the smile of the artist who looks on the completed work.

From MANY INVENTIONS (1893)

'*Bugglesmith*'

This day the ship went down, and all hands was drowned but me.

CLARK RUSSELL

The first officer of the *Breslau* asked me to dinner on board, before the ship went round to Southampton to pick up her passengers. The *Breslau* was lying below London Bridge,° her fore-hatches opened for cargo, and her deck littered with nuts and bolts, and screws and chains. The Black M'Phee° had been putting some finishing touches to his adored engines, and M'Phee is the most tidy of chief engineers. If the leg of a cockroach gets into one of his slide-valves the whole ship knows it, and half the ship has to clean up the mess.

After dinner, which the first officer, M'Phee, and I ate in one little corner of the empty saloon, M'Phee returned to the engine room to attend to some brass-fitters. The first officer and I smoked on the bridge and watched the lights of the crowded shipping till it was time for me to go home. It seemed, in the pauses of our conversation, that I could catch an echo of fearful bellowings from the engine-room, and the voice of M'Phee singing of home and the domestic affections.

'M'Phee has a friend aboard to-night—a man who was a boiler-maker at Greenock when M'Phee was a 'prentice,' said the first officer. 'I didn't ask him to dine with us because—'

'I see—I mean I hear,' I answered. We talked on for a few minutes longer, and M'Phee came up from the engine-room with his friend on his arm.

'Let me present ye to this gentleman,' said M'Phee. 'He's a great admirer o' your wor-rks. He has just hearrd o' them.'

M'Phee could never pay a compliment prettily. The friend sat down suddenly on a bollard, saying that M'Phee had understated the truth. Personally, he on the bollard considered that Shakespeare was trembling in the balance solely on my account, and if the first officer wished to dispute this he was prepared to fight the first officer then or later, 'as per invoice.' 'Man, if ye only knew,' said he, wagging his head, 'the times I've lain in my lonely bunk reading *Vanity Fair*° an' sobbin'—ay, weepin' bitterly at the pure fascination of it.'

He shed a few tears for guarantee of good faith, and the first officer laughed. M'Phee resettled the man's hat, that had tilted over one eyebrow.

'That'll wear off in a little. It's just the smell o' the engine-room,' said M'Phee.

'I think I'll wear off myself,' I whispered to the first officer. 'Is the dinghy ready?'

The dinghy was at the gangway, which was down, and the first officer went forward to find a man to row me to the bank. He returned with a very sleepy Lascar, who knew the river.

'Are you going?' said the man on the bollard. 'Well, I'll just see ye home. M'Phee, help me down the gangway. It has as many ends as a cat-o'-nine-tails, and—losh!—how innumerable are the dinghies!'

'You'd better let him come with you,' said the first officer. 'Muhammad Jan, put the drunk sahib ashore first. Take the sober sahib to the next stairs.'

I had my foot in the bow of the dinghy, the tide was making upstream, when the man cannoned against me, pushed the Lascar back on the gangway, cast loose the painter, and the dinghy began to saw, stern-first, along the side of the *Breslau*.

'We'll have no exter-r-raneous races here,' said the man. 'I've known the Thames for thirty years—'

There was no time for argument. We were drifting under the *Breslau's* stern, and I knew that her propeller was half out of water, in the middle of an inky tangle of buoys, low-lying hawsers, and moored ships, with the tide ripping through them.

'What shall I do?' I shouted to the first officer.

'Find the Police Boat as soon as you can, and for God's sake get some way on the dinghy. Steer with the oar. The rudder's unshipped and—'

I could hear no more. The dinghy slid away, bumped on a mooring-buoy, swung round and jigged off irresponsibly as I hunted for the oar. The man sat in the bow, his chin on his hands, smiling.

'Row, you ruffian,' I said. 'Get her out into the middle of the river—'

'It's a preevilege to gaze on the face o' genius. Let me go on thinking. There was "Little Barnaby Dorrit" and "The Mystery o' the Bleak Druid."° I sailed in a ship called the *Druid* once—badly found she was. It all comes back to me so sweet. It all comes back to me. Man, ye steer like a genius.'

We bumped round another mooring-buoy and drifted on to the bows of a Norwegian timber-ship—I could see the great square holes° on either side of the cut-water. Then we dived into a string of barges and scraped through them by the paint on our planks. It was a consolation to think that the dinghy was being reduced in value at every bump, but the question before me was when she would begin to leak. The man looked ahead into the pitchy darkness and whistled.

'Yon's a Castle liner;° her ties are black. She's swinging across stream. Keep her port light on our starboard bow, and go large,' he said.

'How can I keep anything anywhere? You're sitting on the oars. Row, man, if you don't want to drown.'

He took the sculls, saying sweetly: 'No harm comes to a drunken man. That's why I wished to come wi' *you*. Man, ye're not fit to be alone in a boat.'

He flirted the dinghy round the big ship, and for the next ten minutes I enjoyed—positively enjoyed—an exhibition of first-class steering. We threaded in and out of the mercantile marine of Great Britain as a ferret threads a rabbit-hole, and we, he that is to say, sang joyously to each ship till men looked over bulwarks and cursed us. When we came to some moderately clear water he gave the sculls to me, and said:

'If ye could row as ye write, I'd respect you for all your vices. Yon's London Bridge. Take her through.'

We shot under the dark ringing arch, and came out the other side, going up swiftly with the tide chanting songs of victory. Except that I wished to get home before morning, I was growing reconciled to the jaunt. There were one or two stars visible, and by keeping into the centre of the stream, we could not come to any very serious danger.

The man began to sing loudly:—

'The smartest clipper that you could find,°
Yo ho! Oho!
Was the *Marg'ret Evans* of the Black X Line,
A hundred years ago!

Incorporate that in your next book, which is marvellous.' Here he stood up in the bows and declaimed:—

'Ye Towers o' Julia, London's lasting wrong,°
By mony a foul an' midnight murder fed—

> Sweet Thames run softly till I end my song—
> And yon's the grave as little as my bed.

I'm a poet mysel' an' I can feel for others.'

'Sit down,' said I. 'You'll have the boat over.'

'Ay, I'm settin'—settin' like a hen.' He plumped down heavily, and added, shaking his forefinger at me:—

> 'Lear-rn, prudent, cautious self-control°
> Is wisdom's root.

How did a man o' your parts come to be so drunk? Oh, it's a sinfu' thing, an' ye may thank God on all fours that I'm with you. What's yon boat?'

We had drifted far up the river, and a boat manned by four men, who rowed with a soothingly regular stroke, was overhauling us.

'It's the River Police,' I said, at the top of my voice.

'Oh ay! If your sin do not find you out on dry land, it will find you out in the deep waters.° Is it like they'll give us drink?'

'Exceedingly likely. I'll hail them.' I hailed.

'What are you doing?' was the answer from the boat.

'It's the *Breslau's* dinghy broken loose,' I began.

'It's a vara drunken man broke loose,' roared my companion, 'and I'm taking him home by water, for he cannot stand on dry land.' Here he shouted my name twenty times running, and I could feel the blushes racing over my body three deep.

'You'll be locked up in ten minutes, my friend,' I said, 'and I don't think you'll be bailed either.'

'H'sh, man, h'sh. They think I'm your uncle.' He caught up a scull and began splashing the boat as it ranged alongside.

'You're a nice pair,' said the sergeant at last.

'I am anything you please so long as you take this fiend away. Tow us in to the nearest station, and I'll make it worth your while,' I said.

'Corruption—corruption,' roared the man, throwing himself flat in the bottom of the boat. 'Like unto the worms that perish,° so is man! And all for the sake of a filthy half-crown to be arrested by the river police at my time o' life!'

'For pity's sake, row,' I shouted. 'The man's drunk.'

They rowed us to a flat°—a fire or a police-station; it was too dark to see which. I could feel that they regarded me in no better light than the other man. I could not explain, for I was holding the far end of the painter, and feeling cut off from all respectability.

We got out of the boat, my companion falling flat on his wicked face, and the sergeant asked us rude questions about the dinghy. My companion washed his hands of all responsibility. He was an old man; he had been lured into a stolen boat by a young man—probably a thief—he had saved the boat from wreck (this was absolutely true), and now he expected salvage in the shape of hot whisky and water. The sergeant turned to me. Fortunately I was in evening dress, and had a card to show. More fortunately still, the sergeant happened to know the *Breslau* and M'Phee. He promised to send the dinghy down next tide, and was not beyond accepting my thanks, in silver.

As this was satisfactorily arranged, I heard my companion say angrily to a constable, 'If you will not give it to a dry man, ye maun to a drookit.'° Then he walked deliberately off the edge of the flat into the water. Somebody stuck a boat-hook into his clothes and hauled him out.

'Now,' said he triumphantly, 'under the rules o' the R-royal Humane Society, ye must give me hot whisky and water.° Do not put temptation before the laddie. He's my nephew an' a good boy i' the main. Tho' why he should masquerade as Mister Thackeray on the high seas is beyond my comprehension. Oh the vanity o' youth! M'Phee told me ye were as vain as a peacock. I mind that now.'

'You had better give him something to drink and wrap him up for the night. I don't know who he is,' I said desperately, and when the man had settled down to a drink supplied on my representations, I escaped and found that I was near a bridge.

I went towards Fleet Street, intending to take a hansom and go home. After the first feeling of indignation died out, the absurdity of the experience struck me fully and I began to laugh aloud in the empty streets, to the scandal of a policeman. The more I reflected the more heartily I laughed, till my mirth was quenched by a hand on my shoulder, and turning I saw him who should have been in bed at the river police-station. He was damp all over; his wet silk hat rode far at the back of his head, and round his shoulders hung a striped yellow blanket, evidently the property of the State.

'The crackling o' thorns under a pot,'° said he, solemnly. 'Laddie, have ye not thought o' the sin of idle laughter? My heart misgave me that ever ye'd get home, an' I've just come to convoy you a piece. They're sore uneducate down there by the river. They wouldna listen to me when I talked o' your worrks, so I e'en left them. Cast the blanket about you, laddie. It's fine and cold.'

I groaned inwardly. Providence evidently intended that I should frolic through eternity with M'Phee's infamous acquaintance.

'Go away,' I said; 'go home, or I'll give you in charge!'

He leaned against a lamp-post and laid his finger to his nose—his dishonourable, carnelian neb.

'I mind now that M'Phee told me ye were vainer than a peacock, an' your castin' me adrift in a boat shows ye were drunker than an owl. A good name is as a savoury bakemeat.° I ha' nane.' He smacked his lips joyously.

'Well, I know that,' I said.

'Ay, but *ye* have. I mind now that M'Phee spoke o' your reputation that you're so proud of. Laddie, if ye gie me in charge—I'm old enough to be your father—I'll bla-ast your reputation as far as my voice can carry; for I'll call you by name till the cows come hame. It's no jestin' matter to be a friend to me. If you discard my friendship, ye must come to Vine Street wi' me for stealin' the *Breslau's* dinghy.'

Then he sang at the top of his voice:—

> 'In the mornin'°
> I' the mornin' by the black van—
> We'll toodle up to Vine Street i' the mornin'!

Yon's my own composeetion, but *I'm* not vain. We'll go home together, laddie, we'll go home together.' And he sang 'Auld Lang Syne' to show that he meant it.

A policeman suggested that we had better move on, and we moved on to the Law Courts near St Clement Danes.° My companion was quieter now, and his speech, which up till that time had been distinct —it was a marvel to hear how in his condition he could talk dialect— began to slur and slide and slummock.° He bade me observe the architecture of the Law Courts and linked himself lovingly to my arm. Then he saw a policeman, and before I could shake him off, whirled me up to the man singing:—

> 'Every member of the Force,°
> Has a watch and chain of course—'

and threw his dripping blanket over the helmet of the Law. In any other country in the world we should have run an exceedingly good chance of being shot, or dirked, or clubbed—and clubbing is worse than being shot. But I reflected in that wet-cloth tangle that this was England, where the police are made to be banged and battered and bruised, that they may the better endure a police-court reprimand next morning. We three fell in a festoon, he calling on me by name—that was the tingling horror of it—to sit on the policeman's head and cut the traces.° I wriggled clear first and shouted to the policeman to kill the blanket-man.

Naturally the policeman answered: 'You're as bad as 'im,' and chased me, as the smaller man, round St Clement Danes into Holywell Street,° where I ran into the arms of another policeman. That flight could not have lasted more than a minute and a half, but it seemed to me as long and as wearisome as the foot-bound flight of a nightmare. I had leisure to think of a thousand things as I ran; but most I thought of the great and god-like man who held a sitting° in the north gallery of St Clement Danes a hundred years ago.° I know that he at least would have felt for me. So occupied was I with these considerations, that when the other policeman hugged me to his bosom and said: 'What are you tryin' to do?' I answered with exquisite politeness: 'Sir, let us take a walk down Fleet Street.' 'Bow Street'll° do *your* business, I think,' was the answer, and for a moment I thought so too, till it seemed I might scuffle out of it. Then there was a hideous scene, and it was complicated by my companion hurrying up with the blanket and telling me—always by name—that he would rescue me or perish in the attempt.

'Knock him down,' I pleaded. 'Club his head open first and I'll explain afterwards.'

The first policement, the one who had been outraged, drew his truncheon and cut at my companion's head. The high silk hat crackled and the owner dropped like a log.

'Now you've done it,' I said. 'You've probably killed him.'

Holywell Street never goes to bed. A small crowd gathered on the spot, and some one of German extraction shrieked: 'You haf killed the man.'

Another cried: 'Take his bloomin' number. I saw him strook cruel 'ard. Yah!'

Now the street was empty when the trouble began, and, saving the two policemen and myself, no one had seen the blow. I said, therefore, in a loud and cheerful voice:—

'The man's a friend of mine. He's fallen down in a fit. Bobby, will you bring the ambulance?' Under my breath I added: 'It's five shillings apiece, and the man didn't hit you.'

'No, but 'im and you tried to scrob° me,' said the policeman.

This was not a thing to argue about.

'Is Dempsey on duty at Charing Cross?' I said.

'Wot d'you know of Dempsey, you bloomin' garrotter?'° said the policeman.

'If Dempsey's there, he knows me. Get the ambulance quick, and I'll take him to Charing Cross.'

'You're coming to Bow Street, *you* are,' said the policeman crisply.

'The man's dying'—he lay groaning on the pavement—'get the ambulance,'° said I.

There is an ambulance at the back of St Clement Danes, whereof I know more than most people. The policeman seemed to possess the keys of the box in which it lived. We trundled it out—it was a three-wheeled affair with a hood—and we bundled the body of the man upon it.

A body in an ambulance looks very extremely dead. The policeman softened at the sight of the stiff boot-heels.

'Now then,' said they, and I fancied that they still meant Bow Street.

'Let me see Dempsey for three minutes if he's on duty,' I answered.

'Very good. He is.'

Then I knew that all would be well, but before we started I put my head under the ambulance-hood to see if the man were alive. A guarded whisper came to my ear.

'Laddie, you maun pay me for a new hat. They've broken it. Dinna desert me, now, laddie. I'm o'er old to go to Bow Street in my gray hairs for a fault of yours. Laddie, dinna desert me.'

'You'll be lucky if you get off under seven years,' I said to the policeman.

Moved by a very lively fear of having exceeded their duty, the two policeman left their beats, and the mournful procession wound down the empty Strand. Once west of the Adelphi,° I knew I should be in my own country; and the policemen had reason to know that too, for as I was pacing proudly a little ahead of the catafalque, another policeman said 'Good-night, sir,' to me as he passed.

'Now, you see,' I said, with condescension, 'I wouldn't be in your shoes for something. On my word, I've a great mind to march you two down to Scotland Yard.'

'If the gentleman's a friend o' yours, per'aps—' said the policeman who had given the blow, and was reflecting on the consequences.

'Perhaps you'd like me to go away and say nothing about it,' I said. Then there hove into view the figure of Constable Dempsey, glittering in his oil-skins, and an angel of light to me. I had known him for months; he was an esteemed friend of mine, and we used to talk together in the early mornings. The fool seeks to ingratiate himself with Princes and Ministers; and courts and cabinets leave him to perish miserably. The wise man makes allies among the police and the hansoms, so that his friends spring up from the round-house and the cab-rank, and even his offences become triumphal processions.

'Dempsey,' said I, 'have the police been on strike again? They've put some things on duty at St Clement Danes that want to take me to Bow Street for garrotting.'

'Lor, sir!' said Dempsey indignantly.

'Tell them I'm not a garrotter, nor a thief. It's simply disgraceful that a gentleman can't walk down the Strand without being man-handled by these roughs. One of them has done his best to kill my friend here; and I'm taking the body home. Speak for me, Demspey.'

There was no time for the much misrepresented policemen to say a word. Dempsey spoke to them in language calculated to frighten. They tried to explain, but Dempsey launched into a glowing catalogue of my virtues as noted by gas in the early hours. 'And,' he concluded vehemently, ''e writes for the papers, too. How'd *you* like to be written for in the papers—in verse, too, which is 'is 'abit. You leave 'im alone. 'Im an' me have been friends for months.'

'What about the dead man?' said the policeman who had not given the blow.

'I'll tell you,' I said relenting, and to the three policemen under the lights of Charing Cross assembled, I recounted faithfully and at length the adventures of the night, beginning with the *Breslau* and ending at St Clement Danes. I described the sinful old ruffian in the ambulance in words that made him wriggle where he lay, and never since the Metropolitan Police was founded did three policemen laugh as those three laughed. The Strand echoed to it, and the unclean birds of the night stood and wondered.

'Oh lor'!' said Dempsey, wiping his eyes, 'I'd ha' given anything to see that old man runnin' about with a wet blanket an' all! Excuse me, sir, but you ought to get took up every night for to make us 'appy.' He dissolved into fresh guffaws.

There was a clinking of silver and the two policemen of St Clement Danes hurried back to their beats, laughing as they ran.

'Take 'im to Charing Cross,' said Demspey between shouts. 'They'll send the ambulance back in the morning.'

'Laddie, ye've misca'ed me shameful names, but I'm o'er old to go to a hospital. Dinna desert me, laddie. Tak me home to my wife,' said the voice in the ambulance.

'He's none so bad. 'Is wife'll comb 'is hair for 'im proper,' said Dempsey, who was a married man.

'Where d'you live?' I demanded.

'Brugglesmith,' was the answer.

'What's that?' I said to Dempsey, more skilled than I in portmanteau-words.

'Brook Green, 'Ammersmith,'° Dempsey translated promptly.

'Of course,' I said. 'That's just the sort of place he would choose to live in. I only wonder that it was not Kew.'

'Are you going to wheel him 'ome, sir?' said Dempsey.

'I'd wheel him home if he lived in—Paradise. He's not going to get out of this ambulance while I'm here. He'd drag me into a murder for tuppence.'

'Then strap 'im up an' make sure,' said Dempsey, and he deftly buckled two straps that hung by the side of the ambulance over the man's body. Brugglesmith—I know not his other name—was sleeping deeply. He even smiled in his sleep.

'That's all right,' said Dempsey, and I moved off, wheeling my devil's perambulator before me. Trafalgar Square was empty except for the few that slept in the open. One of these wretches ranged alongside and begged for money, asserting that he had been a gentleman once.

'So have I,' I said. 'That was long ago. I'll give you a shilling if you'll help me push this thing.'

'Is it a murder?' said the vagabond, shrinking back. 'I've not got to *that* yet.'

'No, it's going to be one,' I answered. 'I have.'

The man slunk back into the darkness and I pressed on, through Cockspur Street, and up to Piccadilly Circus, wondering what I should do with my treasure. All London was asleep, and I had only this drunken carcase to bear me company. It was silent—silent as chaste Piccadilly. A young man of my acquaintance came out of a pink brick club as I passed. A faded carnation drooped from his button-hole; he had been playing cards, and was walking home before the dawn, when he overtook me.

'What are you doing?' he said.

I was far beyond any feeling of shame. 'It's for a bet,' said I. 'Come and help.'

'Laddie, who's yon?' said the voice beneath the hood.

'Good Lord!' said the young man, leaping across the pavement. Perhaps card-losses had told on his nerves. Mine were steel that night.

'The Lord, The Lord?' the passionless, incurious voice went on. 'Dinna be profane, laddie. He'll come in His ain good time.'

The young man looked at me with horror.

'It's all part of the bet,' I answered. 'Do come and push!'

'W—where are you going to?' said he.

'Brugglesmith,' said the voice within. 'Laddie, d'ye ken my wife?'

'No,' said I.

'Well, she's just a tremenjus wumman. Laddie, I want a drink. Knock at one o' those braw houses, laddie, an'—an'—ye may kiss the girrl for your pains.'

'Lie still, or I'll gag you,' I said, savagely.

The young man with the carnation crossed to the other side of Piccadilly, and hailed the only hansom visible for miles. What he thought I cannot tell.

I pressed on—wheeling, eternally wheeling—to Brook Green, Hammersmith. There I would abandon Brugglesmith to the gods of that desolate land. We had been through so much together that I could not leave him bound in the street. Besides, he would call after me, and oh! it is a shameful thing to hear one's name ringing down the emptiness of London in the dawn.

So I went on, pass Apsley House,° even to the coffee-stall, but there was no coffee for Brugglesmith. And into Knightsbridge—respectable Knightsbridge—I wheeled my burden, the body of Brugglesmith.

'Laddie, what are ye going to do wi' me?' he said when opposite the barracks.

'Kill you,' I said briefly, 'or hand you over to your wife. Be quiet.'

He would not obey. He talked incessantly—sliding in one sentence from clear cut dialect to wild and drunken jumble. At the Albert Hall he said that I was the 'Hattle Gardle buggle,' which I apprehend is the Hatton Garden burglar.° At Kensington High Street he loved me as a son, but when my weary legs came to the Addison Road Bridge he implored me with tears to unloose the straps and to fight against the sin of vanity. No man molested us. It was as though a bar had been set between myself and all humanity till I had cleared my account with Brugglesmith. The glimmering of light grew in the sky; the cloudy brown of the wood pavement turned to heather-purple; I made no doubt that I should be allowed vengeance on Brugglesmith ere the evening.

At Hammersmith the heavens were steel-gray, and the day came weeping. All the tides of the sadness of an unprofitable dawning poured into the soul of Brugglesmith. He wept bitterly, because the puddles looked cold and houseless. I entered a half-waked public-house—in evening dress and an ulster, I marched to the bar—and got him whisky on condition that he should cease kicking at the canvas of the ambulance. Then he wept more bitterly, for that he had ever been associated with me, and so seduced into stealing the *Breslau's* dinghy.

The day was white and wan when I reached my long journey's end, and, putting back the hood, bade Brugglesmith declare where he lived. His eyes wandered disconsolately round the red and gray houses till they fell on a villa in whose garden stood a staggering board with the legend 'To Let.' It needed only this to break him down utterly, and with the breakage fled his fine fluency in his guttural northern tongue; for liquor levels all.

'Olely lil while,' he sobbed. 'Olely lil while. Home—falmy—besht of falmies—wife too—*you* dole know my wife! Left them all a lill while ago. Now everything's sold—all sold. Wife—falmy—all sold. Lemmegellup!'

I unbuckled the straps cautiously. Brugglesmith rolled off his resting-place and staggered to the house.

'Wattle I do?' he said.

Then I understood the baser depths in the mind of Mephistopheles.

'Ring,' I said; 'perhaps they are in the attic or the cellar.'

'You do' know my wife. She shleeps on soful in the dorlin' room, waiting meculhome. *You* do' know my wife.'

He took off his boots, covered them with his tall hat, and craftily as a Red Indian picked his way up the garden path and smote the bell marked 'Visitors' a severe blow with the clenched fist.

'Bell sole too. Sole electick bell! Wassor bell this? I can't riggle bell,' he moaned despairingly.

'You pull it—pull it hard,' I repeated, keeping a wary eye down the road. Vengeance was coming and I desired no witnesses.

'Yes, I'll pull it hard.' He slapped his forehead with inspiration. 'I'll pull it out.'

Leaning back he grasped the knob with both hands and pulled. A wild ringing in the kitchen was his answer. Spitting on his hands he pulled with renewed strength, and shouted for his wife. Then he bent his ear to the knob, shook his head, drew out an enormous yellow and red handkerchief, tied it round the knob, turned his back to the door, and pulled over his shoulder.

Either the handkerchief or the wire, it seemed to me, was bound to give way. But I had forgotten the bell. Something cracked in the kitchen, and Brugglesmith moved slowly down the doorsteps, pulling valiantly. Three feet of wire followed him.

'Pull, oh pull!' I cried. 'It's coming now.'

'Qui' ri',' he said. '*I'll* riggle bell.'

He bowed forward, the wire creaking and straining behind him, the bell-knob clasped to his bosom, and from the noises within I fancied the bell was taking away with it half the woodwork of the kitchen and all the basement banisters.°

'Get a purchase on her,' I shouted, and he spun round, lapping that good copper wire about him. I opened the garden gate politely, and he passed out, spinning his own cocoon. Still the bell came up, hand over hand, and still the wire held fast. He was in the middle of the road now, whirling like an impaled cockchafer, and shouting madly for his wife and family. There he met with the ambulance, the bell within the house gave one last peal, and bounded from the far end of the hall to the inner side of the hall-door, where it stayed fast. So did not my friend Brugglesmith. He fell upon his face, embracing the ambulance as he did so, and the two turned over together in the toils of the never-sufficiently-to-be-advertised copper wire.

'Laddie,' he gasped, his speech returning, 'have I a legal remedy?'

'I will go and look for one,' I said, and, departing, found two policemen. These I told that daylight had surprised a burglar in Brook Green while he was engaged in stealing lead from an empty house. Perhaps they had better take care of that bootless thief. He seemed to be in difficulties.

I led the way to the spot, and behold! in the splendour of the dawning, the ambulance, wheels uppermost, was walking down the muddy road on two stockinged feet—was shuffling to and fro in a quarter of a circle whose radius was copper wire, and whose centre was the bell-plate of the empty house.

Next to the amazing ingenuity with which Brugglesmith had contrived to lash himself under the ambulance, the thing that appeared to impress the constables most was the fact of the St Clement Danes ambulance being at Brook Green, Hammersmith.

They even asked me, of all people in the world, whether I knew anything about it!

They extricated him; not without pain and dirt. He explained that he was repelling boarding-attacks by a 'Hattle Gardle buggle' who had sold his house, wife, and family. As to the bell-wire, he offered no explanation, and was borne off shoulder-high between the two policemen. Though his feet were not within six inches of the ground, they paddled swiftly, and I saw that in his magnificent mind he was running—furiously running.

Sometimes I have wondered whether he wished to find me.

'Love-o'-Women'

'A lamentable tale of things
Done long ago, and ill done.'

The horror, the confusion, and the separation of the murderer from his comrades were all over before I came. There remained only on the barrack-square the blood of man calling from the ground.° The hot sun had dried it to a dusky goldbeater-skin° film, cracked lozenge-wise by the heat; and as the wind rose, each lozenge, rising a little, curled up at the edges as if it were a dumb tongue. Then a heavier gust blew all away down wind in grains of dark coloured dust. It was too hot to stand in the sunshine before breakfast. The men were in barracks talking the matter over. A knot of soldiers' wives stood by one of the entrances to the married quarters, while inside a woman shrieked and raved with wicked filthy words.

A quiet and well-conducted sergeant had shot down, in broad daylight just after early parade, one of his own corporals, had then returned to barracks and sat on a cot till the guard came for him. He would, therefore, in due time be handed over to the High Court for trial. Further, but this he could hardly have considered in his scheme of revenge, he would horribly upset my work; for the reporting of that trial would fall on me without a relief. What that trial would be like I knew even to weariness. There would be the rifle carefully uncleaned, with the fouling marks about breech and muzzle, to be sworn to by half a dozen superfluous privates; there would be heat, reeking heat, till the wet pencil slipped sideways between the fingers; and the punkah would swish and the pleaders would jabber in the verandahs, and his Commanding Officer would put in certificates to the prisoner's moral character, while the jury would pant and the summer uniforms of the witnesses would smell of dye and soaps; and some abject barrack-sweeper would lose his head in cross-examination, and the younger barrister who always defended soldiers' cases for the credit that they never brought him, would say and do wonderful things, and would then quarrel with me because I had not reported him correctly. At the last, for he surely would not be hanged, I might meet the prisoner again, ruling blank account-forms in the Central Jail,° and cheer him with the hope of his being made a warder in the Andamans.°

The Indian Penal Code and its interpreters do not treat murder, under any provocation whatever, in a spirit of jest. Sergeant Raines would be very lucky indeed if he got off with seven years, I thought. He had slept the night upon his wrongs, and killed his man at twenty yards before any talk was possible. That much I knew. Unless, therefore, the case was doctored a little, seven years would be his least; and I fancied it was exceedingly well for Sergeant Raines that he had been liked by his Company.

That same evening—no day is so long as the day of a murder—I met Ortheris with the dogs,° and he plunged defiantly into the middle of the matter. 'I'll be one o' the witnesses,' said he. 'I was in the verandah when Mackie come along. 'E come from Mrs Raines's quarters. Quigley, Parsons, an' Trot, they was in the inside verandah so *they* couldn't 'ave 'eard nothing. Sergeant Raines was in the verandah talkin' to me, an' Mackie 'e come along acrost the square an' 'e sez, "Well," sez 'e, "'ave they pushed your 'elmet off yet, Sergeant?"° 'e sez. An' at that Raines 'e catches 'is breath an' 'e sez, "My Gawd, I can't stand this!" sez 'e, an' 'e picks up my rifle an' shoots Mackie. See?'

'But what were you doing with your rifle in the outer verandah an hour after parade?'

'Cleanin' 'er,' said Ortheris, with the sullen brassy stare that always went with his choicer lies.

He might as well have said that he was dancing naked, for at no time did his rifle need hand or rag on her twenty minutes after parade. Still, the High Court would not know his routine.

'Are you going to stick to that—on the Book?' I asked.

'Yes. Like a bloomin' leech.'

'All right, I don't want to know any more. Only remember that Quigley, Parsons, and Trot couldn't have been where you say without hearing something; and there's nearly certain to be a barrack-sweeper who was knocking about the square at the time. There always is.'

''Twasn't the sweeper. It was the beastie.° 'E's all right.'

Then I knew that there was going to be some spirited doctoring, and I felt sorry for the Government Advocate who would conduct the prosecution.

When the trial came on I pitied him more, for he was always quick to lose his temper and made a personal matter of each lost cause. Raines's young barrister had for once put aside his unslaked and welling passion for alibis and insanity, had forsworn gymnastics and fireworks, and worked soberly for his client. Mercifully the hot weather was yet young, and there had been no flagrant cases of barrack-shootings up to the time; and the jury was a good one, even for an Indian jury, where nine men out of every twelve are accustomed to weighing evidence. Ortheris stood firm and was not shaken by any cross-examination. The one weak point in his tale—the presence of his rifle in the outer verandah—went unchallenged by civilian wisdom, though some of the witnesses could not help smiling. The Government Advocate called for the rope, contending throughout that the murder had been a deliberate one. Time had passed, he argued, for that reflection which comes so naturally to a man whose honour is lost. There was also the Law, ever ready and anxious to right the wrongs of the common soldier if, indeed, wrong had been done. But he doubted much whether there had been any sufficient wrong. Causeless suspicion over-long brooded upon had led, by his theory, to deliberate crime. But his attempts to minimise the motive failed. The most disconnected witness knew—had known for weeks—the causes of offence; and the prisoner, who naturally was the last of all to know, groaned in the dock while he listened. The one question that the trial circled round was whether Raines had fired under sudden and blinding provocation given that very morning; and in the summing-up it was clear that Ortheris's evidence told. He had contrived most artistically to suggest that he personally hated the Sergeant, who had come into the verandah to give him a talking to for insubordination. In a weak moment the Government Advocate asked one question too many. 'Beggin' *your* pardon, sir,' Ortheris replied, ''e was callin' me a dam' impudent little lawyer.' The Court shook. The jury brought it in a killing, but with every provocation and extenuation known to God or man, and the Judge put his hand to his brow before giving sentence,° and the Adam's apple in the prisoner's throat went up and down like mercury pumping before a cyclone.

In consideration of all considerations, from his Commanding Officer's certificate of good conduct to the sure loss of pension, service, and honour, the prisoner would get two years, to be served in India, and—there need be no demonstration in Court. The Government Advocate scowled and picked up his papers; the guard wheeled with a clash, and the prisoner was relaxed to the Secular Arm,° and driven to the jail in a broken-down *ticca-gharri*.°

His guard and some ten or twelve military witnesses, being less important, were ordered to wait till what was officially called the cool of the evening before marching back to cantonments. They gathered together in one of the deep red brick verandahs of a disused lock-up and congratulated Ortheris, who bore his honours modestly. I sent my work into the office and joined them. Ortheris watched the Government Advocate driving off to lunch.

'That's a nasty little bald-'eaded little butcher, that is,' he said. ''E don't please me. 'E's got a colley dog wot do, though. I'm goin' up to Murree° in a week. That dawg'll bring fifteen rupees anywheres.'

'You had better spend ut in Masses,"° said Terence, unbuckling his belt; for he had been on the prisoner's guard, standing helmeted and bolt upright for three long hours.

'Not me,' said Ortheris cheerfully. 'Gawd'll put it down to B Comp'ny's barrick-damages one o' these days. You look strapped, Terence.'

'Faith, I'm not so young as I was. That guard-mountin' wears on the sole av the fut, and this'—he sniffed contemptuously at the brick verandah—'is as hard setting as standin'!'

'Wait a minute. I'll get the cushions out of my cart,' I said.

''Strewth—sofies. We're going it gay,' said Ortheris, as Terence dropped himself section by section on the leather cushions, saying prettily, 'May ye niver want a soft place wheriver you go, an' power to share ut wid a frind. Another for yourself? That's good. It lets me sit longways. Stanley, pass me a pipe. Augrrh! An' that's another man gone all to pieces bekaze av a woman. I must ha' been on forty or fifty prisoners' gyards, first an' last; an' I hate ut new ivry time.'

'Let's see. You were on Losson's, Lancey's, Dugard's, and Stebbins's, that I can remember,' I said.

'Ay, an' before that an' before that—scores av thim,' he answered with a worn smile. ''Tis better to die than to live for them, though. Whin Raines comes out—he'll be changin' his kit at the jail now—he'll think that too. He shud ha' shot himself an' the woman by rights an' made a clean bill av all. Now he's left the woman—she tuk tay wid Dinah° Sunday gone last—an' he's left himself. Mackie's the lucky man.'

'He's probably getting it hot where he is,' I ventured, for I knew something of the dead Corporal's record.

'Be sure av that,' said Terence, spitting over the edge of the verandah. 'But fwhat he'll get there is light marchin'-ordher to fwhat he'd ha' got here if he'd lived.'

'Surely not. He'd have gone on and forgotten—like the others.'

'Did ye know Mackie well, sorr?' said Terence.

'He was on the Pattiala guard of honour° last winter, and I went out shooting with him in an *ekka* for the day, and I found him rather an amusing man.'

'Well, he'll ha' got shut av amusemints, excipt turnin' from wan side to the other, these few years to come. I knew Mackie, an' I've seen too many to be mistuk in the muster av wan man. He might ha' gone on an forgot as you say, sorr, but he was a man wid an educashin, an' he used ut for his schames; an' the same educashin, an' talkin', an' all that made him able to do fwhat he had a mind to wid a woman, that same wud turn back again in the long-run an' tear him alive. I can't say fwhat that I mane to say bekaze I don't know how, but Mackie was the spit an' livin' image av a man that I saw march the same march *all but*; an' 'twas worse for him that he did not come by Mackie's ind. Wait while I remember now. 'Twas whin I was in the Black Tyrone,° an' he was drafted us from Portsmouth; an' fwhat was his misbegotten name? Larry—Larry Tighe ut was; an' wan of the draft said he was a gentleman-ranker,° an' Larry tuk an' three-parts killed him for saying so. An' he was a big man, an' a strong man, an' a handsome man, an' that tells heavy in practice wid some women, but, takin' them by an' large, not wid all. Yet 'twas wid all that Larry dealt —*all*—for he cud put the comether on any woman that trod the green earth av God, an' he knew ut. Like Mackie that's roastin' now, he knew ut, an' niver did he put the comether on any woman save an' excipt for the black shame. 'Tis not me that shud be talkin', dear knows, dear knows, but the most av my mis—misallinces was for pure devilry, an' mighty sorry I have been whin harm came; an' time an' again wid a girl, ay, an' a woman too, for the matter av that, whin I have seen by the eyes av her that I was makin' more throuble than I talked, I have hild off an' let be for the sake av the mother that bore me. But Larry, I'm thinkin', he was suckled by a she-devil, for he never let wan go that came nigh to listen to him. 'Twas his business, as if it might ha' ben sinthry-go. He was a good soldier too. Now there was the Colonel's governess—an' he a privit too!—that was never known in barricks; an' wan av the Major's maids, and she was promised to a man; an' some more outside; an' fwhat ut was amongst *us* we'll never know till Judgement Day. 'Twas the nature av the baste to put the comether on the best av thim—not the prettiest by any manner av manes—but the like av such women as you cud lay your hand on the Book an' swear there was niver thought av foolishness in.

An' for that very reason, mark you, he was niver caught. He came close to ut wanst or twice, but caught he niver was, an' that cost him more at the ind than the beginnin'. He talked to me more than most, bekaze he tould me, barrin' the accident av my educashin, I'd av been the same kind av divil he was. "An' is ut like," he wud say, houldin' his head high—"is ut like that I'd iver be thrapped? For fwhat am I when all's said an' done?" he sez. "A damned privit," sez he. "An' is ut like, think you, that thim I know wud be connect wid a privit like me? Number tin thousand four hundred an' sivin," he sez grinnin'. I knew by the turn av his spache when he was not takin' care to talk rough-shod that he was a gentleman-ranker.

'"I do not undherstan' ut at all," I sez; "but I know," sez I, "that the divil looks out av your eyes, an' I'll have no share wid you. A little fun by way av amusemint where 'twill do no harm, Larry, is right and fair, but I am mistook if 'tis any amusemint to you," I sez.

'"You are much mistook," he sez. "An' I counsel you not to judge your betters."

'"My betthers!" I sez. "God help you, Larry. There's no betther in this; 'tis all bad, as ye will find for yoursilf."

'"You're not like me," he says, tossin' his head.

'"Praise the Saints, I am not," I sez. "Fwhat I have done I have done an' been crool sorry for. Fwhin your time comes," sez I, "ye'll remimber fwhat I say."

'"An' whin that time comes," sez he, "I'll come to you for ghostly° consolation, Father Terence," an' at that he wint off afther some more divil's business—for to get expayrience, he tould me. He was wicked —rank wicked—wicked as all Hell! I'm not construct by nature to go in fear av any man, but, begad, I was afraid av Larry. He'd come in to barricks wid his cap on three hairs,° an' lie on his cot and stare at the ceilin', and now an' again he'd fetch a little laugh, the like av a splash in the bottom av a well, an' by that I knew he was schamin' new wickedness, an' I'd be afraid. All this was long an' long ago, but ut hild me straight—for a while.

'I tould you, did I not, sorr, that I was caressed an' pershuaded to lave the Tyrone on account av a throuble?'

'Something to do with a belt and a man's head wasn't it?' Terence had never given the tale in full.

'It was. Faith, ivry time I go on prisoner's gyard in coort I wondher fwhy I was not where the pris'ner is. But the man I struck tuk it in fair fight, an' he had the good sinse not to die. Considher now, fwhat wud ha' come to the Arrmy if he had! I was enthreated to exchange, an' my Commandin' Orf'cer pled wid me. I wint, not to be disobligin', an' Larry tould me he was powerful sorry to lose me, though fwhat I'd done to make him sorry I do not know. So to the Ould Reg'mint° I came, lavin' Larry to go to the divil his own way, an' niver expectin' to see him again excipt as a shootin'-case in barracks. . . . Who's that quittin' the compound?' Terence's quick eye had caught sight of a white uniform skulking behind the hedge.

'The Sergeant's gone visiting,' said a voice.

'Thin I command here, an' I will have no sneakin' away to the bazar, an' huntin' for you wid a pathrol at midnight. Nalson, for I know ut's you, come back to the verandah.'

Nalson, detected, slunk back to his fellows. There was a grumble that died away in a minute or two, and Terence turning on the other side went on:—

'That was the last I saw av Larry for a while. Exchange is the same as death for not thinkin', an' by token I married Dinah, an' that kept me from remimberin' ould times. Thin we went up to the Front,° an' ut tore my heart in tu to lave Dinah at the Depôt in Pindi.° Consequint, whin I was at the Front I fought circumspectuous till I warrmed up, an' thin I fought double tides. You remember fwhat I tould you in the gyard-gate av the fight at Silver's Theatre?'°

'Wot's that about Silver's Theayter?' said Ortheris quickly, over his shoulder.

'Nothin', little man. A tale that ye know. As I was sayin', afther that fight, us av the Ould Rig'mint an' the Tyrone was all mixed together takin' shtock av the dead, an' av coorse I wint about to find if there was any man that remembered me. The second man I came acrost—an' how I'd missed him in the fight I do not know—was Larry, an' a fine man he looked, but oulder, by reason that he had fair call to be. "Larry," sez I, "how is ut wid you?"

'"Ye're callin' the wrong man," he sez, wid his gentleman's smile, "Larry has been dead these three years. They call him 'Love-o'-Women' now," he sez. By that I knew the ould divil was in him yet, but the ind av a fight is no time for the beginnin' av confession, so we sat down an' talked av times.

'"They tell me you're a married man," he sez, puffin' slow at his poipe. "Are ye happy?"

'"I will be whin I get back to Depôt," I sez. "'Tis a reconnaissance-honeymoon now."

'"I'm married too," he sez, puffin' slow an' more slow, an' stopperin' wid his forefinger.

'"Send you happiness," I sez. "That's the best hearin' for a long time."

'"Are ye av that opinion?" he sez; an' thin he began talkin' av the campaign. The sweat av Silver's Theatre was not dhry upon him an' he was prayin' for more work. I was well contint to lie and listen to the cook-pot lids.

'Whin he got up off the ground he shtaggered a little, an' laned over all twisted.

'"Ye've got more than ye bargained for," I sez. "Take an inventory, Larry. 'Tis like you're hurt."

'He turned round stiff as a ramrod an' damned the eyes av me up an' down for an impartinent Irish-faced ape. If that had been in barracks, I'd ha' stretched him an' no more said; but 'twas at the Front, an' afther such a fight as Silver's Theatre I knew there was no callin' a man to account for his tempers. He might as well ha' kissed me. Aftherwards I was well pleased I kept my fists home. Thin our Captain Crook—Cruik-na-bulleen°—came up. He'd been talkin' to the little orf'cer bhoy av the Tyrone. "We're all cut to windystraws,"° he sez, "but the Tyrone are damned short for noncoms. Go you over there, Mulvaney, an' be Deputy-Sergeant, Corp'ral, Lance, an' everything else ye can lay hands on till I bid you stop."

'I wint over an' tuk hould. There was wan sergeant left standin', an' they'd pay no heed to him. The remnint was me, an' 'twas full time I came. Some I talked to, an' some I did not, but before night the bhoys av the Tryone stud to attention, begad, if I sucked on my poipe above a whishpher. Betune you an' me an' Bobs° I was commandin' the Company, an' that was what Crook had thransferred me for; an' the little orf'cer bhoy knew ut, and I knew ut, but the Comp'ny did not. And *there*, mark you, is the vartue that no money an' no dhrill can buy—the vartue av the ould soldier that knows his orf'cer's work an' does ut for him at the salute!

'Thin the Tyrone, wid the Ould Rig'mint in touch, was sint maraudin' an' prowlin' acrost the hills promishcuous an' onsatisfactory. 'Tis my privit opinion that a gin'ral does not know half his time fwhat to do wid three-quarthers his command. So he shquats on his hunkers an' bids them run round an' round forninst him while he considhers on it. Whin by the process av nature they get sejuced into a big fight that was none av their seekin', he sez: "Obsarve my shuperior janius. I meant ut to come so." We ran round an' about, an' all we got was shootin' into the camp at night, an' rushin' empty *sungars*° wid the long bradawl,° an' bein' hit from behind rocks till we night av the day whin I was confirmed Corp'ril, not actin' Lef'tinant, an' my thoughts was not good to me.

'Ye can ondersthand that afther that night we came to talkin' a dale together, an' bit by bit ut came out fwhat I'd suspicioned. The whole av his carr'in's on an' divilments had come back on him hard, as liquor comes back whin you've been on the dhrink for a wake. All he'd said an' all he'd done, an' only he cud tell how much that was, come back, and there was niver a minut's peace in his sowl. 'Twas the Horrors widout any cause to see, an' yet, an' yet—fwhat am I talkin' av? He'd ha' taken the Horrors wid thankfulness. Beyon' the repentince av the man, an' that was beyon' the nature av man—awful, awful, to behould!—there was more that was worse than any repentince. Av the scores an' scores that he called over in his mind (an' they were drivin' him mad), there was, mark you, wan woman av all, an' she was not his wife, that cut him to the quick av his marrow. 'Twas there he said that he'd thrown away di'monds an' pearls past count, an' thin he'd begin again like a blind *byle*° in an oil-mill, walkin' round and round, to considher (him that was beyond all touch av bein' happy this side hell!) how happy he wud ha' been wid *her*. The more he considhered, the more he'd consate° himself that he'd lost mighty happiness, an' thin he wud work ut all backwards, an' cry that he niver cud ha' been happy anyway.

'Time an' time an' again in camp, on p'rade, ay, an' in action, I've seen that man shut his eyes an' duck his head as ye wud duck to the flicker av a bay'nit. For 'twas thin, he tould me, that the thought av al he'd missed came an' stud forninst him like red-hot irons. For what he'd done wid the others he was sorry, but he did not care; but this wan woman that I've tould of, by the Hilts av God,° she made him pay for all the others twice over! Niver did I know that a man cud enjure such tormint widout his heart crackin' in his ribs, an' I have been'—Terence turned the pipe-stem slowly between his teeth—'I have been in some black cells. All I iver suffered tho' was not to be talked of alongside av *him* . . . an' what could I do? Paternosters was no more than peas on plates° for his sorrows.

'Evenshually we finished our prom'nade acrost the hills, and, thanks to me for the same, there was no casualties an' no glory. The campaign was comin' to an ind, an' all the rig'mints was being drawn together for to be sint back home. Love-o'-Women was mighty sorry bekaze he had no work to do, an' all his time to think in. I've heard that man talkin' to his belt-plate an' his side-arms while he was soldierin' thim, all to prevent himself from thinkin', an' ivry time he got up afther he

was wore out—all excipt Love-o'-Women. That puppy-dog business was mate an' dhrink to him. Begad he cud niver get enough av ut. Me well knowin' that it is just this desultorial campaignin' that kills the best men, an' suspicionin' that if I was cut, the little orf'cer bhoy wid expind all his men in thryin' to get out, I wud lie most powerful doggo whin I heard a shot, an' curl my long legs behind a bowlder, an' run like blazes whin the ground was clear. Faith, if I led the Tyrone in rethreat wanst I led thim forty times! Love-o'-Women wud stay pottin' an' pottin' from behind a rock, and wait till the fire was heaviest, an' thin stand up an' fire man-height clear. He wud lie out in camp too at night, snipin' at the shadows, for he never tuk a mouthful av slape. My commandin' orf'cer—save his little soul!—cud not see the beauty av my strategims, an' whin the Ould Rig'mint crossed us, an' that was wanst a week, he'd throt off to Crook, wid his big blue eyes as round as saucers, an' lay an information against me. I heard thim wanst talkin' through the tent-wall, an' I nearly laughed.

'"He runs—runs like a hare," sez the little orf'cer bhoy. "'Tis demoralisin' my men."

'"Ye damned little fool," sez Crook, laughin', "he's larnin' you your business. Have ye been rushed at night yet?"

'"No," sez that child; wishful he had been.

'"Have you any wounded?" sez Crook.

'"No," he sez. "There was no chanst for that. They follow Mulvaney too quick," he sez.

'"Fwhat more do you want, thin?" sez Crook. "Terence is bloodin' you neat an' handy," he sez. "He knows fwhat you do not, an' that's that there's a time for ivrything. He'll not lead you wrong," he sez, "but I'd give a month's pay to larn fwhat he thinks av you."

'That kept the babe quiet, but Love-o'-Women was pokin' at me for ivrything I did, an' specially my manœuvres.

'"Mr Mulvaney," he sez wan evenin', very contempshus, "you're growin' very *jeldy*° on your feet. Among gentlemen," he sez, "among gentlemen that's called no pretty name."

'"Among privits 'tis different," I sez. "Get back to your tent. I'm sergeant here," I sez.

'There was just enough in the voice av me to tell him he was playin' wid his life betune his teeth. He wint off, an' I noticed that this man that was contempshus set off from the halt wid a shunt as tho' he was bein' kicked behind. That same night there was a Paythan picnic in the hills about, an' firin' into our tents fit to wake the livin' dead. "Lie down all," I sez. "Lie down an' kape still. They'll no more than waste ammunition."

'I heard a man's feet on the ground, an' thin a 'Tini° joinin' in the chorus. I'd been lyin' warm, thinkin' av Dinah an' all, but I crup out wid the bugle for to look round in case there was a rush; an' the 'Tini was flashin' at the fore-ind av the camp, an' the hill near by was fair flickerin' wid long-range fire. Undher the starlight I behild Love-o'-Women settin' on a rock wid his belt and helmet off. He shouted wanst or twice, an' thin I heard him say: "They shud ha' got the range long ago. Maybe they'll fire at the flash." Thin he fired again, an' that dhrew a fresh volley, and the long slugs that they chew in their teeth came floppin' among the rocks like tree-toads av a hot night. "That's better," sez Love-o'-Women. "Oh Lord, how long, how long!"° he sez, an' at that he lit a match an' held ut above his head.

'"Mad," thinks I, "mad as a coot," an' I tuk wan stip forward, an' the nixt I knew was the sole av my boot flappin' like a cavalry gydon° —an' the funny-bone av my toes tinglin'. 'Twas a clane-cut shot—a slug—that niver touched sock or hide, but set me barefut on the rocks. At that I tuk Love-o'-Women by the scruff an' threw him under a bowlder, an' whin I sat down I heard the bullets patterin' on that same good stone.

'"Ye may dhraw your own wicked fire," I sez, shakin' him, "but I'm not goin' to be kilt too."

'"Ye've come too soon," he sez. "Ye've come too soon. In another minute they cudn't ha' missed me. Mother av' God," he sez, "fwhy did ye not lave me be? Now 'tis all to do again" an' he hides his face in his hands.

'"So that's it," I sez, shakin' him again. "That's the manin' av your disobeyin' ordhers."

'"I dare not kill meself," he sez, rockin' to and fro. "My own hand wud not let me die, and there's not a bullet this month past wud touch me. I'm to die slow," he sez. "I'm to die slow. But I'm in hell now," he sez, shriekin' like a woman. "I'm in hell now!"

'"God be good to us all," I sez, for I saw his face. "Will ye tell a man the throuble? If 'tis not murder, maybe we'll mend it yet."

'At that he laughed. "D'you remember fwhat I said in the Tyrone barricks about comin' to you for ghostly consolation. I have not forgot," he sez. "That came back, and the rest av my time is on me now, Terence. I've fought ut off for months an' months, but the liquor will not bite any more. Terence," he sez, "I can't get dhrunk!"

'Thin I knew he spoke the truth about bein' in hell, for whin liquor

does not take hould the sowl av a man is rotten in him. But me bein' such as I was, fwhat could I say to him?

'"Di'monds an' pearls," he begins again. "Di'monds an' pearls I have thrown away wid both hands—an' fwhat have I left? Oh, fwhat have I left?"

'He was shakin' an' tremblin' up against my shouldher, an' the slugs were singin' overhead, an' I was wonderin' whether my little bhoy wud have sinse enough to kape his men quiet through all this firin'.

'"So long as I did not think," sez Love-o'-Women, "so long I did not see—I wud not see, but I can now, what I've lost. The time an' the place," he sez, "an' the very words I said whin ut pleased me to go off alone to hell. But thin, even thin," he sez, wrigglin' tremenjous, "I wud not ha' been happy. There was too much behind av me. How cud I ha' believed her sworn oath—me that have bruk mine again an' again for the sport av seein' thim cry? An' there are the others," he sez. "Oh, what will I do—what will I do?" He rocked back an' forward again, an' I think he was cryin' like wan av the women he talked av.

'The full half of fwhat he said was Brigade Ordhers° to me, but from the rest an' the remnint I suspicioned somethin' av his throuble. 'Twas the judgmint av God had grup the heel av him,° as I tould him 'twould in the Tyrone barricks. The slugs was singin' over our rock more an' more, an' I sez for to divart him: "Let bad alone," I sez. "They'll be tryin' to rush the camp in a minut'."

'I had no more than said that whin a Paythan man crep' up on his belly wid his knife betune his teeth, not twinty yards from us. Love-o'-Women jumped up an' fetched a yell, an' the man saw him an' ran at him (he'd left his rifle under the rock) wid the knife. Love-o'-Women niver turned a hair, but by the Living Power, for I saw ut, a stone twisted under the Paythan man's feet an' he came down full sprawl, an' his knife wint tinkling acrost the rocks! "I tould you I was Cain,"° sez Love-o'-Women. "Fwhat's the use av killin' him? He's an honust man—by compare."

'I was not dishputin' about the morils av Paythans that tide, so I dhropped Love-o'-Women's butt acrost the man's face, an' "Hurry into camp," I sez, "for this may be the first av a rush."

'There was no rush after all, though we waited undher arms to give them a chanst. The Paythan man must ha' come alone for the mischief, an' afther a while Love-o'-Women wint back to his tint wid that quare lurchin' sind-off in his walk that I cud niver understand. Begad, I pitied him, an' the more bekaze he made me think for the rest av the

had been settin' down or wint on from the halt, he'd start wid that kick an' traverse that I tould you of—his legs sprawlin' all ways to wanst. He wud niver go see the docthor, tho' I tould him to be wise. He'd curse me up an' down for my advice; but I knew he was no more a man to be reckoned wid than the little bhoy was a commandin' orf'cer, so I let his tongue run if it aised him.

'Wan day—'twas on the way back—I was walkin' round camp wid him, an' he stopped an' struck ground wid his right fut three or four times doubtful. "Fwhat is ut?" I sez. "Is that ground?" sez he; an' while I was thinkin' his mind was goin', up comes the docthor, who'd been anatomisin' a dead bullock. Love-o'-Women starts to go on quick, an' lands me a kick on the knee while his legs was gettin' into marchin' ordher.

'"Hould on there," sez the docthor; an' Love-o'-Women's face, that was lined like a gridiron, turns red as brick.

'"'Tention," says the docthor; an' Love-o'-Women stud so. "Now shut your eyes," sez the docthor. "No, ye must not hould by your comrade."

'"'Tis all up," sez Love-o'-Women, thrying to smile. "I'd fall, docthor, an' you know ut."

'"Fall?" I sez. "Fall at attention wid your eyes shut! Fwhat do you mane?"

'"The docthor knows," he sez. "I've hild up as long as I can, but begad I'm glad 'tis all done. But I will die slow," he sez, "I will die very slow."

'I cud see by the docthor's face that he was mortial sorry for the man, an' he ordered him to hospital. We wint back together, an' I was dumb-struck. Love-o'-Women was cripplin' and crumblin' at ivry step. He walked wid a hand on my shoulder all slued sideways, an' his right leg swingin' like a lame camel. Me not knowin' more than the dead fwhat ailed him, 'twas just as though the docthor's word had done ut all—as if Love-o'-Women had but been waitin' for the word to let go.

'In hospital he sez somethin' to the docthor that I could not catch.

'"Holy Shmoke!" sez the docthor, "an' who are you to be givin' names to your diseases? 'Tis agin all the reg'lations."

'"I'll not be a privit much longer," sez Love-o'-Women in his gentleman's voice, an' the docthor jumped.

'"Thrate me as a study, Doctor Lowndes," he sez; an' that was the first time I'd iver heard a docthor called his name.

'"Good-bye, Terence," sez Love-o'-Women. "'Tis a dead man I

am widout the pleasure av dyin'. You'll come an' set wid me sometimes for the peace av my sowl."

'Now I had been minded for to ask Crook to take me back to the Ould Rig'mint; the fightin' was over, an' I was wore out wid the ways av the bhoys in the Tyrone; but I shifted my will, an' hild on, and wint to set wid Love-o'-Women in the hospital. As I have said, sorr, the man bruk all to little pieces under my hand. How long he had hild up an' forced himself fit to march I cannot tell, but in hospital but two days later he was such as I hardly knew. I shuk hands wid him, an' his grip was fair strong, but his hands wint all ways to wanst, an' he cud not button his tunic.

'"I'll take long an' long to die yet," he sez, "for the wages av sin they're like interest in the rig'mintal savin's-bank—sure, but a damned long time bein' paid."

'The docthor sez to me, quiet one day, "Has Tighe there anythin' on his mind?" he sez. "He's burnin' himself out."

'"How shud I know, sorr?" I sez, as innocint as putty.

'"They call him Love-o'-Women in the Tyrone, do they not?" he sez. "I was a fool to ask. Be wid him all you can. He's houldin' on to your strength."

'"But fwhat ails him, docthor?" I sez.

'"They call ut Locomotus attacks us,"° he sez, "bekaze," sez he, "ut attacks us like a locomotive, if ye know fwhat that manes. An' ut comes," sez he, lookin' at me, "ut comes from bein' called Love-o'-Women."

'"You're jokin', docthor," I sez.

'"Jokin'!" sez he. "If iver you feel that you've got a felt sole in your boot instid av a Government bull's-wool,° come to me," he sez, "an' I'll show you whether 'tis a joke."

'You would not belave ut, sorr, but that, an' seein' Love-o'-Women overtuk widout warnin', put the cowld fear av Attacks us on me so strong that for a week an' more I was kickin' my toes against stones an' stumps for the pleasure av feelin' thim hurt.

'An' Love-o'-Women lay in the cot (he might have gone down wid the wounded before an' before, but he asked to stay wid me), and fwhat there was in his mind had full swing at him night an' day an' ivry hour av the day an' the night, and he shrivelled like beef-rations in a hot sun, an' his eyes was like owls' eyes, an' his hands was mut'nous.

'They was gettin' the rig'mints away wan by wan, the campaign bein' inded, but as ushuil they was behavin' as if niver a rig'mint had been moved before in the mem'ry av man. Now, fwhy is that, sorr? There's fightin', in an' out, nine months av the twelve somewhere in the army. There has been—for years an' years an' years; an' I wud ha' thought they'd begin to get the hang av providin' for throops. But no! Ivry time 'tis like a girls' school meetin' a big red bull whin they're goin' to church; an' "Mother av God," sez the Commissariat an' the Railways an' the Barrick-masters, "fwhat will we do now?" The ordhers came to us av the Tyrone an' the Ould Rig'mint an' half a dozen more to go down, an' there the ordhers stopped dumb. We wint down, by the special grace av God—down the Khaiber anyways. There was sick wid us, an' I'm thinkin' that some av thim was jolted to death in the doolies,° but they was anxious to be kilt so if they cud get to Peshawur alive the sooner. I walked by Love-o'-Women—there was no marchin', an' Love-o'-Women was not in a stew to get on. "If I'd only ha' died up there," sez he through the dooli-curtains, an' thin he'd twist up his eyes an' duck his head for the thoughts that come an' raked him.

'Dinah was in Depôt at Pindi, but I wint circumspectuous, for well I knew 'tis just at the rump-ind av all things that his luck turns on a man. By token I had seen a dhriver of a batthery goin' by at a trot singin' "Home, swate home" at the top av his shout, and takin' no heed to his bridle-hand—I had seen that man dhrop under the gun in the middle of a word, and come out by the limber like—like a frog on a pavestone. No. I wud *not* hurry, though, God knows, my heart was all in Pindi. Love-o'-Women saw fwhat was in my mind, an' "Go on, Terence," he sez, "I know fwhat's waitin' for you." "I will not," I sez. "'Twill kape a little yet."

'Ye know the turn of the pass forninst Jumrood° and the nine-mile road on the flat to Peshawur? All Peshawur was along that road day and night waitin' for frinds—men, women, childer, and bands. Some av the throops was camped round Jumrood, an' some wint on to Peshawur to get away down to their cantonmints. We came through in the early mornin', havin' been awake the night through, and we dhruv sheer into the middle av the mess. Mother av Glory, will I iver forget that comin' back? The light was not fair lifted, and the first we heard was "For 'tis my delight av a shiny night,"° frum a band that thought we was the second four comp'nies av the Lincolnshire. At that we was forced to sind them a yell to say who we was, an' thin up wint "The wearin' av the Green."° It made me crawl all up my backbone, not havin' taken my brequist.° Then right smash into our rear came fwhat was left av the Jock Elliott's°—wid four pipers an' not half a kilt among thim, playin' for the dear life, an' swingin' their rumps like buck-rabbits, an' a native rig'mint shriekin' blue murther. Ye niver heard the like! There was men cryin' like women that did—an' faith I do not blame them! Fwhat bruk me down was the Lancers' Band—shinin' an' spick like angils, wid the ould dhrum-horse at the head° an' the silver kettle-dhrums an' all an' all, waitin' for their men that was behind us. They shtruck up the Cavalry Canter;° an' begad those poor ghosts that had not a sound fut in a throop they answered to ut; the men rockin' in their saddles. We thried to cheer them as they wint by, but ut came out like a big gruntin' cough, so there must have been many that was feelin' like me. Oh, but I'm forgettin'! The Fly-by-Nights° was waitin' for their second battalion, an' whin ut came out, there was the Colonel's horse led at the head—saddle-empty. The men fair worshipped him, an' he'd died at Ali Musjid° on the road down. They waited till the remnint av the battalion was up, and thin—clane against ordhers, for who wanted *that* chune that day?—they wint back to Peshawur slow-time an' tearin' the bowils out av ivry man that heard, wid "The Dead March."° Right acrost our line they wint, an' ye know their uniforms are as black as the Sweeps, crawlin' past like the dead, an' the other bands damnin' them to let be.

'Little they cared. The carpse was wid them, an' they'd ha taken ut so through a Coronation. Our ordhers was to go into Peshawur, an' we wint hot-fut past The Fly-by-Nights, not singin', to lave that chune behind us. That was how we tuk the road of the other corps.

''Twas ringin' in my ears still whin I felt in the bones of me that Dinah was comin', an' I heard a shout, an' thin I saw a horse an' a tattoo latherin' down the road, hell-to-shplit, under women. I knew—I knew! Wan was the Tyrone Colonel's wife—ould Beeker's lady—her gray hair flyin' an' her fat round carkiss rowlin' in the saddle, an' the other was Dinah, that shud ha' been at Pindi. The Colonel's lady she charged the head av our column like a stone wall, an' she all but knocked Beeker off his horse, throwin' her arms round his neck an' blubberin', "Me bhoy! Me bhoy!" an' Dinah wheeled left an' came down our flank, an' I let a yell that had suffered inside av me for months and—Dinah came! Will I iver forget that while I live! She'd come on pass from Pindi, an' the Colonel's lady had lint her the tattoo. They'd been huggin' an' cryin' in each other's arms all the long night.

'So she walked along wid her hand in mine, asking forty questions to wanst, an' beggin' me on the Virgin to make oath that there was no a bullet consaled in me, unbeknownst somewhere, an' thin I remembered Love-o'-Women. He was watchin' us, an' his face was like the face av a divil that has been cooked too long. I did not wish Dinah to see ut, for whin a woman's runnin' over with happiness she's like to be touched, for harm afterwards, by the laste little thing in life. So I dhrew the curtain, an' Love-o'-Women lay back and groaned.

'Whin we marched into Peshawur Dinah wint to barracks to wait for me, an', me feelin' so rich that tide, I wint on to take Love-o'-Women to hospital. It was the last I cud do, an' to save him the dust an' the smother I turned the dooli-men down a road well clear av the rest av the throops, an' we wint along, me talkin' through the curtains. Av a sudden I heard him say:

'"Let me look. For the mercy av Hiven, let me look." I had been so tuk up wid gettin' him out av the dust an' thinkin' av Dinah that I had not kept my eyes about me. There was a woman ridin' a little behind av us; an', talkin' ut over wid Dinah afterwards, that same woman must ha' rid out far on the Jumrood road. Dinah said that she had been hoverin' like a kite on the left flank av the columns.

'I halted the dooli to set the curtains, an' she rode by, walkin' pace, an' Love-o'-Women's eyes wint afther her as if he wud fair haul her down from the saddle.

'"Follow there," was all he sez, but I niver heard a man speak in that voice before or since; an' I knew by those two wan words an' the look in his face that she was Di'monds-an'-Pearls that he'd talked av in his disthresses.

'We followed till she turned into the gate av a little house that stud near the Edwardes' Gate. There was two girls in the verandah, an' they ran in whin they saw us. Faith, at long eye-range it did not take me a wink to see fwhat kind av house ut was. The throops bein' there an' all, there was three or four such; but aftherwards the polis bade thim go. At the verandah Love-o'-Women sez, catchin' his breath, "Stop here," an' thin, an' thin, wid a grunt that must ha' tore the heart up from his stomick, he swung himself out av the dooli, an' my troth he stud up on his feet wid the sweat pourin' down his face! If Mackie was to walk in here now I'd be less tuk back than I was thin. Where he'd dhrawn his power from, God knows—or the Divil—but 'twas a dead man walkin' in the sun, wid the face av a dead man and the breath av a dead man, hild up by the Power, an' the legs an' the arms av the carpse obeyin' ordhers.

'The woman stud in the verandah. She'd been a beauty too, though her eyes was sunk in her head, an' she looked Love-o'-Women up an' down terrible. "An'," she sez, kicking back the tail av her habit,—"An'," she sez, "fwhat are you doin' *here*, married man?"

'Love-o'-Women said nothin', but a little froth came to his lips, an' he wiped ut off wid his hand an' looked at her an' the paint on her, an' looked, an' looked, an' looked.

'"An' yet," she sez, wid a laugh. (Did you hear Raines' wife laugh whin Mackie died? Ye did not? Well for you.) "An' yet," she sez, "who but you have betther right," sez she. "You taught me the road. You showed me the way," she sez. "Ay, look," she sez, "for 'tis your work; you that tould me—d'you remimber it?—that a woman who was false to wan man cud be false to two. I have been that," she sez, "that an' more, for you always said I was a quick learner, Ellis. Look well," she sez, "for it is me that you called your wife in the sight av God long since." An' she laughed.

'Love-o'-Women stud still in the sun widout answerin'. Thin he groaned an coughed to wanst, an' I thought 'twas the death-rattle, but he niver tuk his eyes off her face, not for a blink. Ye cud ha' put her eyelashes through the flies av an E. P. tent, they were so long.

'"Fwhat do you do here?" she sez, word by word, "that have taken away my joy in my man this five years gone—that have broken my rest an' killed my body an' damned my soul for the sake av seein' how 'twas done. Did your expayrience aftherwards bring you acrost any woman that give you more than I did? Wud I not ha' died for you, an' wid you, Ellis? Ye know that, man! If iver your lyin' soul saw truth in uts life ye know that."

'An' Love-o'-Women lifted up his head and said, "I knew," an' that was all. While she was spakin' the Power hild him up parade-set in the sun, an' the sweat dhripped undher his helmet. 'Twas more an' more throuble for him to talk, an' his mouth was running twistways.

'"Fwhat do you do *here*?" she sez, an' her voice wint up. 'Twas like bells tollin' before. "Time was whin you were quick enough wid your words,—you that talked me down to hell. Are ye dumb now?" An' Love-o'-Women got his tongue, an' sez simple, like a little child, "May I come in?" he sez.

'"The house is open day an' night," she sez, wid a laugh; an' Love-o'-Women ducked his head an' hild up his hand as tho' he was gyardin'. The Power was on him still—it hild him up still, for, by my sowl, as I'll never save ut, he walked up the verandah steps that had been a livin' carpse in hospital for a month!

'"An' now?" she sez, lookin' at him; an' the red paint stud lone on the white av her face like a bull's-eye on a target.

'He lifted up his eyes, slow an' very slow, an' he looked at her long an' very long, an' he tuk his spache betune his teeth wid a wrench that shuk him.

'"I'm dyin', Aigypt—dyin'," he sez. Ay, those were his words, for I remimber the name he called her. He was turnin' the death-colour, but his eyes niver rowled. They were set—set on her. Widout word or warnin' she opened her arms full stretch, an' "Here!" she sez. (Oh, fwhat a golden mericle av a voice ut was!) "Die here!" she sez; an Love-o'-Women dhropped forward, an' she hild him up, for she was a fine big woman.

'I had no time to turn, bekaze that minut I heard the sowl quit him —tore out in the death-rattle—an' she laid him back in a long chair, an she sez to me, "Misther soldier," she sez, "will ye not wait an' talk to wan av the girls? This sun's too much for him."

'Well I knew there was no sun he'd iver see, but I cud not spake, so I wint away wid the empty dooli to find the docthor. He'd been breakfastin' an' lunchin' iver since we'd come in, an' he was full as a tick.

'"Faith, ye've got dhrunk mighty soon," he sez, whin I'd tould him, "to see that man walk. Barrin' a puff or two av life, he was a carpse before we left Jumrood. I've a great mind," he sez, "to confine you."

'"There's a dale av liquor runnin' about, docthor," I sez, solemn as a hard-boiled egg. "Maybe 'tis so; but will ye not come an' see the carpse at the house?"

'"'Tis dishgraceful," he sez, "that I would be expected to go to a place like that. Was she a pretty woman?" he sez, an' at that he set off double-quick.

'I cud see that the two was in the verandah where I'd left them, an' I knew by the hang av her head an' the noise av the crows fwhat had happened. 'Twas the first and the last time that I'd iver known woman to use the pistol. They fear the shot as a rule, but Di'monds-an'-Pearls she did not—she did not.

'The docthor touched the long black hair av her head ('twas all loose upon Love-o'-Women's tunic), an' that cleared the liquor out av him. He stud considherin' a long time, his hands in his pockets, an' at last he sez to me, "Here's a double death from naturil causes, most naturil causes; an' in the present state av affairs the rig'mint will be thankful for wan grave the less to dig. *Issiwasti*,"° he sez. "*Issiwasti*, Privit Mulvaney, these two will be buried together in the Civil Cemet'ry at my expinse; an' may the good God," he sez, "make it so much for me whin my time comes. Go you to your wife," he sez. "Go an' be happy. I'll see to this all."

'I left him still considherin'. They was buried in the Civil Cemet'ry together, wid a Church av England service. There was too many buryin's thin to ask questions, an' the docthor—he ran away wid Major—Major Van Dyce's lady that year—he saw to ut all. Fwhat the right an' the wrong av Love-o'-Women an' Di'monds-an'-Pearls was I niver knew, an' I will niver know; but I've tould ut as I came acrost ut—here an' there in little pieces. *So*, being fwhat I am, an' knowin' fwhat I know, that's fwhy I say in this shootin'-case here, Mackie that's dead an' in hell is the lucky man. There are times, sorr, whin 'tis better for the man to die than to live, an' by consequince forty million times betther for the woman.'

'H'up there!' said Ortheris. 'It's time to go.'

The witnesses and guard formed up in the thick white dust of the parched twilight and swung off, marching easy and whistling. Down the road to the green by the church I could hear Ortheris, the black Book-lie still uncleansed on his lips, setting, with a fine sense of the fitness of things, the shrill quickstep that runs—

'Oh, do not despise the advice of the wise,
Learn wisdom from those that are older,
And don't try for things that are out of your reach—
An' that's what the Girl told the Soldier!
Soldier! soldier!
Oh, that's what the Girl told the Soldier!'[10]

From THE DAY'S WORK (1898)

The Bridge-Builders

The least that Findlayson, of the Public Works Department, expected was a C.I.E.; he dreamed of a C.S.I.:° indeed his friends told him that he deserved more. For three years he had endured heat and cold, disappointment, discomfort, danger, and disease, with responsibility almost too heavy for one pair of shoulders; and day by day, through that time, the great Kashi Bridge over the Ganges° had grown under his charge. Now, in less than three months, if all went well, His Excellency the Viceroy would open the bridge in state, an archbishop would bless it, the first train-load of soldiers would come over it, and there would be speeches.

Findlayson, C.E.,° sat in his trolley on a construction-line that ran along one of the main revetments—the huge stone-faced banks that flared away north and south for three miles on either side of the river—and permitted himself to think of the end. With its approaches, his work was one mile and three-quarters in length; a lattice-girder bridge, trussed with the Findlayson truss,° standing on seven-and-twenty brick piers. Each one of those piers was twenty-four feet in diameter, capped with red Agra stone and sunk eighty feet below the shifting sand of the Ganges' bed. Above them ran the railway-line fifteen feet broad; above that, again, a cart-road of eighteen feet, flanked with footpaths. At either end rose towers of red brick, loopholed for musketry and pierced for big guns, and the ramp of the road was being pushed forward to their haunches. The raw earth-ends were crawling and alive with hundreds upon hundreds of tiny asses climbing out of the yawning borrow-pit° below with sackfuls of stuff; and the hot afternoon air was filled with the noise of hooves, the rattle of the drivers' sticks, and the swish and roll-down of the dirt. The river was very low, and on the dazzling white sand between the three centre piers stood squat cribs of railway-sleepers, filled within and daubed without with mud, to support the last of the girders as those were riveted up. In the little deep water left by the drought, an overhead-crane travelled to and fro along its spile-pier,° jerking sections of iron into place, snorting and backing and grunting as an elephant grunts in the timber-yard. Riveters by the hundred swarmed about the lattice side-work and the iron roof of the railway-line, hung from invisible staging under the bellies of the girders, clustered round the throats of the piers, and rode on the overhang of the footpath-stanchions; their fire-pots and the spurts of flame that answered each hammer-stroke showing no more than pale yellow in the sun's glare. East and west and north and south the construction-trains rattled and shrieked up and down the embankments, the piled trucks of brown and white stone banging behind them till the side-boards were unpinned, and with a roar and a grumble a few thousand tons more material were thrown out to hold the river in place.

Findlayson, C.E., turned on his trolley and looked over the face of the country that he had changed for seven miles around. Looked back on the humming village of five thousand workmen; up-stream and down, along the vista of spurs and sand; across the river to the far piers, lessening in the haze; overhead to the guard-towers—and only he knew how strong those were—and with a sigh of contentment saw that his work was good.° There stood his bridge before him in the sunlight, lacking only a few weeks' work on the girders of the three middle piers—his bridge, raw and ugly as original sin, but *pukka*°—permanent—to endure when all memory of the builder, yea, even of the splendid Findlayson truss, had perished. Practically, the thing was done.

Hitchcock, his assistant, cantered along the line on a little switch-tailed Kabuli pony,° who, through long practice, could have trotted securely over a trestle, and nodded to his chief.

'All but,' said he, with a smile.

'I've been thinking about it,' the senior answered. 'Not half a bad job for two men, is it?'

'One—and a half. 'Gad, what a Cooper's Hill° cub I was when I came on the works!' Hitchcock felt very old in the crowded experiences of the past three years, that had taught him power and responsibility.

'You *were* rather a colt,' said Findlayson. 'I wonder how you'll like going back to office work when this job's over.'

'I shall hate it!' said the young man, and as he went on his eye followed Findlayson's, and he muttered, 'Isn't it damned good?'

'I think we'll go up the service together,' Findlayson said to himself. 'You're too good a youngster to waste on another man. Cub thou wast; assistant thou art. Personal assistant, and at Simla,° thou shalt be, if any credit comes to me out of the business!'

Indeed, the burden of the work had fallen altogether on Findlayson and his assistant, the young man whom he had chosen because of his rawness to break to his own needs. There were labour-contractors by the half-hundred—fitters and riveters, European, borrowed from the railway workshops, with perhaps twenty white and half-caste subordinates to direct, under direction, the bevies of workmen—but none knew better than these two, who trusted each other, how the underlings were not to be trusted. They had been tried many times in sudden crises—by slipping of booms, by breaking of tackle, failure of cranes, and the wrath of the river—but no stress had brought to light any man among them whom Findlayson and Hitchcock would have honoured by working as remorselessly as they worked themselves. Findlayson thought it over from the beginning: the months of office work destroyed at a blow when the Government of India, at the last moment, added two feet to the width of the bridge, under the impression that bridges were cut out of paper, and so brought to ruin at least half an acre of calculations—and Hitchcock, new to disappointment, buried his head in his arms and wept; the heart-breaking delays over the filling of the contracts in England; the futile correspondences hinting at great wealth of commission if one, only one, rather doubtful consignment were passed; the war that followed the refusal; the careful, polite obstruction at the other end that followed the war, till young Hitchcock, putting one month's leave to another month, and borrowing ten days from Findlayson, spent his poor little savings of a year in a wild dash to London, and there, as his own tongue asserted and the later consignments proved, put the Fear of God into a man so great that he feared only Parliament, and said so till Hitchcock wrought with him across his own dinner-table, and—he feared the Kashi Bridge and all who spoke in its name. Then there was the cholera that came in the night to the village by the bridge-works; and after the cholera smote the smallpox. The fever they had always with them. Hitchcock had been appointed a magistrate of the third class with whipping powers,° for the better government of the community, and Findlayson watched him wield his powers temperately, learning what to overlook and what to look after. It was a long, long reverie, and it covered storm, sudden freshets, death in every manner and shape, violent and awful rage against red tape half frenzying a mind that knows it should be busy on other things; drought, sanitation, finance; birth, wedding, burial, and riot in the village of twenty warring castes; argument, expostulation, persuasion, and the blank despair that a man goes to bed upon, thankful that his rifle is all in pieces in the gun-case. Behind everything rose the black frame of the Kashi Bridge—plate by plate, girder by girder, span by span—and each pier of it recalled Hitchcock, the all-round man, who had stood by his chief without failing from the very first to this last.

So the bridge was two men's work—unless one counted Peroo, as Peroo certainly counted himself. He was a Lascar, a Kharva from Bulsar,° familiar with every port between Rockhampton° and London, who had risen to the rank of serang° on the British India boats,° but wearying of routine musters and clean clothes had thrown up the service and gone inland, where men of his calibre were sure of employment. For his knowledge of tackle and the handling of heavy weights, Peroo was worth almost any price he might have chosen to put upon his services; but custom decreed the wage of the overhead-men, and Peroo was not within many silver pieces of his proper value. Neither running water nor extreme heights made him afraid; and, as an ex-serang, he knew how to hold authority. No piece of iron was so big or so badly placed that Peroo could not devise a tackle to lift it—a loose-ended, sagging arrangement, rigged with a scandalous amount of talking, but perfectly equal to the work in hand. It was Peroo who had saved the girder of Number Seven Pier from destruction when the new wire rope jammed in the eye of the crane, and the huge plate tilted in its slings, threatening to slide out sideways. Then the native workmen lost their heads with great shoutings, and Hitchcock's right arm was broken by a falling T-plate, and he buttoned it up in his coat and swooned, and came to and directed for four hours till Peroo, from the top of the crane, reported, 'All's well,' and the plate swung home. There was no one like Peroo, serang, to lash and guy and hold, to control the donkey-engines, to hoist a fallen locomotive craftily out of the borrow-pit into which it had tumbled; to strip and dive, if need be, to see how the concrete blocks round the piers stood the scouring of Mother Gunga,° or to adventure up-stream on a monsoon night and report on the state of the embankment-facings. He would interrupt the field-councils of Findlayson and Hitchcock without fear, till his wonderful English, or his still more wonderful *lingua-franca*, half Portuguese and half Malay, ran out and he was forced to take string and show the knots that he would recommend. He controlled his own gang of tacklemen—mysterious relatives from Kutch Mandvi° gathered month by month and tried to the uttermost. No consideration of family or kin allowed Peroo to keep weak hands or a giddy head on the pay-roll. 'My honour is the honour of this bridge,' he would say to the about-to-be-dismissed. 'What do I care for your honour? Go and work on a steamer. That is all you are fit for.'

The little cluster of huts where he and his gang lived centred round the tattered dwelling of a sea-priest—one who had never set foot on Black Water,° but had been chosen as ghostly counsellor by two generations of sea-rovers, all unaffected by port missions or those creeds which are thrust upon sailors by agencies along Thames' bank. The priest of the Lascars had nothing to do with their caste, or indeed with anything at all. He ate the offerings of his church, and slept and smoked, and slept again, 'for,' said Peroo, who had haled him a thousand miles inland, 'he is a very holy man. He never cares what you eat so long as you do not eat beef, and that is good, because on land we worship Shiva,° we Kharvas; but at sea on the Kumpani's° boats we attend strictly to the orders of the Burra Malum (the first mate), and on this bridge we observe what Finlinson Sahib says.'

Findlayson Sahib had that day given orders to clear the scaffolding from the guard-tower on the right bank, and Peroo with his mates was casting loose and lowering down the bamboo poles and planks as swiftly as ever they had whipped the cargo out of a coaster.

From his trolley he could hear the whistle of the serang's silver pipe° and the creak and clatter of the pulleys. Peroo was standing on the topmost coping of the tower, clad in the blue dungaree of his abandoned service, and as Findlayson motioned to him to be careful, for his was no life to throw away, he gripped the last pole, and, shading his eyes ship-fashion, answered with the long-drawn wail of the fo'c'sle look-out: '*Ham dekhta hai*' ('I am looking out'). Findlayson laughed, and then sighed. It was years since he had seen a steamer, and he was sick for home. As his trolley passed under the tower, Peroo descended by a rope, ape-fashion, and cried: 'It looks well now, Sahib. Our bridge is all but done. What think you Mother Gunga will say when the rail runs over?'

'She has said little so far. It was never Mother Gunga that delayed us.'

'There is always time for her; and none the less there has been delay. Has the Sahib forgotten last autumn's flood, when the stone-boats were sunk without warning—or only a half-day's warning?'

'Yes, but nothing save a big flood could hurt us now. The spurs are holding well on the west bank.'

'Mother Gunga eats great allowances. There is always room for more stone on the revetments. I tell this to the Chota Sahib'°—he meant Hitchcock—'and he laughs.'

'No matter, Peroo. Another year thou wilt be able to build a bridge in thine own fashion.'

The Lascar grinned. 'Then it will not be in this way—with stonework sunk under water, as the *Quetta* was sunk. I like sus-sus-pen-sheen bridges that fly from bank to bank, with one big step, like a gang-plank. Then no water can hurt. When does the Lord Sahib come to open the bridge?'

'In three months, when the weather is cooler.'

'Ho! ho! He is like the Burra Malum. He sleeps below while the work is being done. Then he comes up upon the quarter-deck and touches with his finger, and says: "This is not clean! Dam jiboonwallah!"'°

'But the Lord Sahib does not call me a dam jiboonwallah, Peroo.'

'No, Sahib; but he does not come on deck till the work is all finished. Even the Burra Malum of the *Nerbudda* said once at Tuticorin—'°

'Bah! Go! I am busy.'

'I, also!' said Peroo, with an unshaken countenance. 'May I take the light dinghy now and row along the spurs?'

'To hold them with thy hands? They are, I think, sufficiently heavy.'

'Nay, Sahib. It is thus. At sea, on the Black Water, we have room to be blown up and down without care. Here we have no room at all. Look you, we have put the river into a dock, and run her between stone sills.'

Findlayson smiled at the 'we.'

'We have bitted and bridled her. She is not like the sea, that can beat against a soft beach. She is Mother Gunga—in irons.' His voice fell a little.

'Peroo, thou hast been up and down the world more even than I. Speak true talk, now. How much dost thou in thy heart believe of Mother Gunga?'

'All that our priest says. London is London, Sahib. Sydney is Sydney, and Port Darwin is Port Darwin. Also Mother Gunga is Mother Gunga, and when I come back to her banks I know this and worship. In London I did poojah° to the big temple by the river° for the sake of the God within. . . . Yes, I will not take the cushions in the dinghy.'

Findlayson mounted his horse and trotted to the shed of a bungalow that he shared with his assistant. The place had become home to him in the last three years. He had grilled in the heat, sweated in the rains, and shivered with fever under the rude thatch roof; the limewash beside the door was covered with rough drawings and formulæ, and the sentry-path trodden in the matting of the verandah showed where he had walked alone. There is no eight-hour limit to an engineer's work, and the evening meal with Hitchcock was eaten booted and spurred: over their cigars they listened to the hum of the village as the gangs came up from the river-bed and the lights began to twinkle.

'Peroo has gone up the spurs in your dinghy. He's taken a couple of nephews with him, and he's lolling in the stern like a commodore,' said Hitchcock.

'That's all right. He's got something on his mind. You'd think that ten years in the British India boats would have knocked most of his religion out of him.'

'So it has,' said Hitchcock, chuckling. 'I overheard him the other day in the middle of a most atheistical talk with that fat old *guru*° of theirs. Peroo denied the efficacy of prayer; and wanted the *guru* to go to sea and watch a gale out with him, and see if he could stop a monsoon.'

'All the same, if you carried off his *guru* he'd leave us like a shot. He was yarning away to me about praying to the dome of St Paul's when he was in London.'

'He told me that the first time he went into the engine-room of a steamer, when he was a boy, he prayed to the low-pressure cylinder.'

'Not half a bad thing to pray to, either. He's propitiating his own Gods now, and he wants to know what Mother Gunga will think of a bridge being run across her. Who's there?' A shadow darkened the doorway, and a telegram was put into Hitchcock's hand.

'She ought to be pretty well used to it by this time. Only a *tar*.° It ought to be Ralli's answer about the new rivets. . . . Great Heavens!'° Hitchcock jumped to his feet.

'What is it?' said the senior, and took the form. '*That's* what Mother Gunga thinks, is it,' he said, reading. 'Keep cool, young 'un. We've got all our work cut for us. Let's see. Muir wires, half an hour ago: "*Floods on the Ramgunga.*° *Look out.*" Well, that gives us—one, two—nine and a half for the flood to reach Melipur Ghaut and seven's sixteen and a half to Latodi—say fifteen hours before it comes down to us.'

'Curse that hill-fed sewer of a Ramgunga! Findlayson, this is two months before anything could have been expected, and the left bank is littered up with stuff still. Two full months before the time!'

'That's why it happens. I've only known Indian rivers for five and twenty years, and I don't pretend to understand. Here comes another *tar*'. Findlayson opened the telegram. 'Cockran, this time, from the

Ganges Canal:° "*Heavy rains here. Bad.*" He might have saved the last word. Well, we don't want to know any more. We've got to work the gangs all night and clean up the river-bed. You'll take the east bank and work out to meet me in the middle. Get everything that floats below the bridge: we shall have quite enough river-craft coming down adrift anyhow, without letting the stone-boats ram the piers. What have you got on the east bank that needs looking after?'

'Pontoon, one big pontoon with the overhead crane on it. T'other overhead crane on the mended pontoon, with the cart-road rivets from Twenty to Twenty-three piers—two construction lines, and a turning-spur. The pile-work must take its chance,' said Hitchcock.

'All right. Roll up everything you can lay hands on. We'll give the gang fifteen minutes more to eat their grub.'

Close to the verandah stood a big night-gong, never used except for flood, or fire in the village. Hitchcock had called for a fresh horse, and was off to his side of the bridge when Findlayson took the cloth-bound stick and smote with the rubbing stroke that brings out the full thunder of the metal.

Long before the last rumble ceased every night-gong in the village had taken up the warning. To these were added the hoarse screaming of the conchs° in the little temples; the throbbing of drums and tomtoms' and from the European quarters, where the riveters lived, M'Cartney's bugle, a weapon of offence on Sundays and festivals, brayed desperately, calling to 'Stables.'° Engine after engine toiling home along the spurs after her day's work whistled in answer till the whistles were answered from the far bank. Then the big gong thundered thrice for a sign that it was flood and not fire; conch, drum, and whistle echoed the call, and the village quivered to the sound of bare feet running upon soft earth. The order in all cases was to stand by the day's work and wait instructions. The gangs poured by in the dusk; men stopping to knot a loin-cloth or fasten a sandal; gang-foremen shouting to their subordinates as they ran or paused by the tool-issue sheds for bars and mattocks; locomotives creeping down their tracks wheel-deep in the crowd, till the brown torrent disappeared into the dusk of the river-bed, raced over the pilework, swarmed along the lattices, clustered by the cranes, and stood still, each man in his place.

Then the troubled beating of the gong carried the order to take up everything and bear it beyond high-water mark, and the flare-lamps broke out by the hundred between the webs of dull-iron as the riveters began a night's work racing against the flood that was to come. The girders of the three centre piers—those that stood on the cribs—were all but in position. They needed just as many rivets as could be driven into them, for the flood would assuredly wash out the supports, and the iron-work would settle down on the caps of stone if they were not blocked at the ends. A hundred crowbars strained at the sleepers of the temporary line that fed the unfinished piers. It was heaved up in lengths, loaded into trucks, and backed up the bank beyond flood-level by the groaning locomotives. The tool-sheds on the sands melted away before the attack of shouting armies, and with them went the stacked ranks of Government stores, iron-bound boxes of rivets, pliers, cutters, duplicate parts of the riveting-machines, spare pumps and chains. The big crane would be the last to be shifted, for she was hoisting all the heavy stuff up to the main structure of the bridge. The concrete blocks on the fleet of stone-boats were dropped overside, where there was any depth of water, to guard the piers, and the empty boats themselves were poled under the bridge down-stream. It was here that Peroo's pipe shrilled loudest, for the first stroke of the big gong had brought back the dinghy at racing speed, and Peroo and his people were stripped to the waist, working for the honour and credit which are better than life.

'I knew she would speak,' he cried. '*I* knew, but the telegraph gave us good warning. O sons of unthinkable begetting—children of unspeakable shame—are we here for the look of the thing?' It was two feet of wire rope frayed at the ends, and it did wonders as Peroo leaped from gunnel to gunnel, shouting the language of the sea.

Findlayson was more troubled for the stone-boats than anything else. M'Cartney, with his gangs, was blocking up the ends of the three doubtful spans, but boats adrift, if the flood chanced to be a high one, might endanger the girders; and there was a very fleet in the shrunken channels.

'Get them behind the swell of the guard-tower,' he shouted to Peroo. 'It will be dead-water there; get them below the bridge.'

'*Accha*! [Very good.] *I* know. We are mooring them with wire rope,' was the answer. 'Heh! Listen to the Chota Sahib. He is working hard.'

From across the river came an almost continuous whistling of locomotives, backed by the rumble of stone. Hitchcock at the last minute was spending a few hundred more trucks of Tarakee stone in reinforcing his spurs and embankments.

'The bridge challenges Mother Gunga,' said Peroo, with a laugh. 'But when *she* talks I know whose voice will be the loudest.'

For hours the naked men worked, screaming and shouting under the lights. It was a hot, moonless night; the end of it was darkened by clouds and a sudden squall that made Findlayson very grave.

'She moves!' said Peroo, just before the dawn. 'Mother Gunga is awake! Hear!' He dipped his hand over the side of a boat and the current mumbled on it. A little wave hit the side of a pier with a crisp slap.

'Six hours before her time,' said Findlayson, mopping his forehead savagely. 'Now we can't depend on anything. We'd better clear all hands out of the river-bed.'

Again the big gong beat, and a second time there was the rushing of naked feet on earth and ringing iron; the clatter of tools ceased. In the silence, men heard the dry yawn of water crawling over thirsty sand.

Foreman after foreman shouted to Findlayson, who had posted himself by the guard-tower, that his section of the river-bed had been cleaned out, and when the last voice dropped Findlayson hurried over the bridge till the iron plating of the permanent way gave place to the temporary plank-walk over the three centre piers, and there he met Hitchcock.

''All clear your side?' said Findlayson. The whisper rang in the box of latticework.

'Yes, and the east channel's filling now. We're utterly out of our reckoning. When is this thing down on us?'

'There's no saying. She's filling as fast as she can. Look!' Findlayson pointed to the planks below his feet, where the sand, burned and defiled by months of work, was beginning to whisper and fizz.

'What orders?' said Hitchcock.

'Call the roll—count stores—sit on your hunkers—and pray for the bridge. That's all I can think of. Good-night. Don't risk your life trying to fish out anything that may go down-stream.'

'Oh, I'll be as prudent as you are! 'Night. Heavens, how she's filling! Here's the rain in earnest!' Findlayson picked his way back to his bank, sweeping the last of M'Cartney's riveters before him. The gangs had spread themselves along the embankments, regardless of the cold rain of the dawn, and there they waited for the flood. Only Peroo kept his men together behind the swell of the guard-tower, where the stone-boats lay tied fore and aft with hawsers, wire-rope, and chains.

A shrill wail ran along the line, growing to a yell, half fear and half wonder: the face of the river whitened from bank to bank between the stone facings, and the far-away spurs went out in spouts of foam. Mother Gunga had come bank-high in haste, and a wall of chocolate-coloured water was her messenger. There was a shriek above the roar of the water, the complaint of the spans coming down on their blocks as the cribs were whirled out from under their bellies. The stone-boats groaned and ground each other in the eddy that swung round the abutment, and their clumsy masts rose higher and higher against the dim sky-line.

'Before she was shut between these walls we knew what she would do. Now she is thus cramped God only knows what she will do!' said Peroo, watching the furious turmoil round the guard-tower. 'Ohé! Fight, then! Fight hard, for it is thus that a woman wears herself out.'

But Mother Gunga would not fight as Peroo desired. After the first down-steam plunge there came no more walls of water, but the river lifted herself bodily, as a snake when she drinks in midsummer, plucking and fingering along the revetments, and banking up behind the piers till even Findlayson began to recalculate the strength of his work.

When day came the village gasped. 'Only last night,' men said, turning to each other, 'it was as a town in the river-bed! Look now!'

And they looked and wondered afresh at the deep water, the racing water that licked the throat of the piers. The farther bank was veiled by rain, into which the bridge ran out and vanished; the spurs up-stream were marked by no more than eddies and spoutings, and down-stream the pent river, once freed of her guide-lines, had spread like a sea to the horizon. Then hurried by, rolling in the water, dead men and oxen together, with here and there a patch of thatched roof that melted when it touched a pier.

'Big flood,' said Peroo, and Findlayson nodded. It was as big a flood as he had any wish to watch. His bridge would stand what was upon her now, but not very much more; and if by any of a thousand chances there happened to be a weakness in the embankments, Mother Gunga would carry his honour to the sea with the other raffle.° Worst of all, there was nothing to do except to sit still; and Findlayson sat still under his macintosh till his helmet became pulp° on his head, and his boots were over-ankle in mire. He took no count of time, for the river was marking the hours, inch by inch and foot by foot, along the embankment, and he listened, numb and hungry, to the straining of the stone-boats, the hollow thunder under the piers, and the hundred noises that make the full note of a flood. Once a dripping servant brought him food, but he could not eat; and once he thought that he heard a faint toot from a locomotive across the river, and then he smiled. The bridge's failure would hurt his assistant not a little, but

Hitchcock was a young man with his big work yet to do. For himself the crash meant everything—everything that made a hard life worth the living. They would say, the men of his own profession—he remembered the half-pitying things that he himself had said when Lockhart's big water-works burst and broke down in brick heaps and sludge, and Lockhart's spirit broke in him and he died. He remembered what he himself had said when the Sumao Bridge went out in the big cyclone by the sea;° and most he remembered poor Hartopp's face three weeks later, when the shame had marked it. His bridge was twice the size of Hartopp's, and it carried the Findlayson truss as well as the new pier-shoe—the Findlayson bolted shoe. There were no excuses in his service. Government might listen, perhaps, but his own kind would judge him by his bridge, as that stood or fell. He went over it in his head, plate by plate, span by span, brick by brick, pier by pier, remembering, comparing, estimating, and recalculating, lest there should be any mistake; and through the long hours and through the flights of formulæ that danced and wheeled before him a cold fear would come to pinch his heart. His side of the sum was beyond question; but what man knew Mother Gunga's arithmetic? Even as he was making all sure by the multiplication-table, the river might be scooping pot-holes to the very bottom of any one of those eighty-foot piers that carried his reputation. Again a servant came to him with food, but his mouth was dry, and he could only drink and return to the decimals in his brain. And the river was still rising. Peroo, in a mat shelter-coat, crouched at his feet, watching now his face and now the face of the river, but saying nothing.

At last the Lascar rose and floundered through the mud towards the village, but he was careful to leave an ally to watch the boats.

Presently he returned, most irreverently driving before him the priest of his creed—a fat old man, with a grey beard that whipped the wind with the wet cloth that blew over his shoulder. Never was seen so lamentable a *guru*.

'What good are offerings and little kerosene lamps and dry grain,' shouted Peroo, 'if squatting in the mud is all that thou canst do? Thou hast dealt long with the Gods when they were contented and well-wishing. Now they are angry. Speak to them!'

'What is a man against the wrath of Gods?' whined the priest, cowering as the wind took him. 'Let me go to the temple, and I will pray there.'

'Son of a pig, pray *here!* Is there no return for salt fish and curry powder and dried onions? Call aloud! Tell Mother Gunga we have had enough. Bid her be still for the night. I cannot pray, but I have served in the Kumpani's boats, and when men did not obey my orders I—' A flourish of the wire-rope colt rounded the sentence, and the priest, breaking from his disciple, fled to the village.

'Fat pig!' said Peroo. 'After all that we have done for him! When the flood is down, I will see to it that we get a new *guru*. Finlinson Sahib, it darkens for night now, and since yesterday nothing has been eaten. Be wise, Sahib. No man can endure watching and great thinking on an empty belly. Lie down, Sahib. The river will do what the river will do.'

'The bridge is mine; I cannot leave it.'

'Wilt thou hold it up with thy hands, then?' said Peroo, laughing. 'I was troubled for my boats and sheers° *before* the flood came. Now we are in the hands of the Gods. The Sahib will not eat and lie down? Take these, then. They are meat and good toddy together, and they kill all weariness, besides the fever that follows the rain. I have eaten nothing else today at all.'

He took a small tin tobacco-box from his sodden waist-belt and thrust it into Findlayson's hand, saying, 'Nay, do not be afraid. It is no more than opium—clean Malwa° opium!'

Findlayson shook two or three of the dark-brown pellets into his hand, and hardly knowing what he did, swallowed them. The stuff was at least a good guard against fever—the fever that was creeping upon him out of the wet mud—and he had seen what Peroo could do in the stewing mists of autumn on the strength of a dose from the tin box.

Peroo nodded with bright eyes. 'In a little—in a little the Sahib will find that he thinks well again. I too will—' He dived into his treasure-box, resettled the rain-coat over his head, and squatted down to watch the boats. It was too dark now to see beyond the first pier, and the night seemed to have given the river new strength. Findlayson stood with his chin on his chest, thinking. There was one point about one of the piers—the Seventh—that he had not fully settled in his mind. The figures would not shape themselves to the eye except one by one and at enormous intervals of time. There was a sound, rich and mellow in his ears, like the deepest note of a double-bass—an entrancing sound upon which he pondered for several hours, as it seemed. Then Peroo was at his elbow, shouting that a wire hawser had snapped and the stone-boats were loose. Findlayson saw the fleet open and swing out fanwise to a long-drawn shriek of wire straining across gunnels.

'A tree hit them. They will all go,' cried Peroo. 'The main hawser has parted. What does the Sahib do?'

An immensely complex plan had suddenly flashed into Findlayson's mind. He saw the ropes running from boat to boat in straight lines and angles—each rope a line of white fire. But there was one rope which was the master-rope. He could see that rope. If he could pull it once, it was absolutely and mathematically certain that the disordered fleet would reassemble itself in the backwater behind the guard-tower. But why, he wondered, was Peroo clinging so desperately to his waist as he hastened down the bank? It was necessary to put the Lascar aside, gently and slowly, because it was necessary to save the boats, and, further, to demonstrate the extreme ease of the problem that looked so difficult. And then—but it was of no conceivable importance—a wire rope raced through his hand, burning it, the high bank disappeared, and with it all the slowly dispersing factors of the problem. He was sitting in the rainy darkness—sitting in a boat that spun like a top, and Peroo was standing over him.

'I had forgotten,' said the Lascar slowly, 'that to those fasting and unused the opium is worse than any wine. Those who die in Gunga go to the Gods. Still, I have no desire to present myself before such great ones. Can the Sahib swim?'

'What need? He can fly—fly as swiftly as the wind,' was the thick answer.

'He is mad!' muttered Peroo under his breath. 'And he threw me aside like a bundle of dung-cakes. Well, he will not know his death. The boat cannot live an hour here even if she strike nothing. It is not good to look at death with a clear eye.'

He refreshed himself again from the tin box, squatted down in the bows of the reeling, pegged, and stitched craft,° staring through the mist at the nothing that was there. A warm drowsiness crept over Findlayson, the Chief Engineer, whose duty was with his bridge. The heavy raindrops struck him with a thousand tingling little thrills, and the weight of all time since time was made hung heavy on his eyelids. He thought and perceived that he was perfectly secure, for the water was so solid that a man could surely step out upon it, and, standing still with his legs apart to keep his balance—this was the most important point—would be borne with great and easy speed to the shore. But yet a better plan came to him. It needed only an exertion of will for the soul to hurl the body ashore as wind drives paper; to waft it kite-fashion to the bank. Thereafter—the boat spun dizzily—suppose the high wind got under the freed body? Would it tower up like a kite and pitch headlong on the far-away sands, or would it duck about beyond control through all eternity? Findlayson gripped the gunnel to anchor himself, for it seemed that he was on the edge of taking the flight before he had settled all his plans. Opium has more effect on the white man than the black. Peroo was only comfortably indifferent to accidents. 'She cannot live,' he grunted. 'Her seams open already. If she were even a dinghy with oars we could have ridden it out; but a box with holes is no good. Finlinson Sahib, she fills.'

'*Accha*! I am going away. Come thou also.'

In his mind Findlayson had already escaped from the boat, and was circling high in air to find a rest for the sole of his foot. His body—he was really sorry for its gross helplessness—lay in the stern, the water rushing about its knees.

'How very ridiculous!' he said to himself, from his eyrie; 'that—is Findlayson—chief of the Kashi Bridge. The poor beast is going to be drowned, too. Drowned when it's close to shore. I'm—I'm on shore already. Why doesn't it come along?'

To his intense disgust, he found his soul back in his body again, and that body spluttering and choking in deep water. The pain of the reunion was atrocious, but it was necessary, also, to fight for the body. He was conscious of grasping wildly at wet sand, and striding prodigiously, as one strides in a dream, to keep foot-hold in the swirling water, till at last he hauled himself clear of the hold of the river, and dropped, panting, on wet earth.

'Not this night,' said Peroo in his ear. 'The Gods have protected us.' The Lascar moved his feet cautiously, and they rustled among dried stumps. 'This is some island of last year's indigo crop,° he went on. 'We shall find no men here; but have great care, Sahib; all the snakes of a hundred miles have been flooded out. Here comes the lightning, on the heels of the wind. Now we shall be able to look; but walk carefully.'

Findlayson was far and far beyond any fear of snakes, or indeed any merely human emotion. He saw, after he had rubbed the water from his eyes, with an immense clearness, and trod, so it seemed to himself, with world-encompassing strides. Somewhere in the night of time he had built a bridge—a bridge that spanned illimitable levels of shining seas; but the Deluge had swept it away, leaving this one island under heaven for Findlayson and his companion, sole survivors of the breed of man.

An incessant lightning, forked and blue, showed all that there was to be seen on the little patch in the flood—a clump of thorn, a clump of swaying creaking bamboos, and a grey gnarled peepul° overshadowing a Hindoo shrine, from whose dome floated a tattered red flag. The holy man whose summer resting-place it was had long since abandoned it, and the weather had broken the red-daubed image of his God. The two men stumbled, heavy-limbed and heavy-eyed, over the ashes of a brick-set cooking-place, and dropped down under the shelter of the branches, while the rain and river roared together.

The stumps of the indigo crackled, and there was a smell of cattle, as a huge and dripping Brahminee Bull shouldered his way under the tree. The flashes revealed the trident mark of Shiva° on his flank, the insolence of head and hump, the luminous stag-like eyes, the brow crowned with a wreath of sodden marigold blooms, and the silky dewlap that nigh swept the ground. There was a noise behind him of other beasts coming up from the flood-line through the thicket, a sound of heavy feet and deep breathing.

'Here be more beside ourselves,' said Findlayson, his head against the tree-pole, looking through half-shut eyes, wholly at ease.

'Truly,' said Peroo thickly, 'and no small ones.'

'What are they, then? I do not see clearly.'

'The Gods. Who else? Look!'

'Ah, true! The Gods surely—the Gods.' Findlayson smiled as his head fell forward on his chest. Peroo was eminently right. After the Flood, who should be alive in the land except the Gods that made it—the Gods who were in all men's mouths and about all men's ways? He could not raise his head or stir a finger for the trance that held him, and Peroo was smiling vacantly at the lightning.

The Bull paused by the shrine, his head lowered to the damp earth. A green Parrot in the branches preened his wet wings and screamed against the thunder as the circle under the tree filled with the shifting shadows of beasts. There was a Black-buck at the Bull's heels—such a buck as Findlayson in his far-away life upon earth might have seen in dreams—a buck with a royal head, ebon back, silver belly, and gleaming straight horns. Beside him, her head bowed to the ground, the green eyes burning under the heavy brows, with restless tail switching the dead grass, paced a Tigress, full-bellied and deep-jowled.

The Bull crouched beside the shrine, and there leaped from the darkness a monstrous grey Ape, who seated himself man-wise in the place of the fallen image, and the rain spilled like jewels from the hair of his neck and shoulders.

Other shadows came and went behind the circle, among them a drunken Man flourishing staff and drinking-bottle. Then a hoarse bellow broke out from near the ground. 'The flood lessens even now,' it cried. 'Hour by hour the water falls, and their bridge still stands!'

'My bridge,' said Findlayson to himself. 'That must be very old work now. What have the Gods to do with my bridge?'

His eyes rolled in the darkness following the roar. A Crocodile—the blunt-nosed, ford-haunting Mugger° of the Ganges—draggled herself before the beasts, lashing furiously to right and left with her tail.

'They have made it too strong for me. In all this night I have only torn away a handful of planks. The walls stand! The towers stand! They have chained my flood, and my river is not free any more. Heavenly Ones, take this yoke away! Give me clear water between bank and bank! It is I, Mother Gunga, that speak. The Justice of the Gods! Deal me the Justice of the Gods!'

'What said I?' whispered Peroo. 'This is in truth a Punchayet° of the Gods. Now we know that all the world is dead, save you and I, Sahib.'

The Parrot screamed and fluttered again, and the Tigress, her ears flat to her head, snarled wickedly.

Somewhere in the shadow a great trunk and gleaming tusks swayed to and fro, and a low gurgle broke the silence that followed on the snarl.

'We be here,' said a deep voice, 'the Great Ones. One only and very many. Shiv, my father, is here, with Indra. Kali has spoken already. Hanuman listens also.'

'Kashi is without her Kotwal° to-night,' shouted the Man with the drinking-bottle, flinging his staff to the ground, while the island rang to the baying of hounds. 'Give her the Justice of the Gods.'

'Ye were still when they polluted my waters,' the great Crocodile bellowed. 'Ye made no sign when my river was trapped between the walls. I had no help save my own strength, and that failed—the strength of Mother Gunga failed—before their guard-towers. What could I do? I have done everything. Finish now, Heavenly Ones!'

'I brought the death; I rode the spotted sickness from hut to hut of their workmen, and yet they would not cease.' A nose-slitten,° hide-worn Ass, lame, scissor-legged, and galled, limped forward. 'I cast the death at them out of my nostrils, but they would not cease.'

Peroo would have moved, but the opium lay heavy upon him.

'Bah!' he said, spitting. 'Here is Sitala herself; Mata—the small-pox.° Has the Sahib a handkerchief to put over his face?'

'Small help! They fed me the corpses for a month, and I flung them out on my sand-bars, but their work went forward. Demons they are, and sons of demons! And ye left Mother Gunga alone for their fire-carriage° to make a mock of. The Justice of the Gods on the bridge-builders!'

The Bull turned the cud in his mouth and answered slowly, 'If the Justice of the Gods caught all who made a mock of holy things, there would be many dark altars in the land, mother.'

'But this goes beyond a mock,' said the Tigress, darting forward a griping paw. 'Thou knowest, Shiv, and ye too, Heavenly Ones; ye know that they have defiled Gunga. Surely they must come to the Destroyer. Let Indra judge.'

The Buck made no movement as he answered, 'How long has this evil been?'

'Three years, as men count years,' said the Mugger, close pressed to the earth.

'Does Mother Gunga die, then, in a year, that she is so anxious to see vengeance now? The deep sea was where she runs but yesterday, and to-morrow the sea shall cover her again as the Gods count that which men call time. Can any say that this their bridge endures till to-morrow?' said the Buck.

There was a long hush, and in the clearing of the storm the full moon stood up above the dripping trees.

'Judge ye, then,' said the River sullenly. 'I have spoken my shame. The flood falls still. I can do no more.'

'For my own part'—it was the voice of the great Ape seated within the shrine—'it pleases me well to watch these men, remembering that I also builded no small bridge in the world's youth.'°

'They say, too,' snarled the Tiger, 'that these men came of the wreck of thy armies, Hanuman, and therefore thou hast aided—'

'They toil as my armies toiled in Lanka, and they believe that their toil endures.° Indra is too high, but Shiv, thou knowest how the land is threaded with their fire-carriages.'

'Yea, I know,' said the Bull. 'Their Gods instructed them in the matter.'

A laugh ran round the circle.

'Their Gods! What should their Gods know? They were born yesterday, and those that made them are scarcely yet cold,' said the Mugger. 'Tomorrow their Gods will die.'

'Ho!' said Peroo. 'Mother Gunga talks good talk. I told that to the padre-sahib who preached on the *Mombassa*, and he asked the Burra Malum to put me in irons for a great rudeness.'

'Surely they make these things to please their Gods,' said the Bull again.

'Not altogether,' the Elephant rolled forth. 'It is for the profit of my mahajuns—my fat money-lenders that worship me at each new year, when they draw my image at the head of the account-books. I, looking over their shoulders by lamplight, see that the names in the books are those of men in far places—for all the towns are drawn together by the fire-carriage, and the money comes and goes swiftly, and the account-books grow as fat as—myself. And I, who am Ganesh of Good Luck, I bless my peoples.'

'They have changed the face of the land—which is my land. They have killed and made new towns on my banks,' said the Mugger.

'It is but the shifting of a little dirt. Let the dirt dig in the dirt if it pleases the dirt,' answered the Elephant.

'But afterwards?' said the Tiger. 'Afterwards they will see that Mother Gunga can avenge no insult, and they fall away from her first, and later from us all, one by one. In the end, Ganesh, we are left with naked altars.'

The drunken Man staggered to his feet, and hiccupped vehemently in the face of the assembled Gods.

'Kali lies. My sister lies. Also this my stick is the Kotwal of Kashi, and he keeps tally of my pilgrims. When the time comes to worship Bhairon—and it is always time—the fire-carriages move one by one, and each bears a thousand pilgrims. They do not come afoot any more, but rolling upon wheels, and my honour is increased.'

'Gunga, I have seen thy bed at Pryag° black with the pilgrims,' said the Ape, leaning forward, 'and but for the fire-carriage they would have come slowly and in fewer numbers. Remember.'

'They come to me always,' Bhairon went on thickly. 'By day and night they pray to me, all the Common People in the fields and the roads. Who is like Bhairon today? What talk is this of changing faiths? Is my staff Kotwal of Kashi for nothing? He keeps the tally, and he says that never were so many altars as to-day, and the fire-carriage serves them well. Bhairon am I—Bhairon of the Common People, and the chiefest of the Heavenly Ones to-day. Also my staff says—'

'Peace, thou!' lowed the Bull. 'The worship of the schools is mine, and they talk very wisely, asking whether I be one or many, as is the delight of my people, and ye know what I am. Kali, my wife, thou knowest also.'

'Yea, I know,' said the Tigress, with lowered head.

'Greater am I than Gunga also.° For ye know who moved the minds of men that they should count Gunga holy among the rivers. Who die in that water—ye know how men say—come to us without punishment, and Gunga knows that the fire-carriage has borne to her scores upon scores of such anxious ones; and Kali knows that she has held her chiefest festivals among the pilgrimages that are fed by the fire-carriage. Who smote at Pooree,° under the Image there, her thousands in a day and a night, and bound the sickness to the wheels of the fire-carriages, so that it ran from one end of the land to the other? Who but Kali? Before the fire-carriage came it was a heavy toil. The fire-carriages have served thee well, Mother of Death. But I speak for mine own altars, who am not Bhairon of the Common Folk, but Shiv. Men go to and fro, making words and telling talk of strange Gods, and I listen. Faith follows faith among my people in the schools, and I have no anger; for when the words are said, and the new talk is ended, to Shiv men return at the last.'

'True. It is true,' murmured Hanuman. 'To Shiv and to the others, mother, they return. I creep from temple to temple in the North, where they worship one God and His Prophet;° and presently my image is alone within their shrines.'

'Small thanks,' said the Buck, turning his head slowly. 'I am that One and His Prophet also.'

'Even so, father,' said Hanuman. 'And to the South I go who am the oldest of the Gods as men know the Gods, and presently I touch the shrines of the new faith° and the Woman whom we know is hewn twelve-armed, and still they call her Mary.'

'Small thanks, brother,' said the Tigress. 'I am that Woman.'

'Even so, sister; and I go West among the fire-carriages, and stand before the bridge-builders in many shapes, and because of me they change their faiths and are very wise. Ho! ho! I am the builder of bridges indeed—bridges between this and that, and each bridge leads surely to Us in the end. Be content, Gunga. Neither these men nor those that follow them mock thee at all.'

'Am I alone, then, Heavenly Ones? Shall I smooth out my flood lest unhappily I bear away their walls? Will Indra dry my springs in the hills and make me crawl humbly between their wharfs? Shall I bury me in the sand ere I offend?'

'And all for the sake of a little iron bar with the fire-carriage atop.

Truly, Mother Gunga is always young!' said Ganesh the Elephant. 'A child had not spoken more foolishly. Let the dirt dig in the dirt ere it return to the dirt. I know only that my people grow rich and praise me. Shiv has said that the men of the schools do not forget; Bhairon is content for his crowd of the Common People: and Hanuman laughs.'

'Surely I laugh,' said the Ape. 'My altars are few beside those of Ganesh or Bhairon, but the fire-carriages bring me new worshippers from beyond the Black Water°—the men who believe that their God is toil. I run before them beckoning, and they follow Hanuman.'

'Give them the toil that they desire, then,' said the River. 'Make a bar across my flood and throw the water back upon the bridge. Once thou wast strong in Lanka, Hanuman. Stoop and lift my bed.'

'Who gives life can take life.' The Ape scratched in the mud with a long forefinger.° 'And yet, who would profit by the killing? Very many would die.'

There came up from the water a snatch of a love-song such as the boys sing when they watch their cattle in the noon heats of late spring. The Parrot screamed joyously, sidling along his branch with lowered head as the song grew louder, and in a patch of clear moonlight stood revealed the young herd,° the darling of the Gopis,° the idol of dreaming maids and of mothers ere their children are born—Krishna the Well-beloved. He stooped to knot up his long wet hair, and the Parrot fluttered to his shoulder.

'Fleeting° and singing, and singing and fleeting,' hiccupped Bhairon. 'Those make thee late for the council, brother.'

'And then?' said Krishna, with a laugh, throwing back his head. 'Ye can do little without me or Karma here'. He fondled the Parrot's plumage and laughed again. 'What is this sitting and talking together? I heard Mother Gunga roaring in the dark, and so came quickly from a hut where I lay warm. And what have ye done to Karma, that he is so wet and silent? And what does Mother Gunga here? Are the heavens full that ye must come paddling in the mud beast-wise? Karma, what do they do?'

'Gunga has prayed for a vengeance on the bridge-builders, and Kali is with her. Now she bids Hanuman whelm the bridge, that her honour may be made great,' cried the Parrot. 'I waited here, knowing that thou wouldst come, O my master!'

'And the Heavenly Ones said nothing? Did Gunga and the Mother of Sorrows° out-talk them? Did none speak for my people?'

'Nay,' said Ganesh, moving uneasily from foot to foot; 'I said it was but dirt at play, and why should we stamp it flat?'

'I was content to let them toil—well content,' said Hanuman.

'What had I to do with Gunga's anger?' said the Bull.

'I am Bhairon of the Common Folk, and this my staff is Kotwal of all Kashi. I spoke for the Common People.'

'Thou?' The young God's eyes sparkled.

'Am I not the first of the Gods in their mouths to-day?' returned Bhairon, unabashed. 'For the sake of the Common People I said—very many wise things which I have now forgotten—but this my staff—'

Krishna turned impatiently, saw the Mugger at his feet, and kneeling, slipped an arm round the cold neck. 'Mother,' he said gently, 'get thee to thy flood again. The matter is not for thee. What harm shall thy honour take of this live dirt? Thou hast given them their fields new year after year, and by thy flood they are made strong. They come all to thee at the last. What need to slay them now? Have pity, mother, for a little—and it is only for a little.'

'If it be only for a little—' the slow beast began.

'Are they Gods, then?' Krishna returned with a laugh, his eyes looking into the dull eyes of the River. 'Be certain that it is only for a little. The Heavenly Ones have heard thee, and presently justice will be done. Go now, mother, to the flood again. Men and cattle are thick on the waters—the banks fall—the villages melt because of thee.'

'But the bridge—the bridge stands.' The Mugger turned grunting into the undergrowth as Krishna rose.

'It is ended,' said the Tigress, viciously. 'There is no more justice from the Heavenly Ones. Ye have made shame and sport of Gunga, who asked no more than a few score lives.'

'Of *my* people—who lie under the leaf-roofs of the village yonder—of the young girls, and the young men who sing to them in the dark—of the child that will be born next morn—of that which was begotten to-night,' said Krishna. 'And when all is done, what profit? To-morrow sees them at work. Ay, if ye swept the bridge out from end to end they would begin anew. Hear me! Bhairon is drunk always. Hanuman mocks his people with new riddles.'

'Nay, but they are very old ones,' the Ape said, laughing.

'Shiv hears the talk of the schools and the dreams of the holy men; Ganesh thinks only of his fat traders; but I—I live with these my people, asking for no gifts, and so receiving them hourly.'

'And very tender art thou of thy people,' said the Tigress.

'They are my own. The old women dream of me, turning in their sleep; the maids look and listen for me when they go to fill their lotahs°

by the river. I walk by the young men waiting without the gates at dusk, and I call over my shoulder to the white-beards. Ye know, Heavenly Ones, that I alone of us all walk upon the earth continually, and have no pleasure in our heavens so long as a green blade springs here, or there are two voices at twilight in the standing crops. Wise are ye, but ye live far off, forgetting whence ye came. So do I not forget. And the fire-carriage feeds your shrines, ye say? And the fire-carriages bring a thousand pilgrimages where but ten came in the old years? True. That is true to-day.'

'But to-morrow they are dead, brother,' said Ganesh.

'Peace!' said the Bull, as Hanuman leaned forward again. 'And to-morrow, beloved—what of to-morrow?'

'This only. A new word creeping from mouth to mouth among the Common Folk—a word that neither man nor God can lay hold of—an evil word—a little lazy word among the Common Folk, saying (and none know who set that word afoot) that they weary of ye, Heavenly Ones.'

The Gods laughed together softly. 'And then, beloved?' they said.

'And to cover that weariness they, my people, will bring to thee, Shiv, and to thee, Ganesh, at first greater offerings and a louder noise of worship. But the word has gone abroad, and, after, they will pay fewer dues to your fat Brahmins. Next they will forget your altars, but so slowly that no man can say how his forgetfulness began.'

'I knew—I knew! I spoke this also, but they would not hear,' said the Tigress. 'We should have slain—we should have slain!'

'It is too late now. Ye should have slain at the beginning, when the men from across the water had taught our folk nothing. Now my people see their work, and go away thinking. They do not think of the Heavenly Ones altogether. They think of the fire-carriage and the other things that the bridge-builders have done, and when your priests thrust forward hands asking alms, they give unwillingly a little. That is the beginning, among one or two, or five or ten—for I, moving among my people, know what is in their hearts.'

'And the end, Jester of the Gods?° What shall the end be?' said Ganesh.

'The end shall be as it was in the beginning, O slothful son of Shiv! The flame shall die upon the altars and the prayer upon the tongue till ye become little Gods again—Gods of the jungle°—names that the hunters of rats and noosers of dogs whisper in the thicket and among the caves—rag-Gods, pot Godlings of the tree, and the village-mark, as ye were at the beginning. That is the end, Ganesh, for thee, and for Bhairon—Bhairon of the Common People.'

'It is very far away,' grunted Bhairon. 'Also it is a lie.'

'Many women have kissed Krishna. They told him this to cheer their own hearts when the grey hairs came, and he has told us the tale,' said the Bull, below his breath.

'Their Gods came, and we changed them. I took the Woman and made her twelve-armed. So shall we twist all their Gods,' said Hanuman.

'Their Gods! This is no question of their Gods—one or three—man or woman. The matter is with the people. *They* move, and not the Gods of the bridge-builders,' said Krishna.

'So be it. I have made a man worship the fire-carriage as it stood still breathing smoke, and he knew not that he worshipped me,' said Hanuman the Ape. 'They will only change a little the names of their Gods. I shall lead the builders of the bridges as of old; Shiv shall be worshipped in the schools by such as doubt and despise their fellows; Ganesh shall have his mahajuns, and Bhairon the donkey-drivers, the pilgrims, and the sellers of toys. Beloved, they will do no more than change the names, and that we have seen a thousand times.'

'Surely they will do no more than change the names,' echoed Ganesh: but there was an uneasy movement among the Gods.

'They will change more than the names. Me alone they cannot kill, so long as maiden and man meet together or the spring follows the winter rains. Heavenly Ones, not for nothing have I walked upon the earth. My people know not now what they know; but I, who live with them, I read their hearts. Great Kings, the beginning of the end is born already. The fire-carriages shout the names of new Gods that are *not* the old under new names. Drink now and eat greatly! Bathe your faces in the smoke of the altars before they grow cold! Take dues and listen to the cymbals and the drums, Heavenly Ones, while yet there are flowers and songs. As men count time the end is far off; but as we who know reckon it is to-day. I have spoken.'

The young God ceased, and his brethren looked at each other long in silence.

'This I have not heard before,' Peroo whispered in his companion's ear. 'And yet sometimes, when I oiled the brasses in the engine-room of the *Goorkha*, I have wondered if our priests were so wise—so wise. The day is coming, Sahib. They will be gone by the morning.'

A yellow light broadened in the sky, and the tone of the river changed as the darkness withdrew.

Suddenly the Elephant trumpeted aloud as though man had goaded him.

'Let Indra judge. Father of all, speak thou! What of the things we have heard? Has Krishna lied indeed? Or—'

'Ye know,' said the Buck, rising to his feet. 'Ye know the Riddle of the Gods. When Brahm ceases to dream the Heavens and the Hells and Earth disappear.° Be content. Brahm dreams still. The dreams come and go, and the nature of the dreams changes, but still Brahm dreams. Krishna has walked too long upon earth, and yet I love him the more for the tale he has told. The Gods change, beloved—all save One!'

'Ay, all save one that makes love in the hearts of men,' said Krishna, knotting his girdle. 'It is but a little time to wait, and ye shall know if I lie.'

'Truly it is but a little time, as thou sayest, and we shall know. Get thee to thy huts again, beloved, and make sport for the young things, for still Brahm dreams. Go, my children! Brahm dreams—and till He wakes the Gods die not.'

'Whither went they?' said the Lascar, awe-struck, shivering a little with the cold.

'God knows!' said Findlayson. The river and the island lay in full daylight now, and there was never mark of hoof or pug on the wet earth under the peepul. Only a parrot screamed in the branches, bringing down showers of water-drops as he fluttered his wings.

'Up! We are cramped with cold! Has the opium died out? Canst thou move, Sahib?'

Findlayson staggered to his feet and shook himself. His head swam and ached, but the work of the opium was over, and, as he sluiced his forehead in a pool, the Chief Engineer of the Kashi Bridge was wondering how he had managed to fall upon the island, what chances the day offered of return, and, above all, how his work stood.

'Peroo, I have forgotten much. I was under the guard-tower watching the river; and then—Did the flood sweep us away?'

'No. The boats broke loose, Sahib, and' (if the Sahib had forgotten about the opium, decidedly Peroo would not remind him) 'in striving to retie them, so it seemed to me—but it was dark—a rope caught the Sahib and threw him upon a boat. Considering that we two, with Hitchcock Sahib, built, as it were, that bridge, I came also upon the boat, which came riding on horseback, as it were, on the nose of this island, and so, splitting, cast us ashore. I made a great cry when the boat left the wharf, and without doubt Hitchcock Sahib will come for us. As for the bridge, so many have died in the building that it cannot fall.'

A fierce sun, that drew out all the smell of the sodden land, had followed the storm, and in that clear light there was no room for a man to think of dreams of the dark. Findlayson stared up-stream, across the blaze of moving water, till his eyes ached. There was no sign of any bank to the Ganges, much less of a bridge-line.

'We came down far,' he said. 'It was wonderful that we were not drowned a hundred times.'

'That was the least of the wonder, for no man dies before his time. I have seen Sydney, I have seen London, and twenty great ports, but'—Peroo looked at the damp, discoloured shrine under the peepul—'never man has seen that we saw here.'

'What?'

'Has the Sahib forgotten; or do we black men only see the Gods?'

'There was a fever upon me.' Findlayson was still looking uneasily across the water. 'It seemed that the island was full of beasts and men talking, but I do not remember. A boat could live in this water now, I think.'

'Oho! Then it *is* true. "When Brahm ceases to dream, the Gods die." Now I know, indeed, what he meant. Once, too, the *guru* said as much to me; but then I did not understand. Now I am wise.'

'What?' said Findlayson over his shoulder.

Peroo went on as if he were talking to himself. 'Six—seven—ten monsoons since, I was watch on the fo'c'sle of the *Rewah*—the Kumpani's big boat—and there was a big *tufan*,° green and black water beating; and I held fast to the life-lines, choking under the waters. Then I thought of the Gods—of Those whom we saw to-night'—he stared curiously at Findlayson's back, but the white man was looking across the flood. 'Yes, I say of Those whom we saw this night past, and I called upon Them to protect me. And while I prayed, still keeping my look-out, a big wave came and threw me forward upon the ring of the great black bow-anchor, and the *Rewah* rose high and high, leaning towards the left-hand side, and the water drew away from beneath her nose, and I lay upon my belly, holding the ring, and looking down into those great deeps. Then I thought, even in the face of death, if I lose hold I die, and for me neither the *Rewah* nor my place by the galley where the rice is cooked, nor Bombay, nor Calcutta, nor even London, will be any more for me. "How shall I be sure," I said, "that the Gods to whom I pray will abide at all?" This I thought, and the *Rewah* dropped her nose as a hammer falls, and all the sea came in and slid me backwards along the fo'c'sle and over the break of the fo'c'sle, and I very badly bruised my shin against the donkey-engine: but I did not die, and I have seen the Gods. They are good for live men, but for the dead—They have spoken Themselves. Therefore, when I come to the village I will beat the *guru* for talking riddles which are no riddles. When Brahm ceases to dream, the Gods go.'

'Look up-stream. The light blinds. Is there smoke yonder?'

Peroo shaded his eyes with his hands. 'He is a wise man and quick. Hitchcock Sahib would not trust a rowboat. He has borrowed the Rao Sahib's steam-launch, and comes to look for us. I have always said that there should have been a steam-launch on the bridge-works for us.'

The territory of the Rao of Baraon° lay within ten miles of the bridge; and Findlayson and Hitchcock had spent a fair portion of their scanty leisure in playing billiards and shooting Black-buck with the young man. He had been bear-led° by an English tutor of sporting tastes for some five or six years, and was now royally wasting the revenues accumulated during his minority by the Indian Government. His steam-launch, with its silver-plated rails, striped silk awning, and mahogany decks, was a new toy which Findlayson had found horribly in the way when the Rao came to look at the bridge-works.

'It's great luck,' murmured Findlayson, but he was none the less afraid, wondering what news might be of the bridge.

The gaudy blue and white funnel came down-stream swiftly. They could see Hitchcock in the bows, with a pair of opera-glasses, and his face was unusually white. Then Peroo hailed, and the launch made for the tail of the island. The Rao Sahib, in tweed shooting-suit and a seven-hued turban, waved his royal hand, and Hitchcock shouted. But he need have asked no questions, for Findlayson's first demand was for his bridge.

'All serene! 'Gad, I never expected to see you again, Findlayson. You're seven koss° down-stream. Yes, there's not a stone shifted anywhere; but how are you? I borrowed the Rao Sahib's launch, and he was good enough to come along. Jump in.'

'Ah, Finlinson, you are very well, eh? That was most unprecedented calamity last night, eh? My royal palace, too, it leaks like the devil, and the crops will also be short all about my country. Now you shall back her out, Hitchcock. I—I do not understand steam-engines. You are wet? You are cold, Finlinson? I have some things to eat here, and you will take a good drink.'

'I'm immensely grateful, Rao Sahib. I believe you've saved my life. How did Hitchcock—'

'Oho! His hair was upon end. He rode to me in the middle of the night and woke me up in the arms of Morphus.° I was most truly concerned, Finlinson, so I came too. My head-priest he is very angry just now. We will go quick, Mister Hitchcock. I am due to attend at twelve forty-five in the state temple, where we sanctify some new idol. If not so I would have asked you to spend the day with me. They are dam-bore, these religious ceremonies, Finlinson, eh?'

Peroo, well known to the crew, had possessed himself of the wheel, and was taking the launch craftily up-steam. But while he steered he was, in his mind, handling two feet of partially untwisted wire-rope; and the back upon which he beat was the back of his *guru*.

The Devil and the Deep Sea

'All supplies very bad and dear, and there are no facilities for even the smallest repairs.'

SAILING DIRECTIONS

Her nationality was British, but you will not find her house-flag in the list of our mercantile marine. She was a nine-hundred ton, iron, schooner-rigged,° screw cargo-boat, differing externally in no way from any other tramp of the sea. But it is with steamers as it is with men. There are those who will for a consideration sail extremely close to the wind; and, in the present state of a fallen world, such people and such steamers have their use. From the hour that the *Aglaia* first entered the Clyde—new, shiny, and innocent, with a quart of cheap champagne trickling down her cutwater—Fate and her owner, who was also her captain, decreed that she should deal with embarrassed crowned heads, fleeing Presidents, financiers of over-extended ability, women to whom change of air was imperative, and the lesser law-breaking Powers. Her career led her sometimes into the Admiralty Courts, where the sworn statements of her skipper filled his brethren with envy. The mariner cannot tell or act a lie in the face of the sea, or mislead a tempest; but, as lawyers have discovered, he makes up for chances withheld when he returns to shore, an affidavit in either hand.°

The *Aglaia* figured with distinction in the great *Mackinaw* salvage case.° It was her first slip from virtue, and she learned how to change her name, but not her heart, and to run across the sea. As the *Guiding Light* she was very badly wanted in a South American port for the little matter of entering harbour at full speed, colliding with a coal-hulk and the State's only man-of-war, just as that man-of-war was going to coal. She put to sea without explanations, though three forts fired at her for half an hour. As the *Julia M'Gregor* she had been concerned in picking up from a raft certain gentlemen who should have stayed in Noumea,° but who preferred making themselves vastly unpleasant to authority in quite another quarter of the world; and as the *Shah-in-Shah* she had been overtaken on the high seas, indecently full of munitions of war, by the cruiser of an agitated Power at issue with its neighbour. That time she was very nearly sunk, and her riddled hull gave eminent lawyers of two countries great profit. After a season she reappeared as the *Martin Hunt*, painted a dull slate colour, with pure saffron funnel, and boats of sparrow's-egg blue, engaging in the Odessa trade° till she was invited (and the invitation could not well be disregarded) to keep away from Black Sea ports altogether.

She had ridden through many waves of depression. Freights might drop out of sight, Seamen's Unions throw spanners and nuts at certificated masters, or stevedores combine° till cargo perished on the dockhead; but the boat of many names came and went, busy, alert, and inconspicuous always. Her skipper made no complaint of hard times, and port officers observed that her crew signed and signed again with the regularity of Atlantic liner boatswains. Her name she changed as occasion called; her well-paid crew never; and a large percentage of the profits of her voyages was spent with an open hand on her engine-room. She never troubled the underwriters, and very seldom stopped to talk with a signal-station;° for her business was urgent and private.

But an end came to her tradings, and she perished in this manner. Deep peace brooded over Europe, Asia, Africa, America, Australasia, and Polynesia. The Powers dealt together more or less honestly; banks paid their depositors to the hour; diamonds of price came safely to the hands of their owners; republics rested content with their dictators; diplomats found no one whose presence in the least incommoded them; monarchs lived openly with their lawfully wedded wives. It was as though the whole earth had put on its best Sunday bib and tucker; and business was very bad for the *Martin Hunt*. The great, virtuous calm engulfed her, slate sides, yellow funnel, and all, but cast up in another hemisphere the steam-whaler *Haliotis*,° black and rusty, with a manure-coloured funnel, a litter of dingy white boats, and an enormous stove, or furnace, for boiling blubber on her forward well-deck. There could be no doubt that her trip was successful, for she lay at several ports not too well known, and the smoke of her trying-out° insulted the beaches.

Anon she departed, at the speed of the average London four-wheeler,° and entered a semi-inland sea,° warm, still, and blue, which is, perhaps, the most strictly preserved water in the world. There she stayed for a certain time, and the great stars of those mild skies beheld her playing puss-in-the-corner° among islands where whales are never found. All that time she smelt abominably, and the smell, though fishy, was not whalesome. One evening calamity descended upon her from the island of Pygang-Watai, and she fled, while her crew jeered at a fat black-and-brown gunboat puffing far behind. They knew to the last revolution the capacity of every boat, on those seas, that they were anxious to avoid. A British ship with a good conscience does not, as a rule, flee from the man-of-war of a foreign Power, and it is also considered a breach of etiquette to stop and search British ships at sea. These things the skipper of the *Haliotis* did not pause to prove, but held on at an inspiriting eleven knots an hour till nightfall. One thing only he overlooked.

The Power that kept an expensive steam-patrol moving up and down those waters (they had dodged the two regular ships of the station with an ease that bred contempt) had newly brought up a third and a fourteen-knot boat with a clean bottom° to help the work; and that was why the *Haliotis*, driving hard from the east to the west, found herself at daylight in such a position that she could not help seeing an arrangement of four flags,° a mile and a half behind, which read: 'Heave to, or take the consequences!'

She had her choice, and she took it, and the end came when, presuming on her lighter draught, she tried to draw away northward over a friendly shoal. The shell that arrived by way of the Chief Engineer's cabin was some five inches in diameter, with a practice, not a bursting, charge.° It had been intended to cross her bows, and that was why it knocked the framed portrait of the Chief Engineer's wife—and she was a very pretty girl—on to the floor, splintered his wash-hand stand, crossed the alleyway into the engine-room, and striking on a grating, dropped directly in front of the forward engine,° where it burst, neatly fracturing both the bolts that held the connecting-rod to the forward crank.

What follows is worth consideration. The forward engine had no more work to do. Its released piston-rod, therefore, drove up fiercely, with nothing to check it, and started most of the nuts of the cylinder-cover. It came down again, the full weight of the steam behind it, and the foot of the disconnected connecting-rod, useless as the leg of a man with a sprained ankle, flung out to the right and struck the starboard, or right-hand, cast-iron supporting-column of the forward engine, cracking it clean through about six inches above the base, and wedging the upper portion outwards three inches towards the ship's side. There the connecting-rod jammed. Meantime, the after-engine, being as yet unembarrassed, went on with its work, and in so doing brought round at its next revolution the crank of the forward engine, which smote the already jammed connecting-rod, bending it and therewith the piston-rod cross-head—the big cross-piece that slides up and down so smoothly.

The cross-head jammed sideways in the guides, and, in addition to putting further pressure on the already broken starboard supporting column, cracked the port, or left-hand supporting column in two or three places. There being nothing more that could be made to move, the engines brought up, all standing,° with a hiccup that seemed to lift the *Haliotis* a foot out of the water; and the engine-room staff, opening every steam outlet that they could find in the confusion, arrived on deck somewhat scalded, but calm. There was a sound below of things happening—a rushing, clicking, purring, grunting, rattling noise that did not last for more than a minute. It was the machinery adjusting itself, on the spur of the moment, to a hundred altered conditions. Mr Wardrop, one foot on the upper grating,° inclined his ear sideways and groaned. You cannot stop engines working at twelve knots an hour° in three seconds without disorganising them. The *Haliotis* slid forward in a cloud of steam, shrieking like a wounded horse. There was nothing more to do. The five-inch shell with a reduced charge had settled the situation. And when you are full, all three holds, of strictly preserved pearls; when you have cleaned out the Tanna Bank, the Sea-Horse Bank,° and four other banks from one end to the other of the Amanala Sea—when you have ripped out the very heart of a rich Government monopoly so that five years will not repair your wrong-doings—you must smile and take what is in store. But the skipper reflected, as a launch put out from the man-of-war, that he had been bombarded on the high seas, with the British flag—several of them—picturesquely disposed above him, and tried to find comfort in the thought.

'Where,' said the stolid naval lieutenant hoisting himself aboard, 'where are those dam' pearls?'

They were there beyond evasion. No affidavit could do away with the fearful smell of decayed oysters, the diving-dresses, and the shell-littered hatches. They were there to the value of seventy thousand pounds, more or less; and every pound poached.

The man-of-war was annoyed; for she had used up many tons of coal, she had strained her tubes,° and, worse than all, her officers and crew had been hurried. Every one on the *Haliotis* was arrested and rearrested several times, as each officer came aboard; then they were told by what they esteemed to be the equivalent of a midshipman that they were to consider themselves prisoners, and finally were put under arrest.

'It's not the least good,' said the skipper, suavely. 'You'd much better send us a tow—'

'Be still—you are arrest!' was the reply

'Where the devil do you expect we are going to escape to? We're helpless. You've got to tow us into somewhere, and explain why you fired on us. Mr Wardrop, we're helpless, aren't we?'

'Ruined from end to end,' said the man of machinery. 'If she rolls, the forward cylinder will come down and go through her bottom. Both columns are clean cut through. There's nothing to hold anything up.'

The council of war clanked off to see if Mr Wardrop's words were true. He warned them that it was as much as a man's life was worth to enter the engine-room, and they contented themselves with a distant inspection through the thinning steam. The *Haliotis* lifted to the long, easy swell, and the starboard supporting-column ground a trifle, as a man grits his teeth under the knife. The forward cylinder was depending on that unknown force men call the pertinacity of materials, which now and then balances that other heart-breaking power, the perversity of inanimate things.

'You see!' said Mr Wardrop, hurrying them away. 'The engines aren't worth their price as old iron.'

'We tow,' was the answer. 'Afterwards we shall confiscate.'

The man-of-war was short-handed, and did not see the necessity for putting a prize-crew aboard the *Haliotis*. So she sent one sub-lieutenant, whom the skipper kept very drunk, for he did not wish to make the tow too easy, and, moreover, he had an inconspicuous little rope hanging from the stern of his ship.

Then they began to tow at an average speed of four knots an hour. The *Haliotis* was very hard to move, and the gunnery-lieutenant, who had fired the five-inch shell, had leisure to think upon consequences. Mr Wardrop was the busy man. He borrowed all the crew to shore up the cylinders, with spars and blocks, from the bottom and sides of the ship. It was a day's risky work; but anything was better than drowning at the end of a tow-rope; and if the forward cylinder had fallen, it would have made its way to the sea-bed, and taken the *Haliotis* after.

'Where are we going to, and how long will they tow us?' he asked of the skipper.

'God knows! and this prize-lieutenant's drunk. What do you think you can do?'

'There's just the bare chance,' Mr Wardrop whispered, though no one was within hearing—'there's just the bare chance o' repairin' her, if a man knew how. They've twisted the very guts out of her, bringing her up with that jerk; but I'm saying that, with time and patience, there's just the chance of making steam yet. *We* could do it.'

The skipper's eye brightened. 'Do you mean,' he began, 'that she is any good?'

'Oh no,' said Mr Wardrop. 'She'll need three thousand pounds in repairs, at the lowest, if she's to take to sea again, an' that apart from any injury to her structure. She's like a man fallen down five pair o' stairs. We can't tell for months what has happened; but we know she'll never be good again without a new inside. Ye should see the condenser-tubes an' the steam connections to the donkey,° for two things only. I'm not afraid of them repairin' her. I'm afraid of them stealin' things.'

'They've fired on us. They'll have to explain that.'

'Our reputation's not good enough to ask for explanations. Let's take what we have and be thankful. Ye would not have consuls rememberin' the *Guidin' Light*, an' the *Shah-in-Shah*, an' the *Aglaia* at this most alarmin' crisis. We've been no better than pirates these ten years. Under Providence we're no worse than thieves now. We've much to be thankful for—if we e'er get back to her.'

'Make it your own way, then,' said the skipper, 'if there's the least chance—'

'I'll leave none,' said Mr Wardrop—'none that they'll dare to take. Keep her heavy on the tow, for we need time.'

The skipper never interfered with the affairs of the engine-room, and Mr Wardrop—an artist in his profession—turned to and composed a work terrible and forbidding. His background was the dark-grained sides of the engine-room; his material the metals of power and strength, helped out with spars, baulks, and ropes. The man-of-war towed sullenly and viciously. The *Haliotis* behind her hummed like a hive before swarming. With extra and totally unneeded spars her crew blocked up the space round the forward engine till it resembled a statue in its scaffolding, and the butts of the shores° interfered with every view that a dispassionate eye might wish to take. And that the dispassionate mind might be swiftly shaken out of its calm, the well-sunk bolts of the shores were wrapped round untidily with loose ends of ropes, giving a studied effect of most dangerous insecurity. Next, Mr Wardrop took up a collection from the after engine, which, as you will remember, had not been affected in the general wreck. The cylinder escape-valve he abolished with a flogging-hammer. It is difficult in far-off ports to come by such valves, unless, like Mr Wardrop, you keep duplicates in store. At the same time men took off the nuts of two of the great holding-down bolts that serve to keep the engines in place on their solid bed. An engine violently arrested in mid-career may easily jerk off the nut of a holding-down bolt, and this accident looked very natural.

Passing along the tunnel,° he removed several shaft coupling-bolts and nuts, scattering other and ancient pieces of iron under foot. Cylinder-bolts he cut off to the number of six from the after engine cylinder, so that it might match its neighbour, and stuffed the bilge- and feed-pumps° with cotton-waste. Then he made a neat bundle of the various odds and ends that he had gathered from the engines—little things like nuts and valve-spindles, all carefully tallowed°—and retired with them under the floor of the engine-room, where he sighed, being fat, as he passed from manhole to manhole of the double bottom, and in a fairly dry submarine compartment hid them. Any engineer, particularly in an unfriendly port, has a right to keep his spare stores where he chooses; and the foot of one of the cylinder shores blocked all entrance into the regular storeroom, even if that had not been already closed with steel wedges. In conclusion, he disconnected the after engine, laid piston and connecting-rod, carefully tallowed, where it would be most inconvenient to the casual visitor, took out three of the eight collars of the thrust-block,° hid them where only he could find them again, filled the boilers by hand, wedged the sliding doors of the coal-bunkers, and rested from his labours. The engine-room was a cemetery, and it did not need the contents of an ash-lift through the skylight to make it any worse.

He invited the skipper to look at the completed work.

'Saw ye ever such a forsaken wreck as that?' said he proudly. 'It almost frights *me* to go under those shores. Now, what d'you think they'll do to us?'

'Wait till we see,' said the skipper. 'It'll be bad enough when it comes.'

He was not wrong. The pleasant days of towing ended all too soon, though the *Haliotis* trailed behind her a heavily weighted jib stayed out into the shape of a pocket;° and Mr Wardrop was no longer an artist of imagination, but one of seven-and-twenty prisoners in a prison full of insects. The man-of-war had towed them to the nearest port, not to the headquarters of the colony, and when Mr Wardrop saw the dismal little harbour, with its ragged line of Chinese junks, its one crazy tug, and the boat-building shed that, under the charge of a philosophical Malay, represented a dockyard, he sighed and shook his head.

'I did well,' he said. 'This is the habitation o' wreckers an' thieves. We're at the uttermost ends of the earth. Think you they'll ever know in England?'

'Doesn't look like it,' said the skipper.

They were marched ashore with what they stood up in, under a generous escort, and were judged according to the customs of the country, which, though excellent, are a little out of date. There were the pearls; there were the poachers; and there sat a small but hot Governor. He consulted for a while, and then things began to move with speed, for he did not wish to keep a hungry crew at large on the beach, and the man-of-war had gone up the coast. With a wave of his hand—a stroke of the pen was not necessary—he consigned them to the *blakgang-tana*, the back country, and the hand of the Law removed them from his sight and the knowledge of men. They were marched into the palms, and the back country swallowed them up—all the crew of the *Haliotis*.

Deep peace continued to brood over Europe, Asia, Africa, America, Australasia, and Polynesia.

It was the firing that did it. They should have kept their counsel; but when a few thousand foreigners are bursting with joy over the fact that a ship under the British flag had been fired at on the high seas, news travels quickly; and when it came out that the pearl-stealing crew had not been allowed access to their consul (there was no consul within a few hundred miles of that lonely port) even the friendliest of Powers has a right to ask questions. The great heart of the British public was beating furiously on account of the performance of a notorious race-horse,° and had not a throb to waste on distant accidents; but somewhere deep in the hull of the ship of State there is machinery which more or less accurately takes charge of foreign affairs. That machinery began to revolve, and who so shocked and surprised as the Power that had captured the *Haliotis*? It explained that colonial governors and far-away men-of-war were difficult to control, and promised that it would most certainly make an example both of the Governor and the vessel. As for the crew, reported to be pressed into military service in tropical climes, it would produce them as soon as possible, and it would apologise, if necessary. Now, no apologies were needed. When one nation apologises to another, millions of amateurs who have no earthly concern with the difficulty hurl themselves into the strife and embarrass the trained specialist. It was requested that the crew be found if they were still alive—they had been eight months beyond knowledge—and it was promised that all would be forgotten.

The little Governor of the little port was pleased with himself. Seven-and-twenty white men made a very compact force to throw away on a war that had neither beginning nor end—a jungle-and-stockade fight that flickered and smouldered through the wet, hot years in the hills a hundred miles away, and was the heritage of every wearied official. He had, he thought, deserved well of his country; and if only some one would buy the unhappy *Haliotis*, moored in the harbour below his verandah, his cup would be full. He looked at the neatly silvered lamps that he had taken from her cabins, and thought of much that might be turned to account. But his countrymen in that moist climate had no spirit. They would peep into the silent engine-room, and shake their heads. Even the men-of-war would not tow her farther up the coast, where the Governor believed that she could be repaired. She was a bad bargain; but her cabin carpets were undeniably beautiful, and his wife approved of her mirrors.

Three hours later cables were bursting round him like shells, for, though he knew it not, he was being offered as a sacrifice by the nether to the upper mill-stone, and his superiors had no regard for his feelings. He had, said the cables, grossly exceeded his power, and failed to report on events. He would, therefore,—at this he cast himself back in his hammock—produce the crew of the *Haliotis*. He would send for them, and, if that failed, he would put his dignity on a pony and fetch them himself. He had no conceivable right to make pearl-poachers serve in any war. He would be held responsible.

Next morning the cables wished to know whether he had found the crew of the *Haliotis*. They were to be found, freed and fed—he was to feed them—till such time as they could be sent to the nearest English port in a man-of-war. If you abuse a man long enough in great words flashed over the sea-beds, things happen. The Governor sent inland swiftly for his prisoners, who were also soldiers; and never was a militia regiment more anxious to reduce its strength. No power short of death could make these mad men wear the uniform of their service. They would not fight, except with their fellows, and it was for that reason the regiment had not gone to war, but stayed in a stockade, reasoning with the new troops. The autumn campaign had been a fiasco, but here were the Englishmen. All the regiment marched back to guard them, and the hairy enemy, armed with blow-pipes, rejoiced in the forest. Five of the crew had died, but there lined up on the Governor's verandah two-and-twenty men marked about the legs with the scars of leech-bites. A few of them wore fringes that had once been trousers; the others used loin-cloths of gay patterns; and they existed beautifully but simply in the Governor's verandah; and when he came out they sang at him. When you have lost seventy thousand pounds' worth of pearls, your pay, your ship, and all your clothes, and have lived in bondage for eight months beyond the faintest pretences of civilisation, you know what true independence means, for you become the happiest of created things—natural man.

The Governor told the crew that they were evil, and they asked for food. When he saw how they ate, and when he remembered that none of the pearl patrol-boats were expected for two months, he sighed. But the crew of the *Haliotis* lay down in the verandah, and said that they were pensioners of the Governor's bounty. A grey-bearded man, fat and bald-headed, his one garment a green and yellow loin-cloth, saw the *Haliotis* in the harbour, and bellowed with joy. The men crowded to the verandah-rail, kicking aside the long cane chairs. They pointed, gesticulated, and argued freely, without shame. The militia regiment sat down in the Governor's garden. The Governor retired to his hammock—it was as easy to be killed lying as standing—and his women squeaked from the shuttered rooms.

'She sold?' said the grey-bearded man, pointing to the *Haliotis*. He was Mr Wardrop.

'No good,' said the Governor, shaking his head. 'No one come buy.'

'He's taken my lamps, though,' said the skipper. He wore one leg of a pair of trousers, and his eye wandered along the verandah. The Governor quailed. There were cuddy° camp-stools and the skipper's writing-table in plain sight.

'They've cleaned her out, o' course,' said Mr Wardrop. 'They would. We'll go aboard and take an inventory. See!' He waved his hands over the harbour. 'We—live—there—now. Sorry?'

The Governor smiled a smile of relief.

'He's glad of that,' said one of the crew, reflectively. 'I don't wonder.'

They flocked down to the harbour-front, the militia regiment clattering behind, and embarked themselves in what they found—it happened to be the Governor's boat. Then they disappeared over the bulwarks of the *Haliotis*, and the Governor prayed that they might find occupation inside.

Mr Wardrop's first bound took him to the engine-room; and when the others were patting the well-remembered decks, they heard him giving God thanks that things were as he had left them. The wrecked engines stood over his head untouched; no inexpert hand had meddled with his shores; the steel wedges of the storeroom were rusted home; and, best of all, the hundred and sixty tons of good Australian coal in the bunkers had not diminished.

'I don't understand it,' said Mr Wardrop. 'Any Malay knows the use o' copper. They ought to have cut away the pipes. And with Chinese junks coming here, too. It's a special interposition o' Providence.'

'You think so,' said the skipper, from above. 'There's only been one thief here, and he's cleaned her out of all *my* things, anyhow.'

Here the skipper spoke less than the truth, for under the planking of his cabin, only to be reached by a chisel, lay a little money which never drew any interest—his sheet-anchor to windward. It was all in clean sovereigns that pass current the world over, and might have amounted to more than a hundred pounds.

'He's left me alone. Let's thank God,' repeated Mr Wardrop.

'He's taken everything else; look!'

The *Haliotis*, except as to her engine-room, had been systematically and scientifically gutted from one end to the other, and there was strong evidence that an unclean guard had camped in the skipper's cabin to regulate that plunder. She lacked glass, plate, crockery, cutlery, mattresses, cuddy carpets and chairs, all boats, and her copper ventilators. These things had been removed, with her sails and as much of the wire rigging as would not imperil the safety of the masts.

'He must have sold those,' said the skipper. 'The other things are in his house, I suppose.'

Every fitting that could be prized or screwed out was gone. Port, starboard, and masthead lights; teak gratings; sliding sashes of the deck-house; the captain's chest of drawers, with charts and chart-table; photographs, brackets, and looking-glasses; cabin doors; rubber cuddy-mats; hatch irons; half the funnel-stays; cork fenders; carpenter's grindstone and tool-chest; holy-stones, swabs, squeegees; all cabin and pantry lamps; galley fittings *en bloc*; flags and flag-locker; clocks, chronometers; the forward compass and the ship's bell and belfry, were among the missing.

There were great scarred marks on the deck-planking, over which the cargo derricks had been hauled. One must have fallen by the way, for the bulwark-rails were smashed and bent and the side-plates bruised.

'It's the Governor,' said the skipper. 'He's been selling her on the instalment plan.'

'Let's go up with spanners and shovels, and kill 'em all,' shouted the crew. 'Let's drown him, and keep the woman!'

'Then we'll be shot by that black-and-tan regiment°—*our* regiment. What's the trouble ashore? They've camped our regiment on the beach.'

'We're cut off, that's all. Go and see what they want,' said Mr Wardrop. 'You've the trousers.'

In his simple way the Governor was a strategist. He did not desire that the crew of the *Haliotis* should come ashore again, either singly or in detachments, and he proposed to turn their steamer into a convict-hulk. They would wait—he explained this from the quay to the skipper in the barge—and they would continue to wait till the man-of-war came along, exactly where they were. If one of them set foot ashore, the entire regiment would open fire, and he would not scruple to use the two cannon of the town. Meantime food would be sent daily in a boat under an armed escort. The skipper, bare to the waist, and rowing, could only grind his teeth; and the Governor improved the occasion, and revenged himself for the bitter words in the cables, by telling what he thought of the morals and manners of the crew. The barge returned to the *Haliotis* in silence, and the skipper climbed aboard, white on the cheekbones and blue about the nostrils.

'I knew it,' said Mr Wardrop; 'and they won't give us good food, either. We shall have bananas morning, noon, and night, an' a man can't work on fruit. *We* know that.'

Then the skipper cursed Mr Wardrop for importing frivolous side-issues into the conversation; and the crew cursed one another, and the *Haliotis*, the voyage, and all that they knew or could bring to mind.

They sat down in silence on the empty decks, and their eyes burned in their heads. The green harbour water chuckled at them overside. They looked at the palm-fringed hills inland, at the white houses above the harbour road, at the single tier of native craft by the quay, at the stolid soldiery sitting round the two cannon, and, last of all, at the blue bar of the horizon. Mr Wardrop was buried in thought, and scratched imaginary lines with his untrimmed finger-nails on the planking.

'I make no promise,' he said at last, 'for I can't say what may or may not have happened to them. But here's the ship, and here's us.'

There was a little scornful laughter at this, and Mr Wardrop knitted his brows. He recalled that in the days when he wore trousers he had been chief engineer of the *Haliotis*.

'Harland, Mackesy, Noble, Hay, Naughton, Fink, O'Hara, Trumbull.'

'Here, sir!' The instinct of obedience waked to answer the roll-call of the engine-room.

'Below!'

They rose and went.

'Captain, I'll trouble you for the rest of the men as I want them. We'll get my stores out, and clear away the shores we don't need, and then we'll patch her up. *My* men will remember that they're in the *Haliotis*—under me.'

He went into the engine-room, and the others stared. They were used to the accidents of the sea, but this was beyond their experience. None who had seen the engine-room believed that anything short of new engines from end to end could stir the *Haliotis* from her moorings.

The engine-room stores were unearthed, and Mr Wardrop's face, red with the filth of the bilges and the exertion of travelling on his stomach, lit with joy. The spare gear of the *Haliotis* had been unusually complete, and two-and-twenty men, armed with screw-jacks, differential blocks, tackle, vices, and a forge or so, can look Kismet° between the eyes without winking. The crew were ordered to replace the holding-down and shaft-bearing bolts, and return the collars of the thrust-block. When they had finished, Mr Wardrop delivered a lecture on repairing compound engines without the aid of the shops, and the men sat about on the cold machinery. The cross-head jammed in the guides leered at them drunkenly, but offered no help. They ran their fingers hopelessly into the cracks of the starboard supporting-column, and picked at the ends of the ropes round the shores, while Mr

Wardrop's voice rose and fell echoing, till the quick tropic night closed down over the engine-room skylight.

Next morning the work of reconstruction began.

It has been explained that the foot of the connecting-rod was forced against the foot of the starboard supporting-column, which it had cracked through and driven outward towards the ship's skin. To all appearance the job was more than hopeless, for rod and column seemed to have been welded into one. But herein Providence smiled on them for one moment to hearten them through the weary weeks ahead. The second eningeer—more reckless than resourceful—struck at random with a cold chisel into the cast-iron of the column, and a greasy, grey flake of metal flew from under the imprisoned foot of the connecting-rod, while the rod itself fell away slowly,° and brought up with a thunderous clang somewhere in the dark of the crank-pit.° The guide-plates above were still jammed fast in the guides, but the first blow had been struck. They spent the rest of the day grooming the cargo-winch, which stood immediately forward of the engine-room hatch. Its tarpaulin, of course, had been stolen, and eight warm months had not improved the working parts. Further, the last dying hiccup of the *Haliotis* seemed—or it might have been the Malay from the boat-house°—to have lifted the thing bodily on its bolts, and set it down inaccurately as regarded its steam connections.

'If we only had one single cargo-derrick!' Mr Wardrop sighed. 'We can take the cylinder-cover off by hand, if we sweat; but to get the rod out o' the piston's not possible unless we use steam. Well, there'll be steam the morn, if there's nothing else. She'll fizzle!'

Next morning men from the shore saw the *Haliotis* through a cloud, for it was as though the decks smoked. Her crew were chasing steam through the shaken and leaky pipes to its work in the forward donkey-engine; and where oakum failed to plug a crack, they stripped off their loin-cloths for lapping,° and swore, half-boiled and mother-naked. The donkey-engine worked—at a price—the price of constant attention and furious stoking—worked long enough to allow a wire rope (it was made up of a funnel and a foremast-stay) to be led into the engine-room and made fast on the cylinder-cover of the forward engine. That rose easily enough, and was hauled through the sky-light and on to the deck; many hands assisting the doubtful steam. Then came the tug of war,° for it was necessary to get to the piston and the jammed piston-rod. They removed two of the piston junk-ring studs,° screwed in two strong iron eye-bolts by way of handles, doubled the wire rope, and set half-a-dozen men to smite with an extemporised battering-ram at the end of the piston-rod, where it peered through the piston, while the donkey-engine hauled upwards on the piston itself. After four hours of this killing work the piston-rod suddenly slipped, and the piston rose with a jerk, knocking one or two men over into the engine-room. But when Mr Wardrop declared that the piston had not split, they cheered, and thought nothing of their wounds; and the donkey-engine was hastily stopped; its boiler was no thing to tamper with.

And day by day their supplies reached them by boat. The skipper humbled himself once more before the Governor, and as a concession had leave to get drinking-water from the Malay boat-builder on the quay. It was not good drinking-water, but the Malay was anxious to supply anything in his power, if he were paid for it.

Now, when the jaws of the forward engine stood, as it were, stripped and empty, they began to wedge up the shores of the cylinder itself. That work alone filled the better part of three days—warm and sticky days, when the hands slipped and sweat ran into the eyes. When the last wedge was hammered home there was no longer an ounce of weight on the supporting-columns; and Mr Wardrop rummaged the ship for boiler-plate three-quarters of an inch thick, where he could find it. There was not much available, but what there was was more than beaten gold to him. In one desperate forenoon the entire crew, naked and lean, haled back, more or less to place, the starboard supporting-column, which, as you remember, was cracked clean through. Mr Wardrop found them asleep where they had finished the work, and gave them a day's rest, smiling upon them as a father while he drew chalk-marks about the cracks. They woke to new and more trying labour; for over each one of those cracks a plate of three-quarter-inch boiler-iron was to be worked hot, the rivet-holes being drilled by hand. All that time they were fed on fruits, chiefly bananas, with some sago.

Those were the days when men swooned over the ratchet-drill and the hand-forge, and where they fell they had leave to lie unless their bodies were in the way of their fellows' feet. And so, patch upon patch, and a patch over all, the starboard supporting-column was clouted; but when they thought all was secure, Mr Wardrop decreed that the noble patchwork would never support working engines: at the best, it could only hold the guide-bars approximately true. The dead weight of the cylinders must be borne by vertical struts; and, therefore, a gang would repair to the bows, and take out, with files, the big bow-anchor davits,° each of which was some three inches in diameter. They threw hot coals at Wardrop, and threatened to kill him, those who did not weep (they were ready to weep on the least provocation); but he hit them with iron bars heated at the end, and they limped forward, and the davits came with them when they returned. They slept sixteen hours on the strength of it, and in three days two struts were in place, bolted from the foot of the starboard supporting-column to the under side of the cylinder. There remained now the port, or condenser-column, which, though not so badly cracked as its fellow, had also been strengthened in four places with boiler-plate patches, but needed struts. They took away the main stanchions of the bridge for that work, and, crazy with toil, did not see till all was in place that the rounded bars of iron must be flattened from top to bottom to allow the air-pump levers to clear them. It was Wardrop's oversight, and he wept bitterly before the men as he gave the order to unbolt the struts and flatten them with hammer and the flame. Now the broken engine was under-pinned firmly, and they took away the wooden shores from under the cylinders, and gave them to the robbed bridge, thanking God for even half a day's work on gentle, kindly wood instead of the iron that had entered into their souls.° Eight months in the back country among the leeches, at a temperature of 85° moist, is very bad for the nerves.

They had kept the hardest work to the last, as boys save Latin prose,° and, worn though they were, Mr Wardrop did not dare to give them rest. The piston-rod and connecting-rod were to be straightened, and this was a job for a regular dockyard with every appliance. They fell to it, cheered by a little chalk-showing of work done and time consumed which Mr Wardrop wrote up on the engine-room bulk-head. Fifteen days had gone—fifteen days of killing labour—and there was hope before them.

It is curious that no man knows how the rods were straightened. The crew of the *Haliotis* remember that week very dimly, as a fever patient remembers the delirium of a long night. There were fires everywhere, they say; the whole ship was one consuming furnace, and the hammers were never still. Now, there could not have been more than one fire at the most, for Mr Wardrop distinctly recalls that no straightening was done except under his own eye. They remember, too, that for many years voices gave orders which they obeyed with their bodies, but their minds were abroad on all the seas. It seems to them that they stood through days and nights slowly sliding a bar backwards and forwards through a white glow that was part of the ship. They remember an intolerable noise in their burning heads from the walls of the stoke-hole, and they remember being savagely beaten by men whose eyes seemed asleep. When their shift was over they would draw straight lines in the air, anxiously and repeatedly, and would question one another in their sleep, crying, 'Is she straight?'

At last—they do not remember whether this was by day or by night—Mr Wardrop began to dance clumsily, and wept the while; and they too danced and wept, and went to sleep twitching all over; and when they woke, men said that the rods were straightened, and no one did any work for two days, but lay on the decks and ate fruit. Mr Wardrop would go below from time to time, and pat the two rods where they lay, and they heard him singing hymns.

Then his trouble of mind went from him, and at the end of the third day's idleness he made a drawing in chalk upon the deck, with letters of the alphabet at the angles. He pointed out that, though the piston-rod was more or less straight, the piston-rod cross-head—the thing that had been jammed sideways in the guides—had been badly strained, and had cracked the lower end of the piston-rod. He was going to forge and shrink a wrought-iron collar on the neck of the piston-rod where it joined the cross-head, and from the collar he would bolt a Y-shaped piece of iron whose lower arms should be bolted into the cross-head. If anything more were needed, they could use up the last of the boiler-plate.

So the forges were lit again, and men burned their bodies, but hardly felt the pain. The finished connection was not beautiful, but it seemed strong enough—at least, as strong as the rest of the machinery; and with that job their labours came to an end. All that remained was to connect up the engines, and to get food and water. The skipper and four men dealt with the Malay boat-builder—by night chiefly; it was no time to haggle over the price of sago and dried fish. The others stayed aboard and replaced piston, piston-rod, cylinder-cover, cross-head, and bolts, with the aid of the faithful donkey-engine. The cylinder-cover was hardly steam-proof, and the eye of science might have seen in the connecting-rod a flexure something like that of a Christmas-tree candle which has melted and been straightened by hand over a stove, but, as Mr Wardrop said, 'She didn't hit anything.'

As soon as the last bolt was in place, men tumbled over one another in their anxiety to get to the hand turning-gear, the wheel and the worm, by which some engines can be moved when there is no steam aboard. They nearly wrenched off the wheel, but it was evident to the blindest eye that the engines stirred. They did not revolve in their orbits with any enthusiasm, as good machines should; indeed, they groaned not a little; but they moved over and came to rest in a way which proved that they still recognised man's hand. Then Mr Wardrop sent his slaves into the darker bowels of the engine-room and the stoke-hole, and followed them with a flare-lamp. The boilers were sound, but would take no harm from a little scaling and cleaning. Mr Wardrop would not have any one over-zealous, for he feared what the next stroke of the tool might show. 'The less we know about her now,' said he, 'the better for us all, I'm thinkin'. Ye'll understand me when I say that this is in no sense regular engineerin'.'

As his raiment, when he spoke, was his grey beard and uncut hair, they believed him. They did not ask too much of what they met, but polished and tallowed and scraped it to a false brilliancy.

'A lick of paint would make me easier in my mind,' said Mr Wardrop, plaintively. 'I know half the condenser-tubes are started;° and the propeller-shaftin' 's God knows how far out of the true, and we'll need a new air-pump, an' the main-steam leaks like a sieve, and there's worse each way I look; but—paint's like clothes to a man, an' ours is near all gone.'

The skipper unearthed some stale ropy paint of the loathsome green that they used for the galleys of sailing-ships, and Mr Wardrop spread it abroad lavishly to give the engines self-respect.

His own was returning day by day, for he wore his loin-cloth continuously; but the crew, having worked under orders, did not feel as he did. The completed work satisfied Mr Wardrop. He would at the last have made shift to run to Singapore, and gone home, without vengeance taken, to show his engines to his brethren in the craft; but the others and the captain forbade him. They had not yet recovered their self-respect.

'It would be safer to make what ye might call a trial trip, but beggars mustn't be choosers; an' if the engines will go over to the hand gear, the probability—I'm only saying it's a probability—the chance is that they'll hold up when we put steam on her.'

'How long will you take to get steam?' said the skipper.

'God knows! Four hours—a day—half a week. If I can raise sixty pound° I'll not complain.'

'Be sure of her first; we can't afford to go out half a mile, and break down.'

'My soul and body, man, we're one continuous breakdown, fore an' aft! We might fetch Singapore, though.'

'We'll break down at Pygang-Watai, where we can do good,' was the answer, in a voice that did not allow argument. 'She's *my* boat, and—I've had eight months to think in.'

No man saw the *Haliotis* depart, though many heard her. She left at two in the morning, having cut her moorings, and it was none of her crew's pleasure that the engines should strike up a thundering half-seas-over chanty that echoed among the hills. Mr Wardrop wiped away a tear as he listened to the new song.

'She's gibberin'—she's just gibberin',' he whimpered. 'Yon's the voice of a maniac.'

And if engines have any soul, as their masters believe, he was quite right. There were outcries and clamours, sobs and bursts of chattering laughter, silences where the trained ear yearned for the clear note, and torturing reduplications where there should have been one deep voice. Down the screw-shaft ran murmurs and warnings, while a heart-diseased flutter without told that the propeller needed re-keying.°

'How does she make it?' said the skipper.

'She moves, but—but she's breakin' my heart. The sooner we're at Pygang-Watai, the better. She's mad, and we're waking the town.'

'Is she at all near safe?'

'What do *I* care how safe she is! She's mad. Hear that, now! To be sure, nothing's hittin' anything, and the bearin's are fairly cool, but—can ye not hear?'

'If she goes,' said the skipper, 'I don't care a curse. And she's *my* boat, too.'

She went, trailing a fathom of weed behind her. From a slow two knots an hour she crawled up to a triumphant four. Anything beyond that made the struts quiver dangerously, and filled the engine-room with steam. Morning showed her out of sight of land, and there was a visible ripple under her bows; but she complained bitterly in her bowels, and, as though the noise had called it, there shot along across the purple sea a swift, dark proa,° hawk-like and curious, which presently ranged alongside and wished to know if the *Haliotis* were helpless. Ships, even the steamers of the white men, had been known to break down in those waters, and the honest Malay and Javanese traders would sometimes aid them in their own peculiar way. But this ship was not full of lady passengers and well-dressed officers. Men, white, naked and savage, swarmed down her sides—some with red-hot iron bars and others with large hammers—threw themselves upon those innocent inquiring strangers, and, before any man could say what had happened, were in full possession of the proa, while the lawful owners bobbed in the water overside. Half an hour later the proa's cargo of sago and tripang,° as well as a doubtful-minded compass, was in the *Haliotis*. The two huge triangular mat sails, with their seventy-foot yards, had followed the cargo, and were being fitted to the stripped masts of the steamer.

They rose, they swelled, they filled, and the empty steamer visibly laid over as the wind took them. They gave her nearly three knots an hour, and what better could men ask? But if she had been forlorn before, this new purchase made her horrible to see. Imagine a respectable charwoman in the tights of a ballet-dancer rolling drunk along the streets, and you will come to some faint notion of the appearance of that nine-hundred-ton well-decked once schooner-rigged cargo-baot as she staggered under her new help, shouting and raving across the deep. With steam and sail that marvellous voyage continued; and the bright-eyed crew° looked over the rail, desolate, unkempt, unshorn, shamelessly clothed—beyond the decencies.

At the end of the third week she sighted the island of Pygang-Watai, whose harbour is the turning-point of a pearling sea-patrol. Here the gunboats stay for a week ere they retrace their line. There is no village at Pygang-Watai, only a stream of water, some palms, and a harbour safe to rest in till the first violence of the south-east monsoon has blown itself out. They opened up the low coral beach, with its mound of whitewashed coal ready for supply, the deserted huts for the sailors, and the flagless flagstaff.

Next day there was no *Haliotis*—only a little proa rocking in the warm rain at the mouth of the harbour, whose crew watched with hungry eyes the smoke of a gunboat on the horizon.

Months afterwards there were a few lines in an English newspaper to the effect that some gunboat of some foreign Power had broken her back at the mouth of some far-away harbour by running at full speed into a sunken wreck.

My Sunday at Home

If the Red Slayer thinks he slays,
Or if the slain thinks he is slain,
They know not well the subtle ways.
I keep and pass and turn again.

EMERSON

It was the unreproducible slid *r*, as he said this was his 'fy-ist' visit to England, that told me he was a New Yorker from New York; and when, in the course of our long, lazy journey westward from Waterloo, he enlarged upon the beauties of his city, I, professing ignorance, said no word. He had, amazed and delighted at the man's civility, given the London porter a shilling for carrying his bag nearly fifty yards; he had thoroughly investigated the first-class lavatory compartment, which the London and South-Western sometimes supply without extra charge; and now, half awed, half contemptuous, but wholly interested, he looked out upon the ordered English landscape wrapped in its Sunday peace, while I watched the wonder grow upon his face. Why were the cars so short and stilted? Why had every other freight car a tarpaulin drawn over it? What wages would an engineer° get now? Where was the swarming population of England he had read so much about? What was the rank of all those men on tricycles along the roads? When were we due at Plymouth?

I told him all I knew, and very much that I did not. He was going to Plymouth to assist in a consultation upon a fellow-countryman who had retired to a place called The Hoe°—was that up town or down town?—to recover from nervous dyspepsia. Yes, he himself was a doctor by profession, and how any one in England could retain any nervous disorder passed his comprehension. Never had he dreamed of an atmosphere so soothing. Even the deep rumble of London traffic was monastical by comparison with some cities he could name; and the country—why, it was Paradise. A continuance of it, he confessed, would drive him mad; but for a few months it was the most sumptuous rest cure in his knowledge.

'I'll come over every year after this,' he said, in a burst of delight, as we ran between two ten-foot hedges of pink and white may. 'It's seeing all the things I've ever read about. Of course it doesn't strike you that way. I presume you belong here? What a finished land it is! It's arrived. Must have been born this way. Now, where I used to live —Hello! what's up?'

The train stopped in a blaze of sunshine at Framlynghame Admiral,° which is made up entirely of the nameboard, two platforms, and an overhead bridge, without even the usual siding. I had never known the slowest of locals stop here before; but on Sunday all things are possible to the London and South-Western. One could hear the drone of conversation along the carriages, and, scarcely less loud, the drone of the bumblebees in the wallflowers up the bank. My companion thrust his head through the window and sniffed luxuriously.

'Where are we now?' said he.

'In Wiltshire,' said I.

'Ah! A man ought to be able to write novels with his left hand in a country like this. Well, well! And so this is about Tess's country,° ain't it? I feel just as if I were in a book. Say, the conduc—the guard has something on his mind. What's he getting at?'

The splendid badged and belted guard was striding up the platform at the regulation official pace, and in the regulation official voice was saying at each door—

'Has any gentleman here a bottle of medicine? A gentleman has taken a bottle of poison (laudanum) by mistake.'

Between each five paces he looked at an official telegram in his hand, refreshed his memory, and said his say. The dreamy look on my companion's face—he had gone far away with Tess—passed with the speed of a snap-shutter.° After the manner of his countrymen, he had risen to the situation, jerked his bag down from the overhead rail, opened it, and I heard the click of bottles. 'Find out where the man is,' he said briefly. 'I've got something here that will fix him—if he can swallow still.'

Swiftly I fled up the line of carriages in the wake of the guard. There was clamour in a rear compartment—the voice of one bellowing to be let out, and the feet of one who kicked. With the tail of my eye I saw the New York doctor hastening thither, bearing in his hand a blue and brimming glass from the lavatory compartment. The guard I found scratching his head unofficially, by the engine, and murmuring: 'Well, I put a bottle of medicine off at Andover,° I'm sure I did.'

'Better say it again, any'ow,' said the driver. 'Orders is orders. Say it again.'

Once more the guard paced back, I, anxious to attract his attention, trotting at his heels.

'In a minute—in a minute, sir,' he said, waving an arm capable of starting all the traffic on the London and South-Western Railway at a wave. 'Has any gentleman here got a bottle of medicine? A gentleman has taken a bottle of poison (laudanum) by mistake.'

'Where's the man?' I gasped.

'Woking. 'Ere's my orders.' He showed me the telegram, on which were the words to be said. ''E must have left 'is bottle in the train, an' took another by mistake. 'E's been wirin' from Woking awful, an', now I come to think of it, I'm nearly sure I put a bottle of medicine off at Andover.'

'Then the man that took the poison isn't in the train?'

'Lord, no, sir. No one didn't take poison *that* way. 'E took it away with 'im, in 'is 'ands. 'E's wirin' from Wokin'. My orders was to ask everybody in the train, and I 'ave, an' we're four minutes late now. Are you comin' on, sir? No? Right be'ind!'

There is nothing, unless, perhaps, the English language, more terrible than the workings of an English railway line. An instant before it seemed as though we were going to spend all eternity at Framlynghame Admiral, and now I was watching the tail of the train disappear round the curve of the cutting.

But I was not alone. On the one bench of the down platform sat the largest navvy I have ever seen in my life, softened and made affable (for he smiled generously) with liquor. In his huge hands he nursed an empty tumbler marked 'L.S.W.R.'—marked also, internally, with streaks of blue-gray sediment. Before him, a hand on his shoulder, stood the doctor, and as I came within earshot this is what I heard him say: 'Just you hold on to your patience for a minute or two longer, and you'll be as right as ever you were in your life. *I'll* stay with you till you're better.'

'Lord! I'm comfortable enough,' said the navvy. 'Never felt better in my life.'

Turning to me, the doctor lowered his voice. 'He might have died while that fool conduct—guard was saying his piece. I've fixed him, though. The stuff's due in about five minutes, but there's a heap *to* him. I don't see how we can make him take exercise.'

For a moment I felt as though seven pounds of crushed ice had been neatly applied in the form of a compress to my lower stomach.

'How—how did you manage it?' I gasped.

'I asked him if he'd have a drink. He was knocking spots out of the car—strength of his constitution, I suppose. He said he'd go 'most anywhere for a drink, so I lured him on to the platform, and loaded him up. Cold-blooded people you Britishers are. That train's gone, and no one seemed to care a cent.'

'We've missed it,' I said.

He looked at me curiously.

'We'll get another before sundown, if that's your only trouble. Say, porter, when's the next train down?'

'Seven forty-five,' said the one porter, and passed out through the wicket-gate into the landscape. It was then three-twenty of a hot and sleepy afternoon. The station was absolutely deserted. The navvy had closed his eyes, and now nodded.

'That's bad,' said the doctor. 'The man, I mean, not the train. We must make him walk somehow—walk up and down.'

Swiftly as might be, I explained the delicacy of the situation, and the doctor from New York turned a full bronze-green. Then he swore comprehensively at the entire fabric of our glorious Constitution, cursing the English language, root, branch, and paradigm, through its most obscure derivatives. His coat and bag lay on the bench next to the sleeper. Thither he edged cautiously, and I saw treachery in his eye.

What devil of delay possessed him to slip on his spring overcoat, I cannot tell. They say a slight noise rouses a sleeper more surely than a heavy one, and scarcely had the doctor settled himself in his sleeves than the giant waked and seized that silk-faced collar in a hot right hand. There was rage in his face—rage and the realisation of new emotions.

'I'm—I'm not so comfortable as I were,' he said from the deeps of his interior. 'You'll wait along o' me, *you* will.' He breathed heavily through shut lips.

Now, if there was one thing more than another upon which the doctor had dwelt in his conversation with me, it was upon the essential law-abidingness, not to say gentleness, of his much-misrepresented country. And yet (truly, it may have been no more than a button that irked him) I saw his hand travel backwards to his right hip, clutch at something, and come away empty.

'He won't kill you,' I said. 'He'll probably sue you in court, if I know my own people. Better give him some money from time to time.'

'If he keeps quiet till the stuff gets in its work,' the doctor answered, 'I'm all right. If he doesn't . . . my name is Emory—Julian B. Emory—193 'Steenth Street, corner of Madison and—'

'I feel worse than I've ever felt,' said the navvy, with suddenness. 'What—did—you—give—me—the—drink—for?'

The matter seemed to be so purely personal that I withdrew to a strategic position on the overhead bridge, and, abiding in the exact centre, looked on from afar.

I could see the white road that ran across the shoulder of Salisbury Plain, unshaded for mile after mile, and a dot in the middle distance, the back of the one porter returning to Framlynghame Admiral, if such a place existed, till seven forty-five. The bell of a church invisible clanked softly. There was a rustle in the horse-chestnuts to the left of the line, and the sound of sheep cropping close.

The peace of Nirvana lay upon the land, and, brooding in it, my elbow on the warm iron girder of the footbridge (it is a forty-shilling fine to cross by any other means), I perceived, as never before, how the consequences of our acts run eternal through time and through space. If we impinge never so slightly upon the life of a fellow-mortal, the touch of our personality, like the ripple of a stone cast into a pond, widens and widens in unending circles across the æons, till the far-off gods themselves cannot say where action ceases. Also, it was I who had silently set before the doctor the tumbler of the first-class lavatory compartment now speeding Plymouthward. Yet I was, in spirit at least, a million leagues removed from that unhappy man of another nationality, who had chosen to thrust an inexpert finger into the workings of an alien life. The machinery was dragging him up and down the sunlit platform. The two men seemed to be learning polka-mazurkas together, and the burden of their song, borne by one deep voice, was: 'What did you give me the drink for?'

I saw the flash of silver in the doctor's hand. The navvy took it and pocketed it with his left; but never for an instant did his strong right leave the doctor's coat-collar, and as the crisis approached, louder and louder rose his bull-like roar: 'What did you give me the drink for?'

They drifted under the great twelve-inch pinned timbers of the footbridge towards the bench, and, I gathered, the time was very near at hand. The stuff was getting in its work. Blue, white, and blue again, rolled over the navvy's face in waves, till all settled to one rich clay-bank yellow and—that fell which fell.

I thought of the blowing-up of Hell Gate;° of the geysers in the Yellowstone Park;° of Jonah and his whale;° but the lively original, as I watched it foreshortened from above, exceeded all these things. He staggered to the bench, the heavy wooden seat cramped with iron cramps into the enduring stone, and clung there with his left hand. It quivered and shook, as a breakwater-pile quivers to the rush of landward-racing seas; nor was there lacking when he caught his breath, the 'scream of a maddened beach dragged down by the tide.'° His right hand was upon the doctor's collar, so that the two shook to one paroxysm, pendulums vibrating together, while I, apart, shook with them.

It was colossal—immense; but of certain manifestations the English language stops short. French only, the caryatid French° of Victor Hugo, would have described it; so I mourned while I laughed, hastily shuffling and discarding inadequate adjectives. The vehemence of the shock spent itself, and the sufferer half fell, half knelt, across the bench. He was calling now upon God and his wife, huskily, as the wounded bull calls upon the unscathed herd to stay. Curiously enough, he used no bad language: that had gone from him with the rest. The doctor exhibited gold. It was taken and retained. So, too, was the grip on the coat-collar.

'If I could stand,' boomed the giant desparingly, 'I'd smash you—you an' your drinks. I'm dyin'—dyin'—dyin'!'

'That's what you think,' said the doctor. 'You'll find it will do you a lot of good'; and, making a virtue of a somewhat imperative necessity, he added: 'I'll stay by you. If you'd let go of me a minute I'd give you something that would settle you.'

'You've settled me now, you damned anarchist.° Takin' the bread out of the mouth of an English workin' man! But I'll keep 'old of you till I'm well or dead. I never did you no harm. S'pose I *were* a little full. They pumped me out once at Guy's° with a stummick-pump. I could see *that*, but I can't see this 'ere, an' it's killin' of me by slow degrees.'

'You'll be all right in half an hour. What do you suppose I'd want to kill you for?' said the doctor, who came of a logical breed.

''Ow do *I* know? Tell 'em in court. You'll get seven years for this, you body-snatcher.° That's what you are—a bloomin' body-snatcher. There's justice, I tell you, in England; and my Union'll prosecute, too. We don't stand no tricks with people's insides 'ere. They gave a woman ten years for a sight less than this. An' you'll 'ave to pay 'undreds an' 'undreds o' pounds, besides a pension to the missus. *You*'ll see, you physickin' furriner. Where's your licence to do such? *You*'ll catch it, I tell you!'

Then I observed, what I had frequently observed before, that a man who is but reasonably afraid of an altercation with an alien has a most poignant dread of the operations of foreign law. The doctor's voice was flute-like in its exquisite politeness, as he answered:

'But I've given you a very great deal of money—fif°—three pounds, I think.'

'An' what's three pounds for poisonin' the likes o' *me*? They told me at Guy's I'd fetch twenty—cold—on the slates. Ouh! It's comin' again.'

A second time he was cut down by the foot, as it were, and the straining bench rocked to and fro as I averted my eyes.

It was the very point of perfection in the heart of an English May-day. The unseen tides of the air had turned, and all nature was setting its face with the shadows of the horse-chestnuts towards the peace of the coming night. But there were hours yet, I knew—long, long hours of the eternal English twilight—to the ending of the day. I was well content to be alive—to abandon myself to the drift of Time and Fate;

to absorb great peace through my skin, and to love my country with the devotion that three thousand miles of intervening sea bring to fullest flower. And what a garden of Eden it was, this fatted, clipped, and washen land! A man could camp in any open field with more sense of home and security than the stateliest buildings of foreign cities could afford. And the joy was that it was all mine inalienably—groomed hedgerow, spotless road, decent greystone cottage, serried spinney, tasselled copse, apple-bellied hawthorn, and well-grown tree. A light puff of wind—it scattered flakes of may over the gleaming rails—gave me a faint whiff as it might have been of fresh cocoanut, and I knew that the golden gorse was in bloom somewhere out of sight. Linnæus° had thanked God on his bended knees when he first saw a field of it; and, by the way, the navvy was on his knees too. But he was by no means praying. He was purely disgustful.

The doctor was compelled to bend over him, his face towards the back of the seat, and from what I had seen I supposed the navvy was now dead. If that were the case it would be time for me to go; but I knew that so long as a man trusts himself to the current of Circumstance, reaching out for and rejecting nothing that comes his way, no harm can overtake him. It is the contriver, the schemer, who is caught by the law, and never the philosopher. I knew that when the play was played, Destiny herself would move me on from the corpse; and I felt very sorry for the doctor.

In the far distance, presumably upon the road that led to Framlynghame Admiral, there appeared a vehicle and a horse—the one ancient fly° that almost every village can produce at need. This thing was advancing, unpaid by me, towards the station; would have to pass along the deep-cut lane, below the railway-bridge, and come out on the doctor's side. I was in the centre of things, so all sides were alike to me. Here, then, was my machine from the machine.° When it arrived, something would happen, or something else. For the rest, I owned my deeply interested soul.

The doctor, by the seat, turned so far as his cramped position allowed, his head over his left shoulder, and laid his right hand upon his lips. I threw back my hat and elevated my eyebrows in the form of a question. The doctor shut his eyes and nodded his head slowly twice or thrice, beckoning me to come. I descended cautiously, and it was as the signs had told. The navvy was asleep, empty to the lowest notch; yet his hand clutched still the doctor's collar, and at the lightest movement (the doctor was really very cramped) tightened mechanically, as the hand of a sick woman tightens on that of the watcher. He had dropped, squatting almost upon his heels, and, falling lower, had dragged the doctor over to the left.

The doctor thrust his right hand, which was free, into his pocket, drew forth some keys, and shook his head. The navvy gurgled in his sleep. Silently I dived into my pocket, took out one sovereign, and held it up between finger and thumb. Again the doctor shook his head. Money was not what was lacking to his peace. His bag had fallen from the seat to the ground. He looked towards it, and opened his mouth—O-shape.° The catch was not a difficult one, and when I had mastered it, the doctor's right forefinger was sawing the air. With an immense caution, I extracted from the bag such a knife as they use for cutting collops off legs. The doctor frowned, and with his first and second fingers imitated the action of scissors. Again I searched, and found a most diabolical pair of cock-nosed° shears, capable of vandyking° the interiors of elephants. The doctor then slowly lowered his left shoulder till the navvy's right wrist was supported by the bench, pausing a moment as the spent volcano rumbled anew. Lower and lower the doctor sank, kneeling now by the navvy's side, till his head was on a level with, and just in front of the great hairy fist, and—there was no tension on the coat-collar. Then light dawned on me.

Beginning a little to the right of the spinal column, I cut a huge demilune out of his new spring overcoat, bringing it round as far under his left side (which was the right side of the navvy) as I dared. Passing thence swiftly to the back of the seat, and reaching between the splines, I sawed through the silk-faced front on the left hand side of the coat till the two cuts joined.

Cautiously as the box-turtle of his native heath,° the doctor drew away sideways and to the right, with the air of a frustrated burglar coming out from under a bed, and stood up free, one black diagonal shoulder projecting through the gray of his ruined overcoat. I returned the scissors to the bag, snapped the catch, and held all out to him as the wheels of the fly rang hollow under the railway arch.

It came at a footpace past the wicket-gate of the station, and the doctor stopped it with a whisper. It was going some five miles across country to bring home from church some one—I could not catch the name—because his own carriage-horses were lame. Its destination happened to be the one place in all the world that the doctor was most burningly anxious to visit, and he promised the driver untold gold to drive to some ancient flame of his—Helen Blazes, she was called.

'Aren't you coming, too?' he said, bundling his overcoat into his bag.

Now the fly had been so obviously sent to the doctor, and to no one else, that I had no concern with it. Our roads, I saw, divided, and there was, further, a need upon me to laugh.

'I shall stay here,' I said. 'It's a very pretty country.'

'My God!' he murmured, as softly as he shut the door, and I felt that it was a prayer.

Then he went out of my life, and I shaped my course for the railway-bridge. It was necessary to pass by the bench once more, but the wicket was between us. The departure of the fly had waked the navvy. He crawled on to the seat, and with malignant eyes watched the driver flog down the road.

'The man inside o' that,' he called, ''as poisoned me. 'E's a body-snatcher. 'E's comin' back again when I'm cold. 'Ere's my evidence!'

He waved his share of the overcoat, and I went my way, because I was hungry. Framlynghame Admiral village is a good two miles from the station, and I waked the holy calm of the evening every step of that way with shouts and yells, casting myself down in the flank of the good green hedge when I was too weak to stand. There was an inn,—a blessed inn with a thatched roof, and peonies in the garden,—and I ordered myself an upper chamber in which the Foresters held their courts,° for the laughter was not all out of me. A bewildered woman brought me ham and eggs, and I leaned out of the mullioned window, and laughed between mouthfuls. I sat long above the beer and the perfect smoke that followed, till the light changed in the quiet street, and I began to think of the seven forty-five down, and all that world of the *Arabian Nights* I had quitted.

Descending, I passed a giant in moleskins who filled the low-ceiled tap-room. Many empty plates stood before him, and beyond them a fringe of the Framlynghame Admiralty, to whom he was unfolding a wondrous tale of anarchy, of body-snatching, of bribery, and the Valley of the Shadow from the which he was but newly risen. And as he talked he ate, and as he ate he drank, for there was much room in him; and anon he paid royally, speaking of justice and the law, before whom all Englishmen are equal, and all foreigners and anarchists vermin and slime.

On my way to the station he passed me with great strides, his head high among the low-flying bats, his feet firm on the packed road metal, his fists clenched, and his breath coming sharply. There was a beautiful smell in the air—the smell of white dust, bruised nettles, and smoke, that brings tears to the throat of a man who sees his country but seldom—a smell like the echoes of the lost talk of lovers;

the infinitely suggestive odour of an immemorial civilisation. It was a perfect walk; and, lingering on every step, I came to the station just as the one porter lighted the last of a truck-load of lamps,° and set them back in the lamp-room, while he dealt tickets to four or five of the population, who, not contented with their own peace, thought fit to travel. It was no ticket that the navvy seemed to need. He was sitting on a bench wrathfully grinding a tumbler into fragments with his heel. I abode in obscurity at the end of the platform, interested as ever, thank heaven, in my surroundings. There was a jar of wheels on the road. The navvy rose as they approached, strode through the wicket, and laid a hand on the horse's bridle that brought the beast up on his hireling hind-legs. It was the providential fly coming back, and for a moment I wondered whether the doctor had been mad enough to revisit his practice.

'Get away; you're drunk,' said the driver.

'I'm not,' said the navvy. 'I've been waitin' 'ere hours and hours. Come out, you beggar inside there.'

'Go on, driver,' said a voice I did not know—a crisp, clear, English voice.

'All right,' said the navvy. 'You wouldn't 'ear me when I was polite. *Now* will you come?'

There was a chasm in the side of the fly, for he had wrenched the door bodily off its hinges, and was feeling within purposely. A well-booted leg rewarded him, and there came out, not with delight, hopping on one foot, a round and gray-haired Englishman, from whose armpits dropped hymn-books, but from his mouth an altogether different service of song.

'Come on, you bloomin' body-snatcher! You thought I was dead, did you?' roared the navvy. And the respectable gentleman came accordingly, inarticulate with rage.

''Ere's a man murderin' the Squire,' the driver shouted, and fell from his box upon the navvy's neck.

To do them justice, the people of Framlynghame Admiral, so many as were on the platform, rallied to the call in the best spirit of feudalism. It was the one porter who beat the navvy on the nose with a ticket-punch, but it was the three third-class tickets who attached themselves to his legs and freed the captive.

'Send for a constable! lock him up!' said that man, adjusting his collar; and unitedly they cast him into the lamp-room, and turned the key, while the driver mourned over the wrecked fly.

Till then the navvy, whose only desire was justice, had kept his temper nobly. Then he went Berserk before our amazed eyes. The door of the lamp-room was generously constructed, and would not give an inch, but the window he tore from its fastenings and hurled outwards. The one porter counted the damage in a loud voice, and the others, arming themselves with agricultural implements from the station garden, kept up a ceaseless winnowing before the window, themselves backed close to the wall, and bade the prisoner think of the gaol. He answered little to the point, so far as they could understand; but seeing that his exit was impeded, he took a lamp and hurled it through the wrecked sash. It fell on the metals and went out. With inconceivable velocity, the others, fifteen in all, followed looking like rockets in the gloom, and with the last (he could have had no plan) the Berserk rage left him as the doctor's deadly brewage waked up, under the stimulus of violent exercise and a very full meal, to one last cataclysmal exhibition, and—we heard the whistle of the seven forty-five down.

They were all acutely interested in as much of the wreck as they could see, for the station smelt to heaven of oil, and the engine skittered over broken glass like a terrier in a cucumber frame. The guard had to hear of it, and the Squire had his version of the brutal assault, and heads were out all along the carriages as I found me a seat.

'What is the row?' said a young man, as I entered. 'Man drunk?'

'Well, the symptoms, so far as my observation has gone, more resemble those of Asiatic cholera than anything else,' I answered, slowly and judicially, that every word might carry weight in the appointed scheme of things. Till then, you will observe, I had taken no part in that war.°

He was an Englishman, but he collected his belongings as swiftly as had the American, ages before, and leaped upon the platform, crying, 'Can I be of any service? I'm a doctor.'

From the lamp-room I heard a wearied voice wailing: 'Another bloomin' doctor!'

And the seven forty-five carried me on, a step nearer to Eternity, by the road that is worn and seamed and channelled with the passions, and weaknesses, and warring interests of man who is immortal and master of his fate.°

From JUST SO STORIES (1902)

The Cat that Walked by Himself

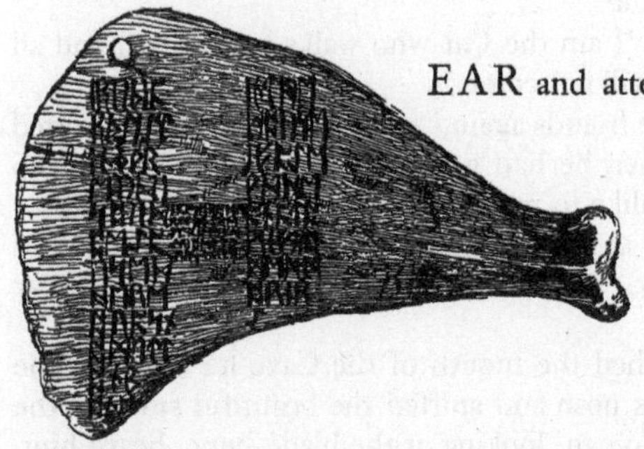

EAR and attend° and listen; for this befell and behappened and became and was, O my Best Beloved, when the Tame animals were wild. The Dog was wild, and the Horse was wild, and the Cow was wild, and the Sheep was wild, and the Pig was wild—as wild as wild could be—and they walked in the Wet Wild Woods by their wild lones. But the wildest of all the wild animals was the Cat. He walked by himself, and all places were alike to him.

Of course the Man was wild too. He was dreadfully wild. He didn't even begin to be tame till he met the Woman, and she told him that she did not like living in his wild ways. She picked out a nice dry Cave, instead of a heap of wet leaves, to lie down in; and she strewed clean sand on the floor; and she lit a nice fire of wood at the back of the Cave; and she hung a dried wild-horse skin, tail-down, across the opening of the Cave; and she said, 'Wipe your feet, dear, when you come in, and now we'll keep house.'

That night, Best Beloved, they ate wild sheep roasted on the hot stones, and flavoured with wild garlic and wild pepper; and wild duck stuffed with wild rice and wild fenugreek and wild coriander; and marrow-bones of wild oxen; and wild cherries, and wild grenadillas. Then the Man went to sleep in front of the fire ever so happy; but the Woman sat up, combing her hair. She took the bone of the shoulder of mutton—the big flat blade-bone—and she looked at the wonderful marks on it, and she threw more wood on the fire, and she made a Magic. She made the First Singing Magic in the world.

Out in the Wet Wild Woods all the wild animals gathered together where they could see the light of the fire a long way off, and they wondered what it meant.

Then Wild Horse stamped with his wild foot and said, 'O my Friends and O my Enemies, why have the Man and the Woman made that great light in that great Cave, and what harm will it do us?'

Wild Dog lifted up his wild nose and smelled the smell of the roast mutton, and said, 'I will go up and see and look, and say; for I think it is good. Cat, come with me.'

'Nenni!' said the Cat. 'I am the Cat who walks by himself, and all places are alike to me. I will not come.'

'Then we can never be friends again,' said Wild Dog, and he trotted off to the Cave. But when he had gone a little way the Cat said to himself, 'All places are alike to me. Why should I not go too and see and look and come away at my own liking?' So he slipped after Wild Dog softly, very softly, and hid himself where he could hear everything.

When Wild Dog reached the mouth of the Cave he lifted up the dried horse-skin with his nose and sniffed the beautiful smell of the roast mutton, and the Woman, looking at the blade-bone, heard him, and laughed, and said, 'Here comes the first. Wild Thing out of the Wild Woods, what do you want?'

Wild Dog said, 'O my Enemy and Wife of my Enemy, what is this that smells so good in the Wild Woods?'

Then the Woman picked up a roasted mutton-bone and threw it to Wild Dog, and said, 'Wild Thing out of the Wild Woods, taste and try.' Wild Dog gnawed the bone, and it was more delicious than anything he had ever tasted, and he said, 'O my Enemy and Wife of my Enemy, give me another.'

The Woman said, 'Wild Thing out of the Wild Woods, help my Man to hunt through the day and guard this Cave at night, and I will give you as many roast bones as you need.'

'Ah!' said the Cat, listening. 'This is a very wise Woman, but she is not so wise as I am.'

Wild Dog crawled into the Cave and laid his head on the Woman's lap, and said, 'O my Friend and Wife of my Friend, I will help your Man to hunt through the day, and at night I will guard your Cave.'

'Ah!' said the Cat, listening. 'That is a very foolish Dog.' And he went back through the Wet Wild Woods waving his wild tail, and walking by his wild lone. But he never told anybody.

When the Man waked up he said, 'What is Wild Dog doing here?'

And the Woman said, 'His name is not Wild Dog any more, but the First Friend, because he will be our friend for always and always and always. Take him with you when you go hunting.'

Next night the Woman cut great green armfuls of fresh grass from the water-meadows, and dried it before the fire, so that it smelt like new-mown hay, and she sat at the mouth of the Cave and plaited a halter out of horse-hide, and she looked at the shoulder-of-mutton bone—at the big broad blade-bone—and she made a Magic. She made the Second Singing Magic in the world.

Out in the Wild Woods all the wild animals wondered what had happened to Wild Dog, and at last Wild Horse stamped with his foot and said, 'I will go and see and say why Wild Dog has not returned. Cat, come with me.'

'Nenni!' said the Cat. 'I am the Cat who walks by himself, and all places are alike to me. I will not come.' But all the same he followed Wild Horse softly, very softly, and hid himself where he could hear everything.

When the Woman heard Wild Horse tripping and stumbling on his long mane,° she laughed and said, 'Here comes the second. Wild Thing out of the Wild Woods, what do you want?'

Wild Horse said, 'O my Enemy and Wife of my Enemy, where is Wild Dog?'

The Woman laughed, and picked up the blade-bone and looked at it, and said, 'Wild Thing out of the Wild Woods, you did not come here for Wild Dog, but for the sake of this good grass.'

And Wild Horse, tripping and stumbling on his long mane, said, 'That is true; give it me to eat.'

The Woman said, 'Wild Thing out of the Wild Woods, bend your wild head and wear what I give you, and you shall eat the wonderful grass three times a day.'

'Ah!' said the Cat, listening. 'This is a clever Woman, but she is not so clever as I am.'

Wild Horse bent his wild head, and the Woman slipped the plaited-hide halter over it, and Wild Horse breathed on the Woman's feet and said, 'O my Mistress, and Wife of my Master, I will be your servant for the sake of the wonderful grass.'

'Ah!' said the Cat, listening. 'That is a very foolish Horse.' And he went back through the Wet Wild Woods, waving his wild tail and walking by his wild lone. But he never told anybody.

When the Man and the Dog came back from hunting, the Man said, 'What is Wild Horse doing here?' And the Woman said, 'His

This is the picture of the Cave where the Man and the Woman lived first of all. It was really a very nice Cave, and much warmer than it looks. The Man had a canoe. It is on the edge of the river, being soaked in water to make it swell up. The tattery-looking thing across the river is the Man's salmon-net to catch salmon with. There are nice clean stones leading up from the river to the mouth of the Cave, so that the Man and the Woman could go down for water without getting sand between their toes. The things like black-beetles far down the beach are really trunks of dead trees that floated down the river from the Wet Wild Woods on the other bank. The Man and the Woman used to drag them out and dry them and cut them up for firewood. I haven't drawn the horse-hide curtain at the mouth of the Cave, because the Woman has just taken it down to be cleaned. All those little smudges on the sand between the Cave and the river are the marks of the Woman's feet and the Man's feet.

The Man and the Woman are both inside the Cave eating their dinner. They went to another cosier Cave when the Baby came, because the Baby used to crawl down to the river and fall in, and the Dog had to pull him out.

name is not Wild Horse any more, but the First Servant, because he will carry us from place to place for always and always and always. Ride on his back when you go hunting.'

Next day, holding her wild head high that her wild horns should not catch in the wild trees, Wild Cow came up to the Cave, and the Cat followed, and hid himself just the same as before; and everything happened just the same as before; and the Cat said the same things as before; and when Wild Cow had promised to give her milk to the Woman every day in exchange for the wonderful grass, the Cat went back through the Wet Wild Woods waving his wild tail and walking by his wild lone, just the same as before. But he never told anybody. And when the Man and the Horse and the Dog came home from hunting and asked the same questions same as before, the Woman said, 'Her name is not Wild Cow any more, but the Giver of Good Food. She will give us the warm white milk for always and always and always, and I will take care of her while you and the First Friend and the First Servant go hunting.'

Next day the Cat waited to see if any other Wild Thing would go up to the Cave, but no one moved in the Wet Wild Woods, so the Cat walked there by himself; and he saw the Woman milking the Cow, and he saw the light of the fire in the Cave, and he smelt the smell of the warm white milk.

Cat said, 'O my Enemy and Wife of my Enemy, where did Wild Cow go?'

The Woman laughed and said, 'Wild Thing out of the Wild Woods, go back to the Woods again, for I have braided up my hair, and I have put away the magic blade-bone, and we have no more need of either friends or servants in our Cave.'

Cat said, 'I am not a friend, and I am not a servant. I am the Cat who walks by himself, and I wish to come into your Cave.'

Woman said, 'Then why did you not come with First Friend on the first night?'

Cat grew very angry and said, 'Has Wild Dog told tales of me?'

Then the Woman laughed and said, 'You are the Cat who walks by himself, and all places are alike to you. You are neither a friend nor a servant. You have said it yourself. Go away and walk by yourself in all places alike.'

Then Cat pretended to be sorry and said, 'Must I never come into the Cave? Must I never sit by the warm fire? Must I never drink the warm white milk? You are very wise and very beautiful. You should not be cruel even to a Cat.'

Woman said, 'I knew I was wise, but I did not know I was beautiful. So I will make a bargain with you. If ever I say one word in your praise, you may come into the Cave.'

'And if you say two words in my praise?' said the Cat.

'I never shall,' said the Woman, 'but if I say two words in your praise, you may sit by the fire in the Cave.'

'And if you say three words?' said the Cat.

'I never shall,' said the Woman, 'but if I say three words in your praise, you may drink the warm white milk three times a day for always and always and always.'

Then the Cat arched his back and said, 'Now let the Curtain at the Mouth of the Cave, and the Fire at the back of the Cave, and the Milk-pots that stand beside the Fire, remember what my Enemy and the Wife of my Enemy has said.' And he went away through the Wet Wild Woods waving his wild tail and walking by his wild lone.

That night when the Man and the Horse and the Dog came home from hunting, the Woman did not tell them of the bargain that she had made with the Cat, because she was afraid that they might not like it.

Cat went far and far away and hid himself in the Wet Wild Woods by his wild lone for a long time till the Woman forgot all about him. Only the Bat—the little upside-down Bat—that hung inside the Cave knew where Cat hid; and every evening Bat would fly to Cat with news of what was happening.

One evening Bat said, 'There is a Baby in the Cave. He is new and pink and fat and small, and the Woman is very fond of him.'

'Ah,' said the Cat, listening, 'but what is the Baby fond of?'

'He is fond of things that are soft and tickle,' said the Bat. 'He is fond of warm things to hold in his arms when he goes to sleep. He is fond of being played with. He is fond of all those things.'

'Ah,' said the Cat, listening, 'then my time has come.'

Next night Cat walked through the Wet Wild Woods and hid very near the Cave till morning-time, and Man and Dog and Horse went hunting. The Woman was busy cooking that morning, and the Baby cried and interrupted. So she carried him outside the Cave and gave him a handful of pebbles to play with. But still the Baby cried.

Then the Cat put out his paddy paw and patted the Baby on the cheek, and it cooed; and the Cat rubbed against its fat knees and tickled it under its fat chin with his tail. And the Baby laughed; and the Woman heard him and smiled.

Then the Bat—the little upside-down Bat—that hung in the mouth

This is the picture of the Cat that Walked by Himself, walking by his wild lone through the Wet Wild Woods and waving his wild tail. There is nothing else in the picture except some toadstools. They had to grow there because the woods were so wet. The lumpy thing on the low branch isn't a bird. It is moss that grew there because the Wild Woods were so wet.

Underneath the truly picture is a picture of the cosy Cave that the Man and Woman went to after the Baby came. It was their summer Cave, and they planted wheat in front of it. The man is riding on the Horse to find the Cow and bring her back to the Cave to be milked. He is holding up his hand to call the Dog, who has swum across to the other side of the river, looking for rabbits.

of the Cave said, 'O my Hostess and Wife of my Host and Mother of my Host's Son, a Wild Thing from the Wild Woods is most beautifully playing with your Baby.'

'A blessing on that Wild Thing whoever he may be,' said the Woman straightening her back, 'for I was a busy woman this morning and he has done me a service.'

That very minute and second, Best Beloved, the dried horse-skin Curtain that was stretched tail-down at the mouth of the Cave fell down—*woosh!*—because it remembered the bargain she had made with the Cat; and when the Woman went to pick it up—lo and behold!— the Cat was sitting quite comfy inside the Cave.

'O my Enemy and Wife of my Enemy and Mother of my Enemy,' said the Cat, 'it is I: for you have spoken a word in my praise, and now I can sit within the Cave for always and always and always. But still I am the Cat who walks by himself, and all places are alike to me.'

The Woman was very angry, and shut her lips tight and took up her spinning-wheel and began to spin.

But the Baby cried becuase the Cat had gone away, and the Woman could not hush it, for it struggled and kicked and grew black in the face.

'O my Enemy and Wife of my Enemy and Mother of my Enemy,' said the Cat, 'take a strand of the thread that you are spinning and tie it to your spinning-whorl and drag it along the floor, and I will show you a Magic that shall make your Baby laugh as loudly as he is now crying.'

'I will do so,' said the Woman, 'because I am at my wits' end; but I will not thank you for it.'

She tied the thread to the little clay spindle-whorl and drew it across the floor, and the Cat ran after it and patted it with his paws and rolled head over heels, and tossed it backward over his shoulder and chased it between his hind-legs and pretended to lose it, and pounced down upon it again, till the Baby laughed as loudly as it had been crying, and scrambled after the Cat and frolicked all over the Cave till it grew tired and settled down to sleep with the Cat in its arms.

'Now,' said Cat, 'I will sing the Baby a song that shall keep him asleep for an hour.' And he began to purr, loud and low, low and loud, till the Baby fell fast asleep. The Woman smiled as she looked down upon the two of them, and said, 'That was wonderfully done. No question but you are very clever, O Cat.'

That very minute and second, Best Beloved, the smoke of the Fire at the back of the Cave came down in clouds from the roof—*puff!*—because it remembered the bargain she had made with the Cat; and when it had cleared away—lo and behold!—the Cat was sitting quite comfy close to the fire.

'O my Enemy and Wife of my Enemy and Mother of my Enemy,' said the Cat, 'it is I: for you have spoken a second word in my praise, and now I can sit by the warm fire at the back of the Cave for always and always and always. But still I am the Cat who walks by himself, and all places are alike to me.'

Then the Woman was very very angry, and let down her hair and put more wood on the fire and brought out the broad blade-bone of the shoulder of mutton and began to make a Magic that should prevent her from saying a third word in praise of the Cat. It was not a Singing Magic, Best Beloved, it was a Still Magic; and by and by the Cave grew so still that a little wee-wee mouse crept out of a corner and ran across the floor.

'O my Enemy and Wife of my Enemy and Mother of my Enemy,' said the Cat, 'is that little mouse part of your Magic?'

'Ouh! Chee! No indeed!' said the Woman, and she dropped the blade-bone and jumped upon the footstool in front of the fire and braided up her hair very quick for fear that the mouse should run up it.

'Ah,' said the Cat, watching, 'then the mouse will do me no harm if I eat it?'

'No,' said the Woman, braiding up her hair, 'eat it quickly and I will ever be grateful to you.'

Cat made one jump and caught the little mouse, and the Woman said, 'A hundred thanks. Even the First Friend is not quick enough to catch little mice as you have done. You must be very wise.'

That very moment and second, O Best Beloved, the Milk-pot that stood by the fire cracked in two pieces—*ffft!*—because it remembered the bargain she had made with the Cat; and when the Woman jumped down from the footstool—lo and behold!—the Cat was lapping up the warm white milk that lay in one of the broken pieces.

'O my Enemy and Wife of my Enemy and Mother of my Enemy,' said the Cat, 'it is I: for you have spoken three words in my praise, and now I can drink the warm white milk three times a day for always and always and always. But *still* I am the Cat who walks by himself, and all places are alike to me.'

Then the Woman laughed and set the Cat a bowl of the warm white milk and said, 'O Cat, you are as clever as a man, but remember that your bargain was not made with the Man or the Dog, and I do not know what they will do when they come home.'

'What is that to me?' said the Cat. 'If I have my place in the Cave by the fire and my warm white milk three times a day I do not care what the Man or the Dog can do.'

That evening when the Man and the Dog came into the Cave, the Woman told them all the story of the bargain, while the Cat sat by the fire and smiled. Then the Man said, 'Yes, but he has not made a bargain, with *me* or with all proper Men after me.' Then he took off his two leather boots and he took up his little stone axe (that makes three) and he fetched a piece of wood and a hatchet (that is five altogether), and he set them out in a row and he said, 'Now we will make *our* bargain. If you do not catch mice when you are in the Cave for always and always and always, I will throw these five things at you whenever I see you, and so shall all proper Men do after me.'

'Ah,' said the Woman, listening, 'this is a very clever Cat, but he is not so clever as my Man.'

The Cat counted the five things (and they looked very knobby) and he said, 'I will catch mice when I am in the Cave for always and always and always; but *still* I am the Cat who walks by himself, and all places are alike to me.'

'Not when I am near,' said the Man. 'If you had not said that last I would have put all these things away for always and always and always; but now I am going to throw my two boots and my little stone axe (that makes three) at you whenever I meet you. And so shall all proper Men do after me!'

Then the Dog said, 'Wait a minute. He has not made a bargain with *me* or with all proper Dogs after me.' And he showed his teeth and said, 'If you are not kind to the Baby while I am in the Cave for always and always and always, I will hunt you till I catch you, and when I catch you I will bite you. And so shall all proper Dogs do after me.'

'Ah,' said the Woman, listening, 'this is a very clever Cat, but he is not so clever as the Dog.'

Cat counted the Dog's teeth (and they looked very pointed) and he said, 'I will be kind to the Baby while I am in the Cave, as long as he does not pull my tail too hard, for always and always and always. But *still* I am the Cat that walks by himself, and all places are alike to me.'

'Not when I am near,' said the Dog. 'If you had not said that last I would have shut my mouth for always and always and always; but *now* I am going to hunt you up a tree whenever I meet you. And so shall all proper Dogs do after me.'

Then the Man threw his two boots and his little stone axe (that makes three) at the Cat, and the Cat ran out of the Cave and the Dog chased him up a tree; and from that day to this, Best Beloved, three proper Men out of five will always throw things at a Cat whenever they meet him, and all proper Dogs will chase him up a tree. But the Cat keeps his side of the bargain too. He will kill mice, and he will be kind to Babies when he is in the house, just as long as they do not pull his tail too hard. But when he has done that, and between times, and when the moon gets up and night comes, he is the Cat that walks by himself, and all places are alike to him. Then he goes out to the Wet Wild Woods or up the Wet Wild Trees or on the Wet Wild Roofs, waving his wild tail and walking by his wild lone.

Pussy can sit by the fire and sing,
　Pussy can climb a tree,
Or play with a silly old cork and string
　To 'muse herself, not me.
But I like *Binkie* my dog, because
　He knows how to behave;
So, *Binkie's* the same as the First Friend was,
　And I am the Man in the Cave.

Pussy will play man-Friday till
　It's time to wet her paw
And make her walk on the window-sill
　(For the footprint Crusoe saw);
Then she fluffles her tail and mews,
　And scratches and won't attend.
But *Binkie* will play whatever I choose,
　And he is my true First Friend.

Pussy will rub my knees with her head
　Pretending she loves me hard;
But the very minute I go to my bed
　Pussy runs out in the yard,
And there she stays till the morning-light;
　So I know it is only pretend;
But *Binkie*, he snores at my feet all night,
　And he is my Firstest Friend!

From TRAFFICS AND DISCOVERIES (1904)

The Bonds of Discipline

Poseidon's Law

When the robust and brass-bound man commissioned first for sea°
His fragile raft, Poseidon laughed, and, 'Mariner,' said he,
'Behold, a Law immutable I lay on thee and thine,
That never shall ye act or tell a falsehood at my shrine.

'Let Zeus adjudge your landward kin, whose votive meal and salt
At easy-cheated altars win oblivion for the fault,
But ye the unhoodwinked waves shall test—the immediate gulfs condemn—
Unless ye owe the Fates a jest, be slow to jest with them.

'Ye shall not clear by Greekly speech, nor cozen from your path°
The twinkling shoal, the leeward beach, and Hadria's white-lipped wrath;°
Nor tempt with painted cloth for wood my fraud-avenging hosts;°
Nor make at all or all make good your bulwarks and your boasts.

'Now and henceforward serve unshod through wet and wakeful shifts,°
A present and oppressive God, but take, to aid, my gifts—
The wide and windward-opened eye, the large and lavish hand,
The soul that cannot tell a lie—except upon the land!'

In dromond and in catafract—wet, wakeful, windward-eyed—°
He kept Poseidon's Law intact (his ship and freight beside),
But, once discharged the dromond's hold, the bireme beached once more,
Splendaciously mendacious rolled the brass-bound man ashore.

. . . .

The thranite now and thalamite are pressures low and high,°
And where three hundred blades bit white the twin-propellers ply:
The God that hailed, the keel that sailed, are changed beyond recall,
But the robust and brass-bound man he is not changed at all!

From Punt returned, from Phormio's Fleet, from Javan and Gadire,°
He strongly occupies the seat about the tavern fire,

And, moist with much Falernian or smoked Massilian juice,°
Revenges there the brass-bound man his long-enforced truce!

The Bonds of Discipline

As literature, it is beneath contempt.° It concerns the endurance,° armament, turning-circle, and inner gear of every ship in the British Navy—the whole embellished with profile plates. The Teuton approaches the matter with pagan thoroughness; the Muscovite runs him close; but the Gaul, ever an artist, breaks enclosure to study the morale, at the present day, of the British sailorman.

In this, I conceive, he is from time to time aided by the zealous amateur,° though I find very little in his dispositions to show that he relies on that amateur's hard-won information. There exists—unlike some other publication, it is not bound in lead boards°—a work by one 'M. de C.,'° based on the absolutely unadorned performances of one of our well-known *Acolyte* type of cruisers.° It contains nothing that did not happen. It covers a period of two days; runs to twenty-seven pages of large type exclusive of appendices; and carries as many exclamation points as the average Dumas novel.°

I read it with care, from the adorably finished prologue—it is the disgrace of our Navy that we cannot produce a commissioned officer capable of writing one page of lyric prose—to the eloquent, the joyful, the impassioned end; and my first notion was that I had been cheated.° In this sort of book-collecting you will see how entirely the bibliophile lies at the mercy of his agent.

'M. de C.,' I read, opened his campaign by stowing away in one of her boats what time H.M.S. *Archimandrite*° lay off Funchal.° 'M. de C.' was, always on behalf of his country, a Madeira Portuguese fleeing from the conscription. They discovered him eighty miles at sea and bade him assist the cook. So far this seemed fairly reasonable. Next day, thanks to his histrionic powers and his ingratiating address, he was promoted to the rank of 'supernumerary captain's servant'—a 'post which,' I give his words, 'I flatter myself, was created for me alone, and furnished me with opportunities unequalled for a task in which one word malapropos would have been my destruction.'

From this point onward, earth and water between them held no marvels like to those 'M. de C.' had 'envisaged'—if I translate him correctly. It became clear to me that 'M. de C.' was either a pyramidal liar, or . . .

*

I was not acquainted with any officer, seaman, or marine in the *Archimandrite*; but instinct told me I could not go far wrong if I took a third-class ticket to Plymouth.

I gathered information on the way from a leading stoker, two seaman-gunners, and an odd hand in a torpedo factory. They courteously set my feet on the right path, and that led me through the alleys of Devonport to a public-house not fifty yards from the water. We drank with the proprietor, a huge, yellowish man called Tom Wessels; and when my guides had departed, I asked if he could produce any warrant or petty officer of the *Archimandrite*.

'The *Bedlamite*, d'you mean—'er last commission, when they all went crazy?'

'Shouldn't wonder,' I replied. 'Fetch me a sample and I'll see.'

'You'll excuse me, o' course, but—what d'you want 'im *for*?'

'I want to make him drunk. I want to make you drunk—if you like. I want to make him drunk here.'

'Spoke very 'andsome. I'll do what I can.' He went out towards the water that lapped at the foot of the street. I gathered from the pot-boy that he was a person of influence beyond Admirals.

In a few minutes I heard the noise of an advancing crowd, and the voice of Mr Wessels.

''E only wants to make you drunk at 'is expense. Dessay 'e'll stand you all a drink. Come up an' look at 'im. 'E don't bite.'

A square man, with remarkable eyes, entered at the head of six large bluejackets. Behind them gathered a contingent of hopeful free-drinkers.

''E's the only one I could get. Transferred to the *Postulant* six months back. I found 'im quite accidental.' Mr Wessels beamed.

'I'm in charge o' the cutter.° Our wardroom° is dinin' on the beach *en masse*. They won't be home till mornin',' said the square man with the remarkable eyes.

'Are you an *Archimandrite*?' I demanded.

'That's me. I was, as you might say.'

'Hold on. I'm a *Archimandrite*.' A Red Marine° with moist eyes tried to climb on the table. 'Was you lookin' for a *Bedlamite*? I've—I've been invalided, an' what with that, an' visitin' my family 'ome at Lewes, per'aps I've come late. 'Ave I?'

'You've 'ad all that's good for you,' said Tom Wessels, as the Red Marine sat cross-legged on the floor.

'There are those 'oo haven't 'ad a thing yet!' cried a voice by the door.

'I will take this *Archimandrite*,' I said, 'and this Marine. Will you please give the boat's crew a drink now, and another in half an hour if —if Mr—'

'Pyecroft,' said the square man. 'Emanuel Pyecroft, second-class petty-officer.'

'—Mr Pyecroft doesn't object?'

'He don't. Clear out. Goldin', you picket the hill by yourself, throwin' out a skirmishin'-line in ample time to let me know when Number One's° comin' down from his vittles.'

The crowd dissolved. We passed into the quiet of the inner bar, the Red Marine zealously leading the way.

'And what do you drink, Mr Pyecroft?' I said.

'Only water. Warm water, with a little whisky an' sugar an' per'aps a lemon.'

'Mine's beer,' said the Marine. 'It always was.'

'Look 'ere, Glass. You take an' go to sleep. The picket'll be comin' for you in a little time, an' per'aps you'll 'ave slep' it off by then. What's your ship, now?' said Mr Wessels.

'The Ship o' State—most important!' said the Red Marine magnificently, and shut his eyes.

'That's right,' said Mr Pyecroft. 'He's safest where he is. An' now —here's santy° to us all!—what d'you want o' me?'

'I want to read you something.'

'Tracts again!' said the Marine, never opening his eyes. 'Well. I'm game . . . A little more 'ead to it, miss, please.'

'He thinks 'e's drinkin'—lucky beggar!' said Mr Pyecroft. 'I'm agreeable to be read to. 'Twon't alter my convictions. I may as well tell you beforehand I'm a Plymouth Brother.'

He composed his face with the air of one in the dentist's chair, and I began at the third page of 'M. de C.'

'"*At the moment of asphyxiation, for I had hidden myself under the boat's cover, I heard footsteps upon the superstructure and coughed with empress*"° coughed loudly, Mr Pyecroft. "*By this time I judged the vessel to be sufficiently far from land. A number of sailors extricated me amid language appropriate to their national brutality. I responded that I named myself Antonio, and that I sought to save myself from the Portuguese conscription.*"

'Ho!' said Mr Pyecroft, and the fashion of his countenance changed. Then pensively: 'Ther beggar! What might you have in your hand there?'

'It's the story of Antonio—a stowaway in the *Archimandrite's* cutter.

A French spy when he's at home, I fancy. What do *you* know about it?'

'An' I thought it was tracts! An' yet some'ow I didn't.' Mr Pyecroft nodded his head wonderingly. 'Our old man° was quite right—so was 'Op°—so was I. Ere, Glass!' He kicked the Marine. 'Here's our Antonio 'as written a impromptu book! He *was* a spy all right.'

The Red Marine turned slightly, speaking with the awful precision of the half-drunk. ''As 'e got anythin' in about my 'orrible death an' execution? Ex*cuse* me, but if I open my eyes, I shan't be well. That's where I'm different from *all* other men. Ahem!'

'What about Glass's execution?' demanded Pyecroft.

'The book's in French,' I replied.

'Then it's no good to me.'

'Precisely. Now I want you to tell your story just as it happened. I'll check it by this book. Take a cigar. I know about his being dragged out of the cutter. What I want to know is what was the meaning of all the other things, because they're unusual.'

'They were,' said Mr Pyecroft with emphasis. 'Lookin' back on it as I set here more an' more I see what an 'ighly unusual affair it was. But it happened. It transpired in the *Archimandrite*—the ship you can trust. . . . Antonio! Ther beggar!'

'Take your time, Mr Pyecroft.'

In a few moments we came to it thus—

'The old man was displeased. I don't deny he was quite a little displeased. With the mail-boats trottin' into Madeira every twenty minutes, he didn't see why a lop-eared Portugee had to take liberties with a man-o'-war's first cutter. Any'ow, we couldn't turn ship round for him. We drew him out and took him to our Number One. "Drown 'im," 'e says. "Drown 'im before 'e dirties my fine new decks." But our owner° was tender-hearted. "Take him to the galley," 'e says. "Boil 'im! Skin 'im! Cook 'im! Cut 'is bloomin' hair. Take 'is bloomin' number! We'll have him executed at Ascension."°

'Retallick, our chief cook, an' a Carth'lic, was the on'y one any way near grateful; bein' short-'anded in the galley. He annexes the blighter by the left ear an' right foot an' sets him to work peelin' potatoes. So then, this Antonio that was avoidin' the conscription—'

'*Sub*scription, you pink-eyed matlow!'° said the Marine, with the face of a stone Buddha, and whimpered sadly: 'Pye don't see any fun in it at all.'

'*Con*scription—come to his illegitimate sphere in Her Majesty's

Navy, an' it was just then that Old 'Op, our Yeoman of Signals, an' a fastidious joker, made remarks to me about 'is hands.

'"Those 'ands," says 'Op, "properly considered, never done a day's honest labour in their life. Tell me those hands belong to a blighted Portugee manual labourist, and I won't call you a liar, but I'll say you an' the Admiralty are pretty much unique in your statements." 'Op was always a fastidious joker—in his language as much as anything else. He pursued 'is investigations with the eye of an 'awk outside the galley. He knew better than to advance line-head against Retallick, so he attacked *ong eshlong*,° speakin' his remarks as much as possible into the breech of the starboard four point seven,° an' 'ummin' to 'imself. Our chief cook 'ated 'ummin'. "What's the matter of your bowels?" he says at last, fistin' out the mess-pork agitated like.

'"Don't mind me," says 'Op. "I'm only a mildewed buntin'-tosser,"° 'e says, "but speakin' for my mess, I do hope," 'e says, "you ain't goin' to boil your Portugee friend's boots along o' that pork you're smellin' so gay!"

'"Boots! Boots! Boots!" says Retallick, an' he run round like a earwig in a alder-stalk. "Boots in the galley,"° 'e says. "Cook's mate, cast out an' abolish this cutter-cuddlin' abori*gine's* boots!"

'They was hove overboard in quick time, an' that was what 'Op was lyin' to° for. As subsequently transpired.

'"Fine Arab arch to that cutter-cuddler's hinstep," he says to me. "Run your eye over it, Pye," 'e says. "Nails all present an' correct," 'e says. "Bunion on the little toe, too," 'e says; "which comes from wearin' a tight boot. What do *you* think?"

'"Dook in trouble, per'aps," I says. "He ain't got the hang of spud-skinnin'." No more he 'ad. 'E was simply cannibalizin' 'em.

'"I want to know what 'e 'as got the 'ang of," says 'Op, obstructed-like. "Watch 'im," 'e says. "These shoulders were foreign-drilled somewhere."

'When it comes to "Down 'ammicks!" which is our naval way o' goin' to bye-bye, I took particular trouble over Antonio, 'oo had 'is 'ammick 'ove at 'im with general instructions to sling it an' be sugared. In the ensuin' melly° I pioneered him to the after-'atch, which is a orifice communicatin' with the after-flat an' similar suites of apartments. He havin' navigated at three-fifths power immejit ahead o' me, *I* wasn't goin' to volunteer any assistance, nor he didn't need it.

'"Mong Jew!"° says 'e, sniffin' round. An' twice more, "Mong Jew!"—which is pure French. Then he slings 'is 'ammick, nips in, an' coils down. "Not bad for a Portugee conscript," I says to myself, casts off the tow, abandons him, and reports to 'Op.

'About three minutes later I'm over'auled by our sub-lootenant, navigatin' under forced draught, with his bearin's 'eated. 'E had the temerity to say I'd instructed our Antonio to sling his carcass in the alleyway, an' 'e was peevish about it. O' course, I prevaricated like 'ell. You get to do that in the service. Nevertheless, to oblige Mr Ducane, I went an' readjusted Antonio. You may not 'ave ascertained that there are two ways o' comin' out of an 'ammick when it's cut down. Antonio came out t'other way—slidin' 'andsome to his feet. That showed me two things. First, 'e had been in an 'ammick before, an' next, he hadn't been asleep. Then I reproached 'im for goin' to bed where 'e'd been told to go, instead o' standin' by till some one gave him entirely contradictory orders. Which is the essence o' naval discipline.

'In the middle o' this argument the Gunner protrudes his ram-bow from 'is cabin, an' brings it all to an 'urried conclusion with some remarks suitable to 'is piebald warrant-rank.° Navigatin' thence under easy steam, an' leavin' Antonio to re-sling his little foreign self, my large flat foot comes in detonatin' contact with a small objec' on the deck. Not 'altin' for the obstacle, nor changin' step, I shuffles it along under the ball of the big toe to the foot o' the hatchway, when, lightly stoopin', I catch it in my right hand and continue my evolutions in rapid time till I eventuates under 'Op's lee.

'It was a small moroccer-bound pocket-book, full of indelible pencil writin'—in French, for I could plainly discern the *doodeladays*,° which is about as far as my education runs.

''Op fists it open and peruses. 'E'd known an 'arf-caste Frenchwoman pretty intricate before he was married; when he was trained man in a stinkin' gunboat up the Saigon River.° He understood a lot o' French—domestic brands chiefly—the kind that isn't in print.

'"Pye," he says to me, "you're a tattician o' no mean value. I am a trifle shady about the precise bearin' an' import' 'o this beggar's private log here," 'e says, "but it's evidently a case for the owner. You'll 'ave your share o' the credit," 'e says.

'"Nay, nay, Pauline,"° I says. "You don't catch Emanuel Pyecroft mine-droppin' under any post-captain's bows," I says, "in search of honour," I says. "I've been there oft."

'"Well, if you must, you must," 'e says, takin' me up quick. "But I'll speak a good word for you, Pye."

'"You'll shut your mouth, 'Op," I says, "or you an' me'll part brass-rags.° The owner has his duties, an' I have mine. We will keep station," I says, "nor seek to deviate."

'"Deviate to blazes!" says 'Op. "I'm goin' to deviate to the owner's comfortable cabin direct." So he deviated.'

Mr Pyecroft leaned forward and dealt the Marine a large-pattern Navy kick. ''Ere, Glass! You was sentry when 'Op went to the old man—the first time, with Antonio's washin'-book. Tell us what transpired. You're sober. You don't know how sober you are!'

The Marine cautiously raised his head a few inches. As Mr Pyecroft said, he was sober—after some R.M.L.I.° fashion of his own devising. ''Op bounds in like a startled anteloper, carryin' 'is signal-slate at the ready. The old man was settin' down to 'is bountiful platter—not like you an' me, without anythin' more in sight for an 'ole night an' 'arf a day. Talkin' about food—'

'No! No! No!' cried Pyecroft, kicking again. 'What about 'Op?' I thought the Marine's ribs would have snapped, but he merely hiccupped.

'Oh, 'im! 'E 'ad it written all down on 'is little slate—I think—an' 'e shoves it under the old man's nose. "Shut the door," says 'Op. "For 'Eavin's sake shut the cabin door!" Then the old man must ha' said somethin' 'bout irons. "I'll put 'em on, Sir, in your very presence," says 'Op, "only 'ear my prayer," or—words to that 'fect. . . . It was jus' the same with me when I called our Sergeant a bladder-bellied, lard-'eaded, perspirin' pension-cheater. They on'y put on the charge-sheet "words to that effect." Spoiled the 'ole 'fect.'

''Op! 'Op! 'Op! What about 'Op?' thundered Pyecroft.

''Op? Oh, shame thing. Words t' that 'fect. Door shut. Nushin' more transhpired till 'Op comes out—nose exshtreme angle plungin' fire° or—or words 'that effect. Proud's parrot. "Oh, you prou' old parrot," I says.'

Mr Glass seemed to slumber again.

'Lord! How a little moisture disintegrates, don't it? When we had ship's theatricals off Vigo,° Glass 'ere played Dick Deadeye° to the moral°, though of course the lower deck wasn't pleased to see a leather-neck° interpretin' a strictly maritime part, as you might say. It's only his repartees, which 'e can't contain, that conquers him. Shall I resume my narrative?'

Another drink was brought on this hint, and Mr Pyecroft resumed.

'The essence o' strategy bein' forethought, the essence o' tattics is surprise. Per'aps you didn't know that? My forethought 'avin' secured the initial advantage in attack, it remained for the old man to ladle out the surprise-packets. 'Eavens! What surprises! That night he dines with the wardroom, bein' of the kind—I've told you as we were a 'appy ship?—that likes it, and the wardroom liked it too. This ain't common in the service. They had up the new Madeira—awful undisciplined stuff which gives you a cordite mouth next morning. They told the mess-men° to navigate towards the extreme an' remote 'orizon, an' they abrogated the sentry about fifteen paces out of earshot. Then they had in the Gunner, the Bo'sun,° an' the Carpenter, an' stood them large round drinks. It all come out later—wardroom joints bein' lower-deck hash, as the sayin' is—that our Number One stuck to it that 'e couldn't trust the ship for the job. The old man swore 'e could, 'avin' commanded 'er over two years. He was right. There wasn't a ship, I don't care in what fleet, could come near the *Archimandrites* when we give our mind to a thing. We held the cruiser big-gun records, the sailing-cutter (fancy-rig) championship, an' the challenge-cup row round the fleet. We 'ad the best nigger minstrels, the best football an' cricket teams, an' the best squee-jee band° of anything that ever pushed in front of a brace o' screws. An' *yet* our Number One mistrusted us! 'E said we'd be a floatin' hell in a week, an' it 'ud take the rest o' the commission to stop our way.° They was arguin' it in the wardroom when the bridge reports a light three points off the port bow. We overtakes her, switches on our search-light, an' she discloses herself as a collier o' no mean reputation, makin' about seven knots on 'er lawful occasions—to the Cape most like.

'Then the owner—so we 'eard in good time—broke the boom,° springin' all mines together at close interval.

'"Look 'ere, my jokers," 'e says (I'm givin' the grist° of 'is arguments, remember), "Number One says we can't enlighten this cutter-cuddlin' Gaulish lootenant on the manners an' customs o' the Navy without makin' the ship a market-garden. There's a lot in that," 'e says, "specially if we kept it up lavish, till we reached Ascension. But," 'e says, "the appearance o' this strange sail has put a totally new aspect on the game. We can run to just one day's amusement for our friend, or else what's the good o' discipline? An' then we can turn 'im over to our presumably short-'anded fellow-subject in the small-coal line out yonder. He'll be pleased," says the old man, "an' so will Antonio. M'rover," he says to Number One, "I'll lay you a dozen o' liquorice an' ink"°—it must ha' been that new tawny port—"that I've got a ship I can trust—for one day," 'e says. "Wherefore," he says, "will you have the extreme goodness to reduce speed as requisite for keepin' a proper distance behind this providential tramp till further orders?" Now, that's what I call tattics.

'The other manœuvres developed next day, strictly in accordance with the plans as laid down in the wardroom, where they sat long an' steady. 'Op whispers to me that Antonio was a Number One spy when 'e was in commission, and a French lootenant when 'e was paid off, so I navigated at three 'undred and ninety-six revolutions to the galley, never 'avin' kicked a lootenant up to date. I may as well say that I did not manœuvre against 'im as a Frenchman, because I like Frenchmen, but stric'ly on 'is rank an' ratin' in 'is own navy. I inquired after 'is health from Retallick.

' "Don't ask me," 'e says, sneerin' be'ind his silver spectacles. " 'E's promoted to be captain's second supernumerary servant, to be dressed and addressed as such. If 'e does 'is dooties same as he skinned the spuds, *I* ain't for changin' with the old man."

'In the balmy dawnin' it was given out, all among the 'olystones,° by our sub-lootenant, who was a three-way-discharge devil,° that all orders after eight bells was to be executed in inverse ration to the cube o' the velocity. "The reg'lar routine," he says, "was arrogated for reasons o' state an' policy, an' any flat-foot who presumed to exhibit surprise, annoyance, or amusement, would be slightly but firmly reproached." Then the Gunner mops up a heathenish large detail for some hanky-panky in the magazines, an' led 'em off along with our Gunnery Jack, which is to say, our Gunnery Lootenant.

'That put us on the *viva voce*°—particularly when we understood how the owner was navigatin' abroad in his sword-belt° trustin' us like brothers. We shifts into the dress o' the day, an' we musters, *an'* we prays *ong reggle*,° an' we carries on anticipatory to bafflin' Antonio.

'Then our Sergeant of Marines come to me wringin' his 'ands an' weepin'. 'E'd been talkin' to the sub-lootenant, an' it looked like as if his upper-works were collapsin'.

' "I want a guarantee," 'e says, wringin' 'is 'ands like this. "*I* 'aven't 'ad sunstroke slave-dhowin' in Tajurrah Bay,° an' been compelled to live on quinine an' chlorodyne ever since. *I* don't get the horrors off two glasses o' brown sherry."

' "What 'ave you got now?" I says.

' "*I* ain't an officer," 'e says. "*My* sword won't be handed back to me at the end o' the court-martial on account o' my little weaknesses, an' no stain on my character. I'm only a pore beggar of a Red Marine with eighteen years' service, an' why for," says he, wringin' 'is hands like this all the time, "must I chuck away my pension, sub-lootenant or no sub-lootenant? Look at 'em," he says, "only look at 'em. Marines fallin' in for small-arm drill!"

'The leather-necks was layin' aft at the double, an' a more insanitary set of accidents I never wish to behold. Most of 'em was in their shirts. They had their trousers on, of course—rolled up nearly to the knee, but what I mean is belts over shirts. Three or four 'ad *our* caps, an' them that had drawn helmets wore their chin-straps like Portugee earrings. Oh, yes; an' three of 'em 'ad only one boot! I knew what our bafflin' tattics was goin' to be, but even I was mildly surprised when this gay fantasia of Brazee° drummers halted under the poop, because of an 'ammick in charge of our Navigator, an' a small but 'ighly efficient landin'-party.

'"'Ard astern both screws!" says the Navigator. "Room for the captain's 'ammick!" The captain's servant—Cockburn 'is name was —had one end, an' our newly promoted Antonio, in a blue slop rig,° 'ad the other. They slung it from the muzzle of the port poop quick-firer° thort-ships° to a stanchion. Then the old man flickered up, smokin' a cigarette, an' brought 'is stern to an anchor slow an' oriental.

'"What a blessin' it is, Mr Ducane," 'e says to our sub-lootenant, "to be out o' sight o' the 'ole pack o' blighted admirals! What's an admiral after all?" 'e says. "Why, 'e's only a post-captain with the pip,° Mr Ducane. The drill will now proceed. What O! Antonio, *descendez*° an' get me a split."

'When Antonio came back with the whisky-an'-soda, he was told off to swing the 'ammick in slow time, an' that massacritin' small-arm party went on with their oratorio. The Sergeant had been kindly excused from participatin', an' he was jumpin' round on the poop-ladder, stretchin' 'is leather neck to see the disgustin' exhibition an' cluckin' like a ash-hoist.° A lot of us went on the fore-an'-aft bridge an' watched 'em like "Listen to the Band in the Park."° All these evolutions, I may as well tell you, are highly unusual in the Navy. After ten minutes o' muckin' about, Glass 'ere—pity 'e's so drunk!—says that 'e'd had enough exercise for 'is simple needs an' he wants to go 'ome. Mr Ducane catches him a sanaka-towzer of a smite° over the 'ead with the flat of his sword. Down comes Glass's rifle with language to correspond, and he fiddles with the bolt. Up jumps Maclean—'oo was a Gosport 'ighlander°—an' lands on Glass's neck, thus bringin' him to the deck, fully extended.

'The old man makes a great show o' wakin' up from sweet slumbers. "Mistah Ducane," he says, "what is this painful interregnum?" or words to that effect. Ducane takes one step to the front, an' salutes: "Only 'nother case of attempted assassination, Sir," he says.

'"Is that all?" says the old man, while Maclean sits on Glass's collar button. "Take him away," 'e says; "he knows the penalty."

'Ah! I suppose that is the "invincible *morgue*° Britannic in the presence of brutally provoked mutiny," I muttered, as I turned over the pages of M. de C.

'So, Glass, 'e was led off kickin' an' squealin' an' hove down the ladder into 'is Sergeant's volupshus arms. 'E run Glass forward, an' was all for puttin' 'im in irons as a maniac.

'"You refill your waterjacket° and cool off!" says Glass, sittin' down rather winded. "The trouble with you is you haven't any imagination."

'"Haven't I? I've got the remnants of a little poor authority though," 'e says, lookin' pretty vicious.

'"You 'ave?" says Glass. "Then for pity's sake 'ave some proper feelin' too. I'm goin' to be shot this evenin'. You'll take charge o' the firin'-party."

'Some'ow or other, that made the Sergeant froth at the mouth. 'E 'ad no more play to his intellects than a spit-kid.° 'E just took everything as it come. Well, that was about all, I think. . . . Unless you'd care to have me resume my narrative.'

We resumed on the old terms, but with rather less hot water. The marine on the floor breathed evenly, and Mr Pyecroft nodded.

'I may have omitted to inform you that our Number One took a general row round the situation while the small-arm party was at work, an' o' course he supplied the outlines; but the details we coloured in by ourselves. These were our tattics to baffle Antonio. It occurs to the Carpenter to 'ave the steam-cutter down for repairs. 'E gets 'is cheero-party° together, an' down she comes. You've never seen a steam-cutter let down on the deck, 'ave you? It's not usual, an' she takes a lot o' humourin'. Thus we 'ave the starboard side completely blocked an' the general traffic tricklin' over'ead along the fore-an'-aft bridge. Then Chips° gets into her an' begins balin' out a mess o' small reckonin's on the deck. Simultaneous there come up three o' those dirty engine-room objects which we call "tiffies,"° an' a stoker or two with orders to repair her steamin'-gadgets. *They* get into her an' bale out another young Christmas-treeful of small reckonin's—brass mostly. Simultaneous it hits the Pusser° that 'e'd better serve out mess pork for the poor matlow. These things half shifted Retallick, our chief cook, off 'is bed-plate. Yes, you might say they broke 'im wide open. 'E wasn't at all used to 'em.

'Number One tells off five or six prime, able-bodied seaman-gunners to the pork barrels. You never see pork fisted out of its receptacle, 'ave you? Simultaneous, it hits the Gunner that now's the day an' now's the hour for a non-continuous class in Maxim° instruction. So they all give way together, and the general effect was *non plus ultra*°. There was the cutter's innards spread out like a Fratton° pawnbroker's shop; there was the "tiffies" hammerin' in the stern of 'er, an' *they* ain't antiseptic; there was the Maxim-class in light skirmishin' order among the pork, an' forrard the blacksmith had 'is forge in full blast, makin' 'orse-shoes, I suppose. Well, that accounts for the starboard side. The on'y warrant officer 'oo hadn't a look in so far was the Bosun. So 'e stated, all out of 'is own 'ead, that Chips's reserve o' wood an' timber, which Chips 'ad stole at our last refit, needed restowin'. It was on the port booms°—a young an' healthy forest of it, for Charley Peace° wasn't to be named 'longside o' Chips for burglary.

'"All right," says our Number One. "You can 'ave the whole port watch if you like. Hell's Hell," 'e says, "an' when there study to improve."

'Jarvis was our Bosun's name. He hunted up the 'ole of the port watch by hand, as you might say, callin' 'em by name loud an' lovin', which is not precisely Navy makee-pigeon.° They 'ad that timber-loft off the booms, an' they dragged it up and down like so many sweatin' little beavers. But Jarvis was jealous o' Chips an' went round the starboard side to envy at him.

'"'Tain't enough," 'e says, when he had climbed back. "Chips 'as got his bazaar lookin' like a coal-hulk in a cyclone. We must adop' more drastic measures." Off 'e goes to Number One and communicates with 'im. Number One got the old man's leave, on account of our goin' so slow (we were keepin' be'ind the tramp), to fit the ship with a full set of patent supernumerary sails. Four trysails°—yes, you might call 'em trysails—was our Admiralty allowance in the un'eard-of event of a cruiser breakin' down, but we had our awnin's as well. They was all extricated from the various flats an' 'oles where they was stored, an' at the end o' two hours' hard work Number One 'e made out eleven sails o' different sorts and sizes. I don't know what exact nature of sail you'd call 'em—pyjama-stun'sles° with a touch of Sarah's shimmy, per'aps—but the riggin' of 'em an' all the supernumerary details, as you might say, bein' carried on through an' over an' between the cutter an' the forge an' the pork an' cleanin' guns, an' the Maxim class an' the Bosun's calaboose° *and* the paintwork, was sublime. There's no other word for it. Sub-lime!

'The old man keeps swimmin' up' an' down through it all with the faithful Antonio at 'is side, fetchin' him numerous splits. 'E had eight that mornin', an' when Antonio was detached to get 'is spy-glass, or his gloves, or his lily-white 'andkerchief, the old man would waste 'em down a ventilator. Antonio must ha' learned a lot about our Navy thirst.'

'He did.'

'Ah! Would you kindly mind turnin' to the precise page indicated an' givin' me a *résumé* of 'is tattics?' said Mr Pyecroft, drinking deeply. 'I'd like to know 'ow it looked from 'is side o' the deck.'

'How will this do?' I said. '"*Once clear of the land,*° *like Voltaire's Habakkuk—*"'°

'One o' their new commerce-destroyers, I suppose,' Mr Pyecroft interjected.

'"*—each man seemed veritably capable of all—to do according to his will. The boats, dismantled and forlorn, are lowered upon the planking. One cries 'Aid me!' flourishing at the same time the weapons of his business. A dozen launch themselves upon him in the orgasm of zeal misdirected. He beats them off with the howlings of dogs. He has lost a hammer. This ferocious outcry signifies that only. Eight men seek the utensil, colliding on the way with some many others which, seated in the stern of the boat, tear up and scatter upon the planking the ironwork which impedes their brutal efforts. Elsewhere, one detaches from on high wood, canvas, iron bolts, coal-dust—what do I know?*"'

'That's where 'e's comin' the bloomin' *onjenew*° 'E knows a lot, reely.'

'"*They descend thundering upon the planking, and the spectacle cannot reproduce itself.*° *In my capacity of valet to the captain, whom I have well and beautifully plied with drink since the rising of the sun (behold me also, Ganymede!*°*), I pass throughout observing, it may be not a little. They ask orders. There is none to give them. One sits upon the edge of the vessel and chants interminably the lugubrious 'Roule*° *Britannia'—to endure how long?*"'

'That was me! On'y 'twas "A Life on the Ocean Wave"—which I hate more than any stinkin' tune I know, havin' dragged too many nasty little guns to it. Yes, Number One told me off to that for ten minutes; an' I ain't musical, you might say.'

'"*Then come marines, half-dressed, seeking vainly through this 'tohu-bohu'*"° (that's one of his names for the *Archimandrite*, Mr Pyecroft) "*for a place whence they shall not be dislodged. The captain, heavy with drink, rolls himself from his hammock. He would have his people fire the*

Maxims. They demand which Maxim. That to him is equal.° *The breech-lock indispensable is not there. They demand it of one who opens a barrel of pork, for this Navy feeds at all hours. He refers them to the cook, yesterday my master—*" '

'Yes, an' Retallick nearly had a fit. What a truthful an' observin' little Antonio we 'ave!'

' "*It is discovered in the hands of a boy who says, and they do not rebuke him, that he has found it by hazard.*" I'm afraid I haven't translated quite correctly, Mr Pyecroft, but I've done my best.'

'Why, it's beautiful—you ought to be a Frenchman—you ought. You don't want anything o' *me*. You've got it all there.'

'Yes, but I like your side of it. For instance. Here's a little thing I can't quite see the end of. Listen! "*Of the domain which Britannia rules by sufferance, my gross captain knew nothing, and his Navigator, if possible, less. From the bestial recriminations and the indeterminate chaos of the grand deck,*° *I ascended—always with a whisky-and-soda in my hands—to a scene truly grotesque. Behold my captain in plain sea,*° *at issue with his Navigator! A crisis of nerves due to the enormous quantity of alcohol which he had swallowed up to then, has filled for him the ocean with dangers, imaginary and fantastic. Incapable of judgment, menaced by the phantasms of his brain inflamed, he envisages islands perhaps of the Hesperides beneath his keel—vigias*° *innumerable.*" I don't know what a vigia is, Mr Pyecroft. "*He creates shoals sad and far-reaching of the mid-Atlantic!*" What was that, now?'

'Oh, I see! That come after dinner, when our Navigator threw 'is cap down an' danced on it. Danby was quartermaster. They 'ad a tea-party on the bridge. It was the old man's contribution. Does he say anything about the leadsmen?'

'Is this it? "*Overborne by his superior's causeless suspicion, the Navigator took off the badges of his rank and cast them at the feet of my captain and sobbed. A disgusting and maudlin reconciliation followed. The argument renewed itself, each grasping the wheel, crapulous*" (that means drunk, I think, Mr Pyecroft), "*shouting. It appeared that my captain would chenaler*"° (I don't know what that means, Mr Pyecroft) "*to the Cape. At the end, he placed a sailor with the sound*" (that's the lead, I think) "*in his hand, garnished with suet.*" Was it garnished with suet?'

'He put two leadsmen in the chains, o' course! He didn't know that there mightn't be shoals there, 'e said. Morgan went an' armed his lead, to enter into the spirit o' the thing. They 'eaved it for twenty minutes, but there wasn't any suet—only tallow, o' course.'

' "*Garnished with suet at two thousand metres of profundity. Decidedly the Britannic Navy is well guarded*." Well, that's all right, Mr Pyecroft. Would you mind telling me anything else of interest that happened?'

'There was a good deal, one way an' another. I'd like to know what this Antonio thought of our sails.'

'He merely says that "*the engines having broken down, an officer extemporised a mournful and useless parody of sails*." Oh, yes! he says that some of them looked like "*bonnets in a needlecase*,"° I think.'

'Bonnets in a needlecase! They were stun'sles. That shows the beggar's no sailor. That trick was really the one thing we did. Pho! I thought he was a sailorman, an' 'e hasn't sense enough to see what extemporisin' eleven good an' drawin' sails out o' four trys'les an' a few awnin's means. 'E must have been drunk!'

'Never mind, Mr Pyecroft. I want to hear about your target-practice, and the execution.'

'Oh! We had a special target-practice that afternoon all for Antonio. As I told my crew—me bein' captain of the port-bow quick-firer, though I'm a torpedo man now—it just showed how you can work your gun under any discomforts. A shell—twenty six-inch shells—burstin' inboard couldn't 'ave begun to make the varicose collection o' tit-bits which we had spilled on our deck. It was a lather—a rich, creamy lather!

'We took it very easy—that gun-practice. We did it in a complimentary "Jenny-'ave-another-cup-o'-tea" style, an' the crews was strictly ordered not to rupture 'emselves with unnecessary exertion. This isn't our custom in the Navy when we're *in puris naturalibus*,° as you might say. But we wasn't so then. We was impromptu. An' Antonio was busy fetchin' splits for the old man, and the old man was wastin' 'em down the ventilators. There must 'ave been four inches in the bilges, I should think—wardroom whisky-an'-soda.

'Then I thought I might as well bear a hand as look pretty. So I let my *bundoop*° go at fifteen 'undred—sightin' very particular. There was a sort of 'appy little belch like—no more, I give you my word—an' the shell trundled out maybe fifty feet an' dropped into the deep Atlantic.

'"Government powder, Sir!" sings out our Gunnery Jack to the bridge, laughin' horrid sarcastic; an' then, of course, we all laughs, which we are not encouraged to do *in puris naturalibus*. Then, of course, I saw that our Gunnery Jack 'ad been after with his subcutaneous details° in the magazines all the mornin' watch. He had redooced the charges to a minimum, as you might say. But it made me feel a trifle faint an' sickish notwithstandin', this spit-in-the-eye° business.

Every time such transpired, our Gunnery Lootenant would say somethin' sarcastic about Government stores, an' the old man fair howled. 'Op was on the bridge with 'im an' 'e told me—'cause 'he's a free-knowledge-ist° an' reads character—that Antonio's face was sweatin' with pure joy. 'Op wanted to kick him. Does Antonio say anything about that?'

'Not about the kicking, but he is great on the gun-practice, Mr Pyecroft. He has put all the results into a sort of appendix—a table of shots. He says that the figures will speak more eloquently than words.'

'What? Nothin' about the way the crews flinched an' hopped? Nothin' about the little shells rumblin' out o' the guns so casual?'

'There are a few pages of notes, but they only bear out what you say. He says that these things always happen as soon as one of our ships is out of sight of land. Oh, yes! I've forgotten. He says, "*From the conversation of my captain with his inferiors I gathered that no small proportion of the expense of these nominally efficient cartridges finds itself in his pockets. So much, indeed, was signified by an officer on the deck below, who cried in a high voice: 'I hope, Sir, you are making something out of it. It is rather monotonous.' This insult, so flagrant, albeit well merited, was received with a smile of drunken bonhommy*"—that's cheerfulness, Mr Pyecroft. Your glass is empty.'

'Resumin' afresh,' said Mr Pyecroft, after a well-watered interval, 'I may as well say that the target-practice occupied us two hours, and then we had to dig out° after the tramp. Then we half an' three-quarters cleaned up the decks an' mucked about as requisite, haulin' down the patent awnin' stun'sles which Number One 'ad made. The old man was a shade doubtful of his course, 'cause I 'eard him say to Number One, "You were right. A week o' this would turn the ship into a Hayti bean-feast.° But," he says pathetic, "haven't they backed the band noble?"

'"Oh! it's a picnic for them," says Number One. "But when do we get rid o' this whisky-peddlin' blighter o' yours, Sir?"

'"That's a cheerful way to speak of a *Vis*count," says the old man. "'E's the bluest blood o' France when he's at home."

'"Which is the precise landfall I wish 'im to make," says Number One. "It'll take all 'ands and the Captain of the Head° to clean up after 'im."

'"They won't grudge it," says the old man. "Just as soon as it's dusk we'll overhaul our tramp friend an' waft him over."

'Then a sno—midshipman°—Moorshed was 'is name—come up an' says somethin' in a low voice. It fetches the old man.

'"You'll oblige me," 'e says, "by takin' the wardroom poultry for *that*. I've ear-marked every fowl we've shipped at Madeira, so there can't be any possible mistake. M'rover," 'e says, "tell 'em if they spill one drop of blood on the deck," he says, "they'll not be extenuated, but hung."

'Mr Moorshed goes forward, lookin' unusual 'appy, even for him. The Marines was enjoyin' a committee-meetin' in their own flat.

'After that, it fell dark, with just a little streaky, oily light on the sea—an' anythin' more chronic than the *Archimandrite* I'd trouble you to behold. She looked like a fancy bazaar and a auction-room—yes, she almost looked like a passenger-steamer. We'd picked up our tramp, an' was about four mile be'ind 'er. I noticed the wardroom as a class, you might say, was manœuvrin' *en masse*, an' then come the order to cockbill the yards. We hadn't any yards except a couple o' signallin' sticks, but we cock-billed 'em. I hadn't seen that sight, not since thirteen years in the West Indies, when a post-captain died o' yellow jack.° It means a sign o' mournin', the yards bein' canted opposite ways, to look drunk an' disorderly. They do.

'"An' what might our last giddy-go-round signify?" I asks of 'Op.

'"Good 'Evins!" 'e says, "Are you in the habit o' permittin' leather-necks to assassinate lootenants every morning at drill without immejitly 'avin' 'em shot on the foc'sle in the horrid crawly-crawly twilight?"'

'"Yes," I murmured over my dear book, "*the infinitely lugubrious crepuscule. A spectacle of barbarity unparalleled—hideous—cold blooded, and yet touched with appalling grandeur*."'

'Ho! Was that the way Antonio looked at it? That shows he 'ad feelin's. To resoom. Without anyone givin' us orders to that effect, we began to creep about an' whisper. Things got stiller and stiller, till they was as still as—mushrooms! Then the bugler let off the "Dead March" from the upper bridge. He done it to cover the remarks of a cock-bird bein' killed forrard, but it came out paralysin' in its *tout ensemble*.° You never heard the "Dead March" on a bugle? Then the pipes went twitterin' for both watches to attend public execution,° and' we came up like so many ghosts, the 'ole ship's company. Why, Mucky 'Arcourt, one o' our boys, was that took in he give tongue like a beagle-pup, an' was properly kicked down the ladder for so doin'. Well, there we lay—engines stopped, rollin' to the swell, all dark, yards cock-billed, an' that merry tune yowlin' from the upper bridge. We fell in on the foc'sle, leavin' a large open space by the capstan, where our sail-maker was sittin' sewin' broken firebars° into the foot of an old 'ammick. 'E looked like a corpse, an' Mucky had another fit o' hysterics, an' you could 'ear us breathin' 'ard.° It beat anythin' in the theatrical line that even us *Archimandrites* had done—an' we was the ship you could trust. Then come the doctor an' lit a red lamp which he used for his photographic muckin's an' chocked it on the capstan. That was finally gashly!°

'Then come twelve Marines guardin' Glass 'ere. You wouldn't think to see 'im what a gratooitous an' aboundin' terror he was that evenin'. 'E was in a white shirt 'e'd stole from Cockburn, an' his regulation trousers, bare-footed. 'E'd pipe-clayed 'is 'ands an' face an' feet an' as much of his chest as the openin' of his shirt showed. 'E marched under escort with a firm an' undeviatin' step to the capstan, an' came to attention. The old man, reinforced by an extra strong split—his seventeenth, an' 'e didn't throw *that* down the ventilator—come up on the bridge an' stood like a image. 'Op, 'oo was with 'im, says that 'e heard Antonio's teeth singin', not chatterin'—singin' like funnel-stays in a typhoon. Yes, a moanin' æolian harp,° 'Op said.

'"When you are ready, Sir, drop your 'andkerchief," Number One whispers.

'"Good Lord!" says the old man, with a jump. "Eh! What? What a sight! What a sight!" an' he stood drinkin' it in, I suppose, for quite two minutes.

'Glass never says a word. 'E shoved aside an 'andkerchief which the sub-lootenant proffered 'im to bind 'is eyes with—quiet an' collected; an' if we 'adn't been feelin' so very much as we did feel, his gestures would 'ave brought down the 'ouse.'

'I can't open my eyes, or I'll be sick,' said the Marine with appalling clearness. 'I'm pretty far gone—I know it—but there wasn't anyone could 'ave beaten Edwardo Glass, R.M.L.I., that time. Why, I scared myself nearly into the 'orrors. Go on, Pye. Glass is in support—as ever.'

'Then the old man drops 'is 'andkerchief, an' the firin'-party fires like one man. Glass drops forward, twitchin' an' eavin' horrid natural, into the shotted° 'ammick all spread out before 'im, and the firin' party closes in to guard the remains of the deceased while Sails is stitchin' it up. An' when they lifted that 'ammick it was one wringin' mess o' blood! They on'y expended one wardroom cock-bird, too. Did you know poultry bled that extravagant? *I* never did.

'The old man—so 'Op told me—stayed on the bridge, brought up on a dead centre. Number One was similarly, though lesser, impressed, but o' course 'is duty was to think of 'is fine white decks an' the blood. "Arf a mo', Sir," he says, when the old man was for leavin'. "We have to wait for the burial, which I am informed takes place immejit."

'"It's beyond me," says the owner. "There was general instructions for an execution, but I never knew I had such a dependable push of mountebanks aboard," he says. "I'm all cold up my back, still."

'The Marines carried the corpse below. Then the bugle give us some more "Dead March." Then we 'eard a splash from a bow six-pounder port, an' the bugle struck up a cheerful tune. The whole lower deck was complimentin' Glass, 'oo took it very meek. 'E *is* a good actor, for all 'e's a leather-neck.

'"Now," said the old man, "we must turn over Antonio. He's in what I have 'eard called one perspirin' funk."

'Of course, I'm tellin' it slow, but it all 'appened much quicker. We run down our trampo—without o' course informin' Antonio of 'is 'appy destiny—an' inquired of 'er if she had any use for a free and gratis stowaway. Oh, yes! she said she'd be highly grateful, but she seemed a shade puzzled at our generosity, as you might put it, an' we lay by till she lowered a boat. Then Antonio—who was un'appy, distinctly un'appy—was politely requested to navigate elsewhere, which I don't think he looked for. 'Op was deputed to convey the information, an' 'Op got in one sixteen-inch kick which 'oisted 'im all up the ladder. 'Op ain't really vindictive, an' 'e's fond of the French, especially the women, but his chances o' kicking lootenants was like the cartridge—reduced to a minimum.

'The boat 'adn't more than shoved off before a change, as you might say, came o'er the spirit of our dream.° The old man says, like Elphinstone an' Bruce in the Portsmouth election when I was a boy:° "Gentlemen," he says, "for gentlemen you have shown yourselves to be—from the bottom of my heart I thank you. The status an' position of our late lamented shipmate made it obligato," 'e says, "to take certain steps not strictly included in the regulations. An' nobly," says 'e, "have you assisted me. Now," 'e says, "you hold the false and felonious reputation of bein' the smartest ship in the Service. Pigsties," 'e says, "is plane trigonometry alongside our present disgustin' state. Efface the effects of this indecent orgy," he says. "Jump, you lop-eared, flat-footed, butter-backed Amalekites! Dig out, you briny-eyed beggars!"

'Do captains talk like that in the Navy, Mr Pyecroft?' I asked.

'I've told you once I only give the grist of his arguments. The Bosun's mate translates it to the lower deck, as you may put it, and the lower deck springs smartly to attention. It took us half the night 'fore we got 'er anyway ship-shape; but by sunrise she was beautiful as ever, an' we resoomed. I've thought it over a lot since; yes, an' I've thought a lot of Antonio trimmin' coal in that tramp's bunkers. 'E must 'ave been highly surprised. Wasn't he?'

'He was, Mr Pyecroft,' I responded. 'But now we're talkin' of it, weren't you all a little surprised?'

'It come as a pleasant relief to the regular routine,' said Mr Pyecroft. 'We appreciated it as an easy way o' workin' for your country. But—the old man was right—a week o' similar manœuvres would 'ave knocked our moral double-bottoms bung out. Now, couldn't you oblige with Antonio's account of Glass's execution?'

I obliged for nearly ten minutes. It was at best but a feeble rendering of M. de C.'s magnificent prose, through which the soul of the poet, the eye of the mariner, and the heart of the patriot bore magnificent accord. His account of his descent from the side of the '*infamous vessel consecrated to blood*' in the '*vast and gathering dusk of the trembling ocean*' could only be matched by his description of the dishonoured hammock sinking unnoticed through the depths, while, above, the bugler played music '*of an indefinable brutality*.'

'By the way, what did the bugler play after Glass's funeral?' I asked.

'Him? Oh! 'e played "The Strict Q.T."° It's a very old song. We 'ad it in Fratton nearly fifteen years back,' said Mr Pyecroft sleepily.

I stirred the sugar dregs in my glass. Suddenly entered armed men, wet and discourteous, Tom Wessels smiling nervously in the background.

'Where is that—minutely particularised person—Glass?' said the sergeant of the picket.

''Ere!' The Marine rose to the strictest of attentions. 'An' it's no good smellin' of my breath, because I'm strictly an' ruinously sober.'

'Oh! An' what may you have been doin' with yourself?'

'Listenin' to tracts. You can look! I've 'ad the evenin' of my little life. Lead on to the *Cornucopia's* midmost dunjing-cell. There's a crowd of brass-'atted blighters there which will say I've been absent without leaf. Never mind. I forgive 'em before'and. *The* evenin' of my life, an' please don't forget it.' Then in a tone of most ingratiating apology to me: 'I soaked it all in be'ind my shut eyes. 'Im'—he jerked a contemptuous thumb towards Mr Pyecroft—''e's a flat-foot, a indigo-blue matlow. 'E never saw the fun from first to last. A mournful beggar—most depressin'.' Private Glass departed, leaning heavily on the escort's arm.

Mr Pyecroft wrinkled his brows in thought—the profound and far-reaching meditation that follows five glasses of hot whisky-and-water.

'Well, I don't see anything comical—greatly—except here an' there. Specially about those redooced charges in the guns. Do *you* see anything funny in it?'

There was that in his eye which warned me the night was too wet for argument.

'No, Mr Pyecroft, I don't,' I replied. 'It was a beautiful tale, and I thank you very much.'

'They'

The Return of the Children

Neither the harps nor the crowns amused, nor the cherubs' dove-
winged races—
Holding hands forlornly the Children wandered beneath the Dome;
Plucking the radiant robes of the passers-by, and with pitiful faces
Begging what Princes and Powers refused:—'Ah, please will you let us
go home?'

Over the jewelled floor, nigh weeping, ran to them Mary the Mother,
Kneeled and caressed and made promise with kisses, and drew them
along to the gateway—
Yea, the all-iron unbribeable Door which Peter must guard and none
other.
Straightway She took the Keys from his keeping, and opened and
freed them straightway.

Then to Her Son, Who had seen and smiled, She said: 'On the night
that I bore Thee
What didst Thou care for a love beyond mine or a heaven that was not
my arm?
Didst Thou push from the nipple, O Child, to hear the angels adore
Thee,
When we two lay in the breath of the kine?' And He said:—'Thou
hast done no harm.'

So through the Void the Children ran homeward merrily hand in
hand,
Looking neither to left nor right where the breathless Heavens stood
still
And the Guards of the Void resheathed their swords, for they heard
the Command:
'Shall I that have suffered the children to come to me hold them
against their will?'°

'They'

One view called me to another; one hill top to its fellow, half across the county, and since I could answer at no more trouble than the snapping forward of a lever, I let the county flow under my wheels. The orchid-studded flats of the East gave way to the thyme, ilex, and grey grass of the Downs; these again to the rich cornland and fig-trees of the lower coast, where you carry the beat of the tide on your left hand for fifteen level miles; and when at last I turned inland through a huddle of rounded hills and woods I had run myself clean out of my known marks. Beyond that precise hamlet which stands godmother to the capital of the United States,° I found hidden villages where bees, the only things awake, boomed in eighty-foot lindens that overhung grey Norman churches; miraculous brooks diving under stone bridges built for heavier traffic than would ever vex them again;° tithe-barns larger than their churches, and an old smithy that cried out aloud how it had once been a hall of the Knights of the Temple.° Gipsies I found on a common where the gorse, bracken, and heath fought it out together up a mile of Roman road; and a little farther on I disturbed a red fox rolling dog-fashion in the naked sunlight.

As the wooded hills closed about me I stood up in the car to take the bearings of that great Down whose ringed head is a landmark for fifty miles° across the low countries. I judged that the lie of the country would bring me across some westward-running road that went to his feet, but I did not allow for the confusing veils of the woods. A quick turn plunged me first into a green cutting brim-full of liquid sunshine, next into a gloomy tunnel where last year's dead leaves whispered and scuffled about my tyres. The strong hazel stuff meeting overhead had not been cut for a couple of generations at least, nor had any axe helped the moss-cankered oak and beech to spring above them. Here the road changed frankly into a carpeted ride on whose brown velvet spent primrose-clumps showed like jade, and a few sickly, white-stalked blue-bells nodded together. As the slope favoured I shut off the power and slid over the whirled leaves, expecting every moment to meet a keeper; but I only heard a jay, far off, arguing against the silence under the twilight of the trees.

Still the track descended. I was on the point of reversing and working my way back on the second speed° ere I ended in some swamp, when I saw sunshine through the tangle ahead and lifted the brake.

It was down again at once. As the light beat across my face my fore-wheels took the turf of a great still lawn from which sprang horsemen ten feet high with levelled lances, monstrous peacocks, and sleek round-headed maids of honour—blue, black, and glistening—all of clipped yew. Across the lawn—the marshalled woods besieged it on three sides—stood an ancient house of lichened and weather-worn stone, with mullioned windows and roofs of rose-red tile. It was flanked by semi-circular walls, also rose-red, that closed the lawn on the fourth side, and at their feet a box hedge grew man-high. There were doves on the roof about the slim brick chimneys, and I caught a glimpse of an octagonal dove-house behind the screening wall.

Here, then, I stayed; a horseman's green spear laid at my breast; held by the exceeding beauty of that jewel in that setting.

'If I am not packed off for a trespasser, or if this knight does not ride a wallop at me,' thought I, 'Shakespeare and Queen Elizabeth at least must come out of that half-open garden door and ask me to tea.'

A child appeared at an upper window, and I thought the little thing waved a friendly hand. But it was to call a companion, for presently another bright head showed. Then I heard a laugh among the yew-peacocks, and turning to make sure (till then I had been watching the house only) I saw the silver of a fountain behind a hedge thrown up against the sun. The doves on the roof cooed to the cooing water; but between the two notes I caught the utterly happy chuckle of a child absorbed in some light mischief.

The garden door—heavy oak sunk deep in the thickness of the wall—opened further: a woman in a big garden hat set her foot slowly on the time-hollowed stone step and as slowly walked across the turf. I was forming some apology when she lifted up her head and I saw that she was blind.

'I heard you,' she said. 'Isn't that a motor car?'

'I'm afraid I've made a mistake in my road. I should have turned off up above—I never dreamed—' I began.

'But I'm very glad. Fancy a motor car coming into the garden! It will be such a treat—' She turned and made as though looking about her. 'You—you haven't seen anyone, have you—perhaps?'

'No one to speak to, but the children seemed interested at a distance.'

'Which?'

'I saw a couple up at the window just now, and I think I heard a little chap in the grounds.'

'Oh, lucky you!' she cried, and her face brightened. 'I hear them, of course, but that's all. You've seen them and heard them?'

'Yes,' I answered. 'And if I know anything of children, one of them's having a beautiful time by the fountain yonder. Escaped, I should imagine.'

'You're fond of children?'

I gave her one or two reasons why I did not altogether hate them.

'Of course, of course,' she said. 'Then you understand. Then you won't think it foolish if I ask you to take your car through the gardens, once or twice—quite slowly. I'm sure they'd like to see it. They see so little, poor things. One tries to make their life pleasant, but—' she threw out her hands towards the woods. 'We're so out of the world here.'

'That will be splendid,' I said. 'But I can't cut up your grass.'

She faced to the right. 'Wait a minute,' she said. 'We're at the South gate, aren't we? Behind those peacocks there's a flagged path. We call it the Peacocks' Walk. You can't see it from here, they tell me, but if you squeeze along by the edge of the wood you can turn at the first peacock and get on to the flags.'

It was sacrilege to wake that dreaming house-front with the clatter of machinery, but I swung the car to clear the turf, brushed along the edge of the wood and turned in on the broad stone path where the fountain-basin lay like one star-sapphire.

'May I come too?' she cried. 'No, please don't help me. They'll like it better if they see me.'

She felt her way lightly to the front of the car, and with one foot on the step she called: 'Children, oh, children! Look and see what's going to happen!'

The voice would have drawn lost souls from the Pit, for the yearning that underlay its sweetness, and I was not surprised to hear an answering shout behind the yews. It must have been the child by the fountain, but he fled at our approach, leaving a little toy boat in the water. I saw the glint of his blue blouse among the still horsemen.

Very disposedly we paraded the length of the walk and at her request backed again. This time the child had got the better of his panic, but stood far off and doubting.

'The little fellow's watching us,' I said. 'I wonder if he'd like a ride.'

'They're very shy still. Very shy. But, oh, lucky you to be able to see them! Let's listen.'

I stopped the machine at once, and the humid stillness, heavy with the scent of box, cloaked us deep. Shears I could hear where some gardener was clipping; a mumble of bees and broken voices that might have been the doves.

'Oh, unkind!' she said weariedly.

'Perhaps they're only shy of the motor. The little maid at the window looks tremendously interested.'

'Yes?' She raised her head. 'It was wrong of me to say that. They are really fond of me. It's the only thing that makes life worth living —when they're fond of you, isn't it? I daren't think what the place would be without them. By the way, is it beautiful?'

'I think it is the most beautiful place I have ever seen.'

'So they all tell me. I can feel it, of course, but that isn't quite the same thing.'

'Then have you never—?' I began, but stopped abashed.

'Not since I can remember. It happened when I was only a few months old, they tell me. And yet I must remember something, else how could I dream about colours. I see light in my dreams, and colours, but I never see *them*. I only hear them just as I do when I'm awake.'

'It's difficult to see faces in dreams. Some people can, but most of us haven't the gift,' I went on, looking up at the window where the child stood all but hidden.

'I've heard that too,' she said. 'And they tell me that one never sees a dead person's face in a dream. Is that true?'

'I believe it is—now I come to think of it.'

'But how is it with yourself—yourself?' The blind eyes turned towards me.

'I have never seen the faces of my dead in any dream,' I answered.

'Then it must be as bad as being blind.'

The sun had dipped behind the woods and the long shades were possessing the insolent horsemen one by one. I saw the light die from off the top of a glossy-leaved lance and all the brave hard green turn to soft black. The house, accepting another day at end, as it had accepted an hundred thousand gone, seemed to settle deeper into its rest among the shadows.

'Have you ever wanted to?' she said after the silence.

'Very much sometimes,' I replied. The child had left the window as the shadows closed upon it.

'Ah! So've I, but I don't suppose it's allowed. . . . Where d'you live?'

'Quite the other side of the county—sixty miles and more, and I must be going back. I've come without my big lamp.'

'But it's not dark yet. I can feel it.'

'I'm afraid it will be by the time I get home. Could you lend me someone to set me on my road at first? I've utterly lost myself.'

'I'll send Madden with you to the cross-roads. We are so out of the world, I don't wonder you were lost! I'll guide you round to the front of the house; but you will go slowly, won't you, till you're out of the grounds? It isn't foolish, do you think?'

'I promise you I'll go like this,' I said, and let the car start herself down the flagged path.

We skirted the left wing of the house, whose elaborately cast lead guttering alone was worth a day's journey; passed under a great rose-grown gate in the red wall, and so round to the high front of the house which in beauty and stateliness as much excelled the back as that all others I had seen.

'Is it so very beautiful?' she said wistfully when she heard my raptures. 'And you like the lead-figures too? There's the old azalea garden behind. They say that this place must have been made for children. Will you help me out, please? I should like to come with you as far as the cross-roads, but I mustn't leave them. Is that you, Madden? I want you to show this gentleman the way to the cross-roads. He has lost his way but—he has seen them.'

A butler appeared noiselessly at the miracle of old oak that must be called the front door, and slipped aside to put on his hat. She stood looking at me with open blue eyes in which no sight lay, and I saw for the first time that she was beautiful.

'Remember,' she said quietly, 'if you are fond of them you will come again,' and disappeared within the house.

The butler in the car said nothing till we were nearly at the lodge gates, where catching a glimpse of a blue blouse in a shrubbery I swerved amply lest the devil that leads little boys to play should drag me into child-murder.

'Excuse me,' he asked of a sudden, 'but why did you do that, Sir?'

'The child yonder.'

'Our young gentleman in blue?'

'Of course.'

'He runs about a good deal. Did you see him by the fountain, sir?'

'Oh, yes, several times. Do we turn here?'

'Yes, Sir. And did you 'appen to see them upstairs too?'

'At the upper window? Yes.'

'Was that before the mistress come out to speak to you, Sir?'

'A little before that. Why d'you want to know?'

He paused a little. 'Only to make sure that—that they had seen the car, Sir, because with children running about, though I'm sure you're driving particularly careful, there might be an accident. That was all, Sir. Here are the cross-roads. You can't miss your way from now on. Thank you, Sir, but that isn't *our* custom, not with—'

'I beg your pardon,' I said, and thrust away the British silver.

'Oh, it's quite right with the rest of 'em as a rule. Good-bye, Sir.'

He retired into the armour-plated conning tower of his caste and walked away. Evidently a butler solicitous for the honour of his house, and interested, probably through a maid, in the nursery.

Once beyond the signposts at the cross-roads I looked back, but the crumpled hills interlaced so jealously that I could not see where the house had lain. When I asked its name at a cottage along the road, the fat woman who sold sweetmeats there gave me to understand that people with motor cars had small right to live—much less to 'go about talking like carriage folk.' They were not a pleasant-mannered community.

When I retraced my route on the map that evening I was little wiser. Hawkin's Old Farm appeared to be the Survey title of the place, and the old County Gazetteer, generally so ample, did not allude to it. The big house of those parts was Hodnington Hall, Georgian with early Victorian embellishments, as an atrocious steel engraving attested. I carried my difficulty to a neighbour—a deep-rooted tree of that soil—and he gave me a name of a family which conveyed no meaning.

A month or so later—I went again, or it may have been that my car took the road of her own volition. She over-ran the fruitless Downs, threaded every turn of the maze of lanes below the hills, drew through the high-walled woods, impenetrable in their full leaf, came out at the cross-roads where the butler had left me, and a little farther on developed an internal trouble which forced me to turn her in on a grass way-waste° that cut into a summer-silent hazel wood. So far as I could make sure by the sun and a six-inch Ordnance map, this should be the road flank of that wood which I had first explored from the heights above. I made a mighty serious business of my repairs and a glittering shop of my repair kit, spanners, pump, and the like, which I spread out orderly upon a rug. It was a trap to catch all childhood, for on such a day, I argued, the children would not be far off. When I paused in my work I listened, but the wood was so full of the noises of summer (though the birds had mated) that I could not at first distinguish these from the tread of small cautious feet stealing across the dead leaves. I rang my bell in an alluring manner, but the feet fled, and I repented, for to a child a sudden noise is very real terror. I must have been at work half an hour when I heard in the wood the voice of the blind woman crying: 'Children, oh, children! Where are you?' and the stillness made slow to close on the perfection of that cry. She came towards me, half feeling her way between the tree boles, and though a child it seemed clung to her skirt, it swerved into the leafage like a rabbit as she drew nearer.

'Is that you?' she said, 'from the other side of the county?'

'Yes, it's me from the other side of the county.'

'Then why didn't you come through the upper woods? They were there just now.'

'They were here a few minutes ago. I expect they knew my car had broken down, and came to see the fun.'

'Nothing serious, I hope? How do cars break down?'

'In fifty different ways. Only mine has chosen the fifty first.'

She laughed merrily at the tiny joke, cooed with delicious laughter, and pushed her hat back.

'Let me hear,' she said.

'Wait a moment,' I cried, 'and I'll get you a cushion.'

She set her foot on the rug all covered with spare parts, and stooped above it eagerly. 'What delightful things!' The hands through which she saw glanced in the chequered sunlight. 'A box here—another box! Why you've arranged them like playing shop!'

'I confess now that I put it out to attract them. I don't need half those things really.'

'How nice of you! I heard your bell in the upper wood. You say they were here before that?'

'I'm sure of it. Why are they so shy? That little fellow in blue who was with you just now ought to have got over his fright. He's been watching me like a Red Indian.'

'It must have been your bell,' she said. 'I heard one of them go past me in trouble when I was coming down. They're shy—so shy even with me.' She turned her face over her shoulder and cried again: 'Children, oh, children! Look and see!'

'They must have gone off together on their own affairs,' I suggested, for there was a murmur behind us of lowered voices broken by the sudden squeaking giggles of childhood. I returned to my tinkerings and she leaned forward, her chin on her hand, listening interestedly.

'How many are they?' I said at last. The work was finished, but I saw no reason to go.

Her forehead puckered a little in thought. 'I don't quite know,' she said simply. 'Sometimes more—sometimes less. They come and stay with me because I love them, you see.'

'That must be very jolly,' I said, replacing a drawer, and as I spoke I heard the inanity of my answer.

'You—you aren't laughing at me,' she cried. 'I—I haven't any of my own. I never married. People laugh at me sometimes about them because—because—'

'Because they're savages,' I returned. 'It's nothing to fret for. That sort laugh at everything that isn't in their own fat lives.'

'I don't know. How should I? I only don't like being laughed at about *them*. It hurts; and when one can't see. . . . I don't want to seem silly,' her chin quivered like a child's as she spoke, 'but we blindies have only one skin, I think. Everything outside hits straight at our souls. It's different with you. You've such good defences in your eyes—looking out—before anyone can really pain you in your soul. People forget that with us.'

I was silent reviewing that inexhaustible matter—the more than inherited (since it is also carefully taught) brutality of the Christian peoples, beside which the mere heathendom of the West Coast° nigger is clean and restrained. It led me a long distance into myself.

'Don't do that!' she said of a sudden, putting her hands before her eyes.

'What?'

She made a gesture with her hand.

'That! It's—it's all purple and black. Don't! That colour hurts.'

'But, how in the world do you know about colours?' I exclaimed, for here was a revelation indeed.

'Colours as colours?' she asked.

'No. *Those* Colours which you saw just now.'

'You know as well as I do,' she laughed, 'else you wouldn't have asked that question. They aren't in the world at all. They're in *you*—when you went so angry.'

'D'you mean a dull purplish patch, like port wine mixed with ink?' I said.

'I've never seen ink or port wine, but the colours aren't mixed. They are separate—all separate.'

'Do you mean black streaks and jags across the purple?'

She nodded. 'Yes—if they are like this,' and zig-zagged her finger again, 'but it's more red than purple—that bad colour.'

'And what are the colours at the top of the—whatever you see?'

Slowly she leaned forward and traced on the rug the figure of the Egg itself.°

'I see them so,' she said, pointing with a grass stem, 'white, green, yellow, red, purple, and when people are angry or bad, black across the red—as you were just now.'

'Who told you anything about it—in the beginning?' I demanded.

'About the colours? No one. I used to ask what colours were when I was little—in table-covers and curtains and carpets, you see—because some colours hurt me and some made me happy. People told me; and when I got older that was how I saw people.' Again she traced the outline of the Egg which it is given to very few of us to see.

'All by yourself?' I repeated.

'All by myself. There wasn't anyone else. I only found out afterwards that other people did not see the Colours.'

She leaned against the tree-bole plaiting and unplaiting chance-plucked grass stems. The children in the wood had drawn nearer. I could see them with the tail of my eye frolicking like squirrels.

'Now I am sure you will never laugh at me,' she went on after a long silence. 'Nor at *them*.'

'Goodness! No!' I cried, jolted out of my train of thought. 'A man who laughs at a child—unless the child is laughing too—is a heathen!'

'I didn't mean that, of course. You'd never laugh *at* children, but I thought—I used to think—that perhaps you might laugh about *them*. So now I beg your pardon. . . . What are you going to laugh at?'

I had made no sound, but she knew.

'At the notion of your begging my pardon. If you had done your duty as a pillar of the State and a landed proprietress you ought to have summoned me for trespass when I barged through your woods the other day. It was disgraceful of me—inexcusable.'

She looked at me, her head against the tree trunk—long and steadfastly—this woman who could see the naked soul.

'How curious,' she half whispered. 'How very curious.'

'Why, what have I done?'

'You don't understand . . . and yet you understood about the Colours. Don't you understand?'

She spoke with a passion that nothing had justified, and I faced her bewilderedly as she rose. The children had gathered themselves in a roundel behind a bramble bush. One sleek head bent over something smaller, and the set of the little shoulders told me that fingers were on lips. They, too, had some child's tremendous secret. I alone was hopelessly astray there in the broad sunlight.

'No,' I said, and shook my head as though the dead eyes could note. 'Whatever it is, I don't understand yet. Perhaps I shall later—if you'll let me come again.'

'You will come again,' she answered. 'You will surely come again and walk in the wood.'

'Perhaps the children will know me well enough by that time to let me play with them—as a favour. You know what children are like.'

'It isn't a matter of favour but of right,' she replied, and while I wondered what she meant, a dishevelled woman plunged round the bend of the road, loose-haired, purple, almost lowing with agony as she ran. It was my rude, fat friend of the sweetmeat shop. The blind woman heard and stepped forward. 'What is it, Mrs Madehurst?' she asked.

The woman flung her apron over her head and literally grovelled in the dust, crying that her grandchild was sick to death, that the local doctor was away fishing, that Jenny the mother was at her wits' end, and so forth, with repetitions and bellowings.

'Where's the next nearest doctor?' I asked between paroxysms.

'Madden will tell you. Go round to the house and take him with you. I'll attend to this. Be quick!' She half supported the fat woman into the shade. In two minutes I was blowing all the horns of Jericho under the front of the House Beautiful, and Madden, in the pantry, rose to the crisis like a butler and a man.

A quarter of an hour at illegal speeds caught us a doctor five miles away. Within the half-hour we had decanted him, much interested in motors, at the door of the sweetmeat shop, and drew up the road to await the verdict.

'Useful things cars,' said Madden, all man and no butler. 'If I'd had one when mine took sick she wouldn't have died.'

'How was it?' I asked.

'Croup. Mrs Madden was away. No one knew what to do. I drove eight miles in a tax cart° for the doctor. She was choked when we came back. This car 'd ha' saved her. She'd have been close on ten now.'

'I'm sorry,' I said. 'I thought you were rather fond of children from what you told me going to the cross-roads the other day.'

'Have you seen 'em again, Sir—this mornin'?'

'Yes, but they're well broke to cars. I couldn't get any of them within twenty yards of it.'

He looked at me carefully as a scout considers a stranger—not as a menial should lift his eyes to his divinely appointed superior.

'I wonder why,' he said just above the breath that he drew.

We waited on. A light wind from the sea wandered up and down the long lines of the woods, and the wayside grasses, whitened already with summer dust, rose and bowed in sallow waves.

A woman, wiping the suds off her arms, came out of the cottage next the sweetmeat shop.

'I've be'n listenin' in de back-yard,'° she said cheerily. 'He says Arthur's unaccountable bad. Did ye hear him shruck° just now? Unaccountable bad. I reckon t'will come Jenny's turn to walk in de wood nex' week along, Mr Madden.'

'Excuse me, Sir, but your lap-robe is slipping,' said Madden deferentially. The woman started, dropped a curtsey, and hurried away.

'What does she mean by "walking in the wood"?' I asked.

'It must be some saying they use hereabouts. I'm from Norfolk myself,' said Madden. 'They're an independent lot in this county. She took you for a chauffeur, Sir.'

I saw the Doctor come out of the cottage followed by a draggle-tailed wench who clung to his arm as though he could make treaty for her with Death. 'Dat sort,' she wailed—'dey're just as much to us dat has 'em as if dey was lawful born. Just as much—just as much! An' God he'd be just as pleased if you saved 'un, Doctor. Don't take it from me. Miss Florence will tell ye de very same. Don't leave 'im, doctor!'

'I know, I know,' said the man; 'but he'll be quiet for a while now. We'll get the nurse and the medicine as fast as we can.' He signalled me to come forward with the car, and I strove not to be privy to what followed; but I saw the girl's face, blotched and frozen with grief, and I felt the hand without a ring clutching at my knees when we moved away.

The Doctor was a man of some humour, for I remember he claimed my car under the Oath of Æsculapius,° and used it and me without mercy. First we convoyed Mrs Madehurst and the blind woman° to wait by the sick bed till the nurse should come. Next we invaded a neat county town for prescriptions (the Doctor said the trouble was cerebro-spinal meningitis), and when the County Institute, banked and flanked with scared market cattle, reported itself out of nurses for the moment we literally flung ourselves loose upon the county. We conferred with the owners of great houses—magnates at the ends of overarching avenues whose big-boned womenfolk strode away from their tea-tables to listen to the imperious Doctor. At last a white-haired lady sitting under a cedar of Lebanon and surrounded by a court of magnificient Borzois°—all hostile to motors—gave the Doctor, who received them as from a princess, written orders which we bore many miles at top speed, through a park, to a French nunnery, where we took over in exchange a pallid-faced and trembling Sister. She knelt at the bottom of the tonneau° telling her beads without pause till, by short cuts of the Doctor's invention, we had her to the sweetmeat shop once more. It was a long afternoon crowded with mad episodes that rose and dissolved like the dust of our wheels; cross-sections of remote and incomprehensible lives through which we raced at right angles; and I went home in the dusk, wearied out, to dream of the clashing horns of cattle; round-eyed nuns walking in a garden of graves; pleasant tea-parties beneath shaded trees; the carbolic-scented, grey-painted corridors of the County Institute; the steps of shy children in the wood, and the hands that clung to my knees as the motor began to move.

I had intended to return in a day or two, but it pleased Fate to hold me from that side of the county, on many pretexts, till the elder and the wild rose had fruited. There came at last a brilliant day, swept clear from the south-west, that brought the hills within hand's reach —a day of unstable airs and high filmy clouds. Through no merit of my own I was free, and set the car for the third time on that known road. As I reached the crest of the Downs I felt the soft air change, saw it glaze under the sun; and, looking down at the sea, in that instant beheld the blue of the Channel turn through polished silver and dulled steel to dingy pewter. A laden collier hugging the coast steered outward for deeper water, and, across copper-coloured haze, I saw sails rise one by one on the anchored fishing-fleet. In a deep dene behind me an eddy of sudden wind drummed through sheltered oaks, and spun aloft the first dry sample of autumn leaves. When I reached the beach road the sea-fog fumed over the brickfields, and the tide was telling all the groins of the gale beyond Ushant. In less than an hour summer England vanished in chill grey. We were again the shut island of the North, all the ships of the world bellowing at our perilous gates; and between their outcries ran the piping of bewildered gulls. My cap dripped moisture, the folds of the rug held it in pools or sluiced it away in runnels, and the salt-rime stuck to my lips.

Inland the smell of autumn loaded the thickened fog among the trees, and the drip became a continuous shower. Yet the late flowers —mallow of the wayside, scabious of the field, and dahlia of the garden—showed gay in the mist, and beyond the sea's breath there was little sign of decay in the leaf. Yet in the villages the house doors were all open, and bare-legged, bare-headed children sat at ease on the damp doorsteps to shout 'pip-pip' at the stranger.

I made bold to call at the sweetmeat shop, where Mrs Madehurst met me with a fat woman's hospitable tears. Jenny's child, she said, had died two days after the nun had come. It was, she felt, best out of the way, even though insurance offices, for reasons which she did not pretend to follow, would not willingly insure such stray lives.° 'Not but what Jenny didn't tend to Arthur as though he'd come all proper at de end of de first year—like Jenny herself.' Thanks to Miss Florence, the child had been buried with a pomp which, in Mrs Madehurst's opinion, more than covered the small irregularity of its birth. She described the coffin, within and without, the glass hearse, and the evergreen lining of the grave.

'But how's the mother?' I asked.

'Jenny? Oh, she'll get over it. I've felt dat way with one or two o' my own. She'll get over. She's walkin' in de wood now.'

'In this weather?'

Mrs Madehurst looked at me with narrowed eyes across the counter.

'I dunno but it opens de 'eart like. Yes, it opens de 'eart. Dat's where losin' and bearin' comes so alike in de long run, we do say.'

Now the wisdom of the old wives is greater than that of all the Fathers,° and this last oracle sent me thinking so extendedly as I went up the road, that I nearly ran over a woman and a child at the wooded corner by the lodge gates of the House Beautiful.

'Awful weather!' I cried, as I slowed dead for the turn.

'Not so bad,' she answered placidly out of the fog. 'Mine's used to 'un. You'll find yours indoors, I reckon.'

Indoors, Madden received me with professional courtesy, and kind inquiries for the health of the motor, which he would put under cover.

I waited in a still, nut-brown hall, pleasant with late flowers and warmed with a delicious wood fire—a place of good influence and great peace. (Men and women may sometimes, after great effort, achieve a creditable lie; but the house, which is their temple, cannot say anything save the truth of those who have lived in it.°) A child's cart and a doll lay on the black-and-white floor, where a rug had been kicked back. I felt that the children had only just hurried away—to hide themselves, most like—in the many turns of the great adzed staircase that climbed statelily out of the hall, or to crouch at gaze behind the lions and roses of the carven gallery above. Then I heard her voice above me, singing as the blind sing—from the soul:—

In the pleasant orchard-closes.°

And all my early summer came back at the call.

In the pleasant orchard-closes,
God bless all our gains say we—
But may God bless all our losses,
Better suits with our degree.

She dropped the marring fifth line, and repeated—

Better suits with our degree!

I saw her lean over the gallery, her linked hands white as pearl against the oak.

'Is that you—from the other side of the county?' she called.

'Yes, me—from the other side of the county,' I answered, laughing.

'What a long time before you had to come here again.' She ran down the stairs, one hand lightly touching the broad rail. 'It's two months and four days. Summer's gone!'

'I meant to come before, but Fate prevented.'

'I knew it. Please do something to that fire. They won't let me play with it, but I can feel it's behaving badly. Hit it!'

I looked on either side of the deep fireplace, and found but a half-charred hedge-stake° with which I punched a black log into flame.

'It never goes out, day or night,' she said, as though explaining. 'In case any one comes in with cold toes, you see.'

'It's even lovelier inside than it was out,' I murmured. The red light poured itself along the age-polished dusky panels till the Tudor roses and lions of the gallery took colour and motion. An old eagle-topped convex mirror gathered the picture into its mysterious heart, distorting afresh the distorted shadows, and curving the gallery lines into the curves of a ship. The day was shutting down in half a gale as the fog turned to stringy scud. Through the uncurtained mullions of the broad window I could see valiant horsemen of the lawn rear and recover against the wind that taunted them with legions of dead leaves.

'Yes, it must be beautiful,' she said. 'Would you like to go over it? There's still light enough upstairs.'

I followed her up the unflinching, wagon-wide staircase to the gallery whence opened the thin fluted Elizabethan doors.

'Feel how they put the latch low down for the sake of the children.' She swung a light door inward.

'By the way, where are they?' I asked. 'I haven't even heard them to-day.'

She did not answer at once. Then, 'I can only hear them,' she replied softly. 'This is one of their rooms—everything ready, you see.'

She pointed into a heavily-timbered room. There were little low gate tables and children's chairs. A doll's house, its hooked front half open, faced a great dappled rocking-horse, from whose padded saddle it was but a child's scramble to the broad window-seat overlooking the lawn. A toy gun lay in a corner beside a gilt wooden cannon.

'Surely they've only just gone,' I whispered. In the failing light a door creaked cautiously. I heard the rustle of a frock and the patter of feet—quick feet through a room beyond.

'I heard that,' she cried triumphantly. 'Did you? Children, oh, children! Where are you?'

The voice filled the walls that held it lovingly to the last perfect note, but there came no answering shout such as I had heard in the garden. We hurried on from room to oak-floored room; up a step here, down three steps there; among a maze of passages; always mocked by our quarry. One might as well have tried to work an unstopped warren with a single ferret. There were bolt-holes innumerable—recesses in walls, embrasures of deep slitten windows now darkened, whence they could start up behind us; and abandoned fireplaces, six feet deep in the masonry, as well as the tangle of communicating doors. Above all, they had the twilight for their helper in our game. I had caught one or two joyous chuckles of evasion, and once or twice had seen the silhouette of a child's frock against some darkening window at the end of a passage; but we returned empty-handed to the gallery, just as a middle-aged woman was setting a lamp in its niche.

'No, I haven't seen her either this evening, Miss Florence,' I heard her say, 'but that Turpin he says he wants to see you about his shed.'

'Oh, Mr Turpin must want to see me very badly. Tell him to come to the hall, Mrs Madden.'

I looked down into the hall whose only light was the dulled fire, and deep in the shadow I saw them at last. They must have slipped down while we were in the passages, and now thought themselves perfectly hidden behind an old gilt leather screen. By child's law, my fruitless chase was as good as an introduction, but since I had taken so much trouble I resolved to force them to come forward later by the simple trick, which children detest, of pretending not to notice them. They lay close, in a little huddle, no more than shadows except when a quick flame betrayed an outline.

'And now we'll have some tea,' she said. 'I believe I ought to have offered it you at first, but one doesn't arrive at manners somehow when one lives alone and is considered—h'm—peculiar.' Then with very pretty scorn, 'Would you like a lamp to see to eat by?'

'The firelight's much pleasanter, I think.' We descended into that delicious gloom and Madden brought tea.

I took my chair in the direction of the screen ready to surprise or be surprised as the game should go, and at her permission, since a hearth is always sacred, bent forward to play with the fire.

'Where do you get these beautiful short faggots from?' I asked idly. 'Why, they are tallies!'

'Of course,' she said. 'As I can't read or write I'm driven back on the early English tally for my accounts. Give me one and I'll tell you what it meant.'

I passed her an unburned hazel-tally, about a foot long, and she ran her thumb down the nicks.

'This is the milk-record for the home farm for the month of April last year, in gallons,' said she. 'I don't know what I should have done without tallies. An old forester of mine taught me the system. It's out of date now for every one else; but my tenants respect it. One of them's coming now to see me. Oh, it doesn't matter. He has no business here out of office hours. He's a greedy, ignorant man—very greedy or—he wouldn't come here after dark.'

'Have you much land then?'

'Only a couple of hundred acres in hand, thank goodness. The other six hundred are nearly all let to folk who knew my folk before me, but this Turpin is quite a new man—and a highway robber.'°

'But are you sure I shan't be—'

'Certainly not. You have the right. He hasn't any children.'

'Ah, the children!' I said, and slid my low chair back till it nearly touched the screen that hid them. 'I wonder whether they'll come out for me.'

There was a murmur of voices—Madden's and a deeper note—at the low, dark side door, and a ginger-headed, canvas-gaitered giant of the unmistakable tenant-farmer type stumbled or was pushed in.

'Come to the fire, Mr Turpin,' she said.

'If—if you please, Miss, I'll—I'll be quite as well by the door.' He clung to the latch as he spoke like a frightened child. Of a sudden I realised that he was in the grip of some almost overpowering fear.

'Well?'

'About that new shed for the young stock—that was all. These first autumn storms settin' in . . . but I'll come again, Miss.' His teeth did not chatter much more than the door latch.

'I think not,' she answered levelly. 'The new shed—m'm. What did my agent write you on the 15th?'

'I—fancied p'raps that if I came to see you—ma—man to man like, Miss. But—'

His eyes rolled into every corner of the room wide with horror. He half opened the door through which he had entered, but I noticed it shut again—from without and firmly.

'He wrote what I told him,' she went on. 'You are overstocked already. Dunnett's Farm never carried more than fifty bullocks—even in Mr Wright's time. And *he* used cake.° You've sixty-seven and you don't cake. You've broken the lease in that respect. You're dragging the heart out of the farm.'°

'I'm—I'm getting some minerals—superphosphates—next week. I've as good as ordered a truck-load already. I'll go down to the station tomorrow about 'em. Then I can come and see you man to man like, Miss, in the daylight. . . . That gentleman's not going away, is he?' He almost shrieked.

I had only slid the chair a little farther back, reaching behind me to tap on the leather of the screen, but he jumped like a rat.

'No. Please attend to me, Mr Turpin.' She turned in her chair and faced him with his back to the door. It was an old and sordid little piece of scheming that she forced from him—his plea for the new cow-shed at his landlady's expense, that he might with the covered manure pay his next year's rent out of the valuation after, as she made clear, he had bled the enriched pastures to the bone. I could not but admire the intensity of his greed, when I saw him out-facing for its sake whatever terror it was that ran wet on his forehead.

I ceased to tap the leather—was, indeed, calculating the cost of the shed—when I felt my relaxed hand taken and turned softly between the soft hands of a child. So at last I had triumphed. In a moment I would turn and acquaint myself with those quick-footed wanderers. . . .

The little brushing kiss fell in the centre of my palm—as a gift on which the fingers were, once, expected to close: as the all-faithful half-reproachful signal of a waiting child not used to neglect even when grown-ups were busiest—a fragment of the mute code devised very long ago.

Then I knew. And it was as though I had known from the first day when I looked across the lawn at the high window.

I heard the door shut. The woman turned to me in silence, and I felt that she knew.

What time passed after this I cannot say. I was roused by the fall of a log, and mechanically rose to put it back. Then I returned to my place in the chair very close to the screen.

'Now you understand,' she whispered, across the packed shadows.

'Yes, I understand—now. Thank you.'

'I—I only hear them.' She bowed her head in her hands. 'I have no right, you know—no other right. I have neither borne nor lost—neither borne nor lost!'

'Be very glad then,' said I, for my soul was torn open within me.

'Forgive me!'

She was still, and I went back to my sorrow and my joy.

'It was because I loved them so,' she said at last, brokenly. '*That* was why it was, even from the first—even before I knew that they—they were all I should ever have. And I loved them so!'

She stretched out her arms to the shadows and the shadows within the shadow.

'They came because I loved them—because I needed them. I—I must have made them come. Was that wrong, think you?'

'No—no.'

'I—I grant you that the toys and—and all that sort of thing were nonsense, but—but I used to so hate empty rooms myself when I was little.' She pointed to the gallery. 'And the passages all empty. . . . And how could I ever bear the garden door shut? Suppose—'

'Don't! For pity's sake, don't!' I cried. The twilight had brought a cold rain with gusty squalls that plucked at the leaded windows.

'And the same thing with keeping the fire in all night. *I* don't think it so foolish—do you?'

I looked at the broad brick hearth, saw, through tears I believe, that there was no unpassable iron° on or near it, and bowed my head.

'I did all that and lots of other things—just to make believe. Then they came. I heard them, but I didn't know that they were not mine by right till Mrs Madden told me—'

'The butler's wife? What?'

'One of them—I heard—she saw. And knew. Hers! *Not* for me. I didn't know at first. Perhaps I was jealous. Afterwards, I began to understand that it was only because I loved them, not because— . . . Oh, you *must* bear or lose,' she said piteously. 'There is no other way—and yet they love me. They must! Don't they?'

There was no sound in the room except the lapping voices of the fire, but we two listened intently, and she at least took comfort from what she heard. She recovered herself and half rose. I sat still in my chair by the screen.

'Don't think me a wretch to whine about myself like this, but—but I'm all in the dark, you know, and *you* can see.'

In truth I could see, and my vision confirmed me in my resolve, though that was like the very parting of spirit and flesh. Yet a little longer I would stay since it was the last time.

'You think it is wrong, then?' she cried sharply, though I had said nothing.

'Not for you. A thousand times no. For you it is right. . . . I am grateful to you beyond words. For me it would be wrong. For me only. . . .'

'Why?' she said, but passed her hand before her face as she had done at our second meeting in the wood. 'Oh, I see,' she went on simply as a child. 'For you it would be wrong.' Then with a little indrawn laugh, 'and, d'you remember, I called you lucky—once—at first. You who must never come here again!'

She left me to sit a little longer by the screen, and I heard the sound of her feet die out along the gallery above.

Mrs Bathurst

From Lyden's 'Irenius'°
ACT III. SC. II.

GOW.—Had it been your Prince instead of a groom caught in this noose there's not an astrologer of the city—

PRINCE.—Sacked! Sacked! We were a city yesterday.

GOW.—So be it, but I was not governor. Not an astrologer, but would ha' sworn he'd forseen it at the last versary° of Venus, when Vulcan caught her with Mars in the house of stinking Capricorn. But since 'tis Jack of the Straw that hangs, the forgetful stars had it not on their tablets.

PRINCE.—Another life! Were there any left to die? How did the poor fool come by it?

GOW.—*Simpliciter*° thus. She that damned him to death knew not that she did it, or would have died ere she had done it. For she loved him. He that hangs him does so in obedience to the Duke, and asks no more than 'Where is the rope?' The Duke, very exactly he hath told us, works God's will, in which holy employ he's not to be questioned. We have then left upon this finger, only Jack whose soul now plucks the left sleeve of Destiny in Hell to overtake° why she clapped him up like a fly on a sunny wall. Whuff! Soh!

PRINCE.—Your cloak, Ferdinand. I'll sleep now.

FERDINAND.—Sleep, then . . . He too, loved his life?

GOW.—He was born of woman . . . but at the end threw life from him, like your Prince, for a little sleep . . . 'Have I any look of a King?' said he, clanking his chain—'to be so baited on all sides by Fortune, that I must e'en die now to live with myself one day longer.' I left him railing at Fortune and woman's love.

FERDINAND.—Ah, woman's love!

(*Aside*) Who knows not Fortune, glutted on easy thrones,
Stealing from feasts as rare to coneycatch,°
Privily in the hedgerows for a clown
With that same cruel-lustful hand and eye,
Those nails and wedges, that one hammer and lead,
And the very gerb of long-stored lightnings loosed
Yesterday 'gainst some King.

Mrs Bathurst

The day that I chose to visit H.M.S. *Peridot*° in Simon's Bay° was the day that the Admiral had chosen to send her up the coast. She was just steaming out to sea as my train came in,° and since the rest of the Fleet were either coaling or busy at the rifle-ranges a thousand feet up the hill, I found myself stranded, lunchless, on the sea-front with no hope of return to Cape Town before 5 P.M. At this crisis I had the luck to come across my friend Inspector Hooper,° Cape Government Railways, in command of an engine and a brake-van chalked for repair.

'If you get something to eat,' he said, 'I'll run you down to Glengariff siding° till the goods comes along. It's cooler there than here, you see.'

I got food and drink from the Greeks° who sell all things at a price, and the engine trotted us a couple of miles up the line to a bay of drifted sand and a plank-platform half buried in sand not a hundred yards from the edge of the surf. Moulded dunes, whiter than any snow, rolled far inland up a brown and purple valley of splintered rocks and dry scrub. A crowd of Malays° hauled at a net beside two blue and green boats on the beach; a picnic party danced and shouted barefoot where a tiny river trickled across the flat, and a circle of dry hills, whose feet were set in sands of silver, locked us in against a seven-coloured sea. At either horn of the bay the railway line cut just above high-water mark, ran round a shoulder of piled rocks, and disappeared.

'You see there's always a breeze here,' said Hooper, opening the door as the engine left us in the siding on the sand, and the strong south-easter buffeting under Elsie's Peak° dusted sand into our tickey beer.° Presently he sat down to a file full of spiked documents. He had returned from a long trip up-country, where he had been reporting on damaged rolling-stock, as far away as Rhodesia. The weight of the bland wind on my eyelids; the song of it under the car roof, and high up among the rocks; the drift of fine grains chasing each other musically ashore; the tramp of the surf; the voices of the picnickers; the rustle of Hooper's file, and the presence of the assured sun, joined with the beer to cast me into magical slumber. The hills of False Bay were just dissolving into those of fairyland when I heard footsteps on the sand outside, and the clink of our couplings.

'Stop that!' snapped Hooper, without raising his head from his work. 'It's those dirty little Malay boys, you see: they're always playing with the trucks. . . .'

'Don't be hard on 'em. The railway's a general refuge in Africa,' I replied.

''Tis—up-country at any rate. That reminds me,' he felt in his waistcoat-pocket, 'I've got a curiosity for you from Wankies—beyond Buluwayo.° It's more of a souvenir perhaps than—'

'The old hotel's inhabited,' cried a voice. 'White men, from the language. Marines to the front! Come on, Pritch. Here's your Belmont.° Wha—i—i!'

The last word dragged like a rope as Mr Pyecroft ran round to the open door, and stood looking up into my face. Behind him an enormous Sergeant of Marines trailed a stalk of dried seaweed, and dusted the sand nervously from his fingers.

'What are you doing here?' I asked. 'I thought the *Hierophant*° was down the coast?'

'We came in last Tuesday—from Tristan d'Acunha°—for overhaul, and we shall be in dockyard 'ands for two months, with boiler-seatings.'°

'Come and sit down.' Hooper put away the file.

'This is Mr Hooper of the Railway,' I exclaimed, as Pyecroft turned to haul up the black-moustached sergeant.

'This is Sergeant Pritchard, of the *Agaric*, an old shipmate,' said he. 'We were strollin' on the beach.' The monster blushed and nodded. He filled up one side of the van when he sat down.

'And this is my friend, Mr Pyecroft,' I added to Hooper, already busy with the extra beer which my prophetic soul had bought from the Greeks.

'*Moi aussi*,' quoth Pyecroft, and drew out beneath his coat a labelled quart bottle.

'Why, it's Bass!' cried Hooper.

'It was Pritchard,' said Pycroft. 'They can't resist him.'

'That's not so,' said Pritchard mildly.

'Not *verbatim*° per'aps, but the look in the eye came to the same thing.'

'Where was it?' I demanded.

'Just on beyond here—at Kalk Bay.° She was slappin' a rug in a back verandah. Pritch 'adn't more than brought his batteries to bear, before she stepped indoors an' sent it flyin' over the wall.'

Pyecroft patted the warm bottle.

'It was all a mistake,' said Pritchard. 'I shouldn't wonder if she mistook me for Maclean. We're about of a size.'

I had heard householders of Muizenburg, St James's, and Kalk Bay complain of the difficulty of keeping beer or good servants at the seaside, and I began to see the reason. None the less, it was excellent Bass, and I too drank to the health of that large-minded maid.

'It's the uniform that fetches 'em, an' they fetch it,' said Pyecroft. 'My simple navy blue is respectable, but not fascinatin'. Now Pritch in 'is Number One rig° is always "purr Mary, on the terrace"°—*ex officio*° as you might say.'

'She took me for Maclean, I tell you,' Pritchard insisted. 'Why—why—to listen to him you wouldn't think that only yesterday—'

'Pritch,' said Pyecroft, 'be warned in time. If we begin tellin' what we know about each other we'll be turned out of the pub. Not to mention aggravated desertion on several occasions—'

'Never anything more than absence without leaf—I defy you to prove it,' said the Sergeant hotly. 'An' if it comes to that, how about Vancouver in '87?'

'How about it? Who pulled bow in the gig going ashore? Who told Boy Niven . . .?'

'Surely you were court-martialled for that?' I said. The story of Boy Niven who lured seven or eight able-bodied seamen and marines into the woods of British Columbia used to be a legend of the Fleet.°

'Yes, we were court-martialled to rights,' said Pritchard, 'but we should have been tried for murder if Boy Niven 'adn't been unusually tough. He told us he had an uncle 'oo'd give us land to farm. 'E said he was born at the back o' Vancouver Island, and *all* the time the beggar was a balmy Barnado Orphan!'

'*But* we believed him,' said Pyecroft. 'I did—you did—Paterson did—an' 'oo was the Marine that married the cocoanut-woman° afterwards—him with the mouth?'

'Oh, Jones, Spit-Kid Jones.° I 'aven't thought of 'im in years,' said Pritchard. 'Yes, Spit-Kid believed it, an' George Anstey and Moon. We were very young an' very curious.'

'*But* lovin' an' trustful to a degree,' said Pyecroft.

''Remember when 'e told us to walk in single file for fear o' bears? 'Remember, Pye, when 'e 'opped about in that bog full o' ferns an' sniffed an' said 'e could smell the smoke of 'is uncle's farm? An' *all* the time it was a dirty little outlyin' uninhabited island. We walked round it in a day, an' come back to our boat lyin' on the beach. A whole day Boy Niven kept us walkin' in circles lookin' for 'is uncle's farm! He said his uncle was compelled by the law of the land to give us a farm!'

'Don't get hot, Pritch. We believed,' said Pyecroft.

'He'd been readin' books. He only did it to get a run ashore an' have himself talked of. A day an' a night—eight of us—followin' Boy Niven round an uninhabited island in the Vancouver archipelago! Then the picket came for us an' a nice pack o' idiots we looked!'

'What did you get for it?' Hooper asked.

'Heavy thunder with continuous lightning for two hours. Thereafter sleet-squalls, a confused sea, and cold, unfriendly weather till conclusion o' cruise,' said Pyecroft. 'It was only what we expected, but what we felt—an' I assure you, Mr Hooper, even a sailor-man has a heart to break—was bein' told that we able seamen an' promisin' marines 'ad misled Boy Niven. Yes, we poor back-to-the-landers was supposed to 'ave misled him! He rounded on us, o' course, an' got off easy.'

'Excep' for what we gave him in the steerin'-flat° when we came out o' cells. 'Eard anything of 'im lately, Pye?'

'Signal Boatswain in the Channel Fleet, I believe—Mr L. L. Niven is.'

'An' Anstey died o' fever in Benin,'° Pritchard mused. 'What come to Moon? Spit-Kid we know about.'

'Moon—Moon! Now where did I last . . .? Oh yes, when I was in the *Palladium*. I met Quigley at Buncrana° Station. He told me Moon 'ad run when the *Astrild* sloop was cruising among the South Seas three years back. He always showed signs o' bein a Mormonastic° beggar. Yes, he slipped off quietly an' they 'adn't time to chase 'im round the islands even if the navigatin' officer 'ad been equal to the job.'

'Wasn't he?' said Hooper.

'Not so. Accordin' to Quigley the *Astrild* spent half her commission rompin' up the beach like a she-turtle, an' the other half hatching turtle's eggs on the top o' numerous reefs. When she was docked at Sydney her copper° looked like Aunt Maria's washing on the line—an' her 'midship frames was sprung. The commander swore the dockyard 'ad done it haulin' the pore thing on to the slips. They *do* do strange things at sea, Mr Hooper.'

'Ah! I'm not a taxpayer,' said Hooper, and opened a fresh bottle. The Sergeant seemed to be one who had a difficulty in dropping subjects.

'How it all comes back, don't it?' he said. 'Why, Moon must 'ave 'ad sixteen years' service before he ran.'

'It takes 'em at all ages. Look at—you know,' said Pyecroft.

'Who?' I asked.

'A service man within eighteen months of his pension is the party you're thinkin' of,' said Pritchard. 'A warrant° 'oo's name begins with a V., isn't it?'

'But, in a way o' puttin' it, we can't say that he actually did desert,' Pyecroft suggested.

'Oh no,' said Pritchard. 'It was only permanent absence up-country without leaf. That was all.'

'Up-country?' said Hooper. 'Did they circulate his description?'

'What for?' said Pritchard, most impolitely.

'Because deserters are like columns in the war.° They don't move away from the line, you see. I've known a chap caught at Salisbury that way tryin' to get to Nyassa.° They tell me, but o' course I don't know, that they don't ask questions on the Nyassa Lake Flotilla up there. I've heard of a P. and O. quartermaster in full command of an armed launch there.'

'Do you think Click 'ud ha' gone up that way?' Pritchard asked.

'There's no saying. He was sent up to Bloemfontein to take over some Navy ammunition left in the fort.° We know he took it over and saw it into the trucks. Then there was no more Click—then or thereafter. Four months ago it transpired, and thus the *casus belli*° stands at present,' said Pyecroft.

'What were his marks?' said Hooper again.

'Does the Railway get a reward for returnin' 'em, then?' said Pritchard.

'If I did d'you suppose I'd talk about it?' Hooper retorted angrily.

'You seemed so very interested,' said Pritchard with equal crispness.

'Why was he called Click?' I asked, to tide over an uneasy little break in the conversation. The two men were staring at each other very fixedly.

'Because of an ammunition hoist carryin' away,' said Pyecroft. 'And it carried away four of 'is teeth—on the lower port side, wasn't it, Pritch? The substitutes which he bought weren't screwed home, in a manner o' sayin'. When he talked fast, they used to lift a little on the bed-plate. 'Ence, "Click." They called 'im a superior man, which is what we'd call a long, black-'aired, genteelly speakin', 'alf-bred beggar on the lower deck.'

'Four false teeth in the lower left jaw,' said Hooper, his hand in his waistcoat-pocket. 'What tattoo marks?'

'Look here,' began Pritchard, half rising. 'I'm sure we're very grateful to you as a gentleman for your 'orspitality, but per'aps we may 'ave made an error in—'

I looked at Pyecroft for aid—Hooper was crimsoning rapidly.

'If the fat marine now occupying the foc'sle will kindly bring 'is *status quo* to an anchor° yet once more, we may be able to talk like gentlemen—not to say friends,' said Pyecroft. 'He regards you, Mr Hooper, as a emissary of the Law.'

'I only wish to observe that when a gentleman exhibits such a peculiar, or I should rather say, such a *bloomin'* curiosity in identification marks as our friend here—'

'Mr Pritchard,' I interposed, 'I'll take all the responsibility for Mr Hooper.'

'An' *you*'ll apologise all round,' said Pyecroft. 'You're a rude little man, Pritch.'

'But how was I—' he began, wavering.

'I don't know an' I don't care. Apologise!'

The giant looked round bewildered and took our little hands into his vast grip, one by one.

'I was wrong,' he said meekly as a sheep. 'My suspicions was unfounded. Mr Hooper, I apologise.'

'You did quite right to look out for your own end o' the line,' said Hooper. 'I'd ha' done the same with a gentleman I didn't know, you see. If you don't mind I'd like to hear a little more o' your Mr Vickery. It's safe with me, you see.'

'Why did Vickery run?' I began, but Pyecroft's smile made me turn my question to 'Who was she?'

'She kep' a little hotel at Hauraki—near Auckland,'° said Pyecroft.

'By Gawd!' roared Pritchard, slapping his hand on his leg. 'Not Mrs Bathurst!'

Pyecroft nodded slowly, and the Sergeant called all the powers of darkness to witness his bewilderment.

'So far as I could get at it, Mrs B. was the lady in question.'

'But Click was married,' cried Pritchard.

'An' 'ad a fifteen-year-old daughter. 'E's shown me her photograph. Settin' that aside, so to say, 'ave you ever found these little things make much difference? Because I haven't.'

'Good Lord Alive an' Watchin'! . . . Mrs Bathurst. . . .' Then with another roar: 'You can say what you please, Pye, but you don't make me believe it was any of 'er fault. She wasn't *that*!'

'If I was going to say what I please, I'd begin by callin' you a silly ox an' work up to the higher pressures at leisure. I'm trying to say solely what transpired. M'rover, for once you're right. It wasn't her fault.'

'You couldn't 'aven't made me believe it if it 'ad been,' was the answer.

Such faith in a Sergeant of Marines interested me greatly. 'Never mind about that,' I cried. 'Tell me what she was like.'

'She was a widow,' said Pyecroft. 'Left so very young and never re-spliced. She kep' a little hotel for warrants and non-coms close to Auckland, an' she always wore black silk, and 'er neck—'

'You ask what she was like,' Pritchard broke in. 'Let me give you an instance. I was at Auckland first in '97, at the end o' the *Marroquin's* commission,° an' as I'd been promoted I went up with the others. She used to look after us all, an' she never lost by it—not a penny! "Pay me now," she'd say, "or settle later. I know you won't let me suffer. Send the money from home if you like." Why, gentlemen all, I tell you I've seen that lady take her own gold watch an' chain off her neck in the bar an' pass it to a bosun 'oo'd come ashore without 'is ticker an' 'ad to catch the last boat. "I don't know your name," she said, "but when you've done with it, you'll find plenty that know me on the front.° Send it back by one o' them." And it was worth thirty pounds if it was worth 'arf-a-crown. The little gold watch, Pye, with the blue monogram at the back. But, as I was sayin', in those days she kep' a beer that agreed with me—Slits° it was called. One way an' another I must 'ave punished a good few bottles of it while we was in the bay—comin' ashore every night or so. Chaffin' across the bar like, once when we were alone, "Mrs B.," I said, "when next I call I want you to remember that this is my particular—just as you're my particular." (She'd let you go *that* far!) "Just as you're my particular," I said. "Oh, thank you, Sergeant Pritchard," she says, an' put 'er hand up to the curl be'ind 'er ear. Remember that way she had, Pye?'

'I think so,' said the sailor.

'Yes, "Thank you, Sergeant Pritchard," she says. "The least I can do is to mark it for you in case you change your mind. There's no great demand for it in the Fleet," she says, "but to make sure I'll put it at the back o' the shelf," an' she snipped off a piece of her hair ribbon with that old dolphin cigar-cutter on the bar—remember it, Pye?—an' she tied a bow round what was left—just four bottles. That was '97—no, '96. In '98 I was in the *Resiliant*—China station—full commission. In Nineteen One, mark you, I was in the *Carthusian*, back in Auckland Bay again. Of course I went up to Mrs B.'s with the rest of us to see how things were goin'. They were the same as ever.

(Remember the big tree on the pavement by the side-bar, Pye?) I never said anythin' in special (there was too many of us talkin' to her), but she saw me at once.'

'That wasn't difficult?' I ventured.

'Ah, but wait. I was comin' up to the bar, when, "Ada," she says to her niece, "get me Sergeant Pritchard's particular," and, gentlemen all, I tell you before I could shake 'ands with the lady, there were those four bottles o' Slits, with 'er 'air ribbon in a bow round each o' their necks, set down in front o' me, an' as she drew the cork she looked at me under her eyebrows in that blindish way she had o' lookin', an', "Sergeant Pritchard," she says, "I do 'ope you 'aven't changed your mind about your particulars." That's the kind o' woman she was—after five years!'

'I don't *see* her yet somehow,' said Hooper, but with sympathy.

'She—she never scrupled to feed a lame duck or set 'er foot on a scorpion at any time of 'er life,'° Pritchard added valiantly.

'That don't help me either. My mother's like that for one.'

The giant heaved inside his uniform and rolled his eyes at the car-roof. Said Pyecroft suddenly:—

'How many women have you been intimate with all over the world, Pritch?'

Pritchard blushed plum colour to the short hairs of his seventeen-inch neck.

''Undreds,' said Pyecroft. 'So've I. How many of 'em can you remember in your own mind, settin' aside the first—an' per'aps the last—*and one more*?'

'Few, wonderful few, now I tax myself,' said Sergeant Pritchard relievedly.

'An' how many times might you 'ave been at Auckland?'

'One—two,' he began—'why, I can't make it more than three times in ten years. But I can remember every time that I ever saw Mrs B.'

'So can I—an' I've only been to Auckland twice—how she stood an' what she was sayin' an' what she looked like. That's the secret. 'Tisn't beauty, so to speak, nor good talk necessarily. It's just It.° Some women'll stay in a man's memory if they once walk down a street, but most of 'em you can live with a month on end, an' next commission you'd be put to it to certify whether they talked in their sleep or not, as one might say.'

'Ah!' said Hooper. 'That's more the idea. I've known just two women of that nature.'

'An' it was no fault o' theirs?' asked Pritchard.

'None whatever. I know *that*!'

'An' if a man gets struck with that kind o' woman, Mr Hooper?' Pritchard went on.

'He goes crazy—or just saves himself,' was the slow answer.

'You've hit it,' said the Sergeant. 'You've seen an' known somethin' in the course o' your life, Mr Hooper. I'm lookin' at you!' He set down his bottle.

'And how often had Vickery seen her?' I asked.

'That's the dark an' bloody mystery,' Pyecroft answered. 'I'd never come across him till I come out in the *Hierophant* just now, an' there wasn't anyone in the ship who knew much about him. You see, he was what you call a superior man. 'E spoke to me once or twice about Auckland and Mrs B. on the voyage out. I called that to mind subsequently. There must 'ave been a good deal between 'em, to my way o' thinkin'. Mind you, I'm only giving you my *résumé* of it all, because all I know is second-hand so to speak, or rather I should say more than second-'and.'

'How?' said Hooper peremptorily. 'You must have seen it or heard it.'

'Ye-es,' said Pyecroft. 'I used to think seein' and hearin' was the only regulation aids to ascertainin' facts, but as we get older we get more accommodatin'. The cylinders work easier, I suppose. . . . Were you in Cape Town last December when Phyllis's Circus° came?'

'No—up-country,' said Hooper, a little nettled at the change of venue.

'I ask because they had a new turn of a scientific nature called "Home and Friends for a Tickey."'°

'Oh, you mean the cinematograph—the pictures of prize-fights and steamers. I've seen 'em up-country.'

'Biograph or cinematograph was what I was alludin' to. London Bridge with the omnibuses—a troopship goin' to the war—marines on parade at Portsmouth, an' the Plymouth Express arrivin' at Paddin'ton.'

'Seen 'em all. Seen 'em all,' said Hooper impatiently.

'We *Hierophants* came in just before Christmas week an' leaf was easy.'

'I think a man gets fed up with Cape Town quicker than anywhere else on the station. Why, even Durban's more like Nature. We was there for Christmas,' Pritchard put in.

'Not bein' a devotee of Indian *peeris*,° as our Doctor said to the Pusser, I can't exactly say. Phyllis's was good enough after musketry practice at Mozambique. I couldn't get off the first two or three nights on account of what you might call an imbroglio with our Torpedo Lieutenant in the submerged flat, where some pride of the West country had sugared up a gyroscope;° but I remember Vickery went ashore with our Carpenter Rigdon—old Crocus we called him. As a general rule Crocus never left 'is ship unless an' until he was 'oisted out with a winch, but *when* 'e went 'e would return noddin' like a lily gemmed with dew. We smothered him down below that night, but the things 'e said about Vickery as a fittin' playmate for a Warrant Officer of 'is cubic capacity, before we got him quiet, was what I should call pointed.'

'I've been with Crocus—in the *Redoubtable*,' said the Sergeant. 'He's a character if there is one.'

'Next night I went into Cape Town with Dawson and Pratt; but just at the door of the Circus I came across Vickery. "Oh!" he says, "you're the man I'm looking for. Come and sit next me. This way to the shillin' places!" I went astern at once, protestin' because tickey seats better suited my so-called finances. "Come on," says Vickery, "I'm payin'." Naturally I abandoned Pratt and Dawson in anticipation o' drinks to match the seats. "No," he says, when this was 'inted—"not now. Not now. As many as you please afterwards, but I want you sober for this occasion." I caught 'is face under a lamp just then, an' the appearance of it quite cured me of my thirsts. Don't mistake. It didn't frighten me. It made me anxious. I can't tell you what it was like, but that was the effect which it 'ad on me. If you want to know, it reminded me of those things in bottles in those herbalistic shops at Plymouth—preserved in spirits of wine. White an' crumply things—previous to birth as you might say.'

'You 'ave a beastial mind, Pye,' said the Sergeant, relighting his pipe.

'Perhaps. We were in the front row, an' "Home an' Friends" came on early. Vickery touched me on the knee when the number went up. "If you see anything that strikes you," he says, "drop me a hint"; then he went on clicking. We saw London Bridge an' so forth an' so on, an' it was most interestin'. I'd never seen it before. You 'eard a little dynamo like buzzin', but the pictures were the real thing—alive an' movin'.'

'I've seen 'em,' said Hooper. 'Of course they are taken from the very thing itself—you see.'

'Then the Western Mail came in to Paddin'ton on the big magic lantern sheet. First we saw the platform empty an' the porters standin' by. Then the engine come in, head on, an' the women in the front row jumped: she headed so straight. Then the doors opened and the passengers came out and the porters got the luggage—just like life. Only—only when any one came down too far towards us that was watchin', they walked right out o' the picture, so to speak. I was 'ighly interested, I can tell you. So were all of us. I watched an old man with a rug 'oo'd dropped a book an' was tryin' to pick it up, when quite slowly, from be'ind two porters—carryin' a little reticule° an' lookin' from side to side—comes out Mrs Bathurst. There was no mistakin' the walk in a hundred thousand. She come forward—right forward—she looked out straight at us with that blindish look which Pritch alluded to. She walked on and on till she melted out of the picture—like—like a shadow jumpin' over a candle, an' as she went I 'eard Dawson in the tickey seats be'ind sing out: "Christ! there's Mrs B.!"'

Hooper swallowed his spittle and leaned forward intently.

'Vickery touched me on the knee again. He was clickin' his four false teeth with his jaw down like an enteric at the last kick.° "Are you sure?" says he. "Sure," I says, "didn't you 'ear Dawson give tongue? Why, it's the woman herself." "I was sure before," he says, "but I brought you to make sure. Will you come again with me to-morrow?"

'"Willingly," I says, "it's like meetin' old friends."

'"Yes," he says, openin' his watch, "very like. It will be four-and-twenty hours less four minutes before I see her again. Come and have a drink," he says. "It may amuse you, but it's no sort of earthly use to me." He went out shaking his head an' stumblin' over people's feet as if he was drunk already. I anticipated a swift drink an' a speedy return, because I wanted to see the performin' elephants. Instead o' which Vickery began to navigate the town at the rate o' knots, lookin' in at a bar every three minutes approximate Greenwich time. "I'm not a drinkin' man, though there are those present"—he cocked his unforgetable eye at me—"who may have seen me more or less imbued with the fragrant spirit.° None the less when I drink I like to do it at anchor an' not at an average speed of eighteen knots on the measured mile. There's a tank as you might say at the back o' that big hotel up the hill—what do they call it?"'

'The Molteno Reservoir,' I suggested, and Hooper nodded.

'That was his limit o' drift. We walked there an' we come down through the Gardens—there was a South-Easter blowin'—an' we finished up by the Docks.° Then we bore up the road to Salt River,° and wherever there was a pub Vickery put in sweatin'. He didn't look at what he drunk—he didn't look at the change. He walked an' he drunk an' he perspired in rivers. I understood why old Crocus 'ad come back in the condition 'e did, because Vickery an' I 'ad two an' a half hours o' this gipsy manœuvre, an' when we got back to the station there wasn't a dry atom on or in me.'

'Did he say anything?' Pritchard asked.

'The sum total of 'is conversation from 7.45 P.M. till 11.15 P.M. was "Let's have another." Thus the mornin' an' the evenin' were the first day, as Scripture says.°. . . To abbreviate a lengthy narrative, I went into Cape Town for five consecutive nights with Master Vickery, and in that time I must 'ave logged about fifty knots over the ground an' taken in two gallon o' all the worst spirits south the Equator. The evolution never varied. Two shilling seats for us two; five minutes o' the pictures, an' perhaps forty-five seconds o' Mrs B. walking down towards us with that blindish look in her eyes an' the reticule in her hand. Then out walk—and drink till train time.'

'What did you think?' said Hooper, his hand fingering his waistcoat-pocket.

'Several things,' said Pyecroft. 'To tell you the truth, I aren't quite done thinkin' about it yet. Mad? The man was a dumb lunatic—must 'ave been for months—years p'raps. I know somethin' o' maniacs, as every man in the Service must. I've been shipmates with a mad skipper—an' a lunatic Number One, but never both together I thank 'Eaven. I could give you the names o' three captains now 'oo ought to be in an asylum, but you don't find me interferin' with the mentally afflicted till they begin to lay about 'em with rammers an' winch-handles. Only once I crept up a little into the wind towards Master Vickery. "I wonder what she's doin' in England," I says. "Don't it seem to you she's lookin' for somebody?" That was in the Gardens again, with the South-Easter blowin' as we were makin' our desperate round. "She's lookin' for me," he says, stoppin' dead under a lamp an' clickin'. When he wasn't drinkin', in which case all 'is teeth clicked on the glass, 'e was clickin' is four false teeth like a Marconi ticker.° "Yes! lookin' for me," he said, an' he went on very softly an' as you might say affectionately. "*But*," he went on, "in future, Mr Pyecroft, I should take it kindly of you if you'd confine your remarks to the drinks set before you. Otherwise," he says, "with the best will in the world towards you, I may find myself guilty of murder! Do you understand?" he says. "Perfectly," I says, "but would it at all soothe you to know that in such a case the chances o' your being killed are precisely equivalent to the chances o' me being outed." "Why, no," he says, "I'm almost afraid that 'ud be a temptation." Then I said—we was right under the lamp by that arch at the end o' the Gardens where the trams come round—"Assumin' murder was done—or attempted murder—I put it to you that you would still be left so badly crippled, as one might say, that your subsequent capture by the police—to 'oom you would 'ave to explain—would be largely inevitable." "That's better," 'e says, passin' 'is hands over his forehead. "That's much better, because," he says, "do you know, as I am now, Pye, I'm not so sure if I could explain anything much." Those were the only particular words I had with 'im in our walks as I remember.'

'What walks!' said Hooper. 'Oh my soul, what walks!'

'They were chronic,' said Pyecroft gravely, 'but I didn't anticipate any danger till the Circus left. Then I anticipated that, bein' deprived of 'is stimulant, he might react on me, so to say, with a hatchet. Consequently, after the final performance an' the ensuin' wet walk, I kep' myself aloof from my superior officer on board in the execution of 'is duty, as you might put it. Consequently, I was interested when the sentry informs me while I was passin' on my lawful occasions that Click had asked to see the captain. As a general rule warrant officers don't dissipate much of the owner's time, but Click put in an hour and more be'ind that door. My duties kep' within eyeshot of it. Vickery came out first, an' 'e actually nodded at me an' smiled. This knocked me out o' the boat, because, havin' seen 'is face for five consecutive nights, I didn't anticipate any change there more than a condenser° in hell, so to speak. The owner emerged later. His face didn't read off at all, so I fell back on his cox, 'oo'd been eight years with him and knew him better than boat signals. Lamson—that was the cox's name—crossed 'is bows once or twice at low speeds an' dropped down to me visibly concerned. "He's shipped 'is court-martial face," says Lamson. "Some one's goin' to be 'ung. I've never seen that look but once before when they chucked the gun-sights overboard in the *Fantastic*." Throwin' gun-sights overboard,° Mr Hooper, is the equivalent for mutiny in these degenerate days. It's done to attract the notice of the authorities an' the *Western Mornin' News*—generally by a stoker. Naturally, word went round the lower deck an' we had a private over'aul of our little consciences. But, barrin' a shirt which a second-class stoker said 'ad walked into 'is bag from the marines' flat by itself, nothin' vital transpired. The owner went about flyin' the signal for "attend public execution," so to say, but there was no corpse at the yard-arm. 'E lunched on the beach an' 'e returned with 'is regulation harbour-routine face about 3 P.M. Thus Lamson lost prestige for raising false alarms. The only person 'oo might 'ave connected the epicycloidal gears correctly was one Pyecroft, when he was told that Mr Vickery would go up-country that same evening to take over certain naval ammunition left after the war in Bloemfontein Fort. No details was ordered to accompany Master Vickery. He was told off first person singular—as a unit—by himself.'

The marine whistled penetratingly.

'That's what I thought,' said Pyecroft. 'I went ashore with him in the cutter° an' 'e asked me to walk through the station. He was clickin' audibly, but otherwise seemed happy-ish.

'"You might like to know," he says, stoppin' just opposite the Admiral's front gate,° "that Phyllis's Circus will be performin' at Worcester° tomorrow night. So I shall see 'er yet once again. You've been very patient with me," he says.

'"Look here, Vickery," I said, "this thing's come to be just as much as I can stand. Consume your own smoke.° I don't want to know any more."

'"You!" he said. "What have you got to complain of?—you've only 'ad to watch. I'm *it*," he says, "but that's neither here nor there," he says. "I've one thing to say before shakin' 'ands. Remember," 'e says—we were just by the Admiral's garden-gate° then—"remember, that I am *not* a murderer, because my lawful wife died in childbed six weeks after I came out.° That much at least I am clear of," 'e says.

'"Then what have you done that signifies?" I said. "What's the rest of it?"

'"The rest," 'e says, "is silence,"° an' he shook 'ands and went clickin' into Simonstown station.'

'Did he stop to see Mrs Bathurst at Worcester?' I asked.

'It's not known. He reported at Bloemfontein, saw the ammunition into the trucks, and then 'e disappeared. Went out—deserted, if you care to put it so—within eighteen months of his pension, an' if what 'e said about 'is wife was true he was a free man as 'e then stood. How do you read it off?'

'Poor devil!' said Hooper. 'To see her that way every night! I wonder what it was.'

'I've made my 'ead ache in that direction many a long night.'

'But I'll swear Mrs B. 'ad no 'and in it,' said the Sergeant, unshaken.

'No. Whatever the wrong or deceit was, he did it, I'm sure o' that. I 'ad to look at 'is face for five consecutive nights. I'm not so fond o' navigatin' about Cape Town with a South-Easter blowin' these days. I can hear those teeth click, so to say.'

'Ah, those teeth,' said Hooper, and his hand went to his waistcoat-pocket once more. 'Permanent things false teeth are. You read about 'em in all the murder trials.'

'What d'you suppose the captain knew—or did?' I asked.

'I've never turned my searchlight that way,' Pyecroft answered unblushingly.

We all reflected together, and drummed on empty beer bottles as the picnic-party, sunburned, wet, and sandy, passed our door singing 'The Honeysuckle and the Bee.'°

'Pretty girl under that kapje,'° said Pyecroft.

'They never circulated his description?' said Pritchard.

'I was askin' you before these gentlemen came,' said Hooper to me, 'whether you knew Wankies—on the way to the Zambesi—beyond Buluwayo?'

'Would he pass there—tryin' to get to that lake what's 'is name?' said Pritchard.

Hooper shook his head and went on: 'There's a curious bit o' line there, you see. It runs through solid teak forest—a sort o' mahogany really—seventy-two miles without a curve.° I've had a train derailed there twenty-three times in forty miles. I was up there a month ago relievin' a sick inspector, you see. He told me to look out for a couple of tramps in the teak.'

'Two?' Pyecroft said. 'I don't envy that other man° if—'

'We get heaps of tramps up there since the war. The inspector told me I'd find 'em at M'Bindwe siding° waiting to go North. He'd given 'em some grub and quinine, you see. I went up on a construction train. I looked out for 'em. I saw them miles ahead along the straight, waiting in the teak. One of 'em was standin' up by the dead-end of the siding an' the other was squattin' down lookin' up at 'im, you see.'

'What did you do for 'em?' said Pritchard.

'There wasn't much I could do, except bury 'em. There'd been a bit of a thunderstorm in the teak, you see, and they were both stone dead and as black as charcoal. That's what they really were, you see—charcoal.° They fell to bits when we tried to shift 'em. The man who was standin' up had the false teeth. I saw 'em shinin' against the black. Fell to bits he did too, like his mate squatting down an' watchin' him, both of 'em all wet in the rain. Both burned to charcoal, you see. And —that's what made me ask about marks just now—the false-toother was tattoed on the arms and chest—a crown and foul anchor with M.V. above.'

'I've seen that,' said Pyecroft quickly. 'It was so.'

'But if he was all charcoal-like?' said Pritchard, shuddering.

'You know how writing shows up white on a burned letter? Well, it was like that, you see. We buried 'em in the teak and I kept . . . But he was a friend of you two gentlemen, you see.'

Mr Hooper brought his hand away from his waistcoat-pocket—empty.

Pritchard covered his face with his hands for a moment, like a child shutting out an ugliness.

'And to think of her at Hauraki!' he murmured—'with 'er 'air-ribbon on my beer. "Ada," she said to her niece . . . Oh, my Gawd!' . . .

'On a summer afternoon, when the honeysuckle blooms,
And all Nature seems at rest,
Underneath the bower, 'mid the perfume of the flower,
Sat a maiden with the one she loves the best—'

sang the picnic-party waiting for their train at Glengariff.

'Well, I don't know how you feel about it,' said Pyecroft, 'but 'avin' seen 'is face for five consecutive nights on end, I'm inclined to finish what's left of the beer an' thank Gawd he's dead!'

From A DIVERSITY OF CREATURES (1917)

The Village that Voted the Earth was Flat

(1913)

Our drive till then had been quite a success. The other men in the car were my friend Woodhouse, young Ollyett, a distant connection of his, and Pallant, the M.P. Woodhouse's business was the treatment and cure of sick journals. He knew by instinct the precise moment in a newspaper's life when the impetus of past good management is exhausted and it fetches up on the dead-centre between slow and expensive collapse and the new start which can be given by gold injections—and genius. He was wisely ignorant of journalism; but when he stooped on a carcase there was sure to be meat. He had that week added a half-dead, halfpenny evening paper to his collection, which consisted of a prosperous London daily, one provincial ditto, and a limp-bodied weekly of commercial leanings. He had also, that very hour, planted me with a large block of the evening paper's common shares, and was explaining the whole art of editorship to Ollyett, a young man three years from Oxford, with coir-matting-coloured hair and a face harshly modelled by harsh experiences, who, I understood, was assisting in the new venture. Pallant, the long, wrinkled M.P., whose voice is more like a crane's than a peacock's, took no shares, but gave us all advice.

'You'll find it rather a knacker's yard,' Woodhouse was saying. 'Yes, I know they call me The Knacker; but it will pay inside a year. All my papers do. I've only one motto: Back your luck and back your staff. It'll come out all right.'

Then the car stopped,° and a policeman asked our names and addresses for exceeding the speed-limit.° We pointed out that the road ran absolutely straight for half a mile ahead without even a side-lane. 'That's just what we depend on,' said the policeman unpleasantly.

'The usual swindle,'° said Woodhouse under his breath. 'What's the name of this place?'

'Huckley,' said the policeman. 'H-u-c-k-l-e-y,' and wrote something in his note-book at which young Ollyett protested. A large red man on a grey horse who had been watching us from the other side of the hedge shouted an order we could not catch. The policeman laid his hand on the rim of the right driving-door (Woodhouse carries his spare tyres aft), and it closed on the button of the electric horn. The grey horse at once bolted, and we could hear the rider swearing all across the landscape.

'Damn it, man, you've got your silly fist on it! Take it off!' Woodhouse shouted.

'Ho!' said the constable, looking carefully at his fingers as though we had trapped them. 'That won't do you any good either,' and he wrote once more in his note-book before he allowed us to go.

This was Woodhouse's first brush with motor law, and since I expected no ill consequences to myself, I pointed out that it was very serious. I took the same view myself when in due time I found that I, too, was summonsed on charges ranging from the use of obscene language to endangering traffic.

Judgment was done in a little pale-yellow market-town with a small, Jubilee clock-tower° and a large corn-exchange. Woodhouse drove us there in his car. Pallant, who had not been included in the summons, came with us as moral support. While we waited outside, the fat man on the grey horse rode up and entered into loud talk with his brother magistrates. He said to one of them—for I took the trouble to note it down—'It falls away from my lodge-gates, dead straight, three-quarters of a mile. I'd defy any one to resist it. We rooked seventy pounds out of 'em last month. No car can resist the temptation. You ought to have one your side the county, Mike. They simply can't resist it.'

'Whew!' said Woodhouse. 'We're in for trouble. Don't you say a word—or Ollyett either! I'll pay the fines and we'll get it over as soon as possible. Where's Pallant?'

'At the back of the court somewhere,' said Ollyett. 'I saw him slip in just now.'

The fat man then took his seat on the Bench, of which he was chairman, and I gathered from a bystander that his name was Sir Thomas Ingell, Bart., M.P., of Ingell Park, Huckley. He began with an allocution pitched in a tone that would have justified revolt throughout empires. Evidence, when the crowded little court did not drown it with applause, was given in the pauses of the address. They were all very proud of their Sir Thomas, and looked from him to us, wondering why we did not applaud too.

Taking its time from the chairman, the Bench rollicked with us for seventeen minutes. Sir Thomas explained that he was sick and tired of processions of cads of our type, who would be better employed breaking stones on the road than in frightening horses worth more than themselves or their ancestors. This was after it had been proved that Woodhouse's man had turned on the horn purposely to annoy Sir Thomas, who 'happened to be riding by'! There were other remarks too—primitive enough,—but it was the unspeakable brutality of the tone, even more than the quality of the justice, or the laughter of the audience that stung our souls out of all reason. When we were dismissed—to the tune of twenty-three pounds, twelve shillings and sixpence—we waited for Pallant to join us, while we listened to the next case—one of driving without a licence. Ollyett, with an eye to his evening paper, had already taken very full notes of our own, but we did not wish to seem prejudiced.

'It's all right,' said the reporter of the local paper soothingly. 'We never report Sir Thomas *in extenso*.° Only the fines and charges.'

'Oh, thank you,' Ollyett replied, and I heard him ask who every one in court might be. The local reporter was very communicative.

The new victim, a large, flaxen-haired man in somewhat striking clothes, to which Sir Thomas, now thoroughly warmed, drew public attention, said that he had left his licence at home. Sir Thomas asked him if he expected the police to go to his home address at Jerusalem° to find it for him; and the court roared. Nor did Sir Thomas approve of the man's name, but insisted on calling him 'Mr Masquerader,' and every time he did so, all his people shouted. Evidently this was their established *auto-da-fé*.°

'He didn't summons me—because I'm in the House, I suppose. I think I shall have to ask a Question,' said Pallant, reappearing at the close of the case.

'I think *I* shall have to give it a little publicity too,' said Woodhouse. 'We can't have this kind of thing going on, you know.' His face was set and quite white. Pallant's, on the other hand, was black, and I know that my very stomach had turned with rage. Ollyett was dumb.

'Well, let's have lunch,' Woodhouse said at last. 'Then we can get away before the show breaks up.'

We drew Ollyett from the arms of the local reporter, crossed the Market Square to the Red Lion and found Sir Thomas's 'Mr Masquerader' just sitting down to beer, beef and pickles.

'Ah!' said he, in a large voice. 'Companions in misfortune. Won't you gentlemen join me?'

'Delighted,' said Woodhouse. 'What did you get?'

'I haven't decided. It might make a good turn, but—the public aren't educated up to it yet. It's beyond 'em. If it wasn't, that red dub on the Bench would be worth fifty a week.'

'Where?' said Woodhouse. The man looked at him with unaffected surprise.

'At any one of My places,' he replied. 'But perhaps you live here?'

'Good heavens!' cried young Ollyett suddenly. 'You *are* Masquerier, then? I thought you were!'

'Bat Masquerier.' He let the words fall with the weight of an international ultimatum. 'Yes, that's all I am. But you have the advantage of me, gentlemen.'

For the moment, while we were introducing ourselves, I was puzzled. Then I recalled prismatic music-hall posters—of enormous acreage—that had been the unnoticed background of my visits to London for years past. Posters of men and women, singers, jongleurs, impersonators and audacities of every draped and undraped brand, all moved on and off in London and the Provinces by Bat Masquerier—with the long wedge-tailed flourish following the final 'r.'

'*I* knew you at once,' said Pallant, the trained M.P., and I promptly backed the lie. Woodhouse mumbled excuses. Bat Masquerier was not moved for or against us any more than the frontage of one of his own palaces.

'I always tell My people there's a limit to the size of the lettering,' he said. 'Overdo that and the ret'na doesn't take it in. Advertisin' is the most delicate of all the sciences.'

'There's one man in the world who is going to get a little of it if I live for the next twenty-four hours,' said Woodhouse, and explained how this would come about.

Masquerier stared at him lengthily with gun-metal-blue eyes.

'You mean it?' he drawled; the voice was as magnetic as the look.

'*I* do,' said Ollyett. 'That business of the horn alone ought to have him off the Bench in three months.' Masquerier looked at him even longer than he had looked at Woodhouse.

'He told *me*,' he said suddenly, 'that my home-address was Jerusalem. You heard that?'

'But it was the tone—the tone,' Ollyett cried.

'You noticed that, too, did you?' said Masquerier. 'That's the artistic temperament. You can do a lot with it. And I'm Bat Masquerier,' he went on. He dropped his chin in his fists and scowled straight in front of him. . . . 'I made the Silhouettes°—I made the Trefoil and the Jocunda. I made 'Dal Benzaguen.' Here Ollyett sat straight up, for in common with the youth of that year he worshipped Miss Vidal Benzaguen of the Trefoil immensely and unreservedly. '"*Is* that a dressing-gown, or an ulster you're supposed to be wearing?" You heard *that*? . . . "And I suppose you hadn't time to brush your hair either?" You heard *that*? . . . Now, you hear *me*!' His voice filled the coffee-room, then dropped to a whisper as dreadful as a surgeon's before an operation. He spoke for several minutes. Pallant muttered 'Hear! hear!' I saw Ollyett's eye flash—it was to Ollyett that Masquerier addressed himself chiefly,—and Woodhouse leaned forward with joined hands.

'Are you *with* me?' he went on, gathering us all up in one sweep of the arm. 'When I begin a thing I see it through, gentlemen. What Bat can't break, breaks him! But I haven't struck that thing yet. This is no one-turn turn-it-down show. This is business to the dead finish. Are you with me, gentlemen? Good! Now, we'll pool our assets. One London morning, and one provincial daily, didn't you say? One weekly commercial ditto and one M.P.'

'Not much use, I'm afraid,' Pallant smirked.

'But privileged. *But* privileged,' he returned. 'And we have also my little team—London, Blackburn, Liverpool, Leeds—I'll tell you about Manchester later—and Me! Bat Masquerier.' He breathed the name reverently into his tankard. 'Gentlemen, when our combination has finished with Sir Thomas Ingell, Bart., M.P., and everything else that is his, Sodom and Gomorrah will be a winsome bit of Merrie England beside 'em. I must go back to town now, but I trust you gentlemen will give me the pleasure of your company at dinner tonight at the Chop Suey—the Red Amber Room—and we'll block out the scenario.' He laid his hand on young Ollyett's shoulder and added: 'It's your brains I want.' Then he left, in a good deal of astrachan collar and nickel-plated limousine, and the place felt less crowded.

We ordered our car a few minutes later. As Woodhouse, Ollyett and I were getting in, Sir Thomas Ingell, Bart., M.P., came out of the Hall of Justice across the square and mounted his horse. I have sometimes thought that if he had gone in silence he might even then have been saved, but as he settled himself in the saddle he caught sight of us and must needs shout: 'Not off yet? You'd better get away and you'd better be careful.' At that moment Pallant, who had been buying picture-postcards, came out of the inn, took Sir Thomas's eye and very leisurely entered the car. It seemed to me that for one instant there was a shade of uneasiness on the baronet's grey-whiskered face.

'I hope,' said Woodhouse after several miles, 'I hope he's a widower.'

'Yes,' said Pallant. 'For his poor, dear wife's sake I hope that, very much indeed. I suppose he didn't see me in Court. Oh, here's the parish history of Huckley written by the Rector and here's your share of the picture-postcards. Are we all dining with this Mr Masquerier to-night?'

'Yes!' said we all.

If Woodhouse knew nothing of journalism, young Ollyett, who had graduated in a hard school, knew a good deal. Our halfpenny evening paper, which we will call *The Bun* to distinguish her from her prosperous morning sister, *The Cake* was not only diseased but corrupt. We found this out when a man brought us the prospectus of a new oil-field and demanded sub-leaders on its prosperity. Ollyett talked pure Brasenose° to him for three minutes. Otherwise he spoke and wrote trade-English—a toothsome amalgam of Americanisms and epigrams. But though the slang changes the game never alters, and Ollyett and I and, in the end, some others enjoyed it immensely. It was weeks ere we could see the wood for the trees, but so soon as the staff realised that they had proprietors who backed them right or wrong, and specially when they were wrong (which is the sole secret of journalism), and that their fate did not hang on any passing owner's passing mood, they did miracles.

But we did not neglect Huckley. As Ollyett said our first care was to create an 'arresting atmosphere' round it. He used to visit the village of week-ends, on a motor-bicycle with a side-car; for which reason I left the actual place alone and dealt with it in the abstract. Yet it was I who drew first blood. Two inhabitants of Huckley wrote to contradict a small, quite solid paragraph in *The Bun* that a hoopoe had been seen at Huckley and had, 'of course, been shot by the local sportsmen.' There was some heat in their letters, both of which we published. Our version of how the hoopoe got his crest from King Solomon° was, I grieve to say, so inaccurate that the Rector himself—no sportsman as he pointed out, but a lover of accuracy—wrote to us to correct it. We gave his letter good space and thanked him.

'This priest is going to be useful,' said Ollyett. 'He has the impartial mind. I shall vitalise him.'

Forthwith he created M. L. Sigden, a recluse of refined tastes who in *The Bun* demanded to know whether this Huckley-of-the-Hoopoe was the Hugly of his boyhood and whether, by any chance, the fell change of name had been wrought by collusion between a local magnate and the railway, in the mistaken interests of spurious refinement. 'For I knew it and loved it with the maidens of my day—*eheu ab angulo!*°—as Hugly,' wrote M. L. Sigden from Oxford.

Though other papers scoffed, *The Bun* was gravely sympathetic. Several people wrote to deny that Huckley had been changed at birth. Only the Rector—no philosopher as he pointed out, but a lover of accuracy—had his doubts, which he laid publicly before Mr M. L. Sigden, who suggested, through *The Bun*, that the little place might have begun life in Anglo-Saxon days as 'Hogslea' or among the Normans as 'Argilé,' on account of its much clay. The Rector had his own ideas too (he said it was mostly gravel), and M. L. Sigden had a fund of reminiscences. Oddly enough—which is seldom the case with free reading-matter—our subscribers rather relished the correspondence, and contemporaries quoted freely.

'The secret of power,' said Ollyett, 'is not the big stick. It's the liftable stick.' (This means the 'arresting' quotation of six or seven lines.) 'Did you see the *Spec.*° had a middle on "Rural Tenacities" last week. That was all Huckley. I'm doing a "Mobiquity" on Huckley next week.'

Our 'Mobiquities' were Friday evening accounts of easy motor-bike-*cum*-side-car trips round London, illustrated (we could never get that machine to work properly) by smudgy maps. Ollyett wrote the stuff with a fervour and a delicacy which I always ascribed to the side-car. His account of Epping Forest, for instance, was simply young love with its soul at its lips. But his Huckley 'Mobiquity' would have sickened a soap-boiler. It chemically combined loathsome familiarity, leering suggestion, slimy piety and rancid 'social service' in one fuming compost that fairly lifted me off my feet.

'Yes,' said he, after compliments. 'It's the most vital, arresting and dynamic bit of tump° I've done up to date. *Non nobis gloria!*° I met Sir Thomas Ingell in his own park. He talked to me again. He inspired most of it.'

'Which? The "glutinous native drawl," or "the neglected adenoids of the village children"?' I demanded.

'Oh, no! That's only to bring in the panel doctor.° It's the last flight we—I'm° proudest of.'

This dealt with 'the crepuscular penumbra spreading her dim limbs over the boskage'; with 'jolly rabbits'; with a herd of 'gravid polled

Angus'; and with the 'arresting, gipsy-like face of their swart, scholarly owner—as well known at the Royal Agricultural Shows as that of our late King-Emperor."[10]

'"Swart" is good and so's "gravid,"' said I, 'but the panel doctor will be annoyed about the adenoids.'

'Not half as much as Sir Thomas will about his face,' said Ollyett. 'And if you only knew what I've left out!'

He was right. The panel doctor spent his week-end (this is the advantage of Friday articles) in overwhelming us with a professional counterblast of no interest whatever to our subscribers. We told him so, and he, then and there, battered his way with it into the *Lancet* where they are keen on glands, and forgot us altogether. But Sir Thomas Ingell was of sterner stuff. He must have spent a happy week-end too. The letter which we received from him on Monday proved him to be a kinless loon of upright life, for no woman, however remotely interested in a man would have let it pass the home wastepaper-basket. He objected to our references to his own herd, to his own labours in his own village, which he said was a Model Village, and to our infernal insolence; but he objected most to our invoice of his features. We wrote him courteously to ask whether the letter was meant for publication. He, remembering, I presume, the Duke of Wellington, wrote back, 'publish and be damned.'

'Oh! This is too easy,' Ollyett said as he began heading the letter.

'Stop a minute,' I said. 'The game is getting a little beyond us. To-night's the Bat dinner.' (I may have forgotten to tell you that our dinner with Bat Masquerier in the Red Amber Room of the Chop Suey had come to be a weekly affair.) 'Hold it over till they've all seen it.'

'Perhaps you're right,' he said. 'You might waste it.'

At dinner, then, Sir Thomas's letter was handed round. Bat seemed to be thinking of other matters, but Pallant was very interested.

'I've got an idea,' he said presently. 'Could you put something into *The Bun* to-morrow about foot-and-mouth disease in that fellow's herd?'

'Oh, plague if you like,' Ollyett replied. 'They're only five measly Shorthorns. I saw one lying down in the park. She'll serve as a sub-stratum of fact.'

'Then, do that; and hold the letter over mean-while. I think *I* come in here,' said Pallant.

'Why?' said I.

'Because there's something coming up in the House about foot-

and-mouth, and because he wrote me a letter after that little affair when he fined you. 'Took ten days to think it over. Here you are,' said Pallant. 'House of Commons paper, you see.'

We read:

DEAR PALLANT—Although in the past our paths have not lain much together, I am sure you will agree with me that on the floor of the House all members are on a footing of equality. I make bold, therefore, to approach you in a manner which I think capable of a very different interpretation from that which perhaps was put upon it by your friends. Will you let them know that that was the case and that I was in no way swayed by animus in the exercise of my magisterial duties, which as you, as a brother magistrate, can imagine are frequently very distasteful to—Yours very sincerely,

T. INGELL.

P.S.—I have seen to it that the motor vigilance to which your friends took exception has been considerably relaxed in my district.

'What did you answer?' said Ollyett, when all our opinions had been expressed.

'I told him I couldn't do anything in the matter. And I couldn't—then. But you'll remember to put in that foot-and-mouth paragraph. I want something to work upon.'

'It seems to me *The Bun* has done all the work up to date,' I suggested. 'When does *The Cake* come in?'

'*The Cake*,' said Woodhouse, and I remembered afterwards that he spoke like a Cabinet Minister on the eve of a Budget, 'reserves to itself the fullest right to deal with situations as they arise.'

'Ye-eh!' Bat Masquerier shook himself out of his thoughts. '"Situations as they arise." I ain't idle either. But there's no use fishing till the swim's baited. You'—he turned to Ollyett—'manufacture very good ground-bait. . . . I always tell My people— What the deuce is that?'

There was a burst of song from another private dining-room across the landing. 'It ees some ladies from the Trefoil,' the waiter began.

'Oh I know that. What are they singing, though?'

He rose and went out, to be greeted by shouts of applause from that merry company. Then there was silence, such as one hears in the form-room after a master's entry. Then a voice that we loved began again: 'Here we go gathering nuts in May—nuts in May—nuts in May!'

'It's only 'Dal—and some nuts,'[10] he explained when he returned. 'She says she's coming in to dessert.' He sat down, humming the old tune to himself, and till Miss Vidal Benzaguen entered, he held us speechless with tales of the artistic temperament.

We obeyed Pallant to the extent of slipping into *The Bun* a wary paragraph about cows lying down and dripping at the mouth, which might be read either as an unkind libel or, in the hands of a capable lawyer, as a piece of faithful nature-study.

'And besides,' said Ollyett, 'we allude to "gravid polled Angus." I am advised that no action can lie in respect of virgin Shorthorns. Pallant wants us to come to the House to-night. He's got us places for the Strangers' Gallery. I'm beginning to like Pallant.'

'Masquerier seems to like you,' I said.

'Yes, but I'm afraid of him,' Ollyett answered with perfect sincerity. 'I am. He's the Absolutely Amoral Soul. I've never met one yet.'

We went to the House together. It happened to be an Irish afternoon,° and as soon as I had got the cries and the faces a little sorted out, I gathered there were grievances in the air, but how many of them was beyond me.

'It's all right,' said Ollyett of the trained ear. 'They've shut their ports again—oh yes—export of Irish cattle! Foot-and-mouth disease at Ballyhellion. *I* see Pallant's idea!'

The House was certainly all mouth for the moment, but, as I could feel, quite in earnest. A Minister with a piece of typewritten paper seemed to be fending off volleys of insults. He reminded me somehow of a nervous huntsman breaking up a fox in the face of rabid hounds.

'It's question time. They're asking questions,' said Ollyett. 'Look! Pallant's up.'

There was no mistaking it. His voice, which his enemies said was his one parliamentary asset, silenced the hubbub as toothache silences mere singing in the ears. He said:

'Arising out of that, may I ask if any special consideration has recently been shown in regard to any suspected outbreak of this disease on *this* side of the Channel?'

He raised his hand; it held a noon edition of *The Bun*. We had thought it best to drop the paragraph out of the later ones. He would have continued, but something in a grey frock-coat roared and bounded on a bench opposite, and waved another *Bun*. It was Sir Thomas Ingell.

'As the owner of the herd so dastardly implicated—' His voice was drowned in shouts of 'Order!'—the Irish leading.

'What's wrong?' I asked Ollyett. 'He's got his hat on his head,° hasn't he?'

'Yes, but his wrath should have been put as a question.'

'Arising out of that, Mr Speaker, Sirrr!' Sir Thomas bellowed through a lull, 'are you aware that—that all this is a conspiracy—part of a dastardly conspiracy to make Huckley ridiculous—to make *us* ridiculous? Part of a deep-laid plot to make *me* ridiculous, Mr Speaker, Sir!'

The man's face showed almost black against his white whiskers, and he struck out swimmingly with his arms. His vehemence puzzled and held the House for an instant, and the Speaker took advantage of it to lift his pack from Ireland to a new scent. He addressed Sir Thomas Ingell in tones of measured rebuke, meant also, I imagine, for the whole House, which lowered its hackles at the word. Then Pallant, shocked and pained: 'I can only express my profound surprise that in response to my simple question the honourable member should have thought fit to indulge in a personal attack. If I have in any way offended—'

Again the Speaker intervened, for it appeared that he regulated these matters.

He, too, expressed surprise, and Sir Thomas sat back in a hush of reprobation that seemed to have the chill of the centuries behind it. The Empire's work was resumed.

'Beautiful!' said I, and I felt hot and cold up my back.

'And now we'll publish his letter,' said Ollyett.

We did—on the heels of his carefully reported outburst. We made no comment. With that rare instinct for grasping the heart of a situation which is the mark of the Anglo-Saxon, all our contemporaries and, I should say, two-thirds of our correspondents demanded how such a person could be made more ridiculous than he had already proved himself to be. But beyond spelling his name 'Injle,' we alone refused to hit a man when he was down.

'There's no need,' said Ollyett. 'The whole press is on the huckle from end to end.'

Even Woodhouse was a little astonished at the ease with which it had come about, and said as much.

'Rot!' said Ollyett. 'We haven't really begun. Huckley isn't news yet.'

'What do you mean?' said Woodhouse, who had grown to have great respect for his young but by no means distant connection.

'Mean? By the grace of God, Master Ridley,° I mean to have it so that when Huckley turns over in its sleep, Reuters and the Press Association jump out of bed to cable.' Then he went off at score about certain restorations in Huckley Church which, he said—and he seemed to spend his every week-end there—had been perpetrated by the Rector's predecessor, who had abolished a 'leper-window' or a 'squinch-hole'° (whatever these may be) to institute a lavatory in the vestry. It did not strike me as stuff for which Reuters or the Press Association would lose much sleep, and I left him declaiming to Woodhouse about a fourteenth-century font which, he said, he had unearthed in the sexton's tool-shed.

My methods were more on the lines of peaceful penetration.° An odd copy, in *The Bun's* rag-and-bone library, of Hone's *Every-Day Book*° had revealed to me the existence of a village dance founded, like all village dances, on Druidical mysteries connected with the Solar Solstice (which is always unchallengeable) and Midsummer Morning, which is dewy and refreshing to the London eye. For this I take no credit—Hone being a mine any one can work—but that I rechristened that dance, after I had revised it, 'The Gubby' is my title to immortal fame. It was still to be witnessed, I wrote, 'in all its poignant purity at Huckley, that last home of significant mediæval survivals'; and I fell so in love with my creation that I kept it back for days, enamelling and burnishing.

'You'd better put it in,' said Ollyett at last. 'It's time we asserted ourselves again. The other fellows are beginning to poach. You saw that thing in the *Pinnacle* about Sir Thomas's Model Village? He must have got one of their chaps down to do it.'

'Nothing like the wounds of a friend,' I said. 'That account of the non-alcoholic pub alone was—'

'I liked the bit best about the white-tiled laundry and the Fallen Virgins who wash Sir Thomas's dress shirts. Our side couldn't come within a mile of that, you know. We haven't the proper flair for sexual slobber.'

'That's what I'm always saying,' I retorted. 'Leave 'em alone. The other fellows are doing our work for us now. Besides I want to touch up my "Gubby Dance" a little more.'

'No. You'll spoil it. Let's shove it in to-day. For one thing it's Literature. I don't go in for compliments as you know, but, etc. etc.'

I had a healthy suspicion of young Ollyett in every aspect, but though I knew that I should have to pay for it, I fell to his flattery, and my priceless article on the 'Gubby Dance' appeared. Next Saturday he asked me to bring out *The Bun* in his absence, which I naturally assumed would be connected with the little maroon side-car. I was wrong.

On the following Monday I glanced at *The Cake* at breakfast-time to make sure, as usual, of her inferiority to my beloved but unremunerative *Bun*. I opened on a heading: 'The Village that Voted the Earth was Flat.' I read . . . I read that the Geoplanarian Society—a society devoted to the proposition that the earth is flat—had held its Annual Banquet and Exercises at Huckley on Saturday, when after convincing addresses, amid scenes of the greatest enthusiam, Huckley village had decided by an unanimous vote of 438 that the earth was flat. I do not remember that I breathed again till I had finished the two columns of description that followed. Only one man could have written them. They were flawless—crisp, nervous, austere yet human, poignant, vital, arresting—most distinctly arresting—dynamic enough to shift a city—and quotable by whole sticks° at a time. And there was a leader, a grave and poised leader, which tore me in two with mirth, until I remembered that I had been left out—infamously and unjustifiably dropped. I went to Ollyett's rooms. He was breakfasting, and, to do him justice, looked conscience-stricken.

'It wasn't my fault,' he began. 'It was Bat Masquerier. I swear *I* would have asked you to come if—'

'Never mind that,' I said. 'It's the best bit of work you've ever done or will do. Did any of it happen?'

'Happen? Heavens! D'you think even *I* could have invented it?'

'Is it exclusive to *The Cake*?' I cried.

'It cost Bat Masquerier two thousand,' Ollyett replied, 'D'you think he'd let any one else in on that? But I give you my sacred word I knew nothing about it till he asked me to come down and cover it. He had Huckley posted in three colours, "The Geoplanarians' Annual Banquet and Exercises." Yes, he invented "Geoplanarians." He wanted Huckley to think it meant aeroplanes. Yes, I know that there is a real Society that thinks the world's flat°—they ought to be grateful for the lift—but Bat made his own. He did! He created the whole show, I tell you. He swept out half his Halls for the job. Think of that—on a Saturday! They—we went down in motor char-à-bancs—three of 'em—one pink, one primrose, and one forget-me-not blue—twenty people in each one and "The Earth *is* Flat" on each side and across the back. I went with Teddy Rickets and Lafone from the Trefoil, and both the Silhouette Sisters, and—wait a minute!—the Crossleigh Trio. You know the Every-Day Dramas Trio at the Jocunda—Ada Crossleigh, "Bunt" Crossleigh, and little Victorine? Them. And there was Hoke Ramsden, the lightning-change chap in *Morgiana and Drexel*°—and there was Billy Turpeen. Yes, you know him! The

North London Star. "I'm the Referee that got himself disliked at Blackheath." *That* chap! And there was Mackaye—that one-eyed Scotch fellow that all Glasgow is crazy about. Talk of subordinating yourself for Art's sake! Mackaye was the earnest inquirer who got converted at the end of the meeting. And there was quite a lot of girls I didn't know, and—oh, yes—there was 'Dal! 'Dal Benzaguen herself! We sat together, going and coming. She's all the darling there ever was. She sent you her love, and she told me to tell you that she won't forget about Nellie Farren.° She says you've given her an ideal to work for. She? Oh, she was the Lady Secretary to the Geoplanarians, of course. I forget who were in the other brakes—provincial stars mostly—but they played up gorgeously. The art of the music-hall's changed since your day. They didn't overdo it a bit. You see, people who believe the earth is flat don't dress quite like other people. You may have noticed that I hinted at that in my account. It's a rather flat-fronted Ionic style—neo-Victorian, except for the bustles, 'Dal told me,—but 'Dal looked heavenly in it! So did little Victorine. And there was a girl in the blue brake—she's a provincial—but she's coming to town this winter and she'll knock 'em—Winnie Deans. Remember that! She told Huckley how she had suffered for the Cause as a governess in a rich family where they believed that the world is round, and how she threw up her job sooner than teach immoral geography. That was at the overflow meeting outside the Baptist chapel. She knocked 'em to sawdust! We must look out for Winnie. . . . But Lafone! Lafone was beyond everything. Impact, personality—conviction—the whole bag o' tricks! He sweated conviction. Gad, he convinced *me* while he was speaking! (Him? He was President of the Geoplanarians, of course. Haven't you read my account?) It *is* an infernally plausible theory. After all, no one has actually proved the earth is round, have they?"°

'Never mind the earth. What about Huckley?'

'Oh, Huckley got tight. That's the worst of these model villages if you let 'em smell fire-water.° There's one alcoholic pub in the place that Sir Thomas can't get rid of. Bat made it his base. He sent down the banquet in two motor lorries—dinner for five hundred and drinks for ten thousand. Huckley voted all right. Don't you make any mistake about that. No vote, no dinner. A unanimous vote—exactly as I've said. At least, the Rector and the Doctor were the only dissentients. We didn't count them. Oh yes, Sir Thomas was there. He came and grinned at us through his park gates. He'll grin worse to-day. There's an aniline dye that you rub through a stencil-plate that eats about a foot into any stone and wears good to the last. Bat had both the lodge-gates stencilled "The Earth *is* flat!" and all the barns and walls they could get at. . . . Oh Lord, but Huckley was drunk! We had to fill 'em up to make 'em forgive us for not being aeroplanes. Unthankful yokels! D'you realise that Emperors couldn't have commanded the talent Bat decanted on 'em? Why, 'Dal alone was . . . And by eight o'clock not even a bit of paper left! The whole show packed up and gone, and Huckley hoo-raying for the earth being flat.'

'Very good,' I began. 'I am, as you know, a one-third proprietor of *The Bun.*'

'I didn't forget that,' Ollyett interrupted. 'That was uppermost in my mind all the time. I've got a special account for *The Bun* to-day—it's an idyll—and just to show how I thought of you, I told 'Dal, coming home, about your Gubby Dance, and she told Winnie. Winnie came back in our char-à-banc. After a bit we had to get out and dance it in a field. It's quite a dance the way we did it—and Lafone invented a sort of gorilla lockstep procession° at the end. Bat had sent down a film-chap on the chance of getting something. He was the son of a clergyman—a most dynamic personality. He said there isn't anything for the cinema in meetings *qua* meetings—they lack action. Films are a branch of art by themselves.° But he went wild over the Gubby. He said it was like Peter's vision at Joppa.° He took about a million feet of it. Then I photoed it exclusive for *The Bun*. I've sent 'em in already, only remember we must eliminate Winnie's left leg in the first figure. It's too arresting. . . . And there you are! But I tell you I'm afraid of Bat. That man's the Personal Devil. He did it all. He didn't even come down himself. He said he'd distract his people.'

'Why didn't he ask me to come?' I persisted.

'Because he said you'd distract me. He said he wanted my brains on ice. He got 'em. I believe it's the best thing I've ever done.' He reached for *The Cake* and re-read it luxuriously. 'Yes, out and away the best—supremely quotable,' he concluded, and—after another survey—'By God, what a genius I was yesterday!'

I would have been angry, but I had not the time. That morning, Press agencies grovelled to me in *The Bun* office for leave to use certain photos, which, they understood, I controlled, of a certain village dance. When I had sent the fifth man away on the edge of tears, my self-respect came back a little. Then there was *The Bun's* poster to get out. Art being elimination, I fined it down to two words (one too many, as it proved)—'The Gubby!' in red, at which our manager protested; but by five o'clock he told me that I was *the* Napoleon of

Fleet Street. Ollyett's account in *The Bun* of the Geoplanarians' Exercises and Love Feast lacked the supreme shock of his version in *The Cake*, but it bruised more; while the photos of 'The Gubby' (which, with Winnie's left leg, was why I had set the doubtful press to work so early) were beyond praise and, next day, beyond price. But even then I did not understand.

A week later, I think it was, Bat Masquerier telephoned me to come to the Trefoil.

'It's your turn now,' he said. 'I'm not asking Ollyett. Come to the stage-box.'

I went, and, as Bat's guest, was received as Royalty is not. We sat well back and looked out on the packed thousands. It was *Morgiana and Drexel*, that fluid and electric review which Bat—though he gave Lafone the credit—really created.

'Ye-es,' said Bat dreamily, after Morgiana had given 'the nasty jar' to the Forty Thieves in their forty oil 'combinations.' 'As you say, I've got 'em and I can hold 'em. What a man does doesn't matter much; and how he does it don't matter either. It's the *when*—the psychological moment. 'Press can't make up for it; money can't; brains can't. A lot's luck, but all the rest is genius. I'm not speaking about My people now. I'm talking of Myself.'

Then 'Dal—she was the only one who dared—knocked at the door and stood behind us all alive and panting as Morgiana. Lafone was carrying the police-court scene, and the house was ripped up crossways with laughter.

'Ah! Tell a fellow now,' she asked me for the twentieth time, 'did you love Nellie Farren when you were young?'

'Did we love her?' I answered. '"If the earth and the sky and the sea"—There were three million of us, 'Dal, and we worshipped her.'

'How did she get it across?' 'Dal went on.

'She was Nellie. The houses used to coo over her when she came on.'

'I've had a good deal, but I've never been cooed over yet,' said 'Dal wistfully.

'It isn't the how, it's the when,' Bat repeated. 'Ah!'

He leaned forward as the house began to rock and peal full-throatedly. 'Dal fled. A sinuous and silent procession was filing into the police-court to a scarcely audible accompaniment. It was dressed—but the world and all its picture-palaces know how it was dressed. It danced and it danced, and it danced the dance which bit all humanity in the leg for half a year, and it wound up with the lockstep finale that mowed the house down in swathes, sobbing and aching. Somebody in the gallery moaned, 'Oh Gord, the Gubby!' and we heard the word run like a shudder, for they had not a full breath left among them. Then 'Dal came on, an electric star in her dark hair, the diamonds flashing in her three-inch heels—a vision that made no sign for thirty counted seconds while the police-court scene dissolved behind her into Morgiana's Manicure Palace, and they recovered themselves. The star on her forehead went out, and a soft light bathed her as she took—slowly, slowly to the croon of adoring strings—the eighteen paces forward. We saw her first as a queen alone; next as a queen for the first time conscious of her subjects, and at the end, when her hands fluttered, as a woman delighted, awed not a little, but transfigured and illuminated with sheer, compelling affection and goodwill. I caught the broken mutter of welcome—the coo which is more than tornadoes of applause. It died and rose and died again lovingly.

'She's got it across,' Bat whispered. 'I've never seen her like this. I told her to light up the star, but I was wrong, and she knew it. She's an artist.'

''Dal, you darling!' some one spoke, not loudly but it carried through the house.

'Thank *you*!' 'Dal answered, and in that broken tone one heard the last fetter riveted. 'Good evening, boys! I've just come from—now—where the dooce was it I have come from?' She turned to the impassive files of the Gubby dancers, and went on: 'Ah, so good of you to remind me, you dear, bun-faced things. I've just come from the village—The Village that Voted the Earth was Flat.'

She swept into that song with the full orchestra. It devastated the habitable earth for the next six months. Imagine, then, what its rage and pulse must have been at the incandescent hour of its birth! She only gave the chorus once. At the end of the second verse, 'Are you *with* me, boys?' she cried, and the house tore it clean away from her—'*Earth* was flat—*Earth* was flat. Flat as my hat—Flatter than that'—drowning all but the bassoons and double-basses that marked the word.

'Wonderful,' I said to Bat. 'And it's only "Nuts in May" with variations.'

'Yes—but *I* did the variations,' he replied.

At the last verse she gestured to Carlini the conductor, who threw her up his baton. She caught it with a boy's ease. 'Are you *with* me?' she cried once more, and—the maddened house behind her—

abolished all the instruments except the guttural belch of the double-basses on '*Earth*'—'The Village that Voted the *Earth* was flat—*Earth* was flat!' It was delirium. Then she picked up the Gubby dancers and led them in a clattering improvised lockstep thrice round the stage till her last kick sent her diamond-hilted shoe catherine-wheeling to the electrolier.

I saw the forest of hands raised to catch it, heard the roaring and stamping pass through hurricanes to full typhoon; heard the song, pinned down by the faithful double-basses as the bull-dog pins down the bellowing bull, overbear even those; till at last the curtain fell and Bat took me round to her dressing-room, where she lay spent after her seventh call. Still the song, through all those white-washed walls, shook the reinforced concrete of the Trefoil as steam pile-drivers shake the flanks of a dock.

'I'm all out—first time in my life. Ah! Tell a fellow now, did I get it across?' she whispered huskily.

'You know you did,' I replied as she dipped her nose deep in a beaker of barley-water. 'They cooed over you.'

Bat nodded. 'And poor Nellie's dead—in Africa, ain't it?'

'I hope I'll die before they stop cooing,' said 'Dal.

'"*Earth* was flat—*Earth* was flat!"' Now it was more like mine-pumps in flood.

'They'll have the house down if you don't take another,' some one called.

'Bless 'em!' said 'Dal, and went out for her eighth, when in the face of that cataract she said yawning, 'I don't know how *you* feel, children, but *I*'m dead. You be quiet.'

'Hold a minute,' said Bat to me. 'I've got to hear how it went in the provinces. Winnie Deans had it in Manchester, and Ramsden at Glasgow—and there are all the films too. I had rather a heavy week-end.'

The telephones presently reassured him.

'It'll do,' said he. 'And *he* said my home address was Jerusalem.' He left me humming the refrain of 'The Holy City.'[10] Like Ollyett I found myself afraid of that man.

When I got out into the street and met the disgorging picture-palaces capering on the pavements and humming it (for he had put the gramophones on with the films), and when I saw far to the south the red electrics flash 'Gubby' across the Thames, I feared more than ever.

*

A few days passed which were like nothing except, perhaps, a suspense of fever in which the sick man perceives the searchlights of the world's assembled navies in act to converge on one minute fragment of wreckage—one only in all the black and agony-strewn sea. Then those beams focussed themselves. Earth as we knew it—the full circuit of our orb—laid the weight of its impersonal and searing curiosity on this Huckley which had voted that it was flat. It asked for news about Huckley—where and what it might be, and how it talked—it knew how it danced—and how it thought in its wonderful soul. And then, in all the zealous, merciless press, Huckley was laid out for it to look at, as a drop of pond water is exposed on the sheet of a magic-lantern show. But Huckley's sheet was only coterminous with the use of type among mankind. For the precise moment that was necessary, Fate ruled it that there should be nothing of first importance in the world's idle eye.° One atrocious murder, a political crisis, an incautious or heady continental statesman, the mere catarrh of a king, would have wiped out the significance of our message, as a passing cloud annuls the urgent helio.° But it was halcyon weather in every respect. Ollyett and I did not need to lift our little fingers any more than the Alpine climber whose last sentence has unkeyed the arch of the avalanche. The thing roared and pulverised and swept beyond eyesight all by itself—all by itself. And once well away, the fall of kingdoms could not have diverted it.

Ours is, after all, a kindly earth. While The Song ran and raped it° with the cataleptic kick of 'Ta-ra-ra-boom-de-ay,' multiplied by the West African significance of 'Everybody's doing it,' plus twice the infernal elementality of a certain tune in *Dona et Gamma*;° when for all practical purposes, literary, dramatic, artistic, social, municipal, political, commercial, and administrative, the Earth *was* flat, the Rector of Huckley wrote to us—again as a lover of accuracy—to point out that the Huckley vote on 'the alleged flatness of this scene of our labours here below' was *not* unanimous; he and the doctor having voted against it. And the great Baron Reuter himself (I am sure it could have been none other) flashed that letter in full to the front, back, and both wings of this scene of our labours. For Huckley was News. *The Bun* also contributed a photograph which cost me some trouble to fake.

'We are a vital nation,' said Ollyett while we were discussing affairs at a Bat dinner. 'Only an Englishman could have written that letter at this present juncture.'

'It reminded me of a tourist in the Cave of the Winds under

Niagara. Just one figure in a mackintosh. But perhaps you saw our photo?' I said proudly.

'Yes,' Bat replied. 'I've been to Niagara, too. And how's Huckley taking it?'

'They don't quite understand, of course,' said Ollyett. 'But it's bringing pots of money into the place. Ever since the motor-bus excursions were started—'

'I didn't know they had been,' said Pallant.

'Oh yes. Motor char-à-bancs—uniformed guides and key-bugles included. They're getting a bit fed up with the tune there nowadays,' Ollyett added.

'They play it under his windows, don't they?' Bat asked. 'He can't stop the right of way across his park.'

'He cannot,' Ollyett answered. 'By the way, Woodhouse, I've bought that font for you from the sexton. I paid fifteen pounds for it.'

'What am I supposed to do with it?' asked Woodhouse.

'You give it to the Victoria and Albert Museum. It is fourteenth-century work all right. You can trust me.'

'Is it worth it—now?' said Pallant. 'Not that I'm weakening, but merely as a matter of tactics?'

'But this is true,' said Ollyett. 'Besides, it is my hobby, I always wanted to be an architect. I'll attend to it myself. It's too serious for *The Bun* and miles too good for *The Cake*.'

He broke ground in a ponderous architectural weekly, which had never heard of Huckley. There was no passion in his statement, but mere fact backed by a wide range of authorities. He established beyond doubt that the old font at Huckley had been thrown out, on Sir Thomas's instigation, twenty years ago, to make room for a new one of Bath stone adorned with Limoges enamels; and that it had lain ever since in a corner of the sexton's shed. He proved, with learned men to support him, that there was only one other font in all England to compare with it. So Woodhouse bought it and presented it to a grateful South Kensington which said it would see the earth still flatter before it returned the treasure to purblind Huckley. Bishops by the benchful and most of the Royal Academy, not to mention 'Margaritas ante Porcos,'° wrote fervently to the papers. *Punch* based a political cartoon on it; the *Times* a third leader, 'The Lust of Newness'; and the *Spectator* a scholarly and delightful middle, 'Village Hausmania.'° The vast amused outside world said in all its tongues and types: 'Of course! This is just what Huckley would do!' And neither Sir Thomas nor the Rector nor the sexton nor any one else wrote to deny it.

'You see,' said Ollyett, 'this is much more of a blow to Huckley than it looks—because every word of it's true. Your Gubby dance was inspiration, I admit, but it hadn't its roots in—'

'Two hemispheres and four continents so far,' I pointed out.

'Its roots in the hearts of Huckley was what I was going to say. Why don't you ever come down and look at the place? You've never seen it since we were stopped there.'

'I've only my week-ends free,' I said, 'and you seem to spend yours there pretty regularly—with the side-car. I was afraid—'

'Oh, *that's* all right,' he said cheerily. 'We're quite an old engaged couple now. As a matter of fact, it happened after "the gravid polled Angus" business. Come along this Saturday. Woodhouse says he'll run us down after lunch. He wants to see Huckley too.'

Pallant could not accompany us, but Bat took his place.

'It's odd,' said Bat, 'that none of us except Ollyett has ever set eyes on Huckley since that time. That's what I always tell My people. Local colour is all right after you've got your idea. Before that, it's a mere nuisance.' He regaled us on the way down with panoramic views of the success—geographical and financial—of 'The Gubby' and The Song.

'By the way,' said he, 'I've assigned 'Dal all the gramophone rights of "The Earth." She's a born artist. 'Hadn't sense enough to hit me for triple-dubs the morning after. She'd have taken it out in coos.'

'Bless her! And what'll she make out of the gramophone rights?' I asked.

'Lord knows!' he replied. 'I've made fifty-four thousand my little end of the business, and it's only just beginning. Hear *that*!'

A shell-pink motor-brake roared up behind us to the music on a key-bugle of 'The Village that Voted the Earth was Flat.' In a few minutes we overtook another, in natural wood, whose occupants were singing it through their noses.

'I don't know that agency. It must be Cook's,' said Ollyett. 'They *do* suffer.' We were never out of ear-shot of the tune the rest of the way to Huckley.

Though I knew it would be so. I was disappointed with the actual aspect of the spot we had—it is not too much to say—created in the face of the nations. The alcoholic pub; the village green; the Baptist chapel; the church; the sexton's shed; the Rectory whence the so-wonderful letters had come; Sir Thomas's park gate-pillars still violently declaring 'The Earth *is* flat,' were as mean, as average, as ordinary as the photograph of a room where a murder has been committed. Ollyett, who, of course, knew the place specially well, made the most of it to us. Bat, who had employed it as a back-cloth to one of his own dramas, dismissed it as a thing used and emptied, but Woodhouse expressed my feelings when he said: 'Is that all—after all we've done?'

'*I* know,' said Ollyett soothingly. '"Like that strange song° I heard Apollo sing: When Ilion like a mist rose into towers." I've felt the same sometimes, though it has been Paradise for me. But they *do* suffer.'

The fourth brake in thirty minutes had just turned into Sir Thomas's park to tell the Hall that 'The *Earth* was flat'; a knot of obviously American tourists were kodaking° his lodge gates; while the tea-shop opposite the lych-gate was full of people buying postcards of the old font as it had lain twenty years in the sexton's shed. We went to the alcoholic pub and congratulated the proprietor.

'It's bringin' money to the place,' said he. 'But in a sense you can buy money too dear. It isn't doin' us any good. People are laughin' at us. That's what they're doin'. . . . Now, with regard to that Vote of ours you may have heard talk about . . .'

'For Gorze sake, chuck that votin' business,' cried an elderly man at the door. 'Money-gettin' or no money-gettin', we're fed up with it.'

'Well, I do think,' said the publican, shifting his ground, 'I do think Sir Thomas might ha' managed better in some things.'

'He tole me,'—the elderly man shouldered his way to the bar—'he tole me twenty years ago to take an' lay that font in my tool-shed. He *tole* me so himself. An' now, after twenty years, me own wife makin' me out little better than the common 'angman!'

'That's the sexton,' the publican explained. 'His good lady sells the postcards—if you 'aven't got some. But we feel Sir Thomas might ha' done better.'

'What's he got to do with it?' said Woodhouse.

'There's nothin' we can trace 'ome to 'im in so many words, but we think he might 'ave saved us the font business. Now, in regard to that votin' business—'

'Chuck it! Oh, chuck it!' the sexton roared, 'or you'll 'ave me cuttin' my throat at cock-crow. 'Ere's another parcel of fun-makers!'

A motor brake had pulled up at the door and a multitude of men and women immediately descended. We went out to look. They bore rolled banners, a reading-desk in three pieces, and, I specially noticed, a collapsible harmonium, such as is used on ships at sea.

'Salvation Army?' I said, though I saw no uniforms.

Two of them unfurled a banner between poles which bore the legend: 'The Earth *is* flat.' Woodhouse and I turned to Bat. He shook his head. 'No, no! Not me. . . . If I had only seen their costumes in advance!'

'Good Lord!' said Ollyett. 'It's the genuine Society!'

The company advanced on the green with the precision of people well broke to these movements. Scene-shifters could not have been quicker with the three-piece rostrum, nor stewards with the harmonium. Almost before its cross-legs had been kicked into their catches, certainly before the tourists by the lodge-gates had begun to move over, a woman sat down to it and struck up a hymn:

Hear ther truth our tongues are telling,
  Spread ther light from shore to shore,
God hath given man a dwelling
  Flat and flat for evermore.

When ther Primal Dark retreated,
  When ther deeps were undesigned,
He with rule and level meted
  Habitation for mankind!

I saw sick envy on Bat's face. 'Curse Nature,' he muttered. 'She gets ahead of you every time. To think *I* forgot hymns and a harmonium!'

Then came the chorus:

Hear ther truth our tongues are telling,
  Spread ther light from shore to shore—
Oh, be faithful! Oh, be truthful!
  Earth is flat for evermore.

They sang several verses with the fervour of Christians awaiting their lions. Then there were growlings in the air. The sexton, embraced by the landlord, two-stepped out of the pub-door. Each was trying to outroar the other. 'Apologising in advarnce for what he says,' the landlord shouted: 'You'd better go away' (here the sexton began to speak words). 'This isn't the time nor yet the place for—for any more o' this chat.'

The crowd thickened. I saw the village police-sergeant come out of his cottage buckling his belt.

'But surely,' said the woman at the harmonium, 'there must me some mistake. We are not suffragettes.'

'Damn it! They'd be a change,' cried the sexton. 'You get out of this! Don't talk! *I* can't stand it for one! Get right out, or we'll font you!'

The crowd which was being recruited from every house in sight echoed the invitation. The sergeant pushed forward. A man beside the reading-desk said: 'But surely we are among dear friends and sympathisers. Listen to me for a moment.'

It was the moment that a passing char-à-banc chose to strike into The Song. The effect was instantaneous. Bat, Ollyett, and I, who by divers roads have learned the psychology of crowds, retreated towards the tavern door. Woodhouse, the newspaper proprietor, anxious, I presume, to keep touch with the public, dived into the thick of it. Every one else told the Society to go away at once. When the lady at the harmonium (I began to understand why it is sometimes necessary to kill women) pointed at the stencilled park pillars and called them 'the cromlechs of our common faith,' there was a snarl and a rush. The police-sergeant checked it, but advised the Society to keep on going. The Society withdrew into the brake fighting, as it were, a rearguard action of oratory up each step. The collapsed harmonium was hauled in last, and with the perfect unreason of crowds, they cheered it loudly, till the chauffeur slipped in his clutch and sped away. Then the crowd broke up, congratulating all concerned except the sexton, who was held to have disgraced his office by having sworn at ladies. We strolled across the green towards Woodhouse, who was talking to the police-sergeant near the park-gates. We were not twenty yards from him when we saw Sir Thomas Ingell emerge from the lodge and rush furiously at Woodhouse with an uplifted stick, at the same time shrieking: 'I'll teach you to laugh, you——' but Ollyett has the record of the language. By the time we reached them, Sir Thomas was on the ground; Woodhouse, very white, held the walking-stick and was saying to the sergeant:

'I give this person in charge for assault.'

'But, good Lord!' said the sergeant, whiter than Woodhouse. 'It's Sir Thomas.'

'Whoever it is, it isn't fit to be at large,' said Woodhouse. The crowd suspecting something wrong began to reassemble, and all the English horror of a row in public moved us, headed by the sergeant, inside the lodge. We shut both park-gates and lodge-door.

'You saw the assault, sergeant,' Woodhouse went on. 'You can testify I used no more force than was necessary to protect myself. You can testify that I have not even damaged this person's property. (Here! take your stick, you!) You heard the filthy language he used.'

'I—I can't say I did,' the sergeant stammered.

'Oh, but *we* did!' said Ollyett, and repeated it, to the apron-veiled horror of the lodge-keeper's wife.

Sir Thomas on a hard kitchen chair began to talk. He said he had 'stood enough of being photographed like a wild beast,' and expressed loud regret that he had not killed 'that man,' who was 'conspiring with the sergeant to laugh at him.'

''Ad you ever seen 'im before, Sir Thomas?' the sergeant asked.

'No! But it's time an example was made here. I've never seen the sweep in my life.'

I think it was Bat Masquerier's magnetic eye that recalled the past to him, for his face changed and his jaw dropped. 'But I have!' he groaned. 'I remember now.'

Here a writhing man entered by the back door. He was, he said, the village solicitor. I do not assert that he licked Woodhouse's boots, but we should have respected him more if he had and been done with it. His notion was that the matter could be accommodated, arranged and compromised for gold, and yet more gold. The sergeant thought so too. Woodhouse undeceived them both. To the sergeant he said, 'Will you or will you not enter the charge?' To the village solicitor he gave the name of his lawyers, at which the man wrung his hands and cried, 'Oh, Sir T., Sir T.!' in a miserable falsetto, for it was a Bat Masquerier of a firm. They conferred together in tragic whispers.

'I don't dive after Dickens,' said Ollyett to Bat and me by the window, 'but every time *I* get into a row I notice the police-court always fills up with his characters.'

'I've noticed that too,' said Bat. 'But the odd thing is you mustn't give the public straight Dickens—not in My business. I wonder why that is.'

Then Sir Thomas got his second wind and cursed the day that he, or it may have been we, were born. I feared that though he was a Radical he might apologise and, since he was an M.P., might lie his way out of the difficulty. But he was utterly and truthfully beside himself. He asked foolish questions—such as what we were doing in the village at all, and how much blackmail Woodhouse expected to make out of him. But neither Woodhouse nor the sergeant nor the writhing solicitor listened. The upshot of their talk, in the chimney-corner, was that Sir Thomas stood engaged to appear next Monday before his brother magistrates on charges of assault, disorderly conduct, and language calculated, etc.° Ollyett was specially careful about the language.

Then we left. The village looked very pretty in the late light—pretty and tuneful as a nest of nightingales.

'You'll turn up on Monday, I hope,' said Woodhouse, when we reached town. That was his only allusion to the affair.

So we turned up—through a world still singing that the Earth was flat—at the little clay-coloured market-town with the large Corn Exchange and the small Jubilee memorial. We had some difficulty in getting seats in the court. Woodhouse's imported London lawyer was a man of commanding personality, with a voice trained to convey blasting imputations by tone. When the case was called, he rose and stated his client's intention not to proceed with the charge. His client, he went on to say, had not entertained, and, of course, in the circumstances could not have entertained, any suggestion of accepting on behalf of public charities any moneys that might have been offered to him on the part of Sir Thomas's estate. At the same time, no one acknowledged more sincerely than his client the spirit in which those offers had been made by those entitled to make them. But, as a matter of fact—here he became the man of the world colloguing with his equals—certain—er—details had come to his client's knowledge *since* the lamentable outburst, which . . . He shrugged his shoulders. Nothing was served by going into them, but he ventured to say that, had those painful circumstances only been known earlier, his client would—again 'of course'—never have dreamed— A gesture concluded the sentence, and the ensnared Bench looked at Sir Thomas with new and withdrawing eyes. Frankly, as they could see, it would be nothing less than cruelty to proceed further with this—er—unfortunate affair. He asked leave, therefore, to withdraw the charge *in toto*, and at the same time to express his client's deepest sympathy with all who had been in any way distressed, as his client had been, by the fact and the publicity of proceedings which he could, of course, again assure them that his client would never have dreamed of instituting if, as he hoped he had made plain, certain facts had been before his client at the time when . . . But he had said enough. For his fee it seemed to me that he had.

Heaven inspired Sir Thomas's lawyer—all of a sweat lest his client's language should come out—to rise up and thank him. Then, Sir Thomas—not yet aware what leprosy had been laid upon him, but grateful to escape on any terms—followed suit. He was heard in interested silence, and people drew back a pace as Gehazi° passed forth.

'You hit hard,' said Bat to Woodhouse afterwards. 'His own people think he's mad.'

'You don't say so? I'll show you some of his letters to-night at dinner,' he replied.

He brought them to the Red Amber Room of the Chop Suey. We forgot to be amazed, as till then we had been amazed, over The Song or 'The Gubby,' or the full tide of Fate that seemed to run only for our sakes. It did not even interest Ollyett that the verb 'to huckle' had passed into the English leader-writers' language. We were studying the interior of a soul, flash-lighted to its grimiest corners by the dread of 'losing its position.'

'And then it thanked you, didn't it, for dropping the case?' said Pallant.

'Yes, and it sent me a telegram to confirm.' Woodhouse turned to Bat. 'Now d'you think I hit too hard?' he asked.

'No—o!' said Bat. 'After all—I'm talking of every one's business now—one can't ever do anything in Art that comes up to Nature in any game in life. Just think how this thing has—'

'Just let me run through that little case of yours again,' said Pallant, and picked up *The Bun* which had it set out in full.

'Any chance of 'Dal looking in on us to-night?' Ollyett began.

'She's occupied with her Art too,' Bat answered bitterly. 'What's the use of Art? Tell me, some one!' A barrel-organ outside promptly pointed out that the *Earth* was flat. 'The gramophone's killing street organs, but I let loose a hundred-and-seventy-four of those hurdy-gurdys twelve hours after The Song,' said Bat. 'Not counting the Provinces.' His face brightened a little.

'Look here!' said Pallant over the paper. 'I don't suppose you or those asinine J.P.'s knew it—but your lawyer ought to have known that you've all put your foot in it most confoundedly over this assault case.'

'What's the matter?' said Woodhouse.

'It's ludicrous. It's insane. There isn't two penn'orth of legality in the whole thing. Of course, you could have withdrawn the charge, but the way you went about it is childish—besides being illegal. What on earth was the Chief Constable thinking of?'

'Oh, he was a friend of Sir Thomas's. They all were for that matter,' I replied.

'He ought to be hanged. So ought the Chairman of the Bench. I'm talking as a lawyer now.'

'Why, what have we been guilty of? Misprision of treason or compounding a felony—or what?' said Ollyett.

'I'll tell you later.' Pallant went back to the paper with knitted brows, smiling unpleasantly from time to time. At last he laughed.

'Thank you!' he said to Woodhouse. 'It ought to be pretty useful—for us.'

'What d'you mean?' said Ollyett.'

'For our side. They are all Rads who are mixed up in this—from the Chief Constable down. There must be a Question. There must be a Question.'

'Yes, but I wanted the charge withdrawn in my own way,' Woodhouse insisted.

'That's nothing to do with the case. It's the legality of your silly methods. You wouldn't understand if I talked till morning.' He began to pace the room, his hands behind him. 'I wonder if I can get it through our Whip's thick head that it's a chance. . . . That comes of stuffing the Bench with radical tinkers,' he muttered.

'Oh, sit down!' said Woodhouse.

'Where's your lawyer to be found now?' he jerked out.

'At the Trefoil,' said Bat promptly. 'I gave him the stage-box for to-night. He's an artist too.'

'Then I'm going to see him,' said Pallant. 'Properly handled this ought to be a godsend for our side.' He withdrew without apology.

'Certainly, this thing keeps on opening up, and up,' I remarked inanely.

'It's beyond me!' said Bat. 'I don't think if I'd known I'd have ever . . . Yes, I would, though. He said my home address was—'

'It was his tone—his tone!' Ollyett almost shouted. Woodhouse said nothing, but his face whitened as he brooded.

'Well, any way,' Bat went on, 'I'm glad I always believed in God and Providence and all those things. Else I should lose my nerve. We've put it over the whole world—the full extent of the geographical globe. We couldn't stop it if we wanted to now. It's got to burn itself out. I'm not in charge any more. What d'you expect'll happen next? Angels?'

I expected nothing. Nothing that I expected approached what I got. Politics are not my concern, but, for the moment, since it seemed that they were going to 'huckle' with the rest, I took an interest in them. They impressed me as a dog's life without a dog's decencies, and I was confirmed in this when an unshaven and unwashen Pallant called on me at ten o'clock one morning, begging for a bath and a couch.

'Bail too?' I asked. He was in evening dress and his eyes were sunk feet in his head.

'No,' he said hoarsely. 'All night sitting. Fifteen divisions. 'Nother to-night. Your place was nearer than mine, so—' He began to undress in the hall.

When he awoke at one o'clock he gave me lurid accounts of what he said was history, but which was obviously collective hysteria. There had been a political crisis. He and his fellow M.P.'s had 'done things' —I never quite got at the things—for eighteen hours on end, and the pitiless Whips were even then at the telephones to herd 'em up to another dog-fight. So he snorted and grew hot all over again while he might have been resting.

'I'm going to pitch in my question about that miscarriage of justice at Huckley this afternoon, if you care to listen to it,' he said. 'It'll be absolutely thrown away—in our present state. I told 'em so; but it's my only chance for weeks. P'raps Woodhouse would like to come.'

'I'm sure he would. Anything to do with Huckley interests us,' I said.

'It'll miss fire, I'm afraid. Both sides are absolutely cooked. The present situation has been working up for some time. You see the row was bound to come, etc. etc.,' and he flew off the handle once more.

I telephoned to Woodhouse, and we went to the House together. It was a dull, sticky afternoon with thunder in the air. For some reason or other, each side was determined to prove its virtue and endurance to the utmost. I heard men snarling about it all round me. 'If they won't spare us, we'll show 'em no mercy.' 'Break the brutes up from the start. They can't stand late hours.' 'Come on! No shirking! I know *you*'ve had a Turkish bath,' were some of the sentences I caught on our way. The House was packed already, and one could feel the negative electricity of a jaded crowd wrenching at one's own nerves, and depressing the afternoon soul.

'This is bad!' Woodhouse whispered. 'There'll be a row before they've finished. Look at the Front Benches!' And he pointed out little personal signs by which I was to know that each man was on edge. He might have spared himself. The House was ready to snap before a bone had been thrown. A sullen minister rose to reply to a staccato question. His supporters cheered defiantly. 'None o' that! None o' that!' came from the Back Benches. I saw the Speaker's face stiffen like the face of a helmsman as he humours a hard-mouthed yacht after a sudden following sea. The trouble was barely met in time. There came a fresh, apparently causeless gust a few minutes later—savage, threatening, but futile. It died out—one could hear the sigh—in sudden wrathful realisation of the dreary hours ahead, and the ship of state drifted on.

Then Pallant—and the raw House winced at the torture of his voice—rose. It was a twenty-line question, studded with legal technicalities. The gist of it was that he wished to know whether the appropriate Minister was aware that there had been a grave miscarriage of justice on such and such a date, at such and such a place, before such and such justices of the peace, in regard to a case which arose—

I heard one desperate, weary 'damn!' float up from the pit of that torment. Pallant sawed on—'out of certain events which occurred at the village of Huckley.'

The House came to attention with a parting of the lips like a hiccough, and it flashed through my mind . . . Pallant repeated, 'Huckley. The village—'

'That voted the *Earth* was flat.' A single voice from a back Bench sang it once like a lone frog in a far pool.

'*Earth* was flat,' croaked another voice opposite.

'*Earth* was flat.' There were several. Then several more.

It was, you understand, the collective, overstrained nerve of the House, snapping, strand by strand to various notes, as the hawser parts from its moorings.

'The Village that voted the *Earth* was flat.' The tune was beginning to shape itself. More voices were raised and feet began to beat time. Even so it did not occur to me that the thing would—

'The Village that voted the *Earth* was flat!' It was easier now to see who were not singing. There were still a few. Of a sudden (and this proves the fundamental instability of the cross-bench mind) a cross-bencher leaped on his seat and there played an imaginary double-bass with tremendous maestro-like wagglings of the elbow.

The last strand parted. The ship of state drifted out helpless on the rocking tide of melody.

'The Village that voted the *Earth* was flat!
The Village that voted the *Earth* was flat!'

The Irish first conceived the idea of using their order-papers as funnels wherewith to reach the correct '*vroom—vroom*' on '*Earth*.' Labour, always conservative and respectable at a crisis, stood out longer than any other section, but when it came in it was howling syndicalism. Then, without distinction of Party, fear of constituents, desire for office, or hope of emolument, the House sang at the tops and at the bottoms of their voices, swaying their stale bodies and epileptically beating with their swelled feet. They sang 'The Village that Voted the Earth was flat': first, because they wanted to, and secondly—which is the terror of that song—because they could not stop. For no consideration could they stop.

Pallant was still standing up. Some one pointed at him and they laughed. Others began to point, lunging, as it were, in time with the tune. At this moment two persons came in practically abreast from behind the Speaker's chair, and halted appalled. One happened to be the Prime Minister and the other a messenger. The House, with tears running down their cheeks, transferred their attention to the paralysed couple. They pointed six hundred forefingers at them. They rocked, they waved, and they rolled while they pointed, but still they sang. When they weakened for an instant, Ireland would yell: 'Are ye *with* me, bhoys?' and they all renewed their strength like Antaeus.° No man could say afterwards what happened in the Press or the Strangers' Gallery. It was the House, the hysterical and abandoned House of Commons that held all eyes, as it deafened all ears. I saw both Front Benches bend forward, some with their foreheads on their despatch-boxes, the rest with their faces in their hands; and their moving shoulders jolted the House out of its last rag of decency. Only the Speaker remained unmoved. The entire press of Great Britain bore witness next day that he had not even bowed his head. The Angel of the Constitution, for vain was the help of man,° foretold him the exact moment at which the House would have broken into 'The Gubby.' He is reported to have said: 'I heard the Irish beginning to shuffle it. So I adjourned.' Pallant's version is that he added: 'And I was never so grateful to a private member in all my life as I was to Mr Pallant.'

He made no explantion. He did not refer to orders or disorders. He simply adjourned the House till six that evening. And the House adjourned—some of it nearly on all fours.

I was not correct when I said that the Speaker was the only man who did not laugh. Woodhouse was beside me all the time. His face was set and quite white—as white, they told me, as Sir Thomas Ingell's when he went, by request, to a private interview with his Chief Whip.

The Press

The Soldier may forget his sword,
    The Sailorman the sea,

The Mason may forget the Word
  And the Priest his litany:
The maid may forget both jewel and gem,
  And the bride her wedding-dress—
But the Jew shall forget Jerusalem
  Ere we forget the Press!

Who once hath stood through the loaded hour
  Ere, roaring like the gale,
The Harrild and the Hoe devour°
  Their league-long paper bale,
And has lit his pipe in the morning calm
  That follows the midnight stress—
He hath sold his heart to the old Black Art
  We call the daily Press.

Who once hath dealt in the widest game
  That all of a man can play,
No later love, no larger fame
  Will lure him long away.
As the war-horse smelleth the battle afar,
  The entered Soul, no less,
He saith: 'Ha! Ha!' where the trumpets are°
  And the thunders of the Press.

Canst thou number the days that we fulfil,°
  Or the *Times* that we bring forth?
Canst thou send the lightnings to do thy will,
  And cause them reign on earth?
Hast thou given a peacock goodly wings
  To please his foolishness?
Sit down at the heart of men and things,
  Companion of the Press!

The Pope may launch his Interdict,
  The Union its decree,
But the bubble is blown and the bubble is pricked
  By Us and such as We.
Remember the battle and stand aside
  While Thrones and Powers confess
That King over all the children of pride
  Is the Press—the Press—the Press!

In the Presence

(1912)

'So the matter,' the Regimental Chaplain concluded, 'was correct; in every way correct. I am well pleased with Rutton Singh and Attar Singh. They have gathered the fruit of their lives.'

He folded his arms and sat down on the verandah. The hot day had ended, and there was a pleasant smell of cooking along the regimental lines, where half-clad men went back and forth with leaf platters and water-goglets.° The Subadar-Major, in extreme undress, sat on a chair, as befitted his rank; the Havildar-Major,° his nephew, leaning respectfully against the wall. The Regiment was at home and at ease in its own quarters in its own district which takes its name from the great Muhammadan saint Mian Mir,° revered by Jehangir° and beloved by Guru Har Gobind, sixth of the great Sikh Gurus.°

'Quite correct,' the Regimental Chaplain repeated.

No Sikh contradicts his Regimental Chaplain who expounds to him the Holy Book of the Grunth Sahib° and who knows the lives and legends of all the Gurus.

The Subadar-Major bowed his grey head. The Havildar-Major coughed respectfully to attract attention and to ask leave to speak. Though he was the Subadar-Major's nephew, and though his father held twice as much land as his uncle, he knew his place in the scheme of things. The Subadar-Major shifted one hand with an iron bracelet on the wrist.°

'Was there by any chance any woman at the back of it?'° the Havildar-Major murmured. 'I was not here when the thing happened.'

'Yes! Yes! Yes! We all know that thou wast in England eating and drinking with the Sahibs. We are all surprised that thou canst still speak Punjabi.' The Subadar-Major's carefully-tended beard bristled.

'There was no woman,' the Regimental Chaplain growled. 'It was land. Hear, you! Rutton Singh and Attar Singh were the elder of four brothers. These four held land in—what was the village's name?—oh, Pishapur, near Thori, in the Banalu Tehsil of Patiala State,° where men can still recognise right behaviour when they see it. The two younger brothers tilled the land, while Rutton Singh and Attar Singh took service with the Regiment, according to the custom of the family.'

'True, true,' said the Havildar-Major. 'There is the same arrangement in all good families.'

'Then, listen again,' the Regimental Chaplain went on. 'Their kin on their mother's side put great oppression and injustice upon the two younger brothers who stayed with the land in Patiala State. Their mother's kin loosened beasts into the four brothers' crops when the crops were green; they cut the corn by force when it was ripe; they broke down the water-courses; they defiled the wells; and they brought false charges in the law-courts against all four brothers. They did not spare even the cotton-seed,° as the saying is.

'Their mother's kin trusted that the young men would thus be forced by weight of trouble, and further trouble and perpetual trouble, to quit their lands in Pishapur village in Banalu Tehsil in Patiala State. If the young men ran away, the land would come whole to their mother's kin. I am not a regimental schoolmaster, but is it understood, child?'

'Understood,' said the Havildar-Major grimly. 'Pishapur is not the only place where the fence eats the field instead of protecting it. But perhaps there was a woman among their mother's kin?'

'God knows!' said the Regimental Chaplain. 'Woman, or man, or law-courts, the young men would *not* be driven off the land which was their own by inheritance. They made appeal to Rutton Singh and Attar Singh, their brethren who had taken service with *us* in the Regiment, and so knew the world, to help them in their long war against their mother's kin in Pishapur. For that reason, because their own land and the honour of their house was dear to them, Rutton Singh and Attar Singh needs must very often ask for leave to go to Patiala and attend to the lawsuits and cattle-poundings° there.

'It was not, look you, as though they went back to their own village and sat, garlanded with jasmine, in honour, upon chairs before the elders under the trees. They went back always to perpetual trouble, either of lawsuits, or theft, or strayed cattle; and they sat on thorns.'

'I knew it,' said the Subadar-Major. 'Life was bitter for them both. But they were well-conducted men. It was not hard to get them their leave from the Colonel Sahib.'

'They spoke to me also,' said the Chaplain. '"*Let him who desires the four great gifts apply himself to the words of holy men.*" That is written. Often they showed me the papers of the false lawsuits brought against them. Often they wept on account of the persecution put upon them by their mother's kin. Men thought it was drugs when their eyes showed red.'

'They wept in my presence too,' said the Subadar-Major. 'Well-conducted men of nine years' service apiece. Rutton Singh was drill-Naik,° too.'

'They did all things correctly as Sikhs should,' said the Regimental Chaplain. 'When the persecution had endured seven years, Attar Singh took leave to Pishapur once again (that was the fourth time in that year only) and he called his persecutors together before the village elders, and he cast his turban at their feet and besought them by his mother's blood to cease from their persecutions. For he told them earnestly that he had marched to the boundaries of his patience, and that there could be but one end to the matter.

'They gave him abuse. They mocked him and his tears, which was the same as though they had mocked the Regiment. Then Attar Singh returned to the Regiment, and laid this last trouble before Rutton Singh, the eldest brother. But Rutton Singh could not get leave all at once.'

'Because he was drill-Naik and the recruits were to be drilled. I myself told him so,' said the Subadar-Major. 'He was a well-conducted man. He said he could wait.'

'But when permission was granted, those two took four days' leave,' the Chaplain went on.

'I do not think Attar Singh should have taken Baynes Sahib's revolver. He was Baynes Sahib's orderly, and all that Sahib's things were open to him. It was, therefore, as I count it, shame to Attar Singh,' said the Subadar-Major.

'All the words had been said. There was need of arms, and how could soldiers use Government rifles upon mere cultivators in the fields?' the Regimental Chaplain replied. 'Moreover, the revolver was sent back, together with a money-order for the cartridges expended. "*Borrow not; but if thou borrowest, pay back soon!*" That is written in the Hymns. Rutton Singh took a sword, and he and Attar Singh went to Pishapur and, after word given, the four brethren fell upon their persecutors in Pishapur village and slew seventeen, wounding ten. A revolver is better than a lawsuit. I say that these four brethren, the two with *us*, and the two mere cultivators, slew and wounded twenty-seven—all their mother's kin, male and female.

'Then the four mounted to their housetop, and Attar Singh, who was always one of the impetuous, said "My work is done," and he made *shinan* (purification) in all men's sight, and he lent Rutton Singh Baynes Sahib's revolver, and Rutton Singh shot him in the head.

'So Attar Singh abandoned his body, as an insect abandons a blade of grass. But Rutton Singh, having more work to do, went down from the housetop and sought an enemy whom he had forgotten—a Patiala man of this regiment who had sided with the persecutors. When he overtook the man, Rutton Singh hit him twice with bullets and once with the sword.'

'But the man escaped and is now in the hospital here,' said the Subadar-Major. 'The doctor says he will live in spite of all.'

'Not Rutton Singh's fault. Rutton Singh left him for dead. Then Rutton Singh returned to the housetop, and the three brothers together, Attar Singh being dead, sent word by a lad to the police station for an army to be dispatched against them that they might die with honours. But none came. And yet Patiala State is not under English law and they should know virtue there when they see it!

'So, on the third day, Rutton Singh also made *shinan*, and the youngest of the brethren shot him also in the head, and *he* abandoned his body. .

'Thus was all correct. There was neither heat, nor haste, nor abuse in the matter from end to end. There remained alive not one man or woman of their mother's kin which had oppressed them. Of the other villagers of Pishapur, who had taken no part in the persecutions, not one was slain. Indeed, the villagers sent them food on the housetop for those three days while they waited for the police who would not dispatch that army.

'Listen again! I know that Attar Singh and Rutton Singh omitted no ceremony of the purifications, and when all was done Baynes Sahib's revolver was thrown down from the housetop, together with three rupees twelve annas; and order was given for its return by post.'

'And what befell the two younger brethren who were not in the service?' the Havildar-Major asked.

'Doubtless they too are dead, but since they were not in the Regiment their honour concerns themselves only. So far as *we* were touched, see how correctly we came out of the matter! I think the King should be told; for where could you match such a tale except among us Sikhs? *Sri wah guru ji ki Khalsa! Sri wah guru ji ki futteh!*'° said the Regimental Chaplain.

'Would three rupees twelve annas pay for the used cartridges?' said the Havildar-Major.

'Attar Singh knew the just price. All Baynes Sahib's gear was in his charge. They expended one tin box of fifty cartouches, lacking two which were returned. As I said—as I say—the arrangement was made not with heat nor blasphemies as a Mussulman would have made it; not with cries nor caperings as an idolater would have made it; but conformably to the ritual and doctrine of the Sikhs. Hear you! "*Though hundreds of amusements are offered to a child it cannot live without milk.*

If a man be divorced from his soul and his soul's desire he certainly will not stop to play upon the road, but he will make haste with his pilgrimage." That is written. I rejoice in my disciples.'

'True! True! Correct! Correct!' said the Subadar-Major. There was a long, easy silence. One heard a water-wheel creaking somewhere and the nearer sound of meal being ground in a quern.

'But he—' the Chaplain pointed a scornful chin at the Havildar-Major—'*he* has been so long in England that—'

'Let the lad alone,' said his uncle. 'He was but two months there, and he was chosen for good cause.'

Theoretically, all Sikhs are equal. Practically, there are differences, as none know better than well-born, land-owning folk, or long-descended chaplains from Amritsar.°

'Hast thou heard anything in England to match my tale?' the Chaplain sneered.

'I saw more than I could understand, so I have locked up my stories in my own mouth,' the Havildar-Major replied meekly.

'Stories? What stories? I know all the stories about England,' said the Chaplain. 'I know that *terains* run underneath their bazaars there, and as for their streets stinking with *mota-kahars*, only this morning I was nearly killed by Duggan Sahib's *mota-kahar*. That young man is a devil.'

'I expect Grunthi-jee,' said the Subadar-Major, 'you and I grow too old to care for the Kahar-ki-nautch—the Bearer's dance.' He named one of the sauciest of the old-time nautches, and smiled at his own pun. Then he turned to his nephew. 'When I was a lad and came back to my village on leave, I waited the convenient hour, and the elders giving permission, I spoke of what I had seen elsewhere.'

'Ay, my father,' said the Havildar-Major, softly and affectionately. He sat himself down with respect, as behoved a mere lad of thirty with a bare half-dozen campaigns to his credit.

'There were four men in this affair also,' he began, 'and it was an affair that touched the honour, not of one regiment, nor two, but of all the Army in Hind. Some part of it I saw; some I heard; but *all* the tale is true. My father's brother knows, and my priest knows, that I was in England on business with my Colonel, when the King—the Great Queen's son°—completed his life.

'First, there was a rumour that sickness was upon him. Next, we knew that he lay sick in the Palace. A very great multitude stood outside the Palace by night and by day, in the rain as well as the sun, waiting for news.

'Then came out one with a written paper, and set it upon a gate-side—the word of the King's death—and they read, and groaned. This I saw with my own eyes, because the office where my Colonel Sahib went daily to talk with Colonel Forsyth Sahib was at the east end of the very gardens where the Palace stood. They are larger gardens than Shalimar here'—he pointed with his chin up the lines—'or Shahdera° across the river.

'Next day there was a darkness in the streets, because all the city's multitude were clad in black garments, and they spoke as a man speaks in the presence of his dead—all those multitudes. In the eyes, in the air, and in the heart, there was blackness. I saw it. But that is not my tale.

'After ceremonies had been accomplished, and word had gone out to the Kings of the Earth that they should come and mourn, the new King°—the dead King's son—gave commandment that his father's body should be laid, coffined, in a certain Temple° which is near the river. There are no idols in that Temple; neither any carvings, nor paintings, nor gildings. It is all grey stone, of one colour as though it were cut out of the live rock. It is larger than—yes, than the Durbar Sahib at Amritsar, even though the Akal Bunga and the Baba-Atal° were added. How old it may be God knows. It is the Sahibs' most sacred Temple.

'In that place, by the new King's commandment, they made, as it were, a shrine for a saint, with lighted candles at the head and the feet of the Dead, and duly appointed watchers for every hour of the day and the night, until the dead King should be taken to the place of his fathers, which is at Wanidza.°

'When all was in order, the new King said, "Give entrance to all people," and the doors were opened, and O my uncle! O my teacher! all the world entered, walking through that Temple to take farewell of the Dead. There was neither distinction, nor price, nor ranking in the host, except an order that they should walk by fours.

'As they gathered in the streets without—very, very far off—so they entered the Temple, walking by fours: the child, the old man; mother, virgin, harlot, trader, priest; of all colours and faiths and customs under the firmament of God, from dawn till late at night. I saw it. My Colonel gave me leave to go. I stood in the line, many hours, one *koss*, two *koss*,° distant from the temple.'

'Then why did the multitude not sit down under the trees?' asked the priest.

'Because we were still between houses. The city is many *koss* wide,' the Havildar-Major resumed. 'I submitted myself to that slow-moving river and thus—thus—a pace at a time—I made pilgrimage. There were in my rank a woman, a cripple, and a lascar from the ships.

'When we entered the Temple, the coffin itself was as a shoal in the Ravi River,° splitting the stream into two branches, one on either side of the Dead; and the watchers of the Dead, who were soldiers, stood about It, moving no more than the still flame of the candles. Their heads were bowed; their hands were clasped; their eyes were cast upon the ground—thus. They were not men, but images, and the multitude went past them in fours by day, and, except for a little while, by night also.

'No, there was no order that the people should come to pay respect. It was a free-will pilgrimage. Eight kings had been commanded to come—who obeyed—but upon his own Sahibs the new King laid no commandment. Of themselves they came.

'I made pilgrimage twice: once for my Salt's sake,° and once again for wonder and terror and worship. But my mouth cannot declare one thing of a hundred thousand things in this matter. There were *lakhs* of *lakhs*, *crores* of *crores*° of people. I saw them.'

'More than at our great pilgrimages?' the Regimental Chaplain demanded.

'Yes. Those are only cities and districts coming out to pray. This was the world walking in grief. And now, hear you! It is the King's custom that four swords of Our Armies in Hind should stand always before the Presence in case of need.'

'The King's custom, our right,' said the Subadar-Major curtly.

'Also our right. These honoured ones are changed after certain months or years, that the honour may be fairly spread. Now it chanced that when the old King—the Queen's son—completed his days, the four that stood in the Presence were Goorkhas.° Neither Sikhs alas, nor Pathans, Rajputs, nor Jats. Goorkhas, my father.'

'Idolaters,' said the Chaplain.

'But soldiers; for I remember in the Tirah°—' the Havildar-Major began.

'*But* soldiers, for I remember fifteen campaigns. Go on,' said the Subadar-Major.

'And it was their honour and right to furnish one who should stand in the Presence by day and by night till It went out to burial. There were no more than four all told—four old men to furnish that guard.'

'Old? Old? What talk is this of old men?' said the Subadar-Major.

'Nay. My fault! Your pardon!' The Havildar-Major spread a

deprecating hand. 'They were strong, hot, valiant men, and the youngest was a lad of forty-five.'

'That is better,' the Subadar-Major laughed.

'But for all their strength and heat they could not eat strange food from the Sahibs' hands. There was no cooking place in the Temple; but a certain Colonel Forsyth Sahib,° who had understanding, made arrangement whereby they should receive at least a little caste-clean parched grain; also cold rice maybe, and water which was pure. Yet, at best, this was no more than a hen's mouthful, snatched as each came off his guard. They lived on grain and were thankful, as the saying is.

'One hour's guard in every four was each man's burden, for, as I have shown, they were but four all told; and the honour of Our Armies in Hind was on their heads. The Sahibs could draw upon all the armies in England for the other watchers—thousands upon thousands of fresh men—if they needed; but these four were but four.

'The Sahibs drew upon the Granadeers° for the other watchers. Granadeers be very tall men under very tall bearskins, such as Fusilier regiments wear in cold weather. Thus, when a Granadeer bowed his head but a very little over his stock, the bearksin sloped and showed as though he grieved exceedingly. Now the Goorkhas wear flat, green caps—'

'I see, I see,' said the Subadar-Major impatiently.

'They are bull-necked, too; and their stocks are hard, and when they bend deeply—deeply—to match the Granadeers—they come nigh to choking themselves. That was a handicap against them, when it came to the observance of ritual.

'Yet even with their tall, grief-declaring bearskins, the Granadeers could not endure the full hour's guard in the Presence. There was good cause, as I will show, why no man could endure that terrible hour. So for them the hour's guard was cut to one-half. What did it matter to the Sahibs? They could draw on ten thousand Granadeers. Forsyth Sahib, who had comprehension, put this choice also before the four, and they said, "No, ours is the Honour of the Armies of Hind. Whatever the Sahibs do, we will suffer the full hour."

'Forsyth Sahib, seeing that they were°—knowing that they could neither sleep long nor eat much, said, "Is it great suffering?" They said, "It is great honour. We will endure."

'Forsyth Sahib, who loves us, said then to the eldest, "Ho, father, tell me truly what manner of burden it is; for the full hour's watch breaks up our men like water."

'The eldest answered, "Sahib, the burden is the feet of the multitude that pass us on either side. Our eyes being lowered and fixed, we see those feet only from the knee down—a river of feet, Sahib, that never—never—never stops. It is not the standing without any motion; it is not hunger; nor is it the dead part before the dawn when maybe a single one comes here to weep. It is the burden of the unendurable procession of feet from the knee down, that never—never—never stops!"

'Forsyth Sahib said, "By God, I had not considered that! Now I know why our men come trembling and twitching off that guard. But at least, my father, ease the stock a little beneath the bent chin for that one hour."

'The eldest said, "We are in the Presence. Moreover *He* knew every button and braid and hook of every uniform in all His armies."

'Then Forsyth Sahib said no more, except to speak about their parched grain, but indeed they could not eat much after their hour, nor could they sleep much because of eye-twitchings and the renewed procession of the feet before the eyes. Yet they endured each his full hour—not half an hour—his one full hour in each four hours.'

'Correct! correct!' said the Subadar-Major and the Chaplain together. 'We come well out of this affair.'

'But seeing that they were old men,' said the Subadar-Major reflectively, 'very old men, worn out by lack of food and sleep, could not arrangements have been made, or influence have been secured, or a petition presented, whereby a well-born Sikh might have eased them of some portion of their great burden, even though his substantive rank—'

'Then they would most certainly have slain me,' said the Havildar-Major with a smile.

'And they would have done correctly,' said the Chaplain. 'What befell the honourable ones later?'

'This. The Kings of the earth and all the Armies sent flowers and such-like to the dead King's palace at Wanidza, where the funeral offerings were accepted. There was no order given, but all the world made oblation. So the four took counsel—three at a time—and either they asked Forsyth Sahib to choose flowers, or themselves they went forth and bought flowers—I do not know; but, however it was arranged, the flowers were bought and made in the shape of a great drum-like circle weighing half a *maund*.°

'Forsyth Sahib had said, "Let the flowers be sent to Wanidza with the other flowers which all the world is sending." But they said among themselves, "It is not fit that these flowers, which are the offerings of

His Armies in Hind, should come to the Palace of the Presence by the hands of hirelings or messengers, or of any man not in His service."

'Hearing this, Forsyth Sahib, though he was much occupied with office-work, said, "Give me the flowers, and I will steal a time and myself take them to Wanidza."

'The eldest said, "Since when has Forsyth Sahib worn sword?"

'Forsyth Sahib said, "But always. And I wear it in the Presence when I put on uniform. I am a Colonel in the Armies of Hind." The eldest said, "Of what regiment?" And Forsyth Sahib looked on the carpet and pulled the hair of his lip. He saw the trap.'

'Forsyth Sahib's regiment was once the old Forty-sixth Pathans which was called—' the Subadar-Major gave the almost forgotten title, adding that he had met them in such and such campaigns, when Forsyth Sahib was a young captain.

The Havildar-Major took up the tale, saying, 'The eldest knew that also, my father.' He laughed, and presently Forsyth Sahib laughed.

'"It is true," said Forsyth Sahib. "I have no regiment. For twenty years I have been a clerk tied to a thick pen. Therefore I am the more fit to be your orderly and messenger in this business."

'The eldest then said, "If it were a matter of my life or the honour of *any* of my household, it would be easy." And Forsyth Sahib joined his hands together, half laughing, though he was ready to weep, and he said, "Enough! I ask pardon. Which one of you goes with the offering?"

'The eldest said, feigning not to have heard, "Nor must they be delivered by a single sword—as though we were pressed for men in His service," and they saluted and went out.'

'Were these things seen, or were they told thee?' said the Subadar-Major.

'I both saw and heard in the office full of books and papers where my Colonel Sahib consulted Forsyth Sahib upon the business that had brought my Colonel Sahib to England.'

'And what was that business?' the Regimental Chaplain asked of a sudden, looking full at the Havildar-Major, who returned the look without a quiver.

'That was not revealed to me,' said the Havildar-Major.

'I heard it might have been some matter touching the integrity of certain regiments,' the Chaplain insisted.

'The matter was not in any way open to my ears,' said the Havildar-Major.

'Humph!' The Chaplain drew his hard road-worn feet under his robe. 'Let us hear the tale that it is permitted thee to tell,' he said, and the Havildar-Major went on:

'So then the three, having returned to the Temple, called the fourth, who had only forty-five years, when he came off guard, and said, "We go to the Palace at Wanidza with the offerings. Remain thou in the Presence, and take all our guards, one after the other, till we return."

'Within that next hour they hired a large and strong *mota-kahar* for the journey from the Temple to Wanidza, which is twenty *koss* or more, and they promised expedition. But he who took their guards said, "It is not seemly that we should for any cause appear to be in haste. There are eighteen medals with eleven clasps and three Orders° to consider. Go at leisure. I can endure."

'So the three with the offerings were absent three hours and a half, and having delivered the offering at Wanidza in the correct manner they returned and found the lad on guard, and they did not break his guard till his full hour was ended. So *he* endured four hours in the Presence, not stirring one hair, his eyes abased, and the river of feet, from the knee down, passing continually before his eyes. When he was relieved, it was seen that his eyeballs worked like weavers' shuttles.

'And so it was done—not in hot blood, not for a little while, nor yet with the smell of slaughter and the noise of shouting to sustain, but in silence, for a very long time, rooted to one place before the Presence among the most terrible feet of the multitude.'

'Correct!' the Chaplain chuckled.

'But the Goorkhas had the honour,' said the Subadar-Major sadly.

'Theirs was the Honour of His Armies in Hind, and that was Our Honour,' the nephew replied.

'Yet I would one Sikh had been concerned in it—even one low-caste Sikh. And after?'

'They endured the burden until the end—until It went out of the Temple to be laid among the older kings at Wanidza. When all was accomplished and It was withdrawn under the earth, Forsyth Sahib said to the four, "The King gives command that you be fed here on meat cooked by your own cooks. Eat and take ease, my fathers."

'So they loosed their belts and ate. They had not eaten food except by snatches for some long time; and when the meat had given them strength they slept for very many hours; and it was told me that the procession of the unendurable feet ceased to pass before their eyes any more.'

He threw out one hand palm upward to show that the tale was ended.

'We came well and cleanly out of it,' said the Subadar-Major.

'Correct! Correct! Correct!' said the Regimental Chaplain. 'In an evil age it is good to hear such things, and there is certainly no doubt that this is a very evil age.'

Jobson's Amen

'Blessed be the English and all their ways and works.
Cursed be the Infidels, Hereticks, and Turks!'
'Amen,' quo' Jobson, 'but where I used to lie
Was neither Candle, Bell nor Book to curse my brethren by:

'But a palm-tree in full bearing, bowing down, bowing down,
To a surf that drove unsparing at the brown-walled town—
Conches in a temple, oil-lamps in a dome—
And a low moon out of Africa said: "This way home!"'

'Blessed be the English and all that they profess.
Cursed by the Savages that prance in nakedness!'
'Amen,' quo' Jobson, 'but where I used to lie
Was neither shirt nor pantaloons to catch my brethren by:

'But a well-wheel slowly creaking, going round, going round,
By a water-channel leaking over drowned, warm ground—
Parrots very busy in the trellised pepper-vine—
And a high sun over Asia shouting: "Rise and shine!"'

'Blessed be the English and everything they own.
Cursed by the Infidels that bow to wood and stone!'°
'Amen,' quo' Jobson, 'but where I used to lie
Was neither pew nor Gospelleer to save my brethren by:

'But a desert stretched and stricken, left and right, left and right,
Where the piled mirages thicken under white-hot light—
A skull beneath a sand-hill and a viper coiled inside—
And a red wind out of Libya roaring: "Run and hide!"'

'Blessed be the English and all they make or do.
Cursed be the Hereticks who doubt that this is true!'

'Amen,' quo' Jobson, 'but where I mean to die
Is neither rule nor calliper to judge the matter by:

'But Himalaya heavenward-heading, sheer and vast, sheer and vast,°
In a million summits bedding on the last world's past;°
A certain sacred mountain where the scented cedars climb,
And—the feet of my Beloved hurrying back through Time!'

Mary Postgate

(1915)

Of Miss Mary Postgate, Lady McCausland wrote that she was 'thoroughly conscientious, tidy, companionable, and ladylike. I am very sorry to part with her, and shall always be interested in her welfare.'

Miss Fowler engaged her on this recommendation, and to her surprise, for she had had experience of companions, found that it was true. Miss Fowler was nearer sixty than fifty at the time, but though she needed care she did not exhaust her attendant's vitality. On the contrary, she gave out, stimulatingly and with reminiscences. Her father had been a minor Court official in the days when the Great Exhibition of 1851 had just set its seal on Civilisation made perfect. Some of Miss Fowler's tales, none the less, were not always for the young. Mary was not young, and though her speech was as colourless as her eyes or her hair, she was never shocked. She listened unflinchingly to every one; said at the end, 'How interesting!' or 'How shocking!' as the case might be, and never again referred to it, for she prided herself on a trained mind, which 'did not dwell on these things.' She was, too, a treasure at domestic accounts, for which the village tradesmen, with their weekly books, loved her not. Otherwise she had no enemies; provoked no jealousy even among the plainest; neither gossip nor slander had ever been traced to her; she supplied the odd place at the Rector's or the Doctor's table at half an hour's notice; she was a sort of public aunt to very many small children of the village street, whose parents, while accepting everything, would have been swift to resent what they called 'patronage'; she served on the Village Nursing Committee as Miss Fowler's nominee when Miss

Fowler was crippled by rheumatoid arthritis, and came out of six months' fortnightly meetings equally respected by all the cliques.

And when Fate threw Miss Fowler's nephew, an unlovely orphan of eleven, on Miss Fowler's hands, Mary Postgate stood to her share of the business of education as practised in private and public schools. She checked printed clothes-lists, and unitemised bills of extras; wrote to Head and House masters, matrons, nurses and doctors, and grieved or rejoiced over half-term reports. Young Wyndham Fowler repaid her in his holidays by calling her 'Gatepost,' 'Postey,' or 'Packthread,' by thumping her between her narrow shoulders, or by chasing her bleating, round the garden, her large mouth open, her large nose high in air, at a stiff-necked shamble very like a camel's. Later on he filled the house with clamour, argument, and harangues as to his personal needs, likes and dislikes, and the limitations of 'you women,' reducing Mary to tears of physical fatigue, or, when he chose to be humorous, of helpless laughter. At crises, which multiplied as he grew older, she was his ambassadress and his interpretress to Miss Fowler, who had no large sympathy with the young; a vote in his interest at the councils on his future; his sewing-woman, strictly accountable for mislaid boots and garments; always his butt and his slave.

And when he decided to become a solicitor, and had entered an office in London; when his greeting had changed from 'Hullo, Postey, you old beast,' to 'Mornin', Packthread,' there came a war which, unlike all wars that Mary could remember, did not stay decently outside England and in the newspapers, but intruded on the lives of people whom she knew. As she said to Miss Fowler, it was 'most vexatious.' It took the Rector's son who was going into business with his elder brother; it took the Colonel's nephew on the eve of fruit-farming in Canada; it took Mrs Grant's son who, his mother said, was devoted to the ministry; and, very early indeed, it took Wynn Fowler, who announced on a postcard that he had joined the Flying Corps and wanted a cardigan waistcoat.

'He must go, and he must have the waistcoat,' said Miss Fowler. So Mary got the proper-sized needles and wool, while Miss Fowler told the men of her establishment—two gardeners and an odd man, aged sixty—that those who could join the Army had better do so. The gardeners left. Cheape, the odd man, stayed on, and was promoted to the gardener's cottage. The cook, scorning to be limited in luxuries, also left, after a spirited scene with Miss Fowler, and took the housemaid with her. Miss Fowler gazetted Nellie, Cheape's seventeen-year-old daughter, to the vacant post; Mrs Cheape to the rank of cook,° with occasional cleaning bouts; and the reduced establishment moved forward smoothly.

Wynn demanded an increase in his allowance. Miss Fowler, who always looked facts in the face, said, 'He must have it. The chances are he won't live long to draw it, and if three hundred makes him happy—'

Wynn was grateful, and came over, in his tight-buttoned uniform, to say so. His training centre was not thirty miles away, and his talk was so technical that it had to be explained by charts of the various types of machines. He gave Mary such a chart.

'And you'd better study it, Postey,' he said. 'You'll be seeing a lot of 'em soon.' So Mary studied the chart, but when Wynn next arrived to swell and exalt himself before his womenfolk, she failed badly in cross-examination, and he rated her as in the old days.

'You *look* more or less like a human being,' he said in his new Service voice. 'You *must* have had a brain at some time in your past. What have you done with it? Where d'you keep it? A sheep would know more than you do, Postey. You're lamentable. You are less use than an empty tin can, you dowey° old cassowary.'

'I suppose that's how your superior officer talks to *you*?' said Miss Fowler from her chair.

'But Postey doesn't mind,' Wynn replied. 'Do you, Packthread?'

'Why? Was Wynn saying anything? I shall get this right next time you come,' she muttered, and knitted her pale brows again over the diagrams of Taubes, Farmans, and Zeppelins.°

In a few weeks the mere land and sea battles which she read to Miss Fowler after breakfast passed her like idle breath. Her heart and her interest were high in the air with Wynn, who had finished 'rolling' (whatever that might be) and had gone on from a 'taxi'° to a machine more or less his own. One morning it circled over their very chimneys, alighted on Vegg's Heath, almost outside the garden gate, and Wynn came in, blue with cold, shouting for food. He and she drew Miss Fowler's bath-chair, as they had often done, along the Heath foot-path to look at the biplane. Mary observed that 'it smelt very badly.'

'Postey, I believe you think with your nose,' said Wynn. 'I know you don't with your mind. Now, what type's that?'

'I'll go and get the chart,' said Mary.

'You're hopeless! You haven't the mental capacity of a white mouse,' he cried, and explained the dials and the sockets for bomb-dropping till it was time to mount and ride the wet clouds once more.

'Ah!' said Mary, as the stinking thing flared upward. 'Wait till our

Flying Corps gets to work! Wynn says it's much safer than in the trenches.'

'I wonder,' said Miss Fowler. 'Tell Cheape to come and tow me home again.'

'It's all downhill. I can do it,' said Mary, 'if you put the brake on.' She laid her lean self against the pushing-bar and home they trundled.

'Now, be careful you aren't heated and catch a chill,' said over-dressed Miss Fowler.

'Nothing makes me perspire,' said Mary. As she bumped the chair under the porch she straightened her long back. The exertion had given her a colour, and the wind had loosened a wisp of hair across her forehead. Miss Fowler glanced at her.

'What do you ever think of, Mary?' she demanded suddenly.

'Oh, Wynn says he wants another three pairs of stockings—as thick as we can make them.'

'Yes. But I mean the things that women think about. Here you are, more than forty—'

'Forty-four,' said truthful Mary.

'Well?'

'Well?' Mary offered Miss Fowler her shoulder as usual.

'And you've been with me ten years now.'

'Let's see,' said Mary. 'Wynn was eleven when he came. He's twenty now, and I came two years before that. It must be eleven.'

'Eleven! And you've never told me anything that matters in all that while. Looking back, it seems to me that *I*'ve done all the talking.'

'I'm afraid I'm not much of a conversationalist. As Wynn says, I haven't the mind. Let me take your hat.'

Miss Fowler, moving stiffly from the hip, stamped her rubber-tipped stick on the tiled hall floor. 'Mary, aren't you *anything* except a companion? Would you *ever* have been anything except a companion?'

Mary hung up the garden hat on its proper peg. 'No,' she said after consideration. 'I don't imagine I ever should. But I've no imagination, I'm afraid.'

She fetched Miss Fowler her eleven-o-clock glass of Contrexeville.°

That was the wet December when it rained six inches to the month, and the women went abroad as little as might be. Wynn's flying chariot visited them several times, and for two mornings (he had warned her by postcard) Mary heard the thresh of his propellers at dawn. The second time she ran to the window, and stared at the whitening sky. A little blur passed overhead. She lifted her lean arms towards it.

That evening at six o'clock there came an announcement in an official envelope that Second Lieutenant W. Fowler had been killed during a trial flight. Death was instantaneous. She read it and carried it to Miss Fowler.

'I never expected anything else,' said Miss Fowler; 'but I'm sorry it happened before he had done anything.'

The room was whirling round Mary Postgate, but she found herself quite steady in the midst of it.

'Yes,' she said. 'It's a great pity he didn't die in action after he had killed somebody.'

'He was killed instantly. That's one comfort,' Miss Fowler went on.

'But Wynn says the shock of a fall kills a man at once—whatever happens to the tanks,"° quoted Mary.

The room was coming to rest now. She heard Miss Fowler say impatiently, 'But why can't we cry, Mary?' and herself replying, 'There's nothing to cry for. He has done his duty as much as Mrs Grant's son did.'

'And when he died, *she* came and cried all the morning,' said Miss Fowler. 'This only makes me feel tired—terribly tired. Will you help me to bed, please, Mary?—And I think I'd like the hot-water bottle.'

So Mary helped her and sat beside, talking of Wynn in his riotous youth.

'I believe,' said Miss Fowler suddenly, 'that old people and young people slip from under a stroke like this. The middle-aged feel it most.'

'I expect that's true,' said Mary, rising. 'I'm going to put away the things in his room now. Shall we wear mourning?'

'Certainly not,' said Miss Fowler. 'Except, of course, at the funeral. I can't go. You will. I want you to arrange about his being buried here. What a blessing it didn't happen at Salisbury!'

Every one, from the Authorities of the Flying Corps to the Rector, was most kind and sympathetic. Mary found herself for the moment in a world where bodies were in the habit of being despatched by all sorts of conveyances to all sorts of places. And at the funeral two young men in buttoned-up uniforms stood beside the grave and spoke to her afterwards.

'You're Miss Postgate, aren't you?' said one. 'Fowler told me about you. He was a good chap—a first-class fellow—a great loss.'

'Great loss!' growled his companion. 'We're all awfully sorry.'

'How high did he fall from?' Mary whispered.

'Pretty nearly four thousand feet, I should think, didn't he? You were up that day, Monkey?'

'All of that,' the other child replied. 'My bar made three thousand, and I wasn't as high as him by a lot.'

'Then *that's* all right,' said Mary. 'Thank you very much.'

They moved away as Mrs Grant flung herself weeping on Mary's flat chest, under the lych-gate, and cried, '*I* know how it feels! *I* know how it feels!'

'But both his parents are dead,' Mary returned, as she fended her off. 'Perhaps they've all met by now,' she added vaguely as she escaped towards the coach.

'I've thought of that too,' wailed Mrs Grant; 'but then he'll be practically a stranger to them. Quite embarrassing!'

Mary faithfully reported every detail of the ceremony to Miss Fowler, who, when she described Mrs Grant's outburst, laughed aloud.

'Oh, how Wynn would have enjoyed it! He was always utterly unreliable at funerals. D'you remember—' And they talked of him again, each piecing out the other's gaps. 'And now,' said Miss Fowler, 'we'll pull up the blinds and we'll have a general tidy. That always does us good. Have you seen to Wynn's things?'

'Everything—since he first came,' said Mary. 'He was never destructive—even with his toys.'

They faced that neat room.

'It can't be natural not to cry,' Mary said at last. 'I'm *so* afraid you'll have a reaction.'

'As I told you, we old people slip from under the stroke. It's you I'm afraid for. Have you cried yet?'

'I can't. It only makes me angry with the Germans.'

'That's sheer waste of vitality,' said Miss Fowler. 'We must live till the war's finished.' She opened a full wardrobe. 'Now, I've been thinking things over. This is my plan. All his civilian clothes can be given away—Belgian refugees, and so on.'

Mary nodded. 'Boots, collars, and gloves?'

'Yes. We don't need to keep anything except his cap and belt.'

'They came back yesterday with his Flying Corps clothes'—Mary pointed to a roll on the little iron bed.

'Ah, but keep his Service things. Some one may be glad of them later. Do you remember his sizes?'

'Five feet eight and a half; thirty-six inches round the chest. But he told me he's just put on an inch and a half. I'll mark it on a label and tie it on his sleeping-bag.'

'So that disposes of *that*,' said Miss Fowler, tapping the palm of one hand with the ringed third finger of the other. 'What waste it all is! We'll get his old school trunk to-morrow and pack his civilian clothes.'

'And the rest?' said Mary. 'His books and pictures and the games and the toys—and—and the rest?'

'My plan is to burn every single thing,' said Miss Folwer. 'Then we shall know where they are and no one can handle them afterwards. What do you think?'

'I think that would be much the best,' said Mary. 'But there's such a lot of them.'

'We'll burn them in the destructor,' said Miss Fowler.

This was an open-air furnace for the consumption of refuse; a little circular four-foot tower of pierced brick over an iron grating. Miss Fowler had noticed the design in a gardening journal years ago, and had had it built at the bottom of the garden. It suited her tidy soul, for it saved unsightly rubbish-heaps, and the ashes lightened the stiff clay soil.

Mary considered for a moment, saw her way clear, and nodded again. They spent the evening putting away well-remembered civilian suits, underclothes that Mary had marked, and the regiments of very gaudy socks and ties. A second trunk was needed, and, after that, a little packing-case, and it was late next day when Cheape and the local carrier lifted them to the cart. The Rector luckily knew of a friend's son, about five feet eight and a half inches high, to whom a complete Flying Corps outfit would be most acceptable, and sent his gardener's son down with a barrow to take delivery of it. The cap was hung up in Miss Fowler's bedroom, the belt in Miss Postgate's; for, as Miss Fowler said, they had no desire to make tea-party talk of them.

'That disposes of *that*,' said Miss Fowler. 'I'll leave the rest to you, Mary. I can't run up and down the garden. You'd better take the big clothes-basket and get Nellie to help you.'

'I shall take the wheel-barrow and do it myself,' said Mary, and for once in her life closed her mouth.

Miss Fowler, in moments of irritation, had called Mary deadly methodical. She put on her oldest waterproof and gardening-hat and her ever-slipping goloshes, for the weather was on the edge of more rain. She gathered fire-lighters from the kitchen, a half-scuttle of coals, and a faggot of brushwood. These she wheeled in the barrow down the mossed paths to the dank little laurel shrubbery where the destructor stood under the drip of three oaks. She climbed the wire fence into the Rector's glebe just behind, and from his tenant's rick pulled two large armfuls of good hay, which she spread neatly on the fire-bars. Next, journey by journey, passing Miss Fowler's white face at the morning-room window each time, she brought down in the towel-covered clothes-basket, on the wheelbarrow, thumbed and used Hentys, Marryats, Levers, Stevensons, Baroness Orczys, Garvices,° schoolbooks, and atlases, unrelated piles of the *Motor Cyclist*, the *Light Car*, and catalogues of Olympia Exhibitions; the remnants of a fleet of sailing-ships from nine-penny cutters to a three-guinea yacht; a prep.-school dressing-gown; bats from three-and-sixpence to twenty-four shillings; cricket and tennis balls; disintegrated steam and clockwork locomotives with their twisted rails; a grey and red tin model of a submarine; a dumb gramophone and cracked records; golf-clubs that had to be broken across the knee, like his walking-sticks, and an assegai; photographs of private and public school cricket and football elevens, and his O.T.C.° on the line of march; kodaks, and film-rolls; some pewters, and one real silver cup, for boxing competitions and Junior Hurdles; sheaves of school photographs; Miss Fowler's photograph; her own which he had borne off in fun and (good care she took not to ask!) had never returned; a playbox with a secret drawer; a load of flannels, belts, and jerseys, and a pair of spiked shoes unearthed in the attic; a packet of all the letters that Miss Fowler and she had ever written to him, kept for some absurd reason through all these years; a five-day attempt at a diary; framed pictures of racing motors in full Brooklands° career, and load upon load of undistinguishable wreckage of tool-boxes, rabbit-hutches, electric batteries, tin soldiers, fret-saw outfits, and jig-saw puzzles.

Miss Fowler at the window watched her come and go, and said to herself, 'Mary's an old woman. I never realised it before.'

After lunch she recommended her to rest.

'I'm not in the least tired,' said Mary. 'I've got it all arranged. I'm going to the village at two o'clock for some paraffin. Nellie hasn't enough, and the walk will do me good.'

She made one last quest round the house before she started, and found that she had overlooked nothing. It began to mist as soon as she had skirted Vegg's Heath, where Wynn used to descend—it seemed to her that she could almost hear the beat of his propellers overhead, but there was nothing to see. She hoisted her umbrella and lunged into the blind wet till she had reached the shelter of the empty village.

As she came out of Mr Kidd's shop with a bottle full of paraffin in her string shopping-bag, she met Nurse Eden, the village nurse, and fell into talk with her, as usual, about the village children. They were just parting opposite the 'Royal Oak,' when a gun, they fancied, was fired immediately behind the house. It was followed by a child's shriek dying into a wail.

'Accident!' said Nurse Eden promptly, and dashed through the empty bar, followed by Mary. They found Mrs Gerritt, the publican's wife, who could only gasp and point to the yard, where a little cart-lodge was sliding sideways amid a clatter of tiles. Nurse Eden snatched up a sheet drying before the fire, ran out, lifted something from the ground, and flung the sheet round it. The sheet turned scarlet and half her uniform too, as she bore the load into the kitchen. It was little Edna Gerritt, aged nine, whom Mary had known since her perambulator days.

'Am I hurted bad?' Edna asked, and died between Nurse Eden's dripping hands. The sheet fell aside and for an instant, before she could shut her eyes, Mary saw the ripped and shredded body.

'It's a wonder she spoke at all,' said Nurse Eden. 'What in God's name was it?'

'A bomb,' said Mary.

'One o' the Zeppelins?'

'No. An aeroplane. I thought I heard it on the Heath, but I fancied it was one of ours. It must have shut off its engines as it came down. That's why we didn't notice it.'

'The filthy pigs!' said Nurse Eden, all white and shaken. 'See the pickle I'm in! Go and tell Dr Hennis, Miss Postgate.' Nurse looked at the mother, who had dropped face down on the floor. 'She's only in a fit. Turn her over.'

Mary heaved Mrs Gerritt right side up, and hurried off for the doctor. When she told her tale, he asked her to sit down in the surgery till he got her something.

'But I don't need it, I assure you,' said she. 'I don't think it would be wise to tell Miss Fowler about it, do you? Her heart is so irritable in this weather.'

Dr Hennis looked at her admiringly as he packed up his bag.

'No. Don't tell anybody till we're sure,' he said, and hastened to the 'Royal Oak,' while Mary went on with the paraffin. The village behind her was as quiet as usual, for the news had not yet spread. She frowned a little to herself, her large nostrils expanded uglily, and from time to time she muttered a phrase which Wynn, who never restrained himself before his women-folk, had applied to the enemy. 'Bloody pagans! They *are* bloody pagans. But,' she continued, falling back on the teaching that had made her what she was, 'one mustn't let one's mind dwell on these things.'

Before she reached the house Dr Hennis, who was also a special constable, overtook her in his car.

'Oh, Miss Postgate,' he said. 'I wanted to tell you that that accident at the "Royal Oak" was due to Gerritt's stable tumbling down. It's been dangerous for a long time. It ought to have been condemned.'

'I thought I heard an explosion too,' said Mary.

'You might have been misled by the beams snapping. I've been looking at 'em. They were dry-rotted through and through. Of course, as they broke, they would make a noise just like a gun.'

'Yes?' said Mary politely.

'Poor little Edna was playing underneath it,' he went on, still holding her with his eyes, 'and that and the tiles cut her to pieces, you see?'

'I saw it,' said Mary, shaking her head. 'I heard it too.'

'Well, we cannot be sure.' Dr Hennis changed his tone completely. 'I know both you and Nurse Eden (I've been speaking to her) are perfectly trustworthy, and I can rely on you not to say anything—yet at least. It is no good to stir up people unless—'

'Oh, I never do—anyhow,' said Mary, and Dr Hennis went on to the county town.

After all, she told herself, it might, just possibly, have been the collapse of the old stable that had done all those things to poor little Edna. She was sorry she had even hinted at other things, but Nurse Eden was discretion itself. By the time she reached home the affair seemed increasingly remote by its very monstrosity. As she came in, Miss Fowler told her that a couple of aeroplanes had passed half an hour ago.

'I thought I heard them,' she replied. 'I'm going down to the garden now. I've got the paraffin.'

'Yes, but—what *have* you got on your boots? They're soaking wet. Change them at once.'

Not only did Mary obey but she wrapped the boots in a newspaper, and put them into the string bag with the bottle. So, armed with the longest kitchen poker, she left.

'It's raining again,' was Miss Fowler's last word, 'but—I know you won't be happy till that's disposed of.'

'It won't take long. I've got everything down there, and I've put the lid on the destructor to keep the wet out.'

The shrubbery was filling with twilight by the time she had completed her arrangements and sprinkled the sacrificial oil. As she lit the match that would burn her heart to ashes, she heard a groan or a grunt behind the dense Portugal laurels.

'Cheape?' she called impatiently, but Cheape, with his ancient lumbago, in his comfortable cottage would be the last man to profane the sanctuary. 'Sheep,' she concluded, and threw in the fusee. The pyre went up in a roar, and the immediate flame hastened night around her.

'How Wynn would have loved this!' she thought, stepping back from the blaze.

By its light she saw, half hidden behind a laurel not five paces away, a bareheaded man sitting very stiffly at the foot of one of the oaks. A broken branch lay across his lap—one booted leg protruding from beneath it. His head moved ceaselessly from side to side, but his body was as still as the tree's trunk. He was dressed—she moved sideways to look more closely—in a uniform something like Wynn's, with a flap buttoned across the chest. For an instant, she had some idea that it might be one of the young flying men she had met at the funeral. But their heads were dark and glossy. This man's was as pale as a baby's, and so closely cropped that she could see the disgusting pinky skin beneath. His lips moved.

'What do you say?' Mary moved towards him and stooped.

'Laty! Laty! Laty!' he muttered, while his hands picked at the dead wet leaves. There was no doubt as to his nationality. It made her so angry that she strode back to the destructor, though it was still too hot to use the poker there. Wynn's books seemed to be catching well. She looked up at the oak behind the man; several of the light upper and two or three rotten lower branches had broken and scattered their rubbish on the shrubbery path. On the lowest fork a helmet with dependent strings showed like a bird's-nest in the light of a long-tongued flame. Evidently this person had fallen through the tree. Wynn had told her that it was quite possible for people to fall out of aeroplanes. Wynn told her too, that trees were useful things to break an aviator's fall, but in this case the aviator must have been broken or he would have moved from his queer position. He seemed helpless except for his horrible rolling head. On the other hand, she could see a pistol case at his belt—and Mary loathed pistols. Months ago, after reading certain Belgian reports together, she and Miss Fowler had had dealings with one—a huge revolver with flat-nosed bullets, which latter, Wynn said, were forbidden by the rules of war to be used against civilised enemies. 'They're good enough for us,' Miss Fowler had replied. 'Show Mary how it works.' And Wynn, laughing at the mere possibility of any such need, had led the craven winking Mary into the Rector's disused quarry, and had shown her how to fire the terrible machine. It lay now in the top-left-hand drawer of her toilet-table—a memento not included in the burning. Wynn would be pleased to see how she was not afraid.

She slipped up to the house to get it. When she came through the rain, the eyes in the head were alive with expectation. The mouth even tried to smile. But at sight of the revolver its corners went down just like Edna Gerritt's. A tear trickled from one eye, and the head rolled from shoulder to shoulder as though trying to point out something.

'Cassée. Tout cassée,'° it whimpered.

'What do you say?' said Mary disgustedly, keeping well to one side, though only the head moved.

'Cassée,' it repeated. 'Che me rends. Le médicin!° Toctor!'

'Nein!' said she, bringing all her small German to bear with the big pistol. 'Ich haben der todt Kinder gesehn.'°

The head was still. Mary's hand dropped. She had been careful to keep her finger off the trigger for fear of accidents. After a few moments' waiting, she returned to the destructor, where the flames were falling, and churned up Wynn's charring books with the poker. Again the head groaned for the doctor.

'Stop that!' said Mary, and stamped her foot. 'Stop that, you bloody pagan!'

The words came quite smoothly and naturally. They were Wynn's own words, and Wynn was a gentleman who for no consideration on earth would have torn little Edna into those vividly coloured strips and strings. But this thing hunched under the oak-tree had done that thing. It was no question of reading horrors out of newspapers to Miss Fowler. Mary had seen it with her own eyes on the 'Royal Oak' kitchen table. She must not allow her mind to dwell upon it. Now Wynn was dead, and everything connected with him was lumping and rustling and tinkling under her busy poker into red black dust and grey leaves of ash. The thing beneath the oak would die too. Mary had seen death more than once. She came of a family that had a knack of dying under, as she told Miss Fowler, 'most distressing circumstances.' She would stay where she was till she was entirely satisfied that It was dead—dead as dear papa in the late 'eighties; aunt Mary in 'eighty-nine; mamma in 'ninety-one; cousin Dick in 'ninety-five; Lady McCausland's housemaid in 'ninety-nine; Lady McCausland's sister in nineteen hundred and one; Wynn buried five days ago; and Edna Gerritt still waiting for decent earth to hide her. As she thought—her underlip caught up by one faded canine, brows knit and nostrils wide —she wielded the poker with lunges that jarred the grating at the bottom, and careful scrapes round the brick-work above. She looked at her wrist-watch. It was getting on to half-past four, and the rain was coming down in earnest. Tea would be at five. If It did not die before that time, she would be soaked and would have to change. Meantime, and this occupied her, Wynn's things were burning well in spite of the hissing wet, though now and again a book-back with a quite distinguishable title would be heaved up out of the mass. The exercise of stoking had given her a glow which seemed to reach to the marrow of her bones. She hummed—Mary never had a voice—to herself. She had never believed in all those advanced views—though Miss Fowler herself leaned a little that way—of woman's work in the world; but now she saw there was much to be said for them. This, for instance, was *her* work—work which no man, least of all Dr Hennis, would ever have done. A man, at such a crisis, would be what Wynn called a 'sportsman'; would leave everything to fetch help, and would certainly bring It into the house. Now a woman's business was to make a happy home for—for a husband and children.° Failing these—it was not a thing one should allow one's mind to dwell upon—but—

'Stop it!' Mary cried once more across the shadows. 'Nein, I tell you! Ich haben der todt Kinder gesehn.'

But it was a fact. A woman who had missed these things could still be useful—more useful than a man in certain respects. She thumped like a pavior through the settling ashes at the secret thrill of it. The rain was damping the fire, but she could feel—it was too dark to see —that her work was done. There was a dull red glow at the bottom of the destructor, not enough to char the wooden lid if she slipped it half over against the driving wet. This arranged, she leaned on the poker and waited, while an increasing rapture laid hold on her. She ceased to think. She gave herself up to feel. Her long pleasure was broken by a sound that she had waited for in agony several times in her life. She leaned forward and listened, smiling. There could be no mistake. She closed her eyes and drank it in. Once it ceased abruptly.

'Go on,' she muttered, half aloud. 'That isn't the end.'

Then the end came very distinctly in a lull between two rain-gusts. Mary Postgate drew her breath short between her teeth and shivered from head to foot. '*That's* all right,' said she contentedly, and went up to the house, where she scandalised the whole routine by taking a luxurious hot bath before tea, and came down looking, as Miss Fowler said when she saw her lying all relaxed on the other sofa, 'quite handsome!'

The Beginnings

It was not part of their blood,
 It came to them very late
With long arrears to make good,
 When the English began to hate.

They were not easily moved,
 They were icy willing to wait
Till every count should be proved,
 Ere the English began to hate.

Their voices were even and low,
 Their eyes were level and straight.
There was neither sign nor show,
 When the English began to hate.

It was not preached to the crowd,
 It was not taught by the State.
No man spoke it aloud,
 When the English began to hate.

It was not suddenly bred,
 It will not swiftly abate,
Through the chill years ahead,
 When Time shall count from the date
 That the English began to hate.

From DEBITS AND CREDITS (1926)

Sea Constables

The Changelings

Or ever the battered liners sank
With their passengers to the dark,
I was head of a Walworth Bank,
And you were a grocer's clerk.°

I was a dealer in stocks and shares,
And you in butters and teas,
And we both abandoned our own affairs
And took to the dreadful seas.

Wet and worry about our ways—
Panic, onset, and flight—
Had us in charge for a thousand days
And a thousand-year-long night.

We saw more than the nights could hide—
More than the waves could keep—
And—certain faces over the side
Which do not go from our sleep.

We were more tired than words can tell
While the pied° craft fled by,
And the swinging mounds of the Western swell
Hoisted us Heavens-high . . .°

Now there is nothing—not even our rank—
To witness what we have been;
And I am returned to my Walworth Bank,
And you to your margarine!

Sea Constables

A tale of '15

The head-waiter of the Carvoitz° almost ran to meet Portson and his guests as they came up the steps from the palm-court where the string band plays.

'Not seen you since—oh, ever so long,' he began. '*So* glad to get your wire. Quite well—eh?'

'Fair to middling, Henri,' Portson shook hands with him. 'You're looking all right, too. Have you got us our table?'

Henri nodded towards a pink alcove, kept for mixed doubles,° which discreetly commanded the main dining-room's glitter and blaze.

'Good man!' said Portson. 'Now, this is serious, Henri. We put ourselves unreservedly in your hands. We're weather-beaten mariners—though we don't look it, and we haven't eaten a Christian meal in months. Have you thought of all that, Henri, mon ami?'

'The menu, I have composed it myself,' Henri answered with the gravity of a high priest.

It was more than a year since Portson—of Portson, Peake and Ensell, Stock and Share Brokers—had drawn Henri's attention to an apparently extinct Oil Company which, a little later, erupted profitably; and it may be that Henri prided himself on paying all debts in full.

The most recent foreign millionaire and the even more recent foreign actress at a table near the entrance clamoured for his attention while he convoyed the party to the pink alcove. With his own hands he turned out some befrilled electrics and lit four pale rose-candles.

'Bridal!' some one murmured. 'Quite bridal!'

'*So* glad you like. There is nothing too good.' Henri slid away, and the four men sat down. They had the coarse-grained complexions of men who habitually did themselves well, and an air, too, of recent, red-eyed dissipation. Maddingham, the eldest, was a thick-set middle-aged presence, with crisped grizzled hair, of the type that one associates with Board Meetings. He limped slightly. Tegg, who followed him, blinking, was neat, small, and sandy, of unmistakable Navy cut, but sheepish aspect. Winchmore, the youngest, was more on the lines of the conventional pre-war 'nut,'° but his eyes were sunk in his head and his hands black-nailed and roughened. Portson, their host, with Vandyke beard and a comfortable little stomach, beamed upon them as they settled to their oysters.

'*That's* what I mean,' said the carrying voice of the foreign actress, whom Henri had just disabused of the idea that she had been promised the pink alcove. 'They ain't *alive* to the war yet. Now, what's the matter with those four dubs yonder joining the British Army° or—or *doing* something?'

'Who's your friend?' Maddingham asked.

'I've forgotten her name for the minute,' Portson replied, 'but she's the latest thing in imported patriotic piece-goods. She sings "Sons of the Empire, Go Forward!" at the Palemseum. It makes the aunties weep.'

'That's Sidney Latter.° She's not half bad,' Tegg reached for the vinegar. 'We ought to see her some night.'

'Yes. We've a lot of time for that sort of thing,' Maddingham grunted. 'I'll take your oysters, Portson, if you don't want 'em.'

'Cheer up, Papa Maddingham! 'Soon be dead!'° Winchmore suggested.

Maddingham glared at him. 'If I'd had you with me for *one* week, Master Winchmore—'

'Not the least use,' the boy retorted. 'I've just been made a full-lootenant. I have indeed. I couldn't reconcile it with my conscience to take *Etheldreda* out any more as a plain sub.° She's too flat in the floor.'

'Did you get those new washboards of yours fixed?' Tegg cut in.

'Don't talk shop already,' Portson protested. 'This is Vesiga soup.° I don't know what he's arranged in the way of drinks.'

'Pol Roger '04,'° said the waiter.

'Sound man, Henri,' said Winchmore. 'But,' he eyed the waiter doubtfully, 'I don't quite like . . . What's your alleged nationality?'

''Henri's nephew, monsieur,' the smiling waiter replied, and laid a gloved hand on the table. It creaked corkily at the wrist. 'Bethisy-sur-Oise,'° he explained. 'My uncle he buy me *all* the hand for Christmas. It is good to hold plates only.'

'Oh! Sorry I spoke,' said Winchmore.

'Monsieur is right. But my uncle is very careful, even with neutrals.' He poured the champagne.

'Hold a minute,' Maddingham cried. 'First toast of obligation: For what we are going to receive, thank God and the British Navy.'

'Amen!' said the others with a nod toward Lieutenant Tegg, of the Royal Navy afloat, and, occasionally, of the Admiralty ashore.

'Next! "Damnation to all neutrals!"' Maddingham went on.

'Amen! Amen!' they answered between gulps that heralded the sole à la Colbert.° Maddingham picked up the menu.'Suprême of chicken,' he read loudly.° 'Filet béarnaise, Woodcock and Richebourg '74, Pêches Melba, Croûtes Baron.° I couldn't have improved on it myself; though one might,' he went on—'one *might* have substituted quail *en casserole* for the woodcock.'

'Then there would have been no reason for the Burgundy,' said Tegg with equal gravity.

'You're right,' Maddingham replied.

The foreign actress shrugged her shoulders. 'What *can* you do with people like that?' she said to her companion. 'And yet *I*'ve been singing to 'em for a fortnight.'

'I left it all to Henri,' said Portson.

'My Gord!' the eavesdropping woman whispered. 'Get on to that! Ain't it typical? They leave everything to Henri in this country.'

'By the way,' Tegg asked Winchmore after the fish, 'where did you mount that one-pounder of yours after all?'

'Midships. *Etheldreda* won't carry more weight forward. She's wet enough as it is.'

'Why don't you apply for another craft?' Portson put in. 'There's a chap at Southampton just now, down with pneumonia and—'

'No, thank you. I know *Etheldreda*. She's nothing to write home about, but when she feels well she can shift a bit.'

Maddingham leaned across the table. 'If she does more than eleven in a flat calm,' said he, 'I'll—I'll give you *Hilarity*.'

''Wouldn't be found dead in *Hilarity*,' was Winchmore's grateful reply. 'You don't mean to say you've taken her into real wet water, Papa? Where did it happen?'

The others laughed. Maddingham's red face turned brick colour, and the veins on the cheek-bones showed blue through a blurr of short bristles.

'He's been convoying neutrals—in a tactful manner,' Tegg chuckled.

Maddingham filled his glass and scowled at Tegg. 'Yes,' he said, 'and here's special damnation to me Lords of the Admiralty. A more muddle-headed set of brass-bound° apes—'

'My! My! My!' Winchmore chirruped soothingly. 'It don't seem to have done you any good, Papa. Who were you conveyancing?'°

Maddingham snapped out a ship's name and some details of her build.

'Oh, but that chap's a friend of *mine*!' cried Winchmore. 'I ran across him—the—not so long ago, hugging the Scotch coast—out of his course, he said, owing to foul weather and a new type of engine—

a Diesel.° That's him, ain't it—the complete neutral?' He mentioned an outstanding peculiarity of the ship's rig.

'Yes,' said Portson. 'Did you board him, Winchmore?'

'No. There'd been a bit of a blow the day before and old *Ethel's* only dinghy had dropped off the hooks. But he signalled me all his symptons. He was as communicative as—as a lady in the Promenade.° (Hold on, Nephew of my Uncle! I'm going to have some more of that Béarnaise fillet.) His smell attracted me. I chaperoned him for a couple of days.'

'Only two days. *You* hadn't anything to complain of,' said Maddingham wrathfully.

'I didn't complain. If he chose to hug things, 'twasn't any of my business. I'm not a Purity League. 'Didn't care what he hugged, so long as I could lie behind him and give him first chop at any mines that were going. I steered in his wake (I really *can* steer a bit now, Portson) and let him stink up the whole of the North Sea. I thought he might come in useful for bait. No Burgundy, thanks, Nephew of my Uncle. I'm sticking to the Jolly Roger.'

'Go on, then—before you're speechless. Was he any use as bait?' Tegg demanded.

'We never got a fair chance. As I told you, he hugged the coast till dark, and then he scraped round Gilarra Head° and went up the bay nearly to the beach.'

''Lights out?' Maddingham asked.

Winchmore nodded. 'But I didn't worry about that. I was under his stern. As luck 'ud have it, there was a fishing-party° in the bay, and we walked slam into the middle of 'em—a most ungodly collection of local talent. 'First thing I knew a steam-launch fell aboard us, and a boy—a nasty little Navy boy, Tegg—wanted to know what I was doing. I told him, and he cursed me for putting the fish down just as they were rising. Then the two of us (he was hanging on to my quarter with a boat-hook) drifted on to a steam trawler and our friend the Neutral and a ten-oared cutter full of the military, all mixed up. They were subs from the garrison° out for a lark. Uncle Newt explained over the rail about the weather and his engine-troubles, but they were all so keen to carry on with their fishing, they didn't fuss. They told him to clear off.'

'Was there anything on the move round Gilarra at that time?' Tegg inquired.

'Oh, they spun me the usual yarns about the water being thick with 'em, and asked me to help; but I couldn't stop. The cutter's sternsheets were piled up with mines, like lobster-pots, and from the way the soldiers handled 'em I thought I'd better get out. So did Uncle Newt. *He* didn't like it a bit. There were a couple of shots fired at something just as we cleared the Head, and one dropped rather close to him. (These duck-shoots in the dark are dam' dangerous, y'know.) He lit up at once—tail-light, head-light, and side-lights. I had no more trouble with him the rest of the night.'

'But what about the report that you sawed off the steam-launch's boat-hook?' Tegg demanded suddenly.

'What! You don't meant to say that little beast of a snotty° reported it? He was scratchin' poor old *Ethel's* paint to pieces. I never reported what he said to *me*. And he called me a damned amateur, too! Well! Well! War's war. I missed all that fishing-party that time. My orders were to follow Uncle Newt. So I followed—and poor *Ethel* without a dry rag on her.'

Winchmore refilled his glass.

'Well, don't get poetical,' said Portson. 'Let's have the rest of your trip.'

'There wasn't any rest,' Winchmore insisted pathetically. 'There was just good old *Ethel* with her engines missing like sin, and Uncle Newt thumping and stinking half a mile ahead of us, and me eating bread and Worcester sauce. I do when I feel that way.° Besides, I wanted to go back and join the fishing-party. Just before dark I made out *Cordelia*—that Southampton ketch that old Jarrott fitted with oil auxiliaries for a family cruiser last summer. She's a beamy bus,° but she *can* roll, and she was doing an honest thirty degrees each way when I overhauled her. I asked Jarrott if he was busy. He said he wasn't. But he was. He's like me and Nelson° when there's any sea on.'

'But Jarrott's a Quaker. 'Has been for generations. Why does he go to war?' said Maddingham.

'If it comes to that,' Portson said, 'why do any of us?'

'Jarrott's a mine-sweeper,' Winchmore replied with deep feeling. 'The Quaker religion (I'm not a Quaker, but I'm *much* more religious than any of you chaps give me credit for) has decided that mine-sweeping is life-saving. Consequently'—he dwelt a little on the word—'the profession is crowded with Quakers—specially off Scarborough.° 'See? Owin' to the purity of their lives, they "*all* go to Heaven when they die—Roll, Jordan, Roll!"'°

*

'Disgustin',' said the actress audibly as she drew on her gloves. Winchmore looked at her with delight. 'That's a peach-Melba, too,' he said.

'And David Jarrott's a mine-sweeper,' Maddingham mused aloud. 'So you turned our Neutral over to him, Winchmore, did you?'

'Yes, I did. It was the end of my beat—I wish I didn't feel so sleepy—and I explained the whole situation to Jarrott, over the rail. 'Gave him all my silly instructions—those latest ones, y'know. I told him to do nothing to imperil existing political relations. I told him to exercise tact. I—I told him that in my capac'ty as Actin' Lootenant, you see. Jarrott's only a Lootenant-Commander—at fifty-four, too! Yes, I handed my Uncle Newt over to Jarrott to chaperone, and I went back to my—I can say it perfectly—pis-ca-to-rial party in the bay. Now I'm going to have a nap. In ten minutes I shall be on deck again. This is my first civilised dinner in nine weeks, so I don't apologise.'

He pushed his plate away, dropped his chin on his palm and closed his eyes.

'Lyndnoch and Jarrott's Bank, established 1793,' said Maddingham half to himself. 'I've seen old Jarrott in Cowes week° bullied by his skipper and steward till he had to sneak ashore to sleep. And now he's out mine-sweeping with *Cordelia*! What's happened to his—I shall forget my own name next—Belfast-built two-hundred tonner?'

'*Goneril*,' said Portson. 'He turned her over to the Service in October. She's—she was *Culana*.'

'*She* was *Culana*, was she? My God! I never knew that. Where did it happen?'

'Off the same old Irish corner I was watching last month. My young cousin was in her; so was one of the Raikes boys. A whole nest of mines, laid between patrols.'

'I've heard there's some dirty work going on there now,' Maddingham half whispered.

'You needn't tell *me* that,' Portson returned. 'But one gets a little back now and again.'

'What are you two talking about?' said Tegg, who seemed to be dozing too.

'*Culana*,' Portson answered as he lit a cigarette.

'Yes, that was rather a pity. But . . . What about this Newt of ours?'

'*I* took her over from Jarrott next day—off Margate,' said Portson. 'Jarrott wanted to get back to his mine-sweeping.'

'Every man to his taste,' said Maddingham. 'That never appealed to me. Had they detailed you specially to look after the Newt?'

'Me among others,' Portson admitted. 'I was going down Channel when I got my orders, and so I went on with him. Jarrott had been tremendously interested in his course up to date—specially off the Wash. He'd charted it very carefully and he said he was going back to find out what some of the kinks and curves meant. Has he found out, Tegg?'

Tegg thought for a moment. '*Cordelia* was all right up to six o'clock yesterday evening,' he said.

''Glad of that. Then I did what Winchmore did. I lay behind this stout fellow and saw him well into the open.'

'Did you say anything to him?' Tegg asked.

'Not a thing. He kept moving all the time.'

''See anything?' Tegg continued.

'No. He didn't seem to be in demand anywhere in the Channel, and, when I'd got him on the edge of soundings, I dropped him—as per your esteemed orders.'

Tegg nodded again and murmured some apology.

'Where did *you* pick him up, Maddingham?' Portson went on.

Maddingham snorted.

'Well north and west of where you left him heading up the Irish Channel and stinking like a taxi. I hadn't had my breakfast. My cook was seasick; so were four of my hands.'

'I can see that meeting. Did you give him a gun across the bows?' Tegg asked.

'No, no. Not *that* time. I signalled him to heave to. He had his papers ready before I came over the side. You see,' Maddingham said pleadingly, 'I'm new to this business. Perhaps I wasn't as polite to him as I should have been if I'd had my breakfast.'

'He deposed that Maddingham came alongside swearing like a bargee,' said Tegg.

'Not in the least. This is what happened.' Maddingham turned to Portson. 'I asked him where he was bound for and he told me—Antigua.'

'Hi! Wake up, Winchmore. You're missing something.' Portson nudged Winchmore, who was slanting sideways in his chair.

'Right! All right! I'm awake,' said Winchmore stickily. 'I heard every word.'

Maddingham went on. 'I told him that this wasn't his way to Antigua—'

'Antigua. Antigua!' Winchmore finished rubbing his eyes. '"There was a young bride° of Antigua—"'

'Hsh! Hsh!' said Portson and Tegg warningly.

'Why? It's the proper one. "Who said to her spouse, 'What a pig you are!'"'

'Ass!' Maddingham growled and continued: 'He told me that he'd been knocked out of his reckoning by foul weather and engine-trouble, owing to experimenting with a new type of Diesel engine. He was perfectly frank about it.'

'So he was with me,' said Winchmore. 'Just like a real lady. I hope you were a real gentleman, Papa.'

'I asked him what he'd got. He didn't object. He had some fifty thousand gallon of oil for his new Diesel engine, and the rest was coal. He said he needed the oil to get to Antigua with, he was taking the coal as ballast, and he was coming back, so he told me, with coconuts. When he'd quite finished, I said: "What sort of damned idiot do you take me for?" He said: "I haven't decided yet!" Then I said he'd better come into port with me, and we'd arrive at a decision. He said that his papers were in perfect order and that my instructions—mine, please!—were not to imperil political relations. I hadn't received these asinine instructions, so I took the liberty of contradicting him—perfectly politely, as I told them at the Inquiry afterward. He was a small-boned man with a grey beard, in a glengarry, and he picked his teeth a lot. He said: "The last time I met you, Mister Maddingham, you were going to Carlsbad,° and you told me all about your blood-pressures in the wagon-lit before we tossed for upper berth. Don't you think you are a little old to buccaneer about the sea this way?" I couldn't recall his face—he must have been some fellow that I'd travelled with some time or other. I told him I wasn't doing this for amusement—it was business. Then I ordered him into port. He said: "S'pose I don't go?" I said: "Then I'll sink you." Isn't it extraordinary how natural it all seems after a few weeks? If any one had told me when I commissioned *Hilarity* last summer what I'd be doing this spring I'd—I'd . . . God! It *is* mad, isn't it?'

'Quite,' said Portson. 'But not bad fun.'

'Not at all, but that's what makes it all the madder. Well, he didn't argue any more. He warned me I'd be hauled over the coals for what I'd done, and I warned him to keep two cables ahead of me and not to yaw.'

'Jaw?' said Winchmore sleepily.

'No. Yaw,' Maddingham snarled. 'Not to look as if he even wanted to yaw. I warned him that, if he did, I'd loose off into him, end-on. But I was absolutely polite about it. 'Give you my word, Tegg.'

'I believe you. Oh, I believe you,' Tegg replied.

'Well, so I took him into port—and that was where I first ran across our Master Tegg. He represented the Admiralty on that beach.'

The small blinking man nodded. 'The Admiralty had that honour,' he said graciously.

Maddingham turned to the others angrily. 'I'd been rather patting myself on the back for what I'd done, you know. Instead of which, they held a court-martial—'

'*We* called it an Inquiry,' Tegg interjected.

'*You* weren't in the dock. They held a court-martial on me to find out how often I'd sworn at the poor injured Neutral, and whether I'd given him hot-water bottles and tucked him up at night. It's all very fine to laugh, but they treated me like a pickpocket. There were two fat-headed civilian judges and that blackguard Tegg in the conspiracy. A cursed lawyer defended my Neutral and he made fun of *me*. He dragged in everything the Neutral had told him about my blood-pressures on the Carlsbad trip. And that's what you get for trying to serve your country in your old age!' Maddingham emptied and refilled his glass.

'We *did* give you rather a grilling,' said Tegg placidly. 'It's the national sense of fair play.'

'I could have stood it all if it hadn't been for the Neutral. We dined at the same hotel while this court-martial was going on, and he used to come over to my table and sympathise with me! He told me that I was fighting for his ideals and the uplift of democracy, but I must respect the Law of Nations!'

'And we respected 'em,' said Tegg. 'His papers were perfectly correct; the Court discharged him. We had to consider existing political relations. I *told* Maddingham so at the hotel and he—'

Again Maddingham turned to the others. 'I couldn't make up my mind about Tegg at the Inquiry,' he explained. 'He had the air of a decent sailor-man, but he talked like a poisonous politician.'

'I was,' Tegg returned. 'I had been ordered to change into that rig. So I changed.'

Maddingham ran one fat square hand through his crisped hair and looked up under his eyebrows like a shy child, while the others lay back and laughed.

'I suppose I ought to have been on to the joke,' he stammered, 'but I'd blacked myself all over° for the part of Lootenant-Commander R.N.V.R. in time of war, and I'd given up thinking as a banker. If it had been put before me as a business proposition I might have done better.'

'I thought you were playing up to me and the judges all the time,' said Tegg. 'I never dreamed you took it seriously.'

'Well, I've been trained to look on the law as serious. I've had to pay for some of it in my time, you know.'

'I'm sorry,' said Tegg. 'We were obliged to let that oily beggar go —for reasons, but, as I told Maddingham, the night the award was given, *his* duty was to see that he was properly directed to Antigua.'

'Naturally,' Portson observed. 'That being the Neutral's declared destination. And what did Maddingham do? Shut up, Maddingham!'

Said Tegg, with downcast eyes: 'Maddingham took my hand and squeezed it; he looked lovingly into my eyes (he *did*!); he turned a plum-colour, and he said: "I will"—just like a bridegroom at the altar. It makes me feel shy to think of it even now. I didn't see him after that till the evening when *Hilarity* was pulling out of the Basin, and Maddingham was cursing the tug-master.'

'I was in a hurry,' said Maddingham. 'I wanted to get to the Narrows and wait for my Neutral there. I dropped down to Biller and Grove's yard that tide (they've done all my work for years) and I jammed *Hilarity* into the creek behind their slip,° so the Newt didn't spot me when he came down the river. Then I pulled out and followed him over the Bar. He stood nor-west at once.° I let him go till we were well out of sight of land. Then I overhauled him, gave him a gun across the bows and ran alongside. I'd just had my lunch, and I wasn't going to lose my temper *this* time. I said: "Excuse me, but I understand you are bound for Antigua?" He was, he said, and as he seemed a little nervous about my falling aboard him in that swell, I gave *Hilarity* another sheer in—she's as handy as a launch—and I said: "May I suggest that this is not the course for Antigua?" By that time he had his fenders overside, and all hands yelling at me to keep away. I snatched *Hilarity* out and began edging in again. He said: "I'm trying a sample of inferior oil that I have my doubts about. If it works all right I shall lay my course for Antigua, but it will take some time to test the stuff and adjust the engines to it." I said: "Very good, let me know if I can be of any service," and I offered him *Hilarity* again once or twice—he didn't want her—and then I dropped behind and let him go on. Wasn't that proper, Portson?'

Portson nodded. 'I know that game of yours with *Hilarity*,' he said. 'How the deuce do you do it? My nerve always goes at close quarters in any sea.'

'It's only a little trick of steering,' Maddingham replied with a simper of vanity. 'You can almost shave with her when she feels like it. I had to do it again that same evening, to establish a moral ascendancy. He wasn't showing any lights, and I nearly tripped over him. He was a scared Neutral for three minutes, but I got a little of my own back for that damned court-martial. *But* I was perfectly polite. I apologised profusely. I didn't even ask him to show his lights.'

'But did he?' said Winchmore.

'He did—every one; and a flare now and then,' Maddingham replied. 'He held north all that night, with a falling barometer and a rising wind and all the other filthy things. Gad, how I hated him! Next morning we got it, good and tight from the nor-nor-west out of the Atlantic, off Carso Head. He dodged into a squall, and then he went about. We weren't a mile behind, but it was as thick as a wall. When it cleared, and I couldn't see him ahead of me, I went about too, and followed the rain. I picked him up five miles down wind, legging it for all he was worth to the south'ard—nine knots, I should think. *Hilarity* doesn't like a following sea. We got pooped a bit, too, but by noon we'd struggled back to where we ought to have been—two cables astern of him. Then he began to signal, but his flags being end-on to us, of course, we had to creep up on his beam—well abeam—to read 'em. *That* didn't restore his morale either. He made out he'd been compelled to put back by stress of weather before completing his oil tests. I made back I was sorry to hear it, but would be greatly interested in the results. Then I turned in (I'd been up all night) and my lootenant took on. He was a widower (by the way) of the name of Sherrin, aged forty-seven. He'd run a girls' school at Weston-super-Mare after he'd left the Service in 'ninety-five, and he believed the English were the Lost Tribes."°

'What about the Germans?' said Portson.

'Oh, they'd been misled by Austria, who was the Beast with Horns in Revelations.° Otherwise he was rather a dull dog. He set the tops'ls in his watch. *Hilarity* won't steer under any canvas, so we rather sported round our friend that afternoon, I believe. When I came up after dinner, she was biting his behind, first one side, then the other. Let's see—that would be about thirty miles east-sou-east of Harry Island. We were running as near as nothing south. The wind had dropped, and there was a useful cross-rip coming up from the south-east. I took the wheel and, the way I nursed him from starboard, he had to take the sea over his port bow. I had my sciatica on me—buccaneering's no game for a middle-aged man—but I gave that fellow sprudel!° By Jove; I washed him out! He stood it as long as he could, and then he made a bolt for Harry Island. I had to ride in his pocket most of the way there because I didn't know that coast. We had charts, but Sherrin never understood 'em, and I couldn't leave the wheel. So we rubbed along together, and about midnight this Newt dodged in over the tail of Harry Shoals and anchored, if you please, in the lee of the Double Ricks. It was dead calm there, except for the swell, but there wasn't much room to manoeuvre in, and *I* wasn't going to anchor. It looked too like a submarine rendezvous. But first, I came alongside and asked him what his trouble was. He told me he had overheated his something-or-other bulb. I've never been shipmates with Diesel engines, but I took his word for it, and I said I 'ud stand by till it cooled. Then he told me to go to hell.'

'If you were inside the Double Ricks in the dark, you were practically there,' said Portson.

'That's what *I* thought. I was on the bridge, rabid with sciatica, going round and round like a circus-horse in about three acres of water, and wondering when I'd hit something. Ridiculous position. Sherrin saw it. He saved me. He said it was an ideal place for submarine attacks, and we'd better begin to repel 'em at once. As I said, I couldn't leave the wheel, so Sherrrin fought the ship—both quick-firers and the maxims.° He tipped 'em well down into the sea or well up at the Ricks as we went round and round. We made rather a row; and the row the gulls made when we woke 'em was absolutely terrifying. 'Give you my word!'

'And then?' said Winchmore.

'I kept on running in circles through this ghastly din. I took one sheer over toward his stern— I thought I'd cut it too fine, but we missed it by inches. Then I heard his capstan busy, and in another three minutes his anchor was up. He didn't wait to stow. He hustled out as he was—bulb or no bulb. He passed within ten feet of us (I was waiting to fall in behind him) and he shouted over the rail: "You think you've got patriotism. All you've got is uric acid and rotten spite!" I expect he was a little bored. I waited till we had cleared Harry Shoals before I went below, and then I slept till 9 A.M. He was heading north this time, and after I'd had breakfast and a smoke I ran alongside and asked him where he was bound for now. He was wrapped in a comforter, evidently suffering from a bad cold. I couldn't quite catch what he said, but I let him croak for a few minutes and fell back. At 9 P.M. he turned round and headed south (I was getting to know the Irish Channel by then) and I followed. There was no particular sea on.

It was a little chilly, but as he didn't hug the coast I hadn't to take the wheel. I stayed below most of the night and let Sherrin suffer. Well, Mr Newt kept up this game all the next day, dodging up and down the Irish Channel. And it was infernally dull. He threw up the sponge off Cloone Harbour. That was on Friday morning. He signalled: "Developed defects in engine-room. Antigua trip abandoned." Then he ran into Cloone and tied up at Brady's Wharf. You know you can't repair a dinghy at Cloone! I followed, of course, and berthed behind him. After lunch I thought I'd pay him a call. I wanted to look at his engines. I don't understand Diesels, but Hyslop, my engineer, said they must have gone round 'em with a hammer, for they were pretty badly smashed up. Besides that, they had offered all their oil to the Admiralty agent there, and it was being shifted to a tug when I went aboard him. So I'd done my job. I was just going back to *Hilarity* when his steward said he'd like to see me. He was lying in his cabin breathing pretty loud—wrapped up in rugs and his eyes sticking out like a rabbit's. He offered me drinks. I couldn't accept 'em, of course. Then he said: "Well, Mr Maddingham, I'm all in." I said I was glad to hear it. Then he told me he was seriously ill with a sudden attack of bronchial pneumonia, and he asked me to run him across to England to see his doctor in town. I said, of course, that was out of the question, *Hilarity* being a man-of-war in commission. He couldn't see it. He asked what had that to do with it? He thought this war was some sort of joke, and I had to repeat it all over again. He seemed rather afraid of dying (it's no game for a middle-aged man, of course) and he hoisted himself up on one elbow and began calling me a murderer. I explained to him—perfectly politely—that I wasn't in this job for fun. It was business. My orders were to see that he went to Antigua, and now that he wasn't going to Antigua, and had sold his oil to us, that finished it as far as I was concerned. (Wasn't that perfectly correct?) He said: "But that finishes me, too. I can't get any doctor in this God-forsaken hole. I made sure you'd treat me properly as soon as I surrendered." I said there wasn't any question of surrender. If he'd been a wounded belligerent, I might have taken him aboard, though I certainly shouldn't have gone a yard out of my course to land him anywhere; but as it was, he was a neutral—altogether outside the game. You see my point? I tried awfully hard to make him understand it. He went on about his affairs all being at loose ends. He was a rich man—a million and a quarter, he said—and he wanted to redraft his will before he died. I told him a good many people were in his position just now—only they weren't rich. He changed his tack then and appealed to me on the grounds of our common humanity. "Why, if you leave me now, Mr Maddingham," he said, "you condemn me to death, just as surely as if you hanged me."'

'This *is* interesting,' Portson murmured. 'I never imagined you in this light before, Maddingham.'

'I was surprised at myself—'give you my word. But I was perfectly polite. I said to him: "Try to be reasonable, sir. If you had got rid of your oil where it was wanted, you'd have condemned lots of people to death just as surely as if you'd drowned 'em." "Ah, but I didn't," he said. "That ought to count in my favour." "That was no thanks to you," I said. "You weren't given the chance. This is war, sir. If you make up your mind to that, you'll see that the rest follows." "I didn't imagine you'd take it as seriously as all that," he said—and he said it quite seriously, too. "Show a little consideration. Your side's bound to win anyway." I said: "Look here! I'm a middle-aged man, and I don't suppose my conscience is any clearer than yours in many respects, but this is business. I can do nothing for you."'

'You got that a bit mixed, I think,' said Tegg critically.

'*He* saw what I was driving at,' Maddingham replied, 'and he was the only one that mattered for the moment. "Then I'm a dead man, Mr Maddingham," he said. "That's *your* business," I said. "Good afternoon." And I went out.'

'And?' said Winchmore, after some silence.

'He died. I saw his flag half-masted next morning.'

There was another silence. Henri looked in at the alcove and smiled. Maddingham beckoned to him.

'But why didn't you lend him a hand to settle his private affairs?' said Portson.

'Because I wasn't acting in my private capacity. I'd been on the bridge for three nights and—' Maddingham pulled out his watch—'this time to-morrow I shall be there again—confound it! Has my car come, Henri?'

'Yes, Sare Francis. I am sorry.' They all complimented Henri on the dinner, and when the compliments were paid he expressed himself still their debtor. So did the nephew.

'Are you coming with me, Portson?' said Maddingham as he rose heavily.

'No. I'm for Southampton, worse luck! My car ought to be here, too.'

'I'm for Euston and the frigid calculating North,' said Winchmore with a shudder. 'One common taxi, please, Henri.'

Tegg smiled. 'I'm supposed to sleep in just now, but if you don't mind, I'd like to come with you as far as Gravesend, Maddingham.'

'Delighted. There's a glass all round left still,' said Maddingham. 'Here's luck! The usual, I suppose? "Damnation to all neutrals!"'

The Vineyard

At the eleventh hour he came,[°]
But his wages were the same
As ours who all day long had trod
The wine-press of the Wrath of God.[°]

When he shouldered through the lines
Of our cropped and mangled vines,
His unjaded eye could scan
How each hour had marked its man.

(Children of the morning-tide
With the hosts of noon had died;
And our noon contingents lay
Dead with twilight's spent array.)

Since his back had felt no load
Virtue still in him abode;
So he swiftly made his own
Those last spoils we had not won.

We went home, delivered thence,
Grudging him no recompense
Till he portioned praise or blame
To our works before he came.

Till he showed us for our good—
Deaf to mirth, and blind to scorn—
How we might have best withstood
Burdens that he had not borne!

The Bull that Thought

Westward from a town by the Mouths of the Rhône, runs a road° so mathematically straight, so barometrically level, that it ranks among the world's measured miles and motorists use it for records.

I had attacked the distance several times, but always with a Mistral blowing, or the unchancy cattle of those parts on the move. But once, running from the East, into a high-piled, almost Egyptian, sunset, there came a night which it would have been sin to have wasted. It was warm with the breath of summer in advance; moonlit till the shadow of every rounded pebble and pointed cypress wind-break lay solid on that vast flat-floored waste; and my Mr Leggatt,° who had slipped out to make sure, reported that the road-surface was unblemished.

'*Now*,' he suggested, 'we might see what she'll do under strict road-conditions. She's been pullin' like the Blue de Luxe° all day. Unless I'm all off, it's her night out.'

We arranged the trial for after dinner—thirty kilometres as near as might be; and twenty-two of them without even a level crossing.

There sat beside me at table d'hôte an elderly, bearded Frenchman wearing the rosette of by no means the lowest grade of the Legion of Honour, who had arrived in a talkative Citroën. I gathered that he had spent much of his life in the French Colonial Service in Annam and Tonquin.° When the War came, his years barring him from the front line, he had supervised Chinese woodcutters° who, with axe and dynamite, deforested the centre of France for trench-props. He said my chauffeur had told him that I contemplated an experiment. He was interested in cars—had admired mine—would, in short, be greatly indebted to me if I permitted him to assist as an observer.° One could not well refuse; and, knowing my Mr Leggatt, it occurred to me there might also be a bet in the background.

While we went to get his coat, I asked the proprietor his name. 'Voiron—Monsieur André Voiron,' was the reply. 'And his business?' 'Mon Dieu! He is Voiron! He is all those things, there!' The proprietor waved his hands at brilliant advertisements on the dining-room walls, which declared that Voiron Frères dealt in wines, agricultural implements, chemical manures, provisions and produce throughout that part of the globe.

He said little for the first five minutes of our trip, and nothing at all for the next ten—it being, as Leggatt had guessed, Esmeralda's night out. But, when her indicator climbed to a certain figure° and held there for three blinding kilometres, he expressed himself satisfied, and proposed to me that we should celebrate the event at the hotel. 'I keep yonder,' said he, 'a wine on which I should value your opinion.'

On our return, he disappeared for a few minutes, and I heard him rumbling in a cellar. The proprietor presently invited me to the dining-room, where, beneath one frugal light, a table had been set with local dishes of renown. There was, too, a bottle beyond most known sizes, marked black on red, with a date. Monsieur Voiron opened it, and we drank to the health of my car. The velvety, perfumed liquor, between fawn and topaz, neither too sweet nor too dry, creamed in its generous glass. But I knew no wine composed of the whispers of angels' wings, the breath of Eden and the foam and pulse of Youth renewed. So I asked what it might be.

'It is champagne,' he said gravely.

'Then what have I been drinking all my life?'

'If you were lucky, before the War, and paid thirty shillings a bottle, it is possible you may have drunk one of our better-class *tisanes*.'°

'And where does one get this?'

'Here, I am happy to say. Elsewhere, perhaps, it is not so easy. We growers exchange these real wines among ourselves.'

I bowed my head in admiration, surrender, and joy. There stood the most ample bottle, and it was not yet eleven o'clock. Doors locked and shutters banged throughout the establishment. Some last servant yawned on his way to bed. Monsieur Voiron opened a window and the moonlight flooded in from a small pebbled court outside. One could almost hear the town of Chambres breathing in its first sleep. Presently, there was a thick noise in the air, the passing of feet and hooves, lowings, and a stifled bark or two. Dust rose over the courtyard wall, followed by the strong smell of cattle.

'They are moving some beasts,' said Monsieur Voiron, cocking an ear. 'Mine, I think. Yes, I hear Christophe. Our beasts do not like automobiles—so we move at night. You do not know our country—the Crau, here, or the Camargue? I was—I am now, again—of it. All France is good; but this is the best.' He spoke, as only a Frenchman can, of his own loved part of his own lovely land.

'For myself, if I were not so involved in all these affairs'—he pointed to the advertisements—'I would live on our farm with my cattle, and worship them like a Hindu. You know our cattle of the Camargue, Monsieur? No? It is not an acquaintance to rush upon lightly. There are no beasts like them. They have a mentality superior to that of others. They graze and they ruminate, by choice, facing our Mistral, which is more than some automobiles will do. Also they have in them the potentiality of thought—and when cattle think—I have seen what arrives.'

'Are they so clever as all that?' I asked idly.

'Monsieur, when your sportif° chauffeur camouflaged your limousine so that she resembled one of your Army lorries, I would not believe her capacities. I bet him—ah—two to one—she would not touch ninety kilometres. It was proved that she could. I can give you no proof, but will you believe me if I tell you what a beast who thinks can achieve?'

'After the War,' said I spaciously, 'everything is credible.'

'That is true! Everything inconceivable has happened; but still we learn nothing and we believe nothing. When I was a child in my father's house°—before I became a Colonial Administrator—my interest and my affection were among our cattle. We of the old rock° live here—have you seen?—in big farms like castles. Indeed, some of them may have been Saracenic. The barns group round them—great white-walled barns, and yards solid as our houses. One gate shuts all. It is a world apart; an administration of all that concerns beasts. It was there I learned something about cattle. You see, they are our playthings in the Camargue and the Crau. The boy measures his strength against the calf that butts him in play among the manure-heaps. He moves in and out among the cows, who are—not so amiable. He rides with the herdsmen in the open to shift the herds. Sooner or later, he meets as bulls the little calves that knocked him over. So it was with me—till it became necessary that I should go to our Colonies.' He laughed. 'Very necessary. That is a good time in youth, Monsieur, when one does these things which shock our parents. Why is it always Papa who is so shocked and has never heard of such things—and Mamma who supplies the excuses? . . . And when my brother—my elder who stayed and created the business—begged me to return and help him, I resigned my Colonial career gladly enough. I returned to our own lands, and my well-loved, wicked white and yellow cattle of the Camargue and the Crau. My Faith, I could talk of them all night, for this stuff unlocks the heart, without making repentance in the morning. . . . Yes! It was after the War that this happened. There was a calf, among Heaven knows how many of ours—a bull-calf—an infant indistinguishable from his companions. He was sick, and he had been taken up with his mother in the big farmyard at home with us. Naturally the children of our herdsmen practised on him from the first. It is in their blood. The Spaniards make a cult of bull-fighting. Our little devils down here bait bulls as automatically as the English child kicks or throws balls. This calf would chase them with his eyes open, like a cow when she hunts a man. They would take refuge behind our tractors and wine-carts in the centre of the yard: he would chase them in and out as a dog hunts rats. More than that, he would study their psychology, his eyes in their eyes. Yes, he watched their faces to divine which way they would run. He himself, also, would pretend sometimes to charge directly at a boy. Then he would wheel right or left—one could never tell—and knock over some child pressed against a wall who thought himself safe. After this, he would stand over him, knowing that his companions must come to his aid; and when they were all together, waving their jackets across his eyes and pulling his tail, he would scatter them—how he would scatter them! He could kick, too, sideways like a cow. He knew his ranges as well as our gunners, and he was as quick on his feet as our Carpentier.° I observed him often. Christophe—the man who passed just now—our chief herdsman, who had taught me to ride with our beasts when I was ten—Christophe told me that he was descended from a yellow cow of those days that had chased us once into the marshes. "He kicks just like her," said Christophe. "He can side-kick as he jumps. Have you seen, too, that he is not deceived by the jacket when a boy waves it? He uses it to find the boy. They think they are feeling him. He is feeling them always. He thinks, that one." I had come to the same conclusion. Yes—the creature was a thinker along the lines necessary to his sport; and he was a humorist also, like so many natural murderers. One knows the type among beasts as well as among men. It possesses a curious truculent mirth—almost indecent but infallibly significant—'

Monsieur Voiron replenished our glasses with the great wine that went better at each descent.

'They kept him for some time in the yards to practise upon. Naturally he became a little brutal; so Christophe turned him out to learn manners among his equals in the grazing lands, where the Camargue joins the Crau. How old was he then? About eight or nine months, I think. We met again a few months later—he and I. I was riding one of our little half-wild horses, along a road of the Crau, when I found myself almost unseated. It was he! He had hidden himself behind a wind-break till we passed, and had then charged my horse from behind. Yes, he had deceived even my little horse! But I recognised him. I gave him the whip across the nose, and I said:

"Apis,° for this thou goest to Arles!° It was unworthy of thee, between us two." But that creature had no shame. He went away laughing, like an Apache.° If he had dismounted me, I do not think it is I who would have laughed—yearling as he was.'

'Why did you want to send him to Arles?' I asked.

'For the bull-ring. When your charming tourists leave us, we institute our little amusements there. Not a real bull-fight, you understand, but young bulls with padded horns, and our boys from hereabouts and in the city go to play with them. Naturally, before we send them we try them in our yards at home. So we brought up Apis from his pastures. He knew at once that he was among the friends of his youth—he almost shook hands with them—and he submitted like an angel to padding his horns. He investigated the carts and tractors in the yards, to choose his lines of defence and attack. And then—he attacked with an élan, and he defended with a tenacity and forethought that delighted us. In truth, we were so pleased that I fear we trespassed upon his patience. We desired him to repeat himself, which no true artist will tolerate. But he gave us fair warning. He went out to the centre of the yard, where there was some dry earth; he kneeled down and—you have seen a calf whose horns fret him thrusting and rooting into a bank? He did just that, very deliberately, till he had rubbed the pads off his horns. Then he rose, dancing on those wonderful feet that twinkled, and he said: "Now, my friends, the buttons are off the foils. Who begins?" We understood. We finished at once. He was turned out again on the pastures till it should be time to amuse them at our little metropolis. But, some time before he went to Arles—yes, I think I have it correctly—Christophe, who had been out on the Crau, informed me that Apis had assassinated a young bull who had given signs of developing into a rival. That happens, of course, and our herdsmen should prevent it. But Apis had killed in his own style—at dusk, from the ambush of a wind-break—by an oblique charge from behind which knocked the other over. He had then disembowelled him. All very possible, *but*—the murder accomplished—Apis went to the bank of a wind-break, knelt, and carefully, as he had in our yard, cleaned his horns in the earth. Christophe, who had never seen such a thing, at once borrowed (do you know, it is most efficacious when taken that way?) some Holy Water from our little chapel in those pastures, sprinkled Apis (whom it did not affect), and rode in to tell me. It was obvious that a thinker of that bull's type would also be meticulous in his toilette; so, when he was sent to Arles, I warned our consignees to exercise caution with him. Happily, the change of scene, the music, the general attention, and the meeting again with old friends—all our bad boys attended—agreeably distracted him. He became for the time a pure *farceur*° again; but his wheelings, his rushes, his rat-huntings were more superb than ever. There was in them now, you understand, a breadth of technique that comes of reasoned art, and, above all, the passion that arrives after experience. Oh, he had learned, out there on the Crau! At the end of his little turn, he was, according to local rules, to be handled in all respects except for the sword, which was a stick, as a professional bull who must die. He was manœuvred into, or he posed himself in, the proper attitude; made his rush; received the point on his shoulder and then —turned about and cantered toward the door by which he had entered the arena. He said to the world: "My friends, the representation is ended. I thank you for your applause. I go to repose myself." But our Arlesians, who are—not so clever as some, demanded an encore, and Apis was headed back again. We others from his country, we knew what would happen. He went to the centre of the ring, kneeled, and, slowly, with full parade, plunged his horns alternately in the dirt till the pads came off. Christophe shouts: "Leave him alone, you straight-nosed imbeciles! Leave him before you must." But they required emotion; for Rome has always debauched her loved Provincia with bread and circuses.° It was given. Have you, Monsieur, ever seen a servant, with pan and broom, sweeping round the base-board of a room? In a half-minute Apis has them all swept out and over the barrier. Then he demands once more that the door shall be opened to him. It is opened and he retires as though—which, truly, is the case —loaded with laurels.'

Monsieur Voiron refilled the glasses, and allowed himself a cigarette, which he puffed for some time.

'And afterwards?' I said.

'I am arranging it in my mind. It is difficult to do it justice. Afterwards—yes, afterwards—Apis returned to his pastures and his mistresses and I to my business. I am no longer a scandalous old "sportif" in shirt-sleeves howling encouragement to the yellow son of a cow. I revert to Voiron Frères—wines, chemical manures, *et cetera*. And next year, through some chicane which I have not the leisure to unravel, and also, thanks to our patriarchal system of paying our older men out of the increase of the herds, old Christophe possesses himself of Apis. Oh, yes, he proves it through descent from a certain cow that my father had given his father before the Republic.° Beware, Monsieur, of the memory of the illiterate man! An ancestor of Christophe had been a soldier under our Soult against your Beresford,° near Bayonne. He fell into the hands of Spanish guerrillas. Christophe and his wife used to tell me the details on certain Saints' Days when I was a child. Now, as compared with our recent war, Soult's campaign and retreat across the Bidassoa—'

'But did you allow Christophe just to annex the bull?' I demanded.

'You do not know Christophe. He had sold him to the Spaniards before he informed me. The Spaniards pay in coin—douros of very pure silver. Our peasants mistrust our paper. You know the saying: "A thousand francs paper; eight hundred metal, and the cow is yours." Yes, Christophe sold Apis, who was then two and a half years old, and to Christophe's knowledge thrice at least an assassin.'

'How was that?' I said.

'Oh, his own kind only; and always, Christophe told me, by the same oblique rush from behind, the same sideways overthrow, and the same swift disembowelment, followed by this levitical° cleaning of the horns. In human life he would have kept a manicurist—this Minotaur.° And so, Apis disappears from our country. That does not trouble me. I know in due time I shall be advised. Why? Because, in this land, Monsieur, not a hoof moves between Berre and the Saintes Maries° without the knowledge of specialists such as Christophe. The beasts are the substance and the drama of their lives to them. So when Christophe tells me, a little before Easter Sunday, that Apis makes his début in the bull-ring of a small Catalan town on the road to Barcelona, it is only to pack my car and trundle there across the frontier with him. The place lacked importance and manufactures, but it had produced a matador of some reputation, who was condescending to show his art in his native town. They were even running one special train to the place. Now our French railway system is only execrable, but the Spanish—'

'You went down by road, didn't you?' said I.

'Naturally. It was not too good. Villamarti was the matador's name. He proposed to kill two bulls for the honour of his birthplace. Apis, Christophe told me, would be his second. It was an interesting trip, and that little city by the sea was ravishing. Their bull-ring dates from the middle of the seventeenth century. It is full of feeling. The ceremonial too—when the horsemen enter and ask the Mayor in his box to throw down the keys of the bull-ring—that was exquisitely conceived. You know, if the keys are caught in the horseman's hat, it is considered a good omen. They were perfectly caught. Our seats were in the front row beside the gates where the bulls enter, so we saw everything.

'Villamarti's first bull was not too badly killed. The second matador, whose name escapes me, killed his without distinction—a foil to Villamarti. And the third, Chisto, a laborious, middle-aged professional who had never risen beyond a certain dull competence, was equally of the background. Oh, they are as jealous as the girls of the Comédie Française,° these matadors! Villamarti's troupe stood ready for his second bull. The gates opened, and we saw Apis, beautifully balanced on his feet, peer coquettishly round the corner, as though he were at home. A picador—a mounted man with the long lance-goad—stood near the barrier on his right. He had not even troubled to turn his horse, for the capeadors—the men with the cloaks—were advancing to play Apis—to feel his psychology and intentions, according to the rules that are made for bulls who do not think. . . . I did not realise the murder before it was accomplished! The wheel, the rush, the oblique charge from behind, the fall of horse and man were simultaneous. Apis leaped the horse, with whom he had no quarrel, and alighted, all four feet together (it was enough), between the man's shoulders, changed his beautiful feet on the carcass, and was away, pretending to fall nearly on his nose. Do you follow me? In that instant, by that stumble, he produced the impression that his adorable assassination was a mere bestial blunder. Then, Monsieur, I began to comprehend that it was an artist we had to deal with. He did not stand over the body to draw the rest of the troupe. He chose to reserve that trick. He let the attendants bear out the dead, and went on to amuse himself among the capeadors. Now to Apis, trained among our children in the yards, the cloak was simply a guide to the boy behind it. He pursued, you understand, the person, not the propaganda—the proprietor, not the journal. If a third of our electors of France were as wise, my friend! . . . But it was done leisurely, with humour and a touch of truculence. He romped after one man's cloak as a clumsy dog might do, but I observed that he kept the man on his terrible left side. Christophe whispered to me: "Wait for his mother's kick. When he has made the fellow confident it will arrive." It arrived in the middle of a gambol. My God! He lashed out in the air as he frisked. The man dropped like a sack, lifted one hand a little towards his head, and—that was all. So you see, a body was again at his disposition; a second time, Apis refused his grand scene. A second time he acted that his murder was accident and—he convinced his audience! It was as though he had knocked over a bridge-gate in the marshes by mistake. Unbelievable? I saw it.'

The memory sent Monsieur Voiron again to the champagne, and I accompanied him.

'But Apis was not the sole artist present. They say Villamarti comes of a family of actors. I saw him regard Apis with a new eye. He, too, began to understand. He took his cloak and moved out to play him before they should bring on another picador. He had his reputation. Perhaps Apis knew it. Perhaps Villamarti reminded him of some boy with whom he has practised at home. At any rate Apis permitted it—up to a certain point; but he did not allow Villamarti the stage. He cramped him throughout. He dived and plunged clumsily and slowly, but always with menace and always closing in. We could see that the man was conforming to the bull—not the bull to the man; for Apis was playing him towards the centre of the ring, and, in a little while—I watched his face—Villamarti knew it. But I could not fathom the creature's motive. "Wait," said old Christophe. "He wants that picador on the white horse yonder. When he reaches his proper distance he will get him. Villamarti is his cover. He used me once that way." And so it was, my friend! With the clang of one of our own Seventy-fives,° Apis dismissed Villamarti with his chest—breasted him over—and had arrived at his objective near the barrier. The same oblique charge; the head carried low for the sweep of the horns; the immense sideways fall of the horse, broken-legged and half-paralysed; the senseless man on the ground, and—behold Apis between them, backed against the barrier—his right covered by the horse; his left by the body of the man at his feet. The simplicity of it! Lacking the carts and tractors of his early parade-grounds he, being a genius, had extemporised with the materials at hand, and dug himself in. The troupe closed up again, their left wing broken by the kicking horse, their right immobilised by the man's body which Apis bestrode with significance. Villamarti almost threw himself between the horns, but—it was more an appeal than an attack. Apis refused him. He held his base. A picador was sent at him—necessarily from the front, which alone was open. Apis charged—he who, till then, you realise, had not used the horn! The horse went over backwards, the man half beneath him. Apis halted, hooked him under the heart, and threw him to the barrier. We heard his head crack, but he was dead before he hit the wood. There was no demonstration from the audience. They, also, had begun to realise this Foch° among bulls! The arena occupied itself again with the dead. Two of the troupe irresolutely tried to play him—God knows in what hope!—but he moved out to the centre of the ring. "Look!" said Christophe. "Now he goes to clean himself. That always frightened me." He knelt down; he began to clean his horns. The earth was hard. He worried at it in an ecstasy of absorption. As he laid his head along and rattled his ears, it was as though he were interrogating the Devils themselves upon their secrets, and always saying impatiently: "Yes, I know that—and *that*—and *that*! Tell me more—*more*!" In the silence that covered us, a woman cried: "He digs a grave! Oh, Saints, he digs a grave!" Some others echoed this—not loudly—as a wave echoes in a grotto of the sea.

'And when his horns were cleaned, he rose up and studied poor Villamarti's troupe, eyes in eyes, one by one, with the gravity of an equal in intellect and the remote and merciless resolution of a master in his art. This was more terrifying than his toilette.'

'And they—Villamarti's men?' I asked.

'Like the audience, were dominated. They had ceased to posture, or stamp, or address insults to him. They conformed to him. The two other matadors stared. Only Chisto, the oldest, broke silence with some call or other, and Apis turned his head towards him. Otherwise he was isolated, immobile—sombre—meditating on those at his mercy. Ah!

'For some reason the trumpet sounded for the *banderillas*—those gay hooked darts that are planted in the shoulders of bulls who do not think, after their neck-muscles are tired by lifting horses. When such bulls feel the pain, they check for an instant, and, in that instant, the men step gracefully aside. Villamarti's banderillero answered the trumpet mechanically—like one condemned. He stood out, poised the darts and stammered the usual patter of invitation. . . . And after? I do not assert that Apis shrugged his shoulders, but he reduced the episode to its lowest elements, as could only a bull of Gaul. With his truculence was mingled always—owing to the shortness of his tail—a certain Rabelaisian abandon, especially when viewed from the rear. Christophe had often commented upon it. Now, Apis brought that quality into play. He circulated round that boy, forcing him to break up his beautiful poses. He studied him from various angles, like an incompetent photographer. He presented to him every portion of his anatomy except his shoulders. At intervals he feigned to run in upon him. My God, he was cruel! But his motive was obvious. He was playing for a laugh from the spectators which should synchronise with the fracture of the human morale. It was achieved. The boy turned and ran towards the barrier. Apis was on him before the laugh ceased;

passed him; headed him—what do I say?—herded him off to the left, his horns beside and a little in front of his chest: he did not intend him to escape into a refuge. Some of the troupe would have closed in, but Villamarti cried: "If he wants him he will take him. Stand!" They stood. Whether the boy slipped or Apis nosed him over I could not see. But he dropped, sobbing. Apis halted like a car with four brakes, struck a pose, smelt him very completely and turned away. It was dismissal more ignominious than degradation at the head of one's battalion. The representation was finished. Remained only for Apis to clear his stage of the subordinate characters.

'Ah! His gesture then! He gave a dramatic start—this Cyrano° of the Camargue—as though he was aware of them for the first time. He moved. All their beautiful breeches twinkled for an instant along the top of the barrier. He held the stage alone! But Christophe and I, we trembled! For, observe, he had now involved himself in a stupendous drama of which he only could supply the third act. And, except for an audience on the razor-edge of emotion, he had exhausted his material. Molière° himself—we have forgotten, my friend, to drink to the health of that great soul—might have been at a loss. And Tragedy is but a step behind Failure. We could see the four or five Civil Guards, who are sent always to keep order, fingering the breeches of their rifles. They were but waiting a word from the Mayor to fire on him, as they do sometimes at a bull who leaps the barrier among the spectators. They would, of course, have killed or wounded several people—but that would not have saved Apis.'

Monsieur Voiron drowned the thought at once, and wiped his beard.

'At that moment Fate—the Genius of France, if you will—sent to assist in the incomparable finale, none other than Chisto, the eldest, and I should have said (but never again will I judge!) the least inspired of all; mediocrity itself but, at heart—and it is the heart that conquers always, my friend—at heart an artist. He descended stiffly into the arena, alone and assured. Apis regarded him, his eyes in his eyes. The man took stance, with his cloak, and called to the bull as to an equal: "Now, Señor, we will show these honourable caballeros° something together." He advanced thus against this thinker who at a plunge—a kick—a thrust—could, we all knew, have extinguished him. My dear friend, I wish I could convey to you something of the unaffected bonhomie, the humour, the delicacy, the consideration bordering on respect even, with which Apis, the supreme artist, responded to this invitation. It was the Master, wearied after a strenuous hour in the atelier, unbuttoned and at ease with some not inexpert but limited disciple. The telepathy was instantaneous between them. And for good reason! Christophe said to me: "All's well. That Chisto began among the bulls. I was sure of it when I heard him call just now. He has been a herdsman. He'll pull it off." There was a little feeling and adjustment, at first, for mutual distances and allowances.

'Oh, yes! And here occurred a gross impertinence of Villamarti. He had, after an interval, followed Chisto—to retrieve his reputation. My Faith! I can conceive the elder Dumas° slamming his door on an intruder precisely as Apis did. He raced Villamarti into the nearest refuge at once. He stamped his feet outside it, and he snorted: "Go! I am engaged with an artist." Villamarti went—his reputation left behind for ever.

'Apis returned to Chisto saying: "Forgive the interruption. I am not always master of my time, but you were about to observe, my dear confrère° . . . ?" Then the play began. Out of compliment to Chisto, Apis chose as his objective (every bull varies in this respect) the inner edge of the cloak—that nearest to the man's body. This allows but a few millimetres clearance in charging. But Apis trusted himself as Chisto trusted him, and, this time, he conformed to the man, with inimitable judgment and temper. He allowed himself to be played into the shadow or the sun, as the delighted audience demanded. He raged enormously; he feigned defeat; he despaired in statuesque abandon, and thence flashed into fresh paroxysms of wrath—but always with the detachment of the true artist who knows he is but the vessel of an emotion whence others, not he, must drink. And never once did he forget that honest Chisto's cloak was to him the gauge by which to spare even a hair on the skin. He inspired Chisto too. My God! His youth returned to that meritorious beef-sticker—the desire, the grace, and the beauty of his early dreams. One could almost see that girl of the past for whom he was rising, rising to these present heights of skill and daring. It was his hour too—a miraculous hour of dawn returned to gild the sunset. All he knew was at Apis' disposition. Apis acknowledged it with all that he had learned at home, at Arles and in his lonely murders on our grazing-grounds. He flowed round Chisto like a river of death—round his knees, leaping at his shoulders, kicking just clear of one side or the other of his head; behind his back hissing as he shaved by; and once or twice—inimitable!—he reared wholly up before him while Chisto slipped back from beneath the avalanche of that instructed body. Those two, my dear friend, held five thousand people dumb with no sound but of their breathings—regular as pumps. It was unbearable. Beast and man realised together that we needed a change of note—a *détente*. They relaxed to pure buffoonery. Chisto fell back and talked to him outrageously. Apis pretended he had never heard such language. The audience howled with delight. Chisto slapped him; he took liberties with his short tail, to the end of which he clung while Apis pirouetted; he played about him in all postures; he had become the herdsman again—gross, careless, brutal, but comprehending. Yet Apis was always the more consummate clown. All that time (Christophe and I saw it) Apis drew off towards the gates of the *toril*° where so many bulls enter but—have you ever heard of one that returned?° *We* knew that Apis knew that as he had saved Chisto, so Chisto would save him. Life is sweet to us all; to the artist who lives many lives in one, sweetest. Chisto did not fail him. At the last, when none could laugh any longer, the man threw his cape across the bull's back, his arm round his neck. He flung up a hand at the gate, as Villamarti, young and commanding but *not* a herdsman, might have raised it, and he cried: "Gentlemen, open to me and my honourable little donkey." They opened—I have misjudged Spaniards in my time!—those gates opened to the man and the bull together, and closed behind them. And then? From the Mayor to the Guardia Civil they went mad for five minutes, till the trumpets blew and the fifth bull rushed out—an unthinking black Andalusian. I suppose some one killed him. My friend, my very dear friend, to whom I have opened my heart, I confess that I did not watch. Christophe and I, we were weeping together like children of the same Mother.° Shall we drink to Her?'

Alnaschar and the Oxen

There's a pasture in a valley where the hanging woods divide,
 And a Herd lies down and ruminates in peace;
Where the pheasant rules the nooning, and the owl the twilight tide,
 And the war-cries of our world die out and cease.
Here I cast aside the burden that each weary week-day brings
 And, delivered from the shadows I pursue,
On peaceful, postless Sabbaths I consider Weighty Things—
 Such as Sussex Cattle feeding in the dew!

At the gate beside the river where the trouty shallows brawl,
 I know the pride that Lobengula felt,°
When he bade the bars be lowered of the Royal Cattle Kraal,
 And fifteen mile of oxen took the veldt.

From the walls of Bulawayo in unbroken file they came°
  To where the Mount of Council cuts the blue . . .
I have only six and twenty, but the principle's the same
  With my Sussex Cattle feeding in the dew!

To a luscious sound of tearing, where the clovered herbage rips,
  Level-backed and level-bellied watch 'em move—
See those shoulders, guess that heart-girth, praise those loins, admire those hips,
  And the tail set low for flesh to make above!
Count the broad unblemished muzzles, test the kindly mellow skin
  And, where yon heifer lits her head at call,
Mark the bosom's just abundance 'neath the gay and clean-cut chin,
  And those eyes of Juno, overlooking all!°

Here is colour, form and substance! I will put it to the proof
  And, next season, in my lodges shall be born
Some very Bull of Mithras, flawless from his agate hoof°
  To his even-branching, ivory, dusk-tipped horn.
He shall mate with block-square virgins—kings shall seek his like in vain,
  While I multiply his stock a thousandfold,
Till an hungry world extol me, builder of a lofty strain
  That turns one standard ton at two years old!

There's a valley, under oakwood, where a man may dream his dream,
  In the milky breath of cattle laid at ease,
Till the moon o'ertops the alders, and her image chills the stream,
  And the river-mist runs silver round their knees!
Now the footpaths fade and vanish; now the ferny clumps deceive;
  Now the hedgerow-folk possess their fields anew;
Now the Herd is lost in darkness, and I bless them as I leave,
  My Sussex Cattle feeding in the dew!

The Gardener

One grave to me was given,
 One watch till Judgment Day;
And God looked down from Heaven
 And rolled the stone away.

One day in all the years,
 One hour in that one day,
His Angel saw my tears,
 And rolled the stone away!°

Every one in the village knew that Helen Turrell did her duty by all her world, and by none more honourably than by her only brother's unfortunate child. The village knew, too, that George Turrell had tried his family severely since early youth, and were not surprised to be told that, after many fresh starts given and thrown away, he, an Inspector of Indian Police, had entangled himself with the daughter of a retired non-commissioned officer, and had died of a fall from a horse a few weeks before his child was born. Mercifully, George's father and mother were both dead, and though Helen, thirty-five and independent, might well have washed her hands of the whole disgraceful affair, she most nobly took charge, though she was, at the time, under threat of lung trouble which had driven her to the South of France. She arranged for the passage of the child and a nurse from Bombay, met them at Marseilles, nursed the baby through an attack of infantile dysentery due to the carelessness of the nurse, whom she had had to dismiss, and at last, thin and worn but triumphant, brought the boy late in the autumn, wholly restored, to her Hampshire home.

All these details were public property, for Helen was as open as the day, and held that scandals are only increased by hushing them up. She admitted that George had always been rather a black sheep, but things might have been much worse if the mother had insisted on her right to keep the boy. Luckily, it seemed that people of that class would do almost anything for money, and, as George had always turned to her in his scrapes, she felt herself justified—her friends agreed with her—in cutting the whole non-commissioned officer connection, and giving the child every advantage. A christening, by the Rector, under the name of Michael, was the first step. So far as she knew herself, she was not, she said, a child-lover, but, for all his faults, she had been very fond of George, and she pointed out that little Michael had his father's mouth to a line; which made something to build upon.

As a matter of fact, it was the Turrell forehead, broad, low, and well-shaped, with the widely spaced eyes beneath it, that Michael had most faithfully reproduced. His mouth was somewhat better cut than the family type. But Helen, who would concede nothing good to his mother's side, vowed he was a Turrell all over, and, there being no one to contradict, the likeness was established.

In a few years Michael took his place, as accepted as Helen had always been—fearless, philosophical, and fairly good-looking. At six, he wished to know why he could not call her 'Mummy,' as other boys called their mothers. She explained that she was only his auntie, and that aunties were not quite the same as mummies, but that, if it gave him pleasure, he might call her 'Mummy' at bedtime, for a pet-name between themselves.

Michael kept his secret most loyally, but Helen, as usual, explained the fact to her friends; which when Michael heard, he raged.

'Why did you tell? *Why* did you tell?' came at the end of the storm.

'Because it's always best to tell the truth,' Helen answered, her arm round him as he shook in his cot.

'All right, but when the troof's ugly I don't think it's nice.'

'Don't you dear?'

'No, I don't, and'—she felt the small body stiffen—'now you've told, I won't call you "Mummy" any more—not even at bedtimes.'

'But isn't that rather unkind?' said Helen softly.

'I don't care! I don't care! You've hurted me in my insides and I'll hurt you back. I'll hurt you as long as I live!'

'Don't, oh, don't talk like that, dear! You don't know what—'

'I will! And when I'm dead I'll hurt you worse!'

'Thank goodness, I shall be dead long before you, darling.'

'Huh! Emma says, "'Never know your luck."' (Michael had been talking to Helen's elderly, flat-faced maid.) 'Lots of little boys die quite soon. So'll I. *Then* you'll see!'

Helen caught her breath and moved towards the door, but the wail of 'Mummy! Mummy!' drew her back again, and the two wept together.

At ten years old, after two terms at a prep. school, something or somebody gave him the idea that his civil status was not quite regular. He attacked Helen on the subject, breaking down her stammered defences with the family directness.

''Don't believe a word of it,' he said, cheerily, at the end. 'People wouldn't have talked like they did if my people had been married. But don't you bother, Auntie. I've found out all about my sort in English Hist'ry and the Shakespeare bits. There was William the Conqueror to begin with, and—oh, heaps more, and they all got on first-rate. 'Twon't make any difference to you, my being *that*—will it?'

'As if anything could—' she began.

'All right. We won't talk about it any more if it makes you cry.' He never mentioned the thing again of his own will, but when, two years later, he skilfully managed to have measles in the holidays, as his temperature went up to the appointed one hundred and four he muttered of nothing else, till Helen's voice, piercing at last his delirium, reached him with assurance that nothing on earth or beyond could make any difference between them.

The terms at his public school and the wonderful Christmas, Easter, and Summer holidays followed each other, variegated and glorious as jewels on a string; and as jewels Helen treasured them. In due time Michael developed his own interests, which ran their courses and gave way to others; but his interest in Helen was constant and increasing throughout. She repaid it with all that she had of affection or could command of counsel and money; and since Michael was no fool, the War took him just before what was like to have been a most promising career.

He was to have gone up to Oxford, with a scholarship, in October. At the end of August he was on the edge of joining the first holocaust of public-school boys who threw themselves into the Line;° but the captain of his O.T.C.,° where he had been sergeant for nearly a year, headed him off and steered him directly to a commission in a battalion so new that half of it still wore the old Army red,° and the other half was breeding meningitis through living overcrowdedly in damp tents. Helen had been shocked at the idea of direct enlistment.

'But it's in the family,' Michael laughed.

'You don't mean to tell me that you believed that old story all this time?' said Helen. (Emma, her maid, had been dead now several years.) 'I gave you my word of honour—and I give it again—that—that it's all right. It is indeed.'

'Oh, *that* doesn't worry me. It never did,' he replied valiantly. 'What I meant was, I should have got into the show earlier if I'd enlisted—like my grandfather.'

'Don't talk like that! Are you afraid of its ending so soon, then?'

'No such luck. You know what K.° says.'

'Yes. But my banker told me last Monday it couldn't *possibly* last beyond Christmas—for financial reasons.'

''Hope he's right, but our Colonel—and he's a Regular—says it's going to be a long job.'

Michael's battalion was fortunate in that, by some chance which meant several 'leaves,' it was used for coast-defence among shallow trenches on the Norfolk coast; thence sent north to watch the mouth of a Scotch estuary, and, lastly, held for weeks on a baseless rumour of distant service. But, the very day that Michael was to have met Helen for four whole hours at a railway-junction up the line, it was hurled out, to help make good the wastage of Loos,[°] and he had only just time to send her a wire of farewell.

In France luck again helped the battalion. It was put down near the Salient, where it led a meritorious and unexacting life, while the Somme was being manufactured; and enjoyed the peace of the Armentières and Laventie sectors when that battle began. Finding that it had sound views on protecting its own flanks and could dig, a prudent Commander stole it out of its own Division, under pretence of helping to lay telegraphs, and used it round Ypres at large.

A month later, and just after Michael had written Helen that there was nothing special doing and therefore no need to worry, a shell-splinter dropping out of a wet dawn killed him at once. The next shell uprooted and laid down over the body what had been the foundation of a barn wall, so neatly that none but an expert would have guessed that anything unpleasant had happened.

By this time the village was old in experience of war, and, English fashion, had evolved a ritual to meet it. When the postmistress handed her seven-year-old daughter the official telegram to take to Miss Turrell, she observed to the Rector's gardener: 'It's Miss Helen's turn now.' He replied, thinking of his own son: 'Well, he's lasted longer than some.' The child herself came to the front-door weeping aloud, because Master Michael had often given her sweets. Helen, presently, found herself pulling down the house-blinds one after one with great care, and saying earnestly to each: 'Missing *always* means dead.'[°] Then she took her place in the dreary procession that was impelled to go through an inevitable series of unprofitable emotions. The Rector, of course, preached hope and prophesied word, very soon, from a prison camp. Several friends, too, told her perfectly truthful tales, but always about other women, to whom, after months and months of silence, their missing had been miraculously restored. Other people urged her to communicate with infallible Secretaries of organisations who could communicate with benevolent neutrals, who could extract accurate information from the most secretive of Hun prison commandants. Helen did and wrote and signed everything that was suggested or put before her.

Once, on one of Michael's leaves, he had taken her over a munition factory, where she saw the progress of a shell from blank-iron to the all but finished article. It struck her at the time that the wretched thing was never left alone for a single second; and 'I'm being manufactured into a bereaved next of kin,' she told herself, as she prepared her documents.

In due course, when all the organisations had deeply or sincerely regretted their inability to trace, etc., something gave way within her and all sensation—save of thankfulness for the release—came to an end in blessed passivity. Michael had died and her world had stood still and she had been one with the full shock of that arrest. Now she was standing still and the world was going forward, but it did not concern her—in no way or relation did it touch her. She knew this by the ease with which she could slip Michael's name into talk and incline her head to the proper angle, at the proper murmur of sympathy.

In the blessed realisation of that relief, the Armistice with all its bells broke over her and passed unheeded. At the end of another year she had overcome her physical loathing of the living and returned young, so that she could take them by the hand and almost sincerely wish them well. She had no interest in any aftermath, national or personal, of the War, but, moving at an immense distance, she sat on various relief committees and held strong views—she heard herself delivering them—about the site of the proposed village War Memorial.

Then there came to her, as next of kin, an official intimation, backed by a page of a letter to her in indelible pencil, a silver identity-disc, and a watch, to the effect that the body of Lieutenant Michael Turrell had been found, identified, and re-interred in Hagenzeele Third Military Cemetery°—the letter of the row and the grave's number in that row duly given.

So Helen found herself moved on to another process of the manufacture—to a world full of exultant or broken relatives, now strong in the certainty that there was an altar upon earth where they might lay their love. These soon told her, and by means of time-tables made clear, how easy it was and how little it interfered with life's affairs to go and see one's grave.

'*So* different,' as the Rector's wife said, 'if he'd been killed in Mesopotamia, or even Gallipoli.'

The agony of being waked up to some sort of second life drove Helen across the Channel, where, in a new world of abbreviated titles, she learnt that Hagenzeele Third could be comfortably reached by an afternoon train which fitted in with the morning boat, and that there was a comfortable little hotel not three kilometres from Hagenzeele itself, where one could spend quite a comfortable night and see one's grave next morning. All this she had from a Central Authority who lived in a board and tar-paper shed on the skirts of a razed city full of whirling lime-dust and blown papers.

'By the way,' said he, 'you know your grave, of course?'

'Yes, thank you,' said Helen, and showed its row and number typed on Michael's own little typewriter. The officer would have checked it, out of one of his many books; but a large Lancashire woman thrust between them and bade him tell her where she might find her son, who had been corporal in the A.S.C.° His proper name, she sobbed, was Anderson, but, coming of respectable folk,° he had of course enlisted under the name of Smith; and had been killed at Dickiebush,° in early 'Fifteen. She had not his number nor did she know which of his two Christian names he might have used with his alias; but her Cook's tourist ticket expired at the end of Easter week, and if by then she could not find her child she should go mad. Whereupon she fell forward on Helen's breast; but the officer's wife came out quickly from a little bedroom behind the office, and the three of them lifted the woman on to the cot.

'They are often like this,' said the officer's wife, loosening the tight bonnet-strings. 'Yesterday she said he'd been killed at Hooge. Are you sure you know your grave? It makes such a difference.'

'Yes, thank you,' said Helen, and hurried out before the woman on the bed should begin to lament again.

Tea in a crowded mauve and blue striped wooden structure, with a false front, carried her still further into the nightmare. She paid her bill beside a stolid, plain-featured Englishwoman, who, hearing her inquire about the train to Hagenzeele, volunteered to come with her.

'I'm going to Hagenzeele myself,' she explained. 'Not to Hagenzeele Third; mine is Sugar Factory, but they call it La Rosière now. It's just south of Hagenzeele Three. Have you got your room at the hotel there?'

'Oh yes, thank you. I've wired.'

'That's better. Sometimes the place is quite full, and at others there's hardly a soul. But they've put bathrooms into the old Lion d'Or—that's the hotel on the west side of Sugar Factory—and it draws off a lot of people, luckily.'

'It's all new to me. This is the first time I've been over.'

'Indeed! This is my ninth since the Armistice. Not on my own account. *I* haven't lost any one, thank God—but, like every one else, I've a lot of friends at home who have. Coming over as often as I do, I find it helps them to have some one just look at the—the place and tell them about it afterwards. And one can take photos for them, too. I get quite a list of commissions to execute.' She laughed nervously and tapped her slung Kodak. 'There are two or three to see at Sugar Factory this time, and plenty of others in the cemeteries all about. My system is to save them up, and arrange them, you know. And when I've got enough commissions for one area to make it worth while, I pop over and execute them. It *does* comfort people.'

'I suppose so,' Helen answered, shivering as they entered the little train.

'Of course it does. (Isn't it lucky we've got window-seats?) It must do or they wouldn't ask one to do it, would they? I've a list of quite twelve or fifteen commissions here'—she tapped the Kodak again—'I must sort them out to-night. Oh, I forgot to ask you. What's yours?'

'My nephew,' said Helen. 'But I was very fond of him.'

'Ah yes! I sometimes wonder whether *they* know after death? What do you think?'

'Oh, I don't—I haven't dared to think much about that sort of thing,' said Helen, almost lifting her hands to keep her off.

'Perhaps that's better,' the woman answered. 'The sense of loss must be enough, I expect. Well, I won't worry you any more.'

Helen was grateful, but when they reached the hotel Mrs Scarsworth (they had exchanged names) insisted on dining at the same table with her, and after the meal, in the little, hideous salon full of low-voiced relatives, took Helen through her 'commissions' with biographies of the dead, where she happened to know them, and sketches of their next of kin. Helen endured till nearly half-past nine, ere she fled to her room.

Almost at once there was a knock at her door and Mrs Scarsworth entered; her hands, holding the dreadful list, clasped before her.

'Yes—yes—*I* know,' she began. 'You're sick of me, but I want to tell you something. You—you aren't married, are you? Then perhaps you won't . . . But it doesn't matter. I've *got* to tell some one. I can't go on any longer like this.'

'But please—' Mrs Scarsworth had backed against the shut door, and her mouth worked dryly.

'In a minute,' she said. 'You—you know about these graves of mine I was telling you about downstairs, just now? They really *are* commissions. At least several of them are.' Her eye wandered round the room. 'What extraordinary wall-papers they have in Belgium, don't you think? . . . Yes. I swear they are commissions. But there's *one*, d'you see, and—and he was more to me than anything else in the world. Do you understand?'

Helen nodded.

'More than any one else. And, of course, he oughtn't to have been. He ought to have been nothing to me. But he *was*. He *is*. That's why I do the commissions, you see. That's all.'

'But why do you tell me?' Helen asked desperately.

'Because I'm *so* tired of lying. Tired of lying—always lying—year in and year out. When I don't tell lies I've got to act 'em and I've got to think 'em, always. *You* don't know what that means. He was everything to me that he oughtn't to have been—the one real thing—the only thing that ever happened to me in all my life; and I've had to pretend he wasn't. I've had to watch every word I said, and think out what lie I'd tell next, for years and years!'

'How many years?' Helen asked.

'Six years and four months before, and two and three-quarters after. I've gone to him eight times, since. To-morrow'll make the ninth, and—and I can't—I *can't* go to him again with nobody in the world knowing. I want to be honest with some one before I go. Do you understand? It doesn't matter about *me*. I was never truthful, even as a girl. But it isn't worthy of *him*. So—so I—I had to tell you. I can't keep it up any longer. Oh, I can't!'

She lifted her joined hands almost to the level of her mouth, and brought them down sharply, still joined, to full arms' length below her waist. Helen reached forward, caught them, bowed her head over them, and murmured: 'Oh, my dear! My dear!' Mrs Scarsworth stepped back, her face all mottled.

'My God!' said she. 'Is *that* how you take it?'

Helen could not speak, and the woman went out; but it was a long while before Helen was able to sleep.

*

Next morning Mrs Scarsworth left early on her round of commissions, and Helen walked alone to Hagenzeele Third. The place was still in the making, and stood some five or six feet above the metalled road, which it flanked for hundreds of yards. Culverts across a deep ditch served for entrances through the unfinished boundary wall. She climbed a few wooden-faced earthen steps and then met the entire crowded level of the thing in one held breath. She did not know that Hagenzeele Third counted twenty-one thousand dead already. All she saw was a merciless sea of black crosses, bearing little strips of stamped tin at all angles across their faces. She could distinguish no order or arrangement in their mass; nothing but a waist-high wilderness as of weeds stricken dead, rushing at her. She went forward, moved to the left and the right hopelessly, wondering by what guidance she should ever come to her own. A great distance away there was a line of whiteness. It proved to be a block of some two or three hundred graves whose headstones had already been set, whose flowers were planted out, and whose new-sown grass showed green. Here she could see clear-cut letters at the ends of the rows, and, referring to her slip, realised that it was not here she must look.

A man knelt behind a line of headstones—evidently a gardener, for he was firming a young plant in the soft earth. She went towards him, her paper in her hand. He rose at her approach and without prelude or salutation asked: 'Who are you looking for?'

'Lieutenant Michael Turrell—my nephew,' said Helen slowly and word for word, as she had many thousands of times in her life.

The man lifted his eyes and looked at her with infinite compassion before he turned from the fresh-sown grass toward the naked black crosses.

'Come with me,' he said, 'and I will show you where your son lies.'

When Helen left the Cemetery she turned for a last look. In the distance she saw the man bending over his young plants; and she went away, supposing him to be the gardener.°

The Burden

One grief on me is laid
Each day of every year,
Wherein no soul can aid,
Whereof no soul can hear:
Whereto no end is seen
Except to grieve again—
Ah, Mary Magdalene,
Where is there greater pain?

To dream on dear disgrace
Each hour of every day—
To bring no honest face
To aught I do or say:
To lie from morn till e'en—
To know my lies are vain—
Ah, Mary Magdalene,
Where can be greater pain?

To watch my steadfast fear
Attend my every way
Each day of every year—
Each hour of every day:
To burn, and chill between—
To quake and rage again—
Ah, Mary Magdalene,
Where shall be greater pain?

One grave to me was given—
To guard till Judgment Day—
But God looked down from Heaven
And rolled the Stone away!
One day of all my years—
One hour of that one day—
His Angel saw my tears
And rolled the Stone away!

From LIMITS AND RENEWALS (1932)

Dayspring Mishandled

> C'est moi, c'est moi, c'est moi!
> Je suis la Mandragore!
> La fille des beaux jours qui s'éveille à l'aurore—
> Et qui chante pour toi!
>
> *C. Nodier*

In the days beyond compare and before the Judgments, a genius called Graydon° foresaw that the advance of education and the standard of living would submerge all mind-marks in one mudrush of standardised reading-matter, and so created the Fictional Supply Syndicate to meet the demand.

Since a few days' work for him brought them more money than a week's elsewhere, he drew many young men—some now eminent—into his employ. He bade them keep their eyes on the Sixpenny Dream Book, the Army and Navy Stores Catalogue (this for backgrounds and furniture as they changed), and *The Hearthstone Friend*, a weekly publication which specialised unrivalledly in the domestic emotions. Yet, even so, youth would not be denied, and some of the collaborated love-talk in 'Passion Hath Peril,' and 'Ena's Lost Lovers,' and the account of the murder of the Earl in 'The Wickwire Tragedies'—to name but a few masterpieces now never mentioned for fear of blackmail—was as good as anything to which their authors signed their real names in more distinguished years.

Among the young ravens° driven to roost awhile on Graydon's ark was James Andrew Manallace—a darkish, slow northerner of the type that does not ignite, but must be detonated. Given written or verbal outlines of a plot, he was useless; but, with a half-dozen pictures round which to write his tale, he could astonish.

And he adored that woman who afterwards became the mother of Vidal Benzaquen,[1] and who suffered and died because she loved one

[1] 'The Village that Voted the Earth was Flat.' *A Diversity of Creatures*.

unworthy. There was, also, among the company a mannered, bellied person called Alured Castorley, who talked and wrote about 'Bohemia,' but was always afraid of being 'compromised' by the weekly suppers at Neminaka's Café in Hestern Square,° where the Syndicate work was apportioned, and where everyone looked out for himself. He, too, for a time, had loved Vidal's mother, in his own way.

Now, one Saturday at Neminaka's, Graydon, who had given Manallace a sheaf of prints—torn from an extinct children's book called *Philippa's Queen*—on which to improvise, asked for results. Manallace went down into his ulster-pocket, hesitated a moment, and said the stuff had turned into poetry on his hands.

'Bosh!'

'That's what it isn't,' the boy retorted. 'It's rather good.'

'Then it's no use to us,' Graydon laughed. 'Have you brought back the cuts?'

Manallace handed them over. There was a castle in the series; a knight or so in armour; an old lady in a horned head-dress; a young ditto; a very obvious Hebrew; a clerk, with pen and inkhorn, checking wine-barrels on a wharf; and a Crusader. On the back of one of the prints was a note, 'If he doesn't want to go, why can't he be captured and held to ransom?' Graydon asked what it all meant.

'I don't know yet. A comic opera, perhaps,' said Manallace.

Graydon, who seldom wasted time, passed the cuts on to someone else, and advanced Manallace a couple of sovereigns to carry on with, as usual; at which Castorley was angry and would have said something unpleasant but was suppressed. Half-way through supper, Castorley told the company that a relative had died and left him an independence; and that he now withdrew from 'hackwork' to follow 'Literature.' Generally, the Syndicate rejoiced in a comrade's good fortune, but Castorley had gifts of waking dislike. So the news was received with a vote of thanks, and he went out before the end, and, it was said, proposed to 'Dal Benzaquen's mother, who refused him. He did not come back. Manallace, who had arrived a little exalted, got so drunk before midnight that a man had to stay and see him home. But liquor never touched him above the belt, and when he had slept awhile, he recited to the gas-chandelier the poetry he had made out of the pictures; said that, on second thoughts, he would convert it into comic opera; deplored the Upas-tree influence of Gilbert and Sullivan; sang somewhat to illustrate his point; and—after words, by the way, with a negress in yellow satin—was steered to his rooms.

In the course of a few years, Graydon's foresight and genius were rewarded. The public began to read and reason upon higher planes, and the Syndicate grew rich. Later still, people demanded of their printed matter what they expected in their clothing and furniture. So, precisely as the three guinea hand-bag is followed in three weeks by its thirteen and sevenpence ha'penny, indistinguishable sister, they enjoyed perfect synthetic substitutes for Plot, Sentiment, and Emotion. Graydon died before the Cinema-caption school° came in, but he left his widow twenty-seven thousand pounds.

Manallace made a reputation, and, more important, money for Vidal's mother when her husband ran away and the first symptoms of her paralysis showed. His line was the jocundly-sentimental Wardour Street brand of adventure,° told in a style that exactly met, but never exceeded, every expectation.

As he once said when urged to 'write a real book': 'I've got my label, and I'm not going to chew it off. If you save people thinking, you can do anything with 'em.' His output apart, he was genuinely a man of letters. He rented a small cottage in the country and economised on everything, except the care and charges of Vidal's mother.

Castorley flew higher. When his legacy freed him from 'hackwork,' he became first a critic—in which calling he loyally scalped all his old associates as they came up—and then looked for some speciality. Having found it (Chaucer was the prey), he consolidated his position before he occupied it, by his careful speech, his cultivated bearing, and the whispered words of his friends whom he, too, had saved the trouble of thinking. It followed that, when he published his first serious articles on Chaucer, all the world which is interested in Chaucer said: 'This is an authority.' But he was no impostor. He learned and knew his poet and his age; and in a month-long dog-fight in an austere literary weekly, met and mangled a recognised Chaucer expert of the day. He also, 'for old sake's sake,' as he wrote to a friend, went out of his way to review one of Manallace's books with an intimacy of unclean deduction (this was before the days of Freud) which long stood as a record. Some member of the extinct Syndicate took occasion to ask him if he would—for old sake's sake—help Vidal's mother to a new treatment. He answered that he had 'known the lady very slightly and the calls on his purse were so heavy that,' etc. The writer showed the letter to Manallace, who said he was glad Castorley hadn't interfered. Vidal's mother was then wholly paralysed. Only her eyes could move, and those always looked for the husband who had left her. She died thus in Manallace's arms in April of the first year of the War.

During the War he and Castorley worked as some sort of departmental dishwashers° in the Office of Co-ordinated Supervisals. Here Manallace came to know Castorley again. Castorley, having a sweet tooth, cadged lumps of sugar for his tea from a typist, and when she took to giving them to a younger man, arranged that she should be reported for smoking in unauthorised apartments. Manallace possessed himself of every detail of the affair, as compensation for the review of his book. Then there came a night when, waiting for a big air-raid, the two men had talked humanly, and Manallace spoke of Vidal's mother. Castorley said something in reply, and from that hour —as was learned several years later—Manallace's real life-work and interests began

The War over, Castorley set about to make himself Supreme Pontiff on Chaucer by methods not far removed from the employment of poison-gas. The English Pope was silent, through private griefs, and influenza had carried off the learned Hun who claimed continental allegiance. Thus Castorley crowed unchallenged from Upsala to Seville,° while Manallace went back to his cottage with the photo of Vidal's mother over the mantelpiece. She seemed to have emptied out his life, and left him only fleeting interests in trifles. His private diversions were experiments of uncertain outcome, which, he said, rested him after a day's gadzooking and vitalstapping.° I found him for instance, one week-end, in his toolshed-scullery, boiling a brew of slimy barks which were, if mixed with oak-galls, vitriol and wine, to become an ink-powder. We boiled it till the Monday, and it turned into an adhesive stronger than birdlime, and entangled us both.

At other times, he would carry me off, once in a few weeks, to sit at Castorley's feet, and hear him talk about Chaucer. Castorley's voice, bad enough in youth, when it could be shouted down, had, with culture and tact, grown almost insupportable. His mannerisms, too, had multiplied and set. He minced and mouthed, postured and chewed his words throughout those terrible evenings; and poisoned not only Chaucer, but every shred of English literature which he used to embellish him. He was shameless, too, as regarded self-advertisement and 'recognition'—weaving elaborate intrigues; forming petty friendships and confederacies, to be dissolved next week in favour of more promising alliances; fawning, snubbing, lecturing, organising and lying as unrestingly as a politician, in chase of the Knighthood due not to him (he always called on his Maker to forbid such a thought) but as tribute to Chaucer. Yet, sometimes, he could break from his obsession and prove how a man's work will try to save the soul of him. He would tell us charmingly of copyists of the fifteenth century in England and the Low Countries, who had multiplied the Chaucer MSS., of which there remained—he gave us the exact number—and how each scribe could by him (and, he implied, by him alone) be distinguished from every other by some peculiarity of letter-formation, spacing or like trick of pen-work; and how he could fix the dates of their work within five years. Sometimes he would give us an hour of really interesting stuff and then return to his overdue 'recognition.' The changes sickened me, but Manallace defended him, as a master in his own line who had revealed Chaucer to at least one grateful soul.

This, as far as I remembered, was the autumn when Manallace holidayed in the Shetlands or the Faroes, and came back with a stone 'quern'—a hand corn-grinder. He said it interested him from the ethnological standpoint. His whim lasted till next harvest, and was followed by a religious spasm which, naturally, translated itself into literature. He showed me a battered and mutilated Vulgate° of 1485, patched up the back with bits of legal parchments, which he had bought for thirty-five shillings. Some monk's attempt to rubricate chapter-initials had caught, it seemed, his forlorn fancy, and he dabbled in shells of gold and silver paint° for weeks.

That also faded out, and he went to the Continent to get local colour for a love-story, about Alva and the Dutch,° and the next year I saw practically nothing of him. This released me from seeing much of Castorley, but, at intervals, I would go there to dine with him, when his wife—an unappetising, ash-coloured woman—made no secret that his friends wearied her almost as much as he did. But at a later meeting, not long after Manallace had finished his Low Countries' novel, I found Castorley charged to bursting-point with triumph and high information hardly withheld. He confided to me that a time was at hand when great matters would be made plain, and 'recognition' would be inevitable. I assumed, naturally, that there was fresh scandal or heresy afoot in Chaucer circles, and kept my curiosity within bounds.

In time, New York cabled that a fragment of a hitherto unknown Canterbury Tale lay safe in the steel-walled vaults of the seven-million-dollar Sunnapia Collection.° It was news on an international scale—the New World exultant—the Old deploring the 'burden of British taxation which drove such treasures, etc.,' and the lighter-minded journals disporting themselves according to their publics; for 'our Dan,'° as one earnest Sunday editor observed, 'lies closer to the national heart than we wot of.' Common decency made me call on

Castorley, who, to my surprise, had not yet descended into the arena. I found him, made young again by joy, deep in just-passed proofs.

Yes, he said, it was all true. He had, of course, been in it from the first. There had been found one hundred and seven new lines of Chaucer tacked on to an abridged end of *The Persone's*° *Tale*, the whole the work of Abraham Mentzius,° better known as Mentzel of Antwerp (1388–1438/9)—I might remember he had talked about him—whose distinguishing peculiarities were a certain Byzantine formation of his *g*'s, the use of a 'sickle-slanted' reed-pen, which cut into the vellum at certain letters; and, above all, a tendency to spell English words on Dutch lines, whereof the manuscript carried one convincing proof. For instance (he wrote it out for me), a girl praying against an undesired marriage, says:—

'Ah Jesu-Moder, pitie my oe peyne.°
Daiespringe mishandeelt cometh nat agayne.'

Would I, please, note the spelling of 'mishandeelt'? Stark Dutch and Mentzel's besetting sin! But in *his* position one took nothing for granted. The page had been part of the stiffening of the side of an old Bible, bought in a parcel by Dredd, the big dealer,° because it had some rubricated chapter-initials, and by Dredd shipped, with a consignment of similar odds and ends, to the Sunnapia Collection, where they were making a glass-cased exhibit of the whole history of illumination and did not care how many books they gutted for that purpose. There, someone who noticed a crack in the back of the volume had unearthed it. He went on: 'They didn't know what to make of the thing at first. But they knew about *me*! They kept quiet till I'd been consulted. You might have noticed I was out of England for three months.

'I was over there, of course. It was what is called a "spoil"—a page Mentzel had spoiled with his Dutch spelling—I expect he had had the English dictated to him—then had evidently used the vellum for trying out his reeds; and then, I suppose, had put it away. The "spoil" had been doubled, pasted together, and slipped in as stiffening to the old book-cover. I had it steamed open, and analysed the wash. It gave the flour-grains in the paste—coarse, because of the old millstone—and there were traces of the grit itself. What? Oh, possibly a handmill of Mentzel's own time. He may have doubled the spoilt page and used it for part of a pad to steady wood-cuts on. It may have knocked about his workshop for years. That, indeed, is practically certain because a beginner from the Low Countries has tried his reed on a few lines of some monkish hymn—not a bad lilt tho'—which must have been common form. Oh yes, the page may have been used in other books before it was used for the Vulgate. That doesn't matter, but *this* does. Listen! I took a wash, for analysis, from a blot in one corner—that would be after Mentzel had given up trying to make a possible page of it, and had grown careless—and I got the actual *ink* of the period! It's a practically eternal stuff compounded on—I've forgotten his name for the minute—the scribe at Bury St Edmunds, of course—hawthorn bark and wine. Anyhow, on *his* formula. *That* wouldn't interest you either, but, taken with all the other testimony, it clinches the thing. (You'll see it all in my Statement to the Press on Monday.) Overwhelming, isn't it?'

'Overwhelming,' I said, with sincerity. 'Tell me what the tale was about, though. That's more in my line.'

'I know it; but *I* have to be equipped on all sides. The verses are relatively easy for one to pronounce on. The freshness, the fun, the humanity, the fragrance of it all, cries—no, shouts—itself as Dan's work. Why "Daiespringe mishandled" alone stamps it from Dan's mint. Plangent as doom, my dear boy—plangent as doom! It's all in my Statement. Well, substantially, the fragment deals with a girl whose parents wish her to marry an elderly suitor. The mother isn't so keen on it, but the father, an old Knight, is. The girl, of course, is in love with a younger and a poorer man. Common form? Granted. Then the father, who doesn't in the least want to, is ordered off to a Crusade and, by way of passing on the kick, as we used to say during the War, orders the girl to be kept in duresse till his return or her consent to the old suitor. Common form, again? Quite so. That's too much for her mother. She reminds the old Knight of his age and infirmities, and the discomforts of Crusading. Are you sure I'm not boring you?'

'Not at all,' I said, though time had begun to whirl backward through my brain to a red-velvet, pomatum-scented side-room at Neminaka's and Manallace's set face intoning to the gas.

'You'll read it all in my Statement next week. The sum is that the old lady tells him of a certain Knight-adventurer on the French coast, who, for a consideration, waylays Knights who don't relish crusading and holds them to impossible ransoms till the trooping-season is over, or they are returned sick. He keeps a ship in the Channel to pick 'em up and transfers his birds to his castle ashore, where he has a reputation for doing 'em well. As the old lady points out:

'And if perchance thou fall into his honde
By God how canstow ride to Holilonde?'

'You see? Modern in essence as Gilbert and Sullivan, but handled as only Dan could! And she reminds him that "Honour and olde bones" parted company long ago. He makes one splendid appeal for the spirit of chivalry:

Lat all men change as Fortune may send,
But Knighthood beareth service to the end,

and *then*, of course, he gives in:

For what his woman willeth to be don
Her manne must or wauken Hell anon.

'Then she hints that the daughter's young lover, who is in the Bordeaux wine-trade, could open negotiations for a kidnapping without compromising him. And *then* that careless brute Mentzel spoils his page and chucks it! But there's enough to show what's going to happen. You'll see it all in my Statement. Was there ever anything in literary finds to hold a candle to it? . . . And they give grocers Knighthoods for selling cheese!'

I went away before he could get into his stride on that course. I wanted to think, and to see Manallace. But I waited till Castorley's Statement came out. He had left himself no loophole. And when, a little later, his (nominally the Sunnapia people's) 'scientific' account of their analyses and tests appeared, criticism ceased, and some journals began to demand 'public recognition.' Manallace wrote me on this subject, and I went down to his cottage, where he at once asked me to sign a Memorial on Castorley's behalf. With luck, he said, we might get him a K.B.E. in the next Honours List. Had I read the Statement?

'I have,' I replied. 'But I want to ask you something first. Do you remember the night you got drunk at Neminaka's, and I stayed behind to look after you?'

'Oh, *that* time,' said he, pondering. 'Wait a minute! I remember Graydon advancing me two quid. He was a generous paymaster. And I remember—now, who the devil rolled me under the sofa—and what for?'

'We all did,' I replied. 'You wanted to read us what you'd written to those Chaucer cuts.'

'I don't remember that. No! I don't remember anything after the sofa-episode. . . . *You* always said that you took me home—didn't you?'

'I did, and you told Kentucky Kate° outside the old Empire that you had been faithful, Cynara, in your fashion."°

'Did I?' said he. 'My God! Well, I suppose I have.' He stared into the fire. 'What else?'

'Before we left Neminaka's you recited me what you had made out of the cuts—the whole tale! So—you see?'

'Ye-es.' He nodded. 'What are you going to do about it?'

'What are *you*?'

'I'm going to help him get his Knighthood—first.'

'Why?'

'I'll tell you what he said about 'Dal's mother—the night there was that air-raid on the offices.'

He told it.

'That's why,' he said. 'Am I justified?'

He seemed to me entirely so.

'But after he gets his Knighthood?' I went on.

'That depends. There are several things I can think of. It interests me.'

'Good Heavens! I've always imagined you a man without interests.'

'So I was. I owe my interests to Castorley. He gave me every one of 'em except the tale itself.'

'How did *that* come?'

'Something in those ghastly cuts touched off something in me—a sort of possession, I suppose. I was in love too. No wonder I got drunk that night. I'd *been* Chaucer for a week!° Then I thought the notion might make a comic opera. But Gilbert and Sullivan were too strong.'

'So I remember you told me at the time.'

'I kept it by me, and it made me interested in Chaucer—philologically and so on. I worked on it on those lines for years. There wasn't a flaw in the wording even in '14. I hardly had to touch it after that.'

'Did you ever tell it to anyone except me?'

'No, only 'Dal's mother—when she could listen to anything—to put her to sleep. But when Castorley said—what he did about her, I thought I might use it. 'Twasn't difficult. *He* taught me. D'you remember my birdlime experiments, and the stuff on our hands? I'd been trying to get that ink for more than a year. Castorley told me where I'd find the formula. And your falling over the quern, too?'

'That accounted for the stone-dust under the microscope?'

'Yes. I grew the wheat in the garden here, and ground it myself.

Castorley gave me Mentzel complete. He put me on to an MS. in the British Museum which he said was the finest sample of his work. I copied his "Byzantine *g*'s" for months.'

'And what's a "sickle-slanted" pen?' I asked.

'You nick one edge of your reed till it drags and scratches on the curves of the letters. Castorley told me about Mentzel's spacing and margining. I only had to get the hang of his script.'

'How long did that take you?'

'On and off—some years. I was too ambitious at first—I wanted to give the whole poem. That would have been risky. Then Castorley told me about spoiled pages and I took the hint. I spelt "Dayspring mishandeelt" Mentzel's way—to make sure of him. It's not a bad couplet in itself. Did you see how he admires the "plangency" of it?'

'Never mind him. Go on!' I said.

He did. Castorley had been his unfailing guide throughout, specifying in minutest detail every trap to be set later for his own feet. The actual vellum was an Antwerp find, and its introduction into the cover of the Vulgate was begun after a long course of amateur bookbinding. At last, he bedded it under pieces of an old deed, and a printed page (1686) of Horace's *Odes*, legitimately used for repairs by different owners in the seventeenth and eighteenth centuries; and at the last moment, to meet Castorley's theory that spoiled pages were used in workshops by beginners, he had written a few Latin words in fifteenth century script—the Statement gave the exact date—across an open part of the fragment. The thing ran: '*Illa alma Mater ecca, secum afferens me acceptum. Nicolaus Atrib.*'[10] The disposal of the thing was easiest of all. He had merely hung about Dredd's dark bookshop of fifteen rooms, where he was well known, occasionally buying but generally browsing, till, one day, Dredd Senior showed him a case of cheap black-letter stuff, English and Continental—being packed for the Sunnapia people—into which Manallace tucked his contribution, taking care to wrench the back enough to give a lead to an earnest seeker.

'And then?' I demanded.

'After six months or so Castorley sent for me. Sunnapia had found it, and as Dredd had missed it, and there was no money-motive sticking out, they were half convinced it was genuine from the start. But they invited him over. He conferred with their experts, and suggested the scientific tests. *I* put that into his head, before he sailed. That's all. And now, will you sign our Memorial?'

I signed. Before we had finished hawking it round there was a host of influential names to help us, as well as the impetus of all the literary discussion which arose over every detail of the glorious trove. The upshot was a K.B.E.[2] for Castorley in the next Honours List; and Lady Castorley, her cards duly printed, called on friends that same afternoon.

Manallace invited me to come with him, a day or so later, to convey our pleasure and satisfaction to them both. We were rewarded by the sight of a man relaxed and ungirt—not to say wallowing naked—on the crest of Success. He assured us that 'The Title' should not make any difference to our future relations, seeing it was in no sense personal, but, as he had often said, a tribute to Chaucer; 'and, after all,' he pointed out, with a glance at the mirror over the mantelpiece, 'Chaucer was the prototype of the "veray parfit gentil Knight"° of the British Empire so far as that then existed.'

On the way back, Manallace told me he was considering either an unheralded revelation in the baser Press which should bring Castorley's reputation about his own ears some breakfast-time, or a private conversation, when he would make clear to Castorley that he must now back the forgery as long as he lived, under threat of Manallace's betraying it if he flinched.

He favoured the second plan. 'If I pull the string of the shower-bath in the papers,' he said, 'Castorley might go off his veray parfit gentil nut. I want to keep his intellect.'

'What about your own position? The forgery doesn't matter so much. But if you tell this you'll kill him,' I said.

'I intend that. Oh—my position? I've been dead since—April, Fourteen, it was. But there's no hurry. What was it *she* was saying to you just as we left?'

'She told me how much your sympathy and understanding had meant to him. She said she thought that even Sir Alured did not realise the full extent of his obligations to you.'

'She's right, but I don't like her putting it that way.'

'It's only common form—as Castorley's always saying.'

'Not with *her*. She can hear a man think.'

'She never struck me in that light.'

'*You* aren't playing against her.'

''Guilty conscience, Manallace?'

[2] Officially it was on account of his good work in the Department of Co-ordinated Supervisals, but all true lovers of literature knew the real reason, and told the papers so.

'H'm! I wonder. Mine or hers? I *wish* she hadn't said that. "More even than *he* realises it." I won't call again for a while.'

He kept away till we read that Sir Alured, owing to slight indisposition, had been unable to attend a dinner given in his honour.

Inquiries brought word that it was but natural reaction, after strain, which, for the moment, took the form of nervous dyspepsia, and he would be glad to see Manallace at any time. Manallace reported him as rather pulled and drawn, but full of his new life and position, and proud that his efforts should have martyred him so much. He was going to collect, collate, and expand all his pronouncements and inferences into one authoritative volume.

'I must make an effort of my own,' said Manallace. 'I've collected nearly all his stuff about the Find that has appeared in the papers, and he's promised me everything that's missing. I'm going to help him. It will be a new interest.'

'How will you treat it?' I asked.

'I expect I shall quote his deductions on the evidence, and parallel 'em with my experiments—the ink and the paste and the rest of it. It ought to be rather interesting.'

'But even then there will only be your word. It's hard to catch up with an established lie,' I said. 'Especially when you've started it yourself.'

He laughed. 'I've arranged for *that*—in case anything happens to me. Do you remember the "Monkish Hymn"?'

'Oh yes! There's quite a literature about it already.'

'Well, you write those ten words above each other, and read down the first and second letters of 'em; and see what you get."[3] My Bank has the formula.'

He wrapped himself lovingly and leisurely round his new task, and Castorley was as good as his word in giving him help. The two practically collaborated, for Manallace suggested that all Castorley's

[3] *Illa*
alma
Mater
ecca
secum
afferens
me
acceptum
Nicolaus
Atrib.

strictly scientific evidence should be in one place, with his deductions and dithyrambs as appendices. He assured him that the public would prefer this arrangement, and, after grave consideration, Castorley agreed.

'That's better,' said Manallace to me. 'Now I sha'n't have so many hiatuses in my extracts. Dots always give the reader the idea you aren't dealing fairly with your man. I shall merely quote him solid, and rip him up, proof for proof, and date for date, in parallel columns. His book's taking more out of him than I like, though. He's been doubled up twice with tummy attacks since I've worked with him. And he's just the sort of flatulent beast who may go down with appendicitis.'

We learned before long that the attacks were due to gall-stones, which would necessitate an operation. Castorley bore the blow very well. He had full confidence in his surgeon, an old friend of theirs; great faith in his own constitution; a strong conviction that nothing would happen to him till the book was finished, and, above all, the Will to Live.

He dwelt on these assets with a voice at times a little out of pitch and eyes brighter than usual beside a slightly-sharpening nose.

I had only met Gleeag, the surgeon, once or twice at Castorley's house, but had always heard him spoken of as a most capable man. He told Castorley that his trouble was the price exacted, in some shape or other, from all who had served their country; and that, measured in units of strain, Castorley had practically been at the front through those three years he had served in the Office of Co-ordinated Supervisals. However, the thing had been taken betimes, and in a few weeks he would worry no more about it.

'But suppose he dies?' I suggested to Manallace.

'He won't. I've been talking to Gleeag. He says he's all right.'

'Wouldn't Gleeag's talk be common form?'

'I *wish* you hadn't said that. But, surely, Gleeag wouldn't have the face to play with me—or her.'

'Why not? I expect it's been done before.'

But Manallace insisted that, in this case, it would be impossible.

The operation was a success and, some weeks later, Castorley began to recast the arrangement and most of the material of his book. 'Let me have my way,' he said, when Manallace protested. 'They are making too much of a baby of me. I really don't need Gleeag looking in every day now.' But Lady Castorley told us that he required careful watching. His heart had felt the strain, and fret or disappointment of any kind must be avoided. 'Even,' she turned to Manallace, 'though you know ever so much better how his book should be arranged than he does himself.'

'But really,' Manallace began. 'I'm very careful not to fuss—'

She shook her finger at him playfully. 'You don't think you do; but, remember, he tells me everything that you tell him, just the same as he told me everything that he used to tell *you*. Oh, I don't mean the things that men talk about. I mean about his Chaucer.'

'I didn't realise that,' said Manallace, weakly.

'I thought you didn't. He never spares me anything; but *I* don't mind,' she replied with a laugh, and went off to Gleeag, who was paying his daily visit. Gleeag said he had no objection to Manallace working with Castorley on the book for a given time—say, twice a week—but supported Lady Castorley's demand that he should not be over-taxed in what she called 'the sacred hours.' The man grew more and more difficult to work with, and the little check he had heretofore set on his self-praise went altogether.

'He says there has never been anything in the History of Letters to compare with it,' Manallace groaned. 'He wants now to inscribe—he never dedicates, you know—inscribe it to me, as his "most valued assistant." The devil of it is that *she* backs him up in getting it out soon. Why? How much do you think she knows?'

'Why should she know anything at all?'

'You heard her say he had told her everything that he had told me about Chaucer? (I *wish* she hadn't said that!) If she puts two and two together, she can't help seeing that every one of his notions and theories has been played up to. But then—but then . . . Why is she trying to hurry publication? She talks about me fretting him. *She's* at him, all the time, to be quick.'

Castorley must have over-worked, for, after a couple of months, he complained of a stitch in his right side, which Gleeag said was a slight sequel, a little incident of the operation. It threw him back awhile, but he returned to his work undefeated.

The book was due in the autumn. Summer was passing, and his publisher urgent, and—he said to me, when after a longish interval I called—Manallace had chosen this time, of all, to take a holiday. He was not pleased with Manallace, once his indefatigable *aide*, but now dilatory, and full of time-wasting objections. Lady Castorley had noticed it, too.

Meantime, with Lady Castorley's help, he himself was doing the best he could to expedite the book; but Manallace had mislaid (did I think through jealousy?) some essential stuff which had been dictated to him. And Lady Castorley wrote Manallace, who had been delayed by a slight motor accident abroad, that the fret of waiting was prejudicial to her husband's health. Manallace, on his return from the Continent, showed me that letter.

'He has fretted a little, I believe,' I said.

Manallace shuddered. 'If I stay abroad, I'm helping to kill him. If I help him to hurry up the book, I'm expected to kill him. *She* knows,' he said.

'You're mad. You've got this thing on the brain.'

'I have not! Look here! You remember that Gleeag gave me from four to six, twice a week, to work with him. She called them the "sacred hours." You heard her? Well, they *are*! They are Gleeag's and hers. But she's so infernally plain, and I'm such a fool, it took me weeks to find it out.'

'That's their affair,' I answered. 'It doesn't prove she knows anything about the Chaucer.'

'She *does*! He told her everything that he had told me when I was pumping him, all those years. She put two and two together when the thing came out. She saw exactly how I had set my traps. I know it! She's been trying to make me admit it.'

'What did you do?'

''Didn't understand what she was driving at, of course. And then she asked Gleeag, before me, if he didn't think the delay over the book was fretting Sir Alured. He didn't think so. He said getting it out might deprive him of an interest. He had that much decency. *She's* the devil!'

'What do you suppose is her game, then?'

'If Castorley knows he's been had, it'll kill him. She's at me all the time, indirectly, to let it out. I've told you she wants to make it a sort of joke between us. Gleeag's willing to wait. He knows Castorley's a dead man. It slips out when they talk. They say "He was," not "He is." Both of 'em know it. But *she* wants him finished sooner.'

'I don't believe it. What are you going to do?'

'What can I? I'm not going to have him killed, though.'

Manlike, he invented compromises whereby Castorley might be lured up by-paths of interest, to delay publication. This was not a success. As autumn advanced Castorley fretted more, and suffered from returns of his distressing colics. At last, Gleeag told him that he thought they might be due to an overlooked gallstone working down. A second comparatively trivial operation would eliminate the bother once and for all. If Castorley cared for another opinion, Gleeag named a surgeon of eminence. 'And then,' said he, cheerily, 'the two of us can talk you over.' Castorley did not want to be talked over. He was oppressed by pains in his side, which, at first, had yielded to the liver-tonics Gleeag prescribed; but now they stayed—like a toothache—behind everything. He felt most at ease in his bedroom-study, with his proofs round him. If he had more pain than he could stand, he would consider the second operation. Meantime Manallace—'the meticulous Manallace,' he called him—agreed with him in thinking that the Mentzel page-facsimile, done by the Sunnapia Library, was not quite good enough for the great book, and the Sunnapia people were, very decently, having it re-processed. This would hold things back till early spring, which had its advantages, for he could run a fresh eye over all in the interval.

One gathered these news in the course of stray visits as the days shortened. He insisted on Manallace keeping to the 'sacred hours,' and Manallace insisted on my accompanying him when possible. On these occasions he and Castorley would confer apart for half an hour or so, while I listened to an unendurable clock in the drawing-room. Then I would join them and help wear out the rest of the time, while Castorley rambled. His speech, now, was often clouded and uncertain—the result of the 'liver-tonics'; and his face came to look like old vellum.

It was a few days after Christmas—the operation had been postponed till the following Friday—that we called together. She met us with word that Sir Alured had picked up an irritating little winter cough, due to a cold wave, but we were not, therefore, to abridge our visit. We found him in steam perfumed with Friar's Balsam. He waved the old Sunnapia facsimile at us. We agreed that it ought to have been more worthy. He took a dose of his mixture, lay back and asked us to lock the door. There was, he whispered, something wrong somewhere. He could not lay his finger on it, but it was in the air. He felt he was being played with. He did not like it. There was something wrong all round him. Had we noticed it? Manallace and I severally and slowly denied that we had noticed anything of the sort.

With no longer break than a light fit of coughing, he fell into the hideous, helpless panic of the sick—those worse than captives who lie at the judgment and mercy of the hale for every office and hope. He wanted to go away. Would we help him to pack his Gladstone? Or, if that would attract too much attention in certain quarters, help him to dress and go out? There was an urgent matter to be set right, and now that he had The Title and knew his own mind it would all end happily and he would be well again. *Please* would we let him go out, just to speak to—he named her; he named her by her 'little' name out of the old Neminaka days? Manallace quite agreed, and recommended a pull at the 'liver-tonic' to brace him after so long in the house. He took it, and Manallace suggested that it would be better if, after his walk, he came down to the cottage for a week-end and brought the revise with him. They could then re-touch the last chapter. He answered to that drug and to some praise of his work, and presently simpered drowsily. Yes, it *was* good—though he said it who should not. He praised himself awhile till, with a puzzled forehead and shut eyes, he told us that *she* had been saying lately that it was too good—the whole thing, if we understood, was *too* good. He wished us to get the exact shade of her meaning. She had suggested, or rather implied, this doubt. She had said—he would let us draw our own inferences—that the Chaucer find had 'anticipated the wants of humanity.' Johnson, of course. No need to tell *him* that. But what the hell was her implication? Oh God! Life had always been one long innuendo! *And* she had said that a man could do anything with anyone if he saved him the trouble of thinking. What did she mean by that? *He* had never shirked thought. He had thought sustainedly all his life. It *wasn't* too good, was it? Manallace didn't think it was too good—did he? But this pick-pick-picking at a man's brain and work was too bad, wasn't it? *What* did she mean? Why did she always bring in Manallace, who was only a friend—no scholar, but a lover of the game—Eh?—Manallace could confirm this if he were here, instead of loafing on the Continent just when he was most needed.

'I've come back,' Manallace interrupted, unsteadily. 'I can confirm every word you've said. You've nothing to worry about. It's *your* find —*your* credit—*your* glory and—all the rest of it.'

'Swear you'll tell her so then,' said Castorley. 'She doesn't believe a word I say. She told me she never has since before we were married. Promise!'

Manallace promised, and Castorley added that he had named him his literary executor, the proceeds of the book to go to his wife. 'All profits without deduction,' he gasped. 'Big sales if it's properly handled. *You* don't need money. . . . Graydon'll trust *you* to any extent. It 'ud be a long . . .'

He coughed, and, as he caught breath, his pain broke through all the drugs, and the outcry filled the room. Manallace rose to fetch Gleeag, when a full, high, affected voice, unheard for a generation, accompanied, as it seemed, the clamour of a beast in agony, saying: 'I wish to God someone would stop that old swine howling down there!

I can't . . . I was going to tell you fellows that it would be a dam' long time before Graydon advanced *me* two quid.'

We escaped together, and found Gleeag waiting, with Lady Castorley, on the landing. He telephoned me, next morning, that Castorley had died of bronchitis, which his weak state made it impossible for him to throw off. 'Perhaps it's just as well,' he added, in reply to the condolences I asked him to convey to the widow. 'We might have come across something we couldn't have coped with.'

Distance from that house made me bold.

'You knew all along, I suppose? What was it, really?'

'Malignant kidney-trouble—generalised at the end. 'No use worrying him about it. We let him through as easily as possible. Yes! A happy release. . . . What? . . . Oh! Cremation. Friday, at eleven.'

There, then, Manallace and I met. He told me that she had asked him whether the book need now be published; and he had told her this was more than ever necessary, in her interests as well as Castorley's.

'She is going to be known as his widow—for a while, at any rate. Did I perjure myself much with him?'

'Not explicitly,' I answered.

'Well, I have now—with *her*—explicitly,' said he, and took out his black gloves. . . .

As, on the appointed words, the coffin crawled sideways through the noiselessly-closing door-flaps, I saw Lady Castorley's eyes turn towards Gleeag.

Gertrude's Prayer

(*Modernised from the 'Chaucer' of Manallace.*)

That which is marred at birth Time shall not mend,
    Nor water out of bitter well make clean;
All evil thing returneth at the end,
    Or elseway walketh in our blood unseen.
Whereby the more is sorrow in certaine—
Dayspring mishandled cometh not againe.

To-bruized be that slender, sterting spray°
    Out of the oake's rind that should betide°
A branch of girt and goodliness, straightway
    Her spring is turnèd on herself, and wried
And knotted like some gall or veiney wen.—
Dayspring mishandled cometh not agen.

Noontide repayeth never morning-bliss—
  Sith noon to morn is incomparable;
And, so it be our dawning goth amiss,
  None other after-hour serveth well.
Ah! Jesu-Moder, pitie my oe paine—°
Dayspring mishandled cometh not againe!

Fairy-Kist

The Mother's Son

I have a dream—a dreadful dream—
  A dream that is never done,
I watch a man go out of his mind,
  And he is My Mother's Son.

They pushed him into a Mental Home,
  And that is like the grave:
For they do not let you sleep upstairs,
  And you're not allowed to shave.

And it was *not* disease or crime
  Which got him landed there,
But because They laid on My Mother's Son
  More than a man could bear.

What with noise, and fear of death,
  Waking, and wounds and cold,
They filled the Cup for My Mother's Son°
  Fuller than it could hold.

They broke his body and his mind
  And yet They made him live,
And They asked more of My Mother's Son
  Than any man could give.

For, just because he had not died
  Nor been discharged nor sick:
They dragged it out with My Mother's Son
  Longer than he could stick. . . .

And no one knows when he'll get well—
So, there he'll have to be:
And, 'spite of the beard in the looking-glass,
I know that man is me!

Fairy-Kist

The only important society in existence to-day is the E.C.F.—the Eclectic *but* Comprehensive Fraternity for the Perpetuation of Gratitude towards Lesser Lights.° Its founders were William Lemming, of Lemming and Orton, print-sellers; Alexander Hay McKnight, of Ellis and McKnight, provision-merchants; Robert Keede, M.R.C.P.,° physician, surgeon, and accoucheur; Lewis Holroyd Burges, tobacconist and cigar importer—all of the South Eastern postal districts—and its zealous, hard-working, but unappreciated Secretary. The meetings are usually at Mr Lemming's little place in Berkshire, where he raises pigs.

I had been out of England for awhile, missing several dinners, but was able to attend a summer one with none present but ourselves; several red mullets in paper; a few green peas and ducklings; an arrangement of cockscombs with olives, and capers as large as cherries; strawberries and cream; some 1903 Chateau la Tour;° and that locked cabinet of cigars to which only Burges has the key.

It was at the hour when men most gracefully curvet abroad on their hobbies,° and after McKnight had been complaining of systematic pilfering in his three big shops, that Burges told us how an illustrious English astrologer called Lily° had once erected a horoscope to discover the whereabouts of a parcel of stolen fish. The stars led him straight to it and the thief and, incidentally, into a breeze° with a lady over 'seven Portugal onions' also gone adrift, but not included in the periscope.° Then we wondered why detective-story writers so seldom use astrology to help out the local Sherlock Holmes; how many illegitimate children that great original had begotten in magazine form; and so drifted on to murder at large. Keede, whose profession gives him advantages, illustrated the subject.

'I wish I could do a decent detective story,' I said at last. 'I never get further than the corpse.'

'Corpses are foul things,' Lemming mused aloud. 'I wonder what sort of a corpse I shall make.'

'You'll never know,' the gentle, silver-haired Burges replied. 'You won't even know you're dead till you look in the glass and see no reflection. An old woman told me that once at Barnet Horse Fair—and I couldn't have been more than seven at the time.'

We were quiet for a few minutes, while the Altar of the Lesser Lights, which is also our cigar-lighter, came into use. The single burner atop, representing gratitude towards Lesser Lights in general, was of course lit. Whenever gratitude towards a named Lesser Light is put forward and proven, one or more of the nine burners round the base can be thrown into action by pulling its pretty silver draw-chain.

'What will you do for me,' said Keede, puffing, 'if I give you an absolutely true detective yarn?'

'If I can make anything of it,' I replied, 'I'll finish the Millar Gift.'

This meant the cataloguing of a mass of Masonic pamphlets (1831–59), bequeathed by a Brother to Lodge Faith and Works 5836° E.C.—a job which Keede and I, being on the Library Committee, had together shirked for months.

'Promise you won't doctor it if you use it?' said Keede.

'And for goodness' sake don't bring *me* in any more than you can help,' said Lemming.

No practitioner ever comprehends another practitioner's methods; but a promise was given, a bargain struck; and the tale runs here substantially as it was told.

That past autumn, Lemming's pig-man (who had been sitting up with a delicate lady-Berkshire) discovered, on a wet Sunday dawn in October, the body of a village girl called Ellen Marsh lying on the bank of a deep cutting where the road from the village runs into the London Road. Ellen, it seemed, had many friends with whom she used to make evening appointments, and Channet's Ash, as the cross-roads were called, from the big ash that overhung them, was one of her well-known trysting-places. The body lay face down at the highest point of a sloping footpath which the village children had trodden out up the bank, and just where that path turned the corner under Channet's Ash and dropped into the London Road. The pig-man roused the village constable, an ex-soldier called Nicol, who picked up, close to the corpse, a narrow-bladed fern-trowel, its handle wrapped with twine. There were no signs of a struggle, but it had been raining all night. The pig-man then went off to wake up Keede, who was spending the week-end with Lemming. Keede did not disturb his host, Mrs Lemming being ill at the time, but he and the policeman commandeered a builder's handcart from some half-built shops down the London Road; wheeled the body to the nearest inn—the Cup o' Grapes—pushed a car out of a lock-up; took the shove-halfpenny board from the Oddfellows' Room,° and laid the body on it till the regular doctor should arrive.

'He was out,' Keede said, 'so I made an examination on my own. There was no question of assault. She had been dropped by one scientific little jab, just at the base of the skull, by someone who knew his anatomy. That was all. Then Nicol, the Bobby, asked me if I'd care to walk over with him to Jimmy Tigner's house.'

'Who was Jimmy Tigner?' I asked.

'Ellen's latest young man—a believing soul.° He was assistant at the local tinsmith's, living with his mother in a cottage down the street. It was seven o'clock then, and not a soul about. Jimmy had to be waked up. He stuck his head out of the window, and Nicol stood in the garden among the cabbages—friendly as all sin—and asked him what he'd been doing the night before, because someone had been knocking Ellen about. Well, there wasn't much doubt what Jimmy had been up to. He was altogether "the morning after." He began dressing and talking out of the window at the same time, and said he'd kill any man who touched Ellen.'

'Hadn't the policeman cautioned him?' McKnight demanded.

'What for? They're all friends in this village. Then Jimmy said that, on general principles, Ellen deserved anything she might have got. He'd done with her. He told us a few details (some girl must have given her away), but the point he kept coming back to was that they had parted in "high dungeon." He repeated that a dozen times. Nicol let him run on, and when the boy was quite dressed, he said: "Well, you may as well come on up-street an' look at her. She don't bear you any malice now." (Oh, I tell you the War has put an edge on things all round!) Jimmy came down, jumpy as a cat, and, when we were going through the Cup o' Grapes yard, Nicol unlocked the garage and pushed him in. The face hadn't been covered either.'

'Drastic,' said Burges, shivering.

'It was. Jimmy went off the handle at once; and Nicol kept patting him on the back and saying: "That's all right! I'll go bail *you* didn't do it." Then Jimmy wanted to know why the deuce he'd been dragged into it. Nicol said: "Oh, that's what the French call a confrontation. But you're all right." Then Jimmy went for Nicol. So we got him out of the garage, and gave him a drink, and took him back to his mother. But at the inquest he accounted for every minute of his time. He'd left Ellen under Channet's Ash, telling her what he thought of her over his shoulder for a quarter of a mile down the lane (that's what "high dungeon" meant in their language). Luckily two or three of the girls and the bloods of the village had heard 'em. After that, he'd gone to the Cup o' Grapes, filled himself up, and told everybody his grievances against Ellen till closing-time. The interestin' thing was that he seemed to be about the only decent boy of the lot.'

'Then,' Lemming interrupted, 'the reporters began looking for clues. They—they behaved like nothing *I*'ve ever imagined! I was afraid *we*'d be dragged into it.° You see, that wretched Ellen had been our scullery-maid a few months before, and—my wife—as ill as she was . . . But mercifully that didn't come out at the inquest.'

'No,' Keede went on. 'Nicol steered the thing. He's related to Ellen. And by the time Jimmy had broken down and wept, and the reporters had got their sensation, it was brought in "person or persons unknown."'

'What about the trowel?' said McKnight, who is a notable gardener.

'It was a most valuable clue, of course, because it explained the *modus operandi*. The punch—with the handle, the local doctor said—had been delivered through her back hair, with just enough strength to do the job and no more. I couldn't have operated more neatly myself. The Police took the trowel, but they couldn't trace it to anyone, somehow. The main point in the village was that no one who knew her wanted to go into Ellen's character. She was rather popular, you see. Of course the village was a bit disappointed about Jimmy's getting off; and when he broke down again at her funeral, it revived suspicion. Then the Huish poisoning case° happened up in the North; and the reporters had to run off and take charge of it. What did your pig-man say about 'em, Will?'

'Oh, Griffiths said: "'Twas Gawd's own Mercy those young gen'elmen didn't 'ave 'alf of us 'ung before they left. They were that energetic!"'

'They were,' said Keede. 'That's why I kept back my evidence.'

'There was the wife to be considered too,' said Lemming. 'She'd never have stood being connected with the thing, even remotely.'

'I took it upon myself to act upon that belief,' Keede replied gravely. 'Well—now for *my* little bit. I'd come down that Saturday night to spend the week-end with Will here; and I couldn't get here till late. It was raining hard, and the car skidded badly. Just as I turned off the London Road into the lane under Channet's Ash, my lights picked up a motor-bike lying against the bank where they found Ellen; and I saw a man bending over a woman up the bank. Naturally one don't interfere with these little things as a rule; but it occurred to me there might have been a smash. So I called out: "Anything wrong? Can I help?" The man said: "No, thanks. We're all right," or words to that effect, and I went on. *But* the bike's letters happened to be my own initials, and its number was the year I was born in. I wasn't likely to forget 'em, you see.'

'You told the Police?' said McKnight severely.

'Took 'em into my confidence at once, Sandy,' Keede replied. 'There was a Sergeant, Sydenham way, that I'd been treating for Salonika fever.° I told him I was afraid I'd brushed a motor-bike at night coming up into West Wickham, on one of those blind bends up the hill, and I'd be glad to know I hadn't hurt him. He gave me what I wanted in twenty-four hours. The bike belonged to one Henry Wollin—of independent means—livin' near Mitcham.'

'But West Wickham isn't in Berkshire—nor is Mitcham,' McKnight began.

'Here's a funny thing,' Keede went on, without noticing. 'Most men and nearly all women commit murder single-handed; but no man likes to go man-hunting alone. Primitive instinct, I suppose. That's why I lugged Will into the Sherlock Holmes business. You hated it too.'

'I hadn't recovered from those reporters,' said Lemming.

'They *were* rather energetic. But I persuaded Will that we'd call upon Master Wollin and apologise—as penitent motorists—and we went off to Mitcham in my two-seater. Wollin had a very nice little detached villa down there. The old woman—his housekeeper—who let us in, was West Country, talkin' as broad as a pat o' butter. She took us through the hall to Wollin, planting things in his back-garden.'

'A wonderful little garden for that soil,' said Lemming, who considers himself an even greater gardener than McKnight, although he keeps two men less.

'He was a big, strong, darkish chap—middle-aged—wide as a bull between the eyes—no beauty, and evidently had been a very sick man. Will and I apologised to him, and he began to lie at once. He said he'd been at West Wickham at the time (on the night of the murder, you know), and he remembered dodging out of the way of a car. He didn't seem pleased that we should have picked up his number so promptly. Seeing we were helping him to establish an *alibi*, he ought to have been, oughtn't he?'

'Ye mean,' said McKnight, suddenly enlightened, 'that he was committing the murder here in Berkshire on the night that he told you he was in West Wickham, which is in Kent.'

'Which is in Kent. Thank you. It is. And we went on talking about that West Wickham hill till he mentioned he'd been in the War, and that gave me *my* chance to talk. And he was an enthusiastic gardener, he said, and that let Will in. It struck us both that he was nervous in a carneying way that didn't match his build and voice at all. Then we had a drink in his study. Then the fun began. There were four pictures on the wall.'

'Prints—prints,' Lemming corrected professionally.

''Same thing, aren't they, Will? Anyhow, *you* got excited enough over them. At first I thought Will was only playing up. But he was genuine.'

'So were they,' Lemming said. 'Sandy, you remember those four "Apostles" I sold you last Christmas?'

'I have my counterfoil yet,' was the dry answer.

'What sort of prints were they?' Burges demanded.

The moonlike face of Alexander McKnight, who collects prints along certain lines, lit with devout rapture. He began checking off on his fingers.

'The firrst,' said he, 'was the draped one of Ray—the greatest o' them all. Next, yon French print o' Morrison, when he was with the Duke of Orleans at Blois; third, the Leyden print of Grew in his youth; and fourth, that wreathed Oxford print of Hales.° The whole aapostolic succession of them.'

'I never knew Morrison laid out links in France,' I said.

'Morrison? Links? Links? Did you think those four were gowfers then?'

'Wasn't old Tom Morrison° a great golfer?' I ventured.

McKnight turned on me with utter scorn. 'Those prints—' he began. 'But ye'd not understand. They were—we'll say they were just pictures of some garrdeners I happened to be interested in.'

This was rude of McKnight, but I forgave him because of the excellence of his imported groceries. Keede went on.

'After Will had talked the usual buyer's talk, Wollin seemed willin' to part with 'em, and we arranged we'd call again and complete the deal. Will 'ud do business with a criminal on the drop° o' course. He gave Wollin his card, and we left; Wollin carneying and suckin' up to us right to the front door. We hadn't gone a couple of miles when Will found he'd given Wollin his personal card—*not* his business one—with his private address in Berkshire! The murder about ten days old, and the papers still stinkin' with it! I think I told you at the time you were a fool, Will?'

'You did. I never saw how I came to make the mistake. These cards are different sizes too,' poor Lemming said.

'No, we were not a success as man-hunters,' Keede laughed. 'But Will and I had to call again, of course, to settle the sale. That was a week after. And this time, of course, Wollin—not being as big a fool as Will—had hopped it and left no address. The old lady said he was given to going off for weeks at a time. That hung us up; but to do Will justice, which I don't often, he saved the situation by his damned commercial instincts. He said he wanted to look at the prints again. The old lady was agreeable—rather forthcomin' in fact. She let us into the study, had the prints down, and asked if we'd like some tea. While she was getting it, and Will was hanging over the prints, I looked round the room. There was a cupboard, half opened, full of tools, and on top of 'em a new—what did you say it was, Will?—fern-trowel. 'Same pattern as the one Nicol found by Ellen's head. That gave me a bit of a turn. I'd never done any Sherlockin' outside my own profession. Then the old lady came back and I made up to her. When I was a sixpenny doctor at Lambeth, half my great success—'

'Ye can hold that over,' McKnight observed. 'The murrder's what's interestin' me.'

'Wait till your next go of gout. *I'll* interest you, Sandy. Well, she expanded (they all do with me), and, like patients, she wanted advice gratis. So I gave it. Then she began talking about Wollin. She'd been his nurse, I fancy. Anyhow, she'd known him all his life, and she said he was full of virtue and sickness. She said he'd been wounded and gassed and gangrened in the War, and after that—oh, she worked up to it beautifully—he'd been practically off his head. She called it "fairy-kist."'

'That's pretty—very pretty,' said Burges.

'Meanin' he'd been kissed by the fairies?' McKnight inquired.

'It would appear so, Sandy. I'd never heard the word before. 'West Country, I suppose. And she had one of those slow, hypnotic voices, like cream from a jug. Everything she said squared with my own theories up to date. Wollin was on the break of life, and, given wounds, gas, and gangrene just at that crisis, why anything—Jack the Ripper-ism or religious mania—might come uppermost. I knew that, and the old lady was as good as telling it me over again, and putting up a defence for him in advance. 'Wonderful bit of work. Patients' relatives *are* like that sometimes—specially wives.'

'Yes, but what about Wollin?' I said.

'Wait a bit. Will and I went away, and we talked over the fern-trowel and so forth, and we both agreed we ought to release our evidence. There, somehow, we stuck. Man-hunting's a dirty job. So we compromised. I knew a fellow in the C.I.D., who thought he had a floating kidney, and we decided to put the matter before him and let him take charge. He had to go North, however, and he wrote he could not see us before the Tuesday of next week. This would be four or five weeks after the murder. I came down here again that week-end to stay with Will, and on Saturday night Will and I went to his study to put the finishing touches to our evidence. I was trying to keep my own theory out of it as much as I could. Yes, if you want to know, Jack the Ripper *was* my notion, and my theory was that my car had frightened the brute off before he could do anything in that line. And *then*, Will's housemaid shot into the study with Nicol after her, and Jimmy Tigner after him!'

'Luckily my wife was up in town at the time,' said Lemming. 'They all shouted at once too.'

'They did!' said Keede. 'Nicol shouted loudest, though. He was plastered with mud, waving what was left of his helmet, and Jimmy was in hysterics. Nicol yelled:—"Look at me! Look at this! It's all right! Look at me! I've got it!": He *had* got it too! It came out, when they quieted down, that he had been walking with Jimmy in the lane by Channet's Ash. Hearing a lorry behind 'em—you know what a narrow lane it is—they stepped up on to that path on the bank (I told you about it) that the school-children had made. It was a contractor's lorry—Higbee and Norton, a local firm—with two girders for some new shops on the London Road. They were deliverin' late on Saturday evening, so's the men could start on Monday. Well, these girders had been chucked in anyhow on to a brick lorry with a tail-board. Instead of slopin' forward they cocked up backwards like a pheasant's tail, sticking up high and overhanging. They were tied together with a few turns of rope at the far ends. Do you see?'

So far we could see nothing. Keede made it plainer.

'Nicol said he went up the bank first—Jimmy behind him—and after a few steps he found his helmet knocked off. If he'd been a foot higher up the bank his head 'ud have gone. The lorry had skidded on the tar of the London Road, as it turned into it left-handed—her tail swung to the right, and the girders swung with it, just missing braining Nicol up on the bank. The lorry was well in the left-hand gutter when he got his breath again. He went for the driver at once. The man said all the lorries always skidded under Channet's Ash, when it was wet, because of the camber of the road, and they allowed for it as a regular stunt. And he damned the road authorities, and Nicol for being in the light. Then Jimmy Tigner, Nicol told us, caught on to what it meant, and he climbed into the lorry shouting:—"*You* killed Ellen!" It was all Nicol could do to prevent him choking the fellow there and then; but Nicol didn't pull him off till Jimmy got it out of the driver that he had been delivering girders the night Ellen was killed. Of course, he hadn't noticed anything.

'Then Nicol came over to Lemming and me to talk it over. I gave Jimmy a bromide and sent him off to his mother. He wasn't any particular use, except as a witness—and no good after. Then Nicol went over the whole thing again several times, to fix it in our minds. Next morning he and I and Will called on old Higbee before he could get to Church. We made him take out the particular lorry implicated, with the same driver, and a duplicate load packed the same way, and demonstrate for us. We kept her stunting half Sunday morning in the rain, and the skid delivered her into the left-hand gutter of the London Road every time she took that corner; and *every* time her tail with the girders swiped along the bank of that lane like a man topping a golf-ball. And when she did that, there were half-a-dozen paces—not more—along that school-children's path, that meant sure death to anyone on it at the time. Nicol was just climbing into the danger-zone when he stepped up, but he was a foot too low. The girders only brushed through his hair. We got some laths and stuck 'em in along the path (Jimmy Tigner told us Ellen was five foot three) to test our theory. The last lath was as near as could be to where the pig-man had found the body; and that happened to be the extreme end of the lorry's skid. 'See what happened? *We* did. At the end of her skid the lorry's rear wheels 'ud fetch up every time with a bit of a jar against the bank, and the girders 'ud quiver and lash out a few inches—like a golf-club wigglin'. Ellen must have caught just enough of that little sideway flick, at the base of her skull, to drop her like a pithed ox. We worked it all out on the last lath. The rope wrappings on the end of the damned things saved the skin being broken. Hellish, isn't it? And then Jimmy Tigner realised that if she had only gone two paces further she'd have been round the corner of the bank and safe. Then it came back to him that she'd stopped talkin' "in dungeon" rather suddenly, and he hadn't gone back to see! I spent most of the afternoon sitting with him. He'd been tried too high—too high. I had to sign his certificate a few weeks later. No! He won't get better.'

We commented according to our natures, and then McKnight said:—'But—if so—why did Wollin disappear?'

'That comes next on the agenda, Worshipful Sir. Brother Lemming° has *not* the instincts of the real man-hunter. He felt shy. I had to remind him of the prints before he'd call on Wollin again. We'd allow our prey ten days to get the news, while the papers were busy explainin' Ellen's death, and people were writin' to 'em and saying they'd nearly been killed by lorries in the same way in other places. Then old Higbee gave Ellen's people a couple of hundred without prejudice (he wanted to get a higher seat in the Synagogue°—the Squire's pew, I think), and everyone felt that her character had been cleared.'

'But Wollin?' McKnight insisted.

'When Will and I went to call on him he'd come home again. I hadn't seen him for—let's see, it must have been going on for a month—but I hardly recognised him. He was burned out—all his wrinkles gashes, and his eyes re-adjustin' 'emselves after looking into Hell. One gets to know that kind of glare nowadays. But he was immensely relieved to see us. So was the old lady. If he'd been a dog, he'd have been wagging his tail from the nose down. That was rather embarrassing too, because it wasn't our fault we hadn't had him tried for his life. And while we were talking over the prints, he said, quite suddenly: "*I* don't blame you! I'd have believed it against myself on the evidence!" That broke the ice with a brick. He told us he'd almost stepped on Ellen's body that night—dead and stiffening. Then I'd come round the corner and hailed him, and that panicked him. He jumped on his bike and fled, forgetting the trowel. So he'd bought another with some crazy notion of putting the Law off the track. That's what hangs murderers.

'When Will and I first called on him, with our fairy-tales about West Wickham, he had fancied he might be under observation, and Will's mixing up the cards clinched it. . . . So he disappeared. He went down into his own cellar, he said, and waited there, with his revolver, ready to blow his brains out when the warrant came. What a month! Think of it! A cellar and a candle, a file of gardening papers, and a loaded revolver for company! Then I asked why. He said no jury on earth would have believed his explanation of his movements. "Look at it from the prosecution's point of view," he said. "Here's a middle-aged man with a medical record that 'ud account for any loss of controls—and that would mean Broadmoor—fifty or sixty miles from his home in a rainstorm, on the top of a fifteen foot cutting, at night. He leaves behind him, with the girl's body, the very sort of weapon that might have caused her death. I read about the trowel in the papers. Can't you see how the thing 'ud be handled?" he said.

'I asked him then what in the world he really *was* doing that had to be covered up by suicide. He said he was planting things. I asked if he meant stolen goods. After the trouble we'd given him, Will and I wouldn't have peached on him for that, would we, Will?'

'No,' said Lemming. 'His face was enough. It was like—' and he named a picture by an artist called Goya.°

'"Stolen goods be damned," Wollin said to me. "If you *must* have it, I was planting out plants from my garden." What did you say to him then, Will?'

'I asked him what the plants were, of course,' said Lemming, and turned to McKnight. 'They were daffodils, and a sort of red honeysuckle, and a special loosestrife—a hybrid.'° McKnight nodded judicially while Lemming talked incomprehensible horticulture for a minute or two.

'Gardening isn't my line,' Keede broke in, 'but Will's questions acted on Master Wollin like a charm. He dropped his suicide talk, and began on gardening. After that it was Will's operation. I hadn't a look-in for ten minutes. Then I said: "What's there to make a fuss about in all this?" Then he turned away from Will and spoke to me, carneying again—like patients do. He began with his medical record—one shrapnel peppering, and one gassing, with gangrene. He had put in about fourteen months in various hospitals, and he was full of medical talkee-talkee. Just like *you*, Sandy, when you've been seeing your damned specialists. And he'd been doped for pain and pinched nerves, till the wonder was he'd ever pulled straight again. He told us that the only thing that had helped him through the War was his love of gardening. He'd been mad keen on it all his life—and even in the worst of the Somme he used to get comfort out of plants and bot'ny, and that sort of stuff. *I* never did. Well, I saw he was speaking the truth; but next minute he began to hedge. I noticed it, and said something, and then he sweated in rivers. He hadn't turned a hair over his proposed suicide, but now he sweated till he had to wipe it off his forehead.

'Then I told him I was something else besides a G.P., and Will was too,° if that 'ud make things easier for him. And it did. From then on he told the tale on the Square,° in grave distress, you know. At his last hospital he'd been particularly doped, and he fancied that that was where his mind had gone. He told me that he was insane, and had been for more than a year. I asked him not to start on his theories till he'd finished with his symptons. (You patients are all the same.) He said there were Gotha° raids round his hospital, which used to upset the wards. And there was a V.A.D.°—she must have been something of a woman, too—who used to read to him and tell him stories to keep him quiet. He liked 'em because, as far as he remembered, they were all about gardening. *But*, when he grew better, he began to hear Voices—little whispers at first, growing louder and ending in regular uproars—ordering him to do certain things. He used to lie there shaking with horror, because he funked going mad. He wanted to live and be happy again, in his garden—like the rest of us.

'When he was discharged, he said, he left hospital with a whole Army Corps shouting into his ears. The sum and substance of their orders was that he must go out and plant roots and things at large up and down the country-side. Naturally, he suffered a bit, but, after a while, he went back to his house at Mitcham and obeyed orders, because, he said, as long as he was carrying 'em out the Voices stopped. If he knocked off even for a week, he said, they helled him on again. Being a methodical bird, he'd bought a motor-bike and a basket lined with oil-cloth, and he used to skirmish out planting his silly stuff by the wayside, and in coppices and on commons. He'd spy out likely spots by day and attend to 'em after dark. He was working round Channet's Ash that night, and he'd come out of the meadow, and down the school-children's path, right on to Ellen's body. That upset him. I wasn't worryin' about Ellen for the moment. I headed him back to his own symptons. The devil of it was that, left to himself, there was nothing he'd have liked better than this planting job; but the Voices ordering him to do it, scared the soul out of him. Then I asked him if the Voices had worried him much when he was in the cellar with his revolver. He said, comin' to think of it, that they had not; and I reminded him that there was very little seasickness in the boats when submarines were around.'

'You've forgotten,' said Lemming, 'that he stopped fawning as soon as he found out we were on the Square.'

'He did so,' Keede assented. '*And* he insisted on our staying to supper, so's he could tell his symptoms properly. ('Might have been you again, Sandy.) The old lady backed him up. She was clinging to us too, as though we'd done her a favour. And Wollin told us that if he'd been in the dock, he *knew* he'd have come out with his tale of his Voices and night-plantings, just like the Ancient Mariner;° and that would have sent him to Broadmoor. It was Broadmoor, not hanging, that he funked. And so he went on and on about his Voices, and I cross-examined. He said they used to begin with noises in his head like rotten walnuts being smashed;° but he fancied that must have been due to the bombs in the raid. I reminded him again that I didn't want his theories. The Voices were sometimes like his V.A.D.'s, but louder, and they were all mixed up with horrible dope-dreams. For instance, he said, there was a smiling dog° that ran after him and licked his face, and the dog had something to do with being able to read gardening books, and that gave him the notion, as he lay abed in hospital, that he had water on the brain,° and that that 'ud prevent him from root-gatherin' an' obeying his orders.'

'He used the words "root-gathering."° It's an unusual combination nowadays,' said Lemming suddenly. 'That made me take notice, Sandy.'

Keede held up his hand. 'No, you don't, Will! I tell this tale much better than you. Well, then Will cut in, and asked Wollin if he could remember exactly what sort of stuff his V.A.D. had read to him during the raids. He couldn't; except that it was all about gardening, and it made him feel as if he were in Paradise.° Yes, Sandy, he used the word "Paradise." Then Will asked him if he could give us the precise wording of his orders to plant things. He couldn't do that either. Then Will said, like a barrister: "I put it to you, that the Voices ordered you to plant things by the wayside *for such as have no gardens*."° And Will went over it slowly twice. "My God!" said Wollin. 'That's the *ipsissima verba*." "Good," said Will. "Now for your dog. I put it to you that the smiling dog was really a secret friend of yours. What was his colour?" "Dunno," said Wollin. "It was yellow," says Will. "A big yellow bull-terrier."° Wollin thought a bit and agreed. "When he ran after you," says Will, "did you ever hear anyone trying to call him off, in a very loud voice?" "Sometimes," said Wollin. "Better still," says Will. "Now, I put it to you that that yellow bull-terrier came into a library with a Scotch gardener who said it was a great privilege to be able to consult botanical books." Wollin thought a bit, and said that those were some of the exact words that were mixed up with his Voices, and his trouble about not being able to read. I shan't forget his face when he said it, either. My word, he sweated.'

Here Sandy McKnight smiled and nodded across to Lemming, who nodded back as mysteriously as a Freemason or a gardener.

'All this time,' Keede continued, 'Will looked more important than ever I've seen him outside of his shop; and he said to Wollin: "Now I'll tell you the story, Mr Wollin, that your V.A.D. read or told you. Check me where your memory fails, and I'll refresh it." That's what you said, wasn't it, Will? And Will began to spin him a long nursery-yarn about some children who planted flowers out in a meadow that wasn't theirs,° so that such as had no gardens might enjoy them; and one of the children called himself an Honest Root-gatherer, and one of 'em had something like water on the brain;° and there was an old Squire who owned a smiling yellow bull-terrier that was fond of the children, and he kept his walnuts till they were rotten, and then he smashed 'em all.° You ought to have heard Will! He can talk—even when there isn't money in it.'

'*Mary's Meadow*!' Sandy's hand banged the table.

'Hsh!' said Burges, enthralled. 'Go on, Robin.'

'And Wollin checked it all, with the sweat drying on him—remember, Will?—and he put in his own reminiscences—one about a lilac sun-bonnet, I remember.'

'Not lilac—marigold. One string of it was canary-colour and one was white.'° McKnight corrected as though this were a matter of life and death.

'Maybe. And there was a nightingale singing to the Man in the Moon,° and an old Herbal°—not Gerard's, or I'd have known it—"Paradise" something. Wollin contributed that sort of stuff all the time, with ten years knocked off his shoulders and a voice like the Town Crier's. Yes, Sandy, the story *was* called *Mary's Meadow*. It all came back to him—*via* Will.'

'And that helped?' I asked.

'Well,' Keede said slowly, 'a General Practitioner can't much believe in the remission of sins, can he? But if that's possible, I know how a redeemed soul looks. The old lady had pretended to get supper, but she stopped when Will began his yarn, and listened all through. Then Wollin put up his hand, as though he were hearing his dam' Voices. Then he brushed 'em away, and he dropped his head on the table and wept. My God, how he wept! And then she kissed him, *and* me. Did she kiss you, Will?'

'She certainly did not,' said the scandalised Lemming, who has been completely married for a long while.

'You missed something. She has a seductive old mouth still. And Wollin wouldn't let us go—hung on to us like a child. So, after supper, we went over the affair in detail, till all hours. The pain and the dope had made that nursery story stick in one corner of his mind till it took charge—it does sometimes—but all mixed up with bombings and nightmares. As soon as he got the explanation it evaporated like ether and didn't leave a stink.° I sent him to bed full of his own beer, and growing a shade dictatorial. He was a not uncommon cross between a brave bully and an old maid; but a man, right enough, when the pressures were off. The old lady let us out—she didn't kiss me again, worse luck! She was primitive Stone Age—bless her! She looked on us as a couple of magicians who'd broken the spell on him, she said.'

'Well, you had,' said Burges. 'What did he do afterwards?'

'Bought a side-car to his bike, to hold more vegetables—he'll be had up for poaching or trespassing, some day—and he cuts about the Home Counties planting his stuff as happy as—Oh my soul! *What* wouldn't I give to be even one fraction as happy as he is! *But*, mind you, he'd have committed suicide on the nod if Will and I had had him arrested. We aren't exactly first-class Sherlocks.'

McKnight was grumbling to himself. 'Juliaana Horratia Ewing,' said he. 'The best, the kindest, the sweetest, the most eenocent tale ever the soul of a woman gied birth to. I may sell tapioca for a living in the suburbs, but I know *that*. An' as for those prints o' mine,' he turned to me, 'they were not garrdeners. They were the Four Great British Botanists,° an'—an'—I ask your pardon.'

He pulled the draw-chains of all the nine burners round the Altar of the Lesser Lights before we had time to put it to the vote.

From DEPARTMENTAL DITTIES AND OTHER VERSES (1886)

A General Summary

We are very slightly changed
From the semi-apes who ranged
India's prehistoric clay;
He that drew the longest bow
Ran his brother down, you know,
As we run men down to-day.

'Dowb,' the first of all his race,
Met the Mammoth face to face
On the lake or in the cave:
Stole the steadiest canoe,
Ate the quarry others slew,
Died—and took the finest grave.

When they scratched the reindeer-bone,
Some one made the sketch his own,
Filched it from the artist—then,
Even in those early days,
Won a simple Viceroy's praise
Through the toil of other men.
Ere they hewed the Sphinx's visage
Favouritism governed kissage,
Even as it does in this age.

Who shall doubt 'the secret hid
Under Cheops' pyramid'
Was that the contractor did
Cheops out of several millions?
Or that Joseph's sudden rise
To Comptroller of Supplies

Was a fraud of monstrous size
On King Pharaoh's swart Civilians?°

Thus, the artless songs I sing
Do not deal with anything
New or never said before.
As it was in the beginning
Is to-day official sinning,
And shall be for evermore.°

The Story of Uriah

'Now there were two men in one city; the one rich, and the other poor.'°

Jack Barrett went to Quetta°
Because they told him to.
He left his wife at Simla
On three-fourths his monthly screw.
Jack Barrett died at Quetta
Ere the next month's pay he drew.

Jack Barrett went to Quetta.
He didn't understand
The reason of his transfer
From the pleasant mountain-land.
The season was September,
And it killed him out of hand.

Jack Barrett went to Quetta
And there gave up the ghost,
Attempting two men's duty
In that very healthy post;
And Mrs Barrett mourned for him
Five lively months at most.°

Jack Barrett's bones at Quetta
Enjoy profound repose;
But I shouldn't be astonished
If *now* his spirit knows

The reason of his transfer
From the Himalayan snows.

And, when the Last Great Bugle Call
Adown the Hurnai throbs,
And the last grim joke is entered
In the big black Book of Jobs,
And Quetta graveyards give again
Their victims to the air,
I shouldn't like to be the man
Who sent Jack Barrett there.

A Code of Morals

Lest you should think this story true
I merely mention I
Evolved it lately. 'Tis a most
Unmitigated misstatement.

Now Jones had left his new-wed bride to keep his house in order,
And hied away to the Hurrum Hills above the Afghan border,
To sit on a rock with a heliograph; but ere he left he taught
His wife the working of the Code that sets the miles at naught.

And Love had made him very sage, as Nature made her fair;
So Cupid and Apollo linked, *per* heliograph, the pair.°
At dawn, across the Hurrum Hills, he flashed her counsel wise—
At e'en, the dying sunset bore her husband's homilies.

He warned her 'gainst seductive youths in scarlet clad and gold,
As much as 'gainst the blandishments paternal of the old;
But kept his gravest warnings for (hereby the ditty hangs)
That snowy-haired Lothario, Lieutenant-General Bangs.

'Twas General Bangs, with Aide and Staff, who tittupped on the way,
When they beheld a heliograph tempestuously at play.

They thought of Border risings, and of stations sacked and burnt—
So stopped to take the message down—and this is what they learnt—

'Dash dot dot, dot, dot dash, dot dash dot' twice. The General swore.
'Was ever General Officer addressed as "dear" before?
'"My Love," i' faith! "My Duck," Gadzooks! "My darling popsy-wop!"
'Spirit of great Lord Wolseley, *who* is on that mountaintop?"°

The artless Aide-de-camp was mute, the gilded Staff were still,
As, dumb with pent-up mirth, they booked that message from the hill;
For clear as summer lightning-flare, the husband's warning ran:—
'Don't dance or ride with General Bangs—a most immoral man.'

[At dawn, across the Hurrum Hills, he flashed her counsel wise—
But, howsoever Love be blind, the world at large hath eyes.]
With damnatory dot and dash he heliographed his wife
Some interesting details of the General's private life.

The artless Aide-de-camp was mute, the shining Staff were still,
And red and ever redder grew the General's shaven gill.
And this is what he said at last (his feelings matter not):—
'I think we've tapped a private line. Hi! Threes about there! Trot!'

All honour unto Bangs, for ne'er did Jones thereafter know
By word or act official who read off that helio.
But the tale is on the Frontier, and from Michni to Mool*tan*
They know the worthy General as 'that most immoral man.'

The Man Who Could Write

Shun—shun the Bowl! That fatal, facile drink
Has ruined many geese who dipped their quills in 't;
Bribe, murder, marry, but steer clear of Ink
Save when you write receipts for paid-up bills in 't.
There may be silver in the 'blue-black'—all
I *know of is the iron and the gall.*

Boanerges Blitzen, servant of the Queen,°
Is a dismal failure—is a Might-have-been.
In a luckless moment he discovered men
Rise to high position through a ready pen.

Boanerges Blitzen argued therefore—'I,
With the selfsame weapon, can attain as high.'
Only he did not possess when he made the trial,
Wicked wit of Colvin, irony of Lyall.°

[Men who spar with Government need, to back their blows,
Something more than ordinary journalistic prose.]

Never young Civilian's prospects were so bright,
Till an Indian paper found that he could write:
Never young Civilian's prospects were so dark,
When the wretched Blitzen wrote to make his mark.

Certainly he scored it, bold, and black, and firm,
In that Indian paper—made his seniors squirm,
Quoted office scandals, wrote the tactless truth—
Was there ever known a more misguided youth?

When the Rag he wrote for praised his plucky game,
Boanerges Blitzen felt that this was Fame;
When the men he wrote of shook their heads and swore,
Boanerges Blitzen only wrote the more:

Posed as Young Ithuriel, resolute and grim,°
Till he found promotion didn't come to him;
Till he found that reprimands weekly were his lot,
And his many Districts curiously hot.

Till he found his furlough strangely hard to win,
Boanerges Blitzen didn't care a pin:
Then it seemed to dawn on him something wasn't right—
Boanerges Blitzen put it down to 'spite'.

Languished in a District desolate and dry;
Watched the Local Government yearly pass him by;
Wondered where the hitch was; called it most unfair.

. . . .

That was seven years ago—and he still is there!

The Betrothed

'*You must choose between me and your cigar.*' —Breach of Promise Case, circa 1885

Open the old cigar-box, get me a Cuba stout,
For things are running crossways, and Maggie and I are out.

We quarrelled about Havanas—we fought o'er a good cheroot,
And *I* know she is exacting, and she says I am a brute.

Open the old cigar-box—let me consider a space;
In the soft blue veil of the vapour musing on Maggie's face.

Maggie is pretty to look at—Maggie's a loving lass,
But the prettiest cheeks must wrinkle, the truest of loves must pass.

There's peace in a Larranaga, there's calm in a Henry Clay;
But the best cigar in an hour is finished and thrown away—

Thrown away for another as perfect and ripe and brown—
But I could not throw away Maggie for fear o' the talk o' the town!

Maggie, my wife at fifty—grey and dour and old—
With never another Maggie to purchase for love or gold!

And the light of Days that have Been the dark of the Days that
Are,
And Love's torch stinking and stale, like the butt of a dead
cigar—

The butt of a dead cigar you are bound to keep in your
pocket—
With never a new one to light tho' it's charred and black to the
socket!

Open the old cigar-box—let me consider a while.
Here is a mild Manila—there is a wifely smile.

Which is the better portion—bondage bought with a ring,
Or a harem of dusky beauties, fifty tied in a string?

Counsellors cunning and silent—comforters true and tried,
And never a one of the fifty to sneer at a rival bride?

Thought in the early morning, solace in time of woes,
Peace in the hush of the twilight, balm ere my eyelids close,

This will the fifty give me, asking nought in return,
With only a *Suttee's* passion—to do their duty and burn.

This will the fifty give me. When they are spent and dead,
Five times other fifties shall be my servants instead.

The furrows of far-off Java, the isles of the Spanish Main,
When they hear my harem is empty will send me my brides
again.

I will take no heed to their raiment, nor food for their mouths
withal,
So long as the gulls are nesting, so long as the showers fall.

I will scent 'em with best vanilla, with tea will I temper their
hides,
And the Moor and the Mormon shall envy who read of the tale
of my brides.°

For Maggie has written a letter to give me my choice between
The wee little whimpering Love and the great god Nick o'
Teen.

And I have been servant of Love for barely a twelvemonth
 clear,
But I have been Priest of Cabanas a matter of seven year;

And the gloom of my bachelor days is flecked with the cheery
 light
Of stumps that I burned to Friendship and Pleasure and Work
 and Fight.

And I turn my eyes to the future that Maggie and I must prove,
But the only light on the marshes is the Will-o'-the-Wisp of
 Love.

Will it see me safe through my journey or leave me bogged in
 the mire?
Since a puff of tobacco can cloud it, shall I follow the fitful fire?

Open the old cigar-box—let me consider anew—
Old friends, and who is Maggie that I should abandon *you*?

A million surplus Maggies are willing to bear the yoke;°
And a woman is only a woman, but a good Cigar is a Smoke.

Light me another Cuba—I hold to my first-sworn vows.
If Maggie will have no rival, I'll have no Maggie for Spouse!

From BARRACK-ROOM BALLADS AND OTHER VERSES (1892)

Danny Deever

'What are the bugles blowin' for?' said Files-on-Parade.
'To turn you out, to turn you out,' the Colour-Sergeant said.
'What makes you look so white, so white?' said Files-on-Parade.
'I'm dreadin' what I've got to watch,' the Colour-Sergeant said.
For they're hangin' Danny Deever, you can hear the Dead March play,
The Regiment's in 'ollow square—they're hangin' him to-day;
They've taken of his buttons off an' cut his stripes away,
An' they're hangin' Danny Deever in the mornin'.

'What makes the rear-rank breathe so 'ard?' said Files-on-Parade.
'It's bitter cold, it's bitter cold,' the Colour-Sergeant said.
'What makes that front-rank man fall down?' said Files-on-Parade.
'A touch o' sun, a touch o' sun,' the Colour-Sergeant said.
They are hangin' Danny Deever, they are marchin' of 'im round,
They 'ave 'alted Danny Deever by 'is coffin on the ground;
An' 'e'll swing in 'arf a minute for a sneakin' shootin' hound—
O they're hangin' Danny Deever in the mornin'!

''Is cot was right-'and cot to mine,' said Files-on-Parade.
''E's sleepin' out an' far to-night,' the Colour-Sergeant said.
'I've drunk 'is beer a score o' times,' said Files-on-Parade.
''E's drinkin' bitter beer alone,' the Colour-Sergeant said.
They are hangin' Danny Deever, you must mark 'im to 'is place,

For 'e shot a comrade sleepin'—you must look 'im in the face;
Nine 'undred of 'is county an' the Regiment's disgrace,°
While they're hangin' Danny Deever in the mornin'.

'What's that so black agin the sun?' said Files-on-Parade.
'It's Danny fightin' 'ard for life,' the Colour-Sergeant said.
'What's that that whimpers over'ead?' said Files-on-Parade.
'It's Danny's soul that's passin' now,' the Colour-Sergeant said.
For they're done with Danny Deever, you can 'ear the quickstep play,
The Regiment's in column, an' they're marchin' us away;
Ho! the young recruits are shakin', an' they'll want their beer to-day,
After hangin' Danny Deever in the mornin'!

Tommy

I went into a public-'ouse to get a pint o' beer,
The publican 'e up an' sez, 'We serve no red-coats here.'
The girls be'ind the bar they laughed an' giggled fit to die,
I outs into the street again an' to myself sez I:
O it's Tommy this, an' Tommy that, an' 'Tommy, go away'
But it's 'Thank you, Mister Atkins,' when the band begins to play—
The band begins to play, my boys, the band begins to play,
O it's 'Thank you, Mister Atkins,' when the band begins to play.

I went into a theatre as sober as could be,
They gave a drunk civilian room, but 'adn't none for me;
They sent me to the gallery or round the music-'alls,
But when it comes to fightin', Lord! they'll shove me in the stalls!
For it's Tommy this, an' Tommy that, an' 'Tommy, wait outside'
But it's 'Special train for Atkins' when the trooper's on the tide—

The troopship's on the tide, my boys, the troopship's on
the tide,
O it's 'Special train for Atkins' when the trooper's on the
tide.

Yes, makin' mock o' uniforms that guard you while you sleep
Is cheaper than them uniforms, an' they're starvation cheap;
An' hustlin' drunken soldiers when they're goin' large a bit
Is five times better business than paradin' in full kit.
Then it's Tommy this, an' Tommy that, an' 'Tommy,
'ow's yer soul?'
But it's 'Thin red line of 'eroes' when the drums begin to
roll—°
The drums begin to roll, my boys, the drums begin to roll,
O it's 'Thin red line of 'eroes' when the drums begin to
roll.

We aren't no thin red 'eroes, nor we aren't no blackguards too,
But single men in barricks, most remarkable like you;
An' if sometimes our conduck isn't all your fancy paints,
Why, single men in barricks don't grow into plaster saints;
While it's Tommy this, an' Tommy that, an' 'Tommy, fall
be'ind,'
But it's 'Please to walk in front, sir,' when there's trouble
in the wind—
There's trouble in the wind, my boys, there's trouble in
the wind,
O it's 'Please to walk in front, sir,' when there's trouble in
the wind.

You talk o' better food for us, an' schools, an' fires, an' all:
We'll wait for extry rations if you treat us rational.
Don't mess about the cook-room slops, but prove it to our face
The Widow's Uniform is not the soldier-man's disgrace.°
For it's Tommy this, an' Tommy that, an' 'Chuck him
out, the brute!'
But it's 'Saviour of 'is country' when the guns begin to
shoot;
An' it's Tommy this, an' Tommy that, an' anything you
please;
An' Tommy ain't a bloomin' fool—you bet that Tommy
sees!

'Fuzzy-Wuzzy'

We've fought with many men acrost the seas,
An' some of 'em was brave an' some was not:
The Paythan an' the Zulu an' Burmese;
But the Fuzzy was the finest o' the lot.
We never got a ha'porth's change of 'im:
'E squatted in the scrub an' 'ocked our 'orses,
'E cut our sentries up at Suakim,
An' 'e played the cat an' banjo with our forces.
So 'ere's *to* you, Fuzzy-Wuzzy, at your 'ome in the Soudan;
You're a pore benighted 'eathen but a first-class fightin' man;
We gives you your certificate, an' if you want it signed
We'll come an' 'ave a romp with you whenever you're inclined.

We took our chanst among the Kyber 'ills,
The Boers knocked us silly at a mile,
The Burman give us Irriwaddy chills,
An' a Zulu impi dished us up in style:°
But all we ever got from such as they
Was pop to what the Fuzzy made us swaller;
We 'eld our bloomin' own, the papers say,
But man for man the Fuzzy knocked us 'oller.
Then 'ere's *to* you, Fuzzy-Wuzzy, an' the missis and the kid;
Our orders was to break you, an' of course we went an' did.
We sloshed you with Martinis, an' it wasn't 'ardly fair;°
But for all the odds agin' you, Fuzzy-Wuz, you broke the square.

'E 'asn't got no papers of 'is own,
'E 'asn't got no medals nor rewards,
So we must certify the skill 'e's shown
In usin' of 'is long two-'anded swords:
When 'e's 'oppin' in an' out among the bush
With 'is coffin-'eaded shield an' shovel-spear,
An 'appy day with Fuzzy on the rush

Will last an 'ealthy Tommy for a year.
So 'ere's *to* you, Fuzzy-Wuzzy, an' your friends which are no more,
If we 'adn't lost some messmates we would 'elp you to deplore.
But give an' take's the gospel, an' we'll call the bargain fair,
For if you 'ave lost more than us, you crumpled up the square!

'E rushes at the smoke when we let drive,°
An', before we know, 'e's 'ackin' at our 'ead;
'E's all 'ot sand an' ginger when alive,
An' 'e's generally shammin' when 'e's dead.
'E's a daisy, 'e's a ducky, 'e's a lamb!
'E's a injia-rubber idiot on the spree,
'E's the on'y thing that doesn't give a damn
For a Regiment o' British Infantree!
So 'ere's *to* you, Fuzzy-Wuzzy, at your 'ome in the Soudan;
You're a pore benighted 'eathen but a first-class fightin' man;
An' 'ere's *to* you, Fuzzy-Wuzzy, with your 'ayrick 'ead of 'air—
You big black boundin' beggar—for you broke a British square!

Oonts

Wot makes the soldier's 'eart to penk, wot makes 'im to perspire?°
It isn't standin' up to charge nor lyin' down to fire;
But it's everlastin' waitin' on a everlastin' road
For the commissariat camel an' 'is commissariat load.
O the oont,[1] O the oont, O the commissariat oont!
With 'is silly neck a-bobbin' like a basket full o' snakes;
We packs 'im like an idol, an' you ought to 'ear 'im grunt,

[1] Camel: – *oo* is pronounced like *u* in 'bull,' but by Mr Atkins to rhyme with 'front.'

An' when we get 'im loaded up 'is blessed girth-rope
breaks.

Wot makes the rear-guard swear so 'ard when night is drorin'
in,
An' every native follower is shiverin' for 'is skin?
It ain't the chanst o' being rushed by Paythans from the 'ills,
It's the commissariat camel puttin' on 'is bloomin' frills!
O the oont, O the oont, O the hairy scary oont!
A-trippin' over tent-ropes when we've got the night
alarm!
We socks 'im with a stretcher-pole an' 'eads 'im off in
front,
An' when we've saved 'is bloomin' life 'e chaws our
bloomin' arm.

The 'orse 'e knows above a bit, the bullock's but a fool,
The elephant's a gentleman, the battery-mule's a mule;
But the commissariat cam-u-el, when all is said an' done,
'E's a devil an' a ostrich an' a orphan-child in one.
O the oont, O the oont, O the Gawd-forsaken oont!
The lumpy-'umpy 'ummin'-bird a-singin' where 'e lies,
'E's blocked the whole division from the rear-guard to the
front,
An' when we get him up again—the beggar goes an'
dies!

'E'll gall an' chafe an' lame an' fight—'e smells most awful vile.
'E'll lose 'isself for ever if you let 'im stray a mile.
'E's game to graze the 'ole day long an' 'owl the 'ole night
through,
An' when 'e comes to greasy ground 'e splits 'isself in two.
O the oont, O the oont, O the floppin', droppin' oont,
When 'is long legs give from under an' 'is meltin' eye is
dim!
The Tribes is up be'ind us, and the Tribes is out in
front—
It ain't no jam for Tommy, but it's kites an' crows for
'im.

So when the cruel march is done, an' when the roads is blind,
An' when we sees the camp in front an' 'ears the shots be'ind,
Ho! then we strips 'is saddle off, and all 'is woes is past.

'E thinks on us that used 'im so, and gets revenge at last.
O the oont, O the oont, O the floatin', bloatin' oont!
The late lamented camel in the water-cut 'e lies;
We keeps a mile be'ind 'im an' we keeps a mile in front,
But 'e gets into the drinkin'-casks, and then o' course
we dies!

Loot

If you've ever stole a pheasant-egg be'ind the keeper's back,
If you've ever snigged the washin' from the line,°
If you've ever crammed a gander in your bloomin' 'aversack,
You will understand this little song o' mine.
But the service rules are 'ard, an' from such we are debarred,
For the same with English morals does not suit.
(*Cornet*: Toot! toot!)
Why, they call a man a robber if 'e stuffs 'is marchin' clobber
With the—
(*Chorus*) Loo! loo! Lulu! lulu! Loo! loo! Loot! loot! loot!°
Ow, the loot!
Bloomin' loot!
That's the thing to make the boys git up an' shoot!
It's the same with dogs an' men,
If you'd make 'em come again
Clap 'em forward with a Loo! loo! Lulu! Loot!
(*ff*) Whoopee! Tear 'im, puppy! Loo! loo! Lulu!
Loot! loot! loot!

If you've knocked a nigger edgeways when 'e's thrustin' for
your life,
You must leave 'im very careful where 'e fell;
An' may thank your stars an' gaiters if you didn't feel 'is knife
That you ain't told off to bury 'im as well.
Then the sweatin' Tommies wonder as they spade the beggars
under
Why lootin' should be entered as a crime.
So, if my song you'll 'ear, I will learn you plain an' clear
'Ow to pay yourself for fightin' overtime.
(*Chorus*) With the loot, . . .

Now remember when you're 'acking round a gilded Burma god
That 'is eyes is very often precious stones;
An' if you treat a nigger to a dose o' cleanin'-rod
'E's like to show you everything 'e owns.
When 'e won't prodooce no more, pour some water on the floor
Where you 'ear it answer 'ollow to the boot
(*Cornet*: Toot! toot!)—
When the ground begins to sink, shove your baynick down the chink,°
An' you're sure to touch the—
(*Chorus*) Loo! loo! Lulu! Loot! loot! loot!
Ow, the loot! . . .

When from 'ouse to 'ouse you're 'unting, you must always work in pairs—
It 'alves the gain, but safer you will find—
For a single man gets bottled on them twisty-wisty stairs,
An' a woman comes and clobs 'im from be'ind.
When you've turned 'em inside out, an' it seems beyond a doubt
As if there weren't enough to dust a flute
(*Cornet*: Toot! toot!)—
Before you sling your 'ook, at the 'ousetops take a look,
For it's underneath the tiles they 'ide the loot.
(*Chorus*) Ow, the loot! . . .

You can mostly square a Sergint an' a Quartermaster too,
If you only take the proper way to go.
I could never keep my pickin's, but I've learned you all I knew—
But don't you never say I told you so.
An' now I'll bid good-bye, for I'm gettin' rather dry,
An' I see another tunin' up to toot
(*Cornet*: Toot! toot!)—
So 'ere's good-luck to those that wears the Widow's clo'es,
An' the Devil send 'em all they want o' loot!
(*Chorus*) Yes, the loot,
Bloomin' loot!
In the tunic an' the mess-tin an' the boot!
It's the same with dogs an' men,
If you'd make 'em come again

(*fff*) Whoop 'em forward with a Loo! loo! Lulu! Loot! loot! loot!
Heeya! Sick 'im, puppy! Loo! loo! Lulu! Loot! loot! loot!°

The Widow at Windsor

'Ave you 'eard o' the Widow at Windsor
  With a hairy gold crown on 'er 'ead?°
She 'as ships on the foam—she 'as millions at 'ome,
  An' she pays us poor beggars in red.
    (Ow, poor beggars in red!)
There's 'er nick on the cavalry 'orses,
  There's 'er mark on the medical stores—°
An' 'er troopers you'll find with a fair wind be'ind
  That takes us to various wars.
    (Poor beggars!—barbarious wars!)
      Then 'ere's to the Widow at Windsor,
        An' 'ere's to the stores an' the guns,
      The men an' the 'orses what makes up the forces
        O' Missis Victorier's sons.
      (Poor beggars! Victorier's sons!)

Walk wide o' the Widow at Windsor,
  For 'alf o' Creation she owns:
We 'ave bought 'er the same with the sword an' the flame,
  An' we've salted it down with our bones.
    (Poor beggars!—it's blue with our bones!)
Hands off o' the Sons o' the Widow,°
  Hands off o' the goods in 'er shop,
For the Kings must come down an' the Emperors frown
  When the Widow at Windsor says 'Stop!'
    (Poor beggars!—we're sent to say 'Stop!')
      Then 'ere's to the Lodge o' the Widow,
        From the Pole to the Tropics it runs—
      To the Lodge that we tile with the rank an' the file,
        An' open in form with the guns.°
      (Poor beggars!—it's always they guns!)

We 'ave 'eard o' the Widow at Windsor,
It's safest to leave 'er alone:
For 'er sentries we stand by the sea an' the land
Wherever the bugles are blown.
(Poor beggars!—an' don't we get blown!)
Take 'old o' the Wings o' the Mornin',
An' flop round the earth till you're dead;°
But you won't get away from the tune that they play
To the bloomin' old rag over'ead.
(Poor beggars!—it's 'ot over'ead!)
Then 'ere's to the Sons o' the Widow,°
Wherever, 'owever they roam.
'Ere's all they desire, an' if they require
A speedy return to their 'ome.
(Poor beggars!—they'll never see 'ome!)

Gunga Din

You may talk o' gin and beer
When you're quartered safe out 'ere,
An' you're sent to penny-fights an' Aldershot it;°
But when it comes to slaughter
You will do your work on water,
An' you'll lick the bloomin' boots of 'im that's got it.
Now in Injia's sunny clime,
Where I used to spend my time
A-servin' of 'Er Majesty the Queen,
Of all them blackfaced crew
The finest man I knew
Was our regimental bhisti, Gunga Din.°
He was 'Din! Din! Din!
'You limpin' lump o' brick-dust, Gunga Din!
'Hi! Slippy *hitherao*!
'Water, get it! *Panee lao*,[1]
'You squidgy-nosed old idol, Gunga Din.'

The uniform 'e wore
Was nothin' much before,

[1] Bring water swiftly [Kipling's note]

An' rather less than 'arf o' that be'ind,
For a piece o' twisty rag
An' a goatskin water-bag
Was all the field-equipment 'e could find.
When the sweatin' troop-train lay
In a sidin' through the day,
Where the 'eat would make your bloomin' eyebrows crawl,
We shouted 'Harry By!'[2]
Till our throats were bricky-dry,
Then we wopped 'im 'cause 'e couldn't serve us all.
It was 'Din! Din! Din!
'You 'eathen, where the mischief 'ave you been?
'You put some *juldee*[3] in it
'Or I'll *marrow*[4] you this minute
'If you don't fill up my helmet, Gunga Din!'

'E would dot an' carry one
Till the longest day was done;
An' 'e didn't seem to know the use o' fear.
If we charged or broke or cut,°
You could bet your bloomin' nut,
'E'd be waitin' fifty paces right flank rear.
With 'is mussick[5] on 'is back,
'E would skip with our attack,
An' watch us till the bugles made 'Retire,'
An' for all 'is dirty 'ide
'E was white, clear white, inside
When 'e went to tend the wounded under fire!
It was 'Din! Din! Din!'
With the bullets kickin' dust-spots on the green.
When the cartridges ran out,
You could hear the front-ranks shout,
'Hi! ammunition-mules an' Gunga Din!'

I shan't forgit the night
When I dropped be'ind the fight
With a bullet where my belt-plate should 'a' been.

[2] O brother [Kipling's note]
[3] Be quick [Kipling's note]
[4] Hit you [Kipling's note]
[5] Water-skin [Kipling's note]

I was chokin' mad with thirst,
An' the man that spied me first
Was our good old grinnin', gruntin' Gunga Din.
'E lifted up my 'ead,
An' he plugged me where I bled,
An' 'e guv me 'arf-a-pint o' water green.
It was crawlin' and it stunk,
But of all the drinks I've drunk,
I'm gratefullest to one from Gunga Din.
    It was 'Din! Din! Din!
  ''Ere's a beggar with a bullet through 'is spleen;
    'E's chawin' up the ground,
    'An' 'e's kickin' all around:
  'For Gawd's sake git the water, Gunga Din!'

'E carried me away
To where a dooli lay,°
An' a bullet come an' drilled the beggar clean.
'E put me safe inside,
An' just before 'e died,
'I 'ope you liked your drink,' sez Gunga Din.
So I'll meet 'im later on
At the place where 'e is gone—
Where it's always double drill and no canteen.
'E'll be squattin' on the coals
Givin' drink to poor damned souls,
An' I'll get a swig in hell from Gunga Din!
    Yes, Din! Din! Din!
  You Lazarushian-leather Gunga Din!
    Though I've belted you and flayed you,
    By the livin' Gawd that made you,
  You're a better man than I am, Gunga Din!

Mandalay

By the old Moulmein Pagoda, lookin' lazy at the sea,°
There's a Burma girl a-settin', and I know she thinks o' me;
For the wind is in the palm-trees, and the temple-bells they
    say:

'Come you back, you British soldier; come you back to
Mandalay!'
Come you back to Mandalay,
Where the old Flotilla lay:
Can't you 'ear their paddles chunkin' from Rangoon to
Mandalay?
On the road to Mandalay,
Where the flyin'-fishes play,
An' the dawn comes up like thunder outer China 'crost the
Bay!

'Er petticoat was yaller an' 'er little cap was green,
An' 'er name was Supi-yaw-lat—jes' the same as Theebaw's
Queen,°
An' I seed her first a-smokin' of a whackin' white cheroot,
An' a-wastin' Christian kisses on an 'eathen idol's foot:
Bloomin' idol made o' mud—
Wot they called the Great Gawd Budd—°
Plucky lot she cared for idols when I kissed 'er where she
stud!
On the road to Mandalay . . .

When the mist was on the rice-fields an' the sun was droppin'
slow,
She'd git 'er little banjo an' she'd sing 'Kulla-lo-lo!'
With 'er arm upon my shoulder an' 'er cheek agin my cheek
We useter watch the steamers an' the hathis pilin' teak.
Elephints a-pilin' teak
In the sludgy, squdgy creek,
Where the silence 'ung that 'eavy you was 'arf afraid to
speak!
On the road to Mandalay . . .

But that's all shove be'ind me—long ago an' fur away,
An' there ain't no 'buses runnin' from the Bank to Mandalay;
An' I'm learnin' 'ere in London what the ten-year soldier tells:
'If you've 'eard the East a-callin', you won't never 'eed naught
else.'
No! you won't 'eed nothin' else
But them spicy garlic smells,

An' the sunshine an' the palm-trees an' the tinkly temple-bells;
On the road to Mandalay . . .

I am sick o' wastin' leather on these gritty pavin'-stones,
An' the blasted English drizzle wakes the fever in my bones;
Tho' I walks with fifty 'ousemaids outer Chelsea to the Strand,
An' they talks a lot o' lovin', but wot do they understand?
Beefy face an' grubby 'and—
Law! wot do they understand?
I've a neater, sweeter maiden in a cleaner, greener land!
On the road to Mandalay . . .

Ship me somewheres east of Suez, where the best is like the worst,
Where there aren't no Ten Commandments an' a man can raise a thirst;
For the temple-bells are callin', an' it's there that I would be—
By the old Moulmein Pagoda, looking lazy at the sea;
On the road to Mandalay,
Where the old Flotilla lay,
With our sick beneath the awnings when we went to Mandalay!
O the road to Mandalay,
Where the flyin'-fishes play,
An' the dawn comes up like thunder outer China 'crost the Bay!

Gentlemen-Rankers

To the legion of the lost ones, to the cohort of the damned,
To my brethren in their sorrow overseas,
Sings a gentleman of England cleanly bred, machinely crammed,°
And a trooper of the Empress, if you please.
Yes, a trooper of the forces who has run his own six horses,
And faith he went the pace and went it blind,
And the world was more than kin while he held the ready tin,
But to-day the Sergeant's something less than kind.°
We're poor little lambs who've lost our way,

Baa! Baa! Baa!
We're little black sheep who've gone astray,
Baa—aa—aa!
Gentlemen-rankers out on the spree,
Damned from here to Eternity,
God ha' mercy on such as we,
Baa! Yah! Bah!

Oh, it's sweet to sweat through stables, sweet to empty kitchen slops,
And it's sweet to hear the tales the troopers tell,
To dance with blowzy housemaids at the regimental hops
And thrash the cad who says you waltz too well.
Yes, it makes you cock-a-hoop to be 'Rider' to your troop,
And branded with a blasted worsted spur,
When you envy, O how keenly, one poor Tommy living cleanly
Who blacks your boots and sometimes calls you 'Sir.'

If the home we never write to, and the oaths we never keep,
And all we know most distant and most dear,
Across the snoring barrack-room return to break our sleep,
Can you blame us if we soak ourselves in beer?
When the drunken comrade mutters and the great guard-lantern gutters
And the horror of our fall is written plain,
Every secret, self-revealing on the aching whitewashed ceiling,
Do you wonder that we drug ourselves from pain?

We have done with Hope and Honour, we are lost to Love and Truth,
We are dropping down the ladder rung by rung,
And the measure of our torment is the measure of our youth.
God help us, for we knew the worst too young!
Our shame is clean repentance for the crime that brought the sentence,
Our pride it is to know no spur of pride,
And the Curse of Reuben holds us till an alien turf enfolds us°
And we die, and none can tell Them where we died.
We're poor little lambs who've lost our way,
Baa! Baa! Baa!
We're little black sheep who've gone astray,

Baa—aa—aa!
Gentlemen-rankers out on the spree,
Damned from here to Eternity,
God ha' mercy on such as we,
Baa! Yah! Bah!

Ford o' Kabul River

Kabul town's by Kabul river—
Blow the trumpet, draw the sword—°
There I lef' my mate for ever,
Wet an' drippin' by the ford.
Ford, ford, ford o' Kabul river,
Ford o' Kabul river in the dark!
There's the river up and brimmin', an' there's 'arf a squadron swimmin'
'Cross the ford o' Kabul river in the dark.

Kabul town's a blasted place—
Blow the trumpet, draw the sword—
'Strewth I shan't forget 'is face
Wet an' drippin' by the ford!
Ford, ford, ford o' Kabul river,
Ford o' Kabul river in the dark!
Keep the crossing-stakes beside you, an' they will surely guide you
'Cross the ford o' Kabul river in the dark.

Kabul town is sun and dust—
Blow the trumpet, draw the sword—
I'd ha' sooner drownded fust
'Stead of 'im beside the ford.
Ford, ford, ford o' Kabul river,
Ford o' Kabul river in the dark!
You can 'ear the 'orses threshin'; you can 'ear the men a-splashin',
'Cross the ford o' Kabul river in the dark.

Kabul town was ours to take—
Blow the trumpet, draw the sword—
I'd ha' left it for 'is sake—
'Im that left me by the ford.
Ford, ford, ford o' Kabul river,
Ford o' Kabul river in the dark!
It's none so bloomin' dry there; ain't you never comin' nigh there,
'Cross the ford o' Kabul river in the dark?

Kabul town'll go to hell—
Blow the trumpet, draw the sword—
'Fore I see him 'live an' well—
'Im the best beside the ford.
Ford, ford, ford o' Kabul river,
Ford o' Kabul river in the dark!
Gawd 'elp 'em if they blunder, for their boots'll pull 'em under,
By the ford o' Kabul river in the dark.

Turn your 'orse from Kabul town—
Blow the trumpet, draw the sword—
'Im an' 'arf my troop is down,
Down and drownded by the ford.
Ford, ford, ford o' Kabul river,
Ford o' Kabul river in the dark!
There's the river low an' fallin', but it ain't no use a-callin'
'Cross the ford o' Kabul river in the dark!

The Conundrum of the Workshops

When the flush of a new-born sun fell first on Eden's green and gold,
Our father Adam sat under the Tree and scratched with a stick in the mould;
And the first rude sketch that the world had seen was joy to his mighty heart,
Till the Devil whispered behind the leaves, 'It's pretty, but is it Art?'

Wherefore he called to his wife, and fled to fashion his work
anew—
The first of his race who cared a fig for the first, most dread
review;
And he left his lore to the use of his sons—and that was a
glorious gain
When the Devil chuckled 'Is it Art?' in the ear of the branded
Cain.

They builded a tower to shiver the sky and wrench the stars
apart,
Till the Devil grunted behind the bricks: 'It's striking, but is it
Art?'
The stone was dropped at the quarry-side and the idle derrick
swung,
While each man talked of the aims of Art, and each in an alien
tongue.°

They fought and they talked in the North and the South; they
talked and they fought in the West,
Till the waters rose on the pitiful land, and the poor Red Clay
had rest—°
Had rest till that dank blank-canvas dawn when the Dove was
preened to start,°
And the Devil bubbled below the keel: 'It's human, but is it
Art?'

The tale is as old as the Eden Tree—and new as the new-cut
tooth—
For each man knows ere his lip-thatch grows he is master of
Art and Truth;
And each man hears as the twilight nears, to the beat of his
dying heart,
The Devil drum on the darkened pane: 'You did it, but was it
Art?'

We have learned to whittle the Eden Tree to the shape of a
surplice-peg,
We have learned to bottle our parents twain in the yelk of an
addled egg,

We know that the tail must wag the dog, for the horse is drawn
by the cart;°
But the Devil whoops, as he whooped of old: 'It's clever, but is
it Art?'

When the flicker of London sun falls faint on the Club-room's
green and gold,°
The sons of Adam sit them down and scratch with their pens in
the mould—
They scratch with their pens in the mould of their graves, and
the ink and the anguish start,
For the Devil mutters behind the leaves: 'It's pretty, but is it
Art?'

Now, if we could win to the Eden Tree where the Four Great
Rivers flow,
And the Wreath of Eve is red on the turf as she left it long ago,
And if we could come when the sentry slept and softly scurry
through,
By the favour of God we might know as much—as our father
Adam knew!

In the Neolithic Age

In the Neolithic Age savage warfare did I wage
For food and fame and woolly horses' pelt.
I was singer to my clan in that dim, red Dawn of Man,
And I sang of all we fought and feared and felt.

Yea, I sang as now I sing, when the Prehistoric spring
Made the piled Biscayan ice-pack split and shove;
And the troll and gnome and dwerg, and the Gods of Cliff and
Berg°
Were about me and beneath me and above.

But a rival, of Solutré, told the tribe my style was *outré*—°
'Neath a tomahawk, of diorite, he fell.
And I left my views on Art, barbed and tanged, below the heart
Of a mammothistic etcher at Grenelle.°

Then I stripped them, scalp from skull, and my hunting-dogs
  fed full,
 And their teeth I threaded neatly on a thong;
And I wiped my mouth and said, 'It is well that they are dead,
 'For I know my work is right and theirs was wrong.'

But my Totem saw the shame; from his ridgepole-shrine he
  came,
 And he told me in a vision of the night:—
'There are nine and sixty ways of constructing tribal lays,
 'And every single one of them is right!'

. . . .

Then the silence closed upon me till They put new clothing on
  me
 Of whiter, weaker flesh and bone more frail;
And I stepped beneath Time's finger, once again a tribal singer,
 And a minor poet certified by Traill!°

Still they skirmish to and fro, men my messmates on the snow,
 When we headed off the aurochs turn for turn;
When the rich Allobrogenses never kept amanuenses,°
 And our only plots were piled in lakes at Berne.

Still a cultured Christian age sees us scuffle, squeak, and rage,
 Still we pinch and slap and jabber, scratch and dirk;
Still we let our business slide—as we dropped the half-dressed
  hide—
 To show a fellow-savage how to work.

Still the world is wondrous large,—seven seas from marge to
  marge—
 And it holds a vast of various kinds of man;°
And the wildest dreams of Kew are the facts of Khatmandhu,
 And the crimes of Clapham chaste in Martaban.°

Here's my wisdom for your use, as I learned it when the moose
 And the reindeer roamed where Paris roars to-night:—
'There are nine and sixty ways of constructing tribal lays,
 'And—every—single—one—of—them—is—right!'

From THE SEVEN SEAS (1896)

The 'Mary Gloster'

I've paid for your sickest fancies; I've humoured your crackedest whim—
Dick, it's your daddy, dying; you've got to listen to him!
Good for a fortnight, am I? The doctor told you? He lied.
I shall go under by morning, and—Put that nurse outside.
'Never seen death yet, Dickie? Well, now is your time to learn,
And you'll wish you held my record before it comes to your turn.
Not counting the Line and the Foundry, the Yards and the village, too,
I've made myself and a million; but I'm damned if I made you.
Master at two-and-twenty, and married at twenty-three—
Ten thousand men on the pay-roll, and forty freighters at sea!
Fifty years between 'em, and every year of it fight,
And now I'm Sir Anthony Gloster, dying, a baronite:
For I lunched with his Royal 'Ighness—what was it the papers had?
'Not least of our merchant-princes.' Dickie, that's me, your dad!
I didn't begin with askings. *I* took my job and I stuck;
I took the chances they wouldn't, an' now they're calling it luck.
Lord, what boats I've handled—rotten and leaky and old—
Ran 'em, or—opened the bilge-cock, precisely as I was told.
Grub that 'ud bind you crazy, and crews that 'ud turn you grey,
And a big fat lump of insurance to cover the risk on the way.
The others they dursn't do it; they said they valued their life
(They've served me since as skippers). *I* went, and I took my wife.
Over the world I drove 'em, married at twenty-three,
And your mother saving the money and making a man of me.

I was content to be master, but she said there was better behind;
She took the chances I wouldn't, and I followed your mother blind.
She egged me to borrow the money, an' she helped me to clear the loan,
When we bought half-shares in a cheap 'un and hoisted a flag of our own.
Patching and coaling on credit, and living the Lord knew how,
We started the Red Ox freighters—we've eight-and-thirty now.
And those were the days of clippers, and the freights were clipper-freights,°
And we knew we were making our fortune, but she died in Macassar Straits—
By the Little Paternosters, as you come to the Union Bank—°
And we dropped her in fourteen fathom: I pricked it off where she sank.
Owners we were, full owners, and the boat was christened for her,
And she died in the *Mary Gloster*. My heart, how young we were!
So I went on a spree round Java and well-nigh ran her ashore,
But your mother came and warned me and I wouldn't liquor no more:°
Strict I stuck to my business, afraid to stop or I'd think,
Saving the money (she warned me), and letting the other men drink.
And I met M'Cullough in London (I'd saved five 'undred then),
And 'tween us we started the Foundry—three forges and twenty men.
Cheap repairs for the cheap 'uns. It paid, and the business grew;
For I bought me a steam-lathe patent, and that was a gold mine too.
'Cheaper to build 'em than buy 'em,' *I* said, but M'Cullough he shied,
And we wasted a year in talking before we moved to the Clyde.
And the Lines were all beginning, and we all of us started fair,
Building our engines like houses and staying the boilers square.

But M'Cullough 'e wanted cabins with marble and maple and all,
And Brussels an' Utrecht velvet, and baths and a Social Hall,
And pipes for closets all over, and cutting the frames too light,
But M'Cullough he died in the Sixties, and—Well, I'm dying to-night. . . .
I knew—*I* knew what was coming, when we bid on the *Byfleet's* keel—
They piddled and piffled with iron. I'd given my orders for steel!
Steel and the first expansions. It paid, I tell you, it paid,°
When we came with our nine-knot freighters and collared the long-run trade!
And they asked me how I did it, and I gave 'em the Scripture text,
'You keep your light so shining a little in front o' the next!'°
They copied all they could follow, but they couldn't copy my mind,
And I left 'em sweating and stealing a year and a half behind.
Then came the armour-contracts, but that was M'Cullough's side;
He was always best in the Foundry, but better, perhaps, he died.
I went through his private papers; the notes was plainer than print;
And I'm no fool to finish if a man'll give me a hint.
(I remember his widow was angry.) So I saw what his drawings meant,
And I started the six-inch rollers, and it paid me sixty per cent.°
Sixty per cent *with* failures, and more than twice we could do,
And a quarter-million to credit, and I saved it all for you!
I thought—it doesn't matter—you seemed to favour your ma,
But you're nearer forty than thirty, and I know the kind you are.
Harrer an' Trinity College! I ought to ha' sent you to sea—°
But I stood you an education, an' what have you done for me?
The things I knew was proper you wouldn't thank me to give,
And the things I knew was rotten you said was the way to live.
For you muddled with books and pictures, an' china an' etchin's an' fans,

And your rooms at college was beastly—more like a whore's than a man's;
Till you married that thin-flanked woman, as white and as stale as a bone,
An' she gave you your social nonsense; but where's that kid o' your own?
I've seen your carriages blocking the half o' the Cromwell Road,
But never the doctor's brougham to help the missus unload.
(So there isn't even a grandchild, an' the Gloster family's done.)
Not like your mother, she isn't. *She* carried her freight each run.
But they died, the pore little beggars! At sea she had 'em—they died.
Only you, an' you stood it. You haven't stood much beside.
Weak, a liar, and idle, and mean as a collier's whelp
Nosing for scraps in the galley. No help—my son was no help!
So he gets three 'undred thousand, in trust and the interest paid.
I wouldn't give it you, Dickie—you see, I made it in trade.
You're saved from soiling your fingers, and if you have no child,
It all comes back to the business. 'Gad, won't your wife be wild!
'Calls and calls in her carriage, her 'andkerchief up to 'er eye:
'Daddy! dear daddy's dyin'!' and doing her best to cry.
Grateful? Oh, yes, I'm grateful, but keep her away from here.
Your mother 'ud never ha' stood 'er, and, anyhow, women are queer. . . .
There's women will say I've married a second time. Not quite!
But give pore Aggie a hundred, and tell her your lawyers'll fight.
She was the best o' the boiling—you'll meet her before it ends.
I'm in for a row with the mother—I'll leave you settle my friends.
For a man he must go with a woman, which women don't understand—
Or the sort that say they can see it they aren't the marrying brand.
But I wanted to speak o' your mother that's Lady Gloster still;

I'm going to up and see her, without its hurting the will.
Here! Take your hand off the bell-pull. Five thousand's waiting for you,
If you'll only listen a minute, and do as I bid you do.
They'll try to prove me crazy, and, if you bungle, they can;
And I've only you to trust to! (O God, why ain't it a man?)
There's some waste money on marbles, the same as M'Cullough tried—
Marbles and mausoleums—but I call that sinful pride.
There's some ship bodies for burial—we've carried 'em, soldered and packed;
Down in their wills they wrote it, and nobody called *them* cracked.
But me—I've too much money, and people might . . . All my fault:
It come o' hoping for grandsons and buying that Wokin' vault. . . .
I'm sick o' the 'ole dam' business. I'm going back where I came.
Dick, you're the son o' my body, and you'll take charge o' the same!
I want to lie by your mother, ten thousand mile away,
And they'll want to send me to Woking; and that's where you'll earn your pay.
I've thought it out on the quiet, the same as it ought to be done—
Quiet, and decent, and proper—an' here's your orders, my son.
You know the Line? You don't, though. You write to the Board, and tell
Your father's death has upset you an' you're goin' to cruise for a spell,
An' you'd like the *Mary Gloster*—I've held her ready for this—
They'll put her in working order and you'll take her out as she is.
Yes, it was money idle when I patched her and laid her aside
(Thank God, I can pay for my fancies!)—the boat where your mother died,
By the Little Paternosters, as you come to the Union Bank,
We dropped her—I think I told you—and I pricked it off where she sank.
['Tiny she looked on the grating—that oily, treacly sea—]
'Hundred and Eighteen East, remember, and South just Three.

Easy bearings to carry—Three South—Three to the dot;
But I gave McAndrew a copy in case of dying—or not.°
And so you'll write to McAndrew, he's Chief of the Maori Line;
They'll give him leave, if you ask 'em and say it's business o' mine.
I built three boats for the Maoris, an' very well pleased they were,
An' I've known Mac since the Fifties, and Mac knew me—and her.
After the first stroke warned me I sent him the money to keep
Against the time you'd claim it, committin' your dad to the deep;
For you are the son o' my body, and Mac was my oldest friend,
I've never asked 'im to dinner, but he'll see it out to the end.
Stiff-necked Glasgow beggar! I've heard he's prayed for my soul,
But he couldn't lie if you paid him, and he'd starve before he stole.
He'll take the *Mary* in ballast—you'll find her a lively ship;
And you'll take Sir Anthony Gloster, that goes on 'is wedding-trip,
Lashed in our old deck-cabin with all three port-holes wide,
The kick o' the screw beneath him and the round blue seas outside!
Sir Anthony Gloster's carriage—our 'ouse-flag flyin' free—
Ten thousand men on the pay-roll and forty freighters at sea!
He made himself and a million, but this world is a fleetin' show,°
And he'll go to the wife of 'is bosom the same as he ought to go—
By the heel of the Paternosters—there isn't a chance to mistake—
And Mac'll pay you the money as soon as the bubbles break!
Five thousand for six weeks' cruising, the staunchest freighter afloat,
And Mac he'll give you your bonus the minute I'm out o' the boat!
He'll take you round to Macassar, and you'll come back alone;
He knows what I want o' the *Mary*. . . . I'll do what I please with my own.

Your mother 'ud call it wasteful, but I've seven-and-thirty
more;
I'll come in my private carriage and bid it wait at the door....
For my son 'e was never a credit: 'e muddled with books and
art,
And 'e lived on Sir Anthony's money and 'e broke Sir
Anthony's heart.
There isn't even a grandchild, and the Gloster family's done—
The only one you left me—O mother, the only one!
Harrer and Trinity College—me slavin' early an' late—
An' he thinks I'm dying crazy, and you're in Macassar Strait!
Flesh o' my flesh, my dearie, for ever an' ever amen,
That first stroke come for a warning. I ought to ha' gone to you
then.
But—cheap repairs for a cheap 'un—the doctors said I'd do.
Mary, why didn't *you* warn me? I've allus heeded to you,
Excep'—I know—about women; but you are a spirit now;
An', wife, they was only women, and I was a man. That's how.
An' a man 'e must go with a woman, as you *could* not
understand;
But I never talked 'em secrets. I paid 'em out o' hand.
Thank Gawd, I can pay for my fancies! Now what's five
thousand to me,
For a berth off the Paternosters in the haven where I would be?
I believe in the Resurrection, if I read my Bible plain,
But I wouldn't trust 'em at Wokin'; we're safer at sea again.
For the heart it shall go with the treasure—go down to the sea
in ships.°
I'm sick of the hired women. I'll kiss my girl on her lips!
I'll be content with my fountain. I'll drink from my own well,
And the wife of my youth shall charm me—an' the rest can go
to Hell!
(Dickie, *he* will, that's certain.) I'll lie in our standin'-bed,
An' Mac'll take her in ballast—an' she trims best by the
head....
Down by the head an' sinkin', her fires are drawn and cold,
And the water's splashin' hollow on the skin of the empty
hold—
Churning an' choking and chuckling, quiet and scummy and
dark—
Full to her lower hatches and risin' steady. Hark!

That was the after-bulkhead. . . . She's flooded from stem to stern. . . .
'Never seen death yet, Dickie? . . . Well, now is your time to learn!

McAndrew's Hymn

Lord, Thou hast made this world below the shadow of a dream,°
An', taught by time, I tak' it so—exceptin' always Steam.
From coupler-flange to spindle-guide I see Thy Hand, O God—
Predestination in the stride o' yon connectin'-rod.
John Calvin might ha' forged the same—enorrmous, certain, slow—
Ay, wrought it in the furnace-flame—my 'Institutio.'°
I cannot get my sleep to-night; old bones are hard to please;
I'll stand the middle watch up here—alone wi' God an' these
My engines, after ninety days o' race an' rack an' strain
Through all the seas of all Thy world, slam-bangin' home again.
Slam-bang too much—they knock a wee—the crosshead-gibs are loose,
But thirty thousand mile o' sea has gied them fair excuse. . . .
Fine, clear an' dark—a full-draught breeze, wi' Ushant out o' sight,
An' Ferguson relievin' Hay. Old girl, ye'll walk to-night!
His wife's at Plymouth. . . . Seventy—One—Two—Three since he began—°
Three turns for Mistress Ferguson . . . and who's to blame the man?
There's none at any port for me, by drivin' fast or slow,
Since Elsie Campbell went to Thee, Lord, thirty years ago.
(The year the *Sarah Sands* was burned. Oh, roads we used to tread,
Fra' Maryhill to Pollokshaws—fra' Govan to Parkhead!)
Not but they're ceevil on the Board. Ye'll hear Sir Kenneth say:

'Good morrn, McAndrew! Back again? An' how's your bilge to-day?'
Miscallin' technicalities but handin' me my chair
To drink Madeira wi' three Earls—the auld Fleet Engineer
That started as a boiler-whelp—when steam and he were low.
I mind the time we used to serve a broken pipe wi' tow!°
Ten pound was all the pressure then—Eh! Eh!—a man wad drive;
An' here, our workin' gauges give one hunder sixty-five!
We're creepin' on wi' each new rig—less weight an' larger power;
There'll be the loco-boiler next an' thirty mile an hour!
Thirty an' more. What I ha' seen since ocean-steam began
Leaves me na doot for the machine: but what about the man?
The man that counts, wi' all his runs, one million mile o' sea:
Four time the span from earth to moon. . . . How far, O Lord, from Thee
That wast beside him night an' day? Ye mind my first typhoon?
It scoughed the skipper on his way to jock wi' the saloon.°
Three feet were on the stokehold-floor—just slappin' to an' fro—
An' cast me on a furnace-door. I have the marks to show.
Marks! I ha' marks o' more than burns—deep in my soul an' black,
An' times like this, when things go smooth, my wickudness comes back.
The sins o' four an' forty years, all up an' down the seas,
Clack an' repeat like valves half-fed. . . . Forgie's our trespasses!
Nights when I'd come on deck to mark, wi' envy in my gaze,
The couples kittlin' in the dark between the funnel-stays;°
Years when I raked the Ports wi' pride to fill my cup o' wrong—
Judge not, O Lord, my steps aside at Gay Street in Hong-Kong!
Blot out the wastrel hours of mine in sin when I abode—
Jane Harrigan's an' Number Nine, The Reddick an' Grant Road!
An' waur than all—my crownin' sin—rank blasphemy an' wild.
I was not four and twenty then—Ye wadna judge a child?

I'd seen the Tropics first that run—new fruit, new smells, new
air—
How could I tell—blind-fou wi' sun—the Deil was lurkin'
there?
By day like playhouse-scenes the shore slid past our sleepy
eyes;
By night those soft, lasceevious stars leered from those velvet
skies,
In port (we used no cargo-steam) I'd daunder down the
streets—°
An ijjit grinnin' in a dream—for shells an' parrakeets,
An' walkin'-sticks o' carved bamboo an' blowfish stuffed an'
dried—
Fillin' my bunk wi' rubbishry the Chief put overside.
Till, off Sambawa Head, Ye mind, I heard a land-breeze ca',
Milk-warm wi' breath o' spice an' bloom: 'McAndrew, come
awa'!'
Firm, clear an' low—no haste, no hate—the ghostly whisper
went,
Just statin' eevidential facts beyon' all argument:
'Your mither's God's a graspin' deil, the shadow o' yoursel',
'Got out o' books by meenisters clean daft on Heaven an' Hell.
'They mak' him in the Broomielaw, o' Glasgie cold an' dirt,
'A jealous, pridefu' fetich, lad, that's only strong to hurt.
'Ye'll not go back to Him again an' kiss His red-hot rod,°
'But come wi' Us' (Now, who were *They*?) an' know the
Leevin' God,°
'That does not kipper souls for sport or break a life in jest,°
'But swells the ripenin' cocoanuts an' ripes the woman's
breast.'
An' there it stopped—cut off—no more—that quiet, certain
voice—
For me, six months o' twenty-four, to leave or take at choice.
'Twas on me like a thunderclap—it racked me through an'
through—
Temptation past the show o' speech, unnameable an' new—
The Sin against the Holy Ghost? . . . An' under all, our screw.°

That storm blew by but left behind her anchor-shiftin' swell.
Thou knowest all my heart an' mind, Thou knowest, Lord, I
fell—

Third on the *Mary Gloster* then, and first that night in Hell!°
Yet was Thy Hand beneath my head, about my feet Thy Care—
Fra' Deli clear to Torres Strait, the trial o' despair,
But when we touched the Barrier Reef Thy answer to my prayer! . . .
We dared na run that sea by night but lay an' held our fire,
An' I was drowsin' on the hatch—sick—sick wi' doubt an' tire:
'Better the sight of eyes that see than wanderin' o' desire!'°
Ye mind that word? Clear as our gongs—again, an' once again,
When rippin' down through coral-trash ran out our moorin'-chain:
An', by Thy Grace, I had the Light to see my duty plain.
Light on the engine-room—no more—bright as our carbons burn.
I've lost it since a thousand times, but never past return!

. . . .

Obsairve! Per annum we'll have here two thousand souls aboard—
Think not I dare to justify myself before the Lord,
But—average fifteen hunder souls safe-borne fra' port to port—
I *am* o' service to my kind. Ye wadna blame the thought?
Maybe they steam from Grace to Wrath—to sin by folly led—
It isna mine to judge their path—their lives are on my head.
Mine at the last—when all is done it all comes back to me,
The fault that leaves six thousand ton a log upon the sea.
We'll tak' one stretch—three weeks an' odd by ony road ye steer—
Fra' Cape Town east to Wellington—ye need an engineer.
Fail there—ye've time to weld your shaft—ay, eat it, ere ye're spoke;°
Or make Kerguelen under sail—three jiggers burned wi' smoke!
An' home again—the Rio run: it's no child's play to go
Steamin' to bell for fourteen days o' snow an' floe an' blow.°
The bergs like kelpies overside that girn an' turn an' shift°
Whaur, grindin' like the Mills o' God, goes by the big South drift.°
(Hail, Snow and Ice that praise the Lord. I've met them at their work,

An' wished we had anither route or they anither kirk.)
Yon's strain, hard strain, o' head an' hand, for though Thy Power brings
All skill to naught, Ye'll understand a man must think o' things.
Then, at the last, we'll get to port an' hoist their baggage clear—
The passengers, wi' gloves an' canes—an' this is what I'll hear:
'Well, thank ye for a pleasant voyage. The tender's comin' now.'
While I go testin' follower-bolts an' watch the skipper bow.
They've words for every one but me—shake hands wi' half the crew,
Except the dour Scots engineer, the man they never knew.
An' yet I like the wark for all we've dam'-few pickin's here—
No pension, an' the most we'll earn 's four hunder pound a year.
Better myself abroad? Maybe. *I'd* sooner starve than sail
Wi' such as call a snifter-rod *ross*. . . . French for nightingale.°
Commeesion on my stores? Some do; but I cannot afford
To lie like stewards wi' patty-pans. I'm older than the Board.
A bonus on the coal I save? Ou ay, the Scots are close,
But when I grudge the strength Ye gave I'll grudge their food to *those*.
(There's bricks that I might recommend—an' clink the fire-bars cruel.
No! Welsh—Wangarti at the worst—an' damn all patent fuel!)
Inventions? Ye must stay in port to mak' a patent pay.
My Deeferential Valve-Gear taught me how that business lay.
I blame no chaps wi' clearer heads for aught they make or sell.
I found that I could not invent an' look to these as well.
So, wrestled wi' Apollyon—Nah!—fretted like a bairn—
But burned the workin'-plans last run, wi' all I hoped to earn.
Ye know how hard an Idol dies, an' what that meant to me—
E'en tak' it for a sacrifice acceptable to Thee. . . .
Below there! Oiler! What's your wark? Ye find it runnin' hard?
Ye needn't swill the cup wi' oil—this isn't the Cunard!
Ye thought? Ye are not paid to think. Go, sweat that off again!
Tck! Tck! It's deeficult to sweer nor tak' The Name in vain!
Men, ay, an women, call me stern. Wi' these to oversee,
Ye'll note I've little time to burn on social repartee.

The bairns see what their elders miss; they'll hunt me to an' fro,
Till for the sake of—well, a kiss—I tak' 'em down below.
That minds me of our Viscount loon—Sir Kenneth's kin—the chap
Wi' Russia-leather tennis-shoon an' spar-decked yachtin'-cap.
I showed him round last week, o'er all—an' at the last says he:
'Mister McAndrew, don't you think steam spoils romance at sea?'
Damned ijjit! I'd been doon that morn to see what ailed the throws,°
Manholin', on my back—the cranks three inches off my nose.
Romance! Those first-class passengers they like it very well,
Printed an' bound in little books; but why don't poets tell?
I'm sick of all their quirks an' turns—the loves an' doves they dream—
Lord, send a man like Robbie Burns to sing the Song o' Steam!
To match wi' Scotia's noblest speech yon orchestra sublime
Whaurto—uplifted like the Just—the tail-rods mark the time.°
The crank-throws give the double-bass, the feed-pump sobs an' heaves,
An' now the main eccentrics start their quarrel on the sheaves:
Her time, her own appointed time, the rocking link-head bides,
Till—hear that note?—the rod's return whings glimmerin' through the guides.
They're all awa'! True beat, full power, the clangin' chorus goes
Clear to the tunnel where they sit, my purrin' dynamoes.
Interdependence absolute, foreseen, ordained, decreed,
To work, Ye'll note, at ony tilt an' every rate o' speed.
Fra' skylight-lift to furnace-bars, backed, bolted, braced an' stayed,
An' singin' like the Mornin' Stars for joy that they are made;°
While, out o' touch o' vanity, the sweatin' thrust-block says:
'Not unto us the praise, or man—not unto us the praise!'°
Now, a' together, hear them lift their lesson—theirs an' mine:
'Law, Orrder, Duty an' Restraint, Obedience, Discipline!'
Mill, forge an' try-pit taught them that when roarin' they arose,
An' whiles I wonder if a soul was gied them wi' the blows.
Oh for a man to weld it then, in one trip-hammer strain,
Till even first-class passengers could tell the meanin' plain!

But no one cares except mysel' that serve an' understand
My seven thousand horse-power here. Eh, Lord! They're grand—they're grand!
Uplift am I? When first in store the new-made beasties stood,
Were Ye cast down that breathed the Word declarin' all things good?°
Not so! O' that warld-liftin' joy no after-fall could vex,°
Ye've left a glimmer still to cheer the Man—the Arrtifex!°
That holds, in spite o' knock and scale, o' friction, waste an' slip,
An' by that light—now, mark my word—we'll build the Perfect Ship.
I'll never last to judge her lines or take her curve—not I.
But I ha' lived an' I ha' worked. Be thanks to Thee, Most High!
An' I ha' done what I ha' done—judge Thou if ill or well—
Always Thy Grace preventin' me. . . .
    Losh! Yon's the 'Stand-by' bell.
Pilot so soon? His flare it is. The mornin'-watch is set.
Well, God be thanked, as I was sayin', I'm no Pelagian yet.°
Now I'll tak' on. . . .
    'Morrn, Ferguson. Man, have ye ever thought
What your good leddy costs in coal? . . . I'll burn 'em down to port.

The Song of the Banjo

You couldn't pack a Broadwood half a mile—°
  You mustn't leave a fiddle in the damp—
You couldn't raft an organ up the Nile,
  And play it in an Equatorial swamp.
I travel with the cooking-pots and pails—
  I'm sandwiched 'tween the coffee and the pork—
And when the dusty column checks and tails,°
  You should hear me spur the rearguard to a walk!

With my '*Pilly-willy-winky-winky-popp!*'
  [Oh, it's any tune that comes into my head!]
So I keep 'em moving forward till they drop;
  So I play 'em up to water and to bed.

In the silence of the camp before the fight,
  When it's good to make your will and say your prayer,
You can hear my *strumpty-tumpty* overnight,
  Explaining ten to one was always fair.
I'm the Prophet of the Utterly Absurd,
  Of the Patently Impossible and Vain—
And when the Thing that Couldn't has occurred,
  Give me time to change my leg and go again.

  With my '*Tumpa-tumpa-tumpa-tumpa-tump!*'
    In the desert where the dung-fed camp-smoke curled.
  There was never voice before us till I led our lonely
      chorus,
    I—the war-drum of the White Man round the world!

By the bitter road the Younger Son must tread,
  Ere he win to hearth and saddle of his own,—
'Mid the riot of the shearers at the shed,
  In the silence of the herder's hut alone—
In the twilight, on a bucket upside down,
  Hear me babble what the weakest won't confess—
I am Memory and Torment—I am Town!
  I am all that ever went with evening dress!

  With my '*Tunka-tunka-tunka-tunka-tunk!*'
    [So the lights—the London Lights—grow near and
      plain!]
  So I rowel 'em afresh towards the Devil and the Flesh,
    Till I bring my broken rankers home again.°

In desire of many marvels over sea,
  Where the new-raised tropic city sweats and roars,
I have sailed with Young Ulysses from the quay
  Till the anchor rumbled down on stranger shores.
He is blooded to the open and the sky,
  He is taken in a snare that shall not fail,
He shall hear me singing strongly, till he die,
  Like the shouting of a backstay in a gale.

  With my '*Hya! Heeya! Heeya! Hullah! Haul!*'
    [Oh, the green that thunders aft along the deck!]

Are you sick o' towns and men? You must sign and sail again,
For it's 'Johnny Bowlegs, pack your kit and trek!'°

Through the gorge that gives the stars at noon-day clear—
Up the pass that packs the scud beneath our wheel—°
Round the bluff that sinks her thousand fathom sheer—
Down the valley with our guttering brakes asqueal:
Where the trestle groans and quivers in the snow,°
Where the many-shedded levels loop and twine,°
Hear me lead my reckless children from below
Till we sing the Song of Roland to the pine!°

With my '*Tinka-tinka-tinka-tinka-tink!*'
[Oh, the axe has cleared the mountain, croup and crest!]°
And we ride the iron stallions down to drink,°
Through the cañons to the waters of the West!

And the tunes that mean so much to you alone—
Common tunes that make you choke and blow your nose—
Vulgar tunes that bring the laugh that brings the groan—
I can rip your very heartstrings out with those;
With the feasting, and the folly, and the fun—
And the lying, and the lusting, and the drink,
And the merry play that drops you, when you're done,
To the thoughts that burn like irons if you think.

With my '*Plunka-lunka-lunka-lunka-lunk!*'
Here's a trifle on account of pleasure past,
Ere the wit that made you win gives you eyes to see your sin
And—the heavier repentance at the last!

Let the organ moan her sorrow to the roof—
I have told the naked stars the Grief of Man!
Let the trumpet snare the foeman to the proof—
I have known Defeat, and mocked it as we ran!
My bray ye may not alter nor mistake
When I stand to jeer the fatted Soul of Things,
But the Song of Lost Endeavour that I make,
Is it hidden in the twanging of the strings?

With my '*Ta-ra-rara-rara-ra-ra-rrrp!*'
[Is it naught to you that hear and pass me by?]
But the word—the word is mine, when the order moves the line
And the lean, locked ranks go roaring down to die!

The grandam of my grandam was the Lyre—
[Oh, the blue below the little fisher-huts!]
That the Stealer stooping beachward filled with fire,°
Till she bore my iron head and ringing guts!
By the wisdom of the centuries I speak—
To the tune of yestermorn I set the truth—
I, the joy of life unquestioned—I, the Greek—
I, the everlasting Wonder-song of Youth!

With my '*Tinka-tinka-tinka-tinka-tink!*'
[What d'ye lack, my noble masters! What d'ye lack?]°
So I draw the world together link by link:
Yea, from Delos up to Limerick and back!°

From *A Song of the English*

The Song of the Dead

Hear now the Song of the Dead—in the North by the torn berg-edges—
They that look still to the Pole, asleep by their hide-stripped sledges.
Song of the Dead in the South—in the sun by their skeleton horses,
Where the warrigal whimpers and bays through the dust of the sere river-courses.°

Song of the Dead in the East—in the heat-rotted jungle-hollows,°
Where the dog-ape barks in the kloof—in the brake of the buffalo-wallows.°
Song of the Dead in the West—in the Barrens, the pass that betrayed them,°
Where the wolverine tumbles their packs from the camp and the grave-mound they made them;
Hear now the Song of the Dead!

I

We were dreamers, dreaming greatly, in the man-stifled town;
We yearned beyond the sky-line where the strange roads go down.
Came the Whisper, came the Vision, came the Power with the Need,
Till the Soul that is not man's soul was lent us to lead.
As the deer breaks—as the steer breaks—from the herd where they graze,
In the faith of little children we went on our ways.
Then the wood failed—then the food failed—then the last water dried—
In the faith of little children we lay down and died.
On the sand-drift—on the veldt-side—in the fern-scrub we lay,
That our sons might follow after by the bones on the way.
Follow after—follow after! We have watered the root,
And the bud has come to blossom that ripens for fruit!
Follow after—we are waiting, by the trails that we lost,
For the sounds of many footsteps, for the tread of a host.
Follow after—follow after—for the harvest is sown:
By the bones about the wayside ye shall come to your own!

When Drake went down to the Horn
And England was crowned thereby,
'Twixt seas unsailed and shores unhailed
Our Lodge—our Lodge was born
(And England was crowned thereby!)°

Which never shall close again
By day nor yet by night,
While man shall take his life to stake
At risk of shoal or main
(By day nor yet by night)

But standeth even so
As now we witness here,
While men depart, of joyful heart,
Adventure for to know
(As now bear witness here!)

II

We have fed our sea for a thousand years
  And she calls us, still unfed,
Though there's never a wave of all her waves
  But marks our English dead:
We have strawed our best to the weed's unrest,
  To the shark and the sheering gull.
If blood be the price of admiralty,
  Lord God, we ha' paid in full!

There's never a flood goes shoreward now
  But lifts a keel we manned;
There's never an ebb goes seaward now
  But drops our dead on the sand—
But slinks our dead on the sands forlore,
  From the Ducies to the Swin.°
If blood be the price of admiralty,
  If blood be the price of admiralty,
Lord God, we ha' paid it in!

We must feed our sea for a thousand years,
  For that is our doom and pride,
As it was when they sailed with the *Golden Hind*,
Or the wreck that struck last tide—
Or the wreck that lies on the spouting reef
  Where the ghastly blue-lights flare.°
If blood be the price of admiralty,
If blood be the price of admiralty,
If blood be the price of admiralty,
  Lord God, we ha' bought it fair!

The Deep-Sea Cables

The wrecks dissolve above us; their dust drops down from
    afar—
  Down to the dark, to the utter dark, where the blind white
    sea-snakes are.
There is no sound, no echo of sound, in the deserts of the deep,
  Or the great grey level plains of ooze where the shell-burred
    cables creep.°

Here in the womb of the world—here on the tie-ribs of earth
  Words, and the words of men, flicker and flutter and beat—
Warning, sorrow, and gain, salutation and mirth—
  For a Power troubles the Still that has neither voice nor feet.

They have wakened the timeless Things; they have killed their
    father Time;
  Joining hands in the gloom, a league from the last of the sun.
Hush! Men talk to-day o'er the waste of the ultimate slime,
  And a new Word runs between: whispering, 'Let us be one!'

The Three-Decker

'The three-volume novel is extinct.'

Full thirty foot she towered from waterline to rail.
It took a watch to steer her, and a week to shorten sail;
But, spite all modern notions, I've found her first and best—
The only certain packet for the Islands of the Blest.°

Fair held the breeze behind us—'twas warm with lovers'
    prayers.
We'd stolen wills for ballast and a crew of missing heirs.
They shipped as Able Bastards till the Wicked Nurse
    confessed,
And they worked the old three-decker to the Islands of the
    Blest.

By ways no gaze could follow, a course unspoiled of Cook,°
Per Fancy, fleetest in man, our titled berths we took,
With maids of matchless beauty and parentage unguessed,
And a Church of England parson for the Islands of the Blest.

We asked no social questions—we pumped no hidden shame—
We never talked obstetrics when the Little Stranger came:
We left the Lord in Heaven, we left the fiends in Hell.
We weren't exactly Yussufs, but—Zuleika didn't tell.°

No moral doubt assailed us, so when the port we neared,
The villain had his flogging at the gangway, and we cheered.

'Twas fiddle in the foc's'le—'twas garlands on the mast,
For every one got married, and I went ashore at last.

I left 'em all in couples a-kissing on the decks.
I left the lovers loving and the parents signing cheques.
In endless English comfort, by county-folk caressed,
I left the old three-decker at the Islands of the Blest! . . .

That route is barred to steamers: you'll never lift again
Our purple-painted headlands or the lordly keeps of Spain.
They're just beyond your skyline, howe'er so far you cruise
In a ram-you-damn-you liner with a brace of bucking screws.

Swing round your aching searchlight—'twill show no haven's peace.
Ay, blow your shrieking sirens at the deaf, grey-bearded seas!
Boom out the dripping oil-bags to skin the deep's unrest—°
And you aren't one knot the nearer to the Islands of the Blest.

But when you're threshing, crippled, with broken bridge and rail,
At a drogue of dead convictions to hold you head to gale,
Calm as the Flying Dutchman, from truck to taffrail dressed,°
You'll see the old three-decker for the Islands of the Blest.

You'll see her tiering canvas in sheeted silver spread;
You'll hear the long-drawn thunder 'neath her leaping figure-head;
While far, so far above you, her tall poop-lanterns shine
Unvexed by wind or weather like the candles round a shrine!

Hull down—hull down and under—she dwindles to a speck,
With noise of pleasant music and dancing on her deck.
All's well—all's well aboard her—she's left you far behind,
With a scent of old-world roses through the fog that ties you blind.

Her crews are babes or madmen? Her port is all to make?
You're manned by Truth and Science, and you steam for steaming's sake?°
Well, tinker up your engines—you know your business best—
She's taking tired people to the Islands of the Blest!

'When 'Omer Smote 'Is Bloomin' Lyre'

When 'Omer smote 'is bloomin' lyre,
He'd 'eard men sing by land an' sea;
An' what he thought 'e might require,
'E went an' took—the same as me!

The market-girls an' fishermen,
The shepherds an' the sailors, too,
They 'eard old songs turn up again,
But kep' it quiet—same as you!

They knew 'e stole; 'e knew they knowed.
They didn't tell, nor make a fuss,
But winked at 'Omer down the road,
An' 'e winked back—the same as us!

The King

'Farewell, Romance!' the Cave-men said;
'With bone well carved He went away.
'Flint arms the ignoble arrowhead,
'And jasper tips the spear to-day.
'Changed are the Gods of Hunt and Dance,
'And He with these. Farewell, Romance!'

'Farewell, Romance!' the Lake-folk sighed;
'We lift the weight of flatling years;
'The caverns of the mountain-side
'Hold Him who scorns our hutted piers.
'Lost hills whereby we dare not dwell,
'Guard ye His rest. Romance, Farewell!'

'Farewell, Romance!' the Soldier spoke;
'By sleight of sword we may not win,
'But scuffle 'mid uncleanly smoke
'Of arquebus and culverin.
'Honour is lost, and none may tell
'Who paid good blows. Romance, farewell!'

'Farewell, Romance!' the Traders cried;
  'Our keels have lain with every sea.
'The dull-returning wind and tide
  'Heave up the wharf where we would be;
'The known and noted breezes swell
'Our trudging sails. Romance, farewell!'

'Good-bye, Romance!' the Skipper said;
  'He vanished with the coal we burn.
'Our dial marks full-steam ahead,
  'Our speed is timed to half a turn.
'Sure as the ferried barge we ply
''Twixt port and port. Romance, good-bye!'

'Romance!' the season-tickets mourn,
  '*He* never ran to catch His train,
'But passed with coach and guard and horn—
  'And left the local—late again!
'Confound Romance!' . . . And all unseen
Romance brought up the nine-fifteen.

His hand was on the lever laid,
  His oil-can soothed the worrying cranks,
His whistle waked the snowbound grade,
  His fog-horn cut the reeking Banks;
By dock and deep and mine and mill
The Boy-god reckless laboured still!

Robed, crowned and throned, He wove His spell,
  Where heart-blood beat or hearth-smoke curled,
With unconsidered miracle,
  Hedged in a backward-gazing world:
Then taught His chosen bard to say:
'Our King was with us—yesterday!'

That Day

It got beyond all orders an' it got beyond all 'ope;
  It got to shammin' wounded an' retirin' from the 'alt.

'Ole companies was lookin' for the nearest road to slope;
  It were just a bloomin' knock-out—an' our fault!

Now there ain't no chorus 'ere to give,
  Nor there ain't no band to play;
An' I wish I was dead 'fore I done what I did,
  Or seen what I seed that day!

We was sick o' bein' punished, an' we let 'em know it, too;
  An' a company-commander up an' 'it us with a sword,
An' some one shouted ''Ook it!' an' it come to *sove-ki-poo*,°
  An' we chucked our rifles from us—O my Gawd!

There was thirty dead an' wounded on the ground we wouldn't keep—
  No, there wasn't more than twenty when the front begun to go—
But, Christ! along the line o' flight they cut us up like sheep,
  An' that was all we gained by doin' so!

I 'eard the knives be'ind me, but I dursn't face my man,
  Nor I don't know where I went to, 'cause I didn't 'alt to see,
Till I 'eard a beggar squealin' out for quarter as 'e ran,
  An' I thought I knew the voice an'—it was me!

We was 'idin' under bedsteads more than 'arf a march away:
  We was lyin' up like rabbits all about the country-side;
An' the Major cursed 'is Maker 'cause 'e'd lived to see that day,
  An' the Colonel broke 'is sword acrost, an' cried.

We was rotten 'fore we started—we was never disci*plined*;
  We made it out a favour if an order was obeyed.
Yes, every little drummer 'ad 'is rights an' wrongs to mind,
  So we had to pay for teachin'—an' we paid!

The papers 'id it 'andsome, but you know the Army knows;
  We was put to groomin' camels till the regiments withdrew,
An' they gave us each a medal for subduin' England's foes,
  An' I 'ope you like my song—because it's true!

An' there ain't no chorus 'ere to give,
Nor there ain't no band to play;
But I wish I was dead 'fore I done what I did,
Or seen what I seed that day!

From THE FIVE NATIONS (1903)

Recessional

God of our fathers, known of old,°
  Lord of our far-flung battle-line,
Beneath whose awful Hand we hold°
  Dominion over palm and pine—°
Lord God of Hosts, be with us yet,°
Lest we forget—lest we forget!°

The tumult and the shouting dies;°
  The Captains and the Kings depart:°
Still stands Thine ancient sacrifice,
  An humble and a contrite heart.°
Lord God of Hosts, be with us yet,
Lest we forget—lest we forget!

Far-called, our navies melt away;
  On dune and headland sinks the fire:
Lo, all our pomp of yesterday
  Is one with Nineveh and Tyre!°
Judge of the Nations, spare us yet,°
Lest we forget—lest we forget!

If, drunk with sight of power, we loose
  Wild tongues that have not Thee in awe,
Such boastings as the Gentiles use,°
  Or lesser breeds without the Law—°
Lord God of Hosts, be with us yet,
Lest we forget—lest we forget!

For heathen heart that puts her trust
  In reeking tube and iron shard,
All valiant dust that builds on dust,
  And guarding, calls not Thee to guard,
For frantic boast and foolish word—
Thy mercy on Thy People, Lord!

The White Man's Burden

Take up the White Man's burden—
 Send forth the best ye breed—
Go bind your sons to exile
 To serve your captives' need;
To wait in heavy harness
 On fluttered folk and wild—
Your new-caught, sullen peoples,
 Half devil and half child.

Take up the White Man's burden—
 In patience to abide,
To veil the threat of terror
 And check the show of pride;
By open speech and simple,
 An hundred times made plain,
To seek another's profit,
 And work another's gain.

Take up the White Man's burden—
 The savage wars of peace—
Fill full the mouth of Famine
 And bid the sickness cease;
And when your goal is nearest
 The end for others sought,
Watch Sloth and heathen Folly
 Bring all your hope to nought.

Take up the White Man's burden—
 No tawdry rule of kings,
But toil of serf and sweeper—
 The tale of common things.
The ports ye shall not enter,
 The roads ye shall not tread,
Go make them with your living,
 And mark them with your dead!

Take up the White Man's burden—
 And reap his old reward:
The blame of those ye better,

The hate of those ye guard—
The cry of hosts ye humour
(Ah, slowly!) toward the light:—
'Why brought ye us from bondage,
Our loved Egyptian night?'

Take up the White Man's burden—
Ye dare not stoop to less—
Nor call too loud on Freedom
To cloak your weariness;
By all ye cry or whisper,
By all ye leave or do,
The silent, sullen peoples
Shall weigh your Gods and you.

Take up the White Man's burden—
Have done with childish days—
The lightly proffered laurel,
The easy, ungrudged praise.
Comes now, to search your manhood
Through all the thankless years,
Cold-edged with dear-bought wisdom,
The judgment of your peers!

Chant-Pagan

Me that 'ave been what I've been—
Me that 'ave gone where I've gone—
Me that 'ave seen what I've seen—
'Ow can I ever take on
With awful old England again,
An' 'ouses both sides of the street,
And 'edges two sides of the lane,
And the parson an' gentry between,
An' touchin' my 'at when we meet—
Me that 'ave been what I've been?

Me that 'ave watched 'arf a world
'Eave up all shiny with dew,
Kopje on kop to the sun,

An' as soon as the mist let 'em through
Our 'elios winkin' like fun—°
Three sides of a ninety-mile square,
Over valleys as big as a shire—
'Are ye there? Are ye there? Are ye there?'
An' then the blind drum of our fire . . .
An' I'm rollin' 'is lawns for the Squire,
Me!

Me that 'ave rode through the dark
Forty mile, often, on end,
Along the Ma'ollisberg Range,
With only the stars for my mark
An' only the night for my friend,
An' things runnin' off as you pass,
An' things jumpin' up in the grass,
An' the silence, the shine an' the size
Of the 'igh, unexpressible skies—
I am takin' some letters almost
As much as a mile to the post,
An' 'mind you come back with the change!'
Me!

Me that saw Barberton took
When we dropped through the clouds on their 'ead,
An' they 'ove the guns over and fled—
Me that was through Di'mond 'Ill,
An' Pieters an' Springs an' Belfast—
From Dundee to Vereeniging all—
Me that stuck out to the last
(An' five bloomin' bars on my chest)—
I am doin' my Sunday-school best,
By the 'elp of the Squire an' 'is wife
(Not to mention the 'ousemaid an' cook),
To come in an' 'ands up an' be still,
An' honestly work for my bread,
My livin' in that state of life
To which it shall please God to call
Me!°

Me that 'ave followed my trade
In the place where the Lightnin's are made;

'Twixt the Rains and the Sun and the Moon—
Me that lay down an' got up
Three years with the sky for my roof—
That 'ave ridden my 'unger an' thirst
Six thousand raw mile on the hoof,
With the Vaal and the Orange for cup,
An' the Brandwater Basin for dish,—
Oh! it's 'ard to be'ave as they wish
(Too 'ard, an' a little too soon),
I'll 'ave to think over it first—
Me!
I will arise an' get 'ence—°
I will trek South and make sure
If it's only my fancy or not
That the sunshine of England is pale,
And the breezes of England are stale,
An' there's somethin' gone small with the lot.
For I know of a sun an' a wind,
An' some plains and a mountain be'ind,
An' some graves by a barb-wire fence,
An' a Dutchman I've fought 'oo might give
Me a job were I ever inclined
To look in an' offsaddle an' live
Where there's neither a road nor a tree—
But only my Maker an' me,
And I think it will kill me or cure,
So I think I will go there an' see.
Me!

Lichtenberg

Smells are surer than sounds or sights
To make your heart-strings crack—
They start those awful voices o' nights
That whisper, 'Old man, come back!'
That must be why the big things pass
And the little things remain,
Like the smell of the wattle by Lichtenberg,
Riding in, in the rain.

There was some silly fire on the flank
  And the small wet drizzling down—
There were the sold-out shops and the bank
  And the wet, wide-open town;
And we were doing escort-duty
  To somebody's baggage-train,
And I smelt wattle by Lichtenberg—
  Riding in, in the rain.

It was all Australia to me—
  All I had found or missed:
Every face I was crazy to see,
  And every woman I'd kissed:
All that I shouldn't ha' done, God knows!
  (As He knows I'll do it again),
That smell of the wattle round Lichtenberg,
  Riding in, in the rain!

And I saw Sydney the same as ever,
  The picnics and brass-bands;
And my little homestead on Hunter River
  And my new vines joining hands.
It all came over me in one act
  Quick as a shot through the brain—
With the smell of the wattle round Lichtenberg,
  Riding in, in the rain.

I have forgotten a hundred fights,
  But one I shall not forget—
With the raindrops bunging up my sights
  And my eyes bunged up with wet;
And through the crack and the stink of the cordite,
  (Ah, Christ! My country again!)
The smell of the wattle by Lichtenberg,
  Riding in, in the rain!

The Files

(*The Sub-editor speaks*)

Files—
The Files—
Office Files!
Oblige me by referring to the Files.
Every question man can raise,
Every phrase of every phase
Of that question is on record in the Files—
(Threshed out threadbare—fought and finished in the Files).
Ere the Universe at large
Was our new-tipped arrows' targe—
Ere we rediscovered Mammon and his wiles—
Faenza, gentle reader, spent her—five-and-twentieth leader—°
(You will find him, and some others, in the Files).
Warn all coming Robert Brownings and Carlyles,
It will interest them to hunt among the Files
Where unvisited, a-cold,
Lie the crowded years of old
In that Kensal-Green of greatness called the Files
(In our newspaPère-la-Chaise the Office Files),°
Where the dead men lay them down
Meekly sure of long renown,
And above them, sere and swift,
Packs the daily deepening drift
Of the all-recording, all-effacing Files—
The obliterating, automatic Files.
Count the mighty men who slung
Ink, Evangel, Sword, or Tongue
When Reform and you were young—
Made their boasts and spake according in the Files—
(Hear the ghosts that wake applauding in the Files!)
Trace each all-forgot career
From long primer through brevier
Unto Death, a para minion in the Files°
(Para minion—solid—bottom of the Files). . . .
Some successful Kings and Queens adorn the Files.
They were great, their views were leaded,°
And their deaths were triple-headed,°

So they catch the eye in running through the Files
(Show as blazes in the mazes of the Files);
For their 'paramours and priests,'
And their gross, jack-booted feasts,
And their 'epoch-marking actions' see the Files.
Was it Bomba fled the blue Sicilian isles?
Was it Saffi, a professor
Once of Oxford, brought redress or
Garibaldi?° Who remembers
Forty-odd-year-old Septembers?—
Only sextons paid to dig among the Files
(Such as I am, born and bred among the Files).
You must hack through much deposit
Ere you know for sure who was it
Came to burial with such honour in the Files
(Only seven seasons back beneath the Files).
'Very great our loss and grievous—
'So our best and brightest leave us,
'And it ends the Age of Giants,' say the Files;
All the '60—'70—'80—'90 Files
(The open-minded, opportunist Files—
The easy 'O King, live for ever' Files).
It is good to read a little in the Files;
'Tis a sure and sovereign balm
Unto philosophic calm,
Yea, and philosophic doubt when Life beguiles.
When you know Success is Greatness,
When you marvel at your lateness
In apprehending facts so plain to Smiles
(Self-helpful, wholly strenuous Samuel Smiles).°
When your Imp of Blind Desire
Bids you set the Thames afire,
You'll remember men have done so—in the Files.
You'll have seen those flames transpire—in the Files
(More than once that flood has run so—in the Files).
When the Conchimarian horns°
Of the reboantic Norns°
Usher gentlemen and ladies
With new lights on Heaven and Hades,
Guaranteeing to Eternity
All yesterday's modernity;

When Brocken-spectres made by°
Some one's breath on ink parade by,
Very earnest and tremendous,
Let not shows of shows offend us.
When of everything we like we
Shout ecstatic: '*Quod ubique*,
'*Quod ab omnibus* means *semper*!'°
Oh, my brother, keep your temper!
Light your pipe and take a look along the Files.
You've a better chance to guess
At the meaning of Success
(Which is Greatness—*vide* Press)
When you've seen it in perspective in the Files!

The Islanders

No doubt but ye are the People—your throne is above the King's.
Whoso speaks in your presence must say acceptable things:
Bowing the head in worship, bending the knee in fear—
Bringing the word well smoothen—such as a King should hear.

Fenced by your careful fathers, ringed by your leaden seas,°
Long did ye wake in quiet and long lie down at ease;
Till ye said of Strife, 'What is it?' of the Sword, 'It is far from our ken';
Till ye made a sport of your shrunken hosts and a toy of your armèd men.
Ye stopped your ears to the warning—ye would neither look nor heed—
Ye set your leisure before their toil and your lusts above their need.
Because of your witless learning and your beasts of warren and chase,°
Ye grudged your sons to their service and your fields for their camping-place.
Ye forced them glean in the highways the straw for the bricks they brought;°
Ye forced them follow in byways the craft that ye never taught.

Ye hampered and hindered and crippled; ye thrust out of sight and away
Those that would serve you for honour and those that served you for pay.
Then were the judgments loosened; then was your shame revealed,
At the hands of a little people, few but apt in the field.
Yet ye were saved by a remnant (and your land's long-suffering star),
When your strong men cheered in their millions while your striplings went to the war.
Sons of the sheltered city—unmade, unhandled, unmeet—
Ye pushed them raw to the battle as ye picked them raw from the street.
And what did ye look they should compass? Warcraft learned in a breath,
Knowledge unto occasion at the first far view of Death?
So? And ye train your horses and the dogs ye feed and prize?
How are the beasts more worthy than the souls, your sacrifice?
But ye said, 'Their valour shall show them' but ye said, 'The end is close.'
And ye sent them comfits and pictures to help them harry your foes:
And ye vaunted your fathomless power, and ye flaunted your iron pride,
Ere—ye fawned on the Younger Nations for the men who could shoot and ride!°
Then ye returned to your trinkets; then ye contented your souls
With the flannelled fools at the wicket or the muddied oafs at the goals.
Given to strong delusion, wholly believing a lie,
Ye saw that the land lay fenceless, and ye let the months go by
Waiting some easy wonder, hoping some saving sign—°
Idle—openly idle—in the lee of the forespent Line.°
Idle—except for your boasting—and what is your boasting worth
If ye grudge a year of service to the lordliest life on earth?
Ancient, effortless, ordered, cycle on cycle set,
Life so long untroubled, that ye who inherit forget
It was not made with the mountains, it is not one with the deep.

Men, not gods, devised it. Men, not gods, must keep.
Men, not children, servants, or kinsfolk called from afar,
But each man born in the Island broke to the matter of war.
Soberly and by custom taken and trained for the same,
Each man born in the Island entered at youth to the game—
As it were almost cricket, not to be mastered in haste,
But after trial and labour, by temperance, living chaste.
As it were almost cricket—as it were even your play,
Weighed and pondered and worshipped, and practised day and day.
So ye shall bide sure-guarded when the restless lightnings wake
In the womb of the blotting war-cloud, and the pallid nations quake.
So, at the haggard trumpets, instant your soul shall leap
Forthright, accoutred, accepting—alert from the wells of sleep.
So at the threat ye shall summon—so at the need ye shall send
Men, not children or servants, tempered and taught to the end;
Cleansed of servile panic, slow to dread or despise,
Humble because of knowledge, mighty by sacrifice. . . .
But ye say, 'It will mar our comfort.' Ye say, 'It will minish our trade.'
Do ye wait for the spattered shrapnel ere ye learn how a gun is laid?
For the low, red glare to southward when the raided coast-towns burn?
(Light ye shall have on that lesson, but little time to learn.)
Will ye pitch some white pavilion, and lustily even the odds,
With nets and hoops and mallets, with rackets and bats and rods?
Will the rabbit war with your foemen—the red deer horn them for hire?
Your kept cock-pheasant keep you?—he is master of many a shire.
Arid, aloof, incurious, unthinking, unthanking, gelt,
Will ye loose your schools to flout them till their brow-beat columns melt?°
Will ye pray them or preach them, or print them, or ballot them back from your shore?
Will your workmen issue a mandate to bid them strike no more?

Will ye rise and dethrone your rulers? (Because ye were idle
both?
Pride by Insolence chastened? Indolence purged by Sloth?)
No doubt but ye are the People; who shall make you afraid?
Also your gods are many; no doubt but your gods shall aid.
Idols of greasy altars built for the body's ease;
Proud little brazen Baals and talking fetishes;
Teraphs of sept and party and wise wood-pavement gods—
These shall come down to the battle and snatch you from under
the rods?°
From the gusty, flickering gun-roll with viewless salvoes rent,
And the pitted hail of the bullets that tell not whence they were
sent.
When ye are ringed as with iron, when ye are scourged as with
whips,
When the meat is yet in your belly, and the boast is yet on your
lips;
When ye go forth at morning and the noon beholds you broke,
Ere ye lie down at even, your remnant, under the yoke?

No doubt but ye are the People—absolute, strong, and wise;
Whatever your heart has desired ye have not withheld from your
eyes.
On your own heads, in your own hands, the sin and the saving lies!

From SONGS FROM BOOKS and MORE SONGS FROM BOOKS 1912–32

Mother o' Mine

If I were hanged on the highest hill,
Mother o' mine, O mother o' mine!
I know whose love would follow me still,
Mother o' mine, O mother o' mine!

If I were drowned in the deepest sea,
Mother o' mine, O mother o' mine!
I know whose tears would come down to me,
Mother o' mine, O mother o' mine!

If I were damned of body and soul,
I know whose prayers would make me whole,
Mother o' mine, O mother o' mine!

Merrow Down

I

There runs a road by Merrow Down—
  A grassy track to-day it is—
An hour out of Guildford town,
  Above the river Wey it is.

Here, when they heard the horse-bells ring,
  The ancient Britons dressed and rode
To watch the dark Phoenicians bring
  Their goods along the Western Road.

Yes, here, or hereabouts, they met
  To hold their racial talks and such—°
To barter beads for Whitby jet,
  And tin for gay shell torques and such.

But long and long before that time
  (When bison used to roam on it)
Did Taffy and her Daddy climb
  That Down, and had their home on it.

Then beavers built in Broadstonebrook
  And made a swamp where Bramley stands;
And bears from Shere would come and look
  For Taffimai where Shamley stands.

The Wey, that Taffy called Wagai,
  Was more than six times bigger then;
And all the Tribe of Tegumai
  They cut a noble figure then!

II

Of all the Tribe of Tegumai
  Who cut that figure, none remain,—
On Merrow Down the cuckoos cry—
  The silence and the sun remain.

But as the faithful years return
  And hearts unwounded sing again,
Comes Taffy dancing through the fern
  To lead the Surrey spring again.

Her brows are bound with bracken-fronds,
  And golden elf-locks fly above;
Her eyes are bright as diamonds
  And bluer than the sky above.

In mocassins and deer-skin cloak,
  Unfearing, free and fair she flits,
And lights her little damp-wood smoke
  To show her Daddy where she flits.

For far—oh, very far behind,
 So far she cannot call to him,
Comes Tegumai alone to find
 The daughter that was all to him!

'Cities and Thrones and Powers'

Cities and Thrones and Powers
 Stand in Time's eye,
Almost as long as flowers,
 Which daily die:
But, as new buds put forth
 To glad new men,
Out of the spent and unconsidered Earth
 The Cities rise again.

This season's Daffodil,
 She never hears
What change, what chance, what chill,
 Cut down last year's;
But with bold countenance,
 And knowledge small,
Esteems her seven days' continuance
 To be perpetual.

So Time that is o'er-kind
 To all that be,
Ordains us e'en as blind,
 As bold as she:
That in our very death,
 And burial sure,
Shadow to shadow, well persuaded, saith,
 'See how our works endure!'

Harp Song of the Dane Women

What is a woman that you forsake her,
And the hearth-fire and the home-acre,
To go with the old grey Widow-maker?

She has no house to lay a guest in—
But one chill bed for all to rest in,
That the pale suns and the stray bergs nest in.

She has no strong white arms to fold you,
But the ten-times-fingering weed to hold you—
Out on the rocks where the tide has rolled you.

Yet, when the signs of summer thicken,
And the ice breaks, and the birch-buds quicken,
Yearly you turn from our side, and sicken—

Sicken again for the shouts and the slaughters.
You steal away to the lapping waters,
And look at your ship in her winter-quarters.

You forget our mirth, and talk at the tables,
The kine in the shed and the horse in the stables—
To pitch her sides and go over her cables.

Then you drive out where the storm-clouds swallow,
And the sound of your oar-blades, falling hollow,
Is all we have left through the months to follow.

Ah, what is Woman that you forsake her,
And the hearth-fire and the home-acre,
To go with the old grey Widow-maker?

A Smuggler's Song

If you wake at midnight, and hear a horse's feet,
Don't go drawing back the blind, or looking in the street,
Them that asks no questions isn't told a lie.
Watch the wall, my darling, while the Gentlemen go by!
  Five and twenty ponies
  Trotting through the dark—
  Brandy for the Parson,
  'Baccy for the Clerk;
  Laces for a lady, letters for a spy,
And watch the wall, my darling, while the Gentlemen go by!

Running round the woodlump if you chance to find
Little barrels, roped and tarred, all full of brandy-wine,
Don't you shout to come and look, nor use 'em for your play.
Put the brishwood back again—and they'll be gone next day!°

If you see the stable-door setting open wide;
If you see a tired horse lying down inside;
If your mother mends a coat cut about and tore;
If the lining's wet and warm—don't you ask no more!

If you meet King George's men, dressed in blue and red,
You be careful what you say, and mindful what is said.
If they call you 'pretty maid,' and chuck you 'neath the chin,
Don't you tell where no one is, nor yet where no one's been!

Knocks and footsteps round the house—whistles after dark—
You've no call for running out till the house-dogs bark.
Trusty's here, and *Pincher's* here, and see how dumb they lie—
They don't fret to follow when the Gentlemen go by!

If you do as you've been told, 'likely there's a chance,
You'll be give a dainty doll, all the way from France,
With a cap of Valenciennes, and a velvet hood—°
A present from the Gentlemen, along o' being good!
Five and twenty ponies
Trotting through the dark—
Brandy for the Parson,
'Baccy for the Clerk.
Them that asks no questions isn't told a lie—
Watch the wall, my darling, while the Gentlemen go by!

The Four Angels

As Adam lay a-dreaming beneath the Apple Tree
The Angel of the Earth came down, and offered Earth in fee;
But Adam did not need it,
Nor the plough he would not speed it,
Singing:—'Earth and Water, Air and Fire,
What more can mortal man desire?'
(The Apple Tree's in bud.)

As Adam lay a-dreaming beneath the Apple Tree
The Angel of the Waters offered all the Seas in fee;
    But Adam would not take 'em,
    Nor the ships he wouldn't make 'em,
  Singing:—'Water, Earth and Air and Fire,
    What more can mortal man desire?'
      (The Apple Tree's in leaf.)

As Adam lay a-dreaming beneath the Apple Tree
The Angel of the Air he offered all the Air in fee;
    But Adam did not crave it,
    Nor the flight he wouldn't brave it,
  Singing:—'Air and Water, Earth and Fire,
    What more can mortal man desire?'
      (The Apple Tree's in bloom.)

As Adam lay a-dreaming beneath the Apple Tree
The Angel of the Fire rose up and not a word said he;
    But he wished a flame and made it,
    And in Adam's heart he laid it,
  Singing:—'Fire, Fire, burning Fire!
    Stand up and reach your heart's desire!'
      (The Apple Blossom's set.)

As Adam was a-working outside of Eden-Wall,
He used the Earth, he used the Seas, he used the Air and all;
    Till out of black disaster
    He arose to be the master
  Of Earth and Water, Air and Fire,
    But never reached his heart's desire!
      (The Apple Tree's cut down!)

The Way through the Woods

They shut the road through the woods
Seventy years ago.
Weather and rain have undone it again,

And now you would never know
There was once a road through the woods
Before they planted the trees.
It is underneath the coppice and heath
And the thin anemones.
Only the keeper sees
That, where the ring-dove broods,
And the badgers roll at ease,
There was once a road through the woods.

Yet, if you enter the woods
Of a summer evening late,
When the night-air cools on the trout-ringed pools
Where the otter whistles his mate,
(They fear not men in the woods,
Because they see so few)
You will hear the beat of a horse's feet,
And the swish of a skirt in the dew,
Steadily cantering through
The misty solitudes,
As though they perfectly knew
The old lost road through the woods. . . .
But there is no road through the woods.

If—

If you can keep your head when all about you
  Are losing theirs and blaming it on you,
If you can trust yourself when all men doubt you,
  But make allowance for their doubting too;
If you can wait and not be tired by waiting,
  Or being lied about, don't deal in lies,
Or being hated, don't give way to hating,
  And yet don't look too good, nor talk too wise:

If you can dream—and not make dreams your master;
  If you can think—and not make thoughts your aim;
If you can meet with Triumph and Disaster
  And treat those two impostors just the same;

If you can bear to hear the truth you've spoken
Twisted by knaves to make a trap for fools,
Or watch the things you gave your life to, broken,
And stoop and build 'em up with worn-out tools:

If you can make one heap of all your winnings
And risk it on one turn of pitch-and-toss,°
And lose, and start again at your beginnings
And never breathe a word about your loss;
If you can force your heart and nerve and sinew
To serve your turn long after they are gone,
And so hold on when there is nothing in you
Except the Will which says to them: 'Hold on!'

If you can talk with crowds and keep your virtue,
Or walk with Kings—nor lose the common touch,
If neither foes nor loving friends can hurt you,
If all men count with you, but none too much;
If you can fill the unforgiving minute
With sixty seconds' worth of distance run,
Yours is the Earth and everything that's in it,
And—which is more—you'll be a Man, my son!

Dane-geld (A.D. 980–1016)

It is always a temptation to an armed and agile nation
To call upon a neighbour and to say:—
'We invaded you last night—we are quite prepared to fight,
Unless you pay us cash to go away.'

And that is called asking for Dane-geld,
And the people who ask it explain
That you've only to pay 'em the Dane-geld
And then you'll get rid of the Dane!

It is always a temptation to a rich and lazy nation,
To puff and look important and to say:—
'Though we know we should defeat you, we have not the time to meet you.
We will therefore pay you cash to go away.'

And that is called paying the Dane-geld;
  But we've proved it again and again,
That if once you have paid him the Dane-geld
  You never get rid of the Dane.

It is wrong to put temptation in the path of any nation,
  For fear they should succumb and go astray;
So when you are requested to pay up or be molested,
  You will find it better policy to say:—

'We never pay *any*-one Dane-geld,
  No matter how trifling the cost;
For the end of that game is oppression and shame,
  And the nation that plays it is lost!'

Big Steamers

'Oh, where are you going to, all you Big Steamers,
  With England's own coal, up and down the salt seas?'
'We are going to fetch you your bread and your butter,
  Your beef, pork, and mutton, eggs, apples, and cheese.'

'And where will you fetch it from, all you Big Steamers,
  And where shall I write you when you are away?'
'We fetch it from Melbourne, Quebec, and Vancouver—
  Address us at Hobart, Hong-Kong, and Bombay.'

'But if anything happened to all you Big Steamers,
  And suppose you were wrecked up and down the salt sea?'
'Then you'd have no coffee or bacon for breakfast,
  And you'd have no muffins or toast for your tea.'

'Then I'll pray for fine weather for all you Big Steamers,
  For little blue billows and breezes so soft.'
'Oh, billows and breezes don't bother Big Steamers,
  For we're iron below and steel-rigging aloft.'

'Then I'll build a new lighthouse for all you Big Steamers,
  With plenty wise pilots to pilot you through.'

'Oh, the Channel's as bright as a ball-room already,
And pilots are thicker than pilchards at Looe.'°

'Then what can I do for you, all you Big Steamers,
Oh, what can I do for your comfort and good?'
'Send out your big warships to watch your big waters,
That no one may stop us from bringing you food.

'For the bread that you eat and the biscuits you nibble,
The sweets that you suck and the joints that you carve,
They are brought to you daily by all us Big Steamers—
And if any one hinders our coming you'll starve!'

The Children

These were our children who died for our lands: they were dear in our sight.
We have only the memory left of their home-treasured sayings and laughter.
The price of our loss shall be paid to our hands, not another's hereafter.
Neither the Alien nor Priest shall decide on it. That is our right.°
But who shall return us the children?

At the hour the Barbarian chose to disclose his pretences,
And raged against Man, they engaged, on the breasts that they bared for us,
The first felon-stroke of the sword he had long-time prepared for us—
Their bodies were all our defence while we wrought our defences.

They bought us anew with their blood, forbearing to blame us,
Those hours which we had not made good when the Judgment o'ercame us.
They believed us and perished for it. Our statecraft, our learning
Delivered them bound to the Pit and alive to the burning

Whither they mirthfully hastened as jostling for honour—
Not since her birth has our Earth seen such worth loosed upon her.

Nor was their agony brief, or once only imposed on them.
The wounded, the war-spent, the sick received no exemption:
Being cured they returned and endured and achieved our redemption,
Hopeless themselves of relief, till Death, marvelling, closed on them.

That flesh we had nursed from the first in all cleanness was given
To corruption unveiled and assailed by the malice of Heaven—
By the heart-shaking jests of Decay where it lolled on the wires—
To be blanched or gay-painted by fumes—to be cindered by fires—
To be senselessly tossed and retossed in stale mutilation
From crater to crater. For this we shall take expiation.
But who shall return us our children?

The Fabulists

When all the world would keep a matter hid,
Since Truth is seldom friend to any crowd,
Men write in fable, as old Æsop did,
Jesting at that which none will name aloud.
And this they needs must do, or it will fall°
Unless they please they are not heard at all.

When desperate Folly daily laboureth
To work confusion upon all we have,
When diligent Sloth demandeth Freedom's death,
And banded Fear commandeth Honour's grave—
Even in that certain hour before the fall,
Unless men please they are not heard at all.

Needs must all please, yet some not all for need,
Needs must all toil, yet some not all for gain,
But that men taking pleasure may take heed,
Whom present toil shall snatch from later pain.
Thus some have toiled, but their reward was small
Since, though they pleased, they were not heard at all.

This was the lock that lay upon our lips,
This was the yoke that we have undergone,
Denying us all pleasant fellowships
As in our time and generation.
Our pleasures unpursued age past recall,
And for our pains—we are not heard at all.

What man hears aught except the groaning guns?
What man heeds aught save what each instant brings?
When each man's life all imaged life outruns,
What man shall pleasure in imaginings?
So it hath fallen, as it was bound to fall,
We are not, nor we were not, heard at all.

The Survival

HORACE, Bk. V. Ode 22.

Securely, after days
Unnumbered, I behold
Kings mourn that promised praise
Their cheating bards foretold.

Of earth-constricting wars,
Of Princes passed in chains,
Of deeds out-shining stars,
No word or voice remains.

Yet furthest times receive,
And to fresh praise restore,
Mere breath of flutes at eve,
Mere seaweed on the shore.

A smoke of sacrifice;
  A chosen myrtle-wreath;
An harlot's altered eyes;
  A rage 'gainst love or death;

Glazed snow beneath the moon;
  The surge of storm-bowed trees—
The Cæsars perished soon,
  And Rome Herself: But these

Endure while Empires fall
  And Gods for Gods make room. . . .
Which greater God than all
  Imposed the amazing doom?

We and They

Father, Mother, and Me,
  Sister and Auntie say
All the people like us are We,
  And every one else is They.
And They live over the sea,
  While We live over the way,
But — would you believe it? — They look upon We
  As only a sort of They!

We eat pork and beef
  With cow-horn-handled knives.
They who gobble Their rice off a leaf,
  Are horrified out of Their lives;
While They who live up a tree,
  And feast on grubs and clay,
(Isn't it scandalous?) look upon We
  As a simply disgusting They!

We shoot birds with a gun.
  They stick lions with spears.
Their full-dress is un-.
  We dress up to Our ears.

They like Their friends for tea.
  We like Our friends to stay;
And, after all that, They look upon We
  As an utterly ignorant They!

We eat kitcheny food.
  We have doors that latch.
They drink milk or blood,
  Under an open thatch.
We have Doctors to fee.
  They have Wizards to pay.
And (impudent heathen!) They look upon We
  As a quite impossible They!

All good people agree,
  And all good people say,
All nice people, like Us, are We
  And every one else is They:
But if you cross over the sea,
  Instead of over the way,
You may end by (think of it!) looking on We
  As only a sort of They!

The Coiner

(*Circa* 1611)

(To be sung by the unlearned to the tune of 'King John and the Abbot of Canterbury,' and by the learned to 'Tempest-a-brewing.')

Against the Bermudas we foundered, whereby
This Master, that Swabber, yon Bo'sun, and I°
(Our pinnace and crew being drowned in the main)
Must beg for our bread through old England again.

For a bite and a sup, and a bed of clean straw,
We'll tell you such marvels as man never saw,
On a Magical Island which no one did spy
Save this Master, that Swabber, yon Bo'sun, and I.

Seven months among Mermaids and Devils and Sprites,
And Voices that howl in the cedars o' nights,
With further enchantments we underwent there.
Good Sirs, 'tis a tale to draw guts from a bear!

'Twixt Dover and Southwark it paid us our way,
Where we found some poor players were labouring a play;
And, willing to search what such business might be,
We entered the yard, both to hear and to see.

One hailed us for seamen and courteous-ly
Did guide us apart to a tavern near by
Where we told him our tale (as to many of late),
And he gave us good cheer, so we gave him good weight.

Mulled sack and strong waters on bellies well lined
With beef and black pudding do strengthen the mind;
And seeing him greedy for marvels, at last
From plain salted truth to flat leasing we passed.

But he, when on midnight our reckoning he paid,
Says, 'Never match coins with a Coiner by trade,
Or he'll turn your lead pieces to metal as rare
As shall fill him this globe, and leave something to spare. . . .'[10]

We slept where they laid us, and when we awoke
'Was a crown or five shillings in every man's poke.
We bit them and rang them, and, finding them good,
We drank to that Coiner as honest men should!

For a cup and a crust, and a truss, etc.

From THE YEARS BETWEEN (1919)

Gethsemane

The Garden called Gethsemane
  In Picardy it was,
And there the people came to see
  The English soldiers pass.
We used to pass—we used to pass
  Or halt, as it might be,
And ship our masks in case of gas
  Beyond Gethsemane.

The Garden called Gethsemane,
  It held a pretty lass,
But all the time she talked to me
  I prayed my cup might pass.
The officer sat on the chair,
  The men lay on the grass,
And all the time we halted there
  I prayed my cup might pass.

It didn't pass—it didn't pass—
  It didn't pass from me.
I drank it when we met the gas
  Beyond Gethsemane!

The Craftsman

Once, after long-drawn revel at The Mermaid,
He to the overbearing Boanerges°
Jonson, uttered (if half of it were liquor,
      Blessed be the vintage!)

Saying how, at an alehouse under Cotswold,
He had made sure of his very Cleopatra
Drunk with enormous, salvation-contemning
Love for a tinker.

How, while he hid from Sir Thomas's keepers,°
Crouched in a ditch and drenched by the midnight
Dews, he had listened to gipsy Juliet
Rail at the dawning.

How at Bankside, a boy drowning kittens
Winced at the business; whereupon his sister—
Lady Macbeth aged seven—thrust 'em under,
Sombrely scornful.

How on a Sabbath, hushed and compassionate—
She being known since her birth to the townsfolk—
Stratford dredged and delivered from Avon
Dripping Ophelia.

So, with a thin third finger marrying
Drop to wine-drop domed on the table,
Shakespeare opened his heart till the sunrise
Entered to hear him.

London waked and he, imperturbable,
Passed from waking to hurry after shadows . . .
Busied upon shows of no earthly importance?
Yes, but he knew it!

The Female of the Species

When the Himalayan peasant meets the he-bear in his pride,
He shouts to scare the monster, who will often turn aside.
But the she-bear thus accosted rends the peasant tooth and nail.
For the female of the species is more deadly than the male.

When Nag the basking cobra hears the careless foot of man,
He will sometimes wriggle sideways and avoid it if he can.

But his mate makes no such motion where she camps beside the trail.
For the female of the species is more deadly than the male.

When the early Jesuit fathers preached to Hurons and Choctaws,
They prayed to be delivered from the vengeance of the squaws.
'Twas the women, not the warriors, turned those stark enthusiasts pale.
For the female of the species is more deadly than the male.

Man's timid heart is bursting with the things he must not say,
For the Woman that God gave him isn't his to give away;
But when hunter meets with husband, each confirms the other's tale—
The female of the species is more deadly than the male.

Man, a bear in most relations—worm and savage otherwise,—
Man propounds negotiations, Man accepts the compromise.
Very rarely will he squarely push the logic of a fact
To its ultimate conclusion in unmitigated act.

Fear, or foolishness, impels him, ere he lay the wicked low,
To concede some form of trial even to his fiercest foe.
Mirth obscene diverts his anger—Doubt and Pity oft perplex
Him in dealing with an issue—to the scandal of The Sex!

But the Woman that God gave him, every fibre of her frame
Proves her launched for one sole issue, armed and engined for the same;
And to serve that single issue, lest the generations fail,
The female of the species must be deadlier than the male.

She who faces Death by torture for each life beneath her breast
May not deal in doubt or pity—must not swerve for fact or jest.
These be purely male diversions—not in these her honour dwells.
She the Other Law we live by, is that Law and nothing else.

She can bring no more to living than the powers that make her great

As the Mother of the Infant and the Mistress of the Mate.
And when Babe and Man are lacking and she strides unclaimed
to claim
Her right as femme (and baron), her equipment is the same.

She is wedded to convictions—in default of grosser ties;
Her contentions are her children, Heaven help him who
denies!—
He will meet no suave discussion, but the instant, white-hot,
wild,
Wakened female of the species warring as for spouse and child.

Unprovoked and awful charges—even so the she-bear fights,
Speech that drips, corrodes, and poisons—even so the cobra
bites,
Scientific vivisection of one nerve till it is raw
And the victim writhes in anguish—like the Jesuit with the
squaw!

So it comes that Man, the coward, when he gathers to confer
With his fellow-braves in council, dare not leave a place for her
Where, at war with Life and Conscience, he uplifts his erring
hands
To some God of Abstract Justice—which no woman
understands.

And Man knows it! Knows, moreover, that the Woman that
God gave him
Must command but may not govern—shall enthral but not
enslave him.
And *She* knows, because She warns him, and Her instincts
never fail,
That the Female of Her Species is more deadly than the Male.

'For All We Have and Are'

For all we have and are,
For all our children's fate,
Stand up and take the war.

The Hun is at the gate![°]
Our world has passed away,
In wantonness o'erthrown.
There is nothing left to-day
But steel and fire and stone!
  Though all we knew depart,
  The old Commandments stand:—
  'In courage keep your heart,
  In strength lift up your hand.'[°]

Once more we hear the word
That sickened earth of old:—
'No law except the Sword
Unsheathed and uncontrolled.'
Once more it knits mankind,
Once more the nations go
To meet and break and bind
A crazed and driven foe.

Comfort, content, delight,
The ages' slow-bought gain,
They shrivelled in a night.
Only ourselves remain
To face the naked days
In silent fortitude,
Through perils and dismays
Renewed and re-renewed.
  Though all we made depart,
  The old Commandments stand:—
  'In patience keep your heart,
  In strength lift up your hand.'

No easy hope or lies
Shall bring us to our goal,
But iron sacrifice
Of body, will, and soul.
There is but one task for all—
One life for each to give.
What stands if Freedom fall?
Who dies if England live?

My Boy Jack

'Have you news of my boy Jack?'
Not this tide.
'When d'you think that he'll come back?'
Not with this wind blowing, and this tide.

'Has any one else had word of him?'
Not this tide.
For what is sunk will hardly swim,
Not with this wind blowing, and this tide.

'Oh, dear, what comfort can I find?'
None this tide,
Nor any tide,
Except he did not shame his kind—
Not even with that wind blowing, and that tide.

Then hold your head up all the more,
This tide,
And every tide;
Because he was the son you bore,
And gave to that wind blowing and that tide!

Epitaphs of the War

'Equality of Sacrifice'

A. 'I was a Have.' B. 'I was a "have-not."'
(*Together.*) 'What hast thou given which I gave not?'

A Servant

We were together since the War began.
He was my servant—and the better man.°

A Son

My son was killed while laughing at some jest. I would I knew
What it was, and it might serve me in a time when jests are few.

An Only Son

I have slain none except my Mother. She
(Blessing her slayer) died of grief for me.

Ex-clerk

Pity not! The Army gave
Freedom to a timid slave:
In which Freedom did he find
Strength of body, will, and mind:
By which strength he came to prove
Mirth, Companionship, and Love:
For which Love to Death he went:
In which Death he lies content.

The Wonder

Body and Spirit I surrendered whole
To harsh Instructors—and received a soul . . .
If mortal man could change me through and through
From all I was—what may The God not do?

Hindu Sepoy in France

This man in his own country prayed we know not to what Powers.
We pray Them to reward him for his bravery in ours.

The Coward

I could not look on Death, which being known,
Men led me to him, blindfold and alone.

Shock

My name, my speech, my self I had forgot.
My wife and children came—I knew them not.
I died. My Mother followed. At her call
And on her bosom I remembered all.

A Grave near Cairo

Gods of the Nile, should this stout fellow here
Get out—get out! He knows not shame nor fear.

Pelicans in the Wilderness

A Grave near Halfa

The blown sand heaps on me, that none may learn
  Where I am laid for whom my children grieve. . . .
O wings that beat at dawning, ye return
  Out of the desert to your young at eve!

Two Canadian Memorials

I

We giving all gained all.
  Neither lament us nor praise.
Only in all things recall,
  It is Fear, not Death that slays.

II

From little towns in a far land we came,
  To save our honour and a world aflame.
By little towns in a far land we sleep;
  And trust that world we won for you to keep!

The Favour

Death favoured me from the first, well knowing I could not endure
  To wait on him day by day. He quitted my betters and came
Whistling over the fields, and, when he had made all sure,
  'Thy line is at end,' he said, 'but at least I have saved its name.'

The Beginner

On the first hour of my first day
  In the front trench I fell.
(Children in boxes at a play
  Stand up to watch it well.)

R.A.F. (Aged Eighteen)

Laughing through clouds, his milk-teeth still unshed,
Cities and men he smote from overhead.
His deaths delivered, he returned to play
Childlike, with childish things now put away.°

The Refined Man

I was of delicate mind. I stepped aside for my needs,
Disdaining the common office. I was seen from afar and killed. . . .°
How is this matter for mirth? Let each man be judged by his deeds.
I have paid my price to live with myself on the terms that I willed.

Native Water-Carrier (M.E.F.)

Prometheus brought down fire to men.
This brought up water.
The Gods are jealous—now, as then,
Giving no quarter.

Bombed in London

On land and sea I strove with anxious care
To escape conscription. It was in the air!

The Sleepy Sentinel

Faithless the watch that I kept: now I have none to keep.
I was slain because I slept: now I am slain I sleep.
Let no man reproach me again, whatever watch is unkept—
I sleep because I am slain. They slew me because I slept.

Batteries out of Ammunition

If any mourn us in the workshop, say
We died because the shift kept holiday.

Common Form

If any question why we died,
Tell them, because our fathers lied.

A Dead Statesman

I could not dig: I dared not rob:
Therefore I lied to please the mob.
Now all my lies are proved untrue
And I must face the men I slew.

What tale shall serve me here among
Mine angry and defrauded young?

The Rebel

If I had clamoured at Thy Gate
For gift of Life on Earth,
And, thrusting through the souls that wait,
Flung headlong into birth—
Even then, even then, for gin and snare
About my pathway spread,°
Lord, I had mocked Thy thoughtful care
Before I joined the Dead!
But now? . . . I was beneath Thy Hand
Ere yet the Planets came.
And now—though Planets pass, I stand
The witness to Thy shame!

The Obedient

Daily, though no ears attended,
Did my prayers arise.
Daily, though no fire descended,
Did I sacrifice.°
Though my darkness did not lift,
Though I faced no lighter odds,
Though the Gods bestowed no gift,
None the less,
None the less, I served the Gods!

A Drifter off Tarentum

He from the wind-bitten North with ship and companions descended,
Searching for eggs of death spawned by invisible hulls.
Many he found and drew forth. Of a sudden the fishery ended
In flame and a clamorous breath known to the eye-pecking gulls.

Destroyers in Collision

For Fog and Fate no charm is found
To lighten or amend.
I, hurrying to my bride, was drowned—
Cut down by my best friend.

Convoy Escort

I was a shepherd to fools
   Causelessly bold or afraid.
They would not abide by my rules.
   Yet they escaped. For I stayed.

Unknown Female Corpse

Headless, lacking foot and hand,
Horrible I come to land.
I beseech all women's sons
Know I was a mother once.

Raped and Revenged

One used and butchered me: another spied
Me broken—for which thing an hundred died.
So it was learned among the heathen hosts
How much a freeborn woman's favour costs.

Salonikan Grave

I have watched a thousand days
Push out and crawl into night
Slowly as tortoises.
Now I, too, follow these.
It is fever, and not the fight—
Time, not battle,—that slays.

The Bridegroom

Call me not false, beloved,
   If, from thy scarce-known breast
So little time removed,
   In other arms I rest.

For this more ancient bride,
   Whom coldly I embrace,
Was constant at my side
   Before I saw thy face.

Our marriage, often set—
   By miracle delayed—

At last is consummate,
And cannot be unmade.

Live, then, whom Life shall cure,
Almost, of Memory,
And leave us to endure
Its immortality.

V.A.D. (Mediterranean)

Ah, would swift ships had never been, for then we ne'er had found,
These harsh Ægean rocks between, this little virgin drowned,
Whom neither spouse nor child shall mourn, but men she nursed through pain
And—certain keels for whose return the heathen look in vain.

Actors

On a Memorial Tablet in Holy Trinity Church, Stratford-on-Avon

We counterfeited once for your disport
Men's joy and sorrow: but our day has passed.
We pray you pardon all where we fell short—
Seeing we were your servants to this last.

Journalists

On a Panel in the Hall of the Institute of Journalists

We have served our day.

From VERSE (INCLUSIVE EDITION) (1919)

Mine Sweepers

Dawn off the Foreland—the young flood making
  Jumbled and short and steep—
Black in the hollows and bright where it's breaking—
  Awkward water to sweep.
  'Mines reported in the fairway,
  'Warn all traffic and detain.
''Sent up *Unity*, *Claribel*, *Assyrian*, *Stormcock*, and
  Golden Gain.'

Noon off the Foreland—the first ebb making
  Lumpy and strong in the bight.
Boom after boom, and the golf-hut shaking
  And the jackdaws wild with fright!
  'Mines located in the fairway,
  'Boats now working up the chain,
'Sweepers—*Unity*, *Claribel*, *Assyrian*, *Stormcock*, and
  Golden Gain.'

Dusk off the Foreland—the last light going
  And the traffic crowding through,
And five damned trawlers with their syreens blowing
  Heading the whole review!
  'Sweep completed in the fairway.
  'No more mines remain.
''Sent back *Unity*, *Claribel*, *Assyrian*, *Stormcock*, and *Golden Gain*.'

The Gods of the Copybook Headings

As I pass through my incarnations in every age and race,
I make my proper prostrations to the Gods of the Market-Place.
Peering through reverent fingers I watch them flourish and fall,
And the Gods of the Copybook Headings, I notice, outlast them all.

We were living in trees when they met us. They showed us each in turn
That Water would certainly wet us, as Fire would certainly burn:
But we found them lacking in Uplift, Vision and Breadth of Mind,
So we left them to teach the Gorillas while we followed the March of Mankind.

We moved as the Spirit listed. *They* never altered their pace,
Being neither cloud nor wind-borne like the Gods of the Market-Place;
But they always caught up with our progress, and presently word would come
That a tribe had been wiped off its icefield, or the lights had gone out in Rome.

With the Hopes that our World is built on they were utterly out of touch,
They denied that the Moon was Stilton; they denied she was even Dutch.
They denied that Wishes were Horses; they denied that a Pig had Wings.
So we worshipped the Gods of the Market Who promised these beautiful things.

When the Cambrian measures were forming, They promised perpetual peace.
They swore, if we gave them our weapons, that the wars of the tribes would cease.

But when we disarmed They sold us and delivered us bound to our foe,
And the Gods of the Copybook Headings said: '*Stick to the Devil you know.*'

On the first Feminian Sandstones we were promised the Fuller Life
(Which started by loving our neighbour and ended by loving his wife)
Till our women had no more children and the men lost reason and faith,
And the Gods of the Copybook Headings said: '*The Wages of Sin is Death.*'°

In the Carboniferous Epoch we were promised abundance for all,
By robbing selected Peter to pay for collective Paul;
But, though we had plenty of money, there was nothing our money could buy,
And the Gods of the Copybook Headings said: '*If you don't work you die.*'

Then the Gods of the Market tumbled, and their smooth-tongued wizards withdrew,
And the hearts of the meanest were humbled and began to believe it was true
That All is not Gold that Glitters, and Two and Two make Four—
And the Gods of the Copybook Headings limped up to explain it once more.

. . . .

As it will be in the future, it was at the birth of Man—
There are only four things certain since Social Progress began:—
That the Dog returns to his Vomit and the Sow returns to her Mire,
And the burnt Fool's bandaged finger goes wabbling back to the Fire;°

And that after this is accomplished, and the brave new world begins

When all men are paid for existing and no man must pay for his
sins,
As surely as Water will wet us, as surely as Fire will burn,
The Gods of the Copybook Headings with terror and slaughter
return!

POEMS COLLECTED IN EDITIONS AFTER 1919

Hymn of Breaking Strain

The careful text-books measure
(Let all who build beware!)
The load, the shock, the pressure
Material can bear.
So, when the buckled girder
Lets down the grinding span,
The blame of loss, or murder,
Is laid upon the man.
Not on the Stuff—the Man!

But, in our daily dealing
With stone and steel, we find
The Gods have no such feeling
Of justice toward mankind.
To no set gauge they make us,—
For no laid course prepare—
And presently o'ertake us
With loads we cannot bear:
Too merciless to bear.

The prudent text-books give it
In tables at the end—
The stress that shears a rivet
Or makes a tie-bar bend—
What traffic wrecks macadam—
What concrete should endure—
But we, poor Sons of Adam,
Have no such literature,
To warn us or make sure!

We hold all Earth to plunder—
All Time and Space as well—

Too wonder-stale to wonder
  At each new miracle;
Till, in the mid-illusion
  Of Godhead 'neath our hand,
Falls multiple confusion
  On all we did or planned—
    The mighty works we planned.

We only of Creation
  (*Oh, luckier bridge and rail!*)
Abide the twin-damnation—
  To fail and know we fail.
Yet we—by which sole token
  We know we once were Gods—
Take shame in being broken
  However great the odds—
    The Burden or the Odds.

Oh, veiled and secret Power
  Whose paths we seek in vain,
Be with us in our hour
  Of overthrow and pain;
That we—by which sure token
  We know Thy ways are true—
In spite of being broken,
  Because of being broken,
    May rise and build anew.
    Stand up and build anew!

'Tin Fish'

The ships destroy us above
  And ensnare us beneath.
We arise, we lie down, and we move
  In the belly of Death.

The ships have a thousand eyes
  To mark where we come . . .

But the mirth of a seaport dies
When our blow gets home.

The Storm Cone

This is the midnight—let no star
Delude us—dawn is very far.
This is the tempest long foretold—
Slow to make head but sure to hold.

Stand by! The lull 'twixt blast and blast
Signals the storm is near, not past;
And worse than present jeopardy
May our forlorn to-morrow be.

If we have cleared the expectant reef,
Let no man look for his relief.
Only the darkness hides the shape
Of further peril to escape.

It is decreed that we abide
The weight of gale against the tide
And those huge waves the outer main
Sends in to set us back again.

They fall and whelm. We strain to hear
The pulses of her labouring gear,
Till the deep throb beneath us proves,
After each shudder and check, she moves!

She moves, with all save purpose lost,
To make her offing from the coast;
But, till she fetches open sea,
Let no man deem that he is free!

The Appeal

If I have given you delight
By aught that I have done,
Let me lie quiet in that night
Which shall be yours anon:

And for the little, little, span
The dead are borne in mind,
Seek not to question other than
The books I leave behind.

APPENDIX A. KIPLING'S INDIA

Kipling returned to India at the age of 16 to work as sub-editor on the *Civil and Military Gazette*, a newspaper published in Lahore in what is now Pakistan, but was then part of Punjab Province. At this period 'British India' was a patchwork of provinces under direct rule from the Indian Government, and semi-independent Native States whose rulers were influenced, if not controlled, by British 'Residents'. These geographical and political peculiarities were the result of Britain having absorbed, more by accident than design, the hitherto separate fiefdoms of the East India Company in the aftermath of the Mutiny in 1857. In addition, British influence stretched into outlying regions and border territories such as the North-West Frontier with Afghanistan. In 1883 Sir John Seeley, Professor of Modern History at Cambridge, declared in a famous lecture that Britain 'seem[ed], as it were, to have conquered and peopled half the world in a fit of absence of mind'. But by this date some presence of mind had begun to show itself. Queen Victoria had been declared Empress of India in 1877, affirming the coherence and legitimacy of British rule in succession to the Moguls, the last empire to control the whole of the subcontinent (effectively from the mid-sixteenth to the mid-eighteenth century). India was governed by a Viceroy at the head of a central administration based at Calcutta in the winter months and the Himalayan hill-station, Simla, during the hot weather. District administration was in the hands of a Civil Service which by Kipling's time was well developed, with separate departments and entrance by competitive examination on the home model. Legal and constitutional institutions had also grown up, as had a more systematic political opposition to British rule. Although there were many parts of the subcontinent which were unsettled and undeveloped, or in which British influence was tenuous, the 'wild' era of conquest and adventure had ended, as Dravot and Carnehan recognize: 'The Man who would be King' must go beyond the frontier to find his kingdom (see p. 64). The difficulties which beset the British in the years of Kipling's residence, especially the district administrators and soldiers he admired, were those he describes in his stories, poems, journalism, and letters: social and personal isolation, illness, boredom, occasional violence.

Kipling's attitude to British rule is best represented by a long letter which he wrote on the subject to his close friend and cousin Margaret Burne-Jones (nicknamed 'Wop') in November 1885. It is worth quoting at length because it gives the full range of his response on the threshold of his literary career, from the official to the personal, from the spokesman to the artist:

When you write 'native' who do you mean? The Mahommedan who hates the Hindu; the Hindu who hates the Mahommedan; the Sikh who loathes both; or the semi-anglicized product of our Indian colleges who is hated and despised by Sikh,

Hindu, and Mahommedan. Do you mean the Punjabi who will have nothing to do with the Bengali; the Mahrattha to whom the Punjabi's tongue is as incomprehensible as Russian to me; the Parsee who controls the whole trade of Bombay and ranges himself on all questions as an Englishman; the Sindee who is an outsider; the Bhil or the Gond who is an aborigine; the Rajput who despises everything on God's earth but himself; the Delhi traders who control trade to the value of millions; the Afghan who is only kept from looting these same merchants by dread of English interference. Which one of all the thousand conflicting tongues, races, nationalities and peoples between the Khaibar Pass and Ceylon do you mean? There is no such thing as the natives of India, any more than there is the 'People of India' as our friends the Indian delegates would have you believe. You may rest assured Wop that if we didn't hold the land in six months it would be one big cock pit of conflicting princelets. Now 'do the English as a rule feel the welfare of the natives much at heart.' Oh Wop! If you had met some of the men I know you would cross out the sentence and weep. What else are we working in the country for. For what else do the best men of the Commission die from overwork, and disease, if not to keep the people alive in the first place and healthy in the second. We spend our best men on the country like water and if ever a foreign country was made better through 'the blood of the martyrs' India is that country. I couldn't now tell you what the men one knows are doing but you can read for yourself if you will how Englishmen have laboured and died for the peoples of the country. Wop dear have you ever heard of a 'demoralized district'; when tens of thousands of peoples are panic stricken say, with an invasion of cholera—or dying from famine? Do you know how Englishmen, Oxford men expensively educated, are turned off to 'do' that district—to make their own arrangements for the cholera camps; for the prevention of disorder; or for famine relief, to pull the business through or die—whichever God wills. Then another man, or may be boy takes his place. Yes the English in India do do a little for the benefit of the natives and small thanks they get. . . . Then you demand:—Have we any interests in common? *Werry* few dear old Wop—the bulk of us—d——d few. And 'faith if you knew in what inconceivable filth of mind the peoples of India were brought up from their cradle; if you realized the views—or one tenth of the views—they hold about women and their absolute incapacity for speaking the truth as we understand it—the immeasurable gulf that lies between the two races in all things you would see how it comes to pass that the Englishman is prone to despise the natives (I *must* use that misleading term for brevity's sake)—and how, except in the matter of trade, to have little or nothing in common with him. Now this is a wholly wrong attitude of mind but it's one that a Briton who washes, and don't take bribes, and who thinks of other things besides intrigue and seduction most naturally falls into. *When he does*—goodbye to his chances of attempting to understand the people of the land. . . . Underneath our excellent administrative system; under the piles of reports and statistics; the thousands of troops; the doctors; and the civilian[,] runs wholly untouched and unaffected the life of the peoples of the land—a life as full of impossibilities and wonders as the Arabian nights. I don't want to gush over it but I do want you to understand Wop dear that, immediately outside of our own English life, is the dark and crooked and fantastic, and wicked, and awe inspiring life of 'the native'. Our rule, so long as no one steals too flagrantly or murders too openly, affects it in no way whatever—only fences it around and prevents it from being disturbed. I have done my little best to penetrate into it and have put the little I have learnt into the pages of 'Mother Maturin'—Heaven send that she may grow into a full blown novel before I die—My experiences of course are only a queer jumble of opium-dens, night houses, night strolls with natives; evenings spent in their company in their own homes (in the men's quarter of course) and the long yarns that my native friends spin me, and one or two queer things I've come across in my own office experience. The result of it all has been to interest me immensely and keenly in the people and to show me how little an Englishman can hope to understand 'em.

The 'full blown novel' of Indian life which Kipling was planning and drafting in this period never materialized—fortunately for him and for us. Its fragments lie scattered in the Indian fiction and poetry of the years 1885–1901, the date of the publication of *Kim*.

APPENDIX B. THE BRITISH ARMY IN INDIA

Kipling became interested in the British Army in India because his family home was in the Punjab. Most of the British military presence in India was deployed in the north-west of the country, along the frontier with Afghanistan and the supply lines behind it. In particular, Lahore gave Kipling the opportunity to observe and meet the common soldiers, non-commissioned officers, and subalterns who people his early fiction, because Lahore had one of the major military bases in the Punjab, the Mian Mir cantonment on the outskirts of the city.

In ch. 3 of *Something of Myself*, Kipling writes:

I got to meet the soldiery of those days in visits to Fort Lahore and, in a less degree, at Mian Mir Cantonments. My first and best beloved Battalion was the 2nd Fifth Fusiliers, with whom I dined in awed silence a few weeks after I came out. When they left I took up with their successors, the 30th East Lancashire, another North-country regiment; and, last, with the 31st East Surrey—a London recruited confederacy of skilful dog-stealers, some of them my good and loyal friends.[1] There were ghostly dinners too with Subalterns in charge of the Infantry Detachment at Fort Lahore, where, all among marble-inlaid, empty apartments of dead Queens, or under the domes of old tombs, meals began with the regulation thirty grains of quinine in the sherry, and ended—as Allah pleased! . . .

Having no position to consider, and my trade enforcing it, I could move at will in the fourth dimension. I came to realise the bare horrors of the private's life, and the unnecessary torments he endured on account of the Christian doctrine which lays down that 'the wages of sin is death.' It was counted impious that bazaar prostitutes should be inspected; or that the men should be taught elementary precautions in their dealings with them. This official virtue cost our Army in India nine thousand expensive white men a year always laid up from venereal disease. Visits to Lock Hospitals made me desire, as earnestly as I do to-day, that I might have six hundred priests—Bishops of the establishment for choice—to handle for six months precisely as the soldiers of my youth were handled.

The stories and poems which Kipling wrote about army life in barracks and about skirmishes on the frontier differ in one important respect. Whereas the ballads are spoken by generic and anonymous 'Tommies', the stories feature the famous 'soldiers three', or 'Three Musketeers', Privates Terence Mulvaney, Stanley Ortheris, and Jock (i.e. John) Learoyd. Ortheris and Learoyd

[1] Kipling's memory and nomenclature are slightly inaccurate. The regiments concerned were: the 2nd Battalion, the (Royal) Northumberland Fusiliers, 5th Foot (at Lahore 1882–5); the 1st Battalion, the East Surrey Regiment, 31st Foot (at Lahore from 1885); and the 2nd Battalion, the East Lancashire Regiment, 59th Foot (*RG*).

might be characters from the battalions which Kipling mentions above (Ortheris is a Cockney and a dog-stealer, Learoyd a northener); Mulvaney, an Irishman, originally served with a regiment which Kipling calls 'the Black Tyrone' (see below), but later transferred into the same unit as Ortheris and Learoyd, which Kipling never names except as (in Mulvaney's Irishism) 'the Ould Regiment'.

I reproduce here extracts from Charles Carrington's contribution to *RG* on the subject of 'Kipling and the Army in India' (i. 13–16; page references to this edition in square brackets):

Not a scrap of direct or indirect evidence has come to light leading us to suppose that his association with the Three Musketeers for a long period was actual . . . It is indeed extremely unlikely. The first 'Mulvaney' story ('The Three Musketeers', first printed in March 1887, then *Plain Tales from the Hills*, 1888) was written shortly before he left Lahore and it presents the three as comparative strangers to him. The stories are located in or near Lahore and are told of a regiment stationed at the great Lahore cantonment of Mian Mir. There is a detachment at 'Fort Amara' which sometimes seems to be the historic citadel of Lahore (as in 'With the Main Guard' [p. 24]) and sometimes a remote place somewhere else ('His Private Honour', *Many Inventions*, 1893). If Kipling had really been on friendly terms with the three for several years they must have served in the East Lancashires, who were at Mian Mir from 1880 to 1885; if he met them for the first time in 1887 they must have been in the Northumberland Fusiliers, the 'Tyneside Tail-Twisters', who succeeded the East Lancashires at Mian Mir; but the Northumberland Fusiliers were not at the battle of Ahmed Khel which the Three Musketeers refer to more than once. . . . A later story ('The Incarnation of Krishna Mulvaney', *Life's Handicap*, 1891) declares that the three had served together in Afghanistan, in Burma, and on the Northwest Frontier, presumably in the Black Mountain Campaign of 1888, but no British line regiment served in all three of these campaigns. . . .

As for the 'Ould Regiment', we must look at Gladstone's two reorganisations of the Army in 1871 and 1881. The first abolished the old long-service soldiers and the second introduced the county regiments with two linked battalions, one at home and one abroad. The Mulvaney stories reiterate the contempt of the old long-service men for the new short-service men . . . The mythical or real 'Mulvaney' first served in the 18th Royal Irish (the 'Black Tyrone'), then transferred to the 59th (the 'Ould Regiment') . . . After the [Second] Afghan War the regiments were reorganised: the old 30th and the old 59th were amalgamated to form the East Lancashire Regiment, of which a battalion was stationed at Mian Mir from 1880 to 1885. . . .

When we turn to battles it may first be noted that the Army stories and ballads deal mostly with other incidents of military life. The frontier was quiet during the seven years Kipling spent in India and he never saw troops under fire . . . In India he had paid one visit to the mouth of the Khyber Pass in March, 1885, and no more. . . . But when he arrived in India in 1882 all the talk was of the recent Afghan War and the consequent reorganisation of the Army.

NOTES

I have not glossed words and phrases found in the *Concise Oxford Dictionary*, which proved (sometimes surprisingly) adequate: it tells you what 'to go off at score' means (in 'Three and—an Extra' and 'The Village that Voted the Earth was Flat') and it has terms such as 'carneying' ('Fairy-Kist'); it glosses proper names which have found their way into current usage, such as 'Lothario' ('A Code of Morals') and 'Apollyon' ('McAndrew's Hymn'); it also has most common Anglo-Indian terms (such as 'sahib' and 'punkah') and many less common ones (such as 'ekka' and the equine meaning of 'tattoo'). I have not either supplemented or corrected Kipling's own glosses (e.g. 'the *loo*, the red-hot wind from the westward', 'The Man who would be King', p. 62), unless there was some point in fussing.

Like most editors I have relied heavily on the *Readers' Guide to Rudyard Kipling*, but I have not taken its word as gospel in all cases. It is an indispensable, but also erratic and occasionally misleading work. Where it forms my sole authority and is cited more or less verbatim I have appended '(*RG*)' to the note, but this does not mean that I have not drawn on it in other places. I have made considerable use of two other reference works: *Hobson-Jobson*, the 'Glossary of Anglo-Indian Words and Phrases' by Henry Yule and Arthur Burnell, which was enthusiastically reviewed by Kipling himself in the *Civil and Military Gazette* on its first appearance in 1886 (reference here is to the second edition, 1903); and Eric Partridge's *Penguin Dictionary of Historical Slang* (1972), an abridgement by Jacqueline Simpson of Partridge's *Dictionary of Slang and Unconventional English*, 1961).

For the stories, the date of first magazine publication is followed by the title and date of the volume in which the story was collected; intermediate and subsequent dates are not recorded unless there is something special about them.

Lispeth

First pub. *Civil and Military Gazette*, 29 Nov. 1886; coll. *Plain Tales from the Hills*, 1888.

The central character reappears as the 'Woman of Shamlegh' in ch. 14 of *Kim*, though the two stories are inconsistent: in *Kim* Lispeth is still majestic and seductive twelve years after the events of this story, and has two husbands (her tribe is polyandrous) whom she dominates.

Kipling presents the Englishman who deserts Lispeth with good-humoured contempt; his real hostility is reserved for the Christian missionaries. Several years later he seized the opportunity afforded him by the Revd John M. Gillespie, secretary of the Board of Foreign Missionaries of the Presbyterian Church in America, who wrote to him asking for a letter of support:

To tell the honest truth, no letter that I could write would in any way assist your cause . . . It is my fortune to have been born and to a large extent brought up among those whom white men call 'heathen'; and while I recognize the paramount duty of every white man to follow the teachings of his creed and conscience as 'a debtor to do the whole law [Gal. 5: 3],' it seems to me cruel that white men, whose governments are armed with the most murderous weapons known to science, should amaze and confound their fellow creatures with a doctrine of salvation imperfectly understood by themselves and a code of ethics foreign to the climate and instincts of those races whose most cherished customs they outrage and whose gods they insult.

This is a matter that has been very near to my heart and I thank you for having afforded me an opportunity to testify. (*Letters*, ii. 205–6)

The story is Kipling's first major portrayal of the power of love to exalt, to blind, and to wound.

1 *Epigraph*. By Kipling; there is no complete poem called 'The Convert'. Collected in the *Definitive Edition* ('Chapter Headings').

the Sutlej Valley on the Kotgarh side: the Sutlej is a river which rises in Tibet and flows westward through the Himalayas; Kotgarh is above the river on the south side, about 30 miles north-east of Simla on the road to Tibet.

pahari: mountainous or hilly; incorrectly used to qualify an abstract noun like 'pronunciation', according to *RG*. Later in the story it is used to mean 'hill-man'.

Moravian missionaries: the Moravian Brethren were a Protestant sect, associated with the Lutheran Church; founded in Saxony in 1722 (as a renewal and continuation of earlier sects) they were active in missionary work from an early date.

Diana of the Romans: the virgin goddess of hunting.

2 *Simla*: see headnote to 'Three and—an Extra', p. 532.

Narkunda: a local beauty-spot on the Simla–Tibet road about 12 miles south-west of Kotgarh (*RG*).

Bagi: a village in the hills 16 miles east-south-east of Kotgarh (*RG*).

3 *'globe-trotters' . . . the P. & O. fleet*: 'globe-trotter' is first cited in *OED* as a book title of 1875; the derogatory sense of 'extensive and hurried travelling over the world, for the sake of sight-seeing' was established by the mid-1880s. The P. & O. (Peninsular and Oriental) line dates back to 1837.

Dehra Dun: the nearest railhead in the plains to Kotgarh, 70 miles to the south-east (*RG*).

the Muttiani path: the next stage towards Simla from Narkunda (*RG*).

4 *Tarka Devi*: the goddess of the dawn, a local deity (*RG*).

Three and—An Extra

First pub. *Civil and Military Gazette*, 17 Nov. 1886; coll. *Plain Tales from the Hills*, 1888.

This is the first appearance of Mrs Hauksbee, who has a leading role in three other stories in *Plain Tales*: 'The Rescue of Pluffles', 'Consequences', and 'Kidnapped', and a cameo role in 'Venus Annodomini'. She also figures in stories in other collections, notably 'The Education of Otis Yeere' and 'A Second-rate Woman' (*Under the Deodars*, 1888). *Plain Tales* was dedicated to 'the wittiest woman in India', in other words to the original of Mrs Hauksbee, Isabella Burton, the wife of Major F. C. Burton, of the 1st Bengal Cavalry. Kipling met her at Simla, the hill-station in the Himalayas where the imperial administration was based during the hot weather, and which features in *Plain Tales* and *Departmental Ditties* as a place of sexual intrigue, social display, and power-politics (for a superb account of the atmosphere of Simla and other hill-stations, see James Morris's essay in J. Gross (ed.), *Rudyard Kipling: The Man, His Work and His World* (1972)). On 26 Oct. 1887 he wrote to her asking her to accept the dedication, though he later reassigned it to his mother (*Letters*, i. 144 and nn. 1 and 2).

5 *Epigraph*. The proverb is applied in the story by Mrs Bremmil, who lures her husband back rather than reproaching him for his infidelity.

gram: grain, 'specially appropriated to that kind of vetch which is the most general grain- (rather pulse-) food of horses all over India' (*Hobson-Jobson*).

6 *rise up and call her not blessed*: unlike the 'virtuous woman' in Prov. 31, whose 'children arise up, and call her blessed'.

But that is another story: 'The Rescue of Pluffles', which comes four stories later in *Plain Tales*. Mrs Hauksbee fights Mrs Reiver for possession of the conceited young idiot Pluffles, not because she wants him for herself but on behalf of Pluffles's fiancée, who is on her way from England to marry him. She takes Pluffles under her wing, shows him the error of his ways, and persuades him to return to England with his bride instead of staying in India. As *RG* points out, Kipling uses the phrase 'But that is another story' eight times in *Plain Tales*, and it became 'for years the most frequently quoted phrase from Kipling'.

tiffined at Peliti's: tiffin is the Anglo-Indian term for lunch (*Hobson-Jobson* has an enjoyably inconclusive article on its derivation); Peliti's was a well-known café or tea-shop situated on the Mall (the main street) at Simla.

the A.-D.-C. in Waiting: the Bremmils are being invited to an official ball at Peterhoff, the Viceroy's residence on the Mall, one of the premier events of the 'season' at Simla. The 'A.-D.-C.' is the 'Aide-de-Camp', the officer on the Viceroy's staff responsible for making the arrangements. Edward Robert Bulwer Lytton, first earl of Lytton (1831–91), was the son of the novelist and statesman Edward Bulwer-Lytton; he became Viceroy in 1876 and the following year proclaimed Queen Victoria Empress of India. He was succeeded in 1880 by Lord Dufferin, a Kipling family friend—he is 'the gentlest and most affable of Viceroys' in 'The Miracle of Purun Bhagat' (*The Second Jungle Book*, 1895)—and who replaced Peterhoff by the grander Viceregal Lodge on Observatory Hill.

7 *the Club*: the United Services Club.

Phelps's: Phelps and Company, a high-class tailoring and dressmaking firm with branches in Calcutta and Lahore as well as Simla. It was situated on the Mall near the Town Hall.

slight mourning: twelve months of mourning was required by a parent for a child. After six months the mourning could be 'slighted', which meant replacing crape with plain black, with jet ornaments and black gloves; after another two months gold and silver jewelry and grey gloves were allowed (J. Morley, *Death, Heaven and the Victorians* (1971), 68–9, referring to an 1880 issue of *The Queen*).

8 *The Roast Beef of Old England*: announcing supper; the song was written by Fielding to a traditional tune for *The Grub Street Opera* (1713), with the chorus 'Oh! The roast beef of England, | And old England's roast beef.'

dandy . . . 'rickshaw: a dandy is a Himalayan litter, 'consisting of a strong cloth slung like a hammock to a bamboo staff, and carried by two (or more) men' (*Hobson-Jobson*). The 'rickshaw (contraction of what *Hobson-Jobson* lists as 'jennyrickshaw'), a light-wheeled vehicle pulled by a man, was first imported from Japan in the 1880s; Kipling's story 'The Phantom 'Rickshaw' first appeared in 1885 (later collected in *The Phantom 'Rickshaw and Other Stories*, 1888), the same year as one of the illustrative quotations in *Hobson-Jobson*, which comes from Lady Dufferin's *Viceregal Life*.

cloud: a light scarf.

In the House of Suddhoo

First pub. *Civil and Military Gazette*, 30 Nov. 1886, with the title 'Section 420, I.P.C.' (i.e. the Indian Penal Code; see below, p. 14); coll. *Plain Tales from the Hills*, 1888.

Kipling's interest in the occult (especially its exotic, oriental variety: the classic example is 'The Mark of the Beast', *Life's Handicap*, 1890) is interwoven here with his grasp of murderous domestic entanglements; the story is affiliated to Zola as well as to Poe (who is explicitly invoked). At the same time the story belongs to a long comic tradition of rich dupes fooled by cynical pseudo-magicians. The narrator's display of superior knowledge and his reasoning tone mask both fascination and impotence; he is more compromised even than Trejago in 'Beyond the Pale' (p. 15).

The story is set in Lahore, which Kipling knew well and whose intricate streets and secret houses he makes the venue of several other stories in *Plain Tales* and other volumes, as well as the opening chapter of *Kim*. See, in this edition, 'Beyond the Pale' and 'On the City Wall' (p. 37). The most detailed description, though also the most 'written', is the sketch 'The City of Dreadful Night' (*Life's Handicap*, 1891). In chapter 3 of *Something of Myself*, Kipling recalled that in the hot weather he 'would wander till dawn in all manner of odd places—liquor-shops, gambling and opium-dens, which are not a bit mysterious . . . or in and about the narrow gullies under the Mosque of Wazir Khan for the sheer sake of looking. . . . I did not supply my paper with many accounts of these prowls. One would come home, just as the light broke, in some night-hawk of a hired carriage, which stank of hookah-fumes, jasmine-flowers, and sandalwood; and if the driver were moved to talk, he told one a good deal. Much of real Indian life goes on in the hot weather nights.' Kipling's father, John Lockwood Kipling, had helped to revise Thomas Henry Thornton's *A Brief Account of the History and Antiquities of Lahore* (Lahore, 1876) and his help is acknowledged in Syad Mohammad Latif's *Lahore* (see headnote to 'On the City Wall', p. 543).

9 *Epigraph*: Kipling's own composition; there is no complete poem called 'From the Dusk to the Dawn', and the lines here are not related to the uncollected story by that name which appeared in the *Gazette* on 14 Sept. 1886. The lines were collected in the *Definitive Edition* ('Chapter Headings').

Churel: 'the ghost of a woman who has died in childbirth' (Kipling's gloss). *Djinn*: a spirit in Muslim mythology, the 'genie' of the Arabian Nights.

Taksali Gate: in the west wall of Lahore City near the corner of the old Fort.

seal-cutting: 'one of the oldest crafts in the world, earlier perhaps than writing, as the seals were used to prove ownership' (*RG*).

Peshawar: a town near the foot of the Khyber Pass, 20 miles from Lahore; in the 19th century it was the terminus of the telegraph line and the Grand Trunk Road (*RG*).

the Edwardes' Gate: a gate in the wall of Peshawar named after the soldier and administrator Sir Herbert Edwardes (1819–68), a mainstay of British rule and influence in the Punjab; he was Commissioner of Peshawar (1853–9).

the Station: Lahore, in its capacity as an administrative centre.

Bareilly: a large town in the district of Rohilkand, 150 miles east of Delhi (*RG*).

extortionate: i.e. extortioner; the form is not recorded as a noun in the *OED*.

adulterator: 'probably by putting sand in the sugar' (*RG*); I presume there were other opportunities for unscrupulous grocers to cheat their customers.

10 *Ranjit Singh's Tomb*: outside the north-west corner of Lahore city and fort. Ranjit Singh, the founder of the Sikh kingdom, took Lahore as his capital in 1799. After his death in 1839, war broke out between the Sikhs and the British, who eventually annexed the Punjab in 1849.

the Huzuri Bagh: a garden not far away from Ranjit Singh's Tomb.

the Sirkar: Hindu term for the Government, the State.

the Empress of India: Queen Victoria had assumed this title in 1877.

the Financial Statement: the annual budget statement of the Government of India (like all journalists, and everybody else, Kipling had a cynical view of the government's manipulation of its finances).

jadoo: magic.

11 *between one hundred and two hundred rupees*: between £6 10*s*. and £13 (*RG*); an extortionate sum at current values.

huqas: hookahs, tobacco-pipes where the smoke is drawn through water.

12 *thermantidote paddle*: an early air-conditioner, consisting of a rotating fan fixed in a window opening which blew air through moistened cloths.

13 *Poe's account . . . mesmerised dying man*: alluding to 'The Facts in the Case of M. Valdemar' (1845); in this story a patient on his deathbed is mesmerized and kept in a state of suspension until the horrific denouement. The voice is described thus: 'there issued from the distended and motionless jaws a voice—such as it would be madness in me to attempt describing. There are, indeed, two or three epithets which might be considered as applicable to it in part; I might say, for example, that the sound was harsh, and broken and hollow; but the hideous whole is indescribable, for the simple reason that no similar sounds have ever jarred upon the ear of humanity. There were two particulars, nevertheless, which I thought then, and still think, might fairly be stated as characteristic of the intonation—as well adapted to convey some idea of its unearthly peculiarity. In the first place, the voice seemed to reach our ears—at least mine—from a vast distance, or from some deep cavern within the earth. In the second place, it impressed me (I fear, indeed, that it will be impossible to make myself comprehended) as gelatinous or glutinous matters impress the sense of touch.'

The whole thing was a careful reproduction of the Egyptian teraphin: the 'whole thing' presumably refers back to the shrivelled head, which the narrator compares to the figure of a household god or idol; but the word 'teraphim' (*sic*) derives from the Bible and is part of Jewish, not Egyptian religious practice. Kipling is right, however, to suggest an association with magic and divination.

13 *Asli nahin! Fareib*: 'Not genuine! A fraud!' (*RG*).

14 *bunnia*: shopkeeper.

mantras: spells.

purdahnashin: in another *Plain Tales* story, 'Yoked with an Unbeliever', Kipling hyphenates 'purdah-nashin' and glosses it as 'a woman who lives behind the veil'. The sense here is that after her marriage Azizun will live in the respectable seclusion of a Hindu wife, as indeed happens (see below).

cow-devourer: the ultimate insult for a Hindu, to whom cattle are sacred.

the lightning-post: the telegraph.

Beyond the Pale

First pub. *Plain Tales from the Hills*, 1888.

This is arguably the finest of Kipling's stories of interracial desire; I would prefer it even to 'Without Benefit of Clergy' (*Life's Handicap*, 1891), good though that is, because here the story's narrative power and economy exactly match its pitiless design. And this design reaches farther than the narrator knows—at any rate in his guise as wise old sawyer in the opening paragraphs. The achievement of mythic scope in Trejago's Adonis-like wound (effortless in comparison with Love-o'-Women's rather contrived self-identification with Shakespeare's Antony—see p. 161) takes the story, like Trejago himself, 'beyond the pale'.

Kipling had written on the quarter of Lahore in which the story is set in an article called 'Typhoid at Home', about the insanitary conditions in which dairy-cattle were kept, pub. in the *Civil and Military Gazette*, 14 Feb. 1885; see *Kipling's India: Uncollected Sketches 1884–1888*, ed. T. Pinney (1986), 69–77. The cityscape of narrow lanes ending in cul-de-sacs, and of high-walled houses with narrow grated windows, is exactly that of the story, though the tone is one of scandalized disgust. Kipling the reporter noticed that 'the dead walls, the barred and grated windows, and the high storeyed houses, were throbbing and humming with human life', even though he saw it as a 'tide of unclean humanity [which] might burst through its dam of rotten brickwork and filth-smeared wood' (*Kipling's India*, 73). In another article, pub. 1 Oct. 1887, and which is related to 'On the City Wall' (see headnote, p. 543), Kipling was more open to suggestion: 'The City by night, and by moonlight more particularly, supplies one of the most fascinating, if least savoury, walks in the station. The yard-wide gullies into which the moonlight cannot struggle are full of mystery, stories of life and death and intrigue of which we, the Mall abiding, open-windowed, purdahless English know nothing and believe less' (*Kipling's India*, 267).

15 *bustee*: lit. a village, or the inhabited quarter of a town, but *Hobson-Jobson* points out that it is 'applied in Calcutta to the separate groups of huts in the humbler native quarters'; the sense here is probably 'the group of buildings which belong to Jitha Megji'.

Gully: alley.

16 *The Love Song of Har Dyal*: no source has been identified for these verses, but they may still be a translation or pastiche of a real song, since Kipling never specifically claimed them; contrast the lines which Trejago hears at his second visit ('Alone upon the housetops to the north'), supposedly a separate section of the same song, which are by Kipling and which he included in the *Definitive Edition*.

dhak: 'a small bushy tree, *Butea frondosa*, which forms large tracts of jungle in the Punjab . . . Its deep orange flowers give a brilliant aspect to the jungle in the early part of the hot weather, and have suggested the occasional name of "Flame of the Forest"' (*Hobson-Jobson*).

17 *boorka*: a long garment which covers the head as well as the body, with slits for the eyes, usually a woman's costume.

the Vernacular: the native language (here, Hindustani).

18 *know him*: in the sense of 'acknowledge him'; if Trejago's affair were discovered he would be ostracized by British 'polite society' in Lahore.

The Story of Muhammad Din

First pub. *Civil and Military Gazette*, 8 Sept. 1886; coll. *Plain Tales from the Hills*, 1888.

Economy of means, the core of the artistic method of *Plain Tales* (and one source of Kipling's strong influence on the early writing of Hemingway) is taken to an extreme in this tale, in which point of view, tone, pace, and cadence are judged to perfection.

20 *Epigraph*. Peter Peterson (1847–99), Professor of Sanskrit at Elphinstone College, Bombay, discovered and edited many Sanskrit texts.

of what use was a polo-ball to a khitmatgar?: Thomas Pinney points out a possible source for this incident in a small news item which Kipling contributed to the *Civil and Military Gazette*, 11 Jan. 1886, concerning the theft of a cricket ball by a 'virtuous bearer': 'What in the name of everything incongruous can a bearer want with a cricket-ball?' (*Kipling's India*, 140–1). *khitmatgar*: *Hobson-Jobson* states that 'the Anglo-Indian use is peculiar to the Bengal Presidency, where the word is habitually applied to a Musulman servant, whose duties are connected with serving meals and waiting at table', but Imam Din's duties are clearly more general. *RG* suggests 'butler', and in the introduction to the stories of *In Black and White* (1888), which is facetiously attributed to 'Kadir Baksh, Khitmatgar', the servant says of himself: 'I am the head of the *Sahib's* household and hold his purse. Without me he does not know where are his rupees or his clean collars'.

21 *budmash*: rogue.

jail-khana: prison (lit. jailhouse).

22 *The water-man from the well-curb*: the narrator's house has its own well, with a 'water-man' to look after it, a sign of his affluence.

The 'Indian Railway' Library Stories

In 1888, A. H. Wheeler & Co., the publishers of the *Pioneer* of Allahabad, for which Kipling was then working, issued a series of cheap paperback booklets under the title 'The Indian Railway Library'. The first six of these were by Kipling: *Soldiers Three*, *The Story of the Gadsbys*, *In Black and White*, *Under the Deodars*, *The Phantom 'Rickshaw*, and *Wee Willie Winkie*. The following stories in this edition appeared in the Indian Railway Library series:

'With the Main Guard' (*Soldiers Three*)
'On the City Wall' (*In Black and White*)
'The Man who would be King' (*The Phantom 'Rickshaw*)
'Baa, Baa, Black Sheep' (*Wee Willie Winkie*)

A second edition of the series appeared in 1888 and an English edition (from the publishers Sampson Low) in 1890. In 1892 the first three numbers were collected into one volume, and the second three into another. In subsequent collected editions of Kipling, therefore, 'With the Main Guard' and 'On the City Wall' would appear in the volume *Soldiers Three and Other Stories*, and 'The Man who would be King' and 'Baa, Baa, Black Sheep' in the volume *Wee Willie Winkie and Other Stories*. Within these volumes, however, the original series titles were preserved (so that 'With the Main Guard' is in the section called 'Soldiers Three', etc.).

With the Main Guard

First pub. *The Week's News* (Allahabad), 4 Aug. 1888; coll. *Soldiers Three* (see general note, above).

Although the city is not named and the fort is given the fictional name 'Fort Amara', the setting is clearly Lahore (see note on p. 534). The torment of a sleepless night in the hot season is the subject of 'The City of Dreadful Night' (*Life's Handicap*, 1891), though there the emphasis is on the crowded city itself and not the handful of soldiers mounting guard in the fort. See also the note to the last words of the story. For the 'soldiers three' who appear in the story, above all Mulvaney, see Appendix B, pp. 528–9.

The battle which Mulvaney disguises under the name of 'Silver's Theatre' has some features of an engagement at Maiwand, near Kandahar, on 27 July

1880, on which Kipling also drew for 'The Drums of the Fore and Aft' (*Wee Willie Winkie*, 1888). In the latter story the issue is the shameful rout of a British regiment, but here the point is the occurrence of 'an event which is exceedingly rare in modern war: close hand-to-hand fighting with whole companies jammed so tightly together that men could not use their weapons' (*RG*). It is this crush which the Irish soldiers in the story compare with black humour to the drunken brawls at a crowded popular theatre in Dublin. The mêlée is therefore historical, but the way it comes about in the story is militarily unthinkable. At Maiwand it happened because companies were driven back on each other's lines, whereas here Mulvaney's company and the Black Tyrone voluntarily abandon a position on the heights overlooking the ravine where the Pathan reserve is stationed and engage them in hand-to-hand combat instead of firing at them from a safe distance. But Kipling knew perfectly well what he was doing: he makes Captain O'Neil (Crook) recognize that they 'could ha' engaged at long range'. The story is an extreme illustration of Mulvaney's maxim that *there's a dale more done in the field than iver gets into Field Ordhers*.

24 *Epigraph*. From 'Breitman in Bivouac' by the American author, editor, and humorist Charles Godfrey Leland (1824–1903). The Breitmann Ballads are poems in the Pennsylvania German dialect.

jungere: younger, youthful. *Uhlanen*: technically lancers, but here meaning 'cavalrymen'.

in the South: during the American Civil War; Leland was a passionate Unionist.

Himmel: Heaven.

Fort Amara: Kipling's pseudonym for the citadel of Lahore. 'Marah' is the Hebrew word for 'bitterness' (see e.g. Exod. 15: 23). A succession of rulers, from the Moghul emperors to the Sikhs, had added to its fortifications; Kipling described it as 'a mausoleum of ghosts' in ch. 3 of *Something of Myself*.

tivvy-tivvy: from 'dhiv-dhiv', an onomatopoeic Bengali term for the throbbing of the heart (Salman Rushdie (ed.), *Soldiers Three* and *In Black and White*, Penguin edn. (1993), 182).

25 *Gentleman born*: see 'Gentleman-Rankers', p. 446.

Martini: see note on p. 555.

whoile Dinah Shadd's here: Dinah Shadd is Mulvaney's wife; their story is told in 'The Courting of Dinah Shadd' (*Life's Handicap*, 1891).

Machiavel: 'cunning, unscrupulous person', from the popular image of Niccolò Machiavelli, author of the classic treatise on statecraft *The Prince* (1513).

mess-kid: container (for serving out food to the mess); originally a 'kid' or 'kit' meant a circular wooden vessel made of hooped staves.

25 *mint*: meant.

mate: meat.

A bloody war or a— : Mulvaney stops short of saying something like 'a quick death' because he realizes that in the 'sickly season' this would be all too likely.

26 *I remembered . . . the skilful magician Mulvaney*: alluding to the story 'The Madness of Private Ortheris' (*Plain Tales from the Hills*, 1888), in which Ortheris is saved from deserting; but Mulvaney's 'magic' is less in evidence in that story than the narrator's in, for example, 'Black Jack', the final story of *Soldiers Three*, where Mulvaney himself is prevented from going off the rails by being persuaded to tell a story.

Faynians: Fenians, i.e. Irish Nationalists.

the Widdy: the Widow, i.e. Queen Victoria; cf. 'The Widow at Windsor' (p. 441).

wid my belt: army-issue belts, with their heavy metal buckles, often featured in brawls among soldiers: see the poem 'Belts' (*Barrack-Room Ballads*, 1892).

the Black Tyrone . . . the Ould Rig'mint: for Mulvaney's military career, see Appendix B, pp. 528–9.

Ghuzni: Ghazni, a town on the road to Kabul from Kandahar, which the British occupied after the battle at Ahmed Khel in April 1880 during the Second Afghan War. (This battle is not the action which Mulvaney goes on to describe, as the term *after* makes clear.)

Silver's Theayter: later we are told that this is the name of a popular theatre or music-hall in Dublin. It is fictional: Kipling took the name from Silver Street, and the atmosphere from his knowledge of the *lively* behaviour of audiences at such venues whether in Dublin or London. (He had not in fact been to Ireland when he wrote this story.)

gut: pass or defile.

26–7 *Scotchies . . . Gurkys*: the friendship between Scotch and Gurkha soldiers is also depicted in 'The Drums of the Fore and Aft' (*Wee Willie Winkie*). The 2nd and 5th Gurkha Regiments served alongside the 72nd and 92nd Highlanders during the Second Afghan War.

27 *Captain O'Neil—Old Crook—Cruikna-bulleen*: Kipling's footnote referring readers to 'The Ballad of Boh Da Thone' (*Barrack-Room Ballads and Other Verses*, 1892) identifies O'Neil as an officer in the Black Tyrone, whereas here he is explicitly said to be an officer in the 'Old Regiment'. See also O'Neil's appearance in 'Love-o'-Women' (p. 150), an episode of which is set after the end of the fight at Silver's Theatre.

like rats in a pit: 'soldiers used to train their dogs for rat-catching by putting them in a pit together' (*RG*).

a rare pluckt wan: 'plucked' means courageous and is 'usually preceded by *cool-*, *good-*, *rare-*, or *well-*' (Eric Partridge, *Dictionary of Historical Slang*).

28 *Knee to knee . . . breast to breast . . . hand over back*: three of the Five Points of Fellowship of the ceremony of initiation into Freemasonry (the other two are 'hand to hand' and 'foot to foot'). Cf. the lines in the ballad 'With Scindia to Delhi' (*Barrack-Room Ballads and Other Verses*, 1892): 'There was no room to clear a sword—no power to strike a blow, | For foot to foot, ay, breast to breast, the battle held us fast'. Kipling took the subject of this ballad from the historical novel *Lalun the Beragun* which is a source for 'On the City Wall': see headnote to that story, pp. 543–4.

Dromeen Fair: there is a Dromin in Louth, 35 miles north of Dublin, and another near Limerick.

Brother Inner Guard: one of the two doorkeepers of a Masonic Lodge during its ceremonies; the other, who stands on the outside of the Lodge, is known as the 'tyler'.

the Vic.: the Victoria Music Hall, now the Old Vic Theatre, in Waterloo Bridge Road, London.

blindin' an' stiffin': cursing.

guv 'em compot: either 'gave them hell, gave them what for', or 'made it up to them (for my earlier inactivity)'; in both cases Ortheris means that he was able to use his rifle to effect, but the exact meaning of 'compot' is unclear. It may be a variant of 'compo', mid-19th century nautical slang for an advance on wages (Ortheris is giving the enemy more than they bargained for).

hamminition one year in store, to let the powder kiss the bullet: 'this may have been true of early propellants, but it did not apply to those of the Mulvaney period' (*RG*). But Kipling's imaginative insight into what a soldier might think seems to me to be more accurate than an expert's knowledge of what was actually the case.

29 *scutt*: contemptible fellow—as worthless as a rabbit's scut or tail (*RG*).

We've seen our dead: meaning bodies of soldiers who had been tortured or mutilated by the Pathans, a horror which Kipling alludes to in several other stories and poems.

30 *the Haymakers' Lift*: 'for tossing a heavy pitchfork of hay high onto a wagon with a short arm grip' (*RG*).

cow-feed: pasture.

31 *asp on a leaf*: Mulvaney's Irishism for 'aspen leaf': the leaves of the aspen move in the slightest breeze, hence the name 'trembling poplar'.

32 *the performinces of a Roshus*: Roscius was a Roman actor whose skill

became proverbial ('When Roscius was an actor in Rome . . .' as Hamlet says to Polonius in Act II scene ii). See note on p. 575.

34 *on the sharp*: roused (with blood-lust).

the women used to come out afther dhark: cf. the concluding lines of 'The Young British Soldier' (*Barrack-Room Ballads*, 1892): 'When you're wounded and left on Afghanistan's plains, | And the women come out to cut up what remains, | Jest roll to your rifle and blow out your brains, | An' go to your Gawd like a soldier'.

minowderin': coaxing.

bâtman: officer's personal servant (now usually spelled without the accent).

kyart: i.e. a pony-cart, to be hired from the stable mentioned a couple of lines down.

35 *Ho! it's weary waitin' for Ma-ary!*: unidentified popular song of the day.

If any young man should marry you: another popular song, called 'The Sentry Box' or 'Gentleman Soldier'; Mulvaney has softened the chorus, whose third line runs, in bawdier versions, 'That you ever were drilled in a sentry-box'.

36 *Morning Gun*: a gun was fired to signal daybreak and the opening of the gates of the city.

He looked at me wearily: Mulvaney's exhaustion and bitter recoil on himself after a storytelling triumph are depicted again at the end of 'The Courting of Dinah Shadd' (*Life's Handicap*, 1891), when the narrator sees him at dawn, 'the night-dew gemming his moustache, leaning on his rifle at picket, lonely as Prometheus on his rock, with I know not what vultures tearing his liver.'

blandandhered: coaxed, cajoled; formed 'by rhyming reduplication on the stem of *blandish*' (Partridge, *Dictionary of Historical Slang*), influenced also here by the fact that Mulvaney is a master of *blarney*.

broke the pitiless day: Kipling had used this phrase in an article pub. in the *Civil and Military Gazette*, 19 May 1888, describing a night of insomnia in the hot season in Lahore: 'And here with a cessation of the dust-storm and a few drops of tepid rain, breaks the pitiless day' (Pinney, *Kipling's India*, 288).

On the City Wall

First pub. *In Black and White*, 1888 (see general note, p. 538).

Kipling had written about the religious conflict between Hindu and Muslim at the time of the Mohurrum festival in a two-part article in the *Civil and Military Gazette* (19 and 22 Oct. 1885), and returned to the subject in Oct. 1887. On both occasions the title was 'The City of Two Creeds'. The 1885 articles are in *RG*, vol. i (pp. 97–103). Pinney (*Kipling's India*, 266–9) reprints the 1887 piece, where Kipling wrote: 'Because many hundreds of years ago Yezid, son of Mowwajib, first of the Ommeiad Caliphs of Damascus, met, on the plains of Kerbela, west of the Euphrates, and slew Hossain and Hussan, sons of Ali, First or Fourth (as you are Shiah or Sunni) of the Caliphs, and of Fatima, his wife, it is now necessary for every Deputy Commissioner in the Province, once a year, to spend half the night in a native city while the representations of the tombs of the butchered and Blessed Imams stagger up and down the ways' (ibid. 266). There is a lengthy description of the festival in a contemporary book about Lahore by a local author, Syad Muhammad Latif (*Lahore: Its History, Architectural Remains, and Antiquities*, 1892). Latif emphasizes the peculiar magnificence of Mohurrum in the city and says 'The mourning *majlises*, or meetings, are numerous, where elegies, describing the mournful events that took place at Karbala, are read, and eulogiums sung with great fervour. . . . The night of 10th Moharram is called the *Shab-i-Qatl*, or the night of murders, and the *Tazias* make the rounds of the principal streets with lighted torches and *Panchis* carried in the hand. The procession consists of reciters and singers of elegies, bands of music, and players with the *Beneti* (a torch lighted at both ends and whirled round so as to form a double circle of fire), spears, swords, etc. . . . All the *Tazias* from the city have to pass through the Lahori Gate and go to the *Karbala* . . . being joined during their passage by the *Tazias* from Anarkali and Mian Mir. There is a great crush of people from the Lahori Gate to the *Karbala* . . . The *Tazias* of Lahore are noted for their beauty and elegance. They are made of wood, covered with pictures, glasses of different colors and other decorations, or of the bark of bamboos, covered outside with colored or painted paper. They are divided into several storeys . . . Although the festival is not new . . . it has vastly increased in splendour and magnificence during the British period' (pp. 270–1).

The story owes some of its names and atmosphere to a historical novel obscure even in its own day, *Lalun the Beragun* (1879, repr. 1884). The author's name on the title-page, 'Mirza Moorad Alee Beg', is a pseudonym, and his real identity is not known. In 'To Be Filed for Reference' (*Plain Tales from the Hills*, 1888), the dying loafer McIntosh Jellaludin declares that his own epic of native life, the 'Book of Mother Maturin', will surpass this work, and the narrator comments: 'This, as will be conceded by any one who knows Mirza Murad Ali Beg's book, was a sweeping statement.' Besides a detail in the 'song of old days' (see note on p. 546) and the name Lalun, the main bearing of *Lalun the Beragun* on Kipling's story concerns its treatment of the battle of Panipat (7 Jan. 1761), in which the Afghans defeated the Mahrattas. The Mahratta leader, Mohadji Rao Sindhia, fled from the battle to Delhi with (in Alee Beg's romantic version) a courtesan, Lalun, on his saddle; but just before he reached Delhi she slipped from his horse in order to ensure his safety, and fell into the hands of a Muslim pursuer. He himself fell to the ground and fainted from exhaustion. Kipling modelled his ballad 'With

Scindia to Delhi' (*Barrack-Room Ballads and Other Verses*, 1892) on Alee Beg's account of this episode, and refers to it in the course of 'On the City Wall', in which he also appropriates a *laonee* or traditional Mahratta ballad of Alee Beg's own composition (see note on p. 546). What matters most, however, is not the detail of the borrowing but the ironic reversal of its central motif. Lalun, helpless and self-sacrificing in the Mahratta story, is cunning and in control of events in Kipling's tale: her knowledge of 'the heart of the City' and the affairs of state resembles that of Mrs Hauksbee; her singing signals conspiracy and rebellion to the old nationalist hero imprisoned in the fort; her exploitation of the English narrator is the means by which the prisoner escapes. But a further irony defeats her purpose: the old man turns out to be as exhausted, as defeated, as Scindia at the end of his flight to Delhi. The narrator's naivety is matched by Lalun's miscalculation, and they are both outdone by Wali Dad, whose ignorance of his own nature is the hinge of the plot. Doubleness (duplicity, ambivalence, racial and sexual dichotomy) rules the story which is the greatest parable of empire in English writing.

37 *Epigraph.* Joshua, the leader of the Israelites after the death of Moses, sends two spies to Jericho, who 'came to an harlot's house, named Rahab, and lodged there'. Rahab conceals the men from their pursuers and helps them to escape as described in the passage which Kipling quotes, in return for a promise that her life will be spared when the Israelites conquer the city. Rahab has a good grasp of imperial *realpolitik*: as she tells Joshua's agents: 'I know that the Lord hath given you the land, and that your terror is fallen upon us, and that all the inhabitants of the land faint because of you.' Lalun is no Rahab: her view of the imperial English is disrespectful and her actions subversive. The allusion, like much else in the story, works by ironic reversal (a principle which reaches to the level of physical detail, for example the position of Lalun's house in relation to the river, and the fact that she does not let anyone *down* the wall from her house, but drags someone *up*).

Lilith . . . before the days of Eve: the legend that Adam had a wife before Eve is an ancient rabbinical tradition; she came to be identified with Lilith, the name of a female demon in Isa. 34: 14 (this name does not occur in the Authorized Version). The figure of Lilith could be used in opposition to Eve in different ways, though she is always the less respectable or orthodox. *RG* plausibly suggests the influence of D. G. Rossetti's ballad 'Eden Bower', which begins: 'It was Lilith the wife of Adam: | (*Sing Eden Bower!*) | Not a drop of her blood was human, | But she was made like a soft sweet woman.' Cf. also the epigraph to 'The Oldest Song' (*The Years Between*, 1919): 'For before Eve was Lilith', ascribed to an 'Old Tale'.

the east wall facing the river: in Lahore it is the west wall which faces the Ravi River, and the prostitutes' quarters were near the Taksali Gate in the north-west of the city, but south of the Fort (*RG*); the inversion preserves the city's formal incognito, as well as belonging to a larger pattern: see note above.

the red tombs of dead Emperors: in an article in the *Civil and Military Gazette*, 16 Feb. 1887, on Queen Victoria's Golden Jubilee, Kipling described the parade of troops on the plain 'in front of Fort Lahore, between the tomb where the one-eyed Lion of the Punjab sleeps among his eleven wives, and the nobler structure where Jehangir lies under the red minars of Shahdera' (*Kipling's India* 194). These tombs are described by Syad Latif (see note on p. 543 above): the 'one eyed Lion of the Punjab' was Ranjit Singh, the great Sikh ruler whose death in 1839 eventually led to the British annexation of the region. His tomb 'is built of stone in a plain, unpretending style' (*Lahore*, 129); his four legal wives and seven concubines immolated themselves on his funeral pyre. The mausoleum of the Mogul Emperor Jehangir Khan, who died in 1627, is 'a monument of surpassing beauty, the finest ornament of Lahore' (p. 104).

38 *making love to*: in the old-fashioned sense of 'courting, making up to'.

from the Street of the Mutton-Butchers to the Copper-Smiths' ward: cf. the opium house in 'The Gate of the Hundred Sorrows' (*Plain Tales from the Hills*) which 'lies between the Coppersmith's Gully and the pipe-stem sellers' quarter'. These street names are invented.

39 *dream dreams*: Joel 2: 28: 'your old men shall dream dreams, your young men shall see visions'.

Red Sauce: socialist or other radical ideology.

Pax Britannic: more usually Pax Britannica (adapted from 'pax Romana') which expressed the Empire's claim to bring civilized order and the rule of law to its subjects; the *OED*'s first citation of the phrase is dated 1865.

between Peshawar and Cape Comorin: marking the northern and southern boundaries of India; Kipling uses a similar phrase in an article in the *Civil and Military Gazette*, 21 June 1884 (repr. in *Kipling's India*, 43).

Civilian: the term originally described 'the covenanted European servants of the East India Company, not in military employ' (*Hobson-Jobson*); by Kipling's time it designated a member of the Indian Civil Service, whose 'covenant' was with the Secretary of State for India.

got behind: seen through.

40 *the Dil Sagar Lake*: poeticism, 'the ocean of the heart' (*RG*).

the Desert of Kutch: Kutch is a region on the north-west coast of India, part of which is saline marsh and salt desert.

a petty Nawab: the ruler of a small (semi-)independent native state.

chunam: a fine cement made of shell-lime and sea-sand.

squabby pluffy: the general sense is clear: 'small, thick, and plump'. Both words were normally used of people rather than things, meaning respectively 'squat' and 'puffy'.

40 *huqa*: tobacco-pipe (see note on p. 11).

Shiahs: or Shiites, Muslims who take their name from the Shiat Ali, the 'party of Ali', the cousin and son-in-law of Muhammad, whom they regard as the true heir of the Prophet. The martyrdom of Ali's two sons, Hasan and Husain, is commemorated by the 'mourning-festival' of Muhurram (see headnote, p. 543), during which the plot of the story unfolds. The Shiahs form a large minority in the Muslim world, the majority being Sunnis (followers of the Sunna, the traditional record of Muhammad's practice which complements the Koran).

Sufis: Muslim mystics, whose name derives from the simple woollen garment (*suf*) worn by early ascetics. Since the early days of Islam they eschewed formal ritual and orthodox learning in favour of esoteric practices intended to lead the believer to personal communion with God.

Pundits: learned men, teachers (from the Sanskrit *pandita*).

Golden Temple: in Amritsar, 33 miles east of Lahore; the holiest place of the Sikh religion.

from beyond the Border: from Afghanistan.

41 *electic*: Wali Dad means 'eclectic', i.e. varied, non-exclusive (except for Jews: see below); his error allows a pun on Lalun's guests as the 'elect' or élite of political opposition to the 'Supreme Government'.

Outside of a Freemasons' Lodge . . . a Jew: for Kipling's own account of the heterogeneous nature of Freemasonry, see the Introduction, p. xv.

It is like the Athenians: when St Paul visits Athens the people are eager to hear him speak: 'For all the Athenians and strangers which were there spent their time in nothing else, but either to tell, or to hear some new thing' (Acts 17: 21). This passage became proverbial as a description of the frivolity and over-sophistication of urban (esp. intellectual) life.

a Demnition Product: Wali Dad is quoting Dickens, whose character Mr Mantalini pronounces 'damn' and its cognates as 'dem' in *Nicholas Nickleby* (he first says 'demnition' in ch. 17). Mr Mantalini is a *faux*-aristocrat, and Wali Dad is reflecting on his own perceived inauthenticity.

O Peacock, cry again: I have not identified this song.

42 *a song of old days*: for Kipling's source, Mirza Moorad Alee Beg's historical novel *Lalun the Beragun*, see headnote. The *laonee* which Kipling quotes was Alee Beg's own composition, and not, therefore, as old as Kipling makes out. Alee Beg's original refrain runs: 'With them rode he who walks so free | With scarf and turban red, | The soldier-youth who earns his fee | By peril of his head!' The *laonee* refers to the exploits of Chimnajee, the father of Scindia, and it is ironic that it should

be sung on the eve of Scindia's disastrous defeat at Panipat. The Peishwa was a hereditary Mahratta minister.

the Fords of the Jumna: the Jumna rises on the southern slopes of the West Himalayas and flows south past Delhi and Agra to join the Ganges at Allahabad. Cf. the ballad 'With Scindia to Delhi' (see headnote): 'Thereat, as when a sand-bar breaks in clotted spume and spray, | When rain of later autumn sweeps the Jumna water-head, | Before their charge from flank to flank our riven ranks gave way— | But of the waters of that flood the Jumna fords ran red' (ll. 29–32).

Sivaji: Sivaji (*c.*1630–80) was the founder of Mahratta power in India; his name is being used here as a kind of honorific title for his successor Scindia.

a Toorkh stallion at his horse's tail: the Toorkh stallion (from Turkestan in Central Asia) is being ridden by Scindia's Afghan pursuer.

Fort Amara: see note on p. 539. The 'three kings' were four, according to Syad Latif (*Lahore*, 121): the Mogul Emperors Akbar (1542–1605), Jahangir (1569–1627), Shah Jahan (1592–1666), and Aurangzeb (1618–1707); it was also added to by the Sikhs.

43 *He fought you in '46 . . . refought you in '57 . . . tried to fight you in '71*: the 'consistent man', Khem Singh, is a composite figure, with no single original, as his eclectic list of anti-British battle-honours suggests: the First Sikh War of 1846, the Mutiny of 1857, and the Kuka uprising of 1871 (see note on p. 548).

blowing men from guns: the method of executing rebels and mutineers by tying them to the muzzle of a cannon and blowing them apart originated in the Mutiny. See the note on the Kuka uprising (p. 548).

Wahabi: a member of a militant reforming Sunni Muslim sect, founded by Muhammed ibn Abd al-Wahhab (1708–92), which was introduced into India by Saiyid Ahmed (1786–1831). In 1824 the Wahabis launched a *jihad* (holy war) against the Sikhs, which spread to the British and the Hindus.

They kept Khem Singh in Burma: Bahadur Shah II, the King of Delhi, was deposed and exiled for his part in the Mutiny; he was sent first to the Cape Colony in South Africa, but the colonists refused to receive him and he was then transported to Rangoon.

go whoring after strange gods: this exact phrase does not appear in the Bible; the Israelites are warned on several occasions not to 'go whoring after' the gods of their neighbours (e.g. Exod. 34: 15, Lev. 20: 5), and other passages employ the phrase 'strange gods' (e.g. Deut. 32: 16, Josh. 24: 20). T. S. Eliot, who knew his Kipling, may have been influenced by this compound quotation when he repeated it as the title of *After Strange Gods* (1934).

44 *Subadar Sahib*: lit. 'Lord Viceroy', a term of more-than-oriental splendour for the distinguished prisoner.

vain things: Ps. 2: 1: 'Why do the heathen rage, and the people imagine a vain thing?' and Ps. 6: 18: 'An heart that deviseth wicked imaginations'.

45 *of a pleasant countenance*: like the young David, both when Samuel anoints him and when he faces Goliath (1 Sam. 16: 12, 17: 42).

Begums and Ranees tortured to death: when the narrator of 'The Man who would be King' first meets Carnehan, he and Dravot are on their way to blackmail the ruler of one of the native states for such a crime: see p. 59.

Sobraon: the decisive battle in the First Sikh War, fought on 10 Feb. 1846, in which the British army under Sir Hugh Gough attacked the Sikh army on the Sutlej River.

the Kuka rising: the account of this episode in a contemporary reference work is instructive. The Kukas (or Kookas) were 'a warlike reforming sect in North-West India, founded by Baluk Ram in 1845, and after his death, about 1855, headed by Ram Singh, who preached the restoration of the old Sikh religion . . . After several outrages against the Mahometans, an outbreak of the Kookas took place near Loodiana, which was vigorously suppressed, 15 Jan. 1872, by commissioner Cowan, who ordered 49 prisoners to be blown from cannon, 17 Jan. Several others were tried and executed by commissioner Forsyth soon after. For this severity Mr. Cowan was ordered to be dismissed, and Mr. Forsyth removed to another station, April, 1872' (*Haydn's Dictionary of Dates* (25th edn.), 1910).

46 *Dogras*: inhabitants of the Duggar district of north-west India. They were Hindus, which compounds the Captain's ignorant racism.

the heterodox women: courtesans such as Aspasia, the mistress of Pericles and friend of Socrates. Lemprière's *Classical Dictionary* (12th edn., 1823) says of her: 'The behaviour of Pericles towards Aspasia greatly corrupted the morals of the Athenians, and introduced dissipation and lasciviousness into the state. She however possessed the merit of a superior excellence in mind as well as person, and her instructions helped to form the greatest and most eloquent orators of Greece.'

48 *fakements*: strictly speaking, the term means a contrivance or 'dodge', or the trimming of an article of clothing; Kipling means something like 'get-up', 'outfit', with a pejorative implication of 'gaudy, trumpery'.

49 *men from Ladakh . . . such as the Russians sell*: Ladakh is about 400 miles north of Lahore, in Kashmir. Russia is to the north-west, and the implication is that the mysterious visitors are agents from that country, who have an interest either in fomenting religious disturbances in the city, or in arranging for Khem Singh's escape, or both.

brick-tea: tea sold in slabs rather than in leaf form.

Vox Populi is Vox Dei, as the Babus say: Wali Dad uses the Latin tag ('the voice of the people is the voice of God') to convey that the rumour of trouble is likely to be true, but his attribution of it to 'the Babus' suggests its application to politics: India should be governed by popular will, in other words self-determination. 'Babu' or 'Baboo' was originally an honorific but Wali Dad's use of the term carries the 'slight savour of disparagement' noted by *Hobson-Jobson* 'as characterizing a superficially cultivated, but too often effeminate, Bengali'.

Padshahi Gate: the 'King's Gate', an invented name; it probably refers to the gate which Syad Latif calls the 'Raushnai gate' (the 'gate of light'), which is situated between the royal mosque and the citadel, and is the principal entrance from the fort to the city (*Lahore*, 85).

talc: mica or Muscovy glass, a thin sheet of translucent material.

Into thy hands, O Lord: '. . . I commend my spirit', the last words of Jesus on the cross (Luke 23: 46).

Sirkar: Hindu term for the Government, the State.

50 *We shall be gutting kine in their temples to-night!*: since cattle are sacred to the Hindus, this would constitute the grossest conceivable defilement.

sons of burnt fathers: possibly, since the crowd here is Muslim, Hugonin is insulting them by reference to the Hindu practice of cremation; but 'burnt' is also slang for 'infected with venereal disease'.

51 *the Club*: the Punjab Club on the Mall; for its importance to Kipling in his time as a journalist in Lahore, see ch. 3 of *Something of Myself*.

52 *the Main Gate of the City*: probably the Delhi gate, on the eastern side.

the Gate of the Butchers: not identified.

53 *thou-ed*: i.e. addressed in the familiar, intimate form of the second person, as opposed to the more formal 'you'.

the Kumharsen Gate: the 'Potters' gate'; unidentified.

Hutt: recorded in *OED* as an impatient exclamation to a horse.

the iron bangle of the Sikhs: the narrator should realize that Lalun has lied to him about the man being a Muslim. The iron bracelet, or 'kara', is one of five distinguishing marks of the orthodox Sikh.

A lakh of men: a 'lakh' usually meant 100,000 rupees, but the sense here is 'an enormous number'.

54 *Akala*: there is no such place (another clue which the narrator misses).

bunnias: shopkeepers.

lest a worse thing should happen: unbeknownst to them, the Sikh horsemen are quoting Jesus: 'sin no more, lest a worse thing come unto thee' (John 5: 14).

54 *the Square of the Mosque*: the Mosque of Wazir Khan.

It is expedient . . . people: the words of Caiaphas, the high priest and instigator of the conspiracy to have Jesus put to death (John 11: 50).

55 *Two Lovely Black Eyes*: a music-hall song of the 1880s by Charles Coborn. *RG* quotes one verse: 'Two lovely black eyes! | Oh! What a surprise! | Only for telling a man he was wrong, | Two lovely black eyes!'

Those who had employed him: the finger almost certainly points at Russia, suspected by Kipling and others at this period of fomenting Indian nationalism for its own nefarious imperial purposes.

56 *Fort Ooltagarh*: no such fort exists.

The Man who would be King

First pub. *The Phantom 'Rickshaw* (1888); see general note, p. 538.

The frame of the story is closely modelled on Kipling's experience of sub-editing (and on occasion editing) the *Civil and Military Gazette* in Lahore, and of being a correspondent of its larger sister-paper, the *Pioneer*, in Allahabad (the latter appears under the transparent disguise of the *Backwoodsman*). See, for example, his account in ch. 3 of *Something of Myself*, and his letter of 12–14 May 1888 to Mrs Edmonia Hill (*Letters*, i. 172; it was Mrs Hill who suggested the names of 'Carnehan' and 'Dravot' for the two adventurers). A railway journey related in *Letters of Marque* has suggestive parallels with the opening of the story, in particular Kipling's conversation with a 'loafer' with whom he talks politics.

The adventure itself is neither history nor myth, but a historical fantasy, akin to Rider Haggard's *King Solomon's Mines* though more convincing in both its historical and its fantastic features. 'Kafiristan' denotes a region north of the imperial frontier, stretching across parts of what are now Afghanistan and Pakistan, and including tribal areas such as Chitral, where there were just enough facts to stimulate the imagination but not enough to constrain it. As Henry Bellew pointed out in a work published three years after the story appeared, *An Inquiry into the Ethnography of Afghanistan*, 'The Kafir, as they are called, are, and have been for many centuries past, so completely isolated in their inaccessible mountain retreats, and so completely shut off from free intercourse with the outside world, that very little is known about them accurately' (1891; repr. 1973, p. 143; see below, p. 554). In this sense Kipling's enterprise parallels that of Dravot and Carnehan, and their loss is his gain. All three found most of the information they needed in the *Encyclopædia Britannica*, which summarized the state of knowledge at that period.

Kipling gave a strong clue as to the sources of the story in a letter of 3 Jan. 1893 to Edward Lucas White (*Letters*, ii. 77). He asserted that the story was credible in general terms as a back-projection from the early days of imperial conquest: 'men even lower than Peachey and Carnehan [*sic*; it should be

'Dravot and Carnehan', since 'Peachey' is Carnehan's first name] made themselves kings (and kept their kingdoms too) in India not 150 years ago'; see also the note on 'Sar-a-*whack*' (p. 553). He goes on: 'All "king" tales of that kind date back from the Tower of Babel'. This is not an accidental allusion: the story of the Tower of Babel (Gen. 11: 1–9) is one in which building in bricks (the symbolic foundation of Freemasonry) is combined with the existence of a universal language. Dravot and Carnehan uncover in Kafiristan the traces of such a language, which is the ritual of Freemasonry itself, but their grand design, like that of the original builders of the Tower of Babel, is confounded. For the mechanism of divine retribution, Kipling reached for a biblical story earlier even than the Tower of Babel, the story of the world before the flood, when 'the sons of God' mated with 'the daughters of men'—a story which Carnehan himself remembers as a warning (see note on p. 559). Thus the most ancient tale of miscegenation in Western culture comes into play as a tragic irony in the denouement of the story, in which Dravot's mastery of events is turned inside out.

A word about the intricacies of the railway journey with which the story opens, and which according to *RG* is erroneously described. But it is perfectly accurate, and would be clear enough to readers familiar with the Anglo-Indian rail network. The main line from Delhi to Bombay on the west coast passes through Ajmir (or Ajmer), about 200 miles from Delhi; Ajmir is a junction for another line running south through Rajasthan to Indore and Khandwa in Madhya Pradesh; Mhow is just to the south of Indore (about 270 miles south of Ajmir). If you continue on the Delhi–Bombay line after Ajmir, you pass through Marwar Junction (about 75 miles), from which yet another line branches off north to Jodhpore (or Jodhpur), the last stop if you are travelling to the 'Indian Desert' (also known as the Desert of Thar, straddling what is now the India–Pakistan border). When the story opens, the narrator is travelling south from Ajmir in the direction of Mhow (his exact destination is not specified). Carnehan gets on at Nasirabad, the first stop after leaving Ajmir. Although Carnehan is also travelling south, he wants to send a telegram from the next station back to Ajmir, because Dravot will be passing through there on his way from Delhi to Bombay. However, neither Carnehan nor the narrator has enough money for a telegram, so Carnehan suggests another plan. After the narrator finishes his business in the 'small Native States' (it is a journalistic assignment, though Carnehan, believing the narrator to be a 'loafer' like himself, assumes it is some shady matter such as he and Dravot are engaged in) his next assignment will be in the 'Indian Desert'. He will therefore be going back north, and will pass through Marwar Junction, where, if the timing works out, he can meet Dravot travelling from Delhi and give him the message in person. Carnehan gets off at an unnamed 'little roadside station' and the narrator continues his journey. When his assignment is concluded he duly takes 'the night Mail' north (the station is again not named) and is able to fulfil Carnehan's request.

57 *Epigraph*. The formula is Masonic (as is the reference to the 'Law' in the first sentence) and refers to the principle of fellowship in Freemasonry.

a Deficit in the Budget: the narrator has run out of money (the reason is not explained) and will not be able to get any more until he 'resume[s] touch with the Treasury' (p. 58), i.e. is able to borrow from an Englishman (presumably a local administrator, and on the credit of the newspaper). The allusion is also topical: see below, note on 'seventy millions of revenue'. For the railway jouney, see headnote.

a wanderer and a vagabond like myself . . . men like you and me: the narrator is a 'roving correspondent', Carnehan a 'loafer'; each is pretending to be the other.

57–8 *not knowing more than the crows*: a disguised biblical allusion: God's care for the ravens appears in Job 38: 41 ('Who provideth for the raven his food?') and in Luke 12: 24 ('Consider the ravens: for they neither sow nor reap . . . and God feedeth them').

58 *seventy millions of revenue*: Sir Auckland Colvin, the Financial Member (i.e. Treasurer) of the Viceroy's Council, announced budget revenues for 1886–7 of £75,798,700, roughly equivalent to proposed expenditure; the budget for the following year, however, was in severe deficit, and led to a tax on petroleum and an increase in salt duty.

the Backwoodsman: i.e. the *Pioneer*, for which Kipling worked, 1887–9.

the Residents: British representatives at the courts of native rulers, officially diplomats but often exercising considerable power in the state's affairs.

59 *as a stranger—going to the West . . . From the East . . . on the Square—for the sake of my Mother*: cryptic allusions to Freemasonry. All the points of the compass have symbolic value in Masonic philosophy and ritual; the square, both as geometric shape and mason's tool, is one of the most important Masonic symbols, denoting among other things equity and just proportion; hence 'on the Square' in the sense of 'belonging to Freemasonry' also acquired the colloquial sense of 'fair-minded, on the level'. The 'mother' is the 'Mother Lodge', technically the originating authority of Freemasonry in a particular country, but here probably symbolizing the 'craft' itself. Further on (p. 76) Dravot declares the foundation of the 'Mother Lodge' of Kafiristan, though he has no warrant to do so.

Degumber . . . Chortumna: fictional native states.

59–60 *four-in-hand barouches*: a barouche is a four-wheeled carriage, and if it were being driven 'four-in-hand', i.e. with two pairs of horses, it would represent a luxurious and stately ride, akin to a stretch limousine today. The correspondents are being bribed not to report any scandal ('drive them out of their mind' is facetious, like 'choke . . . with champagne').

60 *the days of Harun-al-Raschid*: the Caliph of Baghdad in the *Arabian Nights.*

Politicals: political agents, official British advisers to native rulers (sometimes equivalent to the Residents).

a plate made of leaves: food bought from a roadside hawker (a detail which reappears at the end of ch. 4 of *Kim*).

61 *Zenana-mission*: Christian missionary work among Indian women (the word denotes the women's quarters of a household).

the Grand Trunk Road: the highway from Calcutta to Amritsar, begun in 1839, the 'backbone of all Hind' as it is described in ch. 3 of *Kim*: 'It runs straight, bearing without crowding India's traffic for fifteen hundred miles—such a river of life as nowhere else exists in the world.'

Kings are being killed . . . the British Dominions: the references in the story to political events in Europe are generalized, but are based on historical facts (or, in the case of Gladstone, Kipling's hostile interpretation of such facts). In 1881, for example, Czar Alexander II was assassinated, and an attempt was made to assassinate his successor, Alexander III, in 1887; attempted assassinations were made in 1882 against both Queen Victoria and the Emperor Franz Joseph of Austria. To conservatives, Gladstone's bad faith in relation to the Empire was conclusively proved by his failure to relieve Gordon at Khartoum in 1885. Gladstone's later support for Irish Home Rule did nothing to sweeten Kipling's view of him.

as blank as Modred's shield: *RG* suggests that Kipling may have got this detail from Tennyson's 'Gareth and Lynette' (*Idylls of the King*). A row of sculpted shields runs along the hall of Camelot, carved or blazoned according to the knight's prowess, but blank if he has not yet achieved any 'noble deed'. Modred is King Arthur's nephew (and eventual nemesis) and his shield is 'blank as death' (l. 409). The allusion here links the narrator's occupation with the main plot of the story, which is the downfall of a king.

62 *the Khuda Janta Khan District*: a fictional name; *RG* says it translates as 'God Knows Town'.

A King . . . on the other side of the world: the list makes it clear that no specific reference is meant, but in illustration it may be noted that Bulgaria got a new constitution in August 1887 and that two German Emperors, Frederick II and his son Frederick III, died in 1888, during Kipling's stint at the *Pioneer.*

63 *Brother Peachey . . . Brother Daniel*: the title 'Brother' is a Masonic usage.

64 *Sar-a-whack*: alluding to the career of Sir James Brooke (1803–68), known as 'Rajah Brooke' or 'the White Rajah', a soldier formerly in the service of the East India Company who became ruler of Sarawak (on the north-west coast of Borneo) in 1841 after assisting the Sultan of Brunei

against local rebel tribes; he warred successfully against pirates and opium-smugglers, and founded a dynasty which lasted until Sarawak was ceded to the British in 1946. His near-contemporary exploits provide a model for Carnehan and Peachey, though he is both too recent and too upper-class to be an example of the adventurers whom Kipling claimed had carved out kingdoms for themselves (see headnote).

64 *Kafiristan . . . three hundred miles from Peshawar*: the location and distance are deliberately vague and inaccurate: see headnote.

65 *the big thirty-two-miles-to-the-inch map of India*; a sheet of this map (*A Skeleton Map of India (Punjab)*, India Survey, 1886) is reproduced on pp. 88–9. Jagdallak, a small town about 35 miles east of Kabul in Afghanistan, is not on it, so the map on which Dravot puts his thumb in the following paragraph must be one of the 'smaller Frontier maps', several series of which were issued by the India Survey Department.

volume INF-KAN of the Encyclopædia Britannica: volume xiii of the 9th edition; the article on Kafiristan was by Colonel (later Sir) Henry Yule (1820–89), the soldier, geographer, and member of the Indian Council who was one of the original compilers of *Hobson-Jobson*.

We was there with Roberts' Army: a reference to the Second Afghan War of 1878–80, during which the force commanded by Lord Roberts took the Kurram Valley and attacked Kabul, then marched from Kabul to the relief of Kandahar.

Wood on the Sources of the Oxus: John Wood (1811–71), a captain in the East India Company's naval service, was a member of a commercial mission to Afghanistan in 1836, and in 1841 published *A Journey to the Source of the Oxus*, reissued in 1872.

United Services' Institute: Kipling is almost certainly alluding to the branch of this club in Simla, where lectures and examinations on military matters were held, and which issued bulletins and papers.

Bellew: Henry Walter Bellew (1834–92) had recently retired as surgeon-general of the Indian Medical Service; he had been chief political officer at Kabul, and was the author of several books on Afghanistan, e.g. *From the Indus to the Tigris: A Narrative of a Journey through the Countries of Balochistan, Afghanistan, Khorassan and Iran, in 1872* (pub. 1874) and *The Races of Afghanistan: Being a Brief Account of the Principal Natives inhabiting that Country* (1880).

Raverty: Major Henry George Raverty (1825–1906), a soldier and oriental scholar who published *Notes on Afghanistan and Baluchistan* (1881–8).

the Serai: glossed by Kipling further on as the Kumharsen Serai (for 'Kumharsen' see note on p. 549); in ch. 1 of *Kim* it is called the 'Kashmir Serai', 'that huge open square over against the railway station, surrounded with arched cloisters, where the camel and horse caravans put up on their return from Central Asia.'

66 *to draw eye-teeth*: to fleece; 'to make one suffer loss without seeing the manœuvre by which it was effected' (Brewer's *Dictionary of Phrase and Fable*).

67 *the Shinwaris*: tribesmen from south of the Khyber.

the Pass: the Khyber Pass (Kipling's spelling is 'Khaiber', p. 68).

Eusufzai agent of a Rajputana trading-house: the Eusufzai are tribesmen from the district north of Peshawur.

Roum: Turkey (*Hobson-Jobson*).

Pir Khan: a fictional Muslim name, combining the senses of 'saint' and 'ruler'.

the King of the Roos: the Czar of Russia. The 'madman's' proposal is, in fact, a reflection of the British imperial policy which Kipling would have liked to see implemented, and which Dravot forecasts on p. 78.

Huzrut: a term of respectful address, equivalent to 'your Worship', used here half-ironically.

68 *a Martini*: a Martini–Henry rifle, adopted by the British Army in 1871. The name derives from two gunsmiths, Frederic Martini (1832–97), who invented the breech-loading mechanism, and Alexander Henry (1828–94), who improved the rifling. The original design had a .402 bore, altered to .45 in 1886. The technical specification of the Martini–Henry features in the plot of 'Black Jack' (*Soldiers Three*, 1888).

Half my Kingdom shall you have: this is the oath which Herod swears to his daughter (Salome) after she dances for him: 'Whatsoever thou shalt ask of me, I will give it thee, unto the half of my kingdom' (Mark 6: 23). Prompted by Herodias, she asks for the head of John the Baptist. The allusion prefigures Dravot's own fate.

Give us a memento . . . a small charm compass: Dravot addresses the narrator by the Masonic title 'Brother', and the narrator gives him a Masonic charm (the compass is probably a navigational one, though the geometric compass is if anything even more important as a Masonic symbol).

69 *a real King died in Europe*: see note above, p. 553.

71 *Slap from the bridge fell old Peachey*: it is Dravot who dies in this way (p. 85); Carnehan means that his old self died with him.

71 *odd and even*: a gambling game, like heads or tails.

They was fair men: cf. Dravot's claim on p. 78.

72 *footy*: slight, paltry.

72 *jim-jams*: knick-knacks, trivial articles; *OED* glosses this sense as obsolete by the 17th century.

a woman . . . that was carried off: the quarrel over this village Helen of Troy is another trace-element of epic in the story.

73 *be fruitful and multiply*: God's injunction to mankind in Gen. (1: 28).

sights for the brown: takes aim at the mass, not singling out a particular target (a term from game-bird shooting).

74 *Volunteers*: the predecessors of the Territorial Army reserve, whose level of training would be looked down on by regulars.

'Occupy till I come'; which was scriptural: Luke 19: 13, the parable of the talents. The context is suggestive: 'A certain nobleman went into a far country to receive for himself a kingdom, and to return. And he called his ten servants, and delivered them ten pounds, and said unto them, Occupy till I come. But his citizens hated him, and sent a message after him, saying, We will not have this man to reign over us' (12–14).

Bashkai . . . Er-Heb: these, and the names of all the villages in Kafiristan, are fictional (*RG*).

the son of Alexander by Queen Semiramis: Henry Bellew (see p. 554 and headnote) at the very outset of his *Inquiry into the Ethnography of Afghanistan* speaks of the origin of some of the Afghan tribes in settlements established by Alexander the Great in the 4th century BC, a tradition going back to the Greek geographer Strabo. Since Alexander was also a key figure in Freemasonry, the identification has a double force. Semiramis was a legendary semi-divine Queen of Assyria, like Alexander a conqueror and founder of empire; their conjunction is an emblem of the story's fusion of historical and mythical elements.

75 *The Craft's the trick*: the 'Craft' is the brotherhood of Freemasonry.

Mach on the Bolan: Mach is the railway station at the western end of the Bolan Pass, on the line which runs from Sukkur to Quetta, the great military station in Baluchistan (where Jack Barrett is sent in 'The Story of Uriah': see p. 426). The implication is that Carnehan and Dravot worked on the construction of the railway, which took place in the early 1880s.

the Grip. . . . the Fellow Craft Grip. . . . the Master's Grip: Masonic handshakes in ascending order of the three degrees of Freemasonry, those of the Entered Apprentice, the Fellow Craft, and the Master Mason. The tribesmen have knowledge of the intermediate stage, but are ignorant, or have lost touch with, the superior level, which Dravot and Carnehan will use to awe them (although, as Carnehan points out below, they are not themselves Master Masons).

work a Fellow Craft Lodge: enact the rituals appropriate to the second degree of Freemasonry ('Lodge' denotes a specific group of Freemasons; the building where the group meets; and, as here, it is a metonym for the ritual itself). Dravot goes on to propose himself not just as a Master Mason but a Grand-Master, that is the head of a Grand Lodge, with authority to license the foundation of other Lodges and to 'raise' Masons from the second degree to the third. Carnehan's objection that this is 'against the law' refers to the Masonic law, not the civil or criminal law: he is quite right to imply that Dravot's 'policy' is completely irregular. The fact that Dravot and Carnehan 'have never held office in any Lodge' means that they are a very long way from holding any authority: there are many junior offices in a Lodge below that of Master (let alone Grand-Master).

a four-wheeled bogie: a bogie is a railway undercarriage with two or more wheel-pairs, pivoted below the end of the vehicle.

passed and raised: terms meaning that a candidate for a Masonic degree is examined in the ritual appropriate to that degree and raised to it if his performance is satisfactory.

The women must make aprons: the apron is a traditional feature of Masonic dress and ritual, connecting modern or 'speculative' Freemasonry with its medieval origins in 'operative' Freemasonry, the fraternity of working masons for whom the apron was a working garment. Masonic aprons are embroidered with different symbols ('marks') according to the 'degree' of Freemasonry which the wearer has reached and the rank he holds in his Lodge. Dravot's apron is embroidered with the 'Master's Mark', that is a mark appropriate to the third degree of Freemasonry, knowledge of which the tribesmen have lost. However, as the subsequent passage explains, a few priests know of the existence of a symbol cut into the underside of the 'stone of Imbra', and when this mysterious symbol turns out to be identical to the 'master's Mark', Dravot and Carnehan's fortune is assured.

76 *Past Grand-Masters*: a 'Past Master' in Freemasonry is someone who has held office for the period of at least one year as Master of a Lodge; hence a 'Past Grand-Master' is someone who has held the office of Grand-Master, that is the head of Grand Lodge, the supreme authority in the order.

Bazar-master: a non-commissioned officer detailed to oversee the behaviour of soldiers and white civilians in native quarters of a cantonment or town. The 'Bazar-Sergeant' and his bullying, blubbing son are reviled in 'The Drums of the Fore and Aft' (*Wee Willie Winkie*, 1888).

the Mother Lodge o' the country: see note on p. 552.

Senior Warden: an officer of a Lodge, who assists the Master in the performance of the ritual.

76 *we opens the Lodge in most ample form*: i.e. 'we enacted the formal ritual of declaring the Lodge open'. The opening ritual consists of a series of questions and answers concerning the attendance, security, and correct dispositions of the Lodge members, together with specified prayers and invocations.

77 *raised such as was worthy*: i.e. raised them from the second to the third degree of Freemasonry. The ritual of 'raising', like that of initiation into the order, is intended to be secret, and involves administering an oath to the candidate with terrifying penalties for disobedience. Dravot and Carnehan are ignorant of the precise forms, but know the value in 'scaring the soul' out of their new subjects with an impressively bloodthirsty oath of loyalty.

Communication: a Masonic term signifying a meeting at which the 'working' of a Lodge is scrutinized.

Kafuzelum: a character in a bawdy song (*RG*).

the Ghorband country: about 50 miles north of Kabul.

78 *Herati regiments*: Herat is a city over 400 miles west of Kabul.

Kohat Jezails: long heavy Afghan muskets; there was a factory making them on the Peshawar Road to Kohat (*RG*).

the Lost Tribes: Dravot is confusing the Alexander the Great story with the equally enduring legend of the Lost Tribes of Israel who were supposedly left behind when the Israelites returned from the Babylonian exile.

Rajah Brooke: see note on p. 553.

Tounghoo Jail: in Burma, 110 miles north of Pegu.

Sniders: the predecessor of the Martini–Henry rifle (see note on p. 68), named after the American gunsmith Jacob Snider (1820–66).

worn smooth: the rifling of the barrel, which imparts a rotary motion to the bullet and ensures a gas-tight fit, is worn away: the pressure drops and the weapon becomes less accurate (*RG*).

79 *I take it Kings always feel oppressed that way*: among his other models Dravot now resembles Shakespeare's Henry IV, racked with the cares of kingship ('Uneasy lies the head that wears a crown', *1 Henry IV*, III. i. 31).

like chicken and ham: i.e. white and pink.

80 *Mogul Serai*: Mogul, or Mughal, is near Benares.

Dadur Junction: a long way from Mogul, in Baluchistan, about 60 miles south-east from Quetta; the period referred to is presumably the one in which Carnehan and Dravot were working on the railway (see note on p. 556 above).

The Bible says: Prov. 31: 3: 'Give not thy strength unto women, nor thy ways to that which destroyeth kings'. The advice is given by King Lemuel to his son. But most of the chapter (vv. 10–31) is taken up with the praise of the 'virtuous woman' whose 'price is far above rubies'.

Am I a dog: Goliath's indignant response on seeing David (1 Sam. 17: 43).

81 *I remembered something like that in the Bible*: Gen. 6: 2: 'the sons of God saw the daughters of men that they were fair; and they took them wives of all which they chose'. Verse 4 is also relevant: 'There were giants in the earth in those days; and also after that, when the sons of God came in unto the daughters of men, and they bare children to them, the same became mighty men which were of old, men of renown'.

83 *missionary's-pass-hunting-hound*: someone (a loafer?) who begs for a 'pass' from a missionary, that is a certificate of good conduct.

our Fifty-Seven: the year of the Indian Mutiny.

86 *Right Worshipful Brother*: one of the highest titles in Freemasonry.

the Emperor in his 'abit as he lived: the Ghost in *Hamlet*: 'My father, in his habit as he liv'd!' (III. iv. 135).

The Son of Man goes forth to war: the well-known hymn by Bishop Reginald Heber (1783–1826), no. 439 in the old collection of *Hymns Ancient and Modern*, no. 529 in the new. The second line should read 'kingly' for 'golden'.

Baa Baa, Black Sheep

First pub. in *The Week's News*, Allahabad, 21 Dec. 1888, then *Wee Willie Winkie* in the same month and year; see general note, p. 538.

The story is an autobiographical fiction, based on Kipling's experience in being taken from his birthplace, Bombay, to England, and left by his parents at a boarding house in Southsea. He was then (April 1871) five years and four months old. 'Punch' and 'Judy' are the names he gives himself and his sister, Alice ('Trix'); he used these names again in an uncollected children's story, 'The Potted Princess', pub. in *St Nicholas Magazine*, Jan. 1893, and repr. Sussex Edition, vol. XXX. *RG* gives the real names of 'Uncle Harry' and 'Aunty Rosa' as Captain Pryse Agar Holloway and his wife, Sarah; they had a son, Henry Thomas ('Harry'). The real address of 'Downe Lodge' was Lorne Lodge, at no. 5, Campbell Road, Havelock Park, Southsea. Captain Holloway was born in 1810 and served in the Royal Navy from 1824 to 1829, by which time he was a midshipman. He saw action in the *Brisk*, a sloop of ten guns, at the battle of Navarino (see note on p. 562). When the *Brisk* was paid off he joined the merchant navy; after his retirement from this service he ended his career as Chief Officer of the Coastguard at Southsea. Kipling seems to have given him the title of 'Captain' in error. He died on 20 September 1874. Mrs

Sarah Holloway is last recorded in a Southsea directory in 1896, though whether she died or moved away is not known.

The primary reason why Kipling's parents, in common with many other Anglo-Indian families, decided to separate themselves from their children at so young an age was almost certainly a belief that it would benefit their health; considerations of upbringing and education may have played a secondary role. In Kipling's case it has been suggested that his parents thought he was spoilt and needed a more structured and disciplined environment; certainly his own depictions of the imperious Anglo-Indian toddler bear this out, not just in the first pages of this story but in several others, such as 'Tods' Amendment' in *Plain Tales from the Hills* (1888) and 'Wee Willie Winkie' and 'His Majesty the King' in *Wee Willie Winkie* (1888); the character-type makes a final appearance in 'The Debt' (*Limits and Renewals*, 1932). The question of why the Kipling children were left with strangers rather than with members of their extended family in England (their maternal grandmother, for example, or three aunts, all married sisters of Mrs Kipling) is more vexed, and is compounded by the (surely) bad mistake of giving them not the slightest warning. Charles Carrington rationalizes the matter as best he can in ch. 2 of his biography, but I incline to Lord Birkenhead's sharper judgement: 'we cannot overlook the fact that it was in the parents' power to place the children with relations who knew and loved them, that they jumped at the excuse that the aunts could only take one child each, and insisted on the children being together; that, perhaps to avoid lacerating their own emotions, they failed to prepare the children in any way for this grim separation, which was, said Trix, "like a double death, or rather, like an avalanche that had swept away everything happy and familiar"' (p. 14; Birkenhead is citing Alice Kipling's 'Some Childhood Memories of Rudyard Kipling', *Chambers Journal*, Mar. 1939). Kipling avoids this issue in the story, where no extended family is mentioned: Punch and Judy 'had never heard anything of an animal called an aunt' (p. 94).

Although there is no question about the personal source of the events which Kipling describes, many of which are corroborated by his sister, the story also has literary affiliations: Dickens's *David Copperfield* and *Great Expectations*, for example, or Charlotte Brontë's *Jane Eyre*. The vengeful mother-son combination of Mrs Reed and John Reed in the latter novel strongly resembles that of Aunty Rosa and Harry. And as with Charlotte Brontë's account of Lowood School, Kipling's account of the 'House of Desolation' has been contested. Carrington sums up: 'It would be easy to dismiss "Aunty Rosa" as a tyrant, a cruel foster-mother, and no doubt easy for her friends to defend her character. She must have been a good woman and a good housewife, or the sad story of "Black Sheep" would have ended with exposure and disputation. It did not; even when the wretched Rudyard was released from her domination, there was no breach between the two families. Trix remained in her house several years longer, and Rudyard visited Trix at Southsea as a big boy without, so far as we know, any awkwardness over meeting "Aunty Rosa" again.' That the break between the two families in the story is dramatic and final may be as much the result of artistic design as of wish-fulfilment.

In addition to this story, Kipling wrote about the same period in his life in ch. 1 of *Something of Myself*, and (in a more oblique and fictionalized form) in ch. 1 of his novel *The Light that Failed* (1890). Apart from minor differences of detail and emphasis, the account in *Something of Myself* differs from the story in two main ways. First, the bleakness in the story is unrelieved, whereas in *Something of Myself* Kipling writes of his annual holidays at the house of his aunt Georgiana, the wife of the painter Edward Burne-Jones—'a paradise which I verily believe saved me'. Second, as an old man Kipling looks back at experiences which he now judges to be crucial to his development as a writer. Of the 'calculated torture—religious as well as scientific' to which he was subjected, he drily remarks: 'Yet it made me give attention to the lies I soon found it necessary to tell: and this, I presume, is the foundation of literary effort.' In another passage he says: 'Nor was my life an unsuitable preparation for my future, in that it demanded constant wariness, the habit of observation, and attendance on moods and tempers; the noting of discrepancies between speech and action; a certain reserve of demeanour; and automatic suspicion of sudden favours.' The story offers no such compensating gifts of time and mature reflection. For more on this subject, see the Introduction, pp. xxi–xxii.

One other autobiographical comment about the 'House of Desolation' is significant for Kipling's art, though it is hard to know how to read and apply it. 'In the long run these things,' he says of his persecutions, 'drained me of any capacity for real, personal hate for the rest of my days. So close must any life-filling passion lie to its opposite.' Whether this is a profound truth, or one of the most blatant self-delusions ever recorded, should be left to each reader's judgement.

90 *Epigraph*: the rhyme usually ends with 'One for the little boy who lives down the lane', but Kipling did not invent the variant, which is found in an 18th-century collection, *Mother Goose's Melody*: see Iona and Peter Opie (eds.), *Oxford Dictionary of Nursery Rhymes* (corr. edn. 1980), 88. The song is very old: the division of the bags is said to refer to an export tax on wool imposed in 1275.

The First Bag

When I was in my father's house, I was in a better place: 'my father's house' occurs several times in the Bible, but not in this phrase, which seems rather to derive from Touchstone's words in *As You Like It*, II. iv. 13–14: 'Ay, now am I in Arden; the more fool I; when I was at home I was in a better place'. The quotation concludes: '. . . but travellers must be content.'

ayah: 'a native lady's-maid or nurse-maid. The word has been adopted into most of the Indian vernaculars . . . but it is really Portuguese, from *aia*, a nurse, or governess' (*Hobson-Jobson*). In *Something of Myself* we learn that the ayah was a Portuguese Roman Catholic, which explains the reference to the Catholic Church further on.

90 *hamal*: a porter or bearer (*Hobson-Jobson*, s.v. 'hummaul').

Surti boy: native of Surat, a district and town about 200 miles north of Bombay.

the Ranee: a Hindu queen.

give me put-put: smack me (with a slipper, not a cane as on p. 100).

91 *Up the Ghauts . . . to Nassick*: 'ghaut' or 'ghât' means a mountain pass, but came to refer to 'the mountain ranges parallel to the western and eastern coasts of the Peninsula, through which the *ghâts* or passes lead from the table-lands above down to the coast and lowlands' (*Hobson-Jobson*). It is the western range which is referred to here, starting on the coast near Surat and running south-south-east for 700–800 miles. Nassick was a hill-station about 100 miles from Bombay; Punch is remembering travelling there during the hot weather.

Belait: Indian vernacular for Europe (*Hobson-Jobson*, s.v. 'Bilayut'), the origin of the term 'Blighty' to designate England.

snake-man: cf. the character 'One Three Two' in the late story 'The Debt' (*Limits and Renewals*, 1932), who guards 6-year-old William from snakes in the garden. William is the last incarnation of Punch in Kipling's work.

Parel: a northern suburb of Bombay.

Rocklington: fictitious town, modelled on Southsea (see headnote).

92 *the Apollo Bunder*: the main dock at Bombay, from the Persian word 'bandar', meaning a landing-place or quay. The origin of the name 'Apollo' is the subject of one of *Hobson-Jobson*'s most delightful, and inconsequential, speculations.

broom-gharri: Punch's term for the brougham; 'gharri' is a generic Hindu term for a cart or carriage. *Hobson-Jobson* cites Kipling's father's book *Beast and Man in India* (1892) to illustrate the specific term *brum gari*.

a mysterious rune that he called 'Sonny, my soul': from John Keble's 'Evening', the second poem in *The Christian Year* (1827); Punch remembers its abridged form in *Hymns Ancient and Modern* (no. 24), where it begins with stanza 3: 'Sun of my soul! Thou Saviour dear, | It is not night if Thou be near: | Oh! may no earth-born cloud arise | To hide Thee from Thy servant's eyes.'

94 *the Brisk . . . that day at Navarino*: for the *Brisk*, see headnote; for the ballad which Uncle Harry is humming, see note on p. 564. The battle of Navarino was fought between the combined fleets of England, France, and Russia against those of Turkey and Egypt in 1827.

95 *the Snows*: presumably this refers to a trip taken by the children's parents

to the mountains (perhaps as far as the Himalayas) while they were left behind with the Inveraritys; Inverarity reappears as a *deus* (or doctor) *ex machina* at the end of the story (p. 110).

curse God and die: the advice given to Job by his wife (2: 9).

The Second Bag

97 *Epigraph.* Not from James Thomson's poem (one of Kipling's favourites; he borrowed its title for a sketch of Lahore at night (*Life's Handicap*, 1891); the mistake was pointed out by Andrew Lang and corrected in some edns. after 1892, though not here or in the Sussex Edition. The corrected attribution was 'Easter Day. Naples, 1849', though the author's name was not given, and the quotation was left in its inaccurate form. The poem is by Arthur Hugh Clough, and the lines (78–81) should read: 'Eat, drink, and die, for we are souls bereaved: | Of all the creatures under heaven's wide cope | We are most hopeless, who had once most hope, | And most beliefless, that had most believed.' The poem is about the loss of religious faith (its refrain is 'Christ is not risen!').

98 *a wound-pension*: in *Something of Myself*, Kipling describes Uncle Harry's original, Pryse Holloway, not as having been injured in battle but as having been 'entangled in a harpoon-line while whale-fishing, and dragged down till he miraculously freed himself. But the line had scarred his ankle for life—a dry, black scar, which I used to look at with horrified interest.'

muttering something about 'strangers' children': this exact phrase does not occur in the Bible, which does however exhort us separately to care for strangers and children; but Kipling, if not Uncle Harry, may be remembering a passage in Ezekiel about the division of the land of Israel: 'ye shall divide it by lot for an inheritance unto you, and to the strangers that sojourn among you, which shall beget children among you: and they shall be unto you as born in the country among the children of Israel; they shall have inheritance with you among the tribes of Israel' (47: 22). The insistence on equitable treatment here is as pertinent as more general biblical injunctions to behave charitably.

99 *Sharpe's Magazine*: *RG* identifies the magazine as *Sharpe's London Magazine*, vol. 1; the page in question is not the first, but the one for 7 Mar. 1846, and 'the picture of the griffin flying over the mountains . . . was engraved by Dalziel after a drawing by Selous'. The poem was 'The Shepherd of the Giant Mountains', translated from the German by Menella Bute Smedley (1820–77). The basic plot is as Kipling gives it, with the addition that the griffin-slayer is rewarded by marriage to the daughter of the local duke. *RG* points out that the particular words and phrases cited by Kipling ('falchion', 'ewe-lamb', 'base usurper', 'verdant

mead') do not in fact occur in Smedley's verses, 'though all might easily have been there'.

99 *large store of old books*: *Frank Fairlegh, or Scenes from the Life of a Private Pupil* was serialized in 1849–50, with illustrations by Cruikshank; it was an expanded version of a serial story in *Sharpe's London Magazine*, 1846–8. It was by Menella Bute Smedley's cousin, Frank Smedley (1818–64). John Sutherland describes it as 'a *Bildungsroman* similar to Dickens's *David Copperfield* and Thackeray's *Pendennis*' (*Longman Companion to Victorian Fiction*, 1988).

contributed anonymously: a euphemism for 'pirated'; no early poems by Tennyson appeared by his authority in *Sharpe's London Magazine*. The example cited by *RG*, 'Song—The Owl', which the magazine printed in Feb. 1846, had been pub. in Tennyson's *Poems, Chiefly Lyrical* (1830), and was not repr. by him until he included it in the 'Juvenilia' section of his *Poetical Works* (1870).

'62 Exhibition Catalogues: the 'International Exhibition', which ran from May to November 1862 at South Kensington; parts of the structure in which it was housed, incl. the domes, were used in the building of Alexandra Palace.

Grimm's Fairy Tales: *RG* suggests the 1823 translation by Edgar Taylor, with illustrations by Cruikshank, which is probably the one the 6-year-old Georgie reads in 'The Brushwood Boy' (*The Day's Work*, 1898): 'The princess of his tales was a person of wonderful beauty (she came from an old illustrated edition of Grimm, now out of print)'.

Hans Andersen: Hans Christian Andersen's fairy tales had been available in translation since 1846.

101 *the Valley of Humiliation*: from Bunyan's *Pilgrim's Progress*; Christian meets and overcomes the 'foul fiend', Apollyon, there. Kipling strips the term of its allegorical meaning so that it simply means the infliction of undeserved suffering.

103–4 *Cometh up as a Flower*: a best-selling novel by Rhoda Broughton (1840–1920), one of the 'slightly scandalous romances' on which her enormous popularity was based: 'the heroine, Nell Le Strange (who tells her own story) has to make a marriage of convenience with a rich aristocrat in order to repair her family fortunes. She finally dies pathetically of a convenient consumption' (John Sutherland, *Longman Companion to Victorian Fiction*, 1988). Kipling's choice of this title is influenced by the biblical text from which it derives, and which is apt for Uncle Harry's approaching death: 'Man that is born of a woman is of few days, and full of trouble. He cometh forth like a flower, and is cut down: he fleeth also as a shadow, and continueth not' (Job 14: 1–2).

104 *the song of the Battle of Navarino*: no original for this ballad has been

found. The rough and ready rhythm, together with the listing of the names of the ships, suggests an authentic production close to the date of the battle itself (1827); whether it was ever printed or not, it was, I think, communicated orally to Kipling by 'Uncle Harry'. I do not think that Kipling invented it. *RG* cites Admiral Sir Edward Codrington's official report of the battle, which confirms the ballad's accuracy in the order of ships and other details; 'at one moment the little *Brisk* was certainly "sore exposed", coming to close quarters with one of the biggest of the Turkish ships'.

The Third Bag

Epigraph. Shakespeare, *Twelfth Night*, II. iii (the song 'O mistress mine, where are you roaming').

105 *Some of them were unclean*: as often in Kipling, the word means beyond its literal sense: it carries connotations of biblical uncleanness, though in what this consists we are not told.

hubshi: glossed in *Hobson-Jobson* as deriving from the Arabic word 'Habashi', meaning an Abyssinian or Ethiopian; it had become a generic term for 'negro', though in the mouths of Kipling's characters (both English and Indian) it is closer to 'nigger'. The racism of the Indians towards the Africans, which Punch calls to mind here, features strongly in stories such as 'A Sahibs' War' (*Traffics and Discoveries*, 1904), and 'A Deal in Cotton' (*Actions and Reactions*, 1909).

113 *when the Fear of the Lord was so often the beginning of falsehood*: instead of being 'the beginning of wisdom', as it is said to be in Ps. 111: 10.

pagal: a term 'often used colloquially by Anglo-Indians' (*Hobson-Jobson*, s.v. 'poggle'), meaning 'idiot' or 'madman', though the sense here is more like 'rogue, mischief-maker'.

On Greenhow Hill

First pub. *Harper's Magazine*, 23 Aug. 1890, and *Macmillan's Magazine*, Sept. 1890; coll. *Life's Handicap*, 1891.

For Learoyd, Mulvaney, and Ortheris, see Appendix B, pp. 528–9. This is one of only two stories in which Learoyd is the main narrator; the other is a comic story of dog-stealing, 'Private Learoyd's Story' (*Soldiers Three*, 1888). It is also unusual in that the frame-narrative is in the third person, i.e. the story is not told to a narrator (Kipling) who relays it to us.

Kipling's own family roots were in Yorkshire, as he emphatically made clear in a letter to Butler Wood, the librarian of the Bradford Public Library, who wrote to him about this story in 1896:

If you were not yourself a Yorkshireman it is possible that I might use vigorous language when you suggest that I 'may have Yorkshire blood in my veins.' I have —a little. I am the grandson of Joseph Kipling, Wesleyan Methodist minister to

Pately Brigg in 1857, and son of John Lockwood Kipling born in Skipton in Craven [actually Pickering, though still in Yorkshire]. We used to be small Nidderdale yeomen and I believe that in a humble way few stocks carry back cleaner Yorkshire blood for a longer time. I think we are West Riding for a matter of two hundred year; a thing of which I am not a little proud. Yes, you may fairly say that I have good claim to be called a Yorkshireman, and as a fellow tyke I thank you once more for your kind expression of interest. (*Letters*, ii. 244)

Though the background of north-country mining and chapel-going was remote from his personal experience, he might have learned something about it from his father. In the preface to *Life's Handicap*, Kipling wrote that 'a few, but the very best' of the stories were given to him by his father, and there is evidence that J. L. Kipling passed on to his son a sense both of the power and fervour of sectarian faith, and its oppressiveness and intolerance (features which would have been impressed on Kipling, in any case, by his experiences at Southsea: see 'Baa, Baa, Black Sheep'). A. W. Baldwin points out a passage in a 'magazine romance' by J. L. Kipling called 'Inezilla' which is hostile to all forms of religious excess, including 'the ravings of methodist ranters round weeping and snuffling victims at the "penitent bench"' (in J. Gross (ed.), *Rudyard Kipling: The Man, His Work and His World* (1972), 24). Kipling would also have met men with Learoyd's background in two of the regiments quartered at Lahore and the Mian Mir cantonments during his time as a reporter with the *Civil and Military Gazette*, the Fifth (Northumberland) Fusiliers and the 30th East Lancashire.

Victorian fiction dealt extensively with evangelical religion and its good and bad effects; Kipling's attitude has something in common with e.g. George Eliot's in *Scenes of Clerical Life* (1858) and *Adam Bede* (1859), but in terms of literary history the story also looks forward, to the early fiction of D H. Lawrence.

114 *Title*. See note below, p. 118.

Epigraph. From a poem by Alice Kipling (Kipling's mother).

Snider: a muzzle-loaded gun, converted to a breech-loading rifle; no longer in use by the British Army at the time of the story, it had (as is often the case with obsolescent weapons) descended to that army's irregular enemies. See Dravot's comment in 'The Man who would be King', p. 78.

the Aurangabadis: a fictional name for the native regiment, from Aurungabad, a town in the Mahratta hills in Hyderabad State.

116 *the man of many wiles*: a Homeric phrase, applied to Ulysses.

118 *child av calamity*: the self-awarded title of a cowardly braggart in ch. 3 of Mark Twain's *Life on the Mississippi* (1883), originally an episode intended for inclusion in *Huckleberry Finn* (1884–5). See also headnote to 'My Sunday at Home' (p. 589).

Rumbolds Moor . . . Skipton . . . Greenhow Hill . . . Pately Brig: Rumbolds (or Rombalds, or Rumbles) Moor rises south-eastwards from Skipton; Greenhow Hill rises west of Pately Brig (or Bridge) to a height of 1,300 feet. From Skipton to Pately Bridge is about 14 miles as the crow flies. Kipling spent part of his summer holiday before leaving England for India in September 1882 staying with his paternal grandmother at Skipton.

clickin': clutching.

Leeds Townhall: an icon of Victorian municipal Gothic, opened by Queen Victoria in 1858. Its spaciousness and grandeur were an emblem of the city's industrial energy, self-confidence, and prosperity.

th' big sumph: in the sense of 'pit': Learoyd describes his work further on, p. 125.

120 *th' eight-day clock*: a clock which would go for eight days before needing to be wound up; *OED* cites its first literary appearance in one of Dickens's *Sketches by Boz* (1836; ch. 2, 'The Half-Pay Captain').

Primitive Methodist: a Church founded in 1811 by ministers whose American style of camp-meeting revivalism was disapproved of by the official Methodists. It no longer exists as a separate Church, having joined in 1932 with the United Methodists and the Wesleyan Methodists to form the present Methodist Church.

121 *clemmed*: wasted away.

Nova Zambra: Novaya Zemlya, a Russian island far to the north in the Barents Sea.

Cape Cayenne: on the coast of French Guiana, in South America.

shebeen: an unlicensed drinking establishment, but as *RG* suggests it probably just means 'cottage' here.

122 *th' white choaker*: clerical collar.

fared: seemed.

123 *they couldn't abide th' thought o' soldiering*: with this passage, including the comments of Mulvaney and, especially, Ortheris, compare 'Tommy' (*Barrack-Room Ballads*), p. 434.

Th' sword o' th' Lord and o' Gideon: Judg. 7: 18, the war-cry of the Israelites against the Midianites.

puttin' on th' whole armour o' righteousness: from Eph. 6: 11: 'Put on the whole armour of God, that ye may be able to stand against the wiles of the devil'; in v. 14 the 'breastplate of righteousness' is mentioned as part of this armour.

fightin' the good fight o' faith: from 1 Tim. 6: 12: 'Fight the good fight of faith, lay hold on eternal life, whereunto thou art also called, and hast professed a good profession before many witnesses.'

124 *the Widdy*: see note on p. 26.

arf-license pub: a pub licensed only to sell beer and cider, not wines and spirits (hence a poor establishment).

The Forders: another name for the cab-drivers, from the name of a well-known firm which built two-wheeled hansom cabs.

hullabaloojah choruses: Ortheris's mangling of the 'Hallelujah Chorus' in Handel's *Messiah*.

high seconds: either he had the next-to-highest voice, or he was one of the high voices in the second division of the choir.

125 *th' bowels o' th' earth . . . th' framework o' th' everlastin' hills*: the first phrase is not biblical, but from Shakespeare ('the bowels of the harmless earth', *1 Henry IV* I. iii. 61); it and the following phrase are influenced by Job 38: 4: 'Where wast thou when I laid the foundations of the earth?' The phrase 'the everlasting hills' occurs in Gen. 49: 26, though not in the context of God the creator.

a boggart: a spectre, a goblin or bogy, esp. a local goblin or sprite supposed to haunt a gloomy spot or scene of violence (*OED*).

126 *fresh*: tipsy.

a sparrow, a spout, and a thunder-storm: not identified; sparrows are proverbial for lechery, and 'spout' is a slang word for the penis.

127 *'Liza Roantree's for neither on us, nor for nobody o' this earth*: this situation is repeated in 'Marklake Witches' (*Rewards and Fairies*, 1910) in which the French physician René Lanark and the English Dr Break both love the beautiful Philadelphia, who has consumption and is 'not for any living man'.

128 *took th' Widow's shillin'*: accepting a shilling from the recruiting sergeant constituted a legal obligation to enlist.

'Brugglesmith'

First pub. Oct. 1891 in three periodicals: *The Week's News* (Allahabad), *Black and White Magazine* (England), and *Harper's Weekly* (America); coll. *Many Inventions*, 1893.

The story springs from Kipling's bachelor days in London (1889–91), when he had lodgings in Villiers Street, near the Strand, and walked the streets of London gathering impressions and material; he describes this period in ch. 4 of *Something of Myself*, including a reference to the main prop of the story, the 'ambulance' (see note on p. 137). The selection of 'Brook Green, Hammersmith' as the drunk man's destination (and his name) may, as *RG* suggests, derive from the fact that it was the address of Charles Whibley, 'one of the

Henley-Kipling group of writers who held bachelor dinner parties . . . at Sherry's, a famous restaurant of the time in Regent Street. Whibley has been described as "a scholarly *bon viveur* with a well-earned liver complaint".' But the choice of destination was also dictated by the east–west axis of the plot.

The narrator's anguish at the drunken man's exposure of his name (which the story, with comically blind loyalty, refuses to divulge) reflects on Kipling's phenomenal and very recent success on his return to England. He had 'made his name', and became interested in that name's vulnerability as well as its power. Although 'The Village That Voted the Earth was Flat' (p. 293) is a greater farce in scope and depth, it is not more perfectly planned, and not funnier, than this consummate descent into indignity. The denouement is brought about by a final and grotesque entanglement, a device which looks forward to the involuntary umbrella-dance at the climax of 'The Miracle of Saint Jubanus' (*Limits and Renewals*, 1932). The story is also a period piece in its fascination with London at night (*Dr Jekyll and Mr Hyde*, 1886; *The Picture of Dorian Gray*, 1891; *The Adventures of Sherlock Holmes*, 1892).

130 *Epigraph*: William Clark Russell (1844–1911), American author of nautical adventure novels, of which the most popular was *The Wreck of the Grosvenor* (1877).

below London Bridge: the ship was moored in the Pool of London and the tide was running in (up river) (*RG*).

The Breslau . . . The Black M'Phee: both the ship and her chief engineer (spelled 'McPhee') reappear in 'Bread upon the Waters' (*The Day's Work*, 1898), a revenge tale with a very different tone.

131 *Vanity Fair*: by William Makepeace Thackeray, pub. 1847–8.

'Little Bar-rnaby Dorrit' and 'The Mystery o' the Bleak Druid': Dickens's turn to be mocked: muddling *Barnaby Rudge* (1841) and *Little Dorrit* (1855–7), followed by *Bleak House* (1852–3) and *The Mystery of Edwin Drood* (1870).

132 *square holes*: square ports in the hull to facilitate the loading of timber (*RG*).

a Castle liner: the Castle Line was a steamship line sailing mainly to South Africa; in 1900 it was merged with another company to become the Union Castle Line. The 'ties' are short lengths of rope or canvas used to secure the furled sail to its yard (some of the older steamships would still carry yards and sails) and they would be painted black to make a smart contrast with the white sails (*RG*).

The smartest clipper that you could find: a sea shanty adapted from an American railway song 'Let the bulgine [engine] run' (*RG*).

Ye towers o' Julia [etc.]: the first two lines misquote Thomas Gray's 'The Bard' (1757): 'Ye towers of Julius, London's lasting shame, | With many a foul and midnight murther fed' (ll. 87–8; the Tower of London was popularly believed to have been founded by Julius Caesar). The third line is the (accurately quoted) refrain of Edmund Spenser's 'Prothalamion' (1596). The fourth line is taken with distorting effect from the 'Evening Hymn' ('Glory to Thee My God this Night') by Bishop Thomas Ken (1637–1711): 'Teach me to live, that I may dread | The grave as little as my bed.'

133 *'Learn, prudent* [etc.]: the concluding lines of Robert Burns's 'A Bard's Epitaph' (1786), with 'Learn' for 'Know'. Burns also says of the dead bard that 'thoughtless follies laid him low, | And stain'd his name' (ll. 23–4); cf. the play with the narrator's name which is about to begin.

If your sin . . . deep waters: combining phrases from different parts of the Bible: 'be sure your sin will find you out' (Num. 32: 23) and 'deep waters' from several places, e.g. Ps. 69: 14, where the psalmist prays to be 'delivered from them that hate me, and out of the deep waters'; *RG* also suggests an apt allusion to Ezek. 34: 18: 'Seemeth it a small thing unto you . . . to have drunk of the deep waters?'

Like unto the worms that perish: 'worms' replace 'beasts' in this biblical tag, from Ps. 49: 12; wittily, if the drunk man is thinking of the *un*dying worm of damnation in Mark 9: 44.

flat: landing-stage.

134 *drookit*: soaked, drenched.

under the rules o' the R-royal Humane Society, ye must give me hot whisky and water: the Society was founded in 1744 for the recovery of persons who had apparently drowned.

The crackling o' thorns under a pot: the Bible compares it to 'the laughter of the fool', adding 'this also is vanity' (Eccles. 7: 6).

135 *A good name is as a savoury bakemeat*: not (alas) authentic. 'A good name is rather to be chosen than great riches' (Prov. 22: 1) and 'A good name is better than precious ointment' (Eccles. 7: 1) are the soberer biblical versions; 'savoury meat' appears in Gen. 27: 4, and 'bakemeats' in Gen. 40: 17.

In the mornin' [etc.]: 'a parody of an old Negro song, "In the Morning" or "When Gabriel blows his trumpet"' (*RG*).

St Clement Danes: Wren's church in the Strand, at the east (Fleet Street) end; Dr Johnson (see below) worshipped there and had a pew in the north gallery; his statue stands outside the church facing towards Fleet Street.

slummock: an *English* dialect word, meaning to move about awkwardly or clumsily; Kipling's transferred use of it to describe speech is cited by *OED*.

Every member of the Force [etc.]: from a music-hall song written about

1880 by E. W. Rogers, continuing with the famous refrain 'If you want to know the time, | Ask a P'liceman'. J. D. Lewins (letter in *Kipling Journal*, 67 (Sept. 1993), 48–50) suggests that 'an insultingly ironic implication' was inherent in the song, 'since the subsequent verses represent the Police, quite offensively, as corrupt, lecherous and cowardly'; the fact that every member of the Force had a watch would be attributable to its having been filched from drunks like Brugglesmith himself.

136 *sit on the policeman's head and cut the traces*: as though he were a fallen draught horse (*RG*).

Holywell Street: this street no longer exists; it was on the north side of the Strand, and was demolished to make way for the modern Kingsway.

held a sitting: had a reserved place (in a pew).

the great and god-like man . . . a hundred years ago: Dr Samuel Johnson (1709–84), to whom the remark 'And now, Sir, we will take a walk down Fleet Street' was popularly attributed; it became famous as the motto of the *Temple Bar* magazine.

Bow Street: London's most famous police station, which gave its name to the 'Bow Street runners', the precursors of the modern Police.

scrob: the meaning is clear enough (manhandle, esp. by the neck) but the word seems to be Kipling's invention.

137 *you bloomin' garrotter*: this term came into popular currency from the mid-19th century after a spate of street robberies in which the victims were choked (sometimes to death); it originates with the former mode of public execution in Spain.

ambulance: a 'hand-ambulance', as Kipling describes it in ch. 4 of *Something of Myself*: 'One got to know that ambulance (it lived somewhere at the back of St. Clement Danes) as well as the Police of the E. Division, and even as far as Piccadilly Circus'. At this date there were of course no motorized ambulances; a horse-drawn vehicle would have to be summoned and would in any case have difficulty negotiating the narrow streets of the City of London. Pedestrian ambulances resembling large wheelbarrows were therefore stored at a number of locations in the City. This one has a canvas cover which keeps the body out of sight.

the Adelphi: the Adelphi Theatre. Villiers Street, where Kipling lodged (see headnote) runs along the west side of the theatre.

139 *Brook Green, 'Ammersmith*: see headnote.

140 *Apsley House*: now a museum, then still the residence of the Dukes of Wellington (built by the first Duke), at the west end of Piccadilly.

the Hatton Garden burglar: Hatton Garden, which runs between Holborn

Circus and Clerkenwell, had long been a centre of the diamond business; several burglaries took place there in 1890–1.

142 *from the noises within . . . all the basement banisters*: I must reluctantly quote *RG* on the mechanics of the denouement: 'The flaw in this otherwise perfect story is that the bell could not have behaved in the way described. The non-electric bell was actuated by a system of wires and bell-crank-levers . . . That is to say, there is no straight run of wire from front door to basement, but at every angle traversed by the system is placed a bell-crank-lever and between each lever is a length of wire. So that a violent tug on the front door bell-knob would probably wrench the wire from the lever at the far end of the hall, but the bell itself would stay in the basement kitchen.'

'Love-o'-Women'

First pub. *Many Inventions*, 1893.

For Mulvaney and his comrades, see Appendix B, pp. 528–9. This story involves only Mulvaney and Ortheris, not Learoyd. The barrack-shooting which forms the 'frame' of the story has an original, according to Kipling's account in ch. 3 of *Something of Myself*: 'A soldier of my acquaintance had been sentenced to life-imprisonment for a murder which, on evidence not before the court, seemed to me rather justified.' In the story, the 'evidence not before the court' (i.e. the truth which Ortheris conceals) is what enables the crime to be palliated as much as possible. (See also the note on p. 573 below.) Murder is an understandable, even a forgivable response to the goading of shame and jealousy, from which there is no escape in the crowded, sweltering cantonment; a dishonourable murder is more rigorously punished in 'Danny Deever' (p. 433). Kipling's most sustained treatment of this subject is 'Black Jack' (*Soldiers Three*, 1888), in which Mulvaney himself comes close to murder; he then tells a story of how he thwarted the murder of Sergeant O'Hara (who, it turns out, was killed after all for the same reason that Mackie is killed in this story).

The story which forms the central part of the tale belongs to a group of early tales of sexual passion and obsession, represented in this volume by 'Beyond the Pale' (p. 15) and 'On Greenhow Hill' (p. 114); see also 'Dray Wara Yow Dee' and 'In Flood Time' (*In Black and White*, 1888). Mulvaney's prickly, compassionate, fearful attitude to 'Love-o'-Women' anticipates Pyecroft's feelings about Vickery in 'Mrs Bathurst' (p. 276).

The fate of 'Love-o'-Women' is in part determined by what Kipling saw as the perverse policy of the British authorities towards soldiers' sexual activity. See the passage from ch. 3 of *Something of Myself* quoted in Appendix B, p. 528.

143 *Epigraph*. From John Ford's *The Lover's Melancholy* (1629), IV. ii. 120–1 (Revels Plays, ed. R. F. Hill, 1985). The title, and Kipling's choice of quotation, imply tragedy, but in fact the play is a romantic comedy.

the blood of man calling from the ground: God says to Cain after the murder of Abel: 'What hast thou done? the voice of thy brother's blood crieth unto me from the ground' (Gen. 4: 10).

goldbeater-skin: an animal membrane (generally from the gut of oxen) used to separate the leaves of gold-foil during beating.

144 *ruling blank account-forms in the Central Jail*: in ch. 3 of *Something of Myself*, Kipling writes with reference to Sergeant Raines's original (see headnote): 'I saw him later in Lahore gaol at work on some complicated arrangement of nibs with different coloured inks, stuck into a sort of loom which, drawn over paper, gave the ruling for the blank forms of financial statements. It seemed wickedly monotonous. But the spirit of man is undefeatable. "If I made a mistake of an eighth of an inch in spacing these lines, I'd throw out *all* the accounts of the Upper Punjab," said he.'

the Andamans: the prison-settlement in the Andaman Islands, in the Bay of Bengal; situated at Port Blair, on South Island, it had been established in 1858 in the aftermath of the Mutiny, and by the 1890s held around 14,000 prisoners. Employment there would be the best that Sergeant Raines, as an ex-soldier of good character, could expect after serving his sentence.

Ortheris with the dogs: both Ortheris and Learoyd are fond of dogs (and adept at stealing them).

'ave they pushed your 'elmet off yet, Sergeant?: referring to his cuckold's horns.

the beastie: the 'bhisti' or water-carrier (see 'Gunga Din', p. 442).

145 *the Judge put his hand to his brow before giving sentence*: he is not putting on the black cap which would signify death.

relaxed to the Secular Arm: transferred to the custody of the civilian authorities (in origin a phrase used when prisoners of the Inquisition were delivered to the civil authorities for execution of sentence).

ticca-gharri: hired carriage.

146 *Murree*: a hill station in Kashmir.

spend ut in Masses: as repentance for having lied on oath.

Dinah: Mulvaney's wife; their story is told in 'The Courting of Dinah Shadd' (*Life's Handicap*, 1891).

147 *the Pattiala guard of honour*: Kipling's first assignment as a special correspondent for the *Civil and Military Gazette* was to cover a state visit by the Viceroy, Lord Ripon, to Pattiala, a native (Sikh) state 200 miles south-east of Lahore, in March 1884.

the Black Tyrone: see Appendix B, p. 529.

147 *a gentleman-ranker*: see the poem 'Gentlemen-Rankers' (p. 446).

148 *ghostly*: spiritual.

wid his cap on three hairs: pushed back on his head.

149 *the Ould Reg'mint*: see Appendix B, p. 529.

up to the Front: the North-West Frontier, between what is now Pakistan and Afghanistan.

Pindi: Rawalpindi.

fwhat I tould you in the gyard-gate av the fight at Silver's Theatre: see 'With the Main Guard' (p. 24). Mulvaney refers to a battle in which both the 'Old Regiment' and the Black Tyrone were involved.

150 *our Captain Crook—Cruik-na-bulleen*: see note on p. 27.

windystraws: windlestraws, dry stalks of grass.

Bobs: 'Bobs' was the troops' nickname for Lord Roberts (1832–1914), then Commander-in-Chief in India. See the poem 'Bobs' (1898), which similarly stresses Roberts's short stature and his energetic, practical miltary mind.

sungars: 'a rude stone breastwork, such as is commonly erected for defence by the Afridis and other tribes on the Indian N.W. frontier' (*Hobson-Jobson*).

the long bradawl: i.e. the bayonet.

151 *jeldy*: quick (Hindustani).

152 *a 'Tini*: a Martini-Henry rifle; see note on p. 68.

'Oh Lord, how long, how long!': variants of this phrase are frequent in the Bible, esp. Psalms and the prophetic books.

gydon: guidon, pennant.

153 *Brigade Ordhers to me*: 'over my head', 'beyond me'.

grup the heel av him: from Job 19: 9, a passage concerning the fate of the wicked: 'he is cast into a net by his own feet, and he walketh upon a snare. The gin shall take him by the heel, and the robber shall prevail against him . . . Terrors shall make him afraid on every side . . . His confidence shall be rooted out of his tabernacle, and it shall bring him to the king of terrors.'

I tould you I was Cain: after the killing of Abel, 'the Lord set a mark upon Cain, lest any finding him should kill him' (Gen. 4: 15). The implication is that Love-o'-Women is reserved for divine punishment.

154 *byle*: ox.

consate: conceit, fancy, with the implication that Love-o'-Women is deluding himself.

by the Hilts av God: 'by these hilts' is an oath recorded by *OED* in Shakespeare and Chapman, though it seems to have been obsolute by Kipling's time.

Paternosters was no more than peas on plates: 'prayer was of no use'; the image is that of peas bouncing off plates.

156 *Locomotus attacks us*: locomotive ataxy, or *tabes dorsalis*, a disease affecting the sense of position or balance, is one of the forms taken by syphilis in its tertiary and fatal stage.

bull's-wool: shoe-leather.

157 *doolies*: covered litters.

Jumrood: a fort on the road running nearly due east from Peshawar to the Khyber Pass. In the passage which follows Kipling describes the return of the troops from the Second Afghan War in August 1880 (*RG*).

'For 'tis my delight av a shiny night': from a folk song, 'The Lincolnshire Poacher'.

'The wearin' av the Green': an Irish Nationalist ballad.

brequist: breakfast.

the Jock Elliott's: the King's Own Borderers, later the King's Own Scottish Borderers.

158 *the ould dhrum-horse at the head*: see the story 'The Rout of the White Hussars' (*Plain Tales from the Hills*, 1888): 'The soul of the Regiment lives in the Drum-Horse who carries the silver kettle-drums'.

the Cavalry Canter: 'Bonny Dundee' (words by Walter Scott).

The Fly-by-Nights: *RG* says that this is another regiment, but it may still refer to the Lancers, who would have acquired this nickname among others for their 'rout' as told in 'The Rout of the White Hussars'.

Ali Musjid: about 9 miles from the entrance to the Khyber Pass.

'The Dead March': from Handel's oratorio, *Saul*.

161 *I'm dyin, Aigypt—dyin'*: Antony's words to Cleopatra (IV. xiv. 18, repeated at l. 41). In implying that Mulvaney does not recognize them as Shakespeare, Kipling forgets that Mulvaney quotes *Hamlet* to the narrator in 'The Courting of Dinah Shadd' and tells of seeing many Shakespearian performances in Dublin during his youth.

Issiwasti: for this reason (Hindustani).

162 *'Oh do not despise . . . Soldier!'*: an additional verse from a song by Kipling which appears in a story called 'My Great and Only', pub. in the *Civil and Military Gazette* in 1890 but not coll. until the Sussex Edition (1935); in the story the narrator achieves a one-off triumph by getting one of his songs accepted as a popular music-hall number. See *Early Verse by Rudyard Kipling*, ed. A. Rutherford (1986), 473–5.

The Bridge-Builders

First pub. in the Christmas number of the *Illustrated London News*, 1893; coll. *The Day's Work*, 1898.

The bridge is a lattice-girder type of 28 spans of 330 feet each (an average length; the upper limit of a span would be about 800 feet). The spans are independent, i.e. each span reaches from abutment to pier. The construction involves a series of trusses, a combination of structural members whose basic principle is the rigidity of the triangle: by being connected at their ends the trusses form a rigid frame on which to support the bridge. The elaborate defences of such bridges (by means of guide-banks and channels) against the shifting alluvial rivers of northern India, with their propensity to rapid and severe flooding, are as crucial as the construction of the bridge itself, and help to explain the anger of Mother Gunga (the river goddess) at the indignity she feels she has suffered.

Both the bridge and its builders are composite creations, formed from several real models and treated with Kipling's usual freedom. He knew many engineers; one of the leading prototypes of Findlayson, James Richard Bell, commented that the story was 'a farrago of bridge-building stories told to R.K. at various times'. Kipling wrote an article for the *Civil and Military Gazette* (2 Mar. 1887) on 'The Sutlej Bridge' and another (18 May) on 'The Chak-Nizam Bridge' (both repr. *Kipling's India*, 206–23); the former contains a good deal of technical information which points to the Sutlej Bridge (at Ferozepore) as the principal model for the bridge over the Ganges in the story. The dimensions are the same, and so are the problems confronting the builders—the river's 'pent strength and murderous possibilities' (p. 209)—and the stakes involved, though these are official and collective rather than personal: 'the reputation of the Department, a few hundred thousand cubic feet of masonry and concrete, and some lakhs of the public money, were at the mercy of a reprobate stream' (p. 211). Many other details parallel those in the story, for example the feverish haste with which the work was carried out against the coming flood, and the description of the labourers, the 'ten thousand folk of all kinds, from *changar* earth-workers, to Suratee men learned in ropes, tackles, blocks, and falls, and West Indian creoles controlling the pile-driver' (p. 214). There is no hint of the incompetence, corruption, and maladministration against which Findlayson and Hitchcock have to struggle, though in the second article, on the Chak-Nizam bridge, Kipling reports a speech by the chief engineer, James Ramsay, in which various delays and accidents are mentioned, including 'having to wait for the girder-work not arrived from England' (see p. 165). The figure of Peroo, the guide who conducts Findlayson to the other world where he witnesses the conclave of the Hindu gods, has no place in the *Civil and Military Gazette*. The high seriousness with which this conclave is treated contrasts with the black comedy of another gathering of creatures around a recently-completed bridge, in 'The Undertakers' (*Second Jungle Book*, 1895). In the denouement of that story the bridge-builder comes at daybreak to shoot the crocodile who had feasted on his coolies. The flooding of an Indian river is linked with (erotic) passion and power in a story with a native narrator, 'In Flood Time' (*In Black and White*, 1888); that of an English river in 'My Son's Wife' (*A Diversity of Creatures*, 1917) signals Midmore's conversion to true (rural) Englishness and his marriage to Connie Sperrit; in 'Friendly Brook' (*A Diversity of Creatures*, 1917) the flood is an agent of revenge.

The celebration of 'the day's work' (the phrase occurs here, unobtrusively, on p. 170) is shadowed through all the stories in the volume by Christ's warning in John 9: 4: 'I must work the works of him that sent me, while it is day: the night cometh, when no man can work.' (This verse was carved by Kipling's father above the mantelpiece in Kipling's study at Bateman's.) But the 'night' which engulfs Findlayson is both less than death (since he does not die), and more, since he apprehends in his vision the universal cycle of life and death, a cycle which includes the death of the gods. His work is as significant, and as insignificant, as the cosmos itself. Kipling's tone—awe shot through with irony—brings him close to Thomas Hardy in this story.

163 *a C.I.E. . . . a C.S.I.*: Companion of the Order of the Indian Empire and Companion of the Order of the Star of India. The Order of the Indian Empire was instituted in 1877 when Queen Victoria was proclaimed Empress. The Order of the Star of India had been instituted in 1861. Frederick Walton, the engineer who built the Dufferin Bridge at Benares, was made a C.I.E. when the bridge was opened by the Viceroy in 1887, and Kipling had stayed with Walton while the bridge was under construction.

the great Kashi bridge over the Ganges: a fictional bridge; see headnote.

C.E.: Civil Engineer, a professional qualification rather than a distinction.

the Findlayson truss: see headnote.

borrow-pit: the excavation formed by removing earth for the embankments.

spile-pier: a pier built on piles or large timbers driven into the ground for the crane to work on (*RG*).

164 *saw that his work was good*: echoing God in Gen. 1: 31: 'And God saw everything that he had made, and, behold, it was very good.'

pukka: glossed here as 'permanent', from the general sense of something correct and in order.

Kabuli pony: a hardy breed from north of Kabul, the capital of Afghanistan.

Cooper's Hill: the familiar name of the Royal Indian College of Civil Engineering, which offered a three-year course in engineering subjects of particular interest for India and other colonies; it closed in 1904.

164 *Simla*: see headnote to 'Three and—An Extra', p. 532.

165 *whipping powers*: authority to order corporal punishment for theft and other offences.

166 *a Lascar, a Kharva from Bulsar*: 'lascar' is the generic term for a native sailor, as in 'Brugglesmith' (p. 131); the Kharvas of Kutch (on the north-west coast of India) are a seafaring caste; Bulsar is in the Surat district, north of Bombay (cf. the 'Suratee men' mentioned in Kipling's article on the Sutlej Bridge: see headnote).

Rockhampton: in Queensland, Australia.

serang: boatswain.

the British India boats: a passenger line later amalgamated with the P & O.

Mother Gunga: the goddess personifying the Ganges river, who appears later in the story with the other Indian deities.

Kutch Mandvi: Mandvi is a port on the Gulf of Kutch (see above).

167 *Black Water*: open sea.

Shiva: or Siva, one of the principal gods of the Hindu pantheon, who appears later as the Bull.

Kumpani: i.e. 'Company', the British India line referred to above.

silver pipe: boatswain's whistle.

the Chota Sahib: 'little master'; Findlayson would be the 'Burra Sahib', the 'chief master'.

168 *jiboonwallah*: a made-up word, meaning something like 'good-for-nothing'.

Tuticorin: a port at the southern end of the South Indian Railway, from where, at this period, the British India line ran boats to Colombo in Ceylon.

poojah: rite of worship ('did poojah' here means 'performed an obeisance').

the big temple by the river: St Paul's, as Findlayson tells Hitchcock a little later.

169 *guru*: priest, holy man.

tar: telegram.

Great Heavens!: the flood in the story comes more suddenly and dramatically than in the case of the Sutlej Bridge (see headnote); Kipling describes the engineers waiting anxiously for the expected rise in the river which would test their work, but the ordeal does not come before it is due.

Ramgunga: a tributary of the Ganges.

the Ganges Canal: between Delhi and Cawnpore.

170 *conchs*: horns made out of big sea shells.

calling to 'Stables': a cavalry call, sounding the regiment to retire to barracks; M'Cartney is presumably an ex-cavalryman. *RG* suggests it was the only call he knew, otherwise he would have sounded the 'Alarm', but since he blows (however atrociously) on 'Sundays and festivals' we can assume it was his trade, and that he blew 'Stables' because it was as alarming as anything else in his repertoire.

173 *raffle*: debris, both human and material.

his helmet became pulp: because it is made of pith.

174 *when the Sumao Bridge went out in the big cyclone by the sea*: the name is fictional, and no precise original for this event has been identified.

175 *sheers*: (or shears), sheer-legs, a hoisting apparatus.

Malwa: a region of central India.

176 *pegged, and stitched craft*: a boat whose planks were fastened by wooden pegs and stitches of coconut fibre.

177 *indigo crop*: the indigo plant (*Indigofera tinctoris*) cultivated for its blue dye.

178 *peepul*: an Indian species of fig-tree (*Ficus religiosa*), regarded as sacred.

Brahminee Bull . . . the trident mark of Shiva: the bull is both real and, as the capital letter indicates, a personification of the god Shiva (or Siva), 'the Destroyer', one of the greatest gods in the Hindu pantheon; all the creatures who take shelter on the island have this double identity, constituting what Peroo later calls a 'Punchayet' or council of the gods, assembled to hear the complaint of Mother Gunga against the building of the bridge. The Parrot is Karma (or Kama), the god of love (akin to the Greek Eros), the companion of Krishna. The Buck is Indra, who in early Hinduism was the chief of the gods. The Tigress is Kali, the consort of Shiva, whose shrine is occupied by Purun Bhagat in 'The Miracle of Purun Bhagat' (*The Second Jungle Book*, 1895). The Grey Ape is Hanuman, whose monkey-armies helped Rama in his war against Ravana (the story told in one of the great Hindu epics, the *Ramayana*). The Elephant is Ganesh (he has an elephant's head on a man's body), one of the most popular divinities, loved for his good sense and good nature, the patron deity of both literature and commerce. The Ass is Sitala, the goddess of smallpox. The Crocodile is Mother Gunga, the goddess of the river itself. The 'drunken man flourishing staff and drinking bottle', Bhairon, is a local village god who came to be associated with Shiva. The last to appear, Krishna, is the best-loved of all the gods in popular Hinduism: he represents youth and pleasure, especially sexual love and fertility. One other divinity, Brahm, is alluded to at the climax of the story: see note on p. 581. Kipling's versions of these deities are generally conventional, though he adds some idiosyncratic touches: Bhairon's claim to be a god of the masses, for example, or Hanuman's claim to be the god whom men like Findlayson unknowingly worship.

179 *the blunt-nosed, ford-haunting Mugger*: a man-eating (and male) 'Mugger' is the anti-hero of 'The Undertakers' (*The Second Jungle Book*, 1895), which opens after the completion of a bridge has taken away the crocodile's regular food-supply. Although the Mugger in that story is worshipped as a local deity by the villagers on whom he has preyed, he is not, as here, an incarnation of the river itself.

Punchayet: from Hindu *panch*, 'five', 'a council (properly of 5 persons) assembled as a Court of Arbiters or Jury; or as the committee of the people of a village, or the members of a caste, or what-not, to decide on questions interesting the body generally' (*Hobson-Jobson*).

Kashi is without her Kotwal: 'the bridge is without its caretaker': 'kotwal' means magistrate or guardian (*RG*). The 'drunken Man' refers to himself (he says further on that the 'Kotwal of Kashi' is his staff).

nose-slitten: done in order to soften the donkey's bray; in *Beast and Man in India*, John Lockwood Kipling mentions this practice as 'almost universal in India' and adds that it is ineffective.

180 *Sitala herself; Mata—the small-pox*: also identified with Kali (see note above).

their fire-carriage: the steam locomotive.

I also builded no small bridge in the world's youth: in the *Ramayana*, Hanuman builds a bridge between India and Ceylon ('Lanka' below, as in the modern name of the country, Sri Lanka) for his monkey-armies to cross to the aid of Rama.

they believe that their toil endures: cf. the poem 'Cities and Thrones and Powers' (p. 492).

181 *Pryag*: or Prayag, the ancient Hindu name for Allahabad, given by the Mogul Emperor Akbar in the 16th century.

182 *Greater am I than Gunga also*: alluding perhaps to the legend of the descent of the Ganges from heaven, when Shiva broke the weight of its fall and divided it into seven streams (*Larousse Encyclopedia of Mythology*).

Pooree: or Puri, a town in Orissa, on the north-eastern coast of India. It is the site of a famous shrine, that of Jagannatha, a name of Krishna which means 'Lord of the Universe'. The word 'Juggernaut' derives from Jagannatha, and its associations stem from the belief that frenzied worshippers at the festival of Ratha-yatra would immolate themselves under the wheels of the car on which the idol of the god was dragged in procession. *Hobson-Jobson* suggests that this 'popular impression . . . was greatly exaggerated' and points instead to the 'really great mortality from hardship, exhaustion, and epidemic disease which frequently ravaged the crowds of pilgrims on such occasions'.

the North, where they worship one God and His Prophet: i.e. the Muslim religion (Allah and the prophet, Mohammed).

the new faith: Christianity.

183 *new worshippers from beyond the Black Water*: the English; Findlayson is one of those who 'believe that their God is toil'.

The Ape scratched in the mud with a long forefinger: echoing the action of Jesus when he refuses to condemn the woman taken in adultery: 'Jesus stooped down, and with his finger wrote on the ground, as though he heard them not. So when they continued asking him, he lifted up himself, and said unto them, He that is without sin among you, let him first cast a stone at her. And again he stooped down, and wrote on the ground' (John 8: 6–8).

herd: herdsman.

the Gopis: milkmaids, the traditional companions of Krishna.

Fleeting: wiling away the time, like the 'young gentlemen' in the Forest of Arden, who 'fleet the time carelessly, as they did in the golden world' (*As You Like It*, I. i. 107).

the Mother of Sorrows: one of the titles of Kali.

184 *lotahs*: water-pots.

185 *Jester of the Gods*: alluding to the innumerable stories of Krishna's playfulness and mischief.

little Gods again—Gods of the jungle: cf. the episode in 'Letting in the Jungle' (*Second Jungle Book*, 1895), in which the people of the village which Mowgli is destroying call on a Gond hunter, one of the aboriginal tribesmen of India, to advise them, believing that they have offended one of his gods.

187 *Ye know the Riddle of the Gods. When Brahm ceases to dream the Heavens and the Hells and Earth disappear*: Brahm, or Brahman, is a neutral term for 'the eternal soul which penetrates the whole universe and is its cause' (*Larousse Encyclopedia of Mythology*). The masculine god Brahma is one of the manifestations of Brahm, as creator, who, along with Shiva and Vishnu, forms the 'Trimurti' or Hindu triad of supreme gods. The reference to Brahm's 'dream' suggests that Brahman, not Brahma, is meant, even though the god is denominated as 'he'. The whole cosmos, both material and spiritual, is an illusion, produced and sustained by an act of unconscious imagination; but as long as Brahm continues to dream, his timeless suspension of reality is equivalent to reality itself. What Peroo realizes at the end of the story is that this pattern is replicated in each human life: to live is to figure in Brahm's dream, but death means that

(as far as you are concerned) Brahm has woken up. The gods have no purchase on death, but only on life.

188 *tufan*: typhoon.

189 *the Rao of Baraon*: a 'Rao' is a Rajah (here, of a small native state); 'Baraon' is a fictitious name.

bear-led: from 'bear-leader', the burlesque name formerly given to tutors who conducted young noblemen on the Grand Tour (from the practice of leading bears by a ring through their noses).

seven koss: about 14 miles, though the unit of measurement could vary in different parts of India (*RG*).

190 *in the arms of Morphus*: Morpheus, the god of sleep, a tag from the classical education which the Rao has received from his English tutor—even one with 'sporting tastes'.

The Devil and the Deep Sea

First pub. in the Christmas number of the *Graphic*, 1895; coll. *The Day's Work*, 1898.

Roland Barthes's description of the plates in the *Encyclopédie*, that masterwork of the rational Enlightenment, with their dreamlike, 'exploded' diagrams of parts and functions, the products of the text's 'unconscious', recalls not just this wonderful story but the critical exegesis which has followed it. Yet the attempt to pin down by drawing and exposition what happened to the engine of the *Haliotis* when the shell struck it must be undertaken, delirium-inducing though it is. It is part of the pleasure of the story, though readers are strongly advised to read through, at least once, without notes—especially readers who know nothing about marine engineering.

After stating that the shell burst and fractured 'both the bolts that held the connecting-rod to the forward crank', Kipling remarks: 'What follows is worth consideration.' Indeed it is, and it has got it—from innumerable experts and enthusiasts. I am indebted even more than usually to *RG* for details of the ship's construction and layout. For the nature of the damage to the engine, I rely on Charles Moorhouse's article, 'Mr Wardrop's Problem' (*Kipling Journal*, 61 (Mar. 1987), 10–21). I am grateful to the Editor of the *Kipling Journal*, and to the Kipling Society, for permission to reproduce Professor Moorhouse's diagrams of the engine.

The engine of the *Haliotis* is a compound reciprocating steam engine ('compound' because the steam expands in stages, producing more work from the heat input). Professor Moorhouse opens his account with a general description of the engine-type:

> The engine described in this story was probably an arrangement of two cylinders, with cranks set at right-angles, so that one of them would be in a maximum torque (turning effort) position when the other was in a zero torque position. By means of

valves—operated by "eccentrics" from the main revolving shaft—steam is admitted, first to one side and then to the other side of the piston in each cylinder, pushing it up and then pushing it down. This backward-and-forward ('reciprocating') motion is transformed by piston-rod and connecting-rod and crank, into a rotary motion (which turns the propeller shaft).

The undamaged engine looks like this:

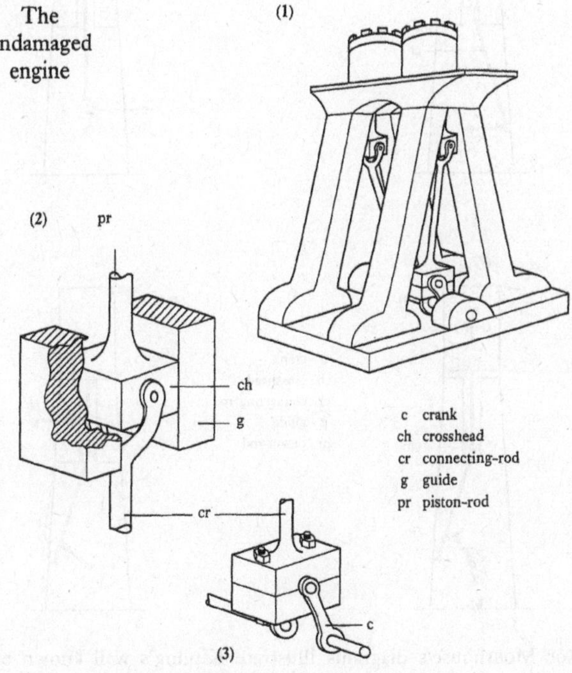

Professor Moorhouse's sketches above illustrate: – (1)The outline configuration of a two-cylinder marine engine such as the *Haliotis* in 'The Devil and the Deep Sea' might be supposed to have, clearly showing how the up-and-down motion of the connecting rods was transformed into a rotary motion capable of turning a propeller-shaft. (2)The top of a connecting-rod and the linkage with its piston-rod. (3)The foot of the connecting-rod, and linkage with the crank: the position of the two vertical retaining bolts in this assembly can be seen: these were broken by the shell—whence all else followed.

The second diagram illustrates the damage done to the engine:

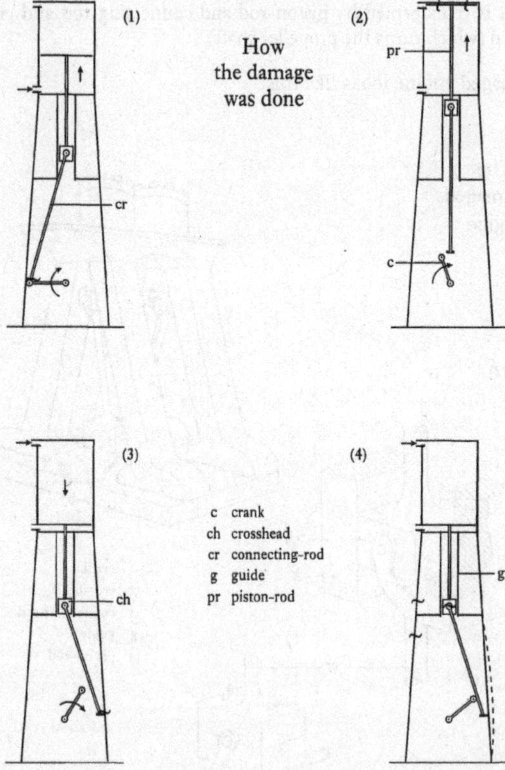

Professor Moorhouse's diagrams illustrate Kipling's well known but little understood account of what happened when the shell fragmented on impact with the forward cylinder, 'fracturing both the bolts that held the connecting-rod to the forward crank'. Marks like a letter 'S' indicate damage. (1) The impact was on the link between the connecting-rod and the crank. (2) The piston-rod, now unrestrained, jarred the cylinder cover. (3) The disconnected connecting-rod, coming down again, cracked the right-hand supporting-column. (4) The crank, continuing to revolve because of the other cylinder, 'smote the already jammed connecting-rod'. Hence three results: – the crosshead jammed in the guides; the additional pressure pushed outward part of the case of the right-hand supporting-column; higher up, the left-hand supporting column was also cracked.

So much for the damage done by the shell. Next comes the process of repair. *RG*'s expert, F. E. Langer, OBE, MRINA, M.I.Mar.E., Principal Technical Adviser to the Royal Fleet Auxiliary Service of the Royal Navy, states flatly: 'The repairs would be technically impossible with the primitive facilities available.' I take his word; the question of whether it makes a difference to the story must be left to each reader's judgement. In my view, Kipling's account is an exercise in hyperbole, the rhetorical equivalent of its subject: the feat performed by the crew of the *Haliotis* transcends matter-of-factness and makes new the old boast about the impossible taking a little longer.

The working of the steam-engine is compared to that of Calvinist predestination in 'McAndrew's Hymn' (p. 460), but the point about the engine in this story is precisely its vulnerability and human capacity for damage. 'The Day's Work' has two stories in which machines themselves are the protagonists, 'The Ship that found Herself' and '.007', both of them uncomfortably slanted and didactic ('.007', besides tormenting Kipling's indexers, is also the unforgivable ancestor of Thomas the Tank-Engine). The engine in 'The Devil and the Deep Sea' is not fully anthropomorphic, but a focus of human states of mind and feeling. This focus is not simple. The story enacts an ironic reversal: as the engine is patched up, the crew become mad; indeed, the frenzied repairing of the engine is an allegory of mental breakdown, and both crew and engine emerge not healed but crazed. Like the crew of the *Pequod* in *Moby-Dick* (it is no coincidence that the *Haliotis* disguises itself as a whaler), they are led by a monomaniac captain to a self-destructive end: they sacrifice the ship itself, the child of their excruciating labour, to a demented idol of revenge. I am uneasy at the engineer, Mr Wardrop, agreeing to this immolation: it isn't like him. His love for his work is human and sane: he is a victim neither of the devil nor the deep sea.

No account of this story that I have read does it full justice. Most critics, even the admirable Joyce Tompkins, have been preoccupied with explaining, or explaining away, its 'riot of bedevilled machinery' (*The Art of Rudyard Kipling*, 125), and have not paid sufficient attention to its geopolitical reach, its sketch (done with swift, sure strokes) of the modern conditions of economic and diplomatic power, exercised by newspaper and telegram as much as by gunfire. (The two preoccupations are brought together in the image of the 'machinery' which lies 'deep in the hull of the ship of State' [p. 198].) Moreover the story pits one kind of collective—the crew of the *Haliotis*, private, piratical, welded into a single entity—against another, the state—whether the British Empire which almost casually (yet not quite casually) rescues them from the jungle, or the rival colonial power which put them there. Inconspicuous, name- and shape-changing, lawless, elusive, the *Haliotis* represents, until her 'arrest', a refuge from the networks and circuits of the modern age. Her final act of revenge (Bacon's 'wild justice') depends for its effectiveness on the appearance, at a given time and place, of a regular patrol.

190 *Epigraph*: the *Sailing Directions*, also known as 'Pilots', are issued by the Admiralty along with navigation charts, and give information about facilities in ports and harbours. The port to which these particular 'Directions' apply is fictional.

schooner-rigged: although the ship is steam-powered, it also carries sail in case of engine failure. Improvised sails are used later in the story (p. 209).

the mariner cannot act or tell a lie . . . in either hand: this maxim is the subject of the poem 'Poseidon's Law', which prefaces 'The Bonds of Discipline' (p. 234).

190–1 *the great Mackinaw salvage case*: a fictional case, presumably one involving an insurance fraud.

191 *certain gentlemen who should have stayed in Noumea*: the capital of New Caledonia, a French dependency in the Pacific, where there was a penal colony until 1896.

engaging in the Odessa trade: Odessa, a port on the Black Sea, was a notorious centre of smuggling and other illicit activities.

combine: i.e. form trades unions (and go on strike).

signal-station: maintained in the principal foreign ports by the underwriters Lloyds of London to report the movements of ships for the *Lloyds List*, the daily register of merchant shipping activity (*RG*).

Haliotis: a genus of mollusc (abalone, ormer, etc.) which produces beautiful mother-of-pearl on the underside of the shell; as *RG* suggests, this may be an oblique allusion to the ship's pearl-fishing activities.

192 *trying-out*: extracting the oil from the whale's blubber by heating it in the 'furnace'.

London four-wheeler: a horse-drawn cab.

a semi-inland sea: later named as the (fictional) Amanala Sea; Kipling evidently has in mind the area of the South Pacific between Indonesia to the south, New Guinea to the east, and the Philippines to the north (the Java Sea, the Celebes Sea, and the Banda Sea are some of the local names); 'Pygang-Watai' is a Malay-sounding name, but the exact locations, and the identity of the foreign power on whose pearl-fishing grounds the *Haliotis* is poaching, do not really matter. It is a European colonial power, and is fighting insurgents in the hinterland of its territory.

puss-in-the-corner: four children stand in the corners of a room, and a fifth in the middle; as the four change places, the fifth tries to snatch one of the vacant corners, sending the loser to the middle to start again. A more elaborate version is a sailors' game in the Navy (*OED*).

a clean bottom: not encrusted by barnacles, weed etc. (as the *Haliotis* itself is later on), and so capable of its maximum speed.

an arrangement of four flags: signal flags, operated according to an internationally recognized code.

a practice, not a bursting, charge: a shell intended for practice firing would contain salt or sand instead of explosive, which explains the fact that it damages the ship without sinking it or causing any casualties.

the forward engine: the usual term would be 'forward cylinder', since Kipling is referring to a component, not a separate machine.

193 *brought up, all standing*: 'came to an abrupt and complete stop'; originally it applied to sailing ships whose masts were still 'standing' after a sudden loss of way.

upper grating: the grated gallery round the upper part of the engine-room, from which the ladders to the machinery spaces descend.

twelve knots an hour: a solecism, *RG* insists; it should just be 'twelve knots', since 'knot' is itself a measure (one nautical mile per hour); but this is a losing battle against the vulgarism by which 'knot' simply means 'nautical mile', and which is recorded as 'pop.' in the *Concise Oxford Dictionary*.

the Tanna Bank, the Sea-Horse Bank: fictional names.

194 *strained her tubes*: her boiler-tubes; the boiler is probably an old-fashioned water-tank boiler, in which the fire passes through a series of tubes inside the boiler.

195 *the donkey*: the donkey (= auxiliary) engine.

196 *the shores*: the planks shoring up the engine.

the tunnel: between the engine-room and the stern, in which the propeller shaft lies.

bilge- and feed-pumps: pumps to clear the bilges (lower spaces of the hull) of water, and to supply water to the boilers.

carefully tallowed: greased to prevent them rusting.

thrust-block: situated at the after-part of the engine, where the propeller shaft begins, this takes the thrust of the propeller as it drives the ship forward.

197 *a heavily weighted jib stayed out into the shape of a pocket*: this is what was trailing from the 'inconspicuous little rope hanging from the stern': dragging a sail through the water would act as a brake and further slow the speed at which the *Haliotis* could be towed.

197–8 *the performance of a notorious race-horse*: no specific allusion is intended; as an example of a famous racehorse of the period, take the Duke of Westminster's 'Ormonde', who was undefeated in 16 races, won the Derby, the St Leger, and the 2,000 Guineas in 1886, and was the subject of a doping scandal in 1892.

199 *cuddy*: a small cabin used for meals.

201 *that black-and-tan regiment*: 'black-and-tan' was slang for a mixture of stout and ale, so the allusion here is to the racial mix; the story was written long before the name was applied to the force recruited to fight Sinn Fein in 1921.

202 *Kismet*: Fate.

203 *the rod itself fell away slowly*: it must have become detached from the piston-rod or crosshead, but we are not told how.

crank-pit: the space below the crankshaft.

the Malay from the boat-house: he has looted the ship's machinery, as the Governor has taken her creature comforts; the winch is one of the few fixtures left, presumably because it was too awkward to remove, though it could hardly be more so than the 'cargo-derricks' for which Mr Wardrop pines, and which were hauled clumsily along the deck (p. 201).

lapping: lagging, to prevent leaks.

Then came the tug of war: a tag from Nathaniel Lee's play *The Rival Queens* (1677): 'When Greeks joined Greeks, then was the tug of war!'

junk-ring studs: the junk-ring is situated at the top of the piston and keeps the piston ring in place. Removing two of the studs which secure it allows screw-holes to be made for the bolts which will be used to get purchase on the jammed piston itself.

204 *bow-anchor davits*: cranes for hoisting the anchor overboard.

205 *the iron that had entered into their souls*: from Ps. 105: 17 (Prayer Book version), referring to Joseph, 'who was sold to be a bond-servant . . . the iron entered into his soul'. The Authorized Version has the more literal 'he was laid in iron'.

Latin prose: translating from English into Latin.

207 *started*: strained (like the tubes of the pursuing gunboat, p. 194).

sixty pound: 60 pounds pressure per square inch; the performance range of a compound engine was 60–100.

208 *the propeller needed re-keying*: the key is a wedge which enables the propeller to grip the shaft.

proa: a boat about 30 feet in length, using oars or sail, with both bow and stern sharp (hence 'hawk-like'); one side is curved and the other straight, a small canoe acting as an outrigger. The design is common in the Malay Archipelago and was used by both traders and pirates.

tripang: more usually 'trepang', a small marine animal (known as the sea-cucumber or sea-slug), a delicacy in Chinese cuisine.

209 *bright-eyed crew*: the crew, collectively, have taken on the identity of the

Ancient Mariner, who is described as 'bright-eyed' in l.20 of Coleridge's poem.

My Sunday at Home

First pub. *The Idler*, Apr. 1895; coll. *The Day's Work*, 1898.

The story was advertised in advance as 'The Child of Calamity', a phrase from Mark Twain (see note on p. 566) which draws attention to its American theme. Kipling had settled in the heart of New England, and some of the vocabulary of the story satirizes New England Transcendentalism, whose leading figure, Ralph Waldo Emerson (1803–82), supplies the epigraph for the story. When the narrator opines that 'so long as a man trusts himself to the current of Circumstance, reaching out for and rejecting nothing that comes his way, no harm can overtake him' (p. 216), he sounds very like Emerson, or Henry David Thoreau. Yet this was a tradition he also admired and followed; the epigraph reminds us that the Transcendentalist love of oriental literature and mysticism connects with the Kipling of 'The Miracle of Purun Bhagat', *Kim*, and 'The Bridge-Builders' (see the note on 'Brahm's dream', p. 581). So the revised title properly focuses on the figure of the narrator and his ambivalent attitude to 'home'. After all, Kipling was still living in America in 1895 and the two events which triggered his departure—his quarrel with his brother-in-law, Beatty Balestier, and the 'Venezualan crisis' of 1895–6, when it looked as though England and America might go to war—had not yet occurred. 'My Sunday at Home' belongs to the *trip* to England which the Kiplings made in 1894, staying at Tisbury in Wiltshire near Kipling's parents; the narrator is an Englishman, but he observes the workings of the language, the railway, and the class-system with a poised irony which belongs neither to the alien nor to the native.

In *The Day's Work* the story follows 'An Error in the Fourth Dimension', also based on Anglo-American misunderstanding and the workings of the English railway. But 'An Error in the Fourth Dimension' is crude by comparison with this story, whose narrator luxuriates in the pleasure of detachment, of artful spectating, as he does in the later story about an escaped swarm of bees, 'The Vortex' ('A Diversity of Creatures', 1917). Although there is farce of the most basic and physical kind (Kipling called it 'viler than "Brugglesmith"', and there can't be many comic tales which so depend on repeated vomiting), there is also a disturbing suspension in the narrative, which corresponds to the intense, dreamy stillness of the landscape and produces what I can only perversely call a kind of melancholia. The rural English scene is phantasmagoric, a theatre of misrule, in which codes and hierarchies are transgressed by mistake or inverted by accident, and in which identity is confused and misattributed. When the story begins the 'ordered English landscape [is] wrapped in its Sunday peace', but the complications produced by the doctor's entanglement with the navvy require violence to be done, from the mutilation of the doctor's coat to the 'Berserk' sacking of the lamp-room at the end. Kipling told Edward Lucas White that writing the story made him laugh for three days, and added: 'I wonder if people get a tithe of the fun out of my tales that I get in doing 'em' (*Letters*, ii. 147). But the 'fun' of this story for the reader lies perhaps in places where Kipling himself could not penetrate.

209 *Epigraph*: from 'Brahma', by Ralph Waldo Emerson (1803–82); see headnote.

210 *an engineer*: engine-driver.

The Hoe: on the seafront at Plymouth; 'hoe' originally meant a promontory.

Framlynghame Admiral: a fictional place.

211 *Tess's country*: Hardy's novel *Tess of the D'Urbervilles* is set in several south-western counties, including Wiltshire, where the climactic scenes on Salisbury Plain and at Stonehenge take place.

snap-shutter: presumably the shutter of a camera, though the compound 'snap-shutter' is not recorded in *OED*.

I put a bottle of medicine off at Andover: with this the clue begins to unravel. When the guard mentions Woking further on the matter is clear, but by then it is too late—for the doctor. He and the narrator wrongly assume that a passenger on the train has *taken poison* and that the guard has been instructed to ask if anyone had any *medicine* to help him. But what the message means is that someone at Woking had *taken away the wrong bottle of medicine by mistake.* In other words, there were two bottles of medicine, one being carried by a passenger who got off at Woking, and the other (containing the laudanum) being dispatched by rail to Andover. (The system of sending small packages by rail in the care of the guard was still commonplace in this period.) When the passenger got off at Woking he took the wrong one, and left his own bottle on the train—which the guard duly put off at Andover, a station forty miles further on. The train has been halted at Framlyngham Admiral because the railway authorities, telegraphing from Woking, do not know that the guard has put the second bottle of medicine off the train, and he has officiously carried out their instructions to ask every passenger whether they have the missing bottle. It is a weak point in the story that no explanation is given as to how the original mix-up could have occurred, but the upshot is that there are no bottles of medicine on the train and no one has been poisoned (yet). But by the time the narrator discovers this, the doctor has administered a powerful emetic to the drunken navvy.

214 *the blowing-up of Hell Gate*: Hell Gate is the passage between Great Barn Island and Long Island, New York; Flood Rock, its most dangerous reef, was blown up in 1876 to make the passage safer.

the geysers in Yellowstone Park: Yellowstone National Park, in the Rocky

Mountains (mainly Wyoming), was founded by Act of Congress in 1872, after exploration had revealed its natural wonders, including the geysers (hot springs which erupt intermittently); the most famous is Old Faithful, which erupts about every hour.

Jonah and his whale: the particular reference is to Jonah 2: 10: 'And the Lord spake unto the fish, and it vomited out Jonah upon the dry land.'

the 'scream of a maddened beach dragged down by the tide': Tennyson, *Maud*, I. iii, l. 99, misquoting 'tide' for 'wave'.

caryatid French: the sense seems to be a language which is sensuous and ornamental, but also powerful and capable of rendering the grotesque; Kipling alludes to the reputation for these qualities of the poet and novelist Victor Hugo (1828–73), the author of *Notre-Dame de Paris* and *Les Misérables*. Kipling knew and admired Hugo's work but had also parodied him in a number of pieces published in the late 1880s (see *RG*, ii. 1054). A caryatid is a supporting column in sculpture, carved in the shape of a bowed female figure. In 'Their Lawful Occasions', the second of the Pyecroft stories and the fourth in *Traffics and Discoveries* (1904), there is a Royal Navy vessel with the (imaginary) name of HMS *Caryatid*.

215 *you damned anarchist*: a topical insult for the date of first publication, 1895, a period in which anarchism had wide political currency and in which the press played up its threat to social order from political assassinations and outrages such as the Greenwich Observatory bomb (1894).

Guy's: Guy's Hospital in London.

body-snatcher: the most famous body-snatchers or 'resurrection-men', who sold corpses for dissection, were Burke and Hare, who murdered their victims rather than disinterring them; their activities came to an end in 1829 when Burke was hanged.

fif—: he is about to say 'fifteen dollars' (at five dollars to the pound, the then rate of exchange).

216 *Linnæus*: Swedish botanist and naturalist (1707–78), famous as a pioneer in the systematic classification of plant and animal species.

fly: a light covered carriage, generally applied to a vehicle hired from a livery-stable.

my machine from the machine: adapting 'deus ex machina', the god from the machine; a theatrical image, as *RG* points out, since it derives from the literal machine which enabled a god to descend to the stage in ancient Greek drama.

217 *He looked towards it, and opened his mouth—O-shape*: like Taffy and Tegumai in 'How the Alphabet was Made' (*Just So Stories*, 1902); then again, the doctor is a precursor of the poor Stranger-man (also the victim

of linguistic misunderstanding) in the preceding story, 'How the First Letter was Written'.

217 *cock-nosed*: with the blades turned up at the ends.

vandyking: cutting in deep, zig-zagged indentations; the term derives from the lace collars or neckerchiefs fashionable in the early 17th century, and frequently depicted in portraits by the Flemish painter Sir Anthony Van Dyck (1599–1641).

the box-turtle of his native heath: the North American Box Turtle can withdraw completely into its shell and close both openings; *OED* cites Emerson's *English Traits* (1856), a passage on the taciturnity of the English on certain subjects: 'The same men . . . shut down their valve, as soon as the conversation approaches the English church. After that, you talk with a box-turtle.' Given the Anglo-American context and the quotation from Emerson in the epigraph to the story, Kipling may have been remembering this occurrence of the term in a book he almost certainly knew.

218 *an upper chamber in which the Foresters held their courts*: alluding to the 'Ancient Order of Foresters', a friendly society incorporated in 1834, whose meetings are called 'courts'.

219 *a truck-load of lamps*: passenger carriages were lit by oil-lamps; they would be ranged in platform trucks, and the station staff would then climb to the roofs of the carriages and insert a lamp in the hole provided for the purpose in the ceiling of each compartment (*RG*). These ones are being prepared for the arrival of the 7.45 down train, because it coincides with dusk.

220 *I had taken no part in that war*: cutting the doctor free doesn't count as 'taking part', apparently.

master of his fate: the story which began with an American verse quotation ends with an allusion to an English poem, W. E. Henley's 'Invictus', which ends: 'I am the master of my fate, | I am the captain of my soul.' For Kipling's friendship with Henley, see p. 640.

The Cat that Walked by Himself

First pub. *Ladies' Home Journal*, July 1902; coll. *Just So Stories*, 1902.

The personal source of the *Just So Stories* is both suggested and concealed by the alterations which Kipling made to the title-page in the 'nursery copy' of the original edition. This reads: 'Just So Stories | for Little Children | by | Rudyard Kipling | Illustrated by the Author'. Kipling crossed out 'Little Children' and wrote the names of his two (surviving) children, 'Elsie and John'; he similarly replaced 'Rudyard Kipling' with 'Their Daddy', and 'the Author' with 'me'. Yet Elsie and John do not figure in these stories as they were later to do in *Puck of Pook's Hill* (1906) and *Rewards and Fairies* (1910), where they appear as Una and Dan. The 'Best Beloved' to whom the *Just So Stories* were originally addressed is Kipling's first-born child, Josephine, who had died in 1899. She is Taffy in 'How the First Letter was Written' and 'How the Alphabet was Made', and the unnamed little girl in 'The Crab that Played with the Sea'; the poem 'Merrow Down' p. 490) commemorates her as movingly as do the tender, near-unbearable lines in 'They' (p. 273). In a note to the first story, 'How the Whale Got His Throat', when it was published in the *St Nicholas Magazine* in 1897, Kipling explained the term 'Just So Stories': 'In the evening there were stories meant to put Effie [Josephine] to sleep, and you were not allowed to alter those by one single little word. They had to be told just so, or Effie would wake up and put back the missing sentence.'

Elsie remembered some of the later-written stories being told to her and John, before they were written down, during the winters they spent at the 'Woolsack', the Kiplings' house in Cape Town (memoir repr. in Carrington, 587). But though 'The Cat that Walked by Himself' was one of the last to be written, probably in January 1902, the story's roots lie in the landscape of New England and the years 1892–6, when Kipling married and began to 'keep house' with Carrie, and in which his first child was born. Elsie added: 'When written, [the stories] were read aloud to us for such suggestions as could be expected from small children. The illustrating of the stories gave their author immense pleasure, and he worked at them (mostly in Indian ink) with meticulous care and was delighted when we approved of the result.' The *Just So Stories* were the only ones solely illustrated by Kipling. For the cryptic content of some of the drawings, see the note to the initial letter 'H' below.

Charles Carrington suggests that the cat was 'perhaps inspired by the gift of a handsome Persian which Carrie had just received' (p. 383), but he is essence of cat, really; he makes most other literary cats look half-realized, yet he is drawn in monochrome. Kipling's account of the making (or, more properly, engendering) of the family is similarly succinct and intense. The flatness and repetitive rhythms which denote a childlike mode of storytelling are primitive without being in the least simple-minded. The cat may be allegorized as many things (the artist's imagination, the Freudian 'id', male sexuality) but the story remains a fable, not an allegory; like all Kipling's best stories, it is meaningful because no single meaning can be extracted from it.

221 *Hear and attend*: the initial 'H' is depicted on a drawing of 'the bone of the shoulder of mutton—the big flat blade-bone' which the Woman uses to make her magic. The 'runes' on the two vertical strokes of the 'H' translate as follows: 'I, Rudyard Kipling, drew this but because there was no mutton bone in the house I faked the anatomy from memory. R.K.' The runes on the cross-piece read: 'I also wrote all of the plays ascribed by Mrs. Gallup.' She was the author of *The Bilateral Cipher of Francis Bacon*, 1900, which claimed that Shakespeare's plays contained a cryptogram revealing that they were really written by Francis Bacon. The point

of Kipling's joke is sharpened by the fact that Mrs Gallup was discredited when it was found that her cipher made Bacon refer to Homer in Pope's (1715) translation (*RG*).

223 *Wild Horse tripping and stumbling on his long mane*: in ch. 4 of *Something of Myself*, Kipling remembers a journey in New Zealand in 1891, 'on great plains where wild horses stared at us, and caught their feet in long blown manes as they stamped and snorted.'

'Pussy can Sit by the Fire and Sing'

Repr. *Definitive Edition* ('Just So Verses'). These include all the poems accompanying the *Just So Stories* except 'Merrow Down', which became a separate poem (see p. 672). In 1903 all the verses (incl. 'Merrow Down') were set to music by Sir Edward German (1862–1936) and published as *The Just So Song Book*.

In the poem, the sex of the cat is female, not male as in the story; I take the child who speaks the verses to be a boy. Kipling's mind is active even in this weak poem, evoking the solitary child who plays at being Robinson Crusoe, and who wants the cat (of all creatures) to share the moment in the story when relationship with another living creature is rediscovered—in the form of subservience. Such dumb loyalty is properly reserved for *Binkie*, who ingratiates himself even in typography.

The Bonds of Discipline

First pub. *Windsor Magazine*, Aug. 1903 (without the accompanying poem 'Poseidon's Law'); coll. *Traffics and Discoveries*, 1904.

'The Bonds of Discipline' is the story in which the narrator (Kipling) first meets Emanuel Pyecroft, though another of the Pyecroft stories, 'Steam Tactics', had already appeared in Dec. 1902. In *Traffics and Discoveries* 'The Bonds of Discipline' was followed by 'Their Lawful Occasions' (parts I and II), 'Steam Tactics', and 'Mrs Bathurst'. One story from this period, 'A Tour of Inspection', was not collected until the Sussex edition; it was placed in vol. vi, 'A Diversity of Creatures', a collection originally published in 1917, and which had included 'The Horse Marines', the last of the Pyecroft stories to be written. Kipling also wrote a one-act play featuring Pyecroft, 'The Harbour Watch', which was performed in 1913 but never published.

Pyecroft was Mulvaney's successor, as the Navy in its home waters succeeded the Indian Army in Kipling's knowledge and affection. In 1897 and 1898 he was the guest of Captain Edward Bayly in HMS *Pelorus*, and in 1898 he published *A Fleet in Being: Notes of Two Trips with the Channel Squadron*. The 'background' of the Pyecroft stories is best traced by reference to this work, in which Kipling describes with characteristic relish 'the new world into which I stepped from a Portsmouth wherry one wonderful summer evening in '97.' Unlike 'M. de C.' in 'The Bonds of Discipline', Kipling was not a stowaway, but an invited guest; but like him, as well as supplying a considerable amount of technical data, he 'breaks enclosure to study the morale, at the present day, of the British sailorman'. The following passage from ch. 1 of *A Fleet in Being* strikes one of the keynotes of the story:

Once forward of the deck torpedo-tubes you enter another and a fascinating world of seamen-gunners, artificers, cooks, Marines (we had twenty and a sergeant), ship's boys, signalmen, and the general democracy. Here the men smoke at the permitted times, and in clubs and coteries gossip and say what they please of each other and their superiors. . . . Their slang borrows from the engine-room, the working parts of guns, the drill-book, and the last music-hall song. It is delivered in a tight-lipped undertone; the more excruciatingly funny parts without a shade of expression. . . . They were men of the world, at once curiously simple and curiously wily (this makes the charm of the Naval man of all ranks), coming and going about their businesses like shadows.

There are similar passages about the 'morale' of the officers, from the junior ranks to captains and admirals, most of which are exemplified by one or another of the Pyecroft stories. But 'The Bonds of Discipline' is concerned mainly with the view from the lower deck. Later in ch. 1 of *A Fleet in Being*, Kipling reports snatches of conversation between a Marine and other members of the crew:

''Ullo! Wot's the matter with *your* condenser?' said the Marine. 'You'd better take your mucky 'ands off them hammick-cloths or you'll be spoke to.'

'Our bunkers,' said the figure, addressing his grievance to the sea-line, 'are stuck all about like a lot o' women's pockets. They're stuck about like a lot o' bunion-plasters. That's what our bunkers are.' He slipped back into the darkness. Presently a signalman pattered by to relieve his mate on the bridge.

'You'll be 'ung,' said the Marine, who was a wit, and by the same token something of a prophet.

'Not if you're anywhere in the crowd I won't,' was the retort, always in a cautious, 'don't-wake-him' undertone. 'Wot are you doin' 'ere?'

'Never you mind. You go on up to the 'igh an' lofty bridge an' persecute your vocation. My Gawd! I wouldn't be a signalman, not for ever so.'

When I met my friend next morning 'persecuting his vocation' as sentry over the lifebuoy aft neither he nor I recognised each other; but I owe him some very nice tales.

This Marine must be the original of Pyecroft's companion, Glass, though his speech (especially the malapropism) also suggests Pyecroft himself; it is possible that among the 'nice tales' was the one that Kipling embroidered into 'The Bonds of Discipline', which needless to say has no official historical event behind it. In a 'letter' to Pyecroft which prefaced the magazine publication of 'Their Lawful Occasions', Kipling remarks: 'You will see, as these stories come out, the care I have taken to disguise your name and rating, and everything else that might reflect upon you. Unless you give yourself away, which I have never known you to do yet, detection is quite impossible' (cited in *RG*, iv. 1758). He goes on to explain why 'The Bonds of Discipline' had not yet been published, despite the fact that it comes chronologically before 'Their Lawful Occasions': 'there has been a hitch about the Antonio tale . . . it being freely alleged that Antonio won't go down, because it is a bit too thick (this shows how much some people know)'. But the question of verisimilitude is complicated by the prefatory poem 'Poseidon's Law', in which Kipling suggests that sailors are such compulsive liars ashore because they dare not lie while they are at sea: the sea's extreme and absolute conditions will not tolerate fantasy. This seems to imply that Pyecroft, the sailor, spins an outrageously improbable yarn to the landsman Kipling (see headnote to 'The Coiner', p. 677). But Pyecroft's story is merely a commentary on a document, the pamphlet by 'M. de C.' which, Kipling emphasizes, 'contains nothing that did not happen'. This pamphlet is a fiction, of course, but it is not Pyecroft's fiction: the 'splendaciously mendacious' storyteller must be Kipling, whose art of lying, like Shakespeare's in 'The Coiner', is a match for any sailor's.

As to the tone of the story, in ch. 5 of *A Fleet in Being* Kipling commented: 'It is in the Navy that you hear the wildest and freest adjectives of any Service, the most blistering characterisation of superiors, the most genuinely comic versions of deeds that elsewhere might be judged heroic.' It must be so, he explained, because

> Things are all too deadly serious and important for any one to insult by taking seriously. Every branch of the Service is forced to be a humourist in spite of itself; and by the time men reach the rank of Captain the least adaptable have some saving sense of fun hammered into them. A Captain remembers fairly well what song the Midshipmen were used to sing about the Lieutenant; what views he held in his own Lieutenancy of his Commander, and what as a Commander he thought of his Captain. If he forgets these matters, as in heat, on lonely stations, or broken with fever some men do, then God help his ship when she comes home with a crop of Court-martials and all hands half-crazy!

The 'Bonds of Discipline', read in this light, is a 'deadly serious' comedy about the preservation of order and sanity by means of a controlled release of disorder and madness, an inoculation (triggered by the 'germ' of a foreigner contaminating the 'body' of the ship) intended to immunize against the actual disease. It is both funny and frightening because the line between artificial chaos and the real thing is so fine: the Captain knows this, and so does Pyecroft, and the story departs from its 'daylight' fidelity to the values which Kipling promotes in *A Fleet in Being* to explore (to indulge) a world of 'all hands half-crazy'.

The identity of 'M. de C.' as a French spy rather than a German or Russian is owing to a seldom-remembered period of diplomatic tension between Britain and France at the turn of the century, caused by friction in Africa both north (the 'Fashoda crisis' in the Sudan) and south (the French were thought to be pro-Boer). Hindsight makes it hard to realize how plausible it seemed in 1900 that France should be Britain's enemy in the next European war; indeed that idea had the virtue of familiarity. The tension between the two countries eased with the *entente cordiale* of 1904; its signing in April may account for Pyecroft's rather awkward insistence that he is not anti-French (p. 243). Of course, the Germans were not neglected: in 1903 Erskine Childers published *The Riddle of the Sands*, in which two British yachtsmen sailing in the Baltic discover a German invasion plot (see also the note on 'zealous amateurs', p. 598).

Kipling's focus on the Navy was also timely. Keith Robbins summarizes recent developments: 'Rapid technological change approximately coincided with the end of unchallenged naval supremacy. By the middle 1880s, the French possessed nearly the same number of first-class battleships as the British. . . . Even Gladstone was forced to make a substantial increase in the estimates both for shipbuilding and ordinance. Continuing friction with France seemed to admit of no relaxation in this programme. When Russia, too, emerged as a naval power, British strategists feared Franco-Russian naval co-operation and the grave threat which it would pose to the British position in the Mediterranean. . . . In 1893–94 the rapid development of cordite-firing guns led to a fresh programme of building, causing considerable problems for the Liberal conscience. The subject became one of abiding press and public interest' (*The Eclipse of a Great Power: Modern Britain 1870–1992* (2nd edn., 1994), 38).

Kipling was to deal with the wartime Navy in soberer fashion, but with equal eloquence, in 'Sea Constables' (p. 351).

Poseidon's Law

234 *Title.* Poseidon was the Greek name for Neptune, the god of the sea, brother of Zeus (Jupiter), the king of the gods. The 'law' is Kipling's invention.

l. 1. *brass-bound*: a 'brass-bounder' is a midshipman in the Navy, or a premium apprentice on board a merchant ship, but the phrase also recalls the 'brass-faced' impudence with which sailors lie.

l. 9. *Greekly speech*: cunning speech, equivocation (for which the Greeks, especially that resourceful sailor Odysseus, were famous).

l. 10. *Hadria*: or Adria, the Italian town from which the Adriatic Sea takes its name.

l. 11. *tempt with painted cloth for wood*: the height of the ship's bulwarks might be raised by canvas screens, which would act as windbreaks but would not be any protection against really rough weather (the 'fraud-avenging hosts' are the waves of a stormy sea).

l. 13. *serve unshod*: seamen traditionally worked bare-footed (for better grip on wooden decks and on the rigging of sailing-ships).

l. 17. *dromond*: large medieval ship for war or commerce, using both oars and sail. *catafract*: or 'cataphract', glossed below as a 'bireme', a

Greek vessel with two banks of oars and bulwarks to protect the upper tier of rowers from attack (*RG*).

234 l. 21. *The thranite . . . low and high*: the thranite is a rower in the upper tier of a trireme, a three-banked vessel; the thalamite rows in the lower tier. In a fanciful image of technological change, the tiers of oars are replaced by the high and low pressure cylinders of a compound steam engine, such as the one minutely described in 'The Devil and the Deep Sea' (see notes and diagrams on pp. 582–4). But, Kipling goes on, modern sailors are as mischievously inventive as their ancient fellows.

l. 25. *Punt . . . Phormio's Fleet . . . Javan and Gadire*: names whose ancient naval associations (especially in the case of the first) overlay contemporary ones. Punt or Puoni was the object of an expedition in search of incense-trees by the Egyptian queen Hatshepshut (*c.*1540–*c.*1481 BC), commemorated in the great temple she built at Deir al Bahri, but in its modern guise of Somaliland was the scene of British (and Italian) expeditionary assaults on the 'Mad Mullah', Muhammad Abdille Sayyid Hasan, who had declared a *jihad* against all colonial powers in 1899. Phormion (*sic*) was an Athenian admiral famous for his exploits against the Spartans and their allies in the Peloponnesian War (5th century BC). Javan is an ancient Hebrew name for the Aegean (Isa. 66: 19). Gadire is the Phoenecian name for the Roman Gades, which became Cadiz in Spain.

l. 27. *Falernian . . . smoked Massilian juice*: wines of ancient Rome (Falernian from Campania in Italy, Massilian from Marseille in France); 'smoked' refers to the practice of subjecting the wine to heat treatment in a *fumarium* in order to stop fermentation.

The Bonds of Discipline

235 *it is beneath contempt*: 'it' refers to the class of foreign publications about the Navy, of which 'M. de C.''s work is one example.

endurance: the ship's 'steaming radius', i.e. the limit which its fuel supply would enable it to reach.

the zealous amateur: but later on we learn that 'M. de C.' is spying for the French Navy, in which he is a lieutenant; it seems odd that he should be called an 'amateur' and be publishing a flamboyantly literary account of his experiences. Kipling's scorn of the 'zealous amateur' may glance at the popularity of Erskine Childers's *The Riddle of the Sands* (1903; see headnote).

bound in lead boards: an official naval intelligence report might be lead-weighted to ensure that it would sink if it had to be thrown overboard in an emergency (*RG*).

M. de C.: i.e. 'Monsieur de C.'

one of our well-known Acolyte type of cruisers: a fictitious name, as are all the subsequent ones; it opens a series of religious/ecclesiastical associations in the names of ships in the story (see note to 'Archimandrite' below). The first-built ship of a class or type usually gave its name to that class: HMS *Pelorus*, the cruiser in which Kipling sailed with the Channel Squadron in 1897 and 1898 (see headnote) was the first, and name ship, of a class of 11 small (3rd class) cruisers.

the average Dumas novel: probably an allusion to the elder Alexandre Dumas (1802–70), the author of *The Three Musketeers* and *The Count of Monte Cristo*, rather than his son (1824–95), best known for *The Lady of the Camelias*.

my first notion was that I had been cheated: the narrator believes that the pamphlet must be fiction, though it has been sold to him as eye-witness reportage. Kipling may be recalling the opening line of Browning's poem 'Childe Roland to the Dark Tower Came': 'My first thought was, he lied in every word'.

Archimandrite: in ch. 5 of *A Fleet in Being*, Kipling describes listening to 'weird yarns in which Chinese Mandarins, West Coast nigger Chiefs, Archimandrites, Turkish Pashas, Calabrian Counts, dignity balls, Chilian beachcombers, and all the queer people of the earth were mingled'. An archimandrite is the superior of a monastery in the Orthodox Church. The significance of the name may lie in its allusion to a closed, all-male community: monks, like sailors, are subject to the 'bonds of discipline', and the sailors in the story exhibit both religious devotion to duty and a saturnalian impulse towards blasphemy. The ship's other name—the *Bedlamite* - is that of another closed community, the madhouse. The name of the ship into which Pyecroft transfers, the *Postulant*, also has monastic connotations: a postulant is a candidate for admission to a religious order. Later still, in 'Mrs Bathurst' (p. 278), Pyecroft's ship is the 'Hierophant' (a priest who initiates others into the sacred mysteries).

Funchal: the principal port on the island of Madeira.

236 *cutter*: a rowing boat used for carrying messages, passengers etc. between ships or between ship and shore. M. de C., or Antonio, stows away in the *Archimandrite*'s cutter and is later called a 'cutter-cuddler'. The *Archimandrite* also has a 'steam-cutter', a larger boat whose engine is later disassembled on deck.

wardroom: i.e. all the ship's officers, equivalent to an army 'mess'.

A Red Marine: soldiers in the Royal Marine Light Infantry wore red uniforms, those in the Royal Marine Artillery wore blue.

237 *Number One*: the first mate.

santy: a health (Fr. *santé*).

empress: translating (in burlesque) the Fr. phrase 'avec empressement', which means literally 'with alacrity' (in order to attract attention).

238 *old man*: the captain.

'Op: the Yeoman of Signals, a petty officer. His name is never given in full: it is presumably something like 'Hopkins'.

our owner: like 'old man', a name for the captain.

Ascension: an island in the mid-Atlantic, near the Equator.

matlow: sailor (Fr. 'matelot').

239 *ong eshlong*: in echelon or staggered formation (Fr. 'en échelon'), meaning indirectly.

four point seven: a gun firing a 4.7 inch calibre shell.

buntin'-tosser: the 'bunting' refers to the flags used in naval signalling.

Boots in the galley: boots were forbidden in the galley (*RG*).

lyin' to: in the naval sense: 'hove to', i.e. 'waiting'.

melly: i.e. melée, another of Pyecroft's burlesque pronunciations of French words, though this one is naturalized in English.

Mong Jew: 'Mon Dieu', 'My God'.

240 *the Gunner . . .'is piebald warrant-rank*: there is nothing dubious about warrant-officers' rank in the regulations, so the imputation here is hard to understand.

the doodeladays: *RG* ingeniously glosses 'du', 'de la', 'des' (from a dimly remembered French grammar lesson).

trained man in a stinkin' gunboat up the Saigon River: in what was then French Indo-China (now Vietnam). The gunboat may have been sent to protect British subjects during the revolt against French rule in 1885, some twenty years before the date of the story, when 'Op would have been a 'trained man', or Able Seaman.

Nay, nay, Pauline: a catchphrase from Edward Bulwer-Lytton's play *The Lady of Lyons* (1838).

240–1 *you an' me'll part brass-rags*: quarrel; 'from the bluejacket's habit of sharing brass cleaning rags with his particular friend' (Partridge, *Dictionary of Historical Slang*).

241 *R.M.L.I.*: Royal Marine Light Infantry.

exshtreme angle plungin' fire: i.e. his nose up in the air; 'plunging fire' is artillery or rifle fire directed downwards from a higher level, and 'Op's nostrils are the gun barrels.

Vigo: a port on the Atlantic coast of north-west Spain.

Dick Deadeye: a one-eyed seaman in Gilbert and Sullivan's *H.M.S. Pinafore* (1878).

to the moral: 'to the life' ('moral' was slang for 'likeness').

a leather-neck: a sailor's derogatory name for a soldier, from the leather stock soldiers used to wear.

242 *mess-men*: the ordinary seamen acting as waiters.

Bo'sun: the boatswain, the warrant officer originally responsible for the sails and rigging; in the age of steam his duties became those of general maintenance.

squee-jee band: an improvised amateur band (jocularly alluding to the noise made by the squeegee, a rubber deck-scraper).

stop our way: a ship's 'way' is its forward momentum, so the sense is 'bring us (the crew) under control again'.

broke the boom: i.e. started the operation abruptly and without further ado.

the grist: this should be 'gist', but Pyecroft is mangling the captain's English; it is uncertain whether the pun is a consequence of his self-consciousness or Kipling's.

liquorice an' ink: rhyming slang—'drink'.

243 *'olystones*: holystones, a soft sandstone used to scour the decks.

a three-way-discharge devil: 'up to any kind of mischief'; a three-way discharge pipe coupled to the ship's fire-main enabled three hoses to be used (*RG*).

put us on the viva voce: mangling 'put us on the *qui vive*', i.e. put us on the alert.

navigatin' abroad in his sword-belt: taking a risk (with his service reputation).

ong reggle: by the book (Fr. *en règle*).

slave-dhowin' in Tajurrah Bay: one of the Navy's tasks was the suppression of the slave-trade in North Africa; Tâjurâ is a Mediterranean port a few miles east of Tripoli.

244 *Brazee*: Brazilian.

slop rig: cheap, ready-made clothing from the ship's stores.

quick-firer: a quick-firing gun such as a Maxim.

thort-ships: 'thwart-ship', i.e. across the length of the ship (a ludicrously inconvenient position).

with the pip: 'in a bad mood'.

descendez: (Fr.) 'go below'.

ash-hoist: a hoist to remove the ashes (of burnt coal) from the vessel's stokehold.

like "Listen to the Band in the Park": a song from the musical comedy *A*

Runaway Girl, by Seymour Hicks and Harry Nicholls, with music by Ivan Carryll and Lionel Monckton, produced at the Gaiety Theatre, London, 2 May 1898.

244 *a sanaka-towzer of a smite*: 'a hell of a blow'; an echoic nonce-word, according to Partridge, who gives the form as 'sanakatowmer' (*Dictionary of Historical Slang*).

Gosport 'ighlander: a Marine (from the barracks at Gosport, across the harbour from Portsmouth).

245 *morgue*: haughty impassivity (a trait of national character supposedly attributed to the British by the French).

waterjacket: a casing filled with water which surrounds the barrel of a gun (e.g. the Maxim, mentioned further on) to provide cooling.

a little poor authority: echoing *Measure for Measure*, II. ii. 117–22: 'man, proud, | Dress'd in a little brief authority . . . Plays such fantastic tricks before high heaven | As makes the angels weep.' The play is also about the 'bonds of discipline'.

spit-kid: shallow wooden tub (spittoon for tobacco-juice, cigarette ends, etc.); cf. the character 'Spit-Kid Jones' in 'Mrs Bathurst' (p. 279).

cheero-party: an organized picnic-party (jocular here for a working-party).

Chips: the carpenter.

tiffies: from 'artificer', naval slang for an engine-room machinist.

Pusser: the Purser, the warrant officer in charge of stores and provisions.

246 *Maxim*: an early type of machine-gun, named after its inventor, Sir Hiram S. Maxim (1840–1916); it had been adopted by the navy in 1892. Maxim, an American who was naturalized in 1900 and knighted the following year, is a model for the character of Laughton O. Zigler, the American military inventor who appears in 'The Captive', the first story in *Traffics and Discoveries*, and again in 'The Edge of the Evening' (*A Diversity of Creatures*).

non plus ultra: a French form of the Latin tag 'ne plus ultra' ('not more beyond'), here used in the sense of 'impossible to improve on'; the legendary origin of the phrase has a nautical flavour, though, since it was said to have been inscribed on the Pillars of Hercules at the mouth of the Mediterranean, meaning 'do not sail beyond this point' and marking the limit of civilized knowledge.

Fratton: a working-class district of Portsmouth; its pawnshops would be well known to sailors and dockers.

booms: a part of the deck reserved for stowage of spare parts, etc.

Charley Peace: a notorious Victorian burglar and murderer, hanged at

Leeds in 1879; he was portrayed in the Chamber of Horrors at Madame Tussaud's (*RG*).

makee-pigeon: practice, custom ('pigeon' is slang for 'business', 'concern').

trysails: a small fore-and-aft sail; on a sailing-ship they would be used in addition to the main sails. Pyecroft's subsequent comment implies that he doesn't think them of much use in any capacity: they *try* to be sails, but can't manage it.

pyjama-stun'sles: a stunsail (itself a contraction of 'studding sail') is another kind of sail extra to the main sail; Pyecroft pictures them as pyjamas hanging on a washing line with a woman's nightdress ('shimmy' = chemise).

calaboose: the usual (American slang) meaning of 'jailhouse' doesn't make sense here; its being a corruption of 'caboose' (ship's kitchen, galley) isn't much more likely, since the Bo'sun has nothing to do with that. It seems to denote the piles of wood whose stowage he is superintending.

247 *Once clear of the land*: the passages in italic which follow represent the narrator's running translation of M. de C.'s French. In many cases (I supply a few to give the flavour) the original can be reconstructed: the comic effect comes (or is intended to come) from renditions of vocabulary and syntax which are either inaccurate or, by contrast, over-literal. Kipling uses this technique with a much finer brush in 'The Bull that Thought' (p. 367) and 'The Miracle of Saint Jubanus' (*Limits and Renewals*).

Voltaire's Habbakuk: 'Habacuc était capable de tout' (Habakkuk was capable of anything) was a saying attributed to Voltaire.

onjenew: (Fr.) 'ingénu', simple-minded person.

the spectacle cannot reproduce itself: 'le spectacle ne peut se reproduire', i.e. words can't do justice to the sight.

Ganymede: in Greek myth, a youth kidnapped by Jupiter for his beauty, and deified as cup-bearer to the gods on Olympus.

Roule: (Fr.) 'wheel'; Kipling implies that the word was mis-spelled in the French text, not that M. de C. doesn't understand what 'rule' means, since his comment implies that British 'rule' at sea is likely to be short-lived if the behaviour of the *Archimandrite* is anything to go by.

tohu-bohu: confusion, hubbub. In French translations of the Bible the term describes the chaos before creation, when 'the earth was without form and void' (Gen. 1: 2).

248 *That to him is equal*: 'cela lui est égal', 'that's a matter of indifference to him'.

the grand deck: 'le grand pont', the main-deck.

in plain sea: 'en pleine mer', 'in mid-ocean'.

248 *vigias*: 'vigies'; the narrator's nautical knowledge oddly fails him here, since there is nothing especially mysterious about the term: a vigia (from the Latin 'vigilia', which also gives 'vigilance') is a warning on a chart to denote some hidden danger. *OED* cites the definition in the *Sailor's Pocket-Book*, by Frederick Bedford (2nd edn., 1875): 'Numerous imaginary dangers are traditionally inserted in all Ocean Charts.'

chenaler: to follow a channel.

249 *bonnets in a needlecase*: 'bonnettes en étui' is French for studding-sails (stun'sles); Antonio's sail-craft is superior to the narrator's command of French idiom.

in puris naturalibus: cod Latin for 'in a state of nature', but meaning 'under ordinary circumstances'.

bundoop: a 'bundook' (*sic*) is an Anglo-Indian term for a musket or matchlock rifle, here facetiously applied to a naval cannon because of its unreliability.

his subcutaneous details: the working-parties who had been burrowing in the ammunition store below-decks ('subcutaneous' means lit. 'below the finger-nails').

spit-in-the-eye: close-range (because the shells were dropping so close to the ship).

250 *a free-knowledge-ist*: burlesque version of 'phrenologist'; the popular science of reading character from the configuration of the cranium was still going strong, and the British Phrenological Society, founded in 1886, had recently (1899) been incorporated as a scientific society.

dig out: hurry on.

a Hayti bean-feast: 'Hayti' was the usual spelling of Haiti at the time; in 1902–3 it underwent a violent period of insurrection and civil war.

the Captain of the Head: the latrine attendant.

sno—midshipman: Pyecroft was on the point of saying 'snotty', the disrespectful term for a midshipman (the most junior officers on board, usually in their teens). Moorshed reappears in 'Their Lawful Occasions', where Pyecroft, who now knows the narrator better, is unabashed about using the word: 'yonder . . . is our Mr Moorshed. He was the second cutter's snotty—*my* snotty—on the *Archimandrite*'. Moorshed's age is there given as 19, and the action takes place a year later from the time of this story.

251 *yellow jack*: yellow fever.

in its tout ensemble: in its entirety, in its complete effect.

attend public execution: this practice had long been discontinued in the Navy; the last recorded instance took place in 1860. The condemned man, a Marine, was hanged from the yardarm, the traditional punishment; the story has Glass 'executed' by firing-squad because a hanging would have been much more difficult to simulate convincingly.

firebars: bars of iron from the boiler furnace (to weigh down the hammock in which the 'corpse' is to be placed).

252 *breathin' 'ard*: as the 'rear-rank' do in 'Danny Deever' (p. 433).

gashly: ghastly.

æolian harp: a musical instrument which makes sounds when the wind passes over its strings, which are fixed on a wooden resonance box (from Aeolus, in Greek mythology the keeper of the winds). The *Oxford Companion to Music* (10th edn.) compares the effect 'to that often heard from telegraph wires', confirming the accuracy of Kipling's image of the 'funnel-stays in a typhoon'.

shotted: weighted (originally with lead shot, hence the term; here with the 'broken firebars' mentioned previously).

253 *a change . . . came o'er the spirit of our dream*: from Byron's *The Dream*, which uses the line 'A change came o'er the spirit of my dream' six times to mark sections III–VIII of the poem.

like Elphinstone an' Bruce in the Portsmouth election when I was a boy: Sir James Elphinstone and the Hon. T. C. Bruce were elected as Conservative members for Portsmouth in the general election of February 1874. After his victory Sir James addressed his supporters from the window of his hotel. Kipling was 8 years old and living in Southsea at the time; perhaps the speech made an impression on him because he heard of it from 'Uncle Harry', who died soon after (see headnote to 'Baa Baa, Black Sheep', p. 559).

254 *"The Strict Q.T."*: 'on the (strict) q.t.' means 'on the quiet'; the phrase appears in the music-hall song 'Ta-ra-ra-boom-de-ay', which appeared in 1891, but has not been found as a separate title; this does not mean that there was no such song, of course (*RG*).

'They'

First pub. *Scribner's Magazine*, Aug. 1904, incl. the prefatory poem; coll. *Traffics and Discoveries*, 1904.

Kipling settled permanently at 'Bateman's', his house in Burwash, Sussex, in September 1902. 'An Habitation Enforced' (*Actions and Reactions*, 1909), 'Friendly Brook' and its accompanying poem 'The Land', and 'My Son's Wife' (*A Diversity of Creatures*, 1917) represent his experience of landowning and his observation of country manners and morals; 'They' represents his 'discovery' of the county and the whole of the south-east of England by means of the new-fangled invention of the motor-car. The sense of freedom which the car gave, combined with its chronic mechanical unreliability, are faithfully reproduced in 'They'. In the same year as the story, Kipling wrote a series of literary pastiches called 'The Muse among the Motors', first pub. in the *Daily Mail* and later considerably expanded, which includes the following (it is of tangential relevance to 'They' and appears here by editorial *Fiat*):

THE IDIOT BOY
(WORDSWORTH)

He wandered down the mountain grade
Beyond the speed assigned—
A youth whom Justice often stayed
And generally fined.

He went alone, that none might know
If he could drive or steer.
Now he is in the ditch, and Oh!
The differential gear!

Much more to the point is the long, passionate, serio-comic letter which Kipling contributed, also in 1904, to the journalist Filson Young's book *The Complete Motorist* (see ch. 13, 'A Packet of Letters', pp. 285–8). He boasts of his sufferings in the cause of motoring ('My agonies, shames, delays, rages, chills, parboilings, road-walkings, water-drawings, burns, and starvations') and of his status as a pioneering spirit: 'Any fool can invent anything, as any fool can wait to buy the invention when it is thoroughly perfected; but the men to reverence, to admire, to write odes and erect statues to, are those Prometheuses and Ixions (maniacs, you used to call us) who chase the inchoate idea to fixity up and down the King's Highway with their red right shoulders to the wheel.' After praising the freedom which the car has given him he goes on:

But the chief end of my car, so far as I am concerned, is the discovery of England. To me it is a land full of stupefying marvels and mysteries; and a day in the car in an English county is a day in some fairy museum where all the exhibits are alive and real and yet none the less delightfully mixed up with books. For instance, in six hours, I can go from the land of the *Ingoldsby Legends* by way of the Norman Conquest and the Barons' War into Richard Jefferies' country, and so through the Regency, one of Arthur Young's less known tours, and *Celia's Arbour*, into Gilbert White's territory. Horses, after all, are only horses; but the car is a time-machine on which one can slide from one century to another at no more trouble than the pushing forward of a lever. On a morning I have seen the Assizes, javelin-men and all, come into a cathedral town; by noon I was skirting a new-built convent for expelled French nuns; before sundown I was watching the Channel Fleet off Selsea Bill, and after dark I nearly broke a fox's back on a Roman road. You who were born and bred in the land naturally take such trifles for granted, but to me it is still miraculous that if I want petrol in a hurry I must either pass the place where Sir John Lade lived, or the garden where Jack Cade was killed. In Africa one has only to put the miles under and go on; but in England the dead, twelve coffin deep, clutch hold of my wheels at every turn, till I sometimes wonder that the very road does not bleed. *That* is the real joy of motoring—the exploration of this amazing England.

The relevance of this passage to 'They' (and not just to the motoring theme) is obvious. It also resembles the story in giving the misleading impression that Kipling was the driver of his cars. For though he was indeed a pioneer car-owner, he was never a driver; he always had a chauffeur, as the narrator has in 'Steam Tactics' (one of the Pyecroft stories: see headnote to 'The Bonds of Discipline', p. 594) and several other stories in which motoring features, e.g. 'The Bull that Thought' (p. 367). The nature of the story of 'They', however, makes it necessary for the narrator to be on his own, and to drive himself.

The climax of the story is the narrator's recognition, in the child's 'little brushing kiss', of the touch of his own dead child, and his realization that the children in the house are ghosts. This moment is an autobiographical fiction: it is not a 'real' event, and does not mean that Kipling believed in ghosts, any more than the appearance of Puck in the stories of *Puck of Pook's Hill* means that he believed in fairies, but it crystallizes an emotional response to the death of his daughter Josephine in 1899. He wrote to his old friend from India, Mrs Edmonia Hill, in July of that year: 'Be thankful that you have never had a child to lose. I thought I knew something of what grief meant till that came to me' (*Letters*, ii. 376). But when he came to write 'They', he changed the emphasis: when the blind woman laments that she has 'neither borne nor lost', the narrator's reply—'Be very glad then'—is a cry of pain, not of truth. It is she who is truly pitiable; he has both sorrow and joy.

Kipling was careful not to compromise his fiction of the supernatural by either affirmative or negative explanations of it. In an undated letter answering questions about the story (cited *RG*, iv. 1926), he wrote: 'You will observe that only those who had lost children themselves . . . saw the children whom the blind woman's longing had drawn to her. . . . Evidently there was an atmosphere around the blind woman which made it possible for these things to happen to people who had lost; and the whole house and grounds were saturated with that atmosphere.' Of the narrator's decision not to return, he comments: 'It was wrong for the man to return to the house because he had really lost his child and it was not his business to continue dabbling among the shadows evoked by the blind woman. But the whole tale is rather difficult to disentangle and I think it is susceptible of several interpretations according as the reader has or has not undergone certain experiences. I don't know that I would apply the word "clairvoyant" to any of the characters; as, in my mind, that always seems to go with "mediums" and suchlike.' Kipling's suspicion of 'mediums' in this context recalls a passage from Browning's poem about 'Mr Sludge, "the Medium"' (*Dramatis Personae*, 1864): Sludge (based on the celebrated American medium D. D. Home) explains that his technique includes playing on people's vulnerability to the suggestion that they might make contact with their lost children: 'Sludge begins | At your entreaty with your dearest dead, | The little voice set lisping once again, | The tiny hand made feel for yours once more, | The poor lost image brought back, plain as dreams' (ll. 471–5). Kipling's sister Alice practised as a medium (under the name 'Mrs Holland') and claimed to have seen the 'Colours' described by the blind woman (see note on p. 609).

The ghosts of children appear in a much darker context, as the victims of German wartime atrocities, in 'Swept and Garnished' (*A Diversity of Creatures*, 1917). See also the headnote to 'Mary Postgate' (p. 626).

The Return of the Children

This is one of the first of Kipling's works in either prose or verse to be set in the afterlife, and to include what became, for him, the most important of its symbols, the 'gateway' presided over by St Peter, who holds the keys to heaven by virtue of Christ's injunction in Matt. 16: 19. See also the poem 'Tomlinson' (*Barrack-Room Ballads*, 1892); 'On the Gate' and the poem 'Jane's Marriage' which follows 'The Janeites' (both *Debits and Credits*, 1926); and 'Uncovenanted Mercies' and the poem 'Dinah in Heaven' which precedes 'The Woman in His Life' (both *Limits and Renewals*, 1932).

256 l. 16. *suffered the children*: Matt. 19: 14: 'Jesus said, Suffer little children, and forbid them not, to come unto me: for of such is the kingdom of heaven.'

'They'

257 *that precise hamlet which stands godmother to the capital of the United States*: Washington, in west Sussex, about 7 miles north of Worthing. In fact the Washington family originated in the county of Durham, and George Washington was descended from a branch of the family which held estates in Northamptonshire.

heavier traffic than would ever vex them again: Lisa Lewis (ed., *Mrs Bathurst and Other Stories*, Oxford University Press (World's Classics), 1991) suggests as an example 'taking guns from Sussex iron-foundries to the Channel ports', a trade which declined with the advent of coalmining in the north and Wales; these foundries are evoked in 'Hal o' the Draft' (*Puck of Pook's Hill*, 1906).

a hall of the Knights of the Temple: Shipley, about 7 miles north of Washington, has a 12th-century church said to have been built by the Templars, though why Kipling should call it a 'smithy' is uncertain.

that great Down whose ringed head is a landmark for fifty miles: Chanctonbury Ring.

on the second speed: in second gear.

262 *way-waste*: a patch of waste ground by the side of the road, a primitive lay-by (Sussex dialect).

264 *the West Coast*: of Africa.

264–5 *Those Colours . . . the figure of the Egg itself*: Kipling's sister Alice, who became a believer in spiritualism and practised as a medium (under the name of 'Mrs Holland'), claimed to have seen these 'colours'; Kipling associates them with 'the Aura or halo around the soul of every human being [which] is seen only by the spiritual eye of those who follow a certain school of psychology' (letter to his French translator Louis Fabulet, 29 June 1905, *Letters*, iii. 185). Apparently the blind woman 'sees' the colours laid in bands across the figure of the Egg, with the gentle or peaceful ones at the top and the violent or disturbed ones at the bottom. A person's emotional state evokes in her an intense perception of one of these bands of colour. But there is a contradiction between her first statement to the narrator that these special colours 'aren't in the world at all', and her subsequent statement that she 'used to ask what colours were when [she] was little . . . because some colours hurt me and some made me happy.' The 'Egg' is unexplained, though it may refer to the 'Mundane Egg', the symbol of the world in Orphic religious mysticism.

266 *tax cart*: or taxed cart, with English perverseness meaning the opposite: a two-wheeled, one-horse vehicle below £21 in value and so exempt from tax.

267 *de back-yard*: Kipling's rendition of the rural Sussex accent softens *t* and *th* to *d*.

shruck: shriek (Sussex dialect).

the Oath of Æsculapius: he was the Greek god of medicine, but no particular oath is ascribed to him; it may be Kipling's variation on the 'Hippocratic Oath' which concerns solidarity among physicians and the observance of medical ethics.

Mrs Madehurst and the blind woman: a small inconsistency: the blind woman had earlier refused to leave the house because she had to stay with the children.

267–8 *a court of magnificent Borzois*: Russian wolf-hounds: 'thin, high, silky coated things like a cross between a deer hound and an Angora goat. They are of the highest aristocracy' (Kipling to Brander Matthews, 7 Aug. 1904, *Letters*, iii. 159).

268 *tonneau*: the rounded back of the car (naturalized from the same word in French, meaning lit. a cask or barrel).

269 *would not willingly insure such stray lives*: the child's funeral expenses might have been covered by insurance (it would not have been legal to insure its life for any greater sum, whether it was born in or out of wedlock). The insurance companies' 'reasons' were probably not moral but actuarial (based on a higher death-rate among illegitimate children), hence Mrs Madehurst's insistence, which confirms what Jenny herself

said to the doctor, that the child was given the same care as if it had 'come all proper'.

269 *the Fathers*: the contraction usually denotes the Church Fathers (such as St Jerome, or St Thomas Aquinas), though the allusion here probably extends beyond them.

the house . . . lived in it: for Kipling's most extended treatment of this idea, see 'The House-Surgeon' (*Actions and Reactions*, 1909). In ch. 7 of *Something of Myself*, Kipling describes his first visit to 'Bateman's': 'We entered and felt her Spirit—her Feng Shui—to be good. We went through every room and found no shadow of ancient regrets, stifled miseries, nor any menace, though the "new" end of her was three hundred years old.'

270 *In the pleasant orchard-closes*: the opening line of Elizabeth Barrett Browning's 'The Lost Bower' (pub. before her marriage, in *Poems*, 1844). The 'marring fifth line' referred to below is: 'Listen, gentle—ay, and simple! listen, children on the knee!' It is not a good line, but the mention of the children probably has as much to do with its omission.

found but a half-charred hedge-stake: the absence of a poker is explained below (see note on *no unpassable iron*).

272 *and a highway robber*: because his name is that of the famous 18th-century highwayman Dick Turpin (who rode to York on Black Bess).

273 *cake*: cattle-cake, concentrated feed.

You're dragging the heart out of the farm: in ch. 7 of *Something of Myself*, Kipling describes becoming a Sussex landowner: 'We began with tenants —two or three small farmers on our very few acres—from whom we learned that farming was a mixture of farce, fraud, and philanthropy that stole the heart out of the land.'

274 *no unpassable iron*: alluding to the widespread superstition that iron wards off spirits; the emphasis is usually on protection from witches, the nightmare, etc., but here the intention is to remove any obstacle to the ghosts appearing, hence the leather screen and the absence of a poker or other metal implement.

Mrs Bathurst

First pub. *Windsor Magazine* (England) and *Metropolitan Magazine* (America), Sept. 1904, in both cases without the prefatory 'scene'; coll. *Traffics and Discoveries*, 1904.

The story is set in South Africa, shortly after the end of the Boer War in 1902. Kipling first went to South Africa in 1891, on a round-the-world trip which also took in New Zealand. He was never to return to New Zealand, whereas South Africa became for many years a second (winter) home; but 'Mrs Bathurst' is based on a flash of memory which fuses the familiar landscape of the Cape with a brief encounter in Auckland. In ch. 4 of *Something of Myself*, he wrote:

All I carried away from the magic town of Auckland was the face and voice of a woman who sold me beer at a little hotel there. They stayed at the back of my head till ten years later when, in a local train of the Cape Town suburbs, I heard a petty officer from Simons Town telling a companion about a woman in New Zealand who 'never scrupled to help a lame duck or put her foot on a scorpion.' Then—precisely as the removal of a key-log in a timber-jam starts the whole pile—those words gave me the key to the face and voice at Auckland, and a tale called 'Mrs. Bathurst' slid into my mind, smoothly and orderly as floating timber on a bank-high river.

The link between these far-flung places is the Navy; this is a naval story not because of what happens on board ship, as in 'The Bonds of Discipline', but because of the accidents of circumstance which belong to navy life and which affect those who take an interest in it. The story begins with one such accident, which leaves the narrator 'stranded', and another accident brings him into company with his old acquaintance Pyecroft. Throughout the story, time and distance are haphazard elements: at one moment Mrs Bathurst leans close over a hotel bar, at another she is distant and ungraspable. Hence the power of her enigmatic appearance at the train station, captured by the newfangled (other-worldly) medium of the cinematograph, a fleeting image which can be repeated again and again, an 'enigma of arrival'.

'Listen, Bill, something really must be done about Kip's "Mrs Bathurst". I read it years ago and didn't understand a word of it. I thought to myself, "Ah, youthful ignorance!" A week ago I re-read it. Result, precisely the same.' P. G. Wodehouse, writing in 1928 (the letter is cited in *Performing Flea*, 1953), is an early witness to the story's capacity to baffle. Indeed 'Mrs Bathurst' has become the most-discussed of Kipling's stories, often to little purpose. A number of puzzles, some of them apparently crucial to the plot, simply cannot be resolved, for example the sequence of events of which Mrs Bathurst's journey to England forms a part (was she looking for Vickery, as he maintains? did they meet subsequently?), or the identity of the second tramp who is found dead with Vickery (is it Mrs Bathurst herself?). The story's indeterminacy is deliberate and radical: as David Lodge points out, it displaces attention onto the process of storytelling itself, and juxtaposes the *mystery* of the central subject (what happened between Vickery and Mrs Bathurst?) with the *suspense* of its narration ('"Mrs Bathurst": Indeterminacy in Modern Narrative', in P. Mallett (ed.), *Kipling Considered* (1989), 71–84). At any rate P. G. Wodehouse is—dare I say it—wrong to exclaim indignantly, after listing several of the plot-puzzles: 'And, above all, how was Kip allowed to get away with six solid pages of padding at the start of the story?' Far from being 'padding', these opening pages are dense with significance—if only we could tell in which direction the signs pointed.

'Mrs Bathurst' represents a deepening of Pyecroft's character comparable to that which Kipling gave Mulvaney's in 'Love-o'-Women' (p. 143) or Learoyd's in 'On Greenhow Hill' (p. 114)—all of them stories of erotic obsession. Like 'Love-o'-Women, the 'gentleman-ranker', Vickery is a 'superior man' in terms of class to the man who tells his story (see p. 281).

276 *From Lyden's 'Irenius'*: part of a pastiche of a Jacobean tragedy, which Kipling never completed; other fragments were attached to other stories, notably 'The Prophet and the Country' and 'A Madonna of the Trenches' (both *Debits and Credits*, 1926), where the play is called 'Gow's Watch'. In the Definitive Edition of Kipling's verse all the fragments appear under the title 'Gow's Watch', with some cuts and some added material. The fragment here is cut with the exception of Ferdinand's last seven lines, and the surrounding context is different.

versary: turning motion; a nonce-word (not rec. in *OED*) playing on the fact that a planet turns or revolves in its orbit to suggest the mutability of women. The story of how Vulcan caught his wife Venus in a net with her lover Mars is told in Homer (*Odyssey* 8. 266–366), though not with the punning astrological twist which Kipling adds by referring to 'the house of stinking Capricorn' (the sign of the goat, an emblem of lust). The allusion to Vulcan, who was amongst other things the god of lightning, foreshadows the manner of Vickery's death, as does the 'gerb of long-stored lightnings' mentioned further on. See also the note to 'consume your own smoke', p. 616.

Simpliciter: 'simply', 'straightforwardly' (Lat.).

overtake: the sense demands something like 'understand', 'get an explanation of', and *OED* does record such a meaning, but the last recorded occurrence was in 1300; it seems unlikely that even Kipling would have known it, and he is probably embroidering on the more common sense of 'take' as 'understand', a phrase found in Elizabethan and Jacobean drama.

coneycatch: to hunt for rabbits; in Elizabethan slang 'coneycatch' meant 'con, deceive', but the metaphor here draws on the literal sense: Fortune abandons her high-born prey to go hunting the common people, with the same cruelty and cunning as she would employ to overthrow a king. 'Clown' is an archaic term for a peasant (there is no implication of a circus clown); the 'gerb' or sheaf of lightnings is associated with Jupiter, the king of the gods. See note to 'versary' above.

Mrs Bathurst

277 *H.M.S. Peridot*: a fictitious name; as *RG* points out, its meaning (a semi-precious mineral) echoes the names of real warships such as the *Amethyst*, *Topaz* etc.

Simon's Bay: on the west side of False Bay; there was a British naval base at Simon's Town.

She was just steaming out to sea as my train came in: David Lodge (see headnote) points out that this detail announces both the theme of frustration and bafflement, and the opposition between land and sea, ship and train, around which the story is structured; ship and train evoke 'resemblance as well as difference, since both are methods of transport that "steam"'; the narrator's friend Hooper takes him by train to the 'plank-platform half buried in sand not a hundred yards from the edge of the surf' where the story will be told.

my friend Inspector Hooper: based on a real South African acquaintance, Teddy Layton, who is said to have contributed the macabre detail of the story's ending (see final note).

Glengariff siding: not identified; *RG* suggests Glencairn, the next station north of Simon's Town.

the Greeks: many café and store owners in South Africa at the time were Greek immigrants.

A crowd of Malays: another immigrant community, less prosperous than the Greeks and mainly engaged in fishing and menial labour.

Elsie's Peak: a hill to the north of Glencairn.

tickey beer: threepenny (cheap, local) beer, hence their pleasure at the sight of a bottle of imported Bass later on.

278 *Wankies—beyond Buluwayo*: Bulawayo (modern spelling) in southern Rhodesia, now Zimbabwe, is over 1,300 miles from Cape Town, and Wankie (the modern name) lies some 180 miles to the north-west of Bulawayo, on the railway line which goes to Victoria Falls.

Here's your Belmont: a British victory in the Boer War (23 Nov. 1899); 'the Royal Marines in fact obtained greater distinction at Graspan, two days after Belmont' (*RG*).

Hierophant: see note on p. 599 (*Archimandrite*).

Tristan d'Acunha: an island in the South Atlantic, about 1,750 miles west of Cape Town.

boiler-seatings: the bed-plates of the boilers, difficult of access and thus liable to corrode (*RG*).

verbatim: lit., 'word for word', but Pyecroft uses it to mean 'verbally, in words'.

Kalk Bay: along with Muizenburg and St James's, places on the coast of False Bay north of Glencairn.

279 *'is Number One rig*: his best outfit.

purr Mary, on the terrace: garbling the Royal Marines' Latin motto, 'per mare per terram' (by sea and by land).

ex officio: a Latin tag meaning 'by virtue of his office'.

279 *The story of Boy Niven . . . used to be a legend of the Fleet*: this 'legend' may be authentic but has not been traced. Desertion at the prospect of land or gold was not uncommon, as *RG* points out. It may seem odd that Kipling should take it lightly, but it occurs in peacetime, and is represented as a youthful folly with a farcical outcome. Vickery, too, deserts in peacetime, but in very different circumstances.

the cocoanut-woman: *RG* suggests that she sold coconuts or ran a fairground coconut-shy stall, but I have always assumed that Jones married a South Sea island woman and that the reference is to her colour.

Spit-Kid Jones: a spit-kid is a spittoon; Jones's mouth is unusually large, or perhaps always open.

280 *steerin'-flat*: a compartment in the after-end of a ship housing the steering gear.

Benin: a punitive naval expedition was mounted against this West African kingdom in 1897 after the massacre of a British mission.

Buncrana: a town on Lough Swilly in Donegal, where there was a British naval base before the advent of the Irish Republic.

Mormonastic: a Carrollian portmanteau word, combining 'Mormon' and 'monastic': the first because Moon intends to adopt the polygamous life of a South Sea islander, and the second because he is seeking a secluded haven.

copper: copper sheathing to protect the wooden hull from the teredo worm (in ships of the 'composite' type, the wooden hull in turn enclosed an iron or steel framework, hence the allusion further on to the 'frames' or ribs of the ship).

281 *A warrant*: a warrant officer.

like columns in the war: the Boer War, in which supply lines were governed by the railway network.

Salisbury . . . Nyassa: Salisbury in northern Rhodesia (now Harare, the capital of Zimbabwe) was at the end of the railway line, with no connection to Lake Nyassa, about 350 miles away in what was then British East Africa (the lake now divides Malawi and Mozambique); the 'flotilla' consisted of gunboats engaged in the suppression of the Arabian slave-trade. Hooper's deserter had presumably stayed close to the railway for as long as he could, even though it would have made more sense to go across country.

He was sent up to Bloemfontein to take over some Navy ammunition left in the fort: Bloemfontein was the capital of the Orange Free State, nearly 600 miles from Cape Town (going inland north and east). Naval Brigades were landed to assist the army in the Boer War, with guns taken from warships and mounted on improvised carriages, hence the presence of Navy ammunition so far inland (*RG*).

casus belli: 'the cause of the quarrel' (Lat.), i.e. 'the matter being discussed'.

282 *bring 'is status quo to an anchor*: Pyecroft's facetious way of telling Pritchard to sit down.

Hauraki—near Auckland: there was no hotel in this small place, which Kipling probably chose because of its closeness to the naval base at Devonport, across the harbour at Auckland.

283 *the Marroquin's commission*: the ship's commission is its period on active service.

on the front: in port, ashore.

Slits: Schlitz, an American beer ('the Beer that made Milawaukee Famous').

284 *she never scrupled to feed a lame duck or set 'er foot on a scorpion at any time of 'er life*: the phrase which triggered the story, in Kipling's account (see headnote); but it does not have the same effect on Hooper.

It's just It: Kipling's comic warning about literary 'borrowing' ('When 'Omer Smote 'Is Bloomin' Lyre', p. 474) may rebound on him here, but as far as can be ascertained he really did invent this famous phrase.

285 *Phyllis's Circus*: there was a real circus-owner called Fillis whose circus was based in Johannesburg.

a Tickey: threepence, as with the 'tickey beer' above (p. 277).

Not bein' a devotee of Indian peeris: Durban had a large Indian population; the allusion here is to Indian women ('peris', or eastern fairies).

286 *I couldn't get off . . . a gyroscope*: Pyecroft has had to stay on board in order to help with the repair of a gyroscope in one of the torpedos, which are lodged in tubes in an underwater compartment; 'sugared up' is a euphemism, as *OED* notes, citing 'Their Lawful Occasions', an earlier Pyecroft story in *Traffics and Discoveries*: '"I'm going on manoeuvres in the *Pedantic*" . . . "War's declared at midnight. *Pedantics* be sugared!"'. The phrase 'some pride of the West country' means either that the defective gyroscope was fitted in the naval dockyard at Plymouth, or, as *RG* suggests, that a clumsy seaman (a west-country bumpkin) had damaged it while on board.

287 *reticule*: a small handbag of woven or netted material.

like an enteric at the last kick: like someone on the point of death from enteric, or typhoid, fever.

more or less imbued with the fragrant spirit: alluding to the way the narrator plied him with drinks during the telling of the story 'The Bonds of Discipline'.

287 *that big hotel up the hill . . . The Molteno Reservoir . . . the Gardens . . . the Docks*: all these details of the geography of Cape Town are accurate, though the docks would have been closer because of subsequent land reclamation (*RG*).

Salt River: an eastern suburb of Cape Town, about 2 miles from the docks.

288 *Thus the mornin' an' the evenin' were the first day, as Scripture says*: but in reverse order, the Jewish day being calculated from sunset to sunset: 'And the evening and the morning were the first day' (Gen. 1: 5).

a Marconi ticker: a telegraph recording instrument, first patented in 1896; Kipling had met its inventor, Guglielmo Marconi, in 1899. 'Wireless', the eighth story in *Traffics and Discoveries*, concerns an early experiment in wireless telegraphy, mixed with elements of the supernatural.

289 *a condenser*: a chamber in a steam-engine in which the vapour is condensed to water.

Throwin' gun-sights overboard: only a few instances of this have actually been recorded, but one took place in 1900, recent enough for Kipling to have heard of it. It is a convincing detail in its demonstrativeness and nuisance-value. The *Western Morning News*, published in Plymouth, would take a particular interest in discontent in the Navy. Pyecroft's dismissive comment about a stoker being responsible reads oddly when set alongside Kipling's appalled testimony to the working conditions of stokers in ch. 6 of *A Fleet in Being* (1899; see headnote to 'The Bonds of Discipline', p. 594).

290 *the cutter*: see note on p. 599.

the Admiral's front gate: Admiralty House in Simon's Town, near the Dockyard; it had big teak gates. Kipling stayed there in 1902 as the guest of Rear-Admiral Sir Arthur Moore (*RG*).

Worcester: east of Cape Town, a station on the line running north-east to Bloemfontein.

Consume your own smoke: attributed in the *Oxford Dictionary of English Proverbs* to Carlyle: 'I see almost nobody. I . . . study to consume my own smoke'. As with the allusions to lightning in the epigraph (see note to 'versary', p. 612), the association of Vickery with soot and smoke prefigures the horrific appearance of his corpse.

the Admiral's garden-gate: they have walked round the side of Admiralty House.

remember, that I am not a murderer, because my lawful wife died in childbed six weeks after I came out: Vickery thinks that if Pyecroft hears of the death of Vickery's wife without knowing the precise date, he will connect it with Vickery's desertion (of her, and of the Navy).

'*The rest, 'e says, is silence*': Hamlet's dying words (v. ii. 350).

291 '*The Honeysuckle and the Bee*': a popular music-hall song by Albert H. Fitz, a verse of which is quoted at the end of the story (*RG*).

kapje: bonnet (Afrikaans).

seventy-two miles without a curve: the 'Dett (or Dete) Straight', accounted for by alternative local legends: (1) 'construction of the line was originally paid for at so much per mile of rail laid, but the first section north from Bulawayo was so devious that the contract was altered to so much per mile as the crow flies'; (2) 'the engineer had the reputation of being fond of the bottle and his friends in the Bulawayo Club, alleging that this was the reason for the sinuosities of the line, bet him that he could not lay a mile without a curve' (*RG*).

that other man: Hooper does not confirm that Vickery's companion was a man; later he calls the second tramp Vickery's 'mate', which is not conclusive; it seems clear that Kipling wanted to suggest the possibility of the second tramp being Mrs Bathurst, but that is as far as his clarity extends. If I had to choose, I would say that the balance of evidence pointed to the second figure being another man, anonymous and otherwise insignificant in the story; but Kipling asks us, and allows us, not to choose.

M'Bindwe siding: there is no place with this name; the closest, M'Benji or Mambanje, is a station beyond the 'Dett Straight'.

That's what they really were, you see—charcoal: the detail of the corpses by the railway line is said to be authentic, and to have been been contributed by Teddy Layton, the original of Inspector Hooper. This does not however mean that Layton vouched for the complete incineration described here, whose scientific plausibility has been questioned. The controversy recalls that over 'spontaneous combustion' in ch. 32 of Dickens's *Bleak House*. Kipling may have had this famous precedent in mind; the combination of grotesque intensity with rational reportage also suggests some of Poe's fiction, for example 'The Facts in the Case of M. Valdemar', which concludes with a disintegrating corpse, and which Kipling had quoted in 'In the House of Suddhoo' (p. 13, and note, p. 535). But Kipling's tone is cooler even than Poe's.

The Village that Voted the Earth was Flat

First pub. *A Diversity of Creatures*, 1917, with the accompanying poem 'The Press'. The date '1913' follows the title in the volume; Kipling actually wrote the story in the spring of 1914, but he presumably wanted to stress that the story belonged to the pre-War world. See also the headnotes to 'In the Presence' (p. 623) and 'Mary Postgate' (p. 626).

The story presents the sour side of Kipling's love of the country (and, indeed, of his country). The ambushed motorists are Londoners and cosmopolitans, who exact revenge using the tools of their city trades and especially the power of the media: the publicity war which destroys Huckley and its squire, Sir Thomas Ingell, is one of Kipling's most accurate prophecies of the tendencies of modern culture. Today the impresario Bat Masquerier would be a television producer, and nemesis would come in the form of a documentary, but the basic technique would be the same. To the farce of a deserved retribution for the highway robber-baron of Huckley and his feudal bumpkins, Kipling adds a dark fable about the passion of revenge, which, in the delirious climax, afflicts the House of Commons with collective madness. His scorn for democracy also comes into play: Parliament is an apt place to give the voters of Huckley their unwanted apotheosis. The story glances at the notion that the nation's legislature is Huckley on a national scale, a 'village' capable of the political equivalent of flat-earthism, and also a music-hall (the term 'house' applies to the House of Commons and to the theatre audience which Bat Marquerier's artistes seduce and manipulate). Certainly the political fate of some of the causes dear to Kipling's heart in the early years of the century (Unionism, in particular—the denouement of the story hinges on the unresolved 'Irish Question') led him to despair of the political system and to identify most politicians as irredeemably malevolent and corrupt. The Conservative Pallant's description of Sir Thomas Ingell as a 'radical tinker' might have been endorsed by Kipling himself, but Pallant himself is in some ways the most sinister character in the story.

The story's lighter side draws on Kipling's love of the music-hall, a love which reaches back to his bachelor days after his move to London in 1889. In ch. 4 of *Something of Myself* he describes his lodgings in Villiers Street, in the Strand: 'from my desk I could look out of my window through the fan-light of Gatti's Music-Hall entrance, across the street, almost on to its stage.' At the music-hall he 'listened to the observed and compelling songs of the Lion and Mammoth Comiques', whose influence found its way into the *Barrack-Room Ballads* (see headnote, 'Danny Deever', p. 651). The music-hall, and Kipling's early literary career in London, come together again in 'Dayspring Mishandled' (p. 391), which also features the (unnamed) mother of the star performer in this story, Vidal Benzaguen.

293 *the car stopped*: none of the named characters is driving; there is a chauffeur, 'Woodhouse's man', referred to later (p. 295).

exceeding the speed-limit: 20 miles per hour at the time (until 1930).

The usual swindle: the perceived injustice of magistrates levying fines on motorists for harmlessly exceeding the speed-limit had been on Kipling's mind for some time: in 'A Deal in Cotton' (*Actions and Reactions*, 1909), the young colonial administrator Adam Strickland, speaking of the limited revenues of his African district, says: 'I tell you I envied your magistrates here hauling money out of motorists every week!' The 'swindle' here is compounded by the odious relish which Sir Thomas takes in tempting passing motorists to speed along the straight stretch of road and then fleecing them, let alone his getting the policeman to sound the horn and make his horse bolt, so that he can add a charge of 'endangering traffic' to the summons.

294 *Jubilee clock-tower*: built either in 1887 or 1897 for Queen Victoria's Golden or Diamond Jubilee, probably the former.

295 *in extenso*: 'at length', 'in full'.

his home address at Jerusalem: an anti-Semitic remark, though there is some doubt about whether Masquerier actually is Jewish: his comment further on, 'He told *me* . . . that my home-address was Jerusalem', might imply that he is not Jewish and takes the imputation as a slur. On balance, however, I think that he is.

auto-da-fé: public execution (from the practice of the Spanish Inquisition); punning on *auto*.

297 *the Silhouettes*: two sisters, we later learn (p. 303), though whether they sing, dance, or strike erotic poses is not revealed. All these names of performers and theatres are fictitious; only the 'Jocunda' suggests a real-life original, the 'Gaiety'.

298 *pure Brasenose*: Brasenose College, Oxford, stands here for the upper-class put-down which Ollyett metes out to the corrupt businessman.

how the hoopoe got his crest from King Solomon: echoing the *Just So Stories* formula; the legend is in the *Koran*.

299 *eheu ab angulo!*: 'alas for that rustic nook!'

the Spec.: the *Spectator*, mentioned later on in unabbreviated form (p. 312).

tump: apparently Kipling's coinage; the context suggests 'rubbish, crap'.

Non nobis gloria!: 'not to us the glory', a Latin tag, from the Vulgate version of Ps. 113: 'Non nobis, Domine, non nobis; sed nomini tuo da gloriam' (Not unto us, Lord, not unto us; but to thy name give glory). See 'McAndrew's Hymn', l. 163 (p. 465). Sir Thomas is the local deity ironically invoked here.

the panel doctor: a doctor who served on the local panel of the Board of Health, a precursor of welfare state provision.

299 *we—I'm*: Ollyett forgets himself and mentions his girlfriend (the occupant of the side-car).

300 *our late King-Emperor*: Edward VII, who had died in 1910.

301 *some nuts*: probably a punning allusion to 'Dal's male companions; see the definition of *the conventional pre-war nut*' on p. 630.

302 *an Irish afternoon*: the date is before partition set up the Irish Free State (1921), so Irish members still sit in the House of Commons, and the day's business is Irish affairs. The Irish Home Rule Bill (the third attempt to legislate) was introduced in 1912 by Asquith's Liberal government; it was bitterly opposed by Unionists in Ulster and by many English Conservatives. In 1913 the bill twice passed the Commons but failed in the Lords. Kipling was a vehement and virulent supporter of Unionism.

Ballyhellion: a fictitious place-name.

He's got his hat on his head: according to parliamentary etiquette of the time, a member's head had to be covered (as a mark of respect to the House) while he asked a question; another rule (still in force) is that during questions to ministers all comments from the floor of the House must be made in the form of questions addressed to the Speaker. It is the second rule which Sir Thomas has broken.

303 *By the grace of God, Master Ridley*: misquoting the famous adjuration of Hugh Latimer to his fellow (former) bishop and Protestant martyr Nicholas Ridley, before they were burnt at the stake for heresy in 1555 during the reign of Bloody Mary: 'Be of good comfort Master Ridley, and play the man. We shall this day light such a candle by God's grace in England, as (I trust) shall never be put out.'

304 *leper-window . . . squinch-hole*: a leper-window allowed lepers, banned from entering a church, to witness the service; it has a more precise meaning than 'squinch', an archaic term for a slit or narrow opening in a building; *OED* cites an 1879 article in *Temple Bar* magazine in which the word is used of churches.

peaceful penetration: a catch-phrase of the time referring to subversion of a country by its (prospective) enemies, through propaganda and the cultivation of political influence.

Hone's Every-Day Book: William Hone (1780–1842), miscellaneous author, journalist, and bookseller; his *Every-Day Book, or Calendar of Popular Amusements, Sports, Pastimes, Ceremonies, Manners, Customs and Events* appeared in 1826–7.

305 *quotable by whole sticks*: as of dynamite, by association with 'dynamic'; or alluding to the line of type in a compositor's 'stick'.

there is a real Society that thinks the world's flat: the Universal Zetetic Society (from a Greek word meaning inquiry or investigation); *OED* cites a book title of 1849, *Zetetic Astronomy: A description of several experiments which prove that the surface of the sea is a perfect plane, and that the Earth is not a Globe!* The contemporary version, the International

Flat Earth Society, is a Christian fundamentalist movement based in California.

Morgiana and Drexel: based on an Arabian Nights burlesque, according to *RG*: Morgiana is the slave-girl who pours the boiling oil over the thieves in the story of Ali Baba; 'Drexel' is a portmanteau name from 'Diesel' and 'electric' (hence 'fluid and electric review', p. 309).

306 *she won't forget about Nellie Farren*: Ellen Farren (1848–1904), the most famous burlesque actress of her day, especially in roles as Principal Boy at the Gaiety Theatre, where she played from its opening in 1868 to her retirement in 1891 (*RG*; see also W. Macqueen-Pope, *Nights of Gladness* (1956), 143–4). It is implied that the narrator has written an appreciation of Nellie Farren which Vidal has seen: see their conversation on p. 308.

no one has actually proved the earth is round, have they?: Stephen Hawking (*A Brief History of Time*, 1988) points out that Aristotle hypothesized as early as 340 BC that the earth was a sphere (the earth's shadow on the moon during a lunar eclipse is round; the North Star appears lower in the sky when viewed in the south than in more northerly regions; the sails of a ship coming over the horizon are seen before the hull). Although the idea was declared heretical by the early Church, it was finally confirmed by the circumnavigations of the 16th century.

That's the worst of these model villages if you let 'em smell fire-water: Kipling treated this theme at much greater length in his (among other things) satire on Prohibition in America, 'The Prophet and the Country' (*Debits and Credits*, 1926).

307 *a sort of gorilla lockstep procession*: the 'lockstep' is a step in military drill; *RG* says it was also the name of a follow-my-leader dance introduced to the London stage about 1910.

Films are a branch of art by themselves: Kipling treated this theme at much greater length in his (among other things) fantasia on American movie-making, 'The Prophet and the Country' (*Debits and Credits*, 1926).

Peter's vision at Joppa: in Acts 10: 9–16, Peter falls into a trance and sees a vision of 'all manner of fourfooted beasts of the earth'.

310 *the refrain of 'The Holy City'*: a drawing-room ballad, words by Frederic E. Weatherley, music by Stephen Adams; the refrain runs: 'Jerusalem! Jerusalem! Lift up your voice and sing! | Hosanna in the highest, Hosanna to your King! | Jerusalem! Jerusalem! Sing for the night is o'er! | Hosanna! Hosanna! To the King for evermore!'

311 *Fate ruled it that there should be nothing of first importance in the world's idle eye*: Kipling here reverses the situation which obtains twice in 'The Man Who Would Be King' (pp. 62 and 69), in which the narrator is waiting for a momentous news event to break.

311 *helio*: heliograph, the signalling apparatus which figures in 'A Code of Morals' (p. 427).

ran and raped it: 'carried all before it'. I think Kipling is adapting the alliterative idiom 'rape and renne', later more usually 'rap and rend', meaning to seize and destroy; there is also an obsolete sense of 'rape' meaning 'hasten', but the last occurrence in *OED* is dated 1430.

the cataleptic kick of 'Ta-ra-ra-boom-de-ay,' multiplied by the West African significance of 'Everybody's doing it' plus twice the infernal elementality of a certain tune in Dona et Gamma: 'Ta-ra-ra-boom-de-ay,' was a popular music-hall song by Henry J. Sayers and B. M. Batchelor; Lottie Collins had a great hit with it in 1891 at the Gaiety Theatre. 'Everybody's Doing It' was a ragtime song which gave its name to a hit musical review of the time (ragtime, like jazz, was a black American art form associated with primitive African origins). I have not identified 'Dona et Gamma'.

312 *Margaritas ante Porcos*: 'Pearls before swine', the waggish pseudonym of a letter-writer.

Hausmania: from Baron Haussman, the French politician who as Prefect of the Seine masterminded the large-scale redevelopment of Paris during the Second Empire (1853–70).

314 *Like that strange song*: Tennyson, 'Tithonus', ll. 62–3. The passage concerns the time when Tithonus was young and happy with the goddess Aurora; Huckley has been the scene of Ollyett's courtship.

kodaking: *OED* first records this as a verb in 1891.

318 *language calculated, etc.*: 'to cause a breach of the King's peace' would follow.

319 *Gehazi*: struck with leprosy by Elisha in 2 Kgs. 5.

323 *renewed their strength like Antaeus*: in Greek myth, a giant, the son of the earth-goddess; he wrestled with Hercules, who threw him repeatedly, but each time he fell he rose refreshed from contact with his mother.

vain was the help of man: 'Give us help from trouble: for vain is the help of man. Through God we shall do valiantly: for he it is that shall tread down our enemies' (Ps. 60: 11–12; the same verses are in Ps. 108: 12–13).

The Press

324 l. 11. *The Harrild and the Hoe*: printing machines.

ll. 21–3. *As the war-horse . . . trumpets are*: from Job 39: 25.

l. 25. *Canst thou number*: this and the following questions parody God's rhetorical questions to Job in chs. 38 and 39, esp. 39: 1–2 ('Knowest thou the time when the wild goats of the rock bring forth? or canst thou mark when the hinds do calve? Canst thou number the months that they fulfil? or knowest thou the time when they bring forth?'); 38: 25–6 ('Who hath divided a water-course for the overflowing of waters, or a way for lightning of thunder; to cause it to rain on the earth, where no man is'); and 39: 13 ('Gavest thou the goodly wings unto the peacocks?').

In the Presence

First pub. *Pearson's Magazine* and *Everybody's Magazine*, March 1912 (without the accompanying poem); coll. *A Diversity of Creatures*, 1917, when the date '1912' was affixed to the story to emphasize its pre-War origin.

King Edward VII died of pneumonia on 6 May 1910. The body lay in state in St George's Hall, Westminster, as described in the story, until 21 May, when it was taken by train for the state funeral at Windsor. The description of the Gurkha soldiers' vigil is historical: see *Kipling Journal*, 129 (1958), repr. *RG* vii. 3084–5, for the verbatim account of one of the participants, Subadar-Major Santbir Gurung. He was accompanied by two other senior officers and by his son. (Kipling transposes this relationship to the Sikh part of the story.) The Subadar-Major says that when the King's body lay in state sentries were posted, among them one Indian officer: 'British Officers were relieved after every hour and so were we . . . Daily from Reveille to Retreat, the public were allowed to come there and pay their respects to their late King. . . . Continuously for four days we were on duty. Did not change our uniform even.'

The story juxtaposes two kinds of honour—one concerning a blood-feud, the other the endurance of physical and psychological strain—and in both cases the honour belongs to Indian subjects of the Empire. But the scope of the story widens as it goes on: for whereas the Subadar-Major and the Chaplain admire the heroic propriety with which men of their own race and regiment have conducted themselves, the Havildar-Major, who has crossed the 'Black Water' and seen sights beyond the knowledge of his seniors, requires them to admire the behaviour of men who are not Sikhs, but 'idolaters' of a different race. The action which he reports is one not of martial valour, but of supreme self-discipline in the observance of a ritual, and it takes place on an international stage, a performance witnessed by hundreds of thousands of people of every race and creed. In the evocation of the bowed figures forced to witness the endless, maddening procession of feet around the coffin of the dead King, Kipling creates one of the most haunting images of psychological stress in literature. Documentary realism and the narrator's even, sober tone unfold a Gothic and urban horror, a nightmare of alienating, multitudinous repetition. The values of courage, caste loyalty, and ruthless determination, exemplified by Rutton Singh and Attar Singh, are also present in the behaviour of the four Gurkhas, who share the Sikhs' unbending meticulousness (the Sikhs' scrupulous accounting for the 'borrowed' cartridges; the Gurkhas' refusal to loosen their high, painfully stiff collars, even though they have to bend their heads twice as low in order to give the same impression of grief as the British grenadiers). But though the Chaplain equates the two 'affairs', the story suggests that the Gurkhas' faith measures, and goes beyond, that of the Sikhs. The context of their heroic loyalty is sharpened by the glancing implication that the 'integrity of certain regiments' in the Indian Army is suspect (p. 335), a matter about which the Havildar-Major evidently knows more than he reveals.

The poem which follows the story, 'Jobson's Amen', is one of Kipling's last, and clearest, expressions of distaste for Imperialism as an extension of Little Englandism.

'The Debt' (*Limits and Renewals*, 1932), in which two Muslims in India discuss the dangerous illness of Edward VII's successor, George V, makes an interesting post-War pendant to this story.

325 *water-goglets*: water-bottles, usually earthenware, of globular body with a long neck (from the Portuguese 'gorgoleta', according to *Hobson-Jobson*).

Subadar-Major . . . Havildar-Major: the rank, respectively, of native commandant of a regiment (under the orders of an English colonel), and sergeant-major.

district which takes its name from the great Muhammadan saint Mian Mir: the Mian Mir cantonment outside Lahore (see Appendix B, p. 528).

Jehangir: Mogul Emperor (1569–1627).

Guru Har Gobind, sixth of the great Sikh Gurus: there are nine of these Gurus, the successors of Guru Nanak (1469–*c.*1539), the founder of the Sikh religion.

the Holy Book of the Grunth Sahib: the *Adi Granth*, compiled in 1604 by Guru Arjun, which contains hymns compiled by the first five Gurus.

one hand with an iron bracelet on the wrist: see note on p. 549.

Was there by any chance any woman at the back of it?: the Havildar-Major agrees with Private Learoyd about such matters: see 'On Greenhow Hill', p. 117.

326 *Pishapur, near Thori, in the Banalu Tehsil of Patiala State*: Patiala is about 150 miles east of Lahore. The other names are fictitious.

even the cotton-seed: the cheapest of all seeds; even in famine time a handful was often spared to make very dry cattle-food a little more palatable (*RG*).

cattle-poundings: impoundings of stray cattle (set loose by the brothers' enemies in the family feud).

327 *drill-Naik*: drill-sergeant.

328 *Sri wah guru . . . futteh!*: these Urdu sentences should read: 'Sri Waheguru ji ka khalsa' and 'Sri Waheguru ji ki fateh'. They are both greetings used by one orthodox Sikh to another. 'Sri Waheguru ji' means 'God'; the first sentence means (roughly) 'God's people' ('khalsa' being a name for the Sikh community), and the second 'God's will prevail' ('fateh' = victory) (*RG*).

329 *Amritsar*: the principal Sikh city in the Punjab, containing the Golden Temple (see below).

330 *the King—the Great Queen's son*: Edward VII (see headnote).

Shalimar . . . Shahdera: the Shalamar Bagh pleasure-gardens in Lahore were laid out by the Mogul Emperor Shah Jahan; they were completed *c.*1642. The Shahdara garden was originally the pleasure-garden of Nur Jahan, wife of the Mogul Emperor Jahangir; after his death in 1627 she redesigned Shahdara as his tomb-garden.

the new King: George V.

a certain Temple: St George's Hall, Westminster, also known as Westminster Hall.

the Durbar Sahib at Amritsar . . . the Akal Bunga and the Baba-Atal: the Golden Temple, the holy centre of the Sikh religion, and adjacent buildings.

Wanidza: Windsor.

331 *one koss, two koss*: 'koss' varies as a measure in different parts of India; the sense here is 'several miles'.

the Ravi River: a tributary of the Sutlej River in the Punjab.

my Salt's sake: out of duty (the Havildar-Major has 'eaten the King's salt', that is taken service under him, and has thus accepted an obligation).

lakhs of lakhs, crores of crores: a lakh is 100,000, a crore 100 lakhs, but the phrase is clearly not intended to be exact: 'hundreds of thousands' is the sense.

Goorkahs: the Gurkhas had dominated Nepal since 1769; after the treaty of 1816 which ended conflict with Britain, regiments of Gurkha soldiers were recruited, becoming renowned for their courage and loyalty (see 'The Drums of the Fore and Aft', *Wee Willie Winkie*, 1888). The religion of Nepal, though it has strong Buddhist elements, is predominantly Hindu, hence the Chaplain's stigma of 'idolaters'.

in the Tirah: on the North-West Frontier, south of the Khyber Pass.

332 *a certain Colonel Forsyth Sahib*: Kipling forgets that the Havildar-Major has already mentioned him as the officer with whom the Colonel was transacting his business.

Granadeers: the Grenadier Guards.

333 *seeing that they were—*: the Havildar-Major stops himself from saying 'old'.

334 *half a maund*: 'maund' is a weight of varying value in different parts of India; again, the sense is probably hyperbolic, not literal—'half a hundredweight'.

335 *eighteen medals with eleven clasps and three Orders*: the decorations on the corpse of the dead monarch.

Jobson's Amen

336 *Title.* No original for 'Jobson' has been found; Nora Crook (*Kipling Journal*, 69 (Dec. 1995), 53–4) is almost certainly right to assume that 'the name is generic and representative, like Plugson in Carlyle's *Past and Present*'. She suggests that Kipling took the name either from the Anglo-Indian term 'Hobson-Jobson' (also the title of the dictionary), or that it is a pun on 'Job's son', i.e. someone who suffers from the ignorant opinions of others.

l. 18. *bow to wood and stone*: such idols are denounced in several places in the Bible, e.g. Deuteronomy 4: 28, Isaiah 37: 19, and Ezekiel 20: 32. The juxtaposition in the poem of religious bigotry and luxuriant pagan landscapes may glance at Bishop Reginald Heber's celebrated hymn, 'From Greenland's Icy Mountains': 'What though the spicy breezes | Blow soft o'er Ceylon's isle; | Though every prospect pleases, | And only man is vile: | In vain with lavish kindness | The gifts of God are strown; | The heathen in his blindness | Bows down to wood and stone.' As against this, note that the last two lines form the opening line of 'The 'Eathen' (*Barrack-Room Ballads*, 1892), where they refer not to pagan pleasures but to military indiscipline: 'The 'eathen in his blindness bows down to wood an' stone; | 'E don't obey no orders unless they is 'is own; | 'E keeps 'is side-arms awful: 'e leaves 'em all about, | An' then comes up the Regiment an' pokes the 'eathen out.'

337 l. 29. *Himalaya*: pronounced 'Himàlya' (so spelled in the Burwash edition, the American equivalent of the Sussex edition).

l. 30. *bedding on the last world's past*: the Himalayas are 'young' mountains, resting on older strata.

Mary Postgate

First pub. *Pall Mall Magazine* and *Century Magazine*, Sept. 1915 (without the accompanying poem); coll. *A Diversity of Creatures*, 1917, when the date '1915' was affixed to the title.

'Mary Postgate' takes pride of place among Kipling's numerous stories of hatred and revenge. Its fearful uncompromising savagery continues to shock readers and critics, many of whom assume with repugnance that Kipling shares Mary's unhallowed sexual relish for the German pilot's death-agony. There are grounds for this belief (though not for the blind certainty with which it has been stated), but there is more to the story than the release of repressed emotion in the form of lurid violence. Boris Ford, one of Kipling's most indignant and scornful critics, impatiently summing up the evidence of the plot so that he can get on to the verdict and sentence, describes the burning of Wynn's belongings as 'one of Kipling's interminable and tasteless inventories' ('A Case for Kipling?' in E. L. Gilbert (ed.), *Kipling and the Critics* (New York, 1965), 71). It is a crass remark (and an unwise one, in an essay devoted to Kipling's crassness) but it is also revealing because it discards without thinking just what the story passionately incorporates into its design. A whole Edwardian world is incinerated in the 'destructor', and behind lies another lost world, the late Victorian world of Mary Postgate's bleak, withering growth to unloved and unlovable maturity. The denuded pathos with which Kipling evokes the familial deathbeds by which Mary has watched (her nurturing has always been that of a Fate, the Spinster who severs the thread of life) is the exact counterpart of the ferocity which he identifies in her nature and of which he demands that we partake. In the same way, the scandal of Mary's cruelty to the fallen pilot must be measured alongside the poignancy of the gesture she makes to Wynn in his airborne glory. Nor is her life isolated from our own: on the contrary, the currents of history pass through it (its minor wars, its village tribulations), and her psychology is rooted in personal and social dispositions for which we bear collective responsibility.

It should be emphasized that the story was written before the death of Kipling's son. John Kipling would not, in any case, be flattered by the identification with the callow and insensitive Wynn Fowler, whose life and death mean everything to Mary and therefore, necessarily, mean nothing to the author or to us.

339 *gazetted . . . the rank of cook*: the official vocabulary is a small sign of the impact of the War on domestic life (the phrase 'home front' dates from this period).

dowey: 'dull and lonely, melancholy, dreary, dismal' (*OED*, which says it is a Scottish and northern dialect word).

Taubes, Farmans, and Zeppelins: the Taube was a German monoplane; the Farman a French biplane; the Zeppelin a German airship. Information about military aircraft in the war was available to the public from an early date, in books such as *Aircraft in the German War* (1914), by H. Massac Buist, the 'aeronautical editor' of the *Morning Post*. This book includes chapters on types of aircraft and diagrams on 'The Anatomy of a Biplane'; Buist also reproduces an official handbill illustrating German aircraft in silhouette so that British and French troops would know which ones to fire at. Both the Taube and the Zeppelin feature on this handbill.

rolling . . . a 'taxi': Kipling's terms are not very accurate: by 'rolling' he seems to mean taxi-ing, and by 'a "taxi"' he seems to mean a flight as a passenger. *The Royal Flying Corps in the War* (1918), by 'Wing Adjutant' (the pseudonym of Wilfred Theodore Blake), has a chapter on training which describes the stages Wynn would have gone through. The British system used instructors and a dual-control system in the initial stages (whereas the French, for example, used a system of graduated solo manœuvres). First the trainee would be taken on a flight as passenger to test his nerves in the air; then 'he is allowed to take control of the engine when the machine is on the ground, "taxi" it after it has landed, and then at last take the machine into the air'. Landing is the most difficult stage to get through; after that the trainee graduates from the passenger seat to that of pilot, and 'At last the novice is strapped in alone, told to fly once round the aerodrome and land'. Cross-country flights of increasing distance and complexity follow. Needless to say, Wynn's unscheduled visits to his aunt would not be countenanced, though 'Wing Adjutant' does comment that a trainee will probably 'have trouble with his engine and be forced to land in strange country' in the course of his cross-country flights.

341 *Contrexeville*: a brand of French mineral water.

the tanks: the fuel tanks. An American pilot, writing to his fiancée in 1918, explains the women's anxiety and need to reassure themselves: 'You've no idea, Izzy dear, how quickly a machine will catch fire and how completely. The gasoline does it. . . . That's the one thing everyone fears —fire' (*A Yankee Ace in the RAF: The World War I Letters of Capt. Bogart Rogers*, ed. John H. Morrow, Jr., and Earl Rogers (Lawrence, Kan., 1996), 93).

344 *Hentys, Marryats, Levers, Stevensons, Baroness Orczys, Garvices*: a typical Victorian and Edwardian list of writers of stories for boys (or rather writers whose stories a boy would like, because none of them in fact wrote exclusively for children): G. A. Henty (1832–1902; historical adventure stories such as *Under Drake's Flag* and *Clive in India*); Captain Frederick Marryat (1792–1848; naval adventures such as *Masterman Ready*, and the enduringly popular *Children of the New Forest*); Charles Lever (1806–72; Irish stories such as *Jack Hinton* and *Tom Burke of Ours* in a series called 'Our Mess'); Robert Louis Stevenson (1850–94; *Treasure Island*, *Kidnapped*, etc.); Baroness Emmuska Orczy (1865–1947; *The Scarlet Pimpernel*); Charles Garvice (1833–1920; romantic fiction such as *Nance*, *Her Heart's Desire*, *A Coronet of Shame*, *Love Decides*, etc.).

O.T.C.: Officer Training Corps (at public school).

Brooklands: the circuit near Weybridge in Surrey, used for motor-racing between 1907 and 1939.

348 *Cassée. Tout cassée*: 'Broken. All broken.' Why the German aviator speaks French at first is not clear. Pedantically: the feminine ending of 'cassée' is incorrect.

Che me rends. Le médicin!: 'I surrender. The doctor!'

Ich haben der todt Kinder gesehn: 'I have seen the dead child', in Mary's approximate German. The correct form would be 'Ich habe das todtes Kind gesehen'. The plural 'Kinder' associates the death of Edna Gerritt with that of other children. In the preceding story, 'Swept and Garnished', the ghosts of several children killed in atrocities in Belgium appear to an elderly German lady.

349 *She had never believed . . . husband and children*: the story becomes a grim exemplification of the principle that 'the female of the species is more deadly than the male': see headnote to 'The Female of the Species' (p. 506), where the principle is linked to Kipling's opposition to the 'advanced views' of feminism and the campaign for women's suffrage.

Sea Constables

First pub. in *Metropolitan Magazine*, Sept. 1915, then *Nash's and Pall Mall Magazine*, Oct. 1915, both without the accompanying poems or subtitle; coll. *Debits and Credits*, 1926.

Germany announced a naval blockade of Britain in February 1915, enforced mainly by U-boats and the laying of mines. Since America had not entered the War, it was open to American 'neutrals' to trade with either side, if they could do so without being intercepted, and the 'neutral' in this story (clearly an American though never named as such) is trying to deliver fuel oil to German vessels, probably submarines. (As *RG* points out, this is an unlikely scenario, 'but rumours of that sort of goings on were common early in the war and Kipling may easily have got the idea of this story from some circumstantial yarn'.) Kipling's scorn for America's neutrality, and then for its late entry into the War, is the subject of several poems, e.g. 'The Question' (1916) and 'The Holy War' (1917); it figures also in his correspondence with Theodore Roosevelt, who shared Kipling's contempt for President Wilson but had a more realistic sense of the political obstacles in the way of American participation in the War. Kipling's attitude towards 'Uncle Newt' in this story differs markedly from his indulgent treatment of Laughton A. Zigler, the American military inventor who fights against the British in the Boer War: see 'The Captive' (*Traffics and Discoveries*, 1904), and also 'The Edge of the Evening' (*A Diversity of Creatures*, 1917, but written 1913) in which Zigler is completely rehabilitated and sides with his British aristocratic hosts in foiling the activity of two (probably German) spies.

The four men who between them tell the story of how they prevented 'Uncle Newt' from making his delivery comprise one member of the Royal Navy (i.e. the regular service) and three members of the Royal Naval Volunteer Reserve, whose own private boats have been commissioned for coastal patrolling and other auxiliary duties. It is on these three 'changelings', as the prefatory poem puts it, translated from their comfortable commercial lives, that the story concentrates. They are not particularly nice people to begin with—they have 'coarse-grained complexions as of men who habitually did themselves well', one of them is not averse to a bit of insider trading, the youngest has the look of a fatuous man-about-town—but the War has precipitated their natures into a heroic and implacable single-mindedness.

Kipling portrays their dedication, their intense professional pride as sailors, their quarrelsome camaraderie, and their conscious abandonment of 'civilian' feeling. With sardonic, and in the end savage, courtesy, they 'escort' the neutral to his death. Maddingham, who finishes the job, remains 'perfectly polite', his dispassionate adherence to regulation masking a ferocity which Kipling identifies as the necessary spirit of this war, if not of war itself.

The Changelings

351 *Or ever . . . clerk*: recalling W. E. Henley's poem 'Or ever the knightly years were gone' (*Echoes*, no. xxxvii, pub. in *A Book of Verses*, 1888), which opens: 'Or ever the knightly years were gone | With the old world to the grave, | I was a King in Babylon | And you were a Christian Slave'. Kipling had used this verse as the epigraph of 'The Finest Story in the World' (Many Inventions, 1893); for his relations with Henley, see note on p. 640). The application of the original poem—or its first two lines—to the story here is that the German policy of total war, including the sinking of civilian ships, means the end of any concept of 'chivalry' in war.

pied: camouflaged.

And the swinging mounds . . . Heaven-high: a glancing allusion to the famous passage in Ps. 108: 23–30, all of which is relevant to the tale, though not all in the same way: 'They that go down to the sea in ships, that do business in great waters; these see the works of the Lord, and his wonders in the deep. For he commandeth, and raiseth the stormy wind, which lifteth up the waves thereof. They mount up to the heaven, they go down again to the depths: their soul is melted because of trouble. They reel to and fro, and stagger like a drunken man, and are at their wit's end. Then they cry unto the Lord in their trouble, and he bringeth them out of their distresses. He maketh the storm a calm, so that the waves thereof are still. Then are they glad because they be quiet; so he bringeth them unto their desired haven.'

Sea Constables

352 *the Carvoitz*: probably, as *RG* suggests, an amalgam of the names of three famous luxury hotels, the Carlton, the Savoy, and the Ritz. The Carlton was destroyed by bombing in the Second World War.

mixed doubles: couples engaged in affairs, who would not wish to be seen in the main dining-room.

the conventional pre-war 'nut': a dandy or fop, a showy or affected young man-about-town. OED's first citation is from 1904.

353 *What's the matter . . . joining the British Army*: it was customary for officers on leave not to wear uniform. The artiste's ignorant comment typifies Kipling's contempt for outsiders.

Sons of the Empire . . . Sidney Latter: fictitious names; Kipling's disparagement of the contribution of music-hall singers to the war effort is the subject of the poem 'A Recantation' (*The Years Between*, 1919). The 'Palemseum', like the 'Carvoitz', is an amalgam, this time of names of music halls: the Palladium, the Empire, and the Coliseum.

Cheer up. . . . 'Soon be dead! from a contemporary comic song with the refrain 'Cheer up, cully, you'll soon be dead! | It's a short life and a gay one!' (*RG*).

a plain sub: sub-lieutenant.

Vesiga soup: vesiga is the spinal cord of the sturgeon, 'usually found commercially in the shape of a dried gelatinous ribbon' (Escoffier's *Complete Guide to the Art of Modern Cookery*, 1921). Escoffier gives guidance as to the soaking and preparation of this grisly ingredient but I have not found a recipe for the soup.

Pol Roger '04: a well-known vintage Champagne. On the subject of Champagne, see M. Voiron's comment in 'The Bull that Thought', p. 368.

Bethisy-sur-Oise: a village north-east of Paris which featured in the Battle of Guise in August 1914, in which the French Fifth Army was engaged. Henri's nephew reassures the men that he is not either a foreigner or a coward, but has been honourably wounded, disabled, and discharged.

sole à la Colbert: fillets of sole dipped in egg and breadcrumbs before frying, and served with a flavoured butter.

354 *he read loudly*: he is naturally loud, but I think he is doing it deliberately to annoy the artiste.

Richebourg . . . Croûtes Baron: Richebourg is a famous Burgundy *appellation*; Pêches Melba the dessert invented by Escoffier for the singer, Dame Nellie Melba, in 1892; I have not identified Croûtes Baron, presumably a savoury in a pastry case.

brass-bound: Maddingham's meaning is clear: the senior officers at the Admiralty are hidebound by rigid adherence to official regulations. The epithet 'brass-bound' applied to naval officers generally (from their brass badges of rank); for another sense, see note on p. 597.

conveyancing: as *RG* points out, Winchmore deliberately misapplies a term from Maddingham's civilian (and business) life as an equivalent of 'convoying'; but the choice is also a shrewd one, because conveyancing means the transfer of property, a central feature of the plot.

355 *a new type of engine—a Diesel*: Diesel (heavy oil) engines had been invented in the 1890s and their use in surface ships was still not widespread. However, they were used generally in submarines—the first

clue as to the neutral's intentions. The distinctive smell of the oil alerts Winchmore and makes him suspicious.

355 *a lady in the Promenade*: the Promenade of the Empire Music Hall in Leicester Square was a well-known haunt of prostitutes.

Gilarra Head: this, and most other locations in the story, are fictitious. *RG* suggests a wartime precaution on Kipling's part, though it is hard to see how any of the details could have been useful to the enemy. The general course of the neutral is from Scotland along the east coast of England, down the Channel, along the south coast and into the Irish Sea, ending at a small port in southern Ireland (still at this period under British rule).

a fishing-party: mine-sweeping; see the poem 'Mine Sweepers', p. 517.

subs from the garrison: subalterns, junior officers.

356 *snotty*: midshipman; see note on p. 604.

when I feel that way: seasick.

a beamy bus: i.e. a vessel with a broad beam, which should therefore be less liable to roll.

like me and Nelson: Nelson suffered from sea-sickness. Jarrott is 'busy' being ill.

specially off Scarborough: Scarborough is a town on the Yorkshire coast, whither Winchmore has followed the neutral, and he facetiously connects his sighting of Jarrott with the fact that Yorkshire is a Quaker heartland. The real reason is that this part of the North Sea was heavily mined, so the Quakers engaged in minesweeping were risking their lives in some of the most dangerous waters of that time.

all go to Heaven . . . Roll! fragments of popular gospel hymns and Negro spirituals.

357 *Cowes week*: the Royal Yacht Club's annual regatta, held in August at Cowes, in the Isle of Wight.

358 *There was a young bride*: the complete limerick is found in Kipling's manuscript of the story, and runs as follows: 'There was a young bride of Antigua, | Who said to her spouse "What a pig you are!" | He replied "Oh my Queen | Is it manners you mean | Or do you refer to my figuar?"'

359 *Carlsbad*: a fashionable spa in Bohemia, whose mineral water was particularly recommended for liver complaints.

360 *blacked myself all over*: like the actor who is supposed to have done this in order to completely identify with the role of Othello (*RG*).

361 *slip*: slipway, ramp for launching or hauling up boats.

He stood nor-west at once: the wrong way for Antigua; presumably the neutral was trying to head back to Scottish waters.

362 *he believed the English were the Lost Tribes*: the ten tribes of Israel which were carried into captivity in Babylon, *c.*720 BC; various nations laid claim to them. See 'The Man who would be King' (p. 78)

the Beast with Horns in Revelations: he appears in ch. 13, and has 'seven heads and ten horns, and upon his horns ten crowns, and upon his heads the name of blasphemy' (v. 1).

363 *sprudel*: one of the Carlsbad mineral springs; the sense is 'a dose of salts' (RG).

both quick-firers and the maxims: see notes on p. 602.

The Vineyard

366 l. 1. *At the eleventh hour he came*: alluding to the parable of the labourers in the vineyard, Matt. 10: 1–16. The owner hires some men in the early morning and others as the day goes on, finally taking on some at 'the eleventh hour', and pays them all the same wage, to the disgruntlement of those who started earliest, and who complain that they have had to endure 'the burden and heat of the day'. The owner rebukes them, pointing out that they have been paid according to their contract, and that he can do what he likes with his own money. The parable illustrates the absolute and unconditional nature of salvation: the kingdom of heaven is open to all, on the same terms, however late they repent. Theologically this is an impeccable position, but as soon as you apply the parable back to earthly matters—as Kipling does here with regard to the late entry of America into the War—the owner's case looks a lot shakier.

l. 4. *the wine-press of the Wrath of God*: this phrase comes not from the parable in Matthew, where the labourers' work is not specified, but from Revelation 19. There is a further twist to the allusion, however, because in Revelation the treading of the winepress is not represented as hard labour, but functions as a figure for the power of God himself: 'And the armies which were in heaven followed him [the Word of God] upon white horses . . . And out of his mouth goeth a sharp sword, that with it he should smite the nations: and he shall rule them with a rod of iron: and he treadeth the winepress of the fierceness and wrath of Almighty God' (vv. 14–15).

The Bull that Thought

First pub. 15 Nov. 1924 in *MacLeans Magazine* and in the December issue of *Cosmopolitan Magazine*, without the accompanying poem; coll. *Debits and Credits*, 1926.

Kipling's love of France, and his delight in transposing French idioms into

English, give this story a glow of good humour which disguises its daemonic face. The figure of Apis—the artist who is god, demon, and sacrifice—is drawn from the narrator's encounter with the worldly-wise, jovial bourgeois, M. Voiron, whose miraculous wine transforms the spectacle of cunning and cruelty, staged in the mind's amphitheatre, into a vision of rapture and comic resolution.

The story moves with unostentatious subtlety from the world of the modern machine to that of the primitive beast, yet the War has brought these worlds into juxtaposition and its presence broods in the shadows of the tale, kept in mind by a constant flicker of allusion ('he knew his ranges as well as our gunners', says M. Voiron of Apis's kicks; his manœuvres in the bullring are likened to those of an army, and M. Voiron calls him 'this Foch among bulls!'). The homicidal violence of the bullfight may be mediated by M. Voiron's sophisticated conceit of the bull's artistic nature (it is this which sharply distinguishes Kipling's treatment from that of Hemingway) but this conceit itself is licensed by the narrator's 'spacious' concession that 'After the War . . . everything is credible'. It is no accident that this story is followed in *Debits and Credits* by 'A Madonna of the Trenches', a supernatural tale whose credibility is also enforced by the extreme conditions and pressures of the War. 'The Miracle of Saint Jubanus' (*Limits and Renewals*, 1932) is another story set in France and concerned with the same question of what human accommodations are possible in the aftermath of unthinkable suffering.

367 *Westward . . . runs a road*: the N113 between the towns of Salon-de-Provence and Arles. For Kipling's passion for motoring, see the headnote to 'They' (p. 605). He had been on frequent motoring tours of France, including the region of the Camargue in which this story is set.

Mr Leggatt: the narrator's driver and mechanic, who figures in several other tales: 'Steam Tactics' and 'The Horse Marines' ('Traffics and Discoveries', 1904), 'The Dog Hervey' (*A Diversity of Creatures*, 1917), and the uncollected story 'A Tour of Inspection' (written 1904, pub. Sussex edn.).

Blue de Luxe: a luxury express running between London and Paris.

Annam and Tonquin: territories in south-east Asia (now mostly modern Vietnam), which became French protectorates in 1883.

Chinese woodcutters: recruited as an auxiliary force; they are referred to in another story in *Debits and Credits*, 'A Friend of the Family'.

assist as an observer: the verb 'assister' in French means not to help but to be present; from here, the language of the story is flavoured with Gallic turns of phrase and idioms. Kipling had used this technique in 'The Bonds of Discipline' (p. 234) to satirize the Gallic flamboyance and gullibility of the French spy 'M. de C.' at a time when France was potentially an enemy rather than an ally of Britain.

368 *a certain figure*: 90 kilometres, as we learn later (p. 369).

tisanes: a 'tisane de champagne' is a light Champagne, but the word also means a herbal infusion. Presumably even the 'Pol Roger '04' which Maddingham and his friends drink in 'Sea Constables' (p. 353) comes under this definition.

369 *sportif*: 'sports-loving' (the 'sport' being motor-racing, and also betting); the term can also mean 'sportsmanlike', by which M. Voiron alludes wryly to Leggatt's having got the better of him by disguising the true quality of the car.

When I was a child in my father's house: 'when I was a child' recalls 2 Cor. 13: 11 ('When I was a child, I spake as a child, I understood as a child, I thought as a child'); 'my father's house' occurs many times in both Old and New Testaments. See also note on p. 561.

We of the old rock: belonging to the original race, and clinging to ancient traditions; a phrase with biblical associations, e.g. Isa. 42: 11, 'inhabitants of the rock' and 51: 1, 'the rock whence ye are hewn'.

370 *Carpentier*: Georges Carpentier (1894–1975), heavyweight champion of France and Europe, defeated in a world title fight by Jack Dempsey in 1921.

371 *Apis*: the Greek form of Hapi, the sacred bull of Egyptian mythology. Hapi was believed to be a reincarnation of the god Ptah, who was the patron of artisans and artists and the inventor of the arts. A black bull with certain sacred markings was worshipped at Memphis: 'Every day at a fixed hour he was let loose in the courtyard attached to his temple, and the spectacle of his frolics attracted crowds of the devout' (*Larousse Encyclopedia of Mythology*).

Arles: a town famous for its Roman remains, including a near-perfect amphitheatre, used among other things for bull-fights; as M. Voiron explains, these are exhibitions of skill which do not end with the death of the bull.

like an Apache: not the Native American, but the French slang term for a street criminal, esp. in Paris.

372 *farceur*: joker, prankster.

Provincia with bread and circuses: Gallia Narbonensis, the territory of south-eastern France which formed the original Roman province of Gaul, centred on the town of Narbonne. The phrase 'bread and circuses' comes from Juvenal (*Satires* 10. 78).

before the Republic: the Third Republic, established in 1871 after defeat in the Franco-Prussian War and the collapse of the Second Empire under Napoleon III. The Third Republic came to a similar end in 1940.

373 *Soult . . . Beresford*: Nicolas-Jean de Dieu Soult (1769–1851), one of Napoleon's Marshals, led the French armies in the Peninsular War;

General William Beresford (1768–1854) defeated him at the battle of Albuera (1811).

373 *levitical*: from the Old Testament book of Leviticus, which contains many injunctions about sacrifice and ritual purification.

Minotaur: in Greek myth, the monster, half-man and half-bull, who inhabited the Cretan Labyrinth and devoured human sacrifices.

between Berre and the Saintes Maries: Berre is north-west of Marseille, on the shores of the lagoon called L'Étang de Berre, and at the easternmost edge of the Camargue; 'les Saintes-Maries-de-la-Mer' is about 38 miles to the west on the Golfe de Beauduc, famous for its anuual Gipsy pilgrimage.

374 *the Comédie Française*: the French national theatre, based at the Théâtre Français in the rue de Richelieu in Paris.

375 *Seventy-fives*: the 75 mm gun, one of the standard pieces of the French Artillery.

Foch: Ferdinand Foch (1851–1929), Marshal of France who commanded the French army at the Somme in 1916, and was General-in-Chief of the Allied armies in the last year of the War; his strategy was based on constant attack and he incarnated a spirit of ruthless national determination which Kipling admired; he would also have supported Foch's opposition to the terms of the post-War settlement.

377 *Cyrano*: Cyrano de Bergerac (1619–55), French playwright and satirist; M. Voiron is almost certainly referring not to the original but to the protagonist of Edmond de Rostand's play (1897), which immortalized Cyrano's wit, swordsmanship, and *panache*.

Molière: French playwright and actor, born Jean-Baptiste Poquelin, 1622–73; he is cited because he wrote comedy, which by definition (however ironic) ends happily.

caballeros: gentlemen.

378 *the elder Dumas*: Alexandre Dumas (1802–70), the dramatist and, most famously, novelist (*The Count of Monte-Cristo*, *The Three Musketeers*); 'elder' to distinguish him from his son (1824–95), also a writer; in French they are Dumas *père* and Dumas *fils*.

confrère: colleague.

379 *toril*: bull-pen.

have you ever heard of one that returned: 'at San Lucat in Andalusia, a bull named Lechuzo was raised to be a fighter. On his first appearance he cleared the ring so quickly that the spectators demanded his freedom. His owners, however, repeated his appearances, and each time he repeated his success. One day he lost interest, sat down in the ring, then rose, jumped a wall and began to graze in the public square. Upon this, a wealthy Andalusian, Snr Juan Silva, bought him and took him home where he lived at ease for 8 years' (*RG*). The fact that the 'fifth bull' at the end of the story is said to be 'an unthinking Andalusian' may be Kipling's way of tipping his hat to the source of his story.

children of the same Mother: Lisa Lewis (ed., *Mrs Bathurst and Other Stories* (1991), 176) glosses this as the Camargue, but I think that Kipling (or M. Voiron) intends the Earth-Goddess or Great Mother, the source of life and death; the ground of this story is as pagan as that of the following story, 'The Gardener', is Christian.

Alnaschar and the Oxen

Title: Alnaschar is the proverbial daydreamer from the *Arabian Nights* (the Tale of the Barber's Fifth Brother).

l. 10. *Lobengula*: last king of the Ndebele or Matabele people (of what is now Zimbabwe); he died in 1894, after being defeated in a war against white settlers, and Matabeleland was incorporated into Southern Rhodesia. Tribal wealth and status in southern Africa were measured in cattle.

l. 13. *Bulawayo*: the capital of Matabeleland; Kipling visited it in 1898.

380 l. 24. *those eyes of Juno*: Juno, wife of Jupiter, king of the gods in classical myth; Homer's epithet for her Greek namesake, Hera, is 'ox-eyed', so Kipling is returning the compliment.

l. 27. *Bull of Mithras*: Mithras was a Persian deity, whose cult, based on sun-worship, involved the ritual sacrifice of a sacred bull. The soldierly ethos of Mithraism made it popular among the Roman legions: Parnesius, the hero of three of the stories in *Puck of Pook's Hill* (1906), is a devotee of Mithras, and speaks of the 'Bull Killing' in 'On the Great Wall', which ends with 'A Song to Mithras'. Valens, the hero of 'The Church that was at Antioch' (*Limits and Renewals*, 1932), is another Roman follower of Mithraism, which in that story is compared to Christianity.

The Gardener

First pub. April 1926 in *McCall's Magazine* and in the May issue of the *Strand Magazine*, in both cases without the accompanying poem; coll. *Debits and Credits*, 1926.

The biblical episode which gives the story its title occurs in John 20: 14–15: see the final note on p. 639. Kipling became a member of the Imperial War Graves Commission in September 1917 at the invitation of Sir Fabian Ware, the former editor of the *Morning Post* who was the leading figure in the progressively greater and more complex task of identifying, burying, and commemorating the hundreds of thousands of war dead. Kipling's arduous and devoted labour on behalf of the Commission, which included devising many of the standard inscriptions in the cemeteries and cathedrals, was driven by his unassuaged grief at not recovering the body of his own son. His profound tender sympathy for Helen Turrell's plight is—not qualified, but accented, we might say—by his unembittered envy of 'a world full of exultant or broken relatives, now strong in the certainty that there was an altar upon earth where they might lay their love'. On this subject see also the poem 'A Nativity' (*The Years Between*, 1919).

Lisa Lewis ('Some Echoes of Austen', *English Literature in Transition*, 29 (1986), 80) acutely remarks the influence of Jane Austen which comes close to pastiche in the opening paragraph of the story (and note that 'The Janeites' belongs to the same volume). *Emma*, in particular, comes to mind in the way the clues to Helen's deception are sown: her trip to the south of France, the story she tells of her dismissal of the nurse, her reasoned insistence on cutting off any ties with the child's mother's family, all form a pattern which many readers, in my experience, do not recognize until the very last, just as Emma fails to spot the liaison between Frank Churchill and Jane Fairfax. It is true that the punishment for deception is grimmer, and more equivocal, than in any of Austen's stories. What complicates the moral equation is the War, since the punishment which Helen undergoes for her lie cannot justifiably include her son's death; yet the manner of that death mimics with appalling symmetry the way in which Helen had covered up the truth about his birth: 'The next shell uprooted and laid down over the body what had been the foundation of a barn wall, so neatly that none but an expert would have guessed that anything unpleasant had happened.' Again, Helen compares the way in which she is 'manufactured into a bereaved next of kin' with the manufacture of a shell 'from blank-iron to the all but finished article', for by a satire of circumstance worthy of Hardy, Michael had taken her on a tour of a munition factory shortly before his death. 'It struck her at the time that the wretched thing was never left alone for a second,' the narrator remarks (it is typical of Kipling not to miss the trick of using the idiom *It struck her* in this context). Only the 'infinite compassion' of the figure at the story's end (whether divine or human) can undo the web of irony in which Helen is caught.

381 *Epigraph.* From 'The Burden', printed complete at the end of the story.

rolled the stone away: as the angel did at the tomb of Jesus (Matt. 28: 2).

383 *who threw themselves into the Line*: that is, enlisted as privates rather than, as befitted their social class, applied for commissions.

O.T.C.: see note on p. 628.

the old Army red: instead of khaki, first introduced in India in the 1870s and which had become the standard uniform for active service; half of Michael's batallion has been equipped with parade-ground uniforms.

K.: evidently Field-Marshal Lord Kitchener, Secretary of State for War; but the initial is also the author's.

384 *the wastage of Loos*: the 'wastage' included the death of John Kipling on 27 Sept. 1915.

Missing always means dead: when John Kipling was reported missing in September 1915, Kipling wrote to Brigadier L. C. Dunsterville (the original of 'Stalky'): 'The wife is standing it wonderfully tho' she, of course, clings to the bare hope of his being a prisoner. I've seen what shells can do, and I don't' (Carrington, 509). See also the headnote to 'My Boy Jack', p. 681.

385 *Hagenzeele Third Military Cemetery*: the name is fictitious, but the details are based on Kipling's observations in the course of his frequent visits on behalf of the Imperial War Graves Commission. He wrote the official booklet of the Commission, *The Graves of the Fallen*, in 1919.

386 *A.S.C.*: the Army Service Corps.

a large Lancashire woman . . . coming of respectable folk: this detail takes us all the way back to Learoyd's bitter remarks about the prejudice against enlistment in 'On Greenhow Hill' (p. 123).

Dickiebush: Dikkebus, a village to the south of Ypres.

389 *supposing him to be the gardener*: from John 20: 14–15; Jesus appears to Mary Magdalene, who is weeping by the empty tomb: 'she turned herself back, and saw Jesus standing, and knew not that it was Jesus. Jesus saith unto her, Woman, why weepest thou? whom seekest thou? She, supposing him to be the gardener, saith unto him, Sir, if thou have borne him hence, tell me where thou hast laid him, and I will take him away.' Jesus then reveals his identity explicitly to Mary, and commands her to tell the disciples about his resurrection and imminent ascension; in Kipling's story there is no such revelation, unless it be to the reader, and even then the suggestion that it is Jesus himself who leads Helen to her son's grave remains no more than that—a suggestion. In any case the man's 'infinite compassion' enables him to guess Helen's secret and respond to it with a tenderness which absolves and heals her.

Dayspring Mishandled

First pub. March 1928 in *McCall's Magazine*, without the epigraph, which first appeared when the story was published in the July issue of *Strand Magazine*; coll. *Limits and Renewals*, 1932. 'Gertrude's Prayer' was published with the story from the beginning, since it has a more necessary connection with the story than is the case with most accompanying poems.

The story presents in multiple forms the diseased personal and social relations which Kipling saw as characterizing the post-War years, yet the causes reach back to what the narrator calls 'the days beyond compare and before the Judgments'. The world of literary London in the 1890s, when the characters in the story were young, is evoked with loving precision (though the names of places and publications are all invented); but it is no Eden, or rather is all too truly Eden—a place of temptation, jealousy, and loss. Nevertheless the War precipitates the natures of both Manallace and Castorley (especially the former) into extremes which are close to madness.

Like Grace Ashcroft in 'The Wish House' (*Debits and Credits*, 1926), Manallace devotes his life—sacrifices himself—for the sake of someone who does not love him in return. But the nature of this sacrifice is different because it involves not the taking of pain upon oneself, but its infliction on another person. That Manallace's self-forgetting love should ultimately express itself as self-blinding hatred is only one of the story's multiple ironies. Another concerns the figure of his deserving victim, Castorley, who starts out with all the opposite qualities to those of Manallace. He is fundamentally mean-spirited, and we are meant to find him odious, but Manallace makes the mistake of assuming that his odiousness means he is not human. On the contrary: he discovers in Castorley a capacity to suffer which equals his own. In the end it is Castorley's wife, against whom Manallace is powerless, who embodies unmitigated evil, and it is her ignoble triumph with which the story closes.

Manallace's soothing behaviour towards Castorley at the end recalls that of Reggie Burke towards the dying accountant Silas Riley in 'A Bank Fraud' (*Plain Tales from the Hills*, 1888), a story which also involves forgery. Kipling himself tested the technique he describes of forging a medieval manuscript, though he did not attempt to pass it off on the experts.

Though 'Dayspring Mishandled' is the opening story of *Limits and Renewals*, its unrelieved bleakness is not the keynote of the volume, which is dominated rather by tales of healing, however partial such healing might be (see the story which follows in this edition, 'Fairy-Kist').

391 *Epigraph.* Charles Nodier (1780–1844) was a novelist and miscellaneous writer, and one of the leading figures of the Romantic movement in France. The lines mean: 'It is I, it is I, it is I! I am the Mandragora! The girl (or, daughter) of fine days who wakes at dawn and who sings for you!' The lines are a fragment recited by a madman in Nodier's fable, *La Fée aux Miettes*, and the mandragora symbolizes poetical delusion (see J. M. S. Tompkins on the significance of Kipling's appropriation of the symbol, *The Art of Rudyard Kipling*, 151–2).

Graydon: a fictional character, but with some resemblance to W. E. Henley (1849–1903), the poet and editor who published the first series of *Barrack-Room Ballads* in the *Scots Observer* in 1890, and who fostered the careers of many young writers of Kipling's generation. Kipling's association with Henley's circle forms part of the background to 'Brugglesmith' (see headnote, p. 568). Around August 1891 Kipling wrote to Henley: 'Touching the influences of men upon each other we two especially are bound up in the queerest chain of give and take and one that I feel sure will last long. At the worst, my very dear man, you can only call me a "bugger" for developing along strange lines, and I shall but love you the more for it' (*Letters*, ii. 40).

the young ravens: Noah sends out a raven from the ark to see if the waters have abated (Gen. 8: 7), but the nourishment of the 'young ravens' suggests rather Job 38: 41: 'Who provideth for the raven his food? when his young ones cry unto God, they wander for lack of meat.'

392 *Neminaka's Café in Hestern Square*: evidently in Soho, but the names are fictitious; Henley used to give bachelor dinner parties at Sherry's in Regent Street, and the atmosphere of these occasions may be evoked here.

393 *the Cinema-caption school*: fiction as basic as the captions in the silent cinema. *RG* suggests that the reference is actually to comics, but I think it more likely that Kipling meant something like 'stories which are no better than comics'.

the jocundly-sentimental Wardour Street brand of adventure: another comparison drawn from cinema, since Wardour Street in Soho housed many film production companies and agents. For Kipling's involvement with the film industry, see Philip French, 'Kipling and the Movies', in J. Gross (ed.), *Rudyard Kipling* (1972).

394 *departmental dishwashers*: lowly clerks.

from Upsala to Seville: i.e. over all of Europe: Uppsala, in Sweden, is one of the northernmost cities of Europe, Seville the southernmost.

gadzooking and vitalstapping: Manallace parodies his own fustian style of historical yarn, full of archaic expletives such as 'gadzooks' and 'stap my vitals'.

395 *Vulgate*: the Latin translation of the Bible by St Jerome, completed in 405, still the official scriptural text of the Roman Catholic Church; its name derives from its having attained the status of 'versio vulgata', the common or standard version.

shells of gold and silver paint: shells were still frequently used as containers for colours at this date.

Alva and the Dutch: the Duke of Alva (1507–82), Regent of Flanders during the Dutch revolt against Spanish rule in the reign of Philip II; he instituted the notorious Council of Blood to try rebels and heretics. A love-story set in this period would contain plenty of gadzooking and vitalstapping.

Sunnapia Collection: a fictitious name; Kipling has in mind the great American collectors of his time such as John D. Rockefeller or J. Pierpont Morgan.

our Dan: from the epithet 'Dan (= Master) Chaucer', applied to him first by Spenser in Book IV of *The Faerie Queene*: 'Dan Chaucer, well of English undefiled' (canto II, stanza xxxii).

396 *Persone's*: Parson's; the earliest spelling rec. in *OED*.

Abraham Mentzius: again, a fictitious figure from an authentic background: some Dutch scribes did work on medieval English manuscripts.

oe: this word is not found in Chaucer and appears not to be authentic; it means something like 'one' or 'own'.

Dredd, the big dealer: an invented figure.

399 *Kentucky Kate*: the 'negress in yellow satin' (p. 392).

you had been faithful, Cynara, in your fashion: the refrain of Ernest Dowson's poem 'Non Sum Qualis Eram Bonae Sub Regno Cynarae'; Dowson (1867–1900) epitomizes the spirit of the 1890s and therefore the narrator's, and Manallace's, lost youth. Dowson's title comes from Horace, *Carmina* IV. i. 3–4: 'I am not now as I was in the reign of the good Cynara', and the first stanza of the poem runs: 'Last night, ah, yesternight, betwixt her lips and mine | There fell thy shadow, Cynara! thy breath was shed | Upon my soul between the kisses and the wine; | And I was desolate and sick of an old passion, | Yea, I was desolate and bowed my head: | I have been faithful to thee, Cynara! in my fashion.'

I'd been Chaucer for a week: cf. 'Wireless' (*Traffics and Discoveries*, 1904) in which a young man is 'possessed' by the spirit of Keats.

400 *Illa alma Mater ecca, secum affarens me acceptum. Nicolaus Atrib.*: the Latin is jumbled, but the sense of the words gives something like 'behold that nourishing mother bringing to me by herself something which I accept—Nicolaus the giver'. The 'alma mater' may be the teacher Castorley who purports to nourish the world with his learning, and *RG* therefore suggests that an expanded and explanatory version would run: 'Behold how the wise preceptor prepared this plot against himself and presented it to me, who accepted and used it—Nicolaus the Avenger'. Manallace's name is not Nicholas, but the sense cannot be too clear or Castorley would spot it. In any case the real coded message is contained in the double acrostic which Manallace reveals to the narrator on p. 402.

401 *veray parfit gentil Knight*: the description of the Knight in the Prologue to the *Canterbury Tales* (l. 72).

402 *see what you get*: 'IAMES A MANALLACE FECIT'. The initial 'I' = 'J' in Latin script, and 'A' is Manallace's second name, Andrew. 'Fecit' means 'made this'. The form of words is common in signatures of paintings and other art-objects; its use here emphasizes the fact that the manuscript is a made thing (a forgery).

Gertrude's Prayer

408 l. 7. *To-bruized be that . . . spray*: 'If that spray is bruised'.

l. 8. *rind*: trunk. betide: grow into.

409 l. 17. *oe*: one.

Fairy-Kist

First pub. 15 Sept. 1927 in *MacLean's Magazine*, and in the October issue of *McCall's Magazine*; coll. *Limits and Renewals*, 1932, where the prefatory poem 'The Mother's Son' first appeared.

A small mystery in the story concerns the identities of the four 'Apostles' mentioned on p. 415. Readers who wish not to be given too many clues on their first reading should skip the headnote.

The 'Eclectic *but* Comprehensive Fraternity for the Perpetuation of Gratitude towards Lesser Lights' is in appearance simply a small dining club which meets on the genial pretext of honouring some lesser-known figure in the arts or sciences. But the term 'Fraternity' suggests that the society has strong resemblances to a Masonic Lodge, as does the phrase 'Lesser Lights' (see note below) and the mention of an 'altar' (p. 410). Its founders, including the narrator, appear in other stories ('In the Interests of the Brethren', 'The Janeites', 'A Madonna of the Trenches', 'A Friend of the Family', all *Debits and Credits*, 1926) as members of the fictitious Lodge 'Faith and Works 5837', whose work is bound up with healing the damage and derangement caused by the War. In these stories the Lodge is the setting for the telling of a story, just as the dinner at Lemming's is here.

Kipling pays affectionate tribute to two pre-War literary genres in this story—detective fiction, as exemplified by the Sherlock Holmes stories, and children's fiction, in the form of *Mary's Meadow*, a story by Juliana Horatia Ewing (1841–85). But the affection for Sherlock Holmes is barbed with irony. The chain of reasoning which leads Keede and Lemming to fasten the guilt of Ellen Marsh's 'murder' on Henry Wollin turns out to be completely misconceived. Wollin is certainly mad, and his madness has been caused by the War, but Keede and Lemming are misled by their 'Sherlocking' into assuming that he is a homicidal maniac, whereas in fact he is a tormented sufferer of what would today be called an 'obsessive-compulsive disorder'. In order to unravel Wollin's neurosis, Keede and Lemming must turn not to the great Conan Doyle but to the 'lesser light' of Mrs Ewing, who holds the key not only to the riddle of Wollin's behaviour and state of mind, but to the partial cure which he achieves at the end of the story.

This key is to do with children, and also with gardens. Mary, the heroine and narrator of *Mary's Meadow*, is a young girl of 13, who makes up a game about gardens to amuse her brothers and sisters. The game brings together names and ideas which she finds in two gardening books: from one she gets the notion of planting flowers in wild and waste places; from the other, a 17th-century work called *Solus in Sole, or The Earthly Paradise*, she gets the phrase which resonates in 'Fairy-Kist'. The author, John Parkinson, says of the honeysuckle: 'The Hunisucle that groweth wilde in euery hedge, although it be very sweete, yet doe I not bring it into my garden, but let it rest in his owne place, to serue their senses that trauell by it, or haue no garden'. So Mary's game consists partly in the creation of an Earthly Paradise by planting flowers *for such as have no gardens*, and it is this utopian task which Wollin's voices order him to undertake. Other episodes from the story feature in Wollin's hallucinations (see notes below). The date of Parkinson's book also connects with the identities of the 'four Apostles' whose portraits Keede and Lemming find in Wollin's house, and who turn out to be the 'apostolic succession' of 'the Four Great British Botanists', all dating from the 17th and 18th centuries. For Kipling as a gardener, and for his knowledge of gardening lore, see Gillian Sheehan, 'Kipling and Gardening', *Kipling Journal*, 66 (Dec. 1992), 11–30. Kipling's admiration for Juliana Horatia Ewing was of long date (on this subject see the Introduction, pp. xxvi–xxvii). He refers to Mrs Ewing in his work more frequently than to any other writer of children's books (*RG*).

The outcome of the story is happy for Wollin, whose war-haunted craziness modulates into benign English eccentricity, in which there is also a touch of Russian holy-foolishness; but his fate is balanced against that of poor Ellen Marsh, the victim of a primitive sacrifice to the gods of blind chance, and her lover Jimmy Tigner, who has reached his 'breaking strain' (see below) and is sentenced by Keede to death-in-life: 'He'd been tried too high—too high. I had to sign his certificate a few weeks later. No! He won't get better.' In all Kipling's writing there are no words of bleaker pathos.

The Mother's Son

The poem is spoken by a man in a mental institution, suffering from a breakdown caused by the War. The phrase 'my mother's son' might conceivably refer to the speaker's brother, but the last line makes clear that it is himself; the grammar is a symbol of his self-alienation.

One of Kipling's abiding interests, in the aftermath of the War, was in the consequences of intolerable stress on mind and body: see, in this edition, 'Hymn of Breaking-Strain' (p. 521).

409 l. 15. *They filled the Cup*: see note to 'Gethsamane', p. 678.

Fairy-Kist

410 *The only important society . . . Lesser Lights*: the phrase 'Lesser Lights' has a Masonic meaning: there are three 'Great Lights' in Freemasonry (the Bible, the Square, and the Compasses) and three Lesser Lights, the symbols of the Sun, the Moon, and the Master of the Lodge, placed respectively at the east, south, and west of the Lodge. The use of the phrase here is more of a pun than an allusion: the 'Lesser Lights'

honoured by the dining-club are people whose fame is, or has become, obscured by time. For the members of the club, see headnote.

M.R.C.P.: Member of the Royal College of Physicians.

several red mullets . . . . Chateau la Tour: the emphasis on the excellence of the food recalls the dinner at the plush hotel in 'Sea Constables' (p. 353). In that story the men's florid self-indulgence deflects the attention of ignorant and impertinent outsiders from their real 'fraternity'; here it is part of the comfort and consolation they derive from each other's company in the aftermath of irretrievable losses (both Burges and the narrator, for example, have lost children in the War; Keede's terrible experiences in the Royal Army Medical Corps come up in another story in *Limits and Renewals*, 'The Tender Achilles').

curvet abroad on their hobbies: the use of the technical term of horsemanship, 'curvet', is explained by the fact that 'hobbies' is a shortening of 'hobby-horses'; to ride one's hobby-horse means to sound off on one's favourite subject.

an illustrious English astrologer called Lily: William Lilly (*sic*; 1602–81), author of immensely popular almanacs; his autobiography was published with the *Memoirs* of his patron and fellow-astrologer Elias Ashmole in 1774.

breeze: a quarrel, a row; *OED*'s last citation for this colloquial term is 1865.

periscope: used here fancifully (to follow 'horoscope') in the sense of a survey or 'look around'.

411 *Lodge Faith and Works 5836 E.C.*: the number should be '5837', as it is in the stories of *Debits and Credits* where it features strongly (see headnote).

412 *the Oddfellows' Room*: the Oddfellows originated in the 18th century as a secret benevolent and social society, and subsequently a friendly benefit society; the name apparently derives from their unusual crossing of social or sectarian boundaries. The resemblance to Freemasonry is confirmed by their meeting in 'lodges' with secret ceremonies, etc. Modern 'Oddfellowship' dates from the foundation of the 'Independent Order of Oddfellows, Manchester Unity' in 1813, which became the governing body of the order. In the early years of the century it had a membership of over a million and 'lodges' in many parts of the country, often, as here, meeting in reserved rooms of inns.

a believing soul: meaning that Jimmy had trusted in Ellen despite her notoriety; as Keede goes on to explain, he had found out she was two-timing him shortly before her death.

413 *I was afraid we'd be dragged into it*: the subsequent reference to Lemming's wife suggests that Lemming was afraid that he would be suspected of being one of Ellen's many lovers.

413 *the Huish poisoning case*: a fictitious case, but *RG* plausibly suggests that Kipling took the name from the character who dies while attempting to throw vitriol in R. L. Stevenson's *The Ebb-Tide* (1894).

414 *Salonika fever*: malaria, associated with campaigns in Greece and the Aegean during the War.

415 *Ray . . . Morrison . . . Grew . . . Hales*: their identities are revealed at the end of the story, where they are glossed; all that McKnight reveals here is that they are 'garrdeners'.

old Tom Morrison: the narrator confuses McKnight's Morrison with Tom Morris (1821–1908), who won the Open Championship four times in the 1860s and was green-keeper of St Andrews golf club (*RG*). The 'mistake' may be deliberate on the part of the narrator, and is certainly a joke on the part of Kipling, who took up golf himself in middle age and was well aware that golfers hold their heroes in religious awe.

on the drop: 'about to be hanged'.

418 *Worshipful Sir. Brother Lemming*: terms of Masonic address.

419 *a higher seat in the Synagogue*: alluding to Matt. 23: 6, where Jesus attacks the scribes and the Pharisees who 'love the uppermost rooms at feasts, and the chief seats in the synagogues'.

420 *a picture by an artist called Goya*: Francisco Goya (1746–1828); *RG* suggests that the picture which Lemming mentions is the one in the National Gallery known as *El Hechizado* (the Bewitched). There are other masters of the Gothic and the macabre, but the choice of Goya may have been influenced by his etchings on the horrors of war, *Los Desastres de la Guerra* (1810–14).

daffodils . . . a special loosestrife—a hybrid: daffodils and honeysuckle are mentioned in *Mary's Meadow*; honeysuckle in particular is associated with a key phrase which triggers Wollin's mania (see headnote). No 'special loosestrife' figures in *Mary's Meadow*.

something else besides a G.P., and Will was too: a Freemason.

on the Square, in grave distress: phrases with Masonic associations, especially the former: see note on p. 552.

Gotha: German aeroplane.

a V.A.D.: a nurse belonging to the Voluntary Aid Detachment, an auxiliary of the Territorial Army.

421 *just like the Ancient Mariner*: in Coleridge's poem, 'The Rime of the Ancient Mariner', the mariner is compelled to tell the story of his killing of the albatross over and over again: 'And till my ghastly tale is told, | This heart within me burns' (ll 584–5). The allusion suggests Wollin's feelings of guilt and terror, caused not by a crime he has committed but by the suffering he has endured.

noises . . . like rotten walnuts being smashed: alluding to something the old squire in *Mary's Meadow* does: see below.

a smiling dog: Saxon the bull-terrier in *Mary's Meadow*: see below.

422 *water on the brain*: alluding to Mary's youngest brother in *Mary's Meadow*: see below.

root-gathering: in *Mary's Meadow*, Mary's brother takes on the role of 'Honest Root-Gatherer' in their game; the name derives from John Parkinson's book (see headnote).

in Paradise: alluding to the title of John Parkinson's book (see headnote).

for such as have no gardens: adapting a phrase in *Mary's Meadow*: see headnote.

a big yellow bull-terrier: he is called Saxon and belongs to the squire who owns the meadow in *Mary's Meadow*, and is indeed friendly to the children: 'He looks very savage, but he is only very funny. His lower jaw sticks out, which makes him grin, and some people think he is gnashing his teeth with rage. We think it looks as if he were laughing' (ch. 1). At one point the squire calls him off in a loud voice (ch. 9). When the children invite the squire's Scotch gardener into the library of their house to consult a botanical dictionary, Saxon 'wanted to come in too, but the gardener was very cross with him, and sent him out'; and the gardener says to Mary's brother Arthur: 'It's a rare privilege, the free entry of a book chamber like this' (ch. 3).

a meadow that wasn't theirs: as part of her game of 'Earthly Paradise' (see headnote), Mary plants flowers in the meadow which belongs to the squire and which he eventually gives to her, at the same time settling a dispute with her father over a right of way.

water on the brain: Mary's youngest brother Christopher, whose 'head is rather large for his body, with some water having got into his brain when he was very little, so that we have to take care of him' (ch. 2).

423 *he kept his walnuts . . . smashed 'em all*: a story told by one of the squire's servants to illustrate his stinginess: 'The Old Zquire he mostly eats ne'er a one now's teeth be so bad. But a counts them every night when desart's done. And a keeps 'em till the karnels be mowldy . . . and when the karnels is dust, a cracks aal the lot of 'em when desart's done, zo's no one mayn't have no good of they walnuts, since they be no good to he' (ch. 1).

a lilac sun-bonnet . . . and one was white: part of the Weeding Woman's costume in Mary's game (ch. 5).

a nightingale singing to the Man in the Moon: in Ludwig Bechstein's fairy tale 'The Man in the Moon, and How He Came There' (1854), the man in the moon is a woodcutter who is banished for gathering wood on Sunday; in *Mary's Meadow* the children's mother makes up 'a new fairy tale about the nightingale in Mary's Meadow being the naughty woodcutter's only child, who was turned into a little brown bird that lives in the woods, and sits on a tree on summer nights, and sings to its father up in the moon' (ch. 1).

423 *an old Herbal*: see headnote.

didn't leave a stink: Kipling may be recalling the superstition that good and evil spirits leave good or bad smells behind them when they vanish; Wollin's obsession is fundamentally benign, though it has got 'mixed up with bombings and nightmares'.

424 *the Four Great British Botanists*: see p. 415. John Ray or Wray (1627–1705), author of *Historia Plantarum* (1686–1704) among other books and treatises, and 'regarded as the father of natural history in this country' (*DNB*); Robert Morison (1620–83), Scottish physician and botanist, who in 1649 was physician to Gaston, duke of Orleans, and in 1660 became senior physician and botanist to Charles II; he was professor of botany at Oxford, and wrote *Praeludia Botanica* (1669) and *Historia Plantarum Oxoniensis* (1680); Nehemiah Grew (1641–1712) studied medicine at Leyden, where he was awarded his MD in 1671; in the same year he became a fellow of the Royal Society, and was its secretary 1677–9; his botanical writings, notably his observations of sex in plants, were collected and published in *The Anatomy of Plants* (1682); Stephen Hales (1677–1761), physiologist and inventor, author of *Vegetable Staticks* (1727), 'the most important contribution of the eighteenth century to plant physiology' (*DNB*).

Departmental Ditties (1886)

A General Summary

First pub. *Departmental Ditties*, 1886.

Although his primary target is 'administrative sinning', Kipling also mentions literary borrowing, bringing the poem closer to home: cf. among other examples 'When 'Omer Smote 'Is Bloomin' Lyre' (p. 474).

425–6 ll. 26–9. *Or that Joseph's . . . swart Civilians*: burlesquing the story of Joseph in Gen. 41.

426 ll. 33–5. *As it was . . . evermore:* based on the familiar concluding phrase from the Litany in the Book of Common Prayer: 'As it was in the beginning, is now, and ever shall be, world without end, amen.'

The Story of Uriah

First pub. *Civil and Military Gazette*, 3 Mar. 1886.

This and the preceding poem demonstrate the two extremes of Kipling's 'light' verse: one frothy and gossipy, its cynicism tempered by an indulgent wit; the other jauntily unforgiving.

The biblical source for the poem is 2 Sam. 11, in which King David arranges for Uriah, Bathsheba's husband, to be killed at the siege of Rabbah: 'And it came to pass in the morning, that David wrote a letter to Joab, and sent it by the hand of Uriah. And he wrote in the letter, saying, Set ye Uriah in the forefront of the hottest battle, and retire ye from him, that he may be smitten, and die' (14–15).

426 *Epigraph*. In 2 Sam. 12, the prophet Nathan rebukes David for his murder of Uriah by means of a parable which begins with these words. The rich man has 'many flocks and herds' while the poor man has only one lamb; nevertheless when a guest visits him, the rich man takes the poor man's lamb to feed him. David angrily denounces the rich man's greed and injustice, only for Nathan to turn the tables on him: 'Thou art the man'.

l. 1 *Quetta*: in what is today western Pakistan, near the Afghan border.

ll. 17–18. *And Mrs Barrett . . . at most*: 'And when the wife of Uriah heard that Uriah her husband was dead, she mourned for her husband. And when the mourning was past, David sent and fetched her to his house' (2 Sam. 11: 26–7).

A Code of Morals

First pub. *Civil and Military Gazette*, 6 Apr. 1886.

The heliograph (a signalling instrument using light reflected from movable mirrors, invented in the 1870s) fascinated Kipling and is referred to many times in poems and stories up to the Boer War, the last conflict in which it played a significant role: cf. the speaker of 'Chant-Pagan' (p. 480) who recalls 'Our 'elios winkin' like fun' (l. 15).

427 l. 6. *Cupid and Apollo*: the god of love working with the god of the sun (apt for the working of the heliograph).

428 l. 20. *Lord Wolseley*: formerly Sir Garnet Wolseley (1833–1913); he had recently (1885) conducted the Nile campaign to relieve General Gordon at Khartoum.

The Man Who Could Write

First pub. 23 Mar. 1886.

Kipling himself, of course, has a claim on the title, and may be commenting obliquely on his (relative) freedom as a journalist; Boanerges is doubly foolish, both as a civil servant who does not know how to get on, and as a writer who does not know that unpalatable truths are best conveyed in fiction.

429 l. 1. *Boanerges*: in the Bible, a plural name given by Jesus to the disciples James and John, meaning 'the sons of thunder' (Mark 3: 17); with 'Blitzen', the name suggests the young man's misguided enthusiasm for

hurling critical thunderbolts. Kipling later gave the name to the 'overbearing' Ben Jonson in 'The Craftsman' (p. 505).

429 l. 8. *Wicked wit of Colvin, irony of Lyall*: Sir Auckland Colvin (1838–1908), whose articles in the *Pall Mall Gazette* influenced British policy in Egypt; at the time of writing he was a financial member of the Viceroy's Council in India; Sir Alfred Comyn Lyall (1835–1911), at the time lieutenant-governor of North-West Provinces and Oudh, had published verse in 1882 later collected as *Verses Written in India* (1889).

l. 23. *Posed as Young Ithuriel*: the angel of the sun in *Paradise Lost*, though Kipling may have been thinking of Abdiel, the angel who refuses to join Satan's rebellion and publicly denounces him (v. 803 ff.).

The Betrothed

First pub. 21 Nov. 1888 in the Allahabad *Pioneer*, and two days later in the *Civil and Military Gazette*; incl. in *Departmental Ditties* (4th edn.), 1890.

431 l. 36. *the Moor and the Mormon*: referring to the fact that polygamy is allowed by Islam and by the Mormon religion, but restricts the number of wives to four.

432 l. 49. *A million surplus Maggies*: the 'surplus' of single women towards the end of the 19th century was a much-debated topic; cf. such fictional treatments as George Gissing's *The Odd Women* (1893). For Kipling's view of this subjet in 1910, see headnote to 'The Female of the Species' (p. 480)

Barrack-Room Ballads and Other Verses

The title was originally given to a series of poems pub. in 1890 in the *Scots Observer*, whose editor, W. E. Hanley, was an early and influential friend and admirer: see note on p. 640. The poems included here appeared as follows: 1. 'Danny Deever', 22 Feb.; 2. 'Tommy', 1 Mar.; 3. 'Fuzzy-Wuzzy', 15 Mar.; 4. 'Oonts', 22 Mar.; 5. 'Loot', 29 Mar.; 7. 'The Widow at Windsor', 26 Apr. (with the title 'The Sons of the Widow'); 9. 'Gunga Din', 7 June. Other poems appeared as noted. All the poems in the series were first coll. in *Departmental Ditties, Barrack-Room Ballads, and Other Verses*, 1890 (1st American edn.) before appearing in the English edn. of *Barrack-Room Ballads*.

Kipling often disclaimed originality in art, his own or others', but these poems were immediately, and rightly, recognized as a new thing. Their lasting virtue comes not simply from the 'voicing', forceful and authentic, of Tommy Atkins, the common soldier, but from Kipling's artistic humility. He does not condescend to his speakers, but assumes that eloquence is native to them, and allows this eloquence to take its native form, the vocal and rhythmic form of popular verse. Very rarely does he strike a false note (the pun on 'rations' and 'rational' in l. 34 of 'Tommy', for example). In ch. 4 of *Something of Myself* he speaks of the origin of the *Ballads* in 'the smoke, the roar, and the good-fellowship of relaxed humanity' at the music-hall, which '"set" the scheme for a certain sort of song. The Private Soldier in India I thought I knew fairly well. His English brother (in the Guards mostly) sat and sang at my elbow any night I chose.'

The emotional range of the *Ballads* marks an awe-inspiring advance on *Departmental Ditties*; Kipling himself must have known this, you can sense (in the opposed extremes of 'Loot' and 'The Widow at Windsor') his own surprise and the exhilaration of someone riding his luck.

I owe a particular debt to the notes in Charles Carrington's edition of *The Complete Barrack-Room Ballads* (1973).

Danny Deever

The question-and-answer format is a feature of many traditional ballads and was used again by Kipling in later poems (see headnote to 'My Boy Jack', p. 681). No original for Danny Deever has been convincingly identified. He is denounced here as a 'sneakin', shootin' hound', but other instances of barrack-shootings in Kipling are not so clear-cut: see the opening of 'Love-o'-Women' (p. 143) and the headnote (p. 572).

Some of the details of the men's reaction to the execution derive from G. R. Gleig's autobiographical novel of the Peninsular War, *The Subaltern* (1826).

434 l. 23. *'is county*: Army regiments were recruited from particular counties, and local pride and loyalty were an important factor in their composition.

Tommy

For popular dislike and scorn of the common soldier, and the common soldier's fierce resentment of it, see 'On Greenhow Hill' (p. 114). The name 'Thomas Atkins' was originally that of a specimen signature on War Office forms, and dates from the early 19th century.

435 l. 22. *Thin red line*: This famous phrase was coined by William Howard Russell, the war correspondent of the *Times* in the Crimea, describing the 93rd Highlanders at the battle of Balaclava in October 1854: 'They [the Russian cavalry] dashed on towards that thin red line tipped with steel.'

l. 36. *the Widow's Uniform*: the Widow is Queen Victoria; see 'The Widow at Windsor', p. 441.

Fuzzy-Wuzzy

Britain was engaged in the Sudan from the time of the Mahdi's rebellion against Egyptian rule in 1881. The poem evokes both set-piece battles and the constant harassing attacks by irregular forces which made the Sudan one of the most feared military postings in the 1880s and beyond. The speaker has nothing to say about heroism, imperialism, Gordon of Khartoum, and the rest; he is interested in his immediate, eye-level enemy.

The 'square' was the standard defensive formation of 19th-century British infantry, and had proved famously impregnable at Waterloo. Tribesmen of the Beggara in western Sudan broke into an infantry square at Abu Klea on 24 December 1884, though the intruders were eventually killed and the square reformed. 'The nickname *Fuzzy-Wuzzy* more properly refers to the Hadedowa tribe of the eastern Sudan, who wore their long hair frizzed out. They repeatedly fought the British near Suakin as described in this ballad, and often had the best of it' (*Complete Barrack-Room Ballads*, ed. Carrington, 160).

436 ll. 13–16. *We took our chanst . . . in style*: Referring to campaigns on the North-West Frontier of India, in the Transvaal (1879–81), in Burma (from 1885), and in what was then Zululand; the Zulus under Cetywayo defeated the British at Isandlwana in 1879. An *impi* is a Zulu regiment.

l. 23. *We sloshed you with Martinis*: 'crushed you by superior firepower'; for the Martini–Henry rifle, see note on p. 555.

437 l. 37. *let drive*: fire a volley.

Oonts

OED records the first appearance in English of the Hindi and Urdu word 'oont' in 1862. Somewhat surprisingly it is not in *Hobson-Jobson*. 'Front' in Kipling's footnote about pronunciation is probably a front for the true rhyme-word. The camel is again treated with disrespect in 'How the Camel Got His Hump' (*Just So Stories*, 1902).

l. 1. *penk*: apparently Kipling's coinage (both examples in *OED* are from his writing, this being the first), evidently meaning 'heave' or 'palpitate'; *OED* suggests that it is a variant of 'pank', a West Country dialect form of 'pant'. It is unlikely to be a misprint since it survived through every edition of the ballads.

Loot

The association between lower-class misbehaviour at home (poaching and petty thievery) and in the army would have been familiar to the poem's original readers; the poem not only confirms, but celebrates, the fact that the army recruited from the dregs of society, and cocks a snook at the disapproval of respectable folk (rather than, as in 'Tommy', attempting to explain and palliate). The mark of this is in the form of the poem, which is addressed to a circle of like-minded associates, rather than to an outside audience. As Carrington remarks (*Complete Barrack Room Ballads*, 160–1), the image of the private soldier here as lawless and brutal (and jolly with it) has hardly changed since *Henry V*. Yet the justification offered by the speaker (that the danger and hardship of soldiering justify 'pay[ing] yourself for fightin' overtime') seems, in the end, less important to Kipling than the music of the human hounds.

439 l. 2. *snigged*: not a slang term, strictly speaking, but Yorkshire dialet; *OED* cites a book on Leeds dialect of 1862: 'to steal after a mean fashion'.

l. 9. *Loo*: is rec. in *OED* as a hunting cry (from 'halloo') in Shakespeare (*King Lear* III. iv. 79) and survived in 19th-century usage, e.g. Richard Jefferies' *Wood Magic* (1881): 'Bevis . . . called "Loo! Loo!" urging the dog on'.

440 l. 34. *baynick*: bayonet.

441 l. 63. *Sick 'im*: to 'sick' a dog is to incite it either to seek (the word from which 'sick' derives) or to attack its quarry.

The Widow at Windsor

The artistry of this poem rests on its two voices, one assertive and jaunty, the other parenthetically plaintive, ironic, and disillusioned. The last line strikes one of the most powerful notes in Kipling's verse, a fusion of the tragic and the knowing which belongs to him alone.

l. 2. *hairy*: splendid, famous (Partridge, *Dictionary of Historical Slang*).

ll. 6–7. *'er nick . . . 'er mark*: the historic crown brand of a broad arrow, ɋ (Carrington, *Complete Barrack-Room Ballads*, 155).

l. 21. *the Sons o' the Widow*: another Masonic allusion; Freemasons refer to themselves by this phrase, derived from 1 Kgs. 7: 14, where Hiram, one of the craftsmen whom Solomon brought from Tyre to build the Temple, is described as a widow's son.

ll. 26–9. *Lodge . . . tile . . . open in form*: Masonic terms: for 'Lodge' and 'open in form' see notes on pp. 75 and 76. To 'tile' a Lodge is to protect it from intruders; the 'tiler' or 'tyler', also known as the 'Outer Guard' is an official stationed outside the entrance to the Lodge.

442 ll. 36–7. *Take 'old . . . till you're dead*: from Ps. 139: 7–10: 'Whither shall I go from thy spirit? or whither shall I flee from thy presence? If I ascend up into heaven, thou art there: if I make my bed in hell, behold, thou art there. If I take the wings of the morning, and dwell in the uttermost parts of the sea; even there shall thy hand lead me, and thy right hand shall hold me.' There may also be an echo of Puck in *A Midsummer Night's Dream*, II. i. 175–6: 'I'll put a girdle round about the earth | In forty minutes'.

Gunga Din

The character is based on a real individual, Juma, water-carrier to the Frontier Force regiment of the Guides at the siege of Delhi in July 1857. He was selected by his comrades as the bravest man in the regiment (*Complete Barrack-*

Room Ballads, ed Carrington, 160, quoting G. F. Younghusband, *Story of the Guides*, 53–4). The figure of the 'native water-carrier' appears again in *Epitaphs of the War*, though the phrase 'better man' is applied not to him but to an officer's servant (see pp. 510 and 513).

The lines in this poem which have caused the most offence (ll. 44–5) are the finest tribute the speaker can imagine; the connotations of 'white' as 'courageous, honourable, manly, upright' were ingrained in English (and American) popular culture in this period, and the verisimilitude of the phrase is matched by Kipling's honesty in using it. Not that this honesty cost him dear: though the poem is a dramatic monologue, and the speaker's point of view is not identical with the author's, we have every reason to think that Kipling endorsed the speaker's racial pride; yet he also takes pride in the same speaker's undermining of his own prejudice, so that 'white' becomes truly and simply a metaphor. It is difficult for a modern readership to accept this, just as Huck's recognition of Jim's greater and more generous humanity in *Huckleberry Finn* is vitiated for many readers by his use of the word 'nigger'. But what other word was Huck to use? On what better foundation than Kipling gives here could the (heretically) redemptive vision of the last lines of this poem have been built?

442 l. 3. *penny-fights an' Aldershot it*: 'when you're called out to deal with minor disturbances and swagger around as you do in barracks'. Aldershot, near Guildford in Surrey, is still an important military base.

l. 12. *bhisti*: water-carrier.

443 l. 35. *dot an' carry one*: 'carry on with his duties (bringing water to one man after another)', from a term used in the teaching of simple arithmetic. This sense seems to be Kipling's coinage; the slang phrase 'a dot and carry one' or 'dot and go one' applies to someone with a wooden leg.

l. 38. *broke*: 'broke ranks' (usually implying a disorderly retreat).
cut: taken with 'broke', this may mean 'fled, ran away', but the emphasis on defeat sounds too strong; it may mean 'advanced rapidly'.

444 l. 70. *dooli*: litter.

ll. 75–80. *So I'll meet . . . from Gunga Din*: a revision of the parable in Luke 16: 19–26; the rich man in hell sees the beggar Lazarus in Abraham's bosom, 'And he cried and said, Father Abraham, have mercy on me, and send Lazarus, that he may dip the tip of his finger in water, and cool my tongue; for I am tormented in this flame.' Abraham refuses, and says that 'there is a great gulf fixed' between the saved and the damned. Kipling's use of the colloquial euphemism 'beggar' in l. 70 artfully anticipates this image, and note the echo of 'Lazarus' in 'Lazarushian', l. 82.

l. 82. *Lazarushian-leather*: 'lazarus' means leprous, and the sense may be 'beggarly-looking (with skin like dirty leather)'.

Mandalay

In ch. 8 of *Something of Myself*, Kipling commented:

I wrote a song called 'Mandalay' which, tacked to a tune with a swing, made one of the waltzes of that distant age. A private soldier reviews his loves and, in the chorus, his experiences in the Burma campaign. One of his ladies lives at Moulmein, which is not on the road to anywhere, and he describes the *amour* with some minuteness, but always in his chorus deals with 'the road to Mandalay,' his golden path to romance. The inhabitants of the United States, to whom I owed most of the bother, 'Panamaed' that song (this was before copyright), set it to their own tunes, and sang it in their own national voices. Not content with this, they took to pleasure cruising, and discovered that Moulmein did not command any view of any sun rising across the Bay of Bengal. They must have interfered too with the navigation of the Irrawaddy Flotilla steamers, for one of the Captains S.O.S.-ed me to give him 'something to tell these somethinged tourists about it.' I forget what word I sent, but I hoped it might help. Had I opened the chorus of the song with 'Oh' instead of 'On the road,' etc., it might have shown that the song was a sort of general mix-up of the singer's Far-Eastern memories against a background of the Bay of Bengal as seen at dawn from a troop-ship taking him there. But 'On' in this case was more singable than 'Oh.' That simple explanation may stand as a warning.

Kipling's emphasis on 'Mandalay' as a song stems from its instant success as a waltz-tune, a music-hall and parlour piece for tenors, and later as a gramophone recording.

The 'Burma campaign' is the third Burma War, which broke out in 1885. The British captured Mandalay and forced King Thibaw into exile, but resistance continued for several years in the jungle, pitting the regular British forces against the 'dacoits', or guerrillas (or bandits) (or both); this phase of the war is depicted in 'The Taking of Lungtungpen' (*Plain Tales from the Hills*, 1888) and 'The Ballad of Boh Da Thone' (*Barrack-Room Ballads*, 1892).

Title. Mandalay was the capital of what was then called Upper Burma. The 'road' to Mandalay is actually a waterway, the great Irrawaddy River (hence the reference in l. 6 to the Flotilla; see Kipling's comments, above).

l. 1. *Moulmein*: a town in what was then called Lower Burma, about 100 miles east of Rangoon across the Gulf of Martaban. As Kipling points out (see above), it would play no part in the river-route from Rangoon to Mandalay.

445 l. 12. *Theebaw*: King Theebaw or Thibaw had ruled Burma since 1878. He surrendered to the British in 1885.

l. 15. *the Great Gawd Budd*: the speaker's confused term for Buddha.

Gentlemen-Rankers

First pub. 15 Dec. 1889 in the New York *Tribune* and 21 Dec. in the Allahabad *Pioneer*, and in the Dec. issue of *Macmillan's Magazine*.

The title refers to men who came from the upper classes in Britain but who had been forced to enlist as private soldiers because of bankruptcy or other social disgrace. The protagonist of 'Love-o'-Women' (p. 143) is a 'gentleman-ranker'.

446 l. 3. *machinely crammed*: qualified to take the army officers' examination by attendance at a 'crammer'.

ll. 7–8. *more than kin . . . less than kind*: from *Hamlet*, I. ii. 65 (the quotation demonstrates the speaker's superior level of education).

447 l. 39. *the Curse of Reuben*: Reuben, the eldest son of Jacob and Leah, is not cursed anywhere in the Bible, and his tribe is associated with cursing only once, in Deut. 27: 13, when he is one of those commanded to pronounce God's curses for disobedience on mount Ebal. These curses are set out in 28: 15–68; it is hard to believe that Kipling intended an allusion to them, but it is equally hard to believe that 'Reuben' could be an error for e.g. Cain.

Ford o' Kabul River

First pub. 22 Nov. 1890 in the *National Observer*.

The poem is based on an incident which took place during the Second Afghan War (1878–80). On 31 Mar. 1879 the 10th Hussars attempted to cross the Kabul river and were overtaken by a flood, with the loss of forty-six men. The poem, one of the greatest love-songs in the language by a man for another man, has a strength and controlled pathos to match the finest of Whitman's poems of the American Civil War. Fittingly, it is an American soldiers' song, 'Tramp, tramp, tramp, the boys are marching' which Kipling adapted for the refrain.

448 l. 2. *trumpet*: in early edns., 'bugle', until it was pointed out to Kipling that British cavalry regiments do not blow bugles but trumpets.

The Conundrum of the Workshops

First pub. 13 Sept. 1890 in the *Scots Observer*; coll. *Departmental Ditties, Barrack-Room Ballads, and Other Verses*, 1890 (the first American edn. of *Departmental Ditties*).

The poem is a response to Kipling's first experiences, when he came from India to London in 1889, of the tensions, anxieties, and jealousies of the metropolitan literary world; its biblical language parallels the mock-evolutionary vocabulary of 'In the Neolithic Age' (p. 451) and 'The Gods of the Copybook Headings' (p. 518).

450 ll. 9–12. *They builded a tower . . . alien tongue*: alluding to the story of the tower of Babel, which resulted in the 'confusion of tongues' (Gen. 11: 1–9), though in the Bible this is God's doing.

l. 14. *Red Clay*: the Hebrew word 'Adam' may mean either 'red' or 'earth'; Adam is formed 'of the dust of the ground' in Gen. 2: 7.

ll. 13–15. *They fought . . . preened to start*: alluding to the story of the Flood and Noah's Ark (Gen. 6–8; the dove is sent forth in 8: 8–12).

450–1 ll. 21–3. *We have learned . . . drawn by the cart*: satirizing modern schools of art, defined by irreligion, scientific naturalism, or perverse aesthetic principles. The sense of l. 21 is that we no longer really believe in Christianity; it has become a trivial convenience (a 'surplice-peg' is a hat-stand).

451 l. 25. *the Club-room's green and gold*: in ch. 4 of *Something of Myself*, Kipling records his pleasure at being elected to the Savile Club in Piccadilly, London's main literary club at that period, in 1890: see below, headnote to 'In the Neolithic Age'.

In the Neolithic Age

First pub. 18 Dec. 1892 in the San Francisco *Examiner* and 31 Dec. in the *Civil and Military Gazette*, and in the Dec. issue of the *Idler*; coll. *Ballads and Barrack-Room Ballads*, 1893 (3rd American edn.).

The background to the poem is the same as for 'The Conundrum of the Workshops' (see headnote above). On the subject of literary rivalries, in ch. 4 of *Something of Myself* Kipling remembers Walter Besant's advice to him to 'keep out of the dog-fight' which he would find at the Savile Club:

> He said that if I were 'in with one lot' I would have to be out with another; and that, at last, 'things would get like a girls' school where they stick out their tongues at each other when they pass.' That was true too. One heard men vastly one's seniors wasting energy and good oaths in recounting 'intrigues' against them, and of men who had 'their knife into' their work, or whom they themselves wished to 'knife'. . . . It seemed best to stand clear of it all. For that reason, I have never directly or indirectly criticised any fellow-craftsman's output, or encouraged any man or woman to do so; nor have I approached any persons that they might be led to comment on my output. My acquaintance with my contemporaries has from first to last been very limited.

Of course this generalization is not entirely accurate, but it is not disingenuous. Kipling's caution about literary-critical partisanship contrasts vividly with his willingness to become politically engaged and to accept the consequences of that fact for his own reputation: on this point see the Introduction, p. xix.

As it happens the 'Neolithic Age' is not quite correct for the period of prehistory which Kipling wants to evoke, that of cave-paintings and the ice age; but it would be inappropriate to introduce critical pedantry into this of all poems.

451 l. 7. *dwerg*: pseudo-archaic form of 'dwarf', from an Old English word (*OED* cites this usage by Kipling and another in 1892).

451 l. 9. *Solutré*: the Solutreans were an early stone age culture in Europe. According to the *Oxford Companion to Art* 'very little art is found during Solutrean times'.

l. 12. *Grenelle*: a district of Paris.

452 l. 24. *Traill*: Henry Duff Traill (1842–1900), author and journalist; in Mar. 1892 he wrote an article in the *Nineteenth Century* listing fifty contemporary writers who had some merit but were still inferior to Tennyson. In a postscript he added Kipling to the list.

l. 27. *Allobrogenses*: The Allobroges were a Celtic tribe occupying the territory of the Modern Dauphiné and Savoy. They took part with Hannibal in the invasion of Italy and were finally subjugated by Rome in 121 BC.

l. 34. *a vast of*: 'a vast amount of', a dialect usage according to *OED*, which records it in a book by R. S. Surtees, one of Kipling's favourite authors.

l. 36. *Martaban*: in Burma.

The Seven Seas

The 'Mary Gloster'

First pub. Aug. 1894 in the *Pall Mall Magazine*.

The theme of the self-made millionaire father with the spoilt worthless son recalls *Captains Courageous*, but here the son has grown up unredeemed, and the father's pride in his achievement is pierced with loss. Accordingly the ending is not that of a young man's comedy which embraces the future, but an old man's tragic and sublime recuperation of the past at the moment of death. The form, that of dramatic monologue, as often in Kipling owes a good deal to Browning (especially 'The Bishop Orders His Tomb at Saint Praxed's Church').

454 l. 31. *clippers*: sailing-ships built for speed, which competed to bring perishable cargoes across the Atlantic in the fastest times. Huge profits were made in the years before steam became reliable enough to supersede the fastest sailing ships.

ll. 32–3. *Macassar Straits— | By the Little Paternosters, as you come to the Union Bank*: the straits between Sulawesi (Celebes) and Borneo; the modern Indonesian name for the Little Paternosters is Kepulauan (= islands, archipelago) Balabalangan. Sir Antony gives the exact co-ordinates, 118°E 3°S, at l. 128.

l. 38. *your mother came*: He means that he saw the ghost of his wife.

455 l. 55. *steel and the first expansions*: steel began to replace wooden or iron-plated hulls in the 1870s. The 'first expansions' refers to the development of double or triple expansion-engines, in which power was increased by

passing the steam through several stages. See the notes to 'The Devil and the Deep Sea' (p. 190).

l. 58. *'You keep . . . the next'*: Prov. 4: 18 is the nearest I can find to this 'Scripture text': 'But the path of the just is as the shining light, that shineth more and more unto the perfect day.'

l. 66. *six-inch rollers*: armour-plating made of six-inch rolled steel.

l. 71. *Harrer an' Trinity College!* 'Harrer' is Harrow School, one of the great English public schools; both Oxford and Cambridge have a Trinity College.

458 l. 130. *McAndrew*: see 'McAndrew's Hymn', l. 77.

l. 147. *this world is a fleetin' show*: a biblical-sounding phrase, though not found in this form in the Bible itself: cf. among others Isa. 24: 4, 'the world languisheth and fadeth away'; Job 9: 25, 'my days are swifter than a post: they flee away, they see no good'; Ps. 144: 4, 'Man is like to vanity: his days are as a shadow that passeth away'; 1 Cor. 7: 31, 'the fashion of this world passeth away'.

459 l. 175. *For the heart it shall go with the treasure—go down to the sea in ships*: combining two biblical texts: Matt. 6: 21, 'where your treasure is, there will your heart be also', and Ps. 107: 23, 'They that go down to the sea in ships, that do business in great waters'.

McAndrew's Hymn

First pub. Dec. 1894 in *Scribner's Magazine*.

The machine as object of desire, and as a figure of human conduct and morality, is evoked here with great power, and considerably more subtlety than Kipling is usually given credit for. McAndrew (a dramatic character, not Kipling's mouthpiece; Kipling's debt to Browning is visible here as it is in 'The "Mary Gloster"') sees the steam-engine as an embodiment of necessity in both the material and theological sense, yet his human sympathy with Ferguson overrides his Scots-Presbyterian zeal for order and economy: he allows Ferguson to burn coal at a profligate rate in order to speed the ship towards the port where his (Ferguson's) wife is waiting. Furthermore, the working of the engine, which we hear and feel in Kipling's masterful deployment of the rhythm of the grand old 'fourteener', is played against the working of McAndrew's memory, the weighing and sifting of his long irregular years.

460 l. 1. *Lord . . . shadow of a dream*: like Sir Antony Gloster, McAndrew is fond of biblical and (as here) quasi-biblical phrases; see above, note to l. 147 of 'The "Mary Gloster"'.

ll. 5–6. *John Calvin . . . my 'Institutio'*: Calvin (1509–64), French reformer and theologian; his major work was *Christianae Religionis Institutio*, written in Latin (its familiar English title is 'the Institutes'), and first pub. 1536. Calvinism rested on four major doctrinal principles: the absolute sovereignty of God; the authority of the Scriptures; justification by faith, not works; and predestination. It was the ideological engine of Puritanism in Britain and America, and became synonymous with the sternest forms of Protestant belief and social practice.

460 l. 15. *Seventy—One—Two—Three*: McAndrew notes the increase in revolutions of the engine since Ferguson took over the watch.

461 l. 26. *serve . . . with tow:* patch up with strands of rope.

l. 36. *scoughed*: not found in dialect dictionaries; the context might suggest either 'soaked' or 'knocked flat'. *jock*: also not found; the sense is 'joke, carouse'.

l. 44. *kittlin'*: courting, embracing.

462 l. 55. *daunder*: saunter.

l. 67. *kiss His red-hot rod*: the phrase 'kiss the rod' comes from Shakespeare, *The Two Gentlemen of Verona*: 'Fie, fie, how wayward is this foolish love, | That like a testy babe will scratch the nurse, | And presently, all humbled, kiss the rod!' (I. ii. 57–9). Given this context, the biblical 'rod' may be that of Prov. 13: 24: 'He that spareth his rod hateth his son', but cf. also Rev. 2: 27: 'he shall rule them with a rod of iron'.

ll. 62–8. *Just statin' . . . Leevin' God*: McAndrew is tempted to abandon his Scottish Presbyterian faith, with its Calvinist emphasis on sin and judgement, as a product of an oppressive and punitive culture, in favour of an undefined hedonistic paganism, superficially attractive but morally lax and irresponsible. 'Leevin'' means easygoing, relaxed, so the implication is of a god of hedonism and 'natural' pleasure, as opposed to the 'living God' of the Bible.

l. 69. *kipper*: roast.

l. 75. *The Sin against the Holy Ghost*: Matt. 12: 31: 'All manner of sin and blasphemy shall be forgiven unto men: but the blasphemy against the Holy Ghost shall not be forgiven unto men'.

l. 78. *Third on the Mary Gloster then*: see 'The "Mary Gloster"', ll. 130 ff.

463 l. 79. *Yet was Thy Hand . . . feet Thy Care*: God is 'the lifter up of mine head' in Ps. 3: 3, but the biblical phrase which comes closest to 'Thy Hand beneath my head' comes in the Song of Solomon 2: 6: 'His left hand is under my head, and his right hand doth embrace me'. God will 'deliver my feet from falling' in Ps. 56: 13. Cf. also such passages as Isa. 41: 10: 'Fear thou not; for I am with thee . . . I will uphold thee with the right hand of my righteousness'.

l. 84. *Better the sight . . .*: Eccles. 6: 9: 'Better is the sight of the eyes than the wandering of the desire: this is also vanity and vexation of spirit.'

l. 100. *spoke*: hailed (by another vessel).

l. 103. *Steamin' to bell*: with the ship's bell ringing at intervals to warn other vessels of its whereabouts in poor visibility.

l. 104. *kelpies*: Scottish name for demonic water-spirits, believed to presage or cause shipwreck and drowning. *girn*: show the teeth, snarl.

l. 105. *the Mills o' God*: a phrase not from the Bible but from an epigram by Friedrich von Logau (1604–55), which Kipling would have known in Longfellow's translation: 'Though the mills of God grind slowly, yet they grind exceeding small; | Though with patience He stands waiting, with exactness grinds he all'.

464 l. 119. *Wi' such as call a snifter-rod ross. . . . French for nightingale*: the French word is 'rossignol'. The term 'snifter-rod' is not rec. in the *OED*, but a 'snifting-valve' is a valve which allows air to be expelled from the cylinder of a steam-engine.

465 l. 146. *the throws*: the cranks.

l. 153. *uplifted like the Just*: Luke 14: 14, 'the resurrection of the just'.

l. 163. *singin' like the Mornin' Stars*: Job 38: 4–7: 'Where wast thou when I laid the foundations of the earth? . . . When the morning stars sang together, and all the sons of God shouted for joy?'

l. 165. *not unto us the praise*: from the opening line of Ps. 115 (in the Prayer Book version): 'Not unto us, O Lord, not unto us, but unto thy Name give the praise.'

466 ll. 174–5. *When first . . . all things good*: Gen. 1: 20–5 records the creation of all the living creatures (except man); the phrase 'God saw that it was good' occurs in vv. 21 and 25.

l. 176. *that warld-liftin' joy no after-fall could vex*: McAndrew's theology is decidedly un-Calvinist here; the suggestion that traces of the divine bliss of creation remain in the creative activity of human beings runs counter to the Calvinist doctrine that the fall of man made all human actions inherently sinful.

l. 177. *the Arrtifex*: the maker.

l. 183. *preventin'*: in the now-archaic sense of 'anticipating' ('prevenient grace' is a recognized term in Calvinist theology).

l. 185. *Pelagian*: 'Theologically, Pelagianism is the heresy which holds that man can take the initial and fundamental steps towards salvation by his own efforts, apart from Divine Grace' (*Oxford Dictionary of the Christian Church*). Pelagius was a 5th-century theologian, an opponent of St Augustine.

The Song of the Banjo

First pub. June 1895 in the *New Review*.

The poem belongs to a group of works in the 1890s (fiction, non-fiction, and verse) in which Kipling celebrated the exploits of white colonists, settlers and pioneers; cf. esp. the passage from *Letters of Travel* in which he celebrates the 'captains courageous' of the New World. But the core of the poem is an artist expressing, and reflecting on, the evocative power of popular songs and tunes, marked by the intense fusions of pleasure with pain which constitute memory and desire. The influence of such songs is evident in Kipling's own work, though his artistic self-consciousness ensures that he differs from what he admires and emulates.

466 l. 1. *a Broadwood*: name of a famous firm of piano-makers, founded by John Broadwood (1732–1812).

l. 7. *tails*: straggles, tails off.

467 l. 36. *broken rankers*: the 'gentlemen-rankers' of Kipling's poem of that name (p. 446), men of good family who were forced to enlist because of bankruptcy or social disgrace.

468 l. 48. *'Johnny Bowlegs, pack your kit and trek!'*: I have not traced this line, evidently from a popular ballad of the period.

l. 49. *Through the gorge that gives the stars at noon-day clear*: the gorge is so deep that the stars can be seen in daylight from its floor.

l. 50. *scud*: loose earth, dirt.

l. 53. *trestle*: timber support shoring up the road.

l. 54. *many-shedded levels*: the banking and terracing of the winding mountain road.

l. 56. *the Song of Roland*: the *Chanson de Roland*, a 12th-century Old French work which recounts one of the heroic myths of Christendom, the death of Charlemagne's companion Roland at the pass of Roncevaux in battle against the Saracens.

l. 58. *croup and crest*: from the bottom to the top.

l. 59. *iron stallions*: railway engines.

469 l. 87. *the Stealer*: Hermes, or Mercury, the patron divinity of thieves, credited in Greek myth with the invention of the lyre. 'Stooping beachward' alludes to the ancient Greek form of the lyre, which was made from a tortoise's shell. 'Stealer' also evokes the figure of Homer: see 'When 'Omer Smote 'Is Bloomin' Lyre', p. 474.

l. 94. *[What d'ye lack, my noble masters! What d'ye lack?]*: the flavour is Elizabethan, the cry of a pedlar like Autolycus in *The Winter's Tale*, though it isn't him.

l. 96. *Yea, from Delos up to Limerick and back!* A figurative encompassing of the Western tradition in time and space: Delos, the mythical birthplace of Apollo, represents the Hellenistic strain; Limerick, in Ireland, stands for the Celtic, the westernmost reach of folk culture.

A Song of the English

First pub. May 1893 in the *English Illustrated Magazine*; a separate issue in 1909 was illustrated by W. Heath Robinson.

Questions of 'Englishness' and national identity feature strongly in late 19th-century culture, and Kipling's literary and personal friendships (notably W. E. Henley's circle) would have encouraged his contributions to this debate; in later years these contributions were influenced by friendships with political figures such as Cecil Rhodes and Theodore Roosevelt, and of course by Kipling's own decision to settle permanently in England. When 'A Song of the English' appeared he had made no such decision, and indeed appeared to the world (and to himself) to have made the opposite choice by marrying an American and settling in America. The tone of the poem divides between the polemical, represented here by 'The Song of the Dead', and the reflective and literary, represented by 'The Deep-Sea Cables', over which Tennyson's poem 'The Kraken' presides: 'Below the thunders of the upper deep; | Far, far beneath in the abysmal sea, | His ancient, dreamless, uninvaded sleep | The Kraken sleepeth . . .'

The Song of the Dead

469 l. 4. *warrigal*: the dingo, the wild dog of Australia.

l. 5. *the East*: covering both India (this line) and Africa (the next).

l. 6. *dog-ape*: baboon. *kloof*: ravine (a South African term).

l. 7. *the West*: the North-West frontier, Afghanistan.

470 ll. 26–30. *When Drake . . . crowned thereby*: Sir Francis Drake's voyage of circumnavigation in the *Golden Hind*, during which he rounded Cape Horn, took place in 1577–80. The reference to the 'Lodge' associates the evolution of the Empire with the brotherhood of Freemansonry.

471 l. 54. *From the Ducies to the Swin*: Ducie Island is in the Pacific, just south of the Tropic of Capricorn, and near Henderson and Pitcairn Islands; the Swina is a channel from the Baltic Sea to the Stettiner Haff between Poland and Germany. The sense of the line is therefore equivalent to 'from one end of the earth to the other'.

l. 63. *blue-lights*: blue flares were used to mark the position of recent wrecks.

The Deep-Sea Cables

471 l. 4. *the shell-burred cables*: the first transatlantic telegraph cable was laid in August 1858, but failed after a month; the most recent (before the date of the poem) was in 1881, giving it plenty of time to become 'shell-burred'.

The Three-Decker

First pub. 14 July 1894 in the *Saturday Review*.

For many years most new Victorian fiction had been published in three octavo volumes costing 31s. 6d., a price which was prohibitive to all but the well-off and meant that circulating libraries bought most of the print-run. This was not the only problem. 'The large expanse of the form led to oversize print, wide margins and relatively few lines on the page. Notoriously, the form encouraged narrative padding, especially a profusion of short-sentenced dialogue by which expanses of white paper could be used up with relatively few words. . . . The three-decker was almost exclusively purchased by libraries, notably the large metropolitan firms of Mudie and W. H. Smith's whose orders could consequently make or break a new novel. This led to de facto censorship and writers such as George Moore and Henry James complained eloquently about the neutered English reading public, as compared to the French. The multi-volume form disappeared abruptly in 1894 when Smith and Mudie agreed not to buy any work of fiction costing more than 4s. a volume. The three-decker was succeeded by the one-volume novel costing 6s., a form of issue that remained essentially in place until 1939' (J. Sutherland, *Longman Companion to Victorian Fiction*, 1988). The awfulness of the 'three-decker' in its death-throes was expounded by George Gissing in *New Grub Street* (1891). Kipling's own two Victorian novels, *The Light That Failed* (1891) and *The Naulahka* (1892) were exceptions to the three-volume rule; both were one-volume novels. Kipling associates the death of the form with the death of the traditional subject-matter and orientation of the novel, so that the poem constructs a nostalgic myth of the pleasures of old-fashioned fiction, and attacks the modern school. In making this attack, exuberant and witty though it is, Kipling was fouling his own nest, as well as going against the spirit of his injunction that 'There are nine and sixty ways of constructing tribal lays, | And every single one of them is right!' ('In the Neolithic Age', ll. 19–20). His motive may be mixed up with his own ambition to write a 'real' novel; he returned to the extended metaphor of the 'three-decker' in ch. 8 of *Something of Myself*, not with indulgent nostalgia but thwarted idealism: 'I dreamed for many years of building a veritable three-decker out of chosen and long-stored timber . . . a vessel ballasted on ingots of pure research and knowledge . . . Nor did I live to see the day when the new three-deckers should hoist themselves over the horizon, quivering to their own power, overloaded with bars, ball-rooms, and insistent chromium plumbing; hellishly noisy from the sports' deck to the barber's shop; but serving their generation as the old craft served theirs.'

472 l. 4. *Islands of the Blest*: or Paradise in both Greek and Celtic myth, here representing the pleasures of fantasy and escapism in fiction. A 'packet' is a mail-boat on a regular run.

l. 9. *a course unspoiled of Cook*: modern travel and tourism are a metaphor for realism, which spoils the glamour of romance. The travel-firm of

Thomas Cook & Son might feel aggrieved at the slight, since they had treated Kipling with great generosity when he lost his savings in a bank crash in 1892 (to be fair he records this episode in ch. 5 of *Something of Myself*).

l. 16. *Yussufs . . . Zuleika*: in Gen. 39: 7–20 the virtuous Joseph (= Yussuf) rejects the advances of Potiphar's wife, who then falsely accuses him of attempting to rape her. The name Zuleika is not in the Bible, but comes from the Koran.

473 l. 31. *dripping oil-bags to skin the deep's unrest*: i.e. 'pour oil on troubled waters' (parodying both the overblown style of some modern fiction, and its lack of success at meeting its readers' needs).

l. 35. *the Flying Dutchman*: legendary ghost-ship, seen in stormy weather off the Cape of Good Hope, and doomed to wander the seas forever because of a curse on the crew.

l. 46. *you're manned . . . for steaming's sake*: a hit at two of the prevailing modern schools, naturalism and aestheticism ('art for art's sake').

'When 'Omer Smote 'Is Bloomin' Lyre'

First pub. in August 1894 in *Pall Mall Magazine*. It formed the prefatory poem in the section of *The Seven Seas* entitled 'Barrack-Room Ballads' (i.e. additional ballads to those collected in 1892).

Kipling's interest (in every sense of the word) in literary borrowing goes back to his very beginnings as a writer, founded on pastiche and parody. 'In our trade we be all felons, more or less,' he says in ch. 8 of *Something of Myself*, adjuring writers to 'bear serenely with imitators'. But there is a line, shifting perhaps but discernible, in Kipling's estimate of strong and weak borrowing. The artist takes what he needs; the plagiarist needs what he takes. In this poem, too, Kipling emphasizes the importance of the collusion between the artist and his audience, whose knowledge and acceptance is vital to the process in which 'old songs' are recreated.

The King

First pub. 1894 in *Under Lochnagar*, a collection ed. R. A. Profeit, with the title 'Romance'.

The non-evolution of art is a recurring theme in Kipling: compare 'In the Neolithic Age' (p. 451) and 'The Conundrum of the Workshops' (p. 449). Kipling's view that romance is alive and well in the conditions of modern life sits oddly with his nostalgic tribute to the 'three-decker' (see above, p. 000), but that poem might be seen as the exemplification of the last lines of this one. The particular complaint that the age of steam has killed romance (ll. 25–30) is rebutted in 'McAndrew's Hymn' (see ll. 142 ff.).

That Day

First pub. 25 Apr. 1895 in the *Pall Mall Gazette*.

Though the poem is not founded on a particular episode, it probably refers, like the story 'The Drums of the Fore-and-Aft' (*Wee Willie Winkie*, 1888) to the breaking of a British regiment (the 66th Foot, the Berkshires) at the battle of Maiwand in July 1880, during the Second Afghan War. Kipling visited the Officers' and Sergeants' Messes of the Berkshires in Bermuda in 1894 (A. Rutherford (ed.), *Rudyard Kipling: War Stories and Poems* (Oxford, 1990), 328).

476 l. 11. *sove-ki-poo*: French 'sauve-qui-peut', 'every man for himself'.

The Five Nations (1903)

Recessional

First pub. 17 July 1897 in *The Times*, and extensively repr. in other newpapers.

In ch. 6 of *Something of Myself* Kipling wrote:

> But at the back of my head there was an uneasiness, based on things that men were telling me about affairs outside England. (The inhabitants of that country never looked further than their annual seaside resorts.) There was trouble too in South Africa after the Jameson Raid [1895–6] which promised, men wrote me, further trouble. Altogether, one had a sense of 'a sound of a going in the tops of the mulberry trees' [2 Sam. 5: 24]—of things moving into position as troops move. And into the middle of it all came the Great Queen's Diamond Jubilee, and a certain optimism that scared me. The outcome, as far as I was concerned, took the shape of a set of verses . . . It was more in the nature of a *nuzzur-wattu* (an averter of the Evil Eye), and—with the conservatism of the English—was used in choirs and places where they sing long after our Navy and Army alike had in the name of 'peace' been rendered innocuous.

The last sour comment refers to Kipling's anger at Britain's failure to rearm in the face of the renewed threat from Nazi Germany in the 1930s. The account in *Something of Myself* is compressed and to some extent warped by time: for a detailed account of the genesis of the poem (including its discussion in the Kipling family conclave) and the public and private responses to its publication, see Carrington, 320–6. Nevertheless in *Something of Myself* Kipling states a truth about the poem which is often ignored in critical accounts, namely its origins in a shared, a collective 'uneasiness': the poet thinks of himself not as a voice crying in the wilderness but as the spokesman for many others whose mood ran counter to the prevailing mood of national complacency. His letter to C. F. Moberly Bell at *The Times*, accompanying the poem, appeals to a reciprocal feeling:

> Enclosed please find my sentiments on things—which I hope are yours. We've been blowing up the Trumpets of the New Moon a little too much for White Men, and it's about time we sobered down.

Sir Walter Besant is representative of many who wrote to him: 'You caught the exact feeling—what all decent people with the Puritanic touch in us wanted to have said and couldn't say'.

Accusations of racism, based on the phrase 'lesser breeds without the Law' (l. 22), have been rebutted by saying that the line does not refer to non-white races but to Germany. (This argument was first made by George Orwell, in the pardonable heat of 1942.) Kipling does use the phrase 'lower breeds' to describe the immigrants from Russia and eastern Europe who were, in his view, 'wiping out' the indigenous Americans (by this Kipling meant the immigrants who had arrived 200 years before, not the Indians whom we now call Native Americans). See his letter of 4 Aug. 1910 (*Letters*, iii. 448) and the parallel passage in ch. 5 of *Something of Myself*.

Contemporary response also focused on Kipling's literary borrowings, which must have given the author of 'When 'Omer Smote 'Is Bloomin' Lyre' a surfeit of ironic pleasure. The major source for the poem is of course the Bible; among many influential passages, see 1 Chron. 29: 10–18, in which David speaks in tones of both celebration and warning of the great temple which Solomon is to complete: 'Now therefore, our God, we thank thee, and praise thy glorious name. But who am I, and what is my people, that we should be able to offer so willingly after this sort? for all things come of thee, and of thine own have we given thee. For we are strangers before thee, and sojourners, as were all our fathers: our days on the earth are as a shadow, and there is none abiding. . . . O Lord God of Abraham, Isaac, and of Israel, our fathers, keep this forever in the imagination of the thoughts of the heart of thy people'.

478 *Title*. The title of the first draft was 'After'; Kipling began writing it on the morning of 23 July 1897, the day after the official Diamond Jubilee celebrations. A 'recessional hymn' is a hymn sung while the clergy and choir retire from the chancel to the vestry after a service.

l. 1. *God of our fathers*: frequent in the Bible from Deut. 26: 7.

l. 3. *awful*: awe-inspiring (the original sense of the word, as opposed to the modern meaning of e.g. 'awful old England' in l. 5. of 'Chant-Pagan', p. 480).

l. 4. *Dominion . . . pine*: cf. Emerson, 'Woodnotes': 'And grant to dwellers with the pine | Dominion o'er the palm and vine'.

l. 5. *Lord God of Hosts*: this phrase occurs in e.g. 2 Sam. 5: 10; there are many occurrences of similar phrases ('God of hosts', 'Lord of hosts').

l. 6. *Lest we forget*: the first occurrence of this phrase, or a variant of it, in the Bible, is Deut. 4: 9: 'Only take heed to thyself, and keep thy soul diligently, lest thou forget the things which thine eyes have seen, and lest they depart from thy heart all the days of thy life: but teach them thy sons, and thy sons' sons'.

l. 7. *The tumult and the shouting dies*: from Amos 2: 2, but deploying the phrases to give a different sense: 'Moab shall die with tumult, with shouting, and with the sound of the trumpet'.

478 l. 8. *Captains and the Kings*: not linked in the Bible, but each has biblical affiliations, e.g. for 'captains', Job 39: 25: 'the thunder of the captains, and the shouting'. For 'depart', cf. Zech. 10: 11: 'the pride of Assyria shall be brought down, and the sceptre of Egypt shall depart away'.

l. 10. *An humble and a contrite heart*: Ps. 51: 17: 'The sacrifices of God are a broken spirit: a broken and a contrite heart, O God, thou wilt not despise'.

l. 16. *Nineveh and Tyre*: the destruction of Nineveh is recorded in the Bible in the book of Nahum; that of Tyre is foretold in Isaiah 23.

l. 17. *Judge of the Nations*: Isa. 2: 4: 'And he shall judge among the nations'.

l. 21. *Gentiles*: those who are not the chosen people, who are outside the covenant.

l. 22. *without the Law*: both in the sense of being without, lacking it, and being outside, not falling within its scope.

The White Man's Burden

First pub. 4 Feb. 1899 in *The Times*, and on 5 Feb. in the *New York Sun* and *Tribune* and the San Francisco *Examiner*.

The poem was addressed to America following its war with Spain in 1898, as a consequence of which it acquired the Spanish colonies of Cuba and the Philippines. Kipling sent an advance copy of the poem to his friend President Theodore Roosevelt, who thought it 'rather poor poetry, but good sense from the expansionist standpoint'—a response to the poem's sense of mission, and to its visionary ideals of service and civilizing power, which the author might not have relished. The continuity of Kipling's thought on this subject—and of his passionate naivety—are striking (see his account of British rule in India, p. 525). Asking for a fair hearing for the poem in our post-colonial age is probably futile, and is made harder by the fact that it is not very good and owes its survival to a notoriety which it does not entirely deserve.

480 ll. 39–40. *Why brought ye . . . Egyptian night*: The complaint of the Israelites in the wilderness against Moses, Exod. 16: 2–3.

Chant-Pagan

First pub. *The Five Nations*.

For a different connection between the Boer War and the social constraints of 'awful old England', see the story 'The Comprehension of Private Copper' (*Traffics and Discoveries*, 1904). Private Copper is captured by a 'burgher', a renegade British colonial fighting on the Boer side, who insults and, worse, patronizes him, and the treatment reminds him of what he had to endure in England from his social superiors.

The vision of fellowship between reconciled enemies at the end of the poem may be contrasted with the ending of another story in *Traffics and Discoveries*, 'A Sahibs' War', which celebrates the vengeance taken on a treacherous Boer family by the total destruction of their farm, so that the very signs of its existence are erased from the landscape.

481 l. 15. *helios*: for more fun with the heliograph, see 'A Code of Morals', p. 427.

ll. 48–50. *My livin' .. Me!*: from the Catechism in the Book of Common Prayer: 'to do my duty in that state of life, unto which it shall please God to call me'.

482 l. 64. *arise an' get 'ence*: Jesus tells his disciples 'Arise, let us go hence' in John 14: 31; elsewhere 'hence' is associated with radical departure, as in Exod. 33: 1: 'And the Lord said unto Moses, Depart, and go up hence . . . unto the land which I sware unto Abraham, to Isaac, and to Jacob, saying, Unto thy seed will I give it'.

Lichtenberg

First pub. *The Five Nations*.

The poem came, according to Kipling, from the rhythm of a chance remark by an Australian soldier: 'I smelt wattle at Lichtenberg, riding in, in the rain.' ('Mrs Bathurst', another story linking South Africa with the Antipodes, also began with an overheard phrase: see headnote, p. 610). Lichtenberg is a town 120 miles west of Johannesburg; the wattle (a variety of acacia, though often called a mimosa) is the Australian national flower. Kipling had made one brief visit to Australia in 1891, and the impressions he evokes here were based on a return train journey from Melbourne to Sydney (Carrington, 237). The Australians who fought in the Boer War come in for high praise in 'A Sahibs' War' (*Traffics and Discoveries*, 1904).

The Files

First pub. 12 Oct. 1901.

In one sense this is a late 'Departmental Ditty', and a return to Kipling's youth, the 'seven years' hard' which he put in on the *Civil and Military Gazette* and the *Pioneer*; but it is a return to a place where this part of his life is buried, as the past is buried in 'the files'. Kipling's last real journalistic assignment had been during the Boer War, and even then the circumstances were special; he was no longer a practising journalist, but his cynical affection for the press had not yet turned sour, and the satire has an indulgent brilliance which recalls some of John Davidson's *Fleet Street Eclogues* (1893). It may be significant that in the final arrangement of his poems Kipling followed 'The Files' with 'The Virginity' which speaks of a man's first profession as his first love: 'Men must keep touch with things they used to use | To earn their living, even when they are free . . . We've only one virginity to lose, | And where we lost it there our hearts will be!'

484 l. 12. *Faenza . . . leader*: Faenza in Italy is the setting for Browning's drama *A Soul's Tragedy*, in which the worldly papal legate Ogniben outwits Chiappino, the radical leader of a popular uprising. Ogniben enters Faenza reflecting that he has seen 'three-and-twenty leaders of revolts', and leaves at the end having added Chiappino to the list: 'I have seen *four*-and-twenty leaders of revolts!'

ll. 18–19. *Kensal-Green . . . newspaPère-la-Chaise*: famous 19th-century cemeteries: Kensal Green in London, Père-la-Chaise in Paris.

ll. 31–3. Referring to sizes of type, in descending order: *long primer* is the biggest, then *brevier*, then *minion*.

l. 36. *leaded*: printed in leaded type, i.e. with the lines separated by a rule for added emphasis.

l. 37. *triple-headed*: printed in headlines three times the usual size.

485 ll. 43–6. *Was it Bomba . . . Garobaldi*: referring to the events of the Risorgimento, the Italian struggle for unification and independence in the first part of the 19th century. It was indeed 'King Bomba' (the nickname of King Ferdinand II of Sicily) who fled after his defeat in 1860 by the nationalist hero Giuseppe Garibaldi; Professor Saffi, who had held the chair of Italian at Oxford, was briefly head of the government before the island was annexed by Sardinia, whose king, Victor Emanuel, was to become ruler of a united Italy in 1861.

ll. 66–7. *Samuel Smiles*: author of *Self-Help* (1859), a byword for earnest, go-getting optimism.

l. 73. *Conchimarian*: conch-shaped (not in *OED*).

l. 74. *reboantic*: re-echoing loudly. *Norns*: the Fates of Scandinavian mythology.

486 l. 79. *Brocken-spectres*: an optical effect in the high mountains by which the magnified shadow of the spectator is projected onto clouds; first observed in the Brocken, the highest of the Harz Mountains in Saxony, which was the traditional location of the witches' revels on Walpurgis-night.

ll. 84–5. *Quod ubique . . . semper*: the sense is, 'That which [is found] everywhere and [is loved] by everyone must endure.' The files teach that fashions change.

The Islanders

First pub. 3 Jan. 1902 in the *Weekly Times* and on 4 Jan. in *The Times* and the *New York Herald*.

Kipling offered the poem to *The Times* as an explicit political statement 'on the matter of compulsory service for the home defense', and asked for the poem to be backed by a leader on the subject: 'Everybody is fighting shy of the blessed word conscription and something has got to be done' (*Letters*, iii. 81). But the poem itself fights shy of the word, using instead the circumlocution of l. 38 ('a year of service to the lordliest life on earth'); moreover its reach goes beyond the bounds of an argument about the merits of compulsory military training. In his opening analysis of the causes of British defeats and difficulties in the Boer War, Kipling attributes technical deficiencies (the Army's lack of training and inexperience in combating small, highly mobile guerrilla forces) to a defective society and culture, but in such violent terms that the poem's rhetorical energy spills over the notional bounds of the argument. The first four lines suggest that democracy is to blame, but the poem goes on to denounce the class system, and the term 'the People' means, in the end, more than the masses: it denotes the whole social order, rulers and ruled being equally 'idle'. The archaic mode of address, together with the tone of prophetic scorn, point to Carlyle as a major influence: the poem is like one of Carlyle's 'latter-day pamphlets', and Kipling here resumes the role of isolated prophet which he had abandoned in 'Recessional'. In another poem, 'The Lesson', Kipling surveyed the Boer War from the standpoint of a collective consciousness ('We have had no end of a lesson: it will do us no end of good') but though the terms of the 'lesson' are the same as here (a denunciation of 'the obese, unchallenged old things that stifle and overlie us') the poem is much less convincing because the prophetic 'we' sounds forced.

Kipling's strong support for compulsory national service continued to figure in his political writings (letters, speeches, etc.); its most elaborate fictional exposition is the two-part futuristic fantasy 'The Army of a Dream' (*Traffics and Discoveries*, 1904) which ends with a *coup de théâtre* of brutal awakening.

486 l. 5. *leaden seas*: pointedly revising the famous image of England in *Richard II*: 'This precious stone set in the silver sea, | Which serves it in the office of a wall (II. i 46–7).

l. 11. *beasts of warren and chase*: the term (originating in feudal times) for animals protected by the hunting and game laws (e.g. deer, pheasants, partridge).

l. 13. *Ye forced them . . . they brought*: as the Israelites are made to do by the Egyptians in Exod. 5: 6–12.

487 l. 30. *the Younger Nations*: Canada and Australia; see headnote to 'Lichtenberg' above, p. 669, and see also another poem in *The Five Nations* not repr. here, 'The Parting of the Columns'.

l. 35. *wonder . . . sign*: cf. Jesus's scorn of those who deemed 'signs and wonders': 'An evil and adulterous generation seeketh after a sign' (Matt. 12: 39).

487 l. 36. *in the lee of the forespent Line*: taking shelter behind a force without acknowledging that it is exhausted ('Line' may refer to 'ships of the line', the old term for the Navy's warships, which would be supported by 'lee'; or, if 'lee' is being used figuratively, 'Line' may refer to the regiments of the regular Army).

488 l. 68. *schools*: schools of thought (the intelligentsia, social and artistic movements) as opposed to education.

489 ll. 74–8. Another poem in *The Five Nations* not repr. here, 'Rimmon', is founded on this identification of delusive social and cultural notions with heathen idols: 'The curtains part, the trumpet blares, | And the eunuch howls aloud; | And the gilt, swag-bellied idol glares, | Insolent over the crowd. || "*This is Rimmon, Lord of the Earth— | Fear Him and bow the knee!*" | And I watch my comrades hide their mirth | That rode to the wars with me.' The 'Teraphs' (teraphim in the Hebrew plural) were images or idols used in divination, equivalent to household gods; Kipling uses them here to denote the leaders of political factions. A 'sept' is a division of a tribe or clan, of Irish, not biblical origin). The 'wood-pavement gods' are ancient, superseded authorities (as obsolete as wooden pavements, which had long disappeared from London); in addition, 'wooden gods' was a slang term in the period for the pieces on a draughts board, so Kipling may be suggesting that these wise oracles are no better than ciphers.

Songs from Books

This section includes poems which appeared in the original volume of 1912, and poems from later volumes of stories which were placed in the section 'More Songs from Books' in collected editions of Kipling's verse.

Mother o' Mine

First pub. in 1891, the dedication to the 15-chapter version of *The Light that Failed* issued by Macmillan.

The strength and intimacy of relations between mothers and sons is a persistent theme in Kipling's work; see, in this edition, 'Baa, Baa, Black Sheep' (p. 90) and 'The Gardener' (p. 381); see also the poem 'A Nativity' (*The Years Between*, 1919).

Merrow Down

First pub. 1902 in *Just So Stories*, where the poem's two parts followed 'How the First Letter was Written' and 'How the Alphabet was Made'; coll. as one poem in *Songs from Books*, 1912.

Kipling's daughter Josephine, the 'Best Beloved' of the first *Just So Stories* and the original of Taffy Tegumai, died in New York in March 1899, age 6. See the headnote to 'They' (p. 606).

The whole poem (but esp. ll. 9–12) is reminiscent of Hardy, whose *Wessex Poems* had been published 1898.

491 l. 10. *racial talks*: tribal gatherings.

'Cities and Thrones and Powers'

First pub. *Puck of Pook's Hill*, 1906, prefacing 'A Centurion of the Thirtieth'.

The metre here is even more short-breathed than the one which Kipling used for his 'Horatian' poems (see 'The Survival', p. 501); its slightly archaic vocabulary marks its affiliation to the verse of the English Renaissance (from Raleigh to Herbert) which influenced Kipling in the same way, though to a lesser extent, as the prose of the Authorized Version.

Harp-Song of the Dane-Women

First pub. *Puck of Pook's Hill*, 1906, prefacing 'The Knights of the Joyous Venture', which describes an adventure in a Danish longboat in the Middle Ages.

The feelings of women who lose their men to the sea are powerfully expressed in ch. 10 of *Captains Courageous*, which describes a remembrance service for men of the New England fishing-fleet. Kipling takes little from the Anglo-Saxon and Norse alliterative tradition in this poem; l. 2 has some affinity with it, as does the circumlocution 'the old grey Widow-maker', but in general the historical element is not strongly coloured by linguistic pastiche, as it is in the story to which the poem is attached (and indeed the other *Puck* stories). The pun on 'home-acre' (= home-maker) in l. 2, and the change from 'a woman' in the first stanza to 'Woman' in the last, are strokes of modern art.

A Smuggler's Song

First pub. 1906 in *Puck of Pook's Hill*, following 'Hal o' the Draft'.

Though the story is set in Tudor times, the accompanying poem belongs to a later period, that of the 18th century when smuggling was rife along the English coastline from Kent to Cornwall. Indeed, 'King George's men' might imply any period from the accession of George I in 1714 to the death of George IV in 1829. J. C. Egerton, vicar of Burwash from 1867 to 1888, writes in *Sussex Folk and Sussex Ways* (1884) that the injunction not to look out of the window if the 'gentlemen' came along was still current in the early part of the century (S. Wintle (ed.), *Puck of Pook's Hill* (1987), 227).

494 l. 14. *brishwood*: brushwood. *OED* has 'brish' as a dialect variant of the verb 'brush', meaning to trim a hedge or tree, citing Kipling's poem 'The Floods' (which accompanies 'My Son's Wife' in *A Diversity of Creatures*,

1917): 'The first wood down is sere and small, | From the hills, the brishings off the hills' (ll. 9–10).

494 l. 29. *Valenciennes*: lace, named after the town in northern France famous for its manufacture.

The Four Angels

First pub. 1909 in *Actions and Reactions*, following 'With the Night Mail'.

The story is a science-fiction or futuristic fantasy in which Kipling predicted the advent of commercial flying (both freight and passengers). The poem suggests that there is nothing special about flight: it is simply one of the three elements which man masters, and which he does not care to master until the fourth, fire, masters him. Kipling, who was so passionate a lover of the materials of life, tells us here that he is the reverse of a materialist. The poem is both a triumphant and a tragic evocation of insatiable human aspiration and its perpetual defeat.

The Way through the Woods

First pub. *Rewards and Fairies*, 1910, prefacing 'Marklake Witches'.

The story, set in the period of the Napoleonic wars, is narrated by Philadelphia, a young and beautiful woman who does not realize that she is dying of consumption. It is her ghost which is heard cantering through the woods (as it is at the end of the story). The poem aptly foreshadows the pathos of Philadelphia's early death, and follows the vanished traces of her beauty and spirit, but it can stand alone and has often been singled out (by T. S. Eliot and Kingsley Amis, for example) as very unusual in Kipling's work. It is tempting to think that both Robert Frost and, especially, Edward Thomas knew and were touched by it.

If—

First pub. Oct. 1910 in the *American Magazine*, and the same year in *Rewards and Fairies*, following 'Brother Square-Toes'.

Though the poem could refer to the hero of the story, or to George Washington who figures in it, it was composed for a contemporary and friend of Kipling's, the colonial statesman Dr Leander Starr Jameson (1853–1917), who visited Bateman's in October 1910. In a letter of 2 Aug. 1909 Kipling described Jameson as 'head and shoulders the noblest Roman of them all' (*Letters*, iii. 384).

Kipling states that the poem was 'drawn from Jameson's character' in ch. 7 of *Something of Myself*, adding that it 'contained counsels of perfection most easy to give'. The note of irony is important—it suggests that Kipling had thought of the analogy between the speaker of the poem and Polonius before his critics—and it goes along with Kipling's uneasiness at the immense popularity of the poem: 'Schools, and places where they teach, took them for the suffering Young—which did me no good with the Young when I met them later. ("Why did you write that stuff? I've had to write it out twice as an impot.") They were printed as cards to hang up in offices and bedrooms; illuminated text-wise and anthologised to weariness. Twenty-seven of the Nations of the Earth translated them into their seven-and-twenty tongues, and printed them on every sort of fabric.' The news that 'If—' was recently voted the nation's favourite poem probably caused Kipling (at his post on the gate) as much anguish as pleasure. Nevertheless the many cheap shots which the poem has taken should be countered by two tributes: one from Lindsay Anderson, whose film *If* (1968) is, as Philip French remarks, 'closer to the central core of Kipling' than any other film treatment of his work; and the other from Craig Raine, who concludes his introduction to the Penguin Poetry Library selection of Kipling with a brilliant defence of the poem's artistry:

> What the sensitive reader responds to is not the particularities of advice but the impossibly stretched rhetorical structure. 'If—' is a single sentence, endlessly burdened by the weight of hypotheticals. The conclusion—'you'll be a Man, my son!'—depends on more qualifications than it seems possible for one sentence to bear. The poem, then, mimics the moral difficulty posed by Kipling—and yet the successful negotiation of the impossibly cumbered sentence to its end demonstrates, in miniature, the possibility of achieving something genuinely difficult. As single-sentence poems go, it is one of the longest, and it possesses all the poetry of the lovingly deferred finale of Dvořák's Cello Concerto. The form tells as much as the substance—and is, indisputably, poetry of a high order.

497 l. 18. *pitch-and-toss*: each player pitches a coin at a mark; the one whose coin lies nearest to the mark then tosses all the coins and keeps those which turn up heads; the one whose coin lay next in order does the same with the remaining coins, until all are gone (*OED*).

Dane-geld

First pub. 1911 in *A History of England* by Kipling and C. R. L. Fletcher, with the title 'What Dane-geld Means'.

Danegeld was first paid in 991 by King Ethelred II (the Unready); it amounted to 10,000 pounds in weight of silver, raised by a land-tax. Later payments rose steeply, to 158,000 pounds in 1012. No further payments were made to the Danes, but the tax continued to be levied to maintain a navy and the royal bodyguard (housecarles), so it ended ironically enough as a means of national defence rather than national subservience.

Big Steamers

First pub. 1911 in *A History of England* by Kipling and C. R. L. Fletcher. The dates '1914–1918' were added later to emphasize the prophetic accuracy of the last lines.

499 l. 20. *Looe*: in Cornwall, an erstwhile centre of the pilchard-fishery.

The Children

First pub. 1917 in *A Diversity of Creatures*, following 'The Honours of War', a story originally pub. 1911; the dates '1914–1918' were added in *Verse* ('Inclusive Edition'), 1919.

Kipling juxtaposes the pre-War story, a light-hearted tale of how an insufferable young prig of a subaltern is humanized and brought within the fold of Army comradeship, with one of the most personally anguished of his utterances on the War, written while its dreadful tide was still flowing. The historical irony ravages the speaker both as a parent and as a guilty accomplice in the 'statecraft' and 'learning' which delivered the children 'bound to the Pit'. In the most piercing of the 'Epitaphs of the War' (p. 513), Kipling was to write: 'If any question why we died, | Tell them, because our fathers lied'. But the lying father here is also the father who suffers, mourns, cries for vengeance, and is pierced again and again by the point of a pointless question.

499 ll. 3–4. *The price of our loss . . . our right*: the promise of retribution in these lines was not satisfied by the terms of the Versailles Treaty; in 'A Friend of the Family' (*Debits and Credits*, 1926) an ex-soldier comments: 'The trouble is there hasn't been any judgment taken or executed. That's why the world is where it is now. We didn't need anything but justice—afterwards. Not gettin' that, the bottom fell out of things, naturally.'

The Fabulists

First pub. 1917 in *A Diversity of Creatures*, prefacing 'The Vortex'; the dates '1914–1918' were added in *Verse* ('Inclusive Edition'), 1919.

'The Vortex' is a farce with a political edge, in which the painful indignities inflicted by a swarm of bees lead a colonial statesman to change his views on the need for imperial solidarity against a common enemy. The story was published in August 1914, which means it was written before the outbreak of the War but, like 'The Edge of Evening', is imbued with knowledge of its coming. The relation between story and poem is no less polemical than in the case of 'The Honours of War' and 'The Children' (see above), and no less bleak; indeed it is despairing, but the despair is directed inward, towards the capacity of art either to accomplish its social purpose or to save the artist himself. The War overwhelms the imagination, and by that very token demonstrates the futility of the artist's hope that he could have helped to prevent it. Yet the poem, densely and darkly reflexive, is itself a protest against 'the groaning guns'.

500 l. 5. *it will fall*: 'it will fall out that', 'the result will be'.

The Survival

First pub. 1926 in *Debits and Credits*, prefacing 'The Janeites'.

Like many of Kipling's post-War stories, 'The Janeites' is preoccupied with the possibilities and limitations of healing; it is set in the fictional Masonic Lodge 'Faith and Works 5837' where a shell-shocked ex-artilleryman tells a strange story of his wartime membership of a secret fraternity devoted to the works of Jane Austen. In contrast to 'The Fabulists', 'The Survival' is able to affirm the power of art by rejecting its political, or ideological, or monumental role—a role which is now assigned to 'cheating bards'.

The poem was later published in *Q. Horati Flacci Carminum Librum Quintum* (Horace, Odes, Bk. V), a collection by Kipling and others of fifteen Latin odes in the style of Horace, purportedly with accompanying English translations (there is no fifth book of Horace's Odes). Kipling contributed three of the English versions, of which 'The Survival' was one, the other two being 'The Pro-Consuls' and 'Lollius'. He also used the conceit in 'A Translation', the poem accompanying 'Regulus' (*A Diversity of Creatures*, 1917). The grave, slightly stilted diction and short-breathed measure of this 'Horatian' style both dignify what is fragile and contingent, and express awe at its endurance.

We and They

First pub. 1926 in *Debits and Credits*, following 'A Friend of the Family'.

The hero of the story is a Queensland drover whose alien social background and undemonstrative personality remain a mystery to the narrator, who witnesses his quiet but utterly ruthless conduct of a feud against the enemies of his dead comrade. The poem is far more playful than the ones which accompany some of the other stories in the collection, and is based on Robert Louis Stevenson's manner in the poems of *A Child's Garden of Verses* (1885), which Kipling also parodied in a section of *The Muse among the Motors*.

The Coiner

First pub. 1932 in *Limits and Renewals*, prefacing 'A Naval Mutiny'.

The story is the anecdote of a farcical episode: the mutineers are parrots belonging to sailors, left in charge of a retired petty-officer. The setting of the story is Bermuda, in the past a source of travellers' tall tales, and the deadpan fashion in which Winter Virgil recounts his quelling of the revolting birds is intended to suggest the kind of elaborate fictional embroidery associated with sailors in 'Poseidon's Law' (p. 234). The poem in turn traces this characteristic to the age of Shakespeare and humorously speculates that a similar tall tale from a Caribbean island gave him the clue to the *Tempest*. Shakespeare turns the tables on the four jolly sailors by transmuting their exotic lies into art—revealing himself to be as consummate a liar as Homer was a borrower: see headnote to 'When 'Omer Smote 'Is Bloomin' Lyre' (p. 665), and for another appearance by Shakespeare see 'The Craftsman' (p. 505).

503 *Subtitle*. The medieval ballad 'King John and the Abbot of Canterbury' begins: 'An ancient story Ile tell you anon | Of a notable prince, that was

called king John; | And he ruled England with maine and with might, | For he did great wrong, and maintein'd little right'. The ballad was included in Thomas Percy's *Reliques of Ancient English Poetry*, 1767, where the tune is said to be 'Derry down', and a note points out that 'about the time of the civil wars, when the cry ran against the bishops, some Puritan worked up the same story into a very doleful ditty, to a solemn tune, concerning "King Henry and a Bishop," with this stinging moral, "Unlearned men hard matters out can find, | When learned bishops princes eyes do blind."' 'Tempest-a-brewing' is a popular song of the day (the irony is that the learned might know the ballad but not the song, and vice-versa).

503 l. 2. From Stephano's song in *The Tempest* II. ii.

504 l. 24. *leasing*: lying (an Elizabethan archaism).

l. 28. *this globe*: punning on the name of Shakespeare's theatre.

The Years Between (1919)

Gethsemane

First pub. in *Twenty Poems from Rudyard Kipling*, 1918.

The title alludes to the ordeal of Jesus in 'the place called Gethsemane' before his arrest and crucifixion, in which he prays: 'O my Father, if it be possible, let this cup pass from me' (Matt. 26: 39); the poem does not take account of the words which follow: 'nevertheless not as I will, but as thou wilt'. Poison gas was first used, by the Germans, at the battle of Ypres in April 1915. The poem is set behind the lines: as Kipling explained to F. N. Doubleday, it refers to 'the horror that overtakes a man when he first ships [puts on] his gas mask', not in battle but amongst civilians: 'What makes war most poignant is the presence of women with whom he can talk and make love, only an hour or so behind the line' (Carrington, 547). Allusive and indirect, the poem haunts the reader with what is not said; compare the savage assault on the senses in Wilfred Owen's 'Gassed'.

The Craftsman

First pub. 18 May 1910 in *The Times* and other newspapers.

The Mermaid Tavern was the home of the Friday Street Club started by Sir Walter Ralegh; Francis Beaumont ('Master Francis Beaumont to Ben Jonson') celebrates its gatherings: 'What things have we seen | Done at the Mermaid! heard words that have been | So nimble, and so full of subtle flame . . .' Kipling almost certainly knew Browning's poem 'At the Mermaid' (*Pacchiarotto . . . and Other Poems*, 1876) in which Shakespeare talks to Jonson about his art, though in very different terms from here. Kipling represents Shakespeare as confiding a secret about his art, though the nature of this secret is not immediately obvious. It is not to do simply with drawing on real life;

John Aubrey makes no mystery about Shakespeare doing this (though his example mixes up two plays): 'The Humour of the Constable in Midsomer-night's Dreame, he happened to take at Grendon, in Bucks (I thinke it was Midsomer night that he happened to lye there) . . . Ben Johnson and he did gather Humours of men dayly where ever they came' (*Aubrey's Brief Lives*, ed. O. Lawson-Dick, 1949; the constable actually comes in *Much Ado About Nothing*). Rather it is to do with Shakespeare's recognition that the passions which govern human life are present in commonplace actions and behaviour and do not have a special dramatic or artistic quality; the quality lies in the artist. The same principle underlies another poem about Shakespeare, 'The Coiner' (p. 503), in which three seamen think they have taken advantage of the poet's good nature by telling him tall stories about their travels in exchange for drink; but he has the better of the bargain, because they have unwittingly supplied him with the story of *The Tempest*.

Ben Jonson and Shakespeare meet at Shakespeare's home in Stratford in the late, uncollected story 'Proofs of Holy Writ'.

505 l. 2. *Boanerges*: see note on p. 649.

506 l. 9. *While he hid from Sir Thomas's keepers*: alluding to the legend that Shakespeare used to poach deer from the estate of Sir Thomas Lucy near Stratford, and that this was the reason for his departure to London.

The Female of the Species

First pub. 20 Oct. 1911 in the *Morning Post* and on 11 Nov. in the *Ladies' Home Journal*.

The movement for women's suffrage had been growing in size and militancy; the poem is a response to this development, yet also affirms beliefs long held and found in many other stories and poems, notably that women were more primitive beings than men, and therefore capable of greater ruthlessness. In the last stanza of 'The Young British Soldier' (*Barrack-Room Ballads*, 1892) it is women who dispatch the wounded, as Mary Postgate does to the German airman (p. 337).

The poem's poise and artful relish (especially the rueful and sharp refrain which has immortalized it) put a gloss on opinions which Kipling could voice in a much more unbalanced and unpleasant way. In August 1905 he began a letter to the classical scholar Gilbert Murray, in response to something Murray had written about Euripides: 'Obviously where the concubine, or polygamy, exists, the most primitive plot of all, originated by one woman and shared by all the others *except one*, is the attack by poison on the male child of the favoured wife or concubine.' In the next paragraph he linked this argument with the way in which 'the unattached women will band together instinctively against the male', offering as an example 'an average country house where there is a match ripening. There you have your chorus (*all* women) communicating by telepathy on strictly Pagan Greek lines; your fool-male blundering about in a maze of delicate intrigue that he don't in the least realize and the girl confiding by signs the progress of her plot to the chorus. . . . *Our* delusion is that after aeons of possession and oppression the woman has suddenly become civilized in the male's sense of the word' (*Letters*, iii. 191–2). In June 1910 he wrote to Andrew Macphail in praise of his essay 'The Psychology of the Suffragette', and stated his theory 'that Nature seeing there are 1,200,000 surplus women in England and being unable to kill 'em as they slay men, is getting 'em to slay themselves. (You can nearly kill a white woman, and totally compromise her issue by making her stand on her feet for consecutive hours). The wreckage after such a suffragette show as we have had is something awful. Women knock up, knock out, go into rest-cures and under the surgeon's hand—disappear from their friends while the evasive husband says they are "not quite well"—and with them goes the promise of increase' (*Letters*, iii. 441).

'For All We Have and Are'

First pub. 2 Sept. 1914 in *The Times*.

War with Germany had been declared on 4 August. The German invasion of Belgium was spectacularly successful at its outset: Liège fell on the 17th, Brussels three days later; on the 23rd the British Expeditionary Force began the retreat from Mons. Kipling's poem is therefore written at a point of crisis, not as a warning but as an exhortation to stand fast. The poem's complex fusion of national resolve and dread distinguishes it, as Ann Parry shrewdly observes, from other contemporary responses to the outbreak of war: 'While Brooke, Grenfell and Sassoon were glorying in the redemptive aspects of battle, the war represented here had more in common with the Hebraic perspective one finds in Rosenberg' (*The Poetry of Rudyard Kipling* (1992), 129).

509 l. 4. *The Hun is at the gate!*: Kingsley Amis defends the line against the charge that it is 'an incitement to racial hatred': 'No: "the Hun" is a metaphor for "the barbarian, the enemy of decent values", and "the gate" is not that of England and the Empire, but that of civilization. If there is a fault here, it is one of overstatement only' (*Rudyard Kipling and His World* (1975), 76–7). Even 'overstatement' may be overstating the case, given the Germans' proclaimed policy of 'shrecklichkeit' ('frightfulness') against Belgian civilians. Kipling's metaphor was to look even more apt in 1915, when Germany became the first combatant to carry out air-raids on civilian towns, declare a policy of unrestricted submarine warfare, and use poison gas in battle.

ll. 11–12. *In courage . . . your hand*: cf. Ps. 27: 14: 'Wait on the Lord: be of good courage, and he shall strengthen thine heart: wait, I say, on the Lord' and 10: 12: 'Arise, O Lord; O God, lift up thine hand'.

My Boy Jack

First pub. 19 Oct. 1916 in the *Daily Telegraph* and *New York Times*, in an article entitled 'Destroyers at Jutland', part of a series of articles collected later in the year as *Sea Warfare*.

This and the following poem are the most direct responses which Kipling made to the death of his son John, killed at the battle of Loos in September 1915. See headnote to 'The Gardener', p. 637. The consolation which the anonymous respondent offers to the questioner in this ballad is both like and unlike that which Kipling offered himself, in a letter of 12 November to Brigadier L. C. Dunsterville (the original of Stalky): 'I'm sorry that all the years' work ended in that one afternoon but—lots of people are in our position—and it's something to have bred a man' (Carrington, 509). In the last line of the poem there is something other than laconic stoicism, something profoundly and permanently shocked, which loads the word *gave* with the burden of sacrifice.

The question-and-answer form, which Kipling also uses in 'Danny Deever' (p. 433), derives from traditional ballads such as 'Edward, Edward' and 'Lord Randal'; asking for news is also traditional, as in 'Jock o' the Side': 'Then up and spoke our gude auld Lord | "What news? what news, sister Downie, to me?" | "Bad news, bad news, my Lord Mangerton; | Michael is killed, and they hae ta'en my son Johnie."'

Epitaphs of the War

First pub. in *The Years Between*, where the title was simply 'Epitaphs'.

Kipling stated that the poems were 'naked cribs from the Greek Anthology' (i.e. the great Palatine Anthology of classical Greek epigrams, section 7 of which consists of a collection of epitaphs). There is also a strong influence from the verse of the late 16th and 17th centuries. The poems treat pathos, tenderness, and righteous fury with equal laconic spareness. They also, as Ann Parry points out, invert the scale of epic while 'convey[ing] an impression of the cultural and geographical magnitude of the war . . . The reader is moved quickly through brief lives in ever-widening geographical dimensions . . . and the effect is to extend the reader's awareness beyond the Western Front to the most far-flung battlefields of this war. The reader commits to memory not only poignant details about the fallen, but becomes the witness of a new historical phenomenon—the first *world* war' (*The Poetry of Rudyard Kipling* (1992), 133–5).

A Servant

510 The phrase 'the better man' recalls the ending of 'Gunga Din' (p. 444). See also 'Native Water-Carrier' (below, p. 513).

Pelicans in the Wilderness

512 *Title*. From Ps. 102: 6: 'I am like a pelican of the wilderness', an image of desolate loneliness which the speaker arrogates to himself: the single pelican becomes 'pelicans' who return to their children.

R.A.F. (Aged Eighteen)

l. 4. *Childlike . . . put away*: from 1 Cor. 13: 11: 'When I was a child, I spake as a child, I understood as a child, I thought as a child: but when I became a man, I put away childish things.'

The Refined Man

513 ll. 1–2. *I stepped aside for my needs, | Disdaining the common office*: he would not use the common latrine ('office' is both an archaism and a euphemism).

Native Water-Carrier (M.E.F.)

Title. 'Mesopotamian Expeditionary Force'. Though this figure recalls 'Gunga Din' (p. 442), the conclusion of that poem is transferred to 'A Servant' (above, p. 510).

The Rebel

514 ll. 5–6. *for gin and snare | About my pathway spread*: from Ps. 140: 5: 'The proud have hid a snare for me, and cords; they have spread a net by the wayside; they have set gins for me.'

The Obedient

ll. 1–4. *Daily . . . Did I sacrifice*: in 1 Kgs. 18: 17–40, the prophet Elijah challenges the priests of Baal to a contest to decide who is the true God. Each builds an altar and sacrifices a bullock, but despite the priests' prayers Baal does nothing, whereas the God of Israel answers Elijah's prayer and consumes his sacrifice with fire. The speaker's faith contrasts sharply here with the gods' silence, as it does in another poem in the volume, 'A Nativity'.

A Drifter off Tarentum

Title. A 'drifter' in this context is a mine. See the poem 'Minesweepers' (p. 517). Tarentum (modern Taranto) is in southern Italy, north of Gallipoli.

V.A.D. (Mediterranean)

516 *Title*. V.A.D. = Volunteer Aid Detachment; see 'Fairy-Kist', p. 420.

Verse ('Inclusive Edition'), 1919

Mine Sweepers

First pub. 23 Nov. 1915, with the title 'The Sweepers', in *The Times* and other British and American newspapers; it accompanied 'The Auxiliary Fleet', the second of a series of articles called 'The Fringes of the Fleet', issued as a pamphlet later in 1915 and then included in *Sea Warfare*, 1916.

Kipling's admiration for the courage of the mine-sweepers is recorded in 'Sea Constables' (p. 356). The litany of names is chanted for protection, as though a magic charm inhered in the charm of the syllables.

The Gods of the Copybook Headings

First pub. 26 Oct. 1919 in the *Sunday Pictorial*.

Copybook headings were specimens in handwriting manuals, and often consisted of pious sayings, proverbs, etc., the idea being to get some moral improvement while practising. The implication is that such maxims would be ineffably trite; *OED* cites Charles Kingsley in 1848: 'A few copy-book headings about benevolence, and industry, and independence'. Kipling himself ruefully records the indignation of young people at being made to copy out the precepts of 'If—: see p. 674. But cf. a passage in the Masonic story 'In the Interests of the Brethren' (*Debits and Credits*, 1926):

> Next the Master delivered a little lecture on the meanings of some pictured symbols and diagrams. His theme was a well-worn one, but his deep holding voice made it fresh.
>
> 'Marvellous how these old copybook-headings persist,' the Doctor said.
>
> '*That's* all right!' the one-footed man spoke cautiously . . . 'But they're the kind o' copy-book headin's we shall find burnin' round our bunks in Hell.'

The 'gods of the copybook headings' therefore represent tried and tested principles of belief and action which cannot be discarded or evaded without retribution, whereas the 'gods of the market-place' represent the comforting illusions in which people mistakenly place their faith. The 'terror and slaughter' of the War had, in Kipling's view, been the result of just such worship of the 'gods of the market-place'; belief in 'social progress', especially that represented by socialist ideas, is a dangerous fantasy. The poem's anti-idealism, and especially its assumption of the prophet's scornful clear-sighted superiority to the infatuations and delusions of the tribe, goes back, like so much of Kipling's social criticism, to Carlyle (see e.g. 'Tomlinson', *Barrack-Room Ballads*, 1892).

The mock-evolutionary vocabulary is one of Kipling's favourite devices for suggesting that things have always been as they are: see 'In the Neolithic Age' (p. 451) and, for a biblical equivalent, 'The Conundrum of the Workshops' (p. 449).

519 l. 24. *The Wages of Sin is Death*: Rom. 6: 23.

519 ll. 33–6. The formula 'There are only four things' borrows from Proverbs, ch. 30, which contains a series of such groupings, e.g. vv. 21–3: 'For three things the earth is disquieted, and for four which it cannot bear: for a servant when he reigneth; and a fool when he is filled with meat; for an odious woman when she is married; and an handmaid that is heir to her mistress.'

l. 36. *wabbling*: an alternative spelling of 'wobbling' still current in the period.

Poems Collected in Editions after 1919

Hymn of Breaking Strain

First pub. 15 Mar. 1935 in the *Daily Telegraph*; coll. Sussex edn. (vol. xxxv), 1939.

Kipling had long been fascinated by the concept of 'breaking strain', the point beyond which human norms collapse. The War had given him multiple examples of such breakdowns, which may be partially healed or lead to permanent madness, as in the case of Jimmy Tigner in 'Fairy-Kist' (see p. 418). But he had treated the subject in his earliest published fiction: 'Thrown Away', for example, in *Plain Tales from the Hills*, or 'At the End of the Passage' (*Life's Handicap*, 1891). In this edition, see esp. 'The Bridge-Builders' (p. 163), in which the endurance of men is juxtaposed, as here, with that of the structure they have made.

'Tin Fish'

First pub., without the title, in the second of two articles on 'Submarines', 27 Nov. 1915 in the *Daily Telegraph*; these articles were subsequently published with others in *Sea Warfare*, 1916. The poem was first separately coll. in *Verse* ('Definitive Edition'), 1940.

RG points out the influence of a poem by Francis William Bourdillon (1852–1921), 'The Night Has a Thousand Eyes', pub. 1890: 'The night has a thousand eyes, | And the day but one; | Yet the light of the bright world dies | With the dying sun || The mind has a thousand eyes, | And the heart but one; | Yet the light of a whole life dies | When love is done.'

The Storm Cone

First pub. 25 May 1932 in the *Morning Post*; coll. *Verse* ('Inclusive Edition', 1885–1932), 1933.

This is Kipling's final poem of prophetic warning. Subsequent events (Hitler's rise to power, the accelerated pace of German rearmament) did nothing to lessen his dread. Yet the poem is hopeful: though it renounces the delusive 'star' of the first lines, it holds to the 'deep throb beneath us', an image which fuses, in a way characteristic of Kipling, the machine with the human body.

The Appeal

First pub. 1939, the final poem in vol. xxxix of the Sussex edn.

Kipling's growing dislike of biography, which he referred to as the 'Higher Cannibalism', is well attested in his last years. The poem functions as the equivalent of the warning verses supposed to have been written by Shakespeare for his tomb at Stratford: 'Good friend, for Jesu's sake forbear | To dig the dust enclosed here. | Blest be the man who spares these stones, | And curst be he that moves my bones.' Needless to say Kipling's final wishes have not been honoured by readers and critics including the present editor. The 'little, little span' is, in another aspect, the subject of 'Cities and Thrones and Powers' (p. 492).

FURTHER READING

Summary of Kipling's Major Publications

(*This list excludes collections and selections, which are recorded separately, and does not record individual items, juvenilia, or privately printed works. Copyright issues are not counted as first editions (e.g.* The Light that Failed *was printed for copyright purposes and deposited in the British Museum in Nov. 1890, but the first commercial edition was issued in Jan. 1891). Volumes are listed according to place and date of first publication, except that the dates of the first English editions of volumes originally published in India or America are also given. The place of publication is London unless otherwise indicated. The contents of volumes are short stories unless otherwise indicated in the title or by the editor; note that most of Kipling's later volumes of short stories also contain verse in the form of accompanying poems. Further details will in many cases be found in the notes to this volume; for a fuller account see the Bibliography by J. McG. Stewart.*)

Departmental Ditties and Other Verses, Lahore 1886; first English edn. 1890.

Plain Tales from the Hills, Calcutta 1888; first English edn. 1890.

Soldiers Three, a collection of stories setting forth certain passages in the lives and adventures of Privates Terence Mulvaney, Stanley Ortheris, and John Learoyd. Done into type and edited by Rudyard Kipling, Allahabad, 1888; first English edn. 1890 when the words 'done into type and edited' were deleted.

The Story of the Gadsbys: A Tale without a Plot (dramatic dialogues), Allahabad 1888; first English edn. 1890.

In Black & White, Allahabad 1888; first English edn. 1890 (with 'and' replacing the ampersand).

Under the Deodars, Allahabad 1888; first English edn. 1890.

The Phantom 'Rickshaw and Other Tales, Allahabad, 1888; first English edn. 1890.

Wee Willie Winkie and Other Child Stories, Allahabad, 1888; first English edn. 1890 when the word 'child' was deleted.

Departmental Ditties, Barrack-Room Ballads, and Other Verses, New York, 1890 (first edn. of 13 of the ballads and 4 of the 'other verses'; for the first separate edn. see below).

The Light that Failed (novel), 1891.

The City of Dreadful Night and Other Places (travel writing, articles and sketches), Allahabad and London, 1891.

Life's Handicap: Being Stories of Mine Own People, 1891.

The Naulahka: A Tale of West and East (with Wolcott Balestier), 1892.

Barrack-Room Ballads and Other Verses, 1892 (first separate edn.).

Many Inventions, 1893.

The Jungle Book, 1894.

The Second Jungle Book, 1895.
The Seven Seas (verse), 1896.
Captains Courageous (novel), 1897.
The Day's Work, 1898.
A Fleet in Being: notes of two trips with the Channel Squadron, 1898.
Stalky & Co., 1899.
From Sea to Sea: Letters of Travel, 2 vols., New York, 1899; first English edn. 1900.
Kim (novel), 1901.
Just So Stories, 1902.
The Five Nations (verse), 1903.
Traffics and Discoveries, 1904.
Puck of Pook's Hill, 1906.
Letters to the Family: Notes of a Journey through Canada, Toronto, 1908.
Actions and Reactions, 1909.
Rewards and Fairies, 1910.
A History of England (with C. R. L. Fletcher; Kipling contributed verse), 1911.
The Fringes of the Fleet (journalism), 1915.
Sea Warfare (journalism; incl. repr. of *The Fringes of the Fleet*), 1916.
A Diversity of Creatures, 1917.
The Years Between (verse), 1919.
Letters of Travel (incl. repr. of *Letters to the Family*), 1920.
Land and Sea Tales for Scouts and Guides, 1923 (in American edns. 'Scouts and Guides' was replaced by 'Boys and Girls').
The Irish Guards in the Great War (history), 2 vols., 1923.
Debits and Credits, 1926.
Thy Servant a Dog, 1930.
Limits and Renewals, 1932.
Souvenirs of France (travel writing), 1933.
Something of Myself for my Friends Known and Unknown (posthumous memoir), 1937.

Reference Works

J. McG. Stewart, *Rudyard Kipling: A Bibliographical Catalogue*, ed. A. W. Yeats, 1959.

W. A. Young and J. H. McGivering, *A Kipling Dictionary*, 1967 (rev. and enlarged edn. of work originally pub. by Young in 1911).

N. Page, *A Kipling Companion*, 1984.

David Alan Richards, *The Books I Leave Behind*, 2007.

David Alan Richards, *Rudyard Kipling: A Bibliography*, 2 vols., 2010 (vol. 1, covering Kipling's sole-authored publications, is a print edition; vol. 2, covering everything else, is a CD-ROM enclosed with vol. 1). Comprehensive and authoritative.

The New Readers' Guide to the works of Rudyard Kipling (ongoing). This web-based guide, hosted by the Kipling Society (http://www.kipling society.co.uk), supersedes *The Readers' Guide to Rudyard Kipling's Work* (privately printed for R. E. Harbord, 1961); it is being continually expanded and updated and will eventually cover all of Kipling's writings, together with biographical and bibliographical information.

Editions

(a) Collections

Works (Uniform Edition), 28 vols., London: Macmillan 1899–1938. Beginning with *Stalky & Co.* (1899), the first English editions of Kipling's prose works appeared in this series. Along with *Stalky & Co.*, Macmillan reissued Kipling's previous volumes in the same format. Eventually the edition comprised twenty-eight volumes, including one anomalous volume of verse: see Stewart, no. 369 (p. 288).

Works (Outward Bound Edition), 36 vols., New York: Charles Scribner's Sons, 1897–1937. The first eleven volumes were issued together in 1897; the others were incorporated in the series shortly after their individual trade publication. Unlike the Uniform Edition, the Outward Bound Edition includes verse as well as prose, and the volumes differ in arrangement and illlustrations.

Complete Works (Sussex Edition), 35 vols., London: Macmillan 1937–39. The edition contains two volumes of uncollected prose (vols. xxix–xxx) and numerous uncollected poems, but is a 'Complete Works' only insofar as it represents Kipling's final authorized version of his œuvre.

Collected Verse, New York: Doubleday, Page & Co., 1907; an English edn. was pub. by Hodder & Stoughton in 1912.

Verse (Inclusive Edition, 1885–1918), 3 vols., London: Hodder & Stoughton 1919. Subsequent 'Inclusive Editions' were issued in 1921 (when it became one volume), 1927 (when the dates were given as '1885–1926'), and 1933 ('1885–1932'). A volume callled *Poems, 1886–1929* was issued in a limited edn. in 1929.

Verse (Definitive Edition), London: Hodder & Stoughton, 1940. Subsuming and supplementing the 'Inclusive Editions'. Like the completeness of the Sussex Edition, the definitiveness of the Definitive Edition is a matter of Kipling's opinion and that of his publishers rather than a matter of fact.

The Cambridge Edition of the Poems of Rudyard Kipling, ed. T. Pinney, 3 vols., 2013. A massive 'completist' project, superseding the Sussex and Definitive Editions as the standard reference text though not without its own flaws and limitations (starting with the title which ignores Kipling's deliberate and consistent use of 'verse' in titles of collections and selections).

(b) Selections

Songs from Books, 1912.
A Book of Words (speeches and addresses), 1928.
All the Mowgli Stories, 1933.
Collected Dog Stories, 1934.
A Kipling Pageant, New York 1935.
A Choice of Kipling's Verse, ed. T. S. Eliot, 1941.
The Complete Barrack-Room Ballads, ed. C. Carrington, 1973.
Kipling's India: Uncollected Sketches 1884–1888, ed. T. Pinney, 1986.
Early Verse by Rudyard Kipling 1879–1889: Unpublished, Uncollected, and Rarely Collected Poems, ed. A. Rutherford, 1986.
War Stories and Poems, ed. A. Rutherford, 1990 (World's Classics).
Something of Myself and Other Autobiographical Writings, ed. T. Pinney, 1991.
Selected Poetry, ed. C. Raine, 1992 (Penguin Poetry Library).
Mrs Bathurst and Other stories, ed. L. Lewis, 1996 (World's Classics).
Writings on Writing by Rudyard Kipling, ed. S. Kemp and L. Lewis, 1996.
Kipling's America: Travel Letters, 1889–1895, ed. D. H. Stewart, 2003.
The Man Who Would be King and Other Stories, ed. Louis L. Cornell, 2008.
Rudyard Kipling's Uncollected Speeches: A Second Book of Words, ed. T. Pinney, 2008.
Kipling Abroad: Traffics and Discoveries from Burma to Brazil, ed. A. Lycett, 2009.
Rudyard Kipling: 100 Poems Old and New, ed. T. Pinney, 2013. A quirky selection with many unpublished poems drawing on the complete *Cambridge Edition* (see above).
The Surprising Mr Kipling: An anthology and re-assessment of the poetry of Rudyard Kipling, ed. B. Harris, 2014.
Kipling and the Sea: Voyages and Discoveries from North Atlantic to South Pacific, ed. A. Lycett, 2014.

(c) Correspondence

Rudyard Kipling to Rider Haggard: The Record of a Friendship, ed. M. N. Cohen, 1965.
'O Beloved Kids!' Rudyard Kipling's Letters to his Children, ed. E. L. Gilbert, 1983.
The Letters of Rudyard Kipling, ed. T. Pinney, 6 vols, 1990–2004. Indispensable work, superbly edited and annotated.

Biographies and Memoirs

Alice Macdonald Fleming, née Kipling, 'Some Childhood Memories of Rudyard Kipling' and 'More Childhood Memories of Rudyard Kipling', *Chambers' Journal*, 8th Series, 8 (1939).
Edmonia Hill, 'The Young Kipling', *Atlantic Monthly*, 157 (1936).

C. Carrington, *Rudyard Kipling: His Life and Work*, 1955 (2nd edn. with revisions 1970; 3rd edn. with additional material in appendices 1978; the official life written with the co-operation of Kipling's surviving daughter, Mrs Elsie Bambridge, replacing the suppressed work by Lord Birkenhead: see below).

J. I. M. Stewart, *Rudyard Kipling*, 1966.

A. Wilson, *The Strange Ride of Rudyard Kipling: His Life and Works*, 1977.

Lord Birkenhead, *Rudyard Kipling*, 1978 (originally the official life, but suppressed by Mrs Bambridge on its completion in 1950 and replaced by Carrington; see above).

H. Orel, *Kipling: Interviews and Recollections*, 1983.

H. Orel, *A Kipling Chronology*, 1989.

M. Seymour-Smith, *Rudyard Kipling*, 1989.

Andrew Lycett, *Rudyard Kipling*, 1999.

Harry Ricketts, *The Unforgiving Minute: A Life of Rudyard Kipling*, 2000.

David Gilmour, *The Long Recessional: The Imperial Life of Rudyard Kipling*, 2002.

Phillip Mallett, *Rudyard Kipling: A Literary Life*, 2003.

Charles Allen, *Kipling Sahib: India and the Making of Rudyard Kipling*, 2007.

Criticism

(a) Collections

W. L. Renwick and A. Rutherford (eds.), *Kipling's Mind and Art*, 1965.

E. L. Gilbert (ed.), *Kipling and the Critics*, 1966.

R. L. Green (ed.), *Kipling: The Critical Heritage*, 1971 (repr. 1997).

J. Gross (ed.), *Rudyard Kipling: The Man, His Work and His World*, 1972.

P. Mallett (ed.), *Kipling Considered*, 1987.

H. Bloom (ed.), *Rudyard Kipling* (Twentieth-Century Views), 1987.

Caroline Rooney and Kaori Nagai (eds.), *Kipling and Beyond: Patriotism, Globalisation and Postcolonialism*, 2010.

Howard Booth (ed.), *The Cambridge Companion to Rudyard Kipling*, 2011.

Janet Montefiore (ed.), *'In Time's eye': Essays on Rudyard Kipling*, 2013.

(b) Books, articles, and essays

Henry James, Introduction to *Mine Own People* (American edn. of *Life's Handicap*), New York, 1891.

Robert Buchanan, *The Voice of the 'Hooligan': A Discussion of Kiplingism*, New York, 1900.

A. M. Weygandt, *Kipling's Reading and Its Influence on His Poetry*, 1939.

E. Wilson, *The Wound and the Bow*, 1941.

G. Orwell, 'Rudyard Kipling', *Horizon*, Feb. 1942 (repr. *Collected Essays, Journalism and Letters*, vol. ii, 1968).

W. H. Auden, 'Rudyard Kipling', *The New Republic*, 109 (1943).

L. Trilling, *The Liberal Imagination*, 1951 (essay originally 1943).
C. S. Lewis, 'Kipling's World', in *They Asked for a Paper*, 1962 (lecture originally 1948).
J. M. S. Tompkins, *The Art of Rudyard Kipling*, 1959.
C. A. Bodelsen, *Aspects of Kipling's Art*, 1964.
R. L. Green, *Kipling and the Children*, 1965.
L. L. Cornell, *Kipling in India*, 1966.
B. Dobrée, *Rudyard Kipling: Realist and Fabulist*, 1967.
E. L. Gilbert, *The Good Kipling: Studies in the Short Story*, 1972.
K. Amis, *Rudyard Kipling and His World*, 1975.
P. Mason, *Kipling: The Glass, the Shadow, and the Fire*, 1975.
J. S. Bratton, 'Kipling's Magic Art' (Chatterton Lecture for 1978), *Proceedings of the British Academy*, 64 (1978), 209–32.
B. J. Moore-Gilbert, *Kipling and 'Orientalism'*, 1986.
S. Kemp, *Kipling's Hidden Narratives*, 1988.
N. Crook, *Kipling's Myths of Love and Death*, 1989.
A. Parry, *The Poetry of Rudyard Kipling: Rousing the Nation*, 1992.
P. Keating, *Kipling the Poet*, 1994.
Helen Pike Bauer, *Rudyard Kipling: A Study of the Short Fiction*, 1994.
John Coates, *The Day's Work: Kipling and the Idea of Sacrifice*, 1997.
John McBratney, *Imperial Subjects, Imperial Space: Rudyard Kipling's Fiction of the Native-Born*, 2004.
William B. Dillingham, *Rudyard Kipling: Hell and Heroism*, 2005.
Kaori Nagai, *Empire of Analogies: Kipling, India & Ireland*, 2006.
Janet Montefiore, *Rudyard Kipling*, 2007. ['Writers and their Work' series]
William B. Dillingham, *Rudyard Kipling: Life, Love and Art*, 2008.
Peter Havholm, *Politics and Awe in Rudyard Kipling's Fiction*, 2008.
Sullivan, Zohreh T., *Narratives of Empire: The Fictions of Rudyard Kipling*, 2008.
David Sergeant, *Kipling's Art of Fiction 1884–1901*, 2013.

INDEX OF TITLES (STORIES)

INDEX OF TITLES AND FIRST LINES (VERSE)

The Oxford World's Classics Website

www.worldsclassics.co.uk

- Browse the full range of Oxford World's Classics online
- Sign up for our monthly e-alert to receive information on new titles
- Read extracts from the Introductions
- Listen to our editors and translators talk about the world's greatest literature with our Oxford World's Classics audio guides
- Join the conversation, follow us on Twitter at OWC_Oxford
- Teachers and lecturers can order inspection copies quickly and simply via our website

www.worldsclassics.co.uk

MORE ABOUT **OXFORD WORLD'S CLASSICS**

American Literature

British and Irish Literature

Children's Literature

Classics and Ancient Literature

Colonial Literature

Eastern Literature

European Literature

Gothic Literature

History

Medieval Literature

Oxford English Drama

Poetry

Philosophy

Politics

Religion

The Oxford Shakespeare

A SELECTION OF OXFORD WORLD'S CLASSICS

JOHN BUCHAN	**Greenmantle** **Huntingtower** **The Thirty-Nine Steps**
JOSEPH CONRAD	**Chance** **Heart of Darkness and Other Tales** **Lord Jim** **Nostromo** **An Outcast of the Islands** **The Secret Agent** **Typhoon and Other Tales** **Under Western Eyes**
ARTHUR CONAN DOYLE	**The Adventures of Sherlock Holmes** **The Case-Book of Sherlock Holmes** **The Hound of the Baskervilles** **The Lost World** **The Memoirs of Sherlock Holmes** **Sherlock Holmes: Selected Stories** **A Study in Scarlet**
FORD MADOX FORD	**The Good Soldier**
JOHN GALSWORTHY	**The Forsyte Saga**
JEROME K. JEROME	**Three Men in a Boat**
JAMES JOYCE	**A Portrait of the Artist as a Young Man** **Dubliners** **Occasional, Critical, and Political Writing** **Ulysses**
RUDYARD KIPLING	**Captains Courageous** **The Complete Stalky & Co** **The Jungle Books** **Just So Stories** **Kim** **The Man Who Would Be King**

A SELECTION OF **OXFORD WORLD'S CLASSICS**

RUDYARD KIPLING	**Plain Tales from the Hills**
	War Stories and Poems
D. H. LAWRENCE	**The Rainbow**
	Sons and Lovers
	Women in Love
WYNDHAM LEWIS	**Tarr**
KATHERINE MANSFIELD	**Selected Stories**
ROBERT FALCON SCOTT	**Journals**
ROBERT TRESSELL	**The Ragged Trousered Philanthropists**
VIRGINIA WOOLF	**Between the Acts**
	Flush
	Jacob's Room
	Mrs Dalloway
	The Mark on the Wall and Other Short Fiction
	Night and Day
	Orlando: A Biography
	A Room of One's Own and Three Guineas
	To the Lighthouse
	The Voyage Out
	The Waves
	The Years
W. B. YEATS	**The Major Works**

A SELECTION OF **OXFORD WORLD'S CLASSICS**

	Late Victorian Gothic Tales
	Literature and Science in the Nineteenth Century
Jane Austen	Emma
	Mansfield Park
	Persuasion
	Pride and Prejudice
	Selected Letters
	Sense and Sensibility
Mrs Beeton	Book of Household Management
Mary Elizabeth Braddon	Lady Audley's Secret
Anne Brontë	The Tenant of Wildfell Hall
Charlotte Brontë	Jane Eyre
	Shirley
	Villette
Emily Brontë	Wuthering Heights
Robert Browning	The Major Works
John Clare	The Major Works
Samuel Taylor Coleridge	The Major Works
Wilkie Collins	The Moonstone
	No Name
	The Woman in White
Charles Darwin	The Origin of Species
Thomas De Quincey	The Confessions of an English Opium-Eater
	On Murder
Charles Dickens	The Adventures of Oliver Twist
	Barnaby Rudge
	Bleak House
	David Copperfield
	Great Expectations
	Nicholas Nickleby

A SELECTION OF **OXFORD WORLD'S CLASSICS**

Charles Dickens	**The Old Curiosity Shop**
	Our Mutual Friend
	The Pickwick Papers
George du Maurier	**Trilby**
Maria Edgeworth	**Castle Rackrent**
George Eliot	**Daniel Deronda**
	The Lifted Veil and Brother Jacob
	Middlemarch
	The Mill on the Floss
	Silas Marner
Edward FitzGerald	**The Rubáiyát of Omar Khayyám**
Elizabeth Gaskell	**Cranford**
	The Life of Charlotte Brontë
	Mary Barton
	North and South
	Wives and Daughters
George Gissing	**New Grub Street**
	The Nether World
	The Odd Women
Edmund Gosse	**Father and Son**
Thomas Hardy	**Far from the Madding Crowd**
	Jude the Obscure
	The Mayor of Casterbridge
	The Return of the Native
	Tess of the d'Urbervilles
	The Woodlanders
James Hogg	**The Private Memoirs and Confessions of a Justified Sinner**
John Keats	**The Major Works**
	Selected Letters
Charles Maturin	**Melmoth the Wanderer**
Henry Mayhew	**London Labour and the London Poor**

A SELECTION OF **OXFORD WORLD'S CLASSICS**

William Morris	**News from Nowhere**
John Ruskin	**Praeterita**
	Selected Writings
Walter Scott	**Ivanhoe**
	Rob Roy
	Waverley
Mary Shelley	**Frankenstein**
	The Last Man
Robert Louis Stevenson	**Strange Case of Dr Jekyll and Mr Hyde and Other Tales**
	Treasure Island
Bram Stoker	**Dracula**
W. M. Thackeray	**Vanity Fair**
Frances Trollope	**Domestic Manners of the Americans**
Oscar Wilde	**The Importance of Being Earnest and Other Plays**
	The Major Works
	The Picture of Dorian Gray
Ellen Wood	**East Lynne**
Dorothy Wordsworth	**The Grasmere and Alfoxden Journals**
William Wordsworth	**The Major Works**
Wordsworth and Coleridge	**Lyrical Ballads**

A SELECTION OF **OXFORD WORLD'S CLASSICS**

A SELECTION OF **OXFORD WORLD'S CLASSICS**

HANS CHRISTIAN ANDERSEN	**Fairy Tales**
J. M. BARRIE	**Peter Pan in Kensington Gardens and Peter and Wendy**
L. FRANK BAUM	**The Wonderful Wizard of Oz**
FRANCES HODGSON BURNETT	**The Secret Garden**
LEWIS CARROLL	**Alice's Adventures in Wonderland and Through the Looking-Glass**
CARLO COLLODI	**The Adventures of Pinocchio**
KENNETH GRAHAME	**The Wind in the Willows**
ANTHONY HOPE	**The Prisoner of Zenda**
THOMAS HUGHES	**Tom Brown's Schooldays**
CHARLES PERRAULT	**The Complete Fairy Tales**
ANNA SEWELL	**Black Beauty**
ROBERT LOUIS STEVENSON	**Kidnapped** **Treasure Island**

TROLLOPE IN OXFORD WORLD'S CLASSICS

ANTHONY TROLLOPE

The American Senator
An Autobiography
Barchester Towers
Can You Forgive Her?
Cousin Henry
Doctor Thorne
The Duke's Children
The Eustace Diamonds
Framley Parsonage
He Knew He Was Right
Lady Anna
The Last Chronicle of Barset
Orley Farm
Phineas Finn
Phineas Redux
The Prime Minister
Rachel Ray
The Small House at Allington
The Warden
The Way We Live Now